CRADLE OF DESTRUCTION

GARETH L. WILLIAMS

Copyright © Gareth L. Williams, 2023

The moral right of the author has been asserted

This is a work of fiction. Names, characters, places and incidents are either the product of the author's imagination or are used fictitiously, and any resemblance to actual persons, living or dead, businesses, companies, events, or locales is entirely coincidental.

BOOK ONE:

HIDDEN WORLDS

PART ONE

THE

DENIAL

Preamble

The immense spacecraft shot back into the void which people call 'Real Space,' entering the outer reaches of the orange-yellow dwarf star system, at a mind-numbing 5,000 kilometres per second. Forged from alloys tougher than diamond the ship resembled nothing less than some sort of gigantic, legless, steel grey insect.

Soon after entering the star system the ship's attitude thrusters would completely turn the beast through an angle of 180°, and then its single, huge, nuclear fusion engine would come to life, its massive engine bell blasting out searingly bright plumes of orange and violet plasma; roiling rivers of energy, flowing far out into the void. That long burn would brake the ship's velocity, slowly, gradually, reducing its dizzying speed, until it decelerated below the escape velocity of the star which lay at the centre of this system. Then it would be forced to be a captive of the star's gravity well, the precise aim of the humans who crewed the ship.

The star ship had come from humanity's origin, the Solar System, but it had now entered the system of a sun which humans had called "Ra"; named after the ancient Egyptian god of the sun, in the ancient theology of that archaic civilisation, back on Earth.

The vessel would remain bound to Ra's own gravity until its great engine was ignited once again, to propel the vessel out of this alien system and return it to its origin.

2

Chapter 1

REBUFFED

Said to be the "sister world" of the Earth, "Oceanus" was the one habitable and naturally life bearing planet in the Ra system – and its surface would die soon. A casual observer from Earth would never think its human colonists were aware of that, judging by the behaviour of the throngs of adults and wide-eyed children, milling and scrambling about, in the cathedral like atrium of their government building. This seat of the administration was situated in central Janitra, the capital city of the human society which now called Oceanus home.

The excited chatter of the crowds reverberated brightly, bell like, in the lofty spaces above their heads, but most of these people existed in a state, not so much of some blissful ignorance of the doom awaiting them, but of a self-satisfied confidence that other people must simply have got it wrong. There were of course, many who had not yet heard the news but just as many who did not pay any serious heed at all to the communique recently brought from faraway Earth to this peaceful, tranquil world.

Most of the crowds in the building today were merely sightseers. Some of the adults were businesspeople while others were political representatives, elected to office by the citizenry of Oceanus. The bustling throng in this place of government was probably a cross-section of the population of Oceanus, who, altogether, made up a relatively small group of around 3.5 million people. The official designation of their world was, "Oceanus Alpha," but most everyday people ignored the letter designation, a leftover from the days of the early pioneers. The name itself was derived from the mythology of the ancient Greek and Classical civilisations of old

Earth and meant, the "worldwide ocean stream", in the middle of which existed the habitable land. There could be no truer description of this wondrous planet.

The original colony's descendants now formed a largely conservative but unashamedly conservationist commonalty; a largely agrarian and, most Earth people would say, unsophisticated population. So, for example, for many, perhaps most, of those in the government building today their only familiarity with sight of its grand, ornate, architecture would have been through looking at photographs; probably old ones.

These were people whose forebears founded the original colony just over 132 Earth-standard years earlier, the first human colony amongst the stars; on a planet slightly smaller than the Earth, with a warmer global climate, and vast oceans which precluded any more than one third of its surface being covered by land. Unusually, for human beings, these pioneers had not begun a process of ruthless exploitation.

Such a "New World" had long been a dream of humanity but had finally been realised; starting a truly unique experiment amongst the stars, forged by settlers from Earth in the early twenty fourth century of the Common Era. The legacy of their struggle to survive was a population now largely self sufficient. They were at peace with the planet and its giant oceans, comfortable with its wild, untamed wildernesses; dedicated to the wide scale preservation of the planet, especially its unsettled parts, which was more than 95% of it. And the descendants of the founders were also, probably uniquely, at peace with themselves – as far as humans can ever be.

All that was about to change.

Radically.

Most observers on Earth and in the many, smaller, colonised worlds of the old Solar System, the place known now and universally, as the "Home System", would have said that in their lifestyles the people of Oceanus had regressed. In some ways, perhaps they had, but the small size of their population had allowed them to make a fresh start. They were aware of the incredible technology, known in the Home System, as "tek", without which their forebears could not have reached Oceanus. But they would say it was no longer a priority and so, the details of that technology had been forgotten.

But this was not a primitive or medieval society, for they still lived with a degree of advanced technology but for the most part the majority simply regarded it as of low importance, preferring to live in a less sophisticated way. Instead, their normal, consistent, state of technology was of a style or form which generous minded Home System commentators had dubbed, "mid-to-late twentieth century simplicity". Others, more cynical, called it, "simple-mindedness", or even worse.

The Oceanus people would have accepted the epithet, "simpler lifestyle" perhaps, but would never consider themselves as innocent, or, despite Home System prejudices, naïve. They were quick to point out that they had recently undergone a hard-fought political struggle with the Allied Home System government, the main governing body for most polities on old Earth and in the Solar System colonies. Oceanus had won the arguments and by this means the planet had been freed from Home System governance and oversight; an achievement secured in a series of landmark political victories, enshrined now in the famed "Treaty of Algarion".

But, for many in the Home System, their preconceptions about the ignorance of the Oceanus populace, were being roundly confirmed by the reception of the Oceanus government and its people, to recent scientific discoveries of dreadful urgency. Most observers outside the Ra system could point to the heedlessness of the population, and its leaders, to the imminent threat to their lives, their homes, everything they knew. For that threat amounted to nothing less than the destruction of most species of animals on the planet, both on the land and in its great seas, and the ravaging of its plant life. It was probably true to say that no-one, or extremely few, understood the full, stark, reality; that a flaming nightmare of annihilation threatened, very soon, to explode into the lives of every single one of them.

***

In a large office, completely panelled with plain, dark stained, wood, but spartanly furnished, the tall and gangly figure of Mike Delenio Tanniss sat and stared at the brilliant, azure, sky of Oceanus, blazing through a large window the other side of the large desk opposite him. He noticed how that beautiful sky was deepening in hue inexorably as the afternoon wore steadily on.

Mike was the 23-year-old official Secretary of the Home System Navy ship, "The Monsoon", recently arrived from the Solar System; a giant interstellar vessel which was a "carrier" ship, and the flagship of the whole fleet; the pride of the Navy. As such it was the 25th century, space-based equivalent of the aircraft carriers of old, which once plied the seas of Earth back in the 20th and early 21st centuries.

The room into which Mike and his distinguished colleague had been ushered was situated at the rear of the Oceanus Government Building, where throngs still milled. Mike felt that the office, on the third floor of that building, smelled of antique mustiness. Freshly arrived from the Home System he felt enveloped, almost swallowed, by the fading upholstery of a once plush, antique armchair, a piece of furniture that had clearly seen better days.

The ship's Secretary made for a tall and willowy figure whose boyish frame was topped with a mein of dark brown, almost black, thatch framing an elliptical face free from the vicissitudes of age. Yet his unlined and slightly quirky countenance gave the impression of a person who has studied hard and long; perhaps too much. Even so, there was a hint of more than mere studiousness there, as Mike had seen many things in his young life that, even in the 25th century, had been glimpsed, for real, by very few.

He had regarded the many worlds he'd seen through piercing silver-grey eyes, and, a central plank of his character, he was well aware that many women were attracted to his sharply featured good looks, particularly those eyes. Though he found the fact amusing, he was nevertheless extremely happy with this good fortune, and had taken full advantage of it. But here, he was far from the familiar surroundings of the ship and the female members of its crew. He sat in the silent, unfamiliar environment of the wood panelled office, perplexed, more than a little aggrieved now and wondering what he was really doing on this world. The office was very warm, reflecting the sultry subtropical environment outside, which did nothing to soothe his feelings of disquiet.

Next to Mike, also sunken into a similarly antique chair, was the person he'd arrived on Oceanus with; someone with a slightly more important function aboard the flagship, for this was none other than the ship's current senior officer, Arkas Aurelius Majorian Tenak. An Admiral of the Home System Navy, Tenak carried the main responsibility for this mission and was, in many, but not necessarily all, ways, Mike's senior officer on board the ship. Mike actually felt, begrudgingly, that Tenak was, sometimes, more like a mentor, at least when he was in the "old man's" good books.

A well-respected figure in the Navy – the space-based force which now protected the Earth and all the colonised worlds of the Solar System – the 58-year-old Admiral regarded the worlds from care-worn but alert eyes set in a weathered yet lightly lined and somewhat square jawed face. An explorer of numerous star systems and a veteran, Tenak had a definite presence and a bearing befitting his rank, not that he was arrogant about it. Far from it. In fact, Mike was constantly amazed by the man's lack of such vices and it even irked him slightly, for he knew deep down *he* would not be like that, were he in his shoes.

Even though Mike was at least 10 centimetres taller than Tenak, the Admiral's presence actually seemed to dwarf him. Well, he was, after all, a lot older, thought Mike. Still, he had to admit, reluctantly, to rather liking this possibly avuncular figure, currently the overall commander of The Monsoon. For the ship had a Captain too, the de-facto, regular, commander. This was the strident and some would say, fierce, Captain Ssanyu Ankh Ebazza who ran the ship in most ways but who, on those occasions when Tenak accompanied her, was required to give precedence to him. As he had accompanied her on most of the ship's missions over the last few years this arrangement was the norm and she, for her part, begrudged it not one iota. But Mike's relationship with her was not like the one he had with Tenak, and he, for one, was grateful for the Admiral's presence on the ship on most occasions.

Part of the older man's appeal to Mike was that Tenak represented a presence which seemed to signal that things would work out, at least most of the time. It was just as well because the rest of the time he just felt he was a pain in the arse.

The true reason for the presence here, of these two, after a bone jarringly long journey, something impossible only a few generations earlier, was a scheduled and vitally important meeting with the President of Oceanus herself, Arbella Nefer-Masterton. But that meeting had been fixed for 45 minutes earlier.

Patience not being one of his virtues Mike fidgeted, hung his head in his hands and sighed long and hard, for what must have been the twentieth time. He surveyed the room once more. No, he thought, nothing seemed to have changed since he had last scanned its entire length, breadth and height, as far back as 3 or 4 minutes ago. The wood panelling had piqued his admiration at first, but it had ceased to claim his interest long ago. He felt it inexplicable that he and the admiral had been left utterly alone for so long. That would not have happened with the government, back on Earth, or in one of the massive orbital stations. Didn't these people appreciate how mind-numbingly far he and Tenak had travelled to get here for this damnatious interview, especially since interstellar travel was not a routine occurrence – for anyone? Why wasn't there a welcoming committee? Something to mark the occasion. Or at least some stimulating kaffee, preferably iced?

Mike was suddenly glad he had Tenak with him, or his sense of frustration might have boiled over, and he'd have just walked. But where to? The shuttle had long since departed for the ship. Even with Tenak present he felt isolated, or more likely, stranded, in a way that simply didn't really happen on The Monsoon, a place where he enjoyed almost continuous social interaction. He surmised that Oceanus was likely to be the sort of place where you could very easily die of boredom. Yet again, he wondered why they were bothering with all this. He knew the Admiral took a dim view of his impatience, so he didn't bother to complain to him, but it didn't stop him glancing sideways at his companion, trying to assess *his* mood.

Tenak was busy radiating his silent but resolute determination routine; his "ambassadorial" persona, or ar least, trying to give that impression. Knowing that Tenak would not have appreciated him making a fuss Mike could only yawn, loudly, for the umpteenth time and stretched his long spindly arms above him, reaching toward the high grey, undecorated ceiling.

He had surprised himself by his original enthusiasm to actually set foot on this planet but ever since then had been having multiple "second thoughts", as he sweltered in the mid-afternoon heat of the Oceanus day. This dammy subtropical world, he thought. The locals seemed not to notice the heat but then they wouldn't, would they? He couldn't see any sign of an airtemp unit or control screen in the room, and he tugged at the stiffly raised collar of his formal white Secretary's uniform tunic, trying to let some air in. In the limpid humidity his midnight blue uniform trousers clung damply to his gangly legs.

He cursed the fact that he hadn't thought to requisition the specialised temperature control undergarments available on the ship, yet he'd known it would be warm down here. But not as hot as this. He stared again out the window, beyond the desk. It didn't look as though it could open and even if it did, he supposed it probably would only have let more warmth in – from out there – in what passed for streets; a place so different from anything back in the Solar System. The lightly urbanised environment outside hardly seemed to keep at bay the huge, wild and intimidating "outdoors" of this planet. And it looked as hot out there as it had been when they had arrived on the planet.

Stretching his spaghetti-like legs out in front of him. His feet could nearly touch the desk, an ornate thing, which he presumed was Nefer-Masterton's "official" desk. He huffed loudly and scanned the room again, for want of something better to do. On the top of the capacious piece of furniture in front of him sat a small, very old-fashioned, lump of a computer unit, or at least he thought that's what it was. Keeping it company was a large, block like thing which he took to be a sort of screen. It had to be an ancient monitor, didn't it? How quaint.

As he shifted his position uncomfortably, he glanced again at Tenak and suddenly caught the man, regarding him with a mixture of amusement and irritation. The Admiral hardly seemed perturbed by the heat at all, despite wearing his full, vivid purple, uniform with its gold braiding and peaked, similarly braided, hat. Mike doubted whether Tenak would even have bothered wearing the temp-control underclothes anyway and, in his head, he could almost hear him berating Mike, with words like, 'You're a ship's Secretary. This kind of thing goes with the territory. Been at it for three years, haven't you?' But Tenak actually said nothing. He didn't have to. With mounting chagrin, he realised that Tenak would be absolutely right.

But there was something else troubling Mike; something infinitely more important. This mission seemed different, somehow. It was something subtle, invisible to the senses, but still there. He wanted to put his finger on it; try to make out its shape in the bright daylight. Whatever it was, it had been a presence since landing here and the prickly feeling it produced continued to elude him. The one thing he was sure of was that it was intimately connected with the very nature of their "mission". Everyone back home, and on the ship, knew this world was existing on a knife-edge but, somehow, down here, he felt that it would lead to his own personal downfall. Maybe, the Admiral's as well. But how? Why? After a few seconds he realised his mistake: overthinking it. Nah, he decided, and dismissed it as arcane musings.

He continued to ponder on what had brought him here, not just the mission but his relatively new career. As ship's Secretary Mike was not strictly a member of the crew, and although he fell under the overall command of the Admiral and, for that matter, the Captain too, this held only up to a point. Beyond that, his position meant that, in many ways he was his own boss. And, although it felt as though the Admiral was his "compadre", he was a friend who had an unfortunate habit of making awkward "requests" of him. And he, for reasons he couldn't fathom, had a habit of complying with them. Up to a point.

Although what Tenak sought usually took the form of asking for his advice on scientific matters, despite the contingent of professional scientists on board the ship, he also asked about more esoteric things. Worse, he frequently made requests which, somehow, came out more as demands; demands Mike sometimes resented, but to which he usually felt obliged to accede. And once he'd agreed to do something he was caught and Tenak knew it. Though the Admiral was normally easy-going he would brook no weaselling out once a request made had been agreed. He was usually capable of dealing with Tenak's awkwardness, but it was not worth upsetting his relationship with the man to withhold assistance. Mike also realised soberly, he didn't want to risk losing the good will that came of being considered Tenak's erstwhile advisor and confidante. The Admiral was a possible way to a secure his career, one he had taken up in place of an abortive academic career.

Ostensibly, the reason for his presence here was the subject of the Admiral's most recent appeal, one for which Tenak had had to cajole him to accompany him to this meeting with the President. Captain Ebazza had stayed on The Monsoon, as it was considered not strictly protocol, and, in fact, very unwise, for the Captain to leave the ship at the same time as the Admiral. In any case, Mike knew, it was, in reality, his *job*, when required, to liaise with third parties, and to lend support to the commanding officer, if warranted. In addition, the Secretary suspected that, on this occasion Tenak wanted someone he knew would not balls up delicate discussions with Nefer-Masterton. Despite his acknowledgement of his own impatience and, he also grudgingly admitted, often precipitous behaviour, he was proud to have the Admiral's reliance on his ability to behave with the proper decorum. And his ability to attend to the minutiae of occasions like this.

He had shown an aptitude for legal and quasi-legal matters, even though his background, before joining the government Secretariat, was in theoretical physics, not law. The current mission, he mused, was more a matter of diplomacy; quintessentially, to find out why Arbella's government had shown an astonishing lack of concern about the findings of the "Pan Solar System Science Consortium". The full details of their conclusions, all four thousand pages of text, had been communicated to Oceanus only three standard months ago.

To say the news had been very bad for Oceanus was an understatement of staggering and genuinely cosmic proportions, and while it was understood that the OA government would need time to digest the news, consider their response and plan for the future, their *actual* response had been mystifying. That was especially so, because the infodata on the probe had set out the clear implications of a failure to heed its dire warnings. The formal reply from Oceanus, also sent by automated probe and received by the Home System weeks later, had been baffling to scientists and politicians alike.

Mike's understanding was that the Oceanus authorities had simply made a bare acknowledgement of the warnings and an obvious reluctance to make any significant comment on them. Mike was astounded, as was nearly everyone else, back home. The news that the world of Arbella's people was under severe threat of destruction, had been acknowledged here as though it were a routine request for a new trade deal.

It was also probably true, mused Mike, that the Oceanus reply had not disputed the Home System findings. It had simply made no significant comment, not even alarm, and said that they would take the news "under so-advisement" and that their own scientists, known here as "natural philosophers" would consider the matter at length. Apart from expressing gratitude for the info-data the reply had been decidedly non-commital.

Tenak, one of only three full Admirals in the whole Navy, had been sent to find out the reasons for the clipped, not to say, laconic, response and to reassure Arbella that the Home System would do all in its power to assist the people of this world. The thought, back home, was that the Oceanus people must have been so overawed, so devastated, by the news, that suitable words had failed them. As a seasoned Admiral, Tenak was classed as a senior envoy, but more than that, he had been empowered by the Allied Government to present the Home System's "rescue plan", itself drawn up in conjunction with the Navy.

This called for Tenak to help the OA government to start drafting their own plan and to help iron out any conflicts between strategies. He could also offer to begin taking Oceanus citizens aboard The Monsoon, to start the process of evacuating them back to the Solar System. But it was not anticipated that large numbers of evacuees would be transported on this initial trip. Time constraints had been such that The Monsoon simply wasn't yet ready for that, even though, under pressure from the Home System government the Navy had already carried out some modification to the flagship. But an ambitious program of modification and refitting of ships, to accommodate evacuees, was already underway.

And of course, Mike realised only too well, that this was the real reason for his presence today, with the Admiral but he just couldn't work out how this had become necessary. Not just that but as far as he was concerned, their behaviour since he and Tenak had contacted them from orbit, before getting permission to land, had been unimpressive to say the least.

The Admiral hadn't said anything for a long time now. Mike wondered if he were thinking, like him, that the authorities' behaviour looked unfavourable, not to say, disrespectful. He pondered whether Tenak had thought it best to refrain from discussing the situation openly in case Arbella's people were listening in, though he had been unable to see any obvious signs of surveillance. They hadn't had the chance to sweep the room with detectors; had not even brought one with them. There was a basic piece of Navy kit designed to detect surveillance and it would have settled the matter in less than a second, but Mike wondered if the Oceanus people would have even bothered to snoop. Not everyone had access to the "hi-tek" accoutrements of such things, and probably not the Oceanus people.

The question of whether they would they be subjected to eavesdropping irked him, so he thought it worth asking Tenak, who seemed, strangely, fixated on the dark stained wooden desk in front of them. Poor guy. He must be feeling the heat after all, thought Mike. And the heat from Ra, the orange-yellow sun of the Oceanus system, was at the very centre of this whole affair; the reason why they were here. The star was causing problems even now, thought Mike, sourly. The thing had not yet swept around fully to this side of the building and its obliquely slanting rays were only now beginning to illuminate the frame of the "picture window". It would soon turn even hotter. He turned to Tenak and started to say,

'Do you think they might be carrying out ….?'

But Tenak cut him off sharply, as if he'd known what he had been thinking. Well, he probably had, thought Mike. The Admiral said curtly, 'No. Not down here,' and looked as if he was going to say something else when the wooden door set in the wall on the other side of Tenak opened and swung inwards. Even as he breathed a sigh of relief that something was at last happening Mike wondered again at the sight of such another old-fashioned thing. These door things down here all seemed to work on some sort of archaic hinge mechanism. How odd. But who was this entering, imperiously? Another minor official, like the silent mouthed ones who had politely shown them here in the first place?

No; in breezed Arbella Nefer-Masterton herself. He recognised her by her picture and brief biog', on The Monsoon's ShipNet. In the flesh, he realised with some surprise, she had definite presence, a charisma, about her, even without the, all too obvious, wide silver braiding which hung around her neck. Good, he thought. Progress at last. However, she said absolutely nothing, not even acknowledging their presence. Mike frowned. Tenak's expression didn't change. What is it with him, mused Mike?

Tenak then stood, out of respect, and surreptitiously tugged at Mike's sleeve. Not necessary, thought his companion, with some resentment, as he was already rising to his feet.

Nefer-Masterton, a slim woman, of medium height and maybe in her mid-50s, had short, bobbed light brown hair, fringed with silver-grey, framing a round face. It was, thought Mike, something that would be called a characterful face, etched with light laughter lines, or maybe they were worry lines? Even so, he mused, not bad. Not bad at all, for a woman of her age. Her plain black dress reached almost to the floor, Nefer-Masterton's only decoration being the silver braid. Plain and simple. How different to most women of power back on the Earth, thought Mike.

She was not accompanied by anyone. There were no aides or "uber-assistants", as they were known back home. She stood with her back to them for a second, as she closed the door, fussed with it for a moment, then turned and made her way, silently, almost bird-like, to the other side of her dark desk, where she sat incredibly easily on a plain wooden chair, an object as ancient looking as everything else here.

And still she said nothing. To Mike's astonishment she began to fiddle with her ancient comp monitor. Tenak continued to stand but Mike began to sit again, until he caught a sharp look from his companion. But he also knew Tenak didn't abide ungracious behaviour from those he was scheduled to meet, but now, as often, the man was unreadable. This is going to be fun, he thought, with the anticipation of someone about to start sucking on a raw lemon.

After a minute or two of peering at her screen, the contents of which were of course hidden from the view of her guests, their host finally sat bolt upright and at last turned her face to her off-world visitors. She finally looked interested, thought Mike.

'Good mid-tidings gentilhomms', she said, with what Mike perceived to be a peculiar mix of the Oceanus vernacular and that the Home System polite way of addressing women and men.

'Please, be sitting yet sitting,' she said.

Pure "Oceanus speak", thought Mike.

Aside from noticing that she gave no apology for the delay Mike was taking in her ruddy cheeks and outdoors complexion, her bright and intelligent eyes. He allowed his own eyes to track down her long neck and follow the swell of her breasts, well-hidden below the dark dress, and found himself wondering if he could talk her into … Nar, of course not. She was way above his league. She was after all the highly respected leader of Oceanus Alpha Independence Party and a shrewd and democratic politician, though what exactly that meant down here was anyone's guess. Even in the Home System it might not necessarily have stood for a great deal, but after the Rebel Wars people had come to learn that it was better than the alternative.

The ship's universal database had indicated that Nefer-Masterton, only the second President of Oceanus since they gained independence, was considered by many to be a difficult person. What they had seen so far didn't dissuade Mike from this. Disrespect could probably be added to her list of attributes. Still, he was her guest here and he knew he'd have to show *her* respect. He found himself mentally rehearsing the fact that on this world this person, this leader, was to be addressed as "Madama President", or, alternatively, though rarely, as "Domina".

Admiral Tenak returned Nefer-Masterton's customary greeting, choosing to use the same mixture of vernaculars. Mike was impressed.

Then Nefer-Masterton said, 'Gentilhomms, I am seeing I have honori of speaking to an Admiral, one of few-such in the Home System Navy. Honori, indeed. Also, I speak to the Secretary ... Tanniss? Assign-ed to The Monsoon?' Arbella glanced at her comp screen again.

Mike continued to regard her with interest. He was intrigued by her continued use of a modified form of Anglo-Span. That was the dominant idiom in the vastly distant Solar System, and the original vernacular of her own people, but the culture of Oceanus and its dialect had grown distinct from the one back home; the result of having developed separately on this planet since the first pioneers had arrived, more than a century earlier. Not that it mattered. Both she and they understood each-other well enough and after all, they had not learnt any Oceanus-speak. To Mike, it just seemed an archaic idiom. Another inconvenience here.

Smiling broadly, Tenak confirmed who they were. Mike remembered the ceaseless, probing questions put to each of them, by officials, when they'd arrived at the "spaceport". They were clearly unused to having visitors from another world. Mike had a vague inkling that Tenak had met this "femna", the Home System word for woman, some years ago, but she didn't seem to recognise him, and he said nothing about it to her. Interesting.

Nefer-Masterton took him by surprise as she suddenly launched into a sort of diatribe, sounding very abrupt and yet she continued to smile in a diplomatic kind of way,

'Gentilhomms, I am sure the surface of our world is not going to explode or catch fire! Or any the like thing. Not so at all. Please now be telling me why it was necessary to send the largest vessel in the Solar System Navy, some 123 light years, to see me in person? You have come extreme long ways for little reward, fraid.'

Mike's mouth virtually dropped open and he heard a sharp intake of breath from his companion, but he could see the Admiral was trying to prevent himself from looking shocked. He wasn't entirely successful. But the President's statement *was* shocking. Yet he knew Tenak would want to retain some semblance of decorum and an ability to exercise at least some control of this situation. To Mike, it pretty much looked as if any such control was way off the menu.

Tenak quickly recovered his composure, saying, 'Madama President, I have to say I am … I find your comment somewhat … troubling. We have indeed come a long way. The longest distance anyone can come from one people, to speak to the leader of another people. And the intention was to discuss a plan for *evacuation,* Madama President. Or at least, the best way to begin such a process. I ask you to …'

'Admiral, sirra,' said Masterton, cutting him off, 'you should be knowing that most citizenry of this planet do not so believe that all life on the surface of our world will be destroy-ed by our star, within the next few years. Nor have they been given such an reason to think as such. So, they are not convince-ed that the entire population needs to evacuate. Nor am I, sirra. So, hear me well.'

Mike could hardly believe what he was hearing. What was up with these people?

'I'm very sorry to hear you say that, Madama President,' said Tenak, 'even though we were aware your Government was … sceptical … of our warnings about your star. But not to *this* extent.' His speech had become even again, and he now paused momentarily, for effect, despite the risk of her jumping in again, then continued, 'Your Government's replies to the messages we sent in the last few auto-probes didn't really indicate this level of ... disagreement. The Home System Allied Government simply felt ... no, hoped, that a face to face meeting would be conducive to a meeting of minds and assurance that we will do all we can to assist in ...'

Interrupting again, Arbella harrumphed at this comment and gazed again at her comp screen, leaving a dangling silence. Mike noticed that Ra had already swung farther around, and its molten rays had begun to flood across the side of Masterton's desk. The heat in the room began to rise in sympathy. The average temperature on this planet was significantly higher than that of Earth. So, why didn't this place use airtemp control? Perhaps they did. Perhaps Arbella was using the climate as a further means to exert pressure on them. She seemed quite unperturbed by the heat. There was no perspiration evident on her face and he was quite intent on that. He felt a little awe by her, and definitely attracted. She was mysterious, as well as powerful and he was interested.

Tenak glanced at Mike, and he realised he should do something to support the man at this point. He remembered that that was why he was here. As impatient and despairing of these people as he felt, he would try to be as tactful as possible, so as not to upset Tenak.

'Domina,' said Mike, as graciously as he could, but firmly, with not too obsequias a tone as he could muster, 'we see that there is much to discuss before we institute the "plan".' He risked glancing at Tenak to check if he approved. They had not discussed the possibility that she would object to *everything.* Tenak shot him a knowing look. Good. He continued, 'We genuinely hoped that we could begin a productive dialogue with your Society of Natural Historians and with the School of Natural Philosophers, to try to come to some sort of consensus. Most Home System scientists are *strongly* of the opinion that the surface layers and atmosphere of your star will suffer a massive upsurge. This would lead, very likely, to the complete extinction of most life on the land surface of Oceanus, within a *maximum* time frame of 10 Earth years.' Mike had wisely resisted the urge to say, "*our* scientists". He paused for a second. Curiously, she hadn't interrupted yet.

'I do not think we have seen any evidence that would contradict that,' he added, wide eyed, tring to avoid sounding smug.

Arbella looked unfazed, apart from a slight curling of her lips, as if she had tasted something like cat's pee, but as far as he and the Admiral were concerned the science was conclusive. The biosphere of this world was at serious risk of destruction. The entire surface of this blue, incredibly beautiful and wild looking world; the planet he had gazed at from orbit, for a long time, from orbit, was doomed.

Tenak had removed his peaked hat and it now sat in his lap, its lopps of braiding, like the decoration on his uniform cuffs, catching a glint of Ra's ruddy afternoon light. His normally neatly groomed, greying, hair was now becoming tousled as he ran his hands through it with evident frustration. Mike could see tiny silvery trails made by sweat, running down the side of his seasoned, chunky face.

'Yes, so I am well aware such of the opinions of your Solar System scientists,' came Arbella's reply. She seemed even more self assured now and continued, 'but I am certaint you are aware also of the opinion of our natural historians – that your prediction is – at best, in extremis, premature, and exaggerated. My understanding is that we now do accept that Ra, our sun, is more variable than we – and all – were believing, but tis certainly not about to "go nova, go erupt, or upsurge," or any such thing.' After pausing a moment, she added, 'And by the way, tis the School of Meta-teleosophists, not "Natural Philosophers."'

The way the President settled back in her chair reminded Mike of the leading professor at one of the Academies he had attended in his late teens, but even more austere.

Tenak started, 'But, Madama Presi...' before Nefer-Masterton again hijacked him.

'Be forgiving of me Admiral but might I be asking why it is that I speak to an Admiral of the Sur-Navy, and with him a member of the Civil Secretariat?'

Internally, Mike bridled. He was surprised at Tenak's apparent tolerance of this situation, but the Admiral persisted, with tact, saying, 'I believe my Secretary has already referred to the dialogue we wish to see between our respective groups of researchers, and I can assure you that we have indeed brought our own team of scientists, our "Natural Philosophers", if you will. It was simply hoped that Secretary Tanniss and I could open an earlier, more diplomatic discussion, a constructive dialogue about the process of evacuation.'

Arbella snorted lightly, 'I am yet sorry, but I cannot see any truefold diplomats, Admiral.'

Mike looked down to hide his shock. Wasn't she aware of Tenak's status? For his part, Tenak hesitated only a moment before replying to the point forcefully, 'Perhaps you should know that both Senior Secretary Tanniss and I have the confidence of the full Home System Allied Government.'

Mike added, 'And it may not have been understood – at home – Madama President, that there would be this level of...' He hesitated, trying to find the right words, but allowed it to become a ruse, giving Nefer-Masterton the chance to supply her own words.

'...this level of opposition, *Mer* Secretary?' she said, using the polite form of title for a man, used both at home and on Oceanus.

'Quite so,' he returned.

'Be not a-worry, Mer Tanniss, I have taken into account your submissions and those of Admiral Tenak. In such particulars, I am also aware of your senior position, Admiral,' she said, now in more conciliatory tones, 'but since you so mentioned diplomatica, I still think that a personal visit by a *full ambassador* or some such senior member of the HS Government Diplomatic Corps would have been much in order. I have no doubt they are thinking it unnecessary,' she said, giving them a swingeing, sideways, glance.

Mike's hoped for bit of down-time on this beautiful world was evaporating fast as he realised the process of trying to convince these people of the dangers they really faced would be a long drawn out affair. But how could he think of down-time at that moment, when the fate of over 3 million people were in the balance? Well, he wasn't to blame for Arbella's intransigence, nor any of the scientists back home, or on the ship. He also reminded himself, conveniently, that the disaster was probably still quite a way off at this point. There was enough time to turn these people around. Surely? Well, maybe. Maybe not. But he also knew that the intervening period wouldn't stop Tenak wanting to "complete the mission", which meant he would look to Mike for answers, ideas and help. Yes, he could see his longed for "vacspell" disappearing fast.

But President Nefer-Masterton was proving to be a foil even for Tenak's erudite attempts at diplomacy. Her intransigence might prove too difficult for both of them. Mike suddenly felt like a fish out of water, acutely embarrassed by the situation into which he had been thrust by this mission. This situation was bigger than both him and Tenak, but they were pretty much stuck with it, because he couldn't envisage the Admiral agreeing to return home as soon as the ship's powerplant had recharged.

Nefer-Masterton gave her guests a wan half smile. Mike thought she actually looked as if she'd swallowed some that old cat's pee. 'Perhaps I am being tinely bit harsh, gentilhomms,' she said, 'and I know you are yet trying very hard to convince me and I am certain you are having the best of intentions.'

Mike couldn't help feeling her tone sounded a little like she was addressing five-year-old children. Nefer-Masterton regarded them in silence, for a moment, and again, using conciliatory tones continued, 'Speaking such of evacuation gentilhomms, I am sure the Sur-Navy has actually done their mathmaticsa on this. It seems to me ... obvious, your word would be, that even if our people are wild-wrong about Ra, the logistical implications of a mass move of our population - a distance of 123 light years - is yet astounding. The social and political ramifications also be stagrinten!' She held her hands out toward them, palms up, as though appealing to their reasonableness. In truth, Mike felt, she was not interested in reason very much. She was interested in politics, and, right now, she was playing a dangerous game which threatened to explode in the faces of all the people on this world.

'The Home System Government *has* done its homework, Domina,' Tenak persisted. He paused for effect, then continued, 'and it is thought that with enough preparation a continuous series of evacuations *would* succeed, but the figures show it would have to begin in earnest *within the next year*, Madama. Even then, it could take nearly ten years. But, we are able to begin preliminary evacuation right now, of small numbers.'

Nefer-Masterton didn't give him a chance to go further, doing her pedagogue thing again, 'Admiral, well aware, I am, of the implications if we are wrong but can you not see why immediate evacuation is out of the question, specialry in view of opposition from *so many* of our scientists and engineers? What am I to do, gentilhomms? I am indeed sorry, but your people will have to come up with far more convincing data than they have unto this date. Besides, I am thinking that not all of your natural philosophers are equally convinced as you, are they Admiral?' Masterton almost spat out those last words with emphasis.

Tenak began, 'Well, no, but…'

'And even those who would support the main conclusions of your study group are yet uncertain about the time scale involved,' she said in perfect Anglo-Span, and, without pausing continued, 'Some of *them* are predicting an upwelling in Ra's photosphere in about 50 of our years. And yet – others are saying 100 or 150 years. Yet others – not at all!'

'Well, most of them agree on 10 years – absolute maximum,' said the Admiral firmly but quietly, 'and, as you say, the implications are much too important to ignore, if they are correct. As we believe them to be.'

'Yes, yes. If indeed,' she snorted, 'but I am sure you mayst be aware that *our* people are saying this explosion – should it e'en happen at all – will not occur for 20 to 30 millenia. *Millenia*, Mer Admiral. By that forward-time we may have moved on to other worlds, other planets, or we might not be in existenz anymore, anywayins,'said Masterton, lapsing again into the vernacular of her world. She raised her hands once more, in apparent exasperation. There was a deadening pause; a humourless lacuna. A voice broke into it, at length.

'Not everyone,' said Mike, very quietly. The effect was dramatic in the circumstances; a fact he was very pleased about.

'Your pardonri?' said Nefer-Masterton, frowning.

'You implied that all your people disagree with our data, but I don't think that's quite correct, is it?' returned the young man.

'Ah. I am supposing you mean Muggredge,' she said with a dismissive roll of the eyes.

'Grand Physica Muggredge, I believe,' said Tenak, softly, using the OA vernacular, 'the *Professier* of the School of Natural History.'

There was an embarrassed silence from Nefer-Masterton while she seemed to gather her thoughts. As they sat for the couple of seconds she took to recover, Mike's attention immediately alighted on the fact that the planet's rotation had now caused the late afternoon sunlight to begin to flood through her picture window. It illuminated the far corner and wall of the room with an orange – yellow glow, wiping away the remaining shadows and adding yet more heat to the room.

'I suppose you are yet right about that, Admiral,' she conceded, 'but I am seeing it makes no real difference. The Grand Physica and his small team is, in this now-time, quite out-voted by the others in the bigger study group, therein being 31 of them, I think. No, I am sorry Admiral, but the Planetary Council for Natural Philosophy is in disagreement with the Home System's findings – and your proposals for soon-time evacuation proceedings. Unless you can point to any dramatic new evidence this day, fraid our discussion must be at an end.'

The two men sat before her, motionless; stunned into silence. That's it, thought Mike?

'I understand you will be staying on Oceanus Alpha for a-whiles?' she said.

'Yes, Domina,' said Tenak, sighing as he did so. 'We would be grateful if our science teams could discuss these issues with your Study Group, and we also have to carry out a schedule of maintenance on our ship before returning. We were unfortunate enough to pick up some unexpected buffering and electrical interference on the way through the Interstellar Conduit.'

The last bit of that was true, anyway, thought Mike.

'Oh, then,' said Arbella, 'wouldst you be so kind as to also carry out your duties under sub-article 1048 of the Home System Charter with Oceanus?'

The two men gave each-other puzzled looks, till Mike suddenly realised what she was talking about. He didn't want to be seen to be reminding Tenak but within a few seconds he could see the Admiral also had it too. That old addendum had set out that the Home System was responsible for maintaining the batteries and engines of the auto-probes stored on satellites in orbit around Oceanus.

The auto-probes were the small, fully powered, automated, vehicles, capable of travelling between Oceanus and the Solar System. In order to avoid unnecessary human travel, they were the means by which all manner of messages, both complex and simple, could be sent back and forth – and that was how the HS had communicated its devastating "news" recently – and how Oceanus had sent their reply, using remote control from the planet's surface. At one time the Oceanus authorities had been able to send the occasional manned spacecraft into orbit itself but Mike guessed it had been a very long time since that happened. Only the OA government had had the technology to do things like that and they were rapidly abandoning such capabilities. It was common knowledge that the "tek" they once had was now largely redundant through lack of use. Regardless, the Article of Agreement was clear that HS ships, both Navy and research vessels, had a duty to carry out maintainance of Oceanus's orbital facilities, if requested.

'We did experience some difficulties when we last did try to operate the autos from here,' Arbella was saying, almost apologetically, a wide smile for once breaking across her features.

'But of course, Madama,' said Tenak, 'we will see to it that maintenance is carried out by our ship.'

'By the sideways,' she said, beginning to look serious again, 'mayst I ask what number are your crew on this occasion? And its make-up?' She almost looked guilty and added as a kind of afterthought, 'Please-so?'

Without the slightest pause Tenak said, 'That's fine Madama. The ship's complement is 48, this trip. Many are engineers, and there are the tek specialists. Then there's a few security guards, the officers of course, and our team of scientists. We have no space marines on this occasion, of course, nor will we or any crew carry any sonic weapons on this planet. And I would assure you our usable landing boats are non-weaponised – all in accordance with your laws. Naturally.'

'Well, then I yet thank you for your open truth-such.'

Mike grinned inwardly. "A few security guards?" The guards made up around twenty-six of the complement, over half of those onboard. That was mostly to keep order with any evacuees they had. Some chance thought Mike. And the ship still had two of the large, armed landing boats, but no Navy officer ever revealed their true strength, even to a supposed ally. Still, in the event of any hostilities neither Tenak nor any officer would ever seek to land an armed boat on a world like Oceanus without direct authority from the Allied Home System Government. And that would only be given in extreme circumstances, as it would constitute, effectively, an act of war; a conflict which Oceanus could never hope to win. The whole thing was completely out of the question here.

Arbella was speaking again. 'Well then yet, Admiral. I must make a request now, which is that you and Mer Secretary are very most welcome to stay on the planet as long as you need. But I would ask that your fellow crewmembers mayst only be allowed in Janitra in no more than groups of five at a time. Any more might be sensed as too much of a Home System presence for our populari. I am sure you yet understand, Admiral. And, Admiral, please do not be allowing your science group to wander thither in the political arena. Such mayst be seen as provocative. No permission has been given for any such to discuss with us formally.'

With as much grace as he thought Tenak could muster Mike heard the Admiral acquiesce to her request.

'That is fine and well then, gentilhomms, thanking you,' said Nefer-Masterton, rising imperiously from her chair, gazing out of her picture window momentarily, before turning to them with a surprisingly genuine smile.

'Thank you, Madama President,' said Tenak graciously.

'Then let me so wish you vastli enjoyable stay here on Oceanus,' said Arbella, 'for both of you. Please yet take advantage of our hospitality and use some time to look around our planet. Perhaps then – you will see the wonderful world-place we have - and why we would need to be absolutely certain of the facts before we would ever so think to abandon it.' She emphasised her last words heavily.

'I should also advise you that we will also need to confer with the heads of the opposition parties here on Oceanus, Domina,' said Tenak, his countenance suddenly dark, as he rose from his chair. Mike observed that he had *not* asked permission this time.

Mike had actually begun to think of that down-time again but now he was guessing what Tenak was going to do. And he wasn't sure he liked it.

'Yes, of course, good Admiral, of course,' she said, 'and so good mid-tidings to you and to Mer Secretary. I am so sorry; do you still say "good afternoon" in the Home System?'

"Thank you, Madama President," Mike said, as he rose, "and yes, we do." He and the Admiral inclined their heads in a polite if perfunctory bow and swept out of the room.

After they had gone Nefer-Masterton stared again out of the picture window and this time she allowed a deeply troubled expression to cloud her face.

*****

Mike and Tenak squeezed through the crowds on their way out through the so called "Great Hall" of the government building. Mike had been impressed by the female official who had escorted them out of Arbella's office, and had it not been for the Admiral's presence, would probably have fed her some sort of chat up routine. Sadly, he felt, it was not to be.

The throngs in the main hall simply added to the heat in the area and the pervading smell reminded Mike of the perspiration, damp towels and polished floors of the exercise gymnasia in his early neonate-school back in the South City State Alliance, on the continent once called Australia.

All sorts of local people milled around them, some eager to take in the sights, others looking tired or care worn. Children abounded. The local modes of dress varied somewhat, but to Mike they all looked dowdy and unadventurous, consisting, mostly, of something akin to boiler suits, or loose-fitting dungarees. Even the colours of their apparel were muted, being various shades of greys, browns or mid blues. How unadventurous and boring, he thought, especially when compared with the flamboyant, though some would say, gaudy, attire currently fashionable all across the Earth, and in many colonies in the Solar System – with some notable exceptions.

He saw a large party of school children following an adult male, presumably their instructor, who explained, in booming tones, the early history of Oceanus, and the origins of this particular building. Much of what he said eluded Mike's comprehension. Curious, he thought, that it had taken such a comparatively short time for such a dialect to develop, but it was a measure of the relative isolation of Oceanus. There was, after all, no way that this world and the Solar System could communicate with each-other directly without the intermediary of crewed or uncrewed spacecraft of some sort. And all such journeys took a long time.

Mike spotted a quiet vestibule to one side of the lobby area, mostly devoid of passers-by. He motioned to Tenak to follow him there. The Admiral looked askance but obliged. He spoke to Tenak in exaggerated whispers, 'You've met her before haven't you, Arkas? Is she always like this? You didn't warn me.'

'Not really,' said Tenak calmly, 'I only met her the once, at a function, here. Long time ago.'

'She didn't seem to recognise you.'

'There were hundreds of VIP's there, Mike. I only got to speak to her for a moment. Seemed very amenable but, of course she wasn't in power then. Just running for nomination in her party. No, I think she's having some sort of pressure put on her right now.'

'By whom?'

'Probably those 'Teleo' boys''

'Huh?'

'The Meta-teleosophist party. Come on Mike, try flying in formation. They're really the main opposition party on Oceanus right now, even though they've got the third largest vote. Not much data on the shipNet about them, or back home, but my guess is they probably have a lot more influence with the people than their share of the vote suggests. Arbella's Independence Party had a very small majority at the last election, Mike. Their lowest since this world attained independence, 14 years ago.'

'I still don't understand any of this,' said Mike in exasperated tones.

'Nor I, Mike. Nor I.' Tenak suddenly seemed to stare into an unfathomable distance.

They were silent then, standing in contemplative silence, watching the churning crowd of sightseers and the official types hurrying about their business. Nefer-Masterton's reaction, to what was probably the most important news ever to reach this world, had stunned them like a sonic gun blast. And Tenak was looking sour faced. Mike broke the silence again, pointing to the slightly comic aspects of the Arbella encounter.

'And what was all that stuff about the "Sur-Navy", he said. 'Does she mean the "Navy *above*"? It hasn't been called that for decades has it?'

'That's not important Mike. Try concentrating on the rest of it.'

'Okay, so what now?'

'It's as we told Arbella. We have to speak to the two main opposition parties, including the Meta-teleos'. Then we need to talk to Muggredge and his team.' Tenak's tones remained calm and measured.

'I don't know what good we can do,' rejoined Mike, sounding as though chewing a spoiled nut, 'cos this place is just weird. And Nefer-Masterton strikes me as being unreasonable – to the point of – of bizarro, Arkas. We're only trying to help her avoid a *little* thing like the *destruction* of her dammy world. Pretty much the next biggest disaster in the whole of human history after the super volcano explosion on Earth.'

'I know Mike. I know that, but I think she actually made one or two very good points,' said Tenak, rather too sagely for Mike's taste.

'Oh really? You think so?'

'Yeah sure. And, by the way, try to be less sarcastic with me. The HS Government *should* have sent a couple of political heavy hitters, not us. Oh, I know I have so-called "Tier 3 envoy" status but, here, now, in real terms, we might as well be mid-line civil servants. Our government should have sent a full-blown ambassador. Might have had more impact.'

'So you think. Then why didn't they?'

'An excess of hubris, Mike. And they never dreamed Arbella's Government would try to argue so strongly against the science. Not like this. It's news to all of us. Things have changed a lot on this planet since I was last here – and not necessarily for the better.'

'Yeah. I think maybe *that's* an understatement. Too early to send a message bouy back home?'

Tenak looked askance, 'And wait for the HS government's response? It could take up to two, maybe three months, before someone gets out here, assuming they have a suitable ambassador. And if we wait, no-one gets evacuated for that whole time.'

'Yeah, well, the autoprobe reply from this place didn't give us any real idea what they were thinking. We can't even let our group of scientists loose on the teleo-whatsits. Perhaps we should have taken some of them to our meeting with Arbella.'

'Wouldn't have made a difference and I don't know if they'd have agreed to see them,' said Tenak and continued, this time gruffly, 'At the moment we're the guys on the duramium lathes, and we're not doing too well, are we?'

Mike was surprised by that. 'That doesn't sound like Arkas Tenak,' he said. 'You actually sounded *negative* then.'

Tenak huffed with impatience. Again, not like him, thought Mike.

'I'm just worried about this planet and its people,' Tenak said, 'and so should you be. We've been given a shit job but I, for one, intend doing it to the best of my ability. You might want to think of something useful. Something that would help me turn this around. I suggest you get that brain of yours into this quick-like.'

There he goes again, thought Mike, expecting me to come up with the answer. That's for the scientists to do, isn't it? he mused. A dark shadow then seemed to move to the forefront of his consciousness. These people have no idea of the scale of what's going to hit them, he thought, *if they don't listen to us ... very soon.*

INTERLUDE

TRANSCENDENCE

The soft glow of multiple energy ribbons streamed past a thick, over-arching, canopy, giving only dim illumination of the habitation cabin's enormous expanse. Coiled metal tentacles glinted in the half-light and cast shadows into the chambers below the deck space, far below the canopy. It filtered into the seemingly fathomless depths below. Ever changing patterns of light and shadow danced across the ship's walls, as the tentacles of the beings harboured within the vast cabin, stirred, and started then to slither, to reanimate and wrap around each-other.

The blue coloured being's huge eyes slipped open but her pendulous upper lids drooped again for several moments before snapping wide once more. The energy ribbons flowing past the cabin were suddenly reflected distortedly in her huge limpid, glass-like eyes. Each of the five cybernetic brains attached to this sentient being's three organic brains streamed sweet thoughts into it, awakening her, then gently chiding it. *Time for organic modules to come back to the Now after so many cycles and consider the preparations we have made for this part of Journey's End,* they urged.

I know, she thought in her most private cerebrum, inwardly shaking the sleepiness of ages from her organic brains.

Mesmerised for a moment by a particularly brilliant ellipsoid of energy which sped toward the outer canopy, then snapped past and, just as suddenly, disappeared, she finally outwardly acknowledged the continuous coaxing.

I know. I awake.

Chapter 2

COMPLACENCY

He stood contemplatively in the top floor room of the hotel, one of two rooms he'd booked for himself and Tenak in an establishment near the central government buildings in Janitra. The name of the city was a Sanskrit word meaning "birthplace", which was certainly appropriate. This was the location of the first, tiny, settlement established by the original pioneers who landed on Oceanus, several generations earlier.

Mike had arranged a room for Tenak on the ground floor, some way from his own. Although he certainly liked the man, he was glad to put a little distance between himself and the Admiral, for a while at least. Mike was in reflective mood, which, he decided, was most unlike him but since the "audience" with Nefer-Masterton this mission had given him more than usual pause for thought. The whole thing was a conundrum and this time he really didn't appreciate the kind of pressure Tenak was placing on him to solve it. Mike usually had an answer, or so Tenak thought, even if they were sometimes half-baked ones, which was doubly unfortunate, because on this particular occasion, he simply didn't have anything to offer.

But then, this situation was unprecedented – for Oceanus, for the Home System, for everyone. In a sudden but unwelcome moment of insight Mike felt the weight of history might somehow be resting on his shoulders. Not just on his of course, more so on Tenak's, but also, for that matter, on the whole crew. How could that have happened? Dammy Home System government, he thought. Dammy Tenak, for that matter. As a ship's secretary this was way above his pay bracket, wasn't it? But how could he maintain his relationship with Tenak, let alone his standing on the ship, if he tried to divest himself of it. This massive burden could end up reflecting badly on the

Navy itself as well as the Allied Home System government, *for whom he worked.* Above all he knew that Tenak would simply not simply pack up and go home. Not this Admiral. Not until he'd tried every means at his disposal to carry out his mission, and he obviously considered Mike to be a part of those means.

And yet strangely, it was also beginning to feel like a worthy challenge. How do you convince scientific illiterates of the veracity of what you are saying? Were these people really scientific illiterates? Surely, yes. It was a terrible irony, Mike realised, that this terrible threat should face a world as beautiful as Oceanus. He was not known for his musings on beauty, other than of the female variety, but Mike had been struck dumb by beguiling loveliness of Oceanus, seen from high orbit. Of course, he had watched many holograms of it, both before and during the journey here, and been suitably awed. But witnessing the reality of the bright blue globe spread out, like a giant marble lying "below" him, was an incomparable vision. Somehow, the planet seemed more vividly blue and brighter than it did in the holo-images. That came as a shock to many, including Mike. As well as its beautiful appearance, the pristine nature of the place; its raw wildness, was a huge attraction to many outsiders, though no kind of "space tourism" of any sort was allowed on Oceanus. And for Mike, who had cause to be there, the wildness was, sadly, not a draw.

The ancient Greek and Roman mythological derivation of the planet seemed appropriate because this world's oceans very nearly straddled the southern, semi-temperate region, blocked by the southern-most part of this world's single large continent. Many said Oceanus was Earth's twin – but this member of the twins, as untamed and mostly unburdened by human depredation had also, so far, been spared the other's excessive population. Mike thought it strange that, if Home System science was right, this world would be ravaged, not by the hand of humanity this time, but by nature herself. And Mike was sure the science was right.

Now, staring out of the large window of his hotel room the ship's Secretary found, ironically, a view totally dominated by the back end of the building next door, which was larger by one floor. But it was just as well, he thought. When he had watched Oceanus from orbit, captivatingly beautiful though it was, it had been quite difficult for him. Seeing the planet's surface from a lower altitude, had been worse. From the "landing boat", the Navy shuttle, which had brought the two of them down to the surface, Mike had observed the landscape getting ever closer. He'd shrunk from that, even though he'd simply watched it as a graphic on the screen in front of him, so he could avoid looking at the real thing through any of the boat's large windows. On just one occasion he'd risked a single glance out of a window, when the ship was still more than 30 kilometres up. It had revealed a frighteningly vast seascape, growing larger, looking like burnished silver, and slowly morphing to a bluish-green landscape as they neared touch down. But Mike didn't suffer from fear of heights. It was, in fact, the sheer vastness, the "openness", of the views, when given scale, which affected him. That's why he'd picked a seat next to one of the boat's wide middle aisleways, far away from the windows.

The landing boats, known to the crew as "LBs", were, outside emergency situations, spacious. The one which brought them down had also been practically empty; he and Tenak being the only passengers. But the boat's roominess actually gave Mike no cause for concern. He was, quite simply, long since used to them and the spaciousness was not exactly "first order". There'd have been no point in becoming a ship's secretary if he couldn't cope with *that*. But, on the other hand, the hugeness of Oceanus's great vistas; the grand sweep of that glittering landscape, had genuinely given him jitters.

His surmised that his malady, whose true origin he could not now guess at, probably derived from something in his childhood. He'd tried various drugs offered by medics but none had worked satisfactorily, or without noticeable side effects. So much for the heady heights of 25th century medicine! "Micro-aperture" brain surgery was a possibility but one which he definitely wished to avoid. He was now very much used to his condition and, as people do in such matters, he had developed various coping strategies.

Despite his qualms he'd still been curious about this world and his scientific inquisitiveness made him want to learn more about it, firsthand. But he had underestimated the effects that coming here would have on him. For now, though, he was stuck with it. And it was, after all, where The Monsoon's assigned mission had taken them. In the vast emptiness of space, where he and the crew spent most of their time, the flagship's confines, though capacious in some places, and therefore once upon a time scary for him, had become familiar and eventually, no longer a problem. But he'd hardly set foot on any of the worlds they'd visited. Most of them were rocky, barren planets anyway, mostly without an atmosphere, or cloaked in dense, poisonous ones; all requiring the use of pressure suits. There were also many massive gaseous giants of course, and they constituted most of the planets they encountered, but it was not possible to land on them, nor desirable.

Mike was usually content to watch small scale holograms of the planets being visited, though he loved to follow the scienctific material which flowed from the encounters. Even looking at the good old Earth itself, from orbit, had originally been a problem for him but one he'd adapted to quickly – except when it came to landing on there.

Upon landing on Oceanus, he recalled the fascinating transit from Janitra "spaceport", a place more properly called an airport, for spacecraft rarely landed there now. He'd left the port in the car of a maglev train running over a single magnetised track; a very old fashioned maglev, if not downright primitive. It had provided some amazing views of Janitra itself. He was okay with urbanised areas. In such places you were normally hemmed in by buildings, not that Janitra really qualified as genuinely urbanised. It was the largest city on this planet, but by Earth standards, absolutely tiny. And Janitra was a touch too "open-plan" for Mike, being practically wild country by comparison with the thick, sprawling, City States on Earth.

Yet he remained curious about the place, his eyes glued to the passing townscape as the maglev had trundled slowly along. He'd witnessed blocks of stone-built, old fashioned, cream or dun-coloured buildings, mostly 3 floors in height but never more than 5 storeys. There was some degree of familiarity about the buildings because they were, after all, simply buildings for people, thought their architecture was definitely antique, most having been built in the early years of colonisation. But there was also an odd and unmistakeable sense of "otherness" about this whole place.

The Capital was a patchwork structure, with extensive areas covered in blue-green plants, very unfamiliar to him, though he recognised many species from the little the ShipNet had on Oceanus. Standing above carpets of smaller shrub-like vegetation were large copses of very tall plants which he knew were effectively this planet's equivalent of trees, though most of these looked more like giant versions of the little horsetail plants found on Earth. And had some others looked like giant replicas of clubmosses? Yet others had had thin trunks stretching straight upwards, ending in fluffy, ungainly looking "leaves", hanging like ringlets and curls. He had examined holos of many of these trees, but they seemed far stranger in reality.

Janitra's built up areas also seemed much cleaner and better planned than most of the City States on Earth, or on Mars. Only the very centre of the place appeared less organised. Could it be called sprawling? No, in comparison to the so called "urbanasia" of the City States back home, that was far too harsh a word. "Random", or "undirected", were perhaps better fits.

As he stood in his room, broiling slowly in the sticky humidity of the Oceanus late afternoon, Mike knew he wouldn't get to see much of the local area, nor the local femnas, unless he left the confines of the hotel, but he was once more frustrated by circumstances. He was obliged to meet Tenak soon, to reconsider the strategy of the mission which, now, was nothing less than to *save the entire population of the planet* – or so it seemed. Ridiculous, he thought, though the Admiral and Nefer-Masterton were right about one thing. The HS government should have sent regular, high-status diplomats, or a full-blown ambassador. Too late right now. He knew Tenak would not scuttle home without trying to meet the current situation head on. The question was how far he would go and how deeply he would drag *him*.

As he filled a tumbler with water Mike flopped down on the only seat in the room, an uncomfortable thing which seemed more like a sack full of flour on legs. He stared out of the window again and suddenly glimpsed some strange creatures flying high up and far away, flapping lazily against a backdrop of bright, fluffy, pinkish, clouds. The creatures looked a bit like bats but, at that distance, they would be too large, surely? He wished he'd brought his electro-binocs. The shipNet's lack of detailed data on the natural life forms of Oceanus was, mused Mike, mostly the result of the reluctance of the OA authorities. But he recalled that these things were probably some of the so called "Rapto-birdles"; large and impressive creatures, like flying reptiles. Some thought them to be like the long extinct pterosaurs of prehistoric Earth, but better-informed opinion was that they differed markedly from them.

The reticence of the Oceanus government, and indeed its people, for the most part, to explicate on the wonders of their world, made classification debates difficult to say the least. Nevertheless, Mike decided he would look up these creatures again, using his wrist device. But not now. Now, he wanted to relax and cool down as he still had a little while before meeting Tenak. He closed his eyes and soon, half-dozing, found himself ruminating on his career up to this point, and the apparent folly which had brought him here. He would try to ignore, for the moment, the obvious conclusion that the current mission was going to get woefully complicated. What was the point of getting worked up?

*

Had he known just what a battle it would become for him, personally, he would not have been able to rest so easily.

*****

The giant spaceship which had brought Mike and the Admiral so unimaginably far from home sailed silently along in orbit around Oceanus; the blue and white marbled hemisphere below it glittering and vast. Next to that the huge ship was effectively microscopic.

The ship's secondary bridge was deep within one of the habitation blocks sited along the inside surface of a huge wheel or ring-like structure, which rotated around the central, axial hub of the ship, to which it was connected by six thick, tubular, spokes. On the bridge Captain Ssanyu Ank Ebazza listened intently to the report being delivered to her by the ship's First officer. He'd tagged it as urgent and decided to deliver it in person, mere seconds after his own subordinate had alerted him to the receipt of incoming sensor readings from one of the ship's "minor AIs". The sensors indicated a massive disturbance on the surface of Ra, an upheaval of a type once known to observers of the Sun in the Solar System, as a Coronal Mass Ejection, now called an "M layer plasma spray event". Ra was baring its teeth and it was much fiercer than anything which ever spawned by the Sun.

"What is a reliable estimate for the arrival of the plasma cloud at this planet?" Ebazza asked, her face a picture of evident but restrained concern. She was a short, yet imposing figure, plump, and immaculate in her vibrant purple uniform. A 38-year-old native of what used to be known as Nigeria, in old Africa; now part of the "Western Africa City State Hegemony", she had, for the most part, retained her regional accent. And that was despite having lived some years in "Eastern Seaboard", the city state which covered what was once the New York and Washington areas, in the old United States. Her bushy hair made her face appear even more imposing and her manner showed she brooked no nonsense, but still, her features were outwardly benign – unless you crossed her.

'Thirty-six hours and 14 minutes, Oceanus time. Best estimate, Captain,' said Lieutenant Commander Gallius Cavo Statton, a tall and wiry African American. in his late twenties, Statton, whose hair was so closely cropped it made his head appear nearly bald, gazed at Ebazza with his trademark "action stations" expression. Its intensity reinforced his reputation as a stickler for duty and for following correct Navy procedure. He had evidently anticipated Ebazza's next question, and probably the one after that, as he advised her that the observed plasma event would set off a very large geomagnetic storm on the planet below. It would be worse in the equatorial and sub-equatorial regions.

'It's also worth noting,' he continued, 'the general increase in Ra's activity we observed before orbital insertion. These make early rogue electrical activity on Oceanus very likely.'

'Explain further,' said Ebazza, her bright brown eyes widening with increasing concern.

'Captain, we've ascertained that Oceanus has a stronger equatorial electro-jet than previously estimated. The electro-jet is about 100 kilometres above the surface. It's a naturally occurring current in the ionosphere…'

'Yes, I remember. Thank you, Commander. It is one like the Earth has,' she interjected, 'but much stronger. So, even relatively small increases in Ra's coronal activity could set off a serious geomagnetic storm on the surface. Correct?'

Statton nodded, 'Precisely Captain. This activity's been building for some time, long before we arrived, so it's likely to cause an electrical storm within the next three to four hours – ship's time.'

'Thank you, Commander,' she said and turning away from him walked briskly to the Captain's Ops interface of her command centre on the secondary command centre. She walked very much as she would have done back on the surface of the Earth, despite the current micro-gravity status of the ship; a situation once known, centuries ago, as "zero-g". The ability to walk "normally", was simply because the ship's "wheel", or torus, a structure over 180 metres in radius, rotated at a speed sufficient to produce, through centripetal motion, a simulated gravity of about 0.89 g. While not quite the value of full gravity on Earth, it was definitely more comfortable to live in and for movement – and the difference from full Earth gravity was not noticeable. The torus only rotated when in the ship was in planetary orbit or on coasting journeys, but as these could be for lengthy periods the facility made for a much healthier and happier crew and, consequently, a more efficient ship. For the similar reasons the secondary bridge itself was routinely used for command ops whilst The Monsoon was in planetary orbit.

As Ebazza marched along she tapped her *wristcom*, a device which looked like an old-style chronometer, or watch, strapped around her left wrist. Nowadays the standard Navy personal communication device, usually pronounced "Riscom", or "Riscum", had a bewildering array of powerful functions, included a facility allowing it to be tuned, very finely, to its owner's voice alone. So, alerting it to her wishes with a mere touch of one finger and without needing to bring it anywhere near her face, she said, 'Contact Admiral Tenak now and tag it, urgent.'

****

As he sat, or rather, slouched, lazily, in his room Mike had begun to doze but he suddenly felt a subtle vibration against the skin of his left wrist. He began to surface from his fitful slumber and realised from the pattern of pulsations that Tenak was summoning him. He just had to stir himself and get downstairs, but he also decided he wouldn't rush. He was not, after all, some rookie tekker on the ship, required to run to Tenak's bidding, and the Admiral was well aware of that too.

It wouldn't do to ignore Tenak for too long, though. He mused that his relationship with that particular "mascla", the current century's fashionable, general term for a man, had been a fruitful one. After all, Mike could be considered, or very nearly so, a senior member of the Secretariat, after a mere 3 years, serving the government on the flagship of the Navy fleet. But it still irked him that a productive career as a physicist had been lost, even though he had a "Primo-Sci", qualification which he'd been able to keep, though it had so nearly denied him by bureaucrats. And it was unconnected to his abilities.

The qualification made him one of the top 250 astrophysicists in the whole Solar System; the vast network of human habitation which now included not only the Earth but colonies on the Moon, Mars, many parts of the asteroid belt, one of Saturn's moons, and the three "tuna can" shaped, entirely artificial habitats orbiting the Sun. He wondered whether the fact that for over a hundred years, humanity had also expanded far beyond the Solar System; firstly to Oceanus and more recently to a second Earth-like world, made any difference to that interesting statistic. Probably not, he generously granted himself.

In the larger scale picture, he was often amazed at the rate that things had changed for humanity as a whole, over the last century and a half. The new renaissance, or "Renewal" had come about since the rediscovery, or rather, redevelopment, of high-level technology, a little over two hundred years after the world-wide devastation on the Earth. That was an event precipitated by the cataclysmic explosion of a supervolcano – Toba, in eastern Asia.

When he thought of the grimness of that cataclysmic event, he once again felt eternal gratitude he had not been born in that era. It had pushed humankind to the limit, into a sort of new medieval dark ages – a time of terrible, world-wide poverty and numerous wars, though mostly small scale, but vicious all the same. There had been terror on a huge scale, deprivation and globally endemic disease, a horror from which humanity had emerged only after much anguish, suffering and *billions* of deaths.

Huge tomes had been written about the re-emergence of humanity from near destruction. But Mike's own take on the main reasons, were that once the environment had begun to recover enough for surpluses of crops to be grown, and after the records of previous knowledge and learning had ben fully retrieved and restudied, tek had begun to take off again. Initially, most of the vital stuff had involved the rediscovery and widescale repair of settlement sanitation systems, the infrastructure of much of it having remained in place anyway. Falteringly, the new city states had been founded and international trade had restarted.

Remarkably, there had been a renewal of the human spirit amid a determination to rebuild, and it had led to a kind of renaissance. An explosion of new learning and the re-expansion of human society had occurred, though, regrettably, but perhaps inevitably, there was a re-emergence of many mistakes which had been made before "the fall".

But pushed by new scientific and engineering endeavour there had eventually been a rediscovery of spaceflight and, more importantly, an iron resolve to avert the threat of global extinction happening again. That in turn led to a determination to colonise the Solar System – or at least parts of it. But when the "conduits" were disovered the "human sphere" had expanded even further.

For the first time, travel to the stars, without using unknown physics or taking thousands of years, making it equally impossible, had became possible. Humans could travel to the nearest stars – and later, to systems further out. It wasn't the instantaneous travel of much science fiction speculation, but it was eminently practical, after decades of experimentation and development. And, despite that fledgling freedom eventually turning out to be more limited than imagined, the new renaissance had continued anabated but, many felt, much of the fire seemed to haved gone out of it in more recent times. It was said that avaricious politics, greed, and social disturbance may have started to reappear. It was never far away, thought Mike, sardonically. Mike hoped humanity wasn't repeating all the old mistakes.

Still, the development of interstellar travel, though currently limited, was surely something to be proud of, Mike felt, but despite owing their existence to that very thing the people of Oceanus seemed to care little for it now. But he believed they would be forced, sooner or later, to accept that they would *all* need to leave here and go back to the Solar System, where their forebears came from – or face extinction here. That would be an extinction more complete than the one which had faced the whole of humanity, long before Oceanus had been founded. The ancestors of these people would have understood this. Why didn't the present population of this crazy planet?

Again, sheer exasperation made Mike wonder why he was here. After the bitterness of a stymied academic career Mike had joined the Secretariat after leaving "Uni-col" in the "South Pacifica Alliance City States", in the territory once known as Australia. He had initially been assigned to a tiny Navy skiff. He felt he had been dumped onto a ship with a tight-bound, tight-arsed, crew of only seven. His femna chasing activities; what would once have been known as "womanising", exacerbated an already poor relationship with the vessel's captain. He'd always been perplexed by the fact that, despite the massive changes in marital and cohabiting norms in human societies, at least on Earth, over the last century, it seemed that most people were now, more than ever, "straight laced", in that one sense. So, he'd put in for a transfer.

In an unusual turn for him, he felt, he'd decided to be as bold as a duralamium ball joint and had applied to join the flagship itself, The Monsoon. Surprisingly, his bosses had allowed it but unsurprisingly, had not put any force behind it. Perhaps they thought he had no chance of beeing accepted. His first "lucky bell" was when Tenak, one of very few active Navy Admirals, had accepted him, after an interview by holographic, 3D, communication. Though completely permissible, it was unusual for an Admiral to involve themselves in recruitment and Tenak had broken one of his own rules by doing it. However, the result had been graciously accepted by the Captain, the person nominally in charge of recruitment.

Tenak had been bullish because of his strong belief in the post, something not shared so completely by Ebazza, and because of an association he'd had with the Secretariat in the past. He'd obviously seen something he'd liked in Mike. But Ebazza definitely held no "friendly lights" for him, though, to be fair, felt Mike, she had been much more amenable when he'd first joined the ship.

His second lucky bell was that he and Tenak had hit it off, though that, as he was finding out, carried its own penalties. He was nevertheless proud that he had actually applied himself assiduously over the last three and a half years and had kept his sexual activities quiescent – well, relatively speaking. The ship's environment and most of the crew were very pleasant. He'd impressed most of the officers aboard and he had many mates amongst the engineers, tekies and security crew. And he had settled into the role. Odd that Tenak seemed more often to look to Mike for his scientific insights than anything else, but still, the older man had been impressed by his grasp of the legalities involved in his work as ship's Secretary.

Mike was certainly aware that behind the relevant "legalese" was the concept that the Secretariat was a way for the Allied Home System government to have a visible, personal, presence in the Navy. It was originally represented by a sizeable contingent placed aboard each and every vessel, ostensibly, to advise on civilian law and government protocols. In reality, it was meant to give the government a heads-up on behaviour on board their vessels and everyone knew it. Understandably, many resented it, but even they had to acknowledge the need to give the billions of the electorate some degree of reassurance that a coup would not descend on them from space – again. It had happened before.

The need for reassurance had arisen out of the tragedy of the Rebel Wars of 2462 – 2464 of the Common Era. For then a sizeable part of the space-based force which had preceded the Navy; the so-called "Solar System Defence Force", had been infiltrated and later taken over by rebel forces late in the struggle. The rebels had added the Defence Force vessels to their own sizeable fleet, assembled in an uninhabited star system over 40 light years from Earth. Then they had attacked the alliance worlds of the Earth, Moon and Mars, aiming to bring down the System's democratically elected Allied Government. And they'd nearly succeeded.

After bitter fighting the embattled and scarred remnants of the Defence Force loyalists had narrowly defeated the aggressors. Eventually a new space-based protection force was created, larger and more powerful than the previous one. *And it was to be much more tightly controlled.* This became the Home System Navy, originally named the "Sur-Navy", as Arbella had referred to it. The wars had ended 28 years ago, and at the same time the new Secretariat was formed and given their role.

Despite some continued controversy the Navy accepted that the new civil force had been set up with the precise objective of calming a jittery public by means of a civilian presence aboard the ships. It was either that – or disbandment. But Mike knew that nowadays the Secretariat and their paymasters no longer regarded the chance of significant disloyalty by Navy personnel a serious proposition. Navy crews were selected rigorously by panels of trusted political and civilian representatives from all the colonised worlds and established naval top brass were consulted.

To be fair, Mike reflected, the Navy had acquitted itself well in its role, which was primarily one of defence of the civilian populations and, to a lesser extent, an exploratory role. It was, ultimately, a peace keeping force, an interplanetary police service, for the whole Solar System. Their remit was later expanded to cover the "new worlds", entirely outside the Solar System, including Oceanus and the small colony on another planet known as "Prithvi". Oceanus was by far the more successful colony, and since achieving independence the Navy's welcome on the planet was dependent on the sufferance of the Oceanus people. That was even though the Treaty of Algarion allowed all Navy ships, and any other government sponsored ships from the Home System, to enter the Ra system. Only Navy ships were automatically authorised to enter into Oceanus orbit; applications had to be made by any others and could be refused on any grounds.

Since the early days the presence of large contingents of "Secretaries" aboard Navy ships had gradually been reduced to just *one* person, representing the interests of the government and the people. Abuse or maltreatment of a ship's Secretary was a serious offence and liable to be tried in Home System, in the ordinary criminal courts, not by the Navy. Mike was only aware of one or two examples of this since the Secretariat had been formed. But, given the strength of the the force commanded by the Navy, if a coup was ever seriously on the cards, people like Mike would have represented no obstacle. For that matter, he thought soberly, neither would the larger contingents of the past, as they were never seriously armed or trained militarily.

As the cerulean of the Oceanus slowly deepened toward twilight Mike reflected on the fact that a Secretary's *modern* role was mainly to maintain comms with the government, when practicable, advising or assist senior officers on matters of protocol, and, generally, representing civilian interests. But woe betide him or her if they themselves did anything which went against the government's own "Directives and Regulations".

But, subject to certain restrictions, a Secreatry was pretty much free to do his or her own thing. Though Mike had to participate in some safety drills he wasn't required to do military training or follow the daily routines of most shipmates. For that he was enormously grateful.

*

He didn't realise it yet, but he would soon experience the very real tribulations of the delicate situations into which Secretaries were placed.

*

Although not what he had wanted as a career, being ship's Secretary had enabled Mike to do much that he'd never thought possible. He'd even been to Prithvi, the fourth planet in the system of a star called "Ishtar". It was 92 light years from the Earth, in what could be described as the 'opposite direction' to Oceanus, from the perspective of the Solar System. Though impressive for its size, Mike hadn't liked Prithvi one little bit. He considered it a very unattractive home for humanity. And it was a failing world. Its half million strong colony was losing a battle with a naturally toxic environment, a phenomenon not identified initially or understood until it was too late. And now people were also leaving there in large numbers, returning to the Home System.

Oceanus was so different. Ironically, Mike had always wanted to come here, to the "great ocean world", with its one large continent, called "Bhumi-Devi" – where the whole population lived, and which extended from about 55° north of the equator, to around 25° south of it. Named after a Sanskrit Goddess – the personification of "Mother Earth", Bhumi-Devi covered an area a little larger than Asia and North America combined, on Earth. There was no equivalent to Africa, South America, Australia or Antarctica. There was only one other significantly large piece of dry land: a large island, about 50% larger than Earth's Greenland. That was "Simurgh", lying in the mid latitudes of the southern hemisphere. Mike marvelled at the fact that there were hundreds of thousands of smaller islands scattered all across the oceans of this planet, many more than on Earth.

Mike was fascinated by the idea of getting to know Oceanus Alpha, but he hadn't realised, till now, how hard it was going to be to adjust to the sparsely populated expanse of Bhumi-Devi. Its sweeping panoramas were anathema to him. He remembered how intimidating he had found Prithvi, a planet *larger* than the Earth by more than half. But Prithvi was cooler, with massive ice caps; a world almost entirely covered with land and most of that was flat and largely featureless bog. He had had to steer well clear of its pancake like and seemingly limitless, but dull, vistas.

Oceanus, although about 10% *smaller* than the Earth, had a bewildering variety of habitats, though little significant arctic land. Its polar regions were tiny and its temperate zones also much smaller than those on Earth. The overriding features of both Prithvi and Oceanus were their sheer emptiness, in the sense of the absence of human habitation. A wonderful thing, thought many. Something to be grateful for? The Earth was considered, by most, to be yet again overburdened with population – despite the terrible, tragic, dying off centuries ago. Its population was steadily recovering and once again starting to boom, currently numbering about 4 billion.

The population of Oceanus was a mere 3.6 million, nearly half living in a few small cities and the rest in small farming communities scattered across the eastern seaboard of the continent, ensconced in small pockets of agriculture. Mike reckoned this population equated to a density similar to that of the whole of England and Wales, on Earth, back in the *early-1200s* of the Common Era.

Mike had read about the controversies and massive debates predating the founding of the colony on Oceanus, especially as it harboured so much complex life and varied habitats. In the end the need to avoid complete extinction and the force of the human dispora had won out. There was still controversy and it was one reason why the modern citizens of Oceanus valued their conservationist and smale scale society so much,

Anyway, he was here, now, his bum actually parked on Oceanus. He wondered what some of his mates aboard ship were doing now. He loved The Monsoon but down here, he had been plunged into something he thought was a stupid game of what – politics? Still, the issue had to be dealt with. And, very much against his better judgement he found himself becoming intrigued by the situation here.

Were the people of Oceanus ever going to be prepared to evacuate? If so, would it be too late? What arguments could they possibly have against common sense and what was really motivating them? Was the proverbial 'fusion shield' being pulled over the eyes' of the citizens, and if so, by whom? Mike had no answers at the moment and he had a feeling they were only going to be hard won. His wristcom buzzed again. He'd made Tenak wait long enough.

***

Arkas Tenak, now wearing "civilian" clothes, basked in the breeze of a floor standing fan while he pored over a number of "flimsi-plex" sheets laid out over the small bits of furniture in his spartan room. The sheets were almost exactly like the ancient material called paper, but were in fact, computers. Although not AI-enabled, they were soft and flexible digital screens, and the the text they showed could change upon verbal command. They enabled a huge variety of data sets to be left fixed in place, for casual perusal, and they could be stacked into sheaves, again like paper. Many found they made a refreshing change from holocom and wristcom projections. Tenak was studying the specs and schematics for the evacuation of Oceanus which the Admiralty had, rather optimistically, drawn up.

His wristcom bleeped momentarily, then gave one hard edged chime, indicating an urgent communique from a colleague. He tapped it twice and a 40-centimetre-tall holographic image of Ssanyu Ebazza seemed to spring out of the device, appearing to "stand" on his left wrist.

'Admiral,' she said, 'we've just detected a PSE coming from Ra's surface. It is estimated to be a force 8 event. That's mega-spray class. The proton storm is estimated to reach OA within the next two and a half days.'

'Doesn't sound good Captain. What's the likely damage?'

'Electro-disrupt to any OA satellite is certain, though the extent will depend on the quality and age of their components - and any buffering system they've used. I thought you might have a better idea about that.'

'Not sure. What else?'

'Heavy ionisation of the upper atmosphere and electrical storms that could wipe out all their ground comms for a while, as well as computer nets – to whatever extent they have them. There will probably be aurorae as far south as the equator. Risk to personal health of anyone on the ground is likely to be very small sir, but I'd recommend the public and the authorities be warned that if they have anyone in high flying aircraft, or in orbit they should land – very soon. Astronauts should stay inboard. We haven't detected any other crewed vessel in space at this time. I don't know if they use anything like that, sir.'

'Very good Captain. Your suggestion about advising the public is going to be a difficult one, given the spread of the population here, let alone the outdated comms. We can only warn the government and let them do the rest. Keep me posted, Captain.'

Ebazza added that low level geomagnetic storms might occur within the next few hours, due to the energising of the electro-jet plasma in the upper atmosphere.

'Thank you, Captain,' replied Tenak, 'we'll watch out for that.'

Ebazza's image disappeared, just as a buzzing sound came from the door. Tenak strode to it and had to operate a rather old-fashioned intercom device, 'Is that you, Mike?' he said, 'you took your time.'

On hearing his colleague's answer, he opened the door.

Mike beamed at him. 'Ready to go to supper? I'm starving.'

'I suppose, but ... I guess it seems almost frivolous in the circumstances,' said Tenak, wrinkling his nose, 'there's trouble brewing.'

'It's not me,' said Mike, knowing full well that Tenak was couldn't really smell anything unsavoury. When Tenak didn't laugh he continued, 'I know, but, well, we've got to eat. It's either that, or starve, or ... go back to the ship, I guess.'

'No. I didn't mean the obvious. Listen, there's more work to do first. I've just heard from Ebazza.' Tenak summarised her news.

Mike thought that grimly of the sad irony here, given the government's position on the stability of their star. The super-flare represented a serious event which gave even him pause, despite the fact that being on the planet's surface was not dangerous – yet – and there was no threat to The Monsoon. Nor would it be for any other large Navy vessel. The carrier vessel was more than a match for it, as it carried extra-large, superconducting coils, a heavily amoured hyper-composite hull, and clusters of electromagnetic deflectors – known popularly as "EM shields".

There could still be a danger to personnel working some distance outside the ship, and to landing boats, but he knew Ebazza would suspend any such activity. Still, he wondered how much worse Ra was going to get - and how quickly?

'Okay, what can we do?' said Mike quietly, almost thinking aloud. 'Contact the government? The Ministry of … of what, environmental affairs? Public announcements and all that? Set onwards?'

'Yeah, I think so,' said Tenak, 'but can you set onwards with that for me, Mike? I need to contact the ship again.'

'If you insist,' said Mike, trying not to look cynical as he watched Tenak turn toward the room's large window. Mike tapped his wristcom and verbally asked it to make contact with the Oceanus government department with responsibility for environmental affairs. As he waited he overheard Tenak quizzing The Monsoon's hyper-comp, "Aleph One", the largest of its contingent of so called Artificial Intelligence nexuses. His attention was broken when his wristcom spoke to him, its voiceprint set to Mike's favourite, a cool and languorous, not to say sexy, female voice. The machine said it might take another few seconds to find the appropriate telephone number and get through. Telephone number? What the feggery was going on here?

While he waited Mike became aware that Tenak was still talking to the ship's AI and he mused again about the Ra system's isolation, his mind wandered back to the journey here, aboard The Monsoon. It was by far the longest distance he'd yet travelled. Out here they were a substantial proportion of the way out toward the current limit that crewed vessels could travel. As such they were very effectively cut off from the Home System. Only solid, integrated matter, such as space vessels and their contents, including their human cargos, could travel through the negative energy tubules, the so called "conduits", the strange, naturally occurring phenomena that had enabled humans to travel between some of the stars for a century and a half now.

No electromagnetic waves, of any sort, could be sent through the enigmatic conduits, theorised to be a network which developed during the early age of the universe, and thought to utilise a fifth dimension of space-time. Anything lacking the coherence of "solid" or integrated, matter, like EM waves were just dissipated and absorbed by the frankly weird, high energy, physics occurring inside the conduits. That physics was still poorly understood, but its results were by now well known, after many thousands of trials, experiments and investigations had been done. These had revealed that crewed ships and non-crewed vessels like the dataprobes, were the *only* means of contact between worlds like the Earth, Oceanus, Prithvi, and all the dozens of other stars which could be reached. And that meant that physical communications were essential, in turn involving, for crewed ships, very long journey times, but not through the conduits themselves.

Mike's wristcom buzzed and pulled him from his reverie. He said he was ready to answer but suddenly remembered, as a child, seeing an old telephone in a museum back in his home City State. He and the other children in his Early-School group had even been allowed to hold such an archaic device. It had felt strange, almost alien. He remembered being told that the person you spoke to was said to be "at the other end of the line". Now, who was really at the end of this line, he wondered.

Daydreaming, he placed his device near his right ear and closed his eyes, recalling the feel of that day, years ago, almost forgotten. Suddenly, his wristcom startled him by bleeping loudly again, straight into his right ear. It announced that comms had been established with a "Mer Monzonite", whose title, it said, was "Assistant to the Minister for Public Safety and Information". It said that Monzonite's voice would be the next thing he would hear.

Mike heard a tinny, scratchy voice say, faintly, 'Hello? Hello? To whom do I yet speak?'

Realising that Monzonite's device had not actually *told him* who was calling him, he said, trying to be helpful, 'This is um, Mike Tanniss. I'm the Secretary of the Home System Navy ship, The Monsoon. You know, the ship that's in orb...'

'Oh, is that so, sir? My name is Monzonite, Assistant to the Minstray for Announcements to the Popularia. How mayst I help?'

'Yes, I know who you are,' said Mike, 'my wristcom told me.'

'Your whatso? Oh, if you do say. You appear from the Home System. Sorrymost, for I do not get to speak to many from there. Not many ships from there. Not these days. Just Navy, like yoursevs.'

'I'm sure you're right Mer Assistant but, with respect, it's really important that you listen to me right now, sir. There's a massive stellar flare on its way toward this planet. It's classed at Force 8, on the interstellar scale of severity and is likely to...'

'Pardonry? Force what? Ah, yes, what you say. I am yet sure there is – as you say so. Look, could you yet stop shouting please? No need for such.'

'I'm sorry Minister. I wasn't sure if you could hear me with that ...your telephone ... thing. I, ... we, are just concerned that you get this message out to your people, on as many channels as possible.'

Tenak came to stand by Mike, having finished his own call. He turned toward Mike's wrist unit and spoke, 'Mer Monzonite, sir, this is Admiral Arkas Tenak, of the HS Navy. I've just been in touch with my ship and have asked them to assist you by broadcasting the news to the whole planet, on all channels and wavelengths. We will, of course, issue appropriate advice to all citizens, to accompany this news. I don't want to supersede your authority sir, of course, so if you think you can deal with this without our assistance, I'm happy to belay that order.'

'Oh, surely, that order will not be necessary Admiral. Please do not alarm our citizenry. We've had quite a few of these Ra flash-events in recent years and I would yet say we are used to such. More still0 than you. We just carry out necessary repairs to lectrics but, as you know, there is not a great deal of reliance on high tek on Oceanus. I didst not yet hear you say there is a risk to life and body, did you yet?'

'No, I did not yet,' said Tenak, 'I mean, there isn't. Not to those on the ground, anyway, sir, but there might be to any pilots or passengers in very high-flying vehicles, or in orbit.'

'I doubt as such Admiral. We are only operating turbo-prop'lar aircraft and e'en so they do not fly so high oft-times. But I will check, for you. As for spacecraft, ... well, only you operate those things today, sirra. I will check of course but we arint in the habit of sending anyone up into space. Not so in years – sept by way of visiting ships like yours.'

'Okay, Minister,' said Tenak, grimacing at Mike, 'I'm sorry to have disturbed you. I just thought you ought to know.'

'No need to apologise Admiral sirra. I am glad that the Navy continues to have our best interests at heart, but as I am saying, we are used to such Ra-flash things.'

The Assistant's voice clicked off and Mike looked at Tenak, his eyes wide with surprise, 'You didn't tell him anything about the likelihood of these "Ra-flashes" getting progressively worse.'

'What's the point, Mike? It's the politicians we need to convince and trying to get our scientists get into some sort of dialogue with this lot.'

'Alright. So, are we still meeting the leaders of the opposition parties tomorrow?'

'Yes, of course. We've got to lay the groundwork, but it isn't any use talking to individuals like Monzonite. I'll have to contact Ebazza and tell her to belay my last order."

'I can't believe that Monzonite fella-me-spod,' Mike said acidly. 'He sounded really ignorant as well as ancient. The "real crabbit gimbo".'

Tenak shot a withering look at Mike and sounded genuinely disapproving. 'I'm surprised at you Mike. I didn't expect to hear something like that from you.'

'Oh, come on Arkas,' said Mike.

'No, I mean it, Mike. I won't have my staff talking like that.' He sounded serious.

Feeling defiant now and slightly hurt, Mike said, 'Okay. Sorry. But you know very well that I'm not your ...'

'Yeah, yeah,' said Tenak, interjecting and giving Mike a playful thump to the chest. Mike knew it was meant in jest and though Tenak may have considered it a light and jocular touch, to Mike it felt hard enough. This sometimes seemingly avuncular figure didn't know his own strength.

Tenak quickly said, 'Okay, but just watch your language. Enough said. I think you're right about one thing, though. It's time we got something to eat. Oceanus food can be quite good. Not what *you're* used to, maybe but we'll see what's on offer. I'm glad at least one of us remembered to bring along the OA credit notes. Come on.'

'Certainly,' said Mike, rubbing his chest lightly, 'It's getting much too hot in this place. And an evening out beckons.'

*

Mike's evening was actually going to get much hotter than he would have wished for.

Chapter 3

TOP LEVEL

Earth Orbital Station Five coasted along in orbit, approximately 300 km above the surface of humanity's planet of origin, and forever its ancestral home; the place where over 98% of humanity still lived. A marvel of human engineering the station was enormous with four massive, habitation rings, larger than those of The Monsoon's torus, rotating slowly around its central hub, connected to it by thick spoke like tubes, hundreds of metres long. The central hub was slimmer than that of The Monsoon's, there being no need for a massive fusion engine module.

And the function of this station was mainly civic, not military or law enforcement. The huge rings contained extensive commercial and administrative offices, but there were also luxurious living quarters, housing semi-permanent residents, together with restaurants, shopping malls, science laboratories, hypercomp suites and security zones. This was the Earth's largest orbital station and it happened to be a semi-permanent platform for the Home System's Allied government. Although not military in function, the need to protect its occupants meant that it had some armaments, being several embedded weapons installations, subtly camouflaged. They could pack a punch which, in some respects, almost rivalled that of The Monsoon's. In addition, a small flotilla of robotic surveillance satellites, some with their own armaments, sped along in the same orbit, flying "in front" of, and "behind" it, but always at a seemly distance, of course. For the democratic institution of the Allied government security came with a heavy price tag in terms of cost and complexity, a regrettable but necessary concomitant in that day and age.

One of the most significant occupants of the station this day was Darik Kunghes Nimio Yorvelt for he was most definitely a "VIP", being none other than the Secretary

General of the entire Allied Home System Government. Yorvelt, a 60-year-old, originally hailed from what had once been the Indian sub-continent but had lived in many City States on Earth during his long career. He was the elected leader of all those worlds and colonies of the Solar System which had chosen to join the Alliance. At present, that was most of them, but the situation was slowly changing. He had been in this post for only three years, yet the rigours of responsibility had already etched deep lines in the otherwise clean-cut features of his round face, from which sharply intelligent eyes beheld the worlds of the human commonwealth.

He walked slowly, along the inside surface of the huge third ring of the station; the central one of its five. His route led along a wide but sparsely furnished corridor, recently cleared of its usual throng of people and the hubbub of daily life. He was accompanied by the obligatory two pairs of uniformed security guards. Yorvelt paused near a large glass like booth projecting from base of a massive tubular structure which was the bottom end of one of the spokes leading to the station's hub. The booth sported a large red, illuminated, sign which announced, "Security Check-through." There Yorvelt waited patiently for the arrival of an elevator car which was descending the last few dozen metres through the spoke.

As he waited he fussed with his long, powder pink, robes adjusting the extra-wide lapels of his light blue under-coat. Robes were very much in fashion right now but Yorvelt preferred muted and subdued colours over the current fad for extremely bright, gaudy ones, for he was not an ostentatious person.

One of the pairs of Navy guards; a sturdy male and female, smartly decked out in dark red uniforms, stood inside the glass booth, one either side of the lift doors and, as the elevator chimed to announce its imminent arrival, they snapped to attention and presented arms. These armaments were not projectile weapons, but standard issue, super-accurate, high power, repeater, sonic, rifles. These used, in effect, amplified and super-focussed sound waves. Bullets could not be risked in the pressurised environment of the station, despite the thickly reinforced bulkheads and the sonic weapons were the match of any such weapons for accuracy, even if not in their overall deadliness. They were completely adequate for the present job of personal protection and on the highest power setting their tightly collimated beams of sonic energy were potentially deadly, being able to punch through the protection of thin "personal armour". As they could buckle even thicker armour, they could cause a serious injury to any such user.

As he glimpsed the outline of the elevator's occupant Yorvelt grinned broadly, anticipating his coming meeting with the Deputy Secretary General of the Allied Government, Indrius Garu Aslar Brocke, who also happened to be his long-time friend; a man 10 years his junior. Brocke would have to clear security first, something not waived even for such as he.

After a few minutes the tall, thin, elegant, figure of Brocke appeared, wearing similar flowing garb to Yorvelt, but with brighter robes sporting vivid red and blue circles and diamonds. He marched, stork-like, toward the shorter, squat figure of the Secretary General and clasped the older man's outstretched hand with both of his, saying, 'So good to see you again Dar',' and chuckling.

'Likewise, likewise, my friend,' said Yorvelt, sounding full of genuine enthusiasm. 'How are your wives and children, Indry? It's been a long time since I saw them.'

'They're fine, fine. Yes,' said the Deputy Secretary General. Yorvelt's protégé, the younger man's sharp nosed, aquiline features normally appeared trouble free but today he exhibited deep, dark bags under his eyes, probably a sign of a sleepless journey; an occupational hazard for those who were frequent passengers on the tedious journeys around the Solar System.

'You look in need of refreshment,' said Yorvelt, 'Come over to the Officials' Suite and have a drink. How about some sweet energia-mint? Our meeting with the others isn't scheduled for another half hour.'

'I think I'll need something stronger than energia-mint, Dar', said Brocke with a good-natured grin, 'so I think I'll leave it till after the official business, if that's okay.'

'Yes, yes, of course. Whatever you want. Was the trip from Mars that bad? I know you don't like these inter-planet transits much.'

'Oh, I'm guess I'm fine, Dar. You're right, of course, but I suppose if I wasn't prepared to do these things I shouldn't have put myself in this position in the first place. So, I'll just have to persevere. Either that, or resign,' he said, sounding anything but serious.

Yorvelt feigned a look of shock. 'Don't you dare do that, Indry. I know you don't like those gee forces on those ships, but what bothers *me* the most is the time factor. Even with the new type 1 fusion engines it still takes about five weeks to get back from Mars, doesn't it? Do you know something, Dar, I don't think I've been out there for at least a full Earth year.'

'Well, the trip back was four and a half, this time, Dar, which isn't so bad really, specially given that they have to match planetary orbits and so on … and on. It's a damnatious inconvenience that the laws of physics mean a more direct course would use up far too much fuel. The ships would have to be massive. Not to mention the hard accelerations and decelerations each end.'

'Precisely, Indry,' Yorvelt added, almost mockingly, 'physics is a real bore isn't it? And those hard accelerations might kill you Indry. And where would that leave me?' He chuckled again and added, 'It's as well that none of us need to get around the Home System *really fast*. There's always the holo-conferences, of course,' he said, curling his lips, 'if you like that sort of thing.' As Brocke chuckled he continued, I'm just old fashioned I think, Indry. I know they're supposed to be almost as good as "actually being there in person" but – for me, not really.'

'So that's why you keep sending me, *in person*, to places like Mars,' Brocke said, grinning amiably. He continued walking but bent down toward Yorvelt's ear and lowered his voice conspiratorially, 'That and the fact that we all know how precious the Mars colonists are about security – because "there might be someone lurking just outside the holo-lightcone. Someone manipulating things. Spying,"' he said, with mock sternness, paraphrasing something often said on the red planet.

They walked slowly toward a large office area more than 100 metres along the gently up-curving corridor, their four guards trailing a couple of meters behind them. A person ignorant of life on a space station would think they were constantly walking uphill; the corridor curving upwards equally much behind them as in front. If the torus was likened to a bicycle wheel they were simply walking along the inside surface of the tyre. And, as on The Monsoon, this was where a kind of artificially induced gravity replicated a full Earth gravity effect. The constantly upcurving floor could be unsettling for the uninitiated but not for these two.

As they arrived at the offices which effectively blocked the next section of the wide corridor ahead, a zone enclosed by security strengthened diamond-glass faced them. From a small aperture in the glass wall the smell of freshly ground Martian kaffee reached them. Similar to traditional Earth-grown coffee, but stronger and much spicier, the aroma drifted from a kitchenette somewhere inside the offices.

'Oh no! Not more kaffee, Dar? What are trying to do, kill me?' said Brocke, holding his right hand to his throat, then laughing heartily.

'I'm sorry my friend. I like it, that's all, but I'll ask them to clear it away right now.'

'Don't be "dampy", my friend. I can put up with the smell - just don't ask me to drink it!'

Yorvelt's wristcom gave them admittance to the glass offices, where they arrived at Yorvelt's private suite. It housed what he liked to call the 'elliptical office', in a lighthearted parody of a certain historically significant office on the world they orbited. He waved away the guards at the entranceway, 'Thank you, officers. Please go and help yourselves to some kaffee. As much as you like. It's "on the bubble",' he said.

'Thank you, sir, but we have to wait for our relief squad to arrive.'

'Alright, that's fine.'

Inside the S G's office, Indrius Brocke ran his eyes around the simply decorated but comfortably furnished office of his old colleague and sighing, sank into one of its deep sofas, breathing out very slowly and whistling as he did so. He closed his eyes and appeared to drift into a slumber - when Yorvelt's wristcom chimed loudly. The Secretary General glanced at the device, 'Oh, she's early,' he said. 'Are you okay Indry? Don't those transit shuttles have decent upholstery these days?'

'No, they make you sit on bare metal plating. Didn't you know? I jest of course but seriously, how long did you say it's been since you went on one, Dar? Oh, the seating is alright. Just not like this, that's all. And they keep you cooped up too much. You should travel more. It would broaden your horizons.' He laughed lightly. 'Anyway, who are you talking about, Dar?'

'Ylesia. I know she wanted to get here early for this one. She's rather keen on the subject matter. They've all had some bedtime reading to do. You as well, Indry?'

'Of course, Dar. How could I forget? I did find some time, en-route to watch the briefing notes you transmitted. I don't know how, but I did. I also know Mariana can make it too, and Soronade, and our guest advisor. That's Sardik …? His fam-name eludes me, I'm afraid.'

'Brevans, Indry. Sardik Alsar Brevans, "Chief Government Science and Tek Advisor". Experienced man, but new to this job.'

'Never heard of him before.'

'He's goodful, Indry. Newly promoted but very astute and straight to the point.'

Brocke looked as though he was going to say something else when the door chimed and seconds later Ylesia Varga-Horgans, the Senior Minister for External Affairs, breezed in. She'd hardly walked three steps into the office when she glanced at Brocke and quipped, 'Going to sleep on the job again, Indrius?'

As she walked past she half turned her head toward him, shooting him a wicked, playful smile, then alighted on a chair as softly yielding as Brocke's sofa. Adjusting her ankle length, brocaded, dress-suit she swept her waist-length dark blue hair back to keep it from covering her piercing, purple eyes and pale, high forehead.

Next to arrive was the Minister for Internal Affairs, Marianas Polonia Jenner-Emblois, from the West African State Alliances, the ebony hues of her cheeks catching the cool glow of the office's interior lighting. Her tall figure swept past the others, her wide green cape billowing in her wake, revealing below a bright red check trouser suit. As she settled gracefully on a plain, hard chair, the next delegate entered on her heels; the man discussed by Brocke and Yorvelt: Sardik Alsar Brevans. Like Horgans, Brevans was from Central City on the Moon, but unlike her he was a singularly undistinguished figure, with a square, ruddy face. He was the only person wearing a one-piece, utilitarian jump-suit, a form of dress now several years out of fashion in the HS, in an age when fashion had become very fashionable again.

There was a good twenty-minute wait for the final delegate to appear, during which the attendees made small talk, whilst Brocke appeared to be doing his best to prevent himself from falling asleep. Then, finally, in sauntered Soronade Kar-Yoonsuh Jae, a young woman hailing from a territory now known, in Anglo-Span, as the North-East Asian City State Hegemony. She was the Allied Government's Minister for Finance. As she entered her glance took in all those present and her dark liquid eyes, set in an unblemished face painted pure white, in accordance with the latest fashion for East Asian people, seemed to flash irritation. She appeared manifestly annoyed at being the last to arrive and, with no words of greeting, plonked herself down next to Brocke. The Deputy Secretary General's eyebrows rose a little but he said nothing.

Yorvelt sat at an enormous rectangular desk, one side of which faced the other delegates, such that the SG was not facing the others over the desk; probably an attempt to reduce formality. He watched Kar-Yoonsuh Jae settle herself. Then he sighed, nearly, but not quite, silently, and opened the proceedings,

'Thank you. Thank you, everyone, for coming. I know you're all very busy and most of you would probably have preferred a holo conference but I felt the current situation has some security demands that make a face to face meeting more … appropriate. Sorry Indry. Shades of Martian sensitivities, I suppose?' He glanced at Brocke who rolled his eyes but smiled placidly.

'You're forgiven, but only because it's you, Dar,' he said, grinning.

At that point, a box at the corner of Yorvelt's desk, furthest from the other delegates, came abruptly to life, a baleful red light starting to shine from its one of its top corners. The light beam swung and focused on a spot between Yorvelt's own desk and Marianas's, whereupon a holo of a human sized, cinnamon coloured, animal shape, very much like a bear, seemed to materialise. Bathed in a pale orange light the figure appeared every bit as real as if physical, solid, matter.

'Hello Xander' said Yorvelt, 'and welcome to the meeting. I think you know almost everyone here?'

Xander nodded once. He looked more like a huge teddy bear, still beloved of small children, rather than a real bear, except that he had a Koala-like head. The irony was probably lost on most of those present because there were no more Koalas left in the wild on Earth and, perhaps only a bare handful of real bears. The holo apparition saluted those present with a furry right arm and it spoke with a clear, mellow, male baritone voice, which issued from a perfectly animated mouth,

'I'm certainly glad to see you all today, gentilhomms, especially you, Professor Brevans, as I don't think we've met before. I'm so glad to make your acquaintance, sir.'

Brevans smiled and nodded, as Xander continued, 'I'm ready to take notes whenever you are ready to proceed, Doctrow Yorvelt. The agenda you set for today is: the Mars situation, with Deputy Brocke to report; security issues and religious extremism, with Madam Jenner-Emblois; tek issues with Prof Brevans and last, but certainly not least; the situation with Oceanus Alpha: open report. I will of course record the proceedings in 3-dimensional AV.'

'Thank you, Xander,' said Brocke. The Deputy S G then reported on his trip to Mars, now a mostly self-governing planet. He explained the unhappiness of many Mars colonists, arising mainly from difficulties left by the terraforming process begun 60 years earlier. There were now nearly seventy million people living and working on the planet, in eleven main cities. "Terraforming", the attempt to turn Mars "green", mostly by means of chemical processes, had made a huge, positive difference and enabled the population capacity of the colony to expand quickly and to prosper – at first. However, as is often the way, with engineering projects on a vast scale, problems had arisen and were increasing. Some contamination was getting into some cities, mainly due to the complexity of the process.

Much had been and was being done, said brocke, to combat the problems but next to interstellar travel, the terraforming process was the biggest engineering process ever attempted by humanity. The latter was not working as successfully as the former. Despite having to repatriate 150,000 people to Earth, while the rectification process was being carried out. Brocke reported that the problems were finally being resolved and it was hoped that many would now be able to return and he invited Brevans to comment.

Appearing almost surprised to be drawn into the discussion so soon the top-level engineer spoke reticently.

'The main environmental issues on Mars,' he said, 'appear to have been contained for now, and most contaminated areas have been isolated and are being reprocessed, but it's bound to take time.'

'I appreciate that, Professor,' said Brocke, 'but the Martian Autonomous Zone Authorities aren't noted for their patience. Some of their unrest is obstinacy and abstruse politics, of course, but I think that many of the issues we're discussing today are feeding into this.'

The Minister for Finance spoke up at this juncture, a harsh edge to her voice,

'I think I have said before, at these very meetings,' said Soronade, 'and find I say yet again, that there should be a representative from Mars on *this* Executive Committee. And still – still it hasn't happened.'

'We are all aware of that Soronade, but I have to remind you of the delicate situation with the Earth,' said Yorvelt.

'Indeed,' said Jenner-Emblois, 'there are still City State Alliances on Earth that have larger populations than Mars but are not part of the Executive Committee, even though they do have representatives on the *General* Committee of the Allied Government.'

'As does Mars,' said Brocke, directing his comment at Kar-Yoonsuh Jae. 'They have two, in fact. More than most Earth City State Territories with equivalent populations can claim.'

Soronade bristled and flashed indignant eyes at Brocke.

Yorvelt interjected then, 'Colleagues, colleagues. We must not lose sight of the fact that Mars may decide to withdraw from the General Committee, if relations with them worsen. That's a situation which would be … undesirable.'

'That was the feeling I got when I was there,' added Brocke, 'but we can't just bow to that sort of pressure. There are whole City State Agglomerates, *on Earth*, that are also threatening to leave the Committee and I'm talking about zone groups with more of a stake-holding than Mars, for us as well. And, as we know, one or two of the larger State groups have either refused to join us at all or have withdrawn over the last three years. We can't lose sight of the bigger vista.'

Kar-Yoonsuh Jae wore a stubbornly unconvinced look on her face but she stayed silent after the group agreed that a proposal for Mars to be given an Executive Seat would have to be discussed fully and at length at the next General Committee convocation. The meeting then turned to the issue of general security, Jenner Emblois reporting that there had been some lawlessness and social unrest in two of the three artificial, "Floating Worldships"; the so-called "Bernal" spheres, which were actually squat cylinders, 6 by 4 kilometres in size, flying in orbit around the Sun. These were independent societies of the same status as City States and so, were important to the government. But the unrest had now abated, though relevant issues continued to be addressed.

Jenner Emblois then said that the main security issue in the Home System as a whole was still thought to be "Ultima", an extremist, fundamentalist, religious faction that had arisen out of the massive disorder, first of all caused by the virus pandemics of 2042, and later, after the super-volcano explosion. They had sought to convert as many societies as possible, by violent evangelism, if necessary. But the faction appeared to have disappeared when human civilisation began to recover. Nothing had been heard of them for many decades but they had popped up again in the 2340s. They continued to practice but had co-existed peacefully with the rest of society for a long time, until the 2450s, when they had joined with other militarised dissidents, in something she described as "an unholy unification called the "Rebel Alliance".

The latter was an essentially anarchistic cabal composed of groups of overtly political, non-religious factions, motivated by a desire to impose their will on all the peoples of the Solar System. Not a great deal was known about this group or its shadowy leaders. Some thought it was mainly a right-wing organisation, but most others believed it to be a neo-Marxist – Leninist paradosus group, or rather a caucus of violent, extremist, identitatarian groups. It was thought that the faction had jumped into bed with Ultima for purely practical reasons, as the religious group seemed to have access to the funding needed for arms and equipment. Ultima probably also brought in many willing members to the rebels. It seemed the organisation and penetration of the Rebels became of use to the Ultima, and the zealousness of Ultima useful to the Rebels. Many of the those who had converted to the religion were thought to have come from Mars, a fact not lost now on the Executive Committee.

No-one at the meeting needed reminding of the costly war fought between the Allied Government and the Ultima backed Rebel Alliance of 28 years ago. Yorvelt and Brocke reminded everyone that the Rebels had been defeated and those perpetrators who were caught, punished as severely as allowed in a modern democracy. Most of their soldiers who were taken prisoner knew little about the group's ultimate aims or their real leaders. The ones who may have known refused to talk, and those assessed as being ring leaders had actually taken nerve poison, rather than reveal anything. The remainder were still serving long prison sentences, either on Mars or the Moon.

Of the current Executive Committee, only Brocke, Brevans and Yorvelt personally remembered those times, and only the Secretary General had held office then, as Vice-President of the Central India-Sub-Continent Agglomerate. All present at the meeting were aware of the constant need for vigilance, even though the rebels, as an organised elite, seemed to have largely disappeared from view for years. But no-one believed they were gone and there were some signs of sympathy being shown for their politics in some parts of the Solar System. Some sources said they now called styled themselves the "New Rebels" but there'd been no real signs of illegal activity.

Brocke gave his opinion that there was currently no need for any alarm, because the colonist unrest on Mars had been largely contained. Jenner-Emblois reminded everyone that the Navy was doing a creditable job in keeping the peace throughout the Home System. She also mentioned the fleets of mini-bot surveillance units, which were "semi- intelligent" listening devices; a semi-covert and unfortunate step to be taken by a democratic government but seen by most current politicians as necessary in the socio-political world of the expanded human sphere.

As many as two hundred thousand mini-bots them had been operating across the Solar System for years, she advised, but none had reported any significant increase in terrorist or dissident e-activity. The "chatter" of vigorously dissident groups on SolNet, SocioNet, EndoNet and the Ultranet, had been quiescent too. Nor had there been many reports of "concern" from any of the 23 Intelligence Agencies which were spread far and wide around the System. All but one of those worked directly for the Allied Government. There had been some interesting indications of sympathy for extremist politics in some of the City States that were normally the staunchest supporters of the HS Government and who often provided civil servants for it. However, it was not currently considered to be an upper level threat.

Yet no-one in the room said they were prepared to be complacent about the situation. Things had ppobably been "quiet" for too long. "The silence before the ion storm" was how many were now describing it.

The Agenda moved on. When giving his report on tek developments, Brevans spoke again and said something that lightened the mood a little.

'At least Fleet Admiral Alisiana Khairie Madraser was pleased,' he said, with a deadpan face, 'to receive the upgrades of the four Type 1A, fusion engines for the Kalahari; the ship which will replace The Monsoon as the new flagship though they haven't been fitted to the vessel yet.' Smiles broke out on everyone's faces, even Kar-Yoonsuh Jae's.

'Thank the nebulas for that!' said Brocke. 'That could have been the worst news of all - if *she,* of all people, hadn't been happy with the upgrades to the Kalahari!' Chuckling broke out across the room like an infection. 'Forgive me Sardik,' added Brocke. 'Kindly continue with your report.'

The Professor said that, as it had been mentioned earlier, he didn't intend talking about terraforming, then continued, 'Of more immediate concern is that efforts to develop the "bullet wave" have hit rock bottom, so to speak. Sorry to bring things down again,' he said, rolling his eyes.

'No need for apologies, Professor. I believe you're talking about a way of sending radio or any sort of EM signals through the negative energy conduits?' said Brocke.

Brevans nodded. 'As you know, only solid matter, "integrated matter", if you like, such as datapods and probes and us, of course – in ships, can travel through the conduits – the negative energy tubules. Even then, because of the frankly weird physics going on the conduits, ship sensors are effectively "blind" as they travel through. So, we have little detail of what really happens to them during the short times in transit. But we all know the journeys can be somewhat … difficult … for human crews, especially untrained ones.'

'Kar-Yoonsuh Jae interjected, 'Yes, yes, we know, Professor. We are not pre-coll students - and some of us have, in fact, been through the conduits. But may we now hear more about the bullet wave experiments? I tried looking up results on SolNet. It wasn't even on the secured networks.'

Yorvelt caught her eye and gave her a severe look. Brevans overlooked the interruption and replied, 'Yes, well, that's because the results are too new to have gone on the secure networks. Only a few minutes ago, I received word that the latest attempt to project a "bundle" of data signals, using the newest type of maser EM sheaths, had failed – spectacularly. You also need to know that, even if eventually successful, satellite emitter units would need to remain in remote orbit, at the distances of the conduit transit zones, on a permanent basis.

'And that is a problem because …?' said Kar-Yoonsuh Jae.

'Well, any ship about to undertake a conduit journey needs to carry on board at least 3 linked, high-qubit, quantum computers so as to calculate, on the best sensor info-data, the precise location of a transit zone; that is, the general region likely to contain a suitable conduit. The ship needs first to locate the general volume of space most likely to have a conduit and they are usually no closer than 9 astronomical units, or "AU", from the inner Solar System. Perhaps I should remind everyone that the AU is the average distance of the Earth from the Sun. That's a huge distance.'

Kar-Yonsuh Jae touched her forehead with barely suppressed impatience. Brevans continued anabashed.

'As you know, the main drawback for current crews aboard starships is not the journey through the conduits, the "hop" from one star system's influence to another, but rather the length of time it takes the ships to get to the transit zones – the conduits themselves. That means that ships travelling out to, say, the Ra system, are isolated – very much. We need to develop a fast form of communication between star systems – without having to send crewed, or uncrewed ships on super-long journeys.

Several delegates began to get impatient but Brocke encouraged the Professor to continue, by smiling and nodding enthusiastically.

'Hence, the "bullet wave" concept,' said Brevans. 'Current work shows that any such signal would need to be enclosed by a sort of collimated "sheath"; a tightly focused beam, that would require the transmitter device to stay very close to a suitable conduit "mouth", within a transit zone. That is why such a device would need to be based in the transit zone opening volume permanently and would need to retain 3 working quantum computers on board.'

Ylesia interjected at this point, 'Otherwise, no advantage would be gained from having such satellites, I guess. If they had to sent one out every time we wanted to send a signal, we might as well just send an ordinary datapod through the conduit?'

'Precisely Madama,' said Brevans, 'and even keeping such a unit in a permanent orbit around the Sun, so far out, would be problematical because we know that transit zones themselves move around, sometimes by distances of up to 3 AU.'

'A disappointing result,' said Brocke, 'but please keep trying, Professor. Is there anything else?'

Brevans said, 'Only that the refitting of most of the Navy ships, to deal with evacuation of Oceanus, was going well but...'

'Was?' interrupted Yorvelt, with concern. 'Why, *was?*'

Jenner Emblois interjected at this point, screwing her face up as though she'd suddenly tasted raw lemon, 'I can fill in here. Sorry. My understanding is that F. A. Madraser is objecting to the refitting of the Kalahari. The new ship is still largely untested, and she thinks the refit will compromise its ability to deal with what she sees as an ongoing terrorist threat. And possible negative developments on Mars.'

Yorvelt spoke sternly, unusually for him. Eyebrows all around the room were raised. 'What is she talking about?' he said, his brown eyes agog, 'I've already said that terrorist Ultranet activity is at an all-time low. We have to be alert, of course, but the problems on Mars don't really allow her to countermand our orders for refits, do they?'

'She's apparently muttering something about the legal framework not allowing civilian objectives to override military ones – in certain circumstances,' said Horgans.

'Who's our Secretary on the Kalahari?' asked Yorvelt, evidently impatient.

Varga-Horgans tapped her wristcom straight away, asked it the question, then a richly toned male voice emanated from the device saying, 'The Secretary on-board is Okrotis Retorridus Pendocris.'

'Oh, *him*,' sighed Yorvelt, sounding exasperated. 'Perhaps I should have known better – but even so, I would have expected more.'

Brocke piped up, 'Madraser comes from a legal family, Dar. Her mother was a Senior Judge and was involved in the Rebel Trials at Tharsis. Her father has been a life-long HS Tribunal lawyer. She probably tied Pendocris up in knots. And you can bet that her protest will hold water.'

'Even so, I wish Pendocris had given us better warning, Indry,' said Yorvelt. 'Ylesia, get our legal people onto this right now, please,' he said, 'I don't want a laser cutter thrown into the plans to evacuate all those people on Oceanus.' Varga-Horgans nodded a silent assent.

'Meanwhile, I'll talk to her,' said Brocke.

'No, Indry. Please!' Jenner pleaded. 'It's my responsibility, as you well know. I should be the one to talk to her.' Brocke considered for a moment, then nodded his approval.

Varga-Horgans said, in sour tones, 'I don't know why the Admiralty placed Madraser ahead of Arkas Tenak, for Fleet Admiral. I find it astonishing that the government didn't express an opinion one way or the other.'

There were some mutterings of sympathy for Varga-Horgans's statement, but Brocke stepped in, 'I know we have some control over the ships, in the form of the Secretariat, Ylesia, but I'm afraid internal promotions, or demotions, have to remain with the Admiralty. Please leave the following off the record, Xander,' he said, turning momentarily to the apparently inert bear, then addressing his colleagues again he continued, 'Off-record, I agree with Ylesia. Tenak has tremendous experience and ability, and his approach is much more … measured.'

'Also "off the record" then,' said Kar-Yoonsuh Jae, 'I happen to think that Tenak isn't dynamic enough. He's actually *too* considered in his approach.'

'I think that's what's needed,' retorted Yorvelt, glancing at the Finance Minister, his brows knitted, 'I suppose this subject brings us on to the final item: Oceanus,' he said. 'I see that no datapod has yet been received from the Ra system.'

'Bit early, Dar,' said Brocke.

'True,' said the Secretary General, then continued, wistfully now, almost seeming lost in faraway thought, 'I've never stopped being amazed that we're talking about periods of a few standard weeks, when Oceanus is 123 light years away. And our best telescopes can only see it as it was all that time ago.' Most of the others turned to each-other with mystified looks. But the S-G seemed to snap out of it quickly and said, 'Anyway, I just hope that Tenak is making some progress with the Oceanus government, and that President of theirs. Am I the only one who's ever met Arbella, by the way?'

Brocke said, 'I did once, but it was on Earth, some years ago. Back when she still took the trouble to come the distance. Of course, OA doesn't have any ships that can get here, anyway.'

'She seemed alright to me,' said Yorvelt, 'but I met her before she won their last election. I would have thought she'd be very amenable to starting an evacuation. Well, we all felt that. But the last datapod we got back from the Oceanus government, wasn't encouraging, was it, Indry?'

'True,' said Brocke, 'but it didn't seem to rule out plans for drawing up evacuation. The OA government's position on the science seems to be sort of ... at odds with some of our best experts but there's little detail in it. And most of our people felt it was nothing other than a "meteor-flash" of injured pride.'

'You could be forgiven for thinking there was almost a denial of some of the predictions we made about the fate of their world,' said Yorvelt, with a deeply troubled look.

'There was no explicit mention of a denial, Dar,' said Brocke, 'just doubt about some of our most recent findings. We all felt that at the time, remember?'

'Well, I've gone over their words from that last datapod recording, Indry, and now I'm not sure if we didn't underestimate the depth of the problem,' said Yorvelt, with a deep frown. After a pause, he continued, with renewed frustration in his voice, 'I sorely wish that we could set up EM communication between our worlds. That would bring the comm lag down to a couple of light days. As it stands, any such signals would take 123 years to get there and another 123 years to get the reply!'

Brevans just shrugged, 'As I think I indicated sir, we're mostly out of options on signals, right now, but we aren't giving up just yet.'

Yorvelt nodded in disconsolate approval as Brevans continued, 'Actually, the Ra system has been continuously observed for about 250 years, and colonisation started 132 years ago, which means that for the last 9 years we've been looking at it as it was when humans first reached it. Strangely, we've not seen much evidence of *our own* arrival there – even with the most powerful telescope built…'

'You're talking about the "Far Edge" telescope, aren't you, Professor?' interjected Varga-Horgans.

'Yes, it's the massive instrument, out beyond Neptune's orbit at present. And of course, there's more bad news about Ra, I'm afraid.' Without stopping he went on to explain, 'The most recent observations, on all relevant wavelengths, show a 20 percent increase in the Karabrandon waves in Ra's deep chi-zone; the main radiative zone, over two hundred thousand kilometres below its surface. They indicate even greater long-term instability than was thought just a few standard weeks ago. A dramatic change.'

There was an audible gasp from the others.

'Now he tells us,' said Yorvelt, with a sigh.

'I'm sorry Secretary General,' said Brevans, looking slightly mystified, 'but this info has been published on the Tek Log part of UltraNet for at least ten hours.'

'Yes of course. Thank you, Professor,' said Brocke, 'but our aides have been a bit busy lately, as have we. But thank you for reminding us, anyway. It is most … relevant.'

'Surely, the scientists on the original expedition to reach the Ra system, the pioneers, would have seen this, wouldn't they?' objected Varga-Horgans.

'Not at all, I'm sorry to say,' said the Professor. 'You see, modern methods of observation, let alone the data accumulated over the time since they went out there, mean our knowledge is many magnitudes greater than theirs was. They wouldn't have noticed any problem and neither did the scientists back here, at the time. Otherwise, they wouldn't have approved any of the missions which established colonisation. I was hoping that ...'

At that point Xander, who had lately gone into a strange sort of crouch in the corner, suddenly stood, his eyes starting to glow with a baleful red light. Yorvelt leaned forward, a look of deep concern on his face, and asked him what was wrong.

The bear marched to centre of the room and said, in unhurried and largely placid tones,

'I am so sorry to alarm you Secretary General. I did not mean to do so. However, I have just received some unfortunate news by way of the Centralised Intelligence Nexus, which they bade me inform you of, urgently. The news is likely to reach The Ultranet and SolNet within minutes anyway ...'

'Damnatious,' said Yorvelt, 'what is it, Xander'

'There has been an explosion at the main plant, on Earth, which processes the elements and alloys used in the interstellar vessel crashcouches. These are used by crew and passengers to enable them to travel safely through ...'

'Yes, yes, we know,' said Kar-Yonsuh Jae, 'please get on with it.'

'As you wish, Madama. The explosion, which may or may not be sabotage, has halted production until the facility on Mars can be brought online. That may be some months.'

There were more gasps at this, but Xander had extra news.

'I am also sorry to advise that there a major strike, has been announced, of specialised workers in the supply chains for components for the civilian yards currently tasked with building the fleet of dedicated ferry vessels for Oceanus. The strike is considered by specialists to be of likely long duration.'

The meeting began to break up into a hubbub of private discussions, till Brocke broke in with, 'Gentilhomms. Please … I have to ask you to listen!'

Yorvelt added, 'Xander isn't finished.'

The bear, still standing in the centre of the room was holding up a little furry arm and was furiously wagging it. There was silence.

As Yorvelt and the others looked on with expressions of trepidation, Xander said, still in his usual mellow way, 'Thank you Secretary General, Deputy Secretary General. The new data has allowed me to complete and amend the updated analysis I was carrying out earlier whilst you were all speaking. My analysis takes account of the 8.2 billion variables that have been resolved out of the accumulated data concerning the state of Ra and the proposed evacuation, as well as the news I just brought. My hypothesis comes with the recommendation that it be tested further by submission to a team of quantum computers. The conclusion concerns the time factors involved in the planned evacuation. The data has included all necessary refits to Navy ships, the conversion of civilian research vessels and the problems posed by ….'

Becoming exasperated again, sighing heavily and rolling his eyes, Yorvelt pleaded, 'Xander! I'm sure you've done everything you can. Please give us your conclusions.'

'I'm so sorry, sir,' said Xander. 'My conclusion is that the proposed evacuation of the human inhabitants of Oceanus Alpha, *cannot* succeed. The plan, as it stands, to rescue *all* the inhabitants, will not work. Many tens of thousands are likely to be left on that world when the star's outer envelope disrupts. I am also assuming that the inhabitants have in fact agreed to institute full evacuation procedures within a matter of weeks. I will break down the details of my analysis for you, Mer Secretary General, over the next few hours.'

After Xander stopped speaking, leaving looks of despair all around, Yorvelt said, quietly, 'I think this meeting's going to have to go on for some time.'

Interlude

THE SHOCK OF EMERGENCE

A giant ball of super-heated plasma, blisteringly bright, comet like in shape, but much larger – many thousands of kilometres across, seemed to flash into existence in the space which humans call "ordinary space". It streaked into the observable Universe at tens of thousands of kilometres per second, issuing a radiant tail more than a million kilometres in length; a searing ribbon of luminosity blazing against the backdrop of deep, cold, space. In a shock wave of bright spectral hues the object began to decelerate, relative to the star background, slowing, as it headed toward one particular star in the jet-black firmament. This sun shone with a rich orange hue, appearing just a little brighter than all the millions of other background suns. It was slightly brighter because it was the one closest to this new, comet-like, object.

As the blazing sphere slowed further, it did something which a human observer might not have expected any comet to do. The brilliant nucleus began to splinter, then seemed to explode in a vast splash of phosphorescence, widening into a shower of sparks; droplets of liquid luminescence in their billions, scintillating, like so many newborn, tiny, stars.

And yet the myriad starry droplets themselves suddenly slowed in their outward rush, decelerating as though being pulled on by invisible, impossibly strong, elastic cords, until they reached an almost stationary point. But in microseconds they began to fall back toward their origin, the whole shower crowding in, coalescing, merging once more, to reform the super-bright nucleus, again a condensing fiery mass. This quickly resolved itself, as though cooling incredibly rapidly into something solid; a structure shaped like a tear drop, quickly spinning, a massive, ruddy coloured, ember. But it was an ember the size of a dwarf planet.

**

Having coalesced out of the quantum foam of "complex space", the great vessel had slid back into the geometrically 'flat' Universe from whence it originally came. This latest phase of the journey of its occupants, an epic sojourn, was nearing its destination.

In their inimitably long history, the occupants of the vessel had undertaken this kind of journey many times before, transitioning from real space to complex space zone and back again. They had travelled unfathomable distances through the cosmos within the galaxy we call "the Milky Way". And inside the vessel the beings; part organic and part cybernetic, stirred anew, their organic elements awaking from the slumber of induced stasis.

The Symphony of Energy sings in our favour. Our destination lies both before and behind us, flowed the minds of Percepticon, her thoughts travelling like a mountain cataract, but millions of times faster, from its organic brains into its non-organic adjuncts, and back again. *Our aeons-long search has ended and borne fruit,* her thoughts continued to flow, in joyous abandon. She had been the first of her kin to be pulled out of her long sleep by her cybernetic brains. A vast tract of time had passed in the ordinary Universe since their last way station.

During that journey Percepticon had sometimes neared the surface of sleep and had felt lonely then, missing her kin, unable to communicate with either them or her adjuncts. Yet her cyber-adjuncts had been aware of her situation and, to ward off stress, had pressed her back into slumber. Hermoptica, one of her kin, relatively nearby, also now awoke. Its thoughts flowed, from both its organic and cybernetic brains, into the vessel's cyber-nexus, and thence into Percepticon, and now regaled her with huge greetings and warm affection.

She reciprocated with her own thoughts of tenderness and together they sensed the awakening of all their near kin; the many others in the vast chamber arout them. There was a feeling of great joy at the ending of this part of the "Great Journey", feelings which stretched through the depths of the ship's humungous sentience capsule. Yet, Hermoptica had also awoken en-route and for all of ten milliseconds; a long time during a stasis period, for such a being. It was now tired and would need to drink deeply of stasis when their business here was done.

Though locked out of the realm of the innermost thoughts of one of Hermoptica's brains, an area it would not wish to share with Percepticon at present, the latter still sensed a sudden change in the flow of information. The thought stream was conveyed mainly from Hermoptica's cybernetic adjuncts. It was clearly stimulated to a state of some excitement, almost alarm. In exchanges with her kin, which, in human terms, would have taken no more than one or two hundred thousandths of a second, Percepticon's thoughts flowed back to her chosen one,

Your adjuncts have fed elements of disturbance into your middle minds - as have mine. How many of your frontal brains have also become disconcerted?

All of them, noted Hermoptica. *What is the exact nature of ....?* But the flow stopped abruptly; a halt lasting all of one ten thousandth of a second. The metal coils of its cybernetic tentacles twitched and tightened around themselves. Then the thought flow resumed but alarmed Percepticon yet further, crashing through her, almost invading the being's middle minds. Hermoptica had thought-flowed, *There is ANOTHER here!*

Yes, yes, I have perceived this flow too, came her reply, *Another? How can this be? How did we not know?*

Their middle minds discussed the discovery and, with quantum qubits boiling and flashing in and out of the vacuum, they shared information, as well as thoughts of consternation and puzzlement. They also exchanged information with their respective cybernetic enhancements, until Percepticon concluded, *We must awaken the Superadjunct.*

Dare we? It is in repose now, flowed Hermoptica.

We must disturb it - of necessity, came the instantaneous reply, *The Superadjunct will need to re-analyse and advise.*

Then we must adjoin its auxiliaries.

I have information that our other kin have also now sensed the Other. Only once has this happened before.

Indeed, once only - and many aeons distance from this locus.

Chapter 4

A SPARK IN TIME

In the heart of Janitra Mike D. Tanniss and Arkas A. Tenak walked the kilometre and a half from the Central Hotel to the restaurant the Admiral had recommended, along wide streets, quiet for the time of evening. Mike was glad to finally stretch his legs. The blocks lining the streets conformed to the pattern he'd seen from the maglev, mostly a mere two or three stories high. Most of them were solid looking buildings made of large cream coloured stone, with relatively small windows and often with quaint flights of steps leading up to large porchways. Mike couldn't think of anywhere on Earth, or Mars, that was quite the same. But that was surely a good thing about travelling, wasn't it, to see different places?

It was still light, and a warm breeze blew up the dusty street toward them, lifting thin wisps of haze around them, allowing a slightly cooling effect to stave off the sticky warmth of early evening. Mike noticed that there were none of the transport mag' tubes which characterised most routeways in most City States on Earth. But the main streets had at least one monorail, sunken into the ground. Curious, he thought. Something else he'd never seen. The rails ran past the larger well-spaced houses and shops.

There were also very small, bubble-like, automated electric cars running very slowly along a single marked lane in many streets. Most of them seemed to be carrying piles of metal boxes, or pulling miniature trailers loaded with boxes. There was hardly any noise from any of the vehicles. Mike assumed the loads were deliveries and supplies.

Though few in number, some cars actually carried passengers. Most individual units carried no more than two people, but Mike occasionally spotted, along some sidestreets, groups of two or three linked cars.

Several blocks they passed had glass enclosed fronts at street level. Tenak said they were called "shops". They apparently sold various types of goods, meaning that you had to physically enter them and buy what you wanted by exchanging monetary units, Oceanus credit notes, for goods. Apparently. the type of goods sold were usually signified by large signs affixed above the premises. There wasn't anything like that on Earth. Mike couldn't help but be fascinated. He understood that things were done like this, back home, hundreds of years ago and for some time after the emergence from the new dark ages.

The shops all appeared to be closed for the day, which Mike thought was a pity. He'd have loved to explore them. That would have to wait. Some "Devians"; the name all these people living on Bhumi-Devi called themselves, made their way along the road, often sauntering, like them, others hurrying, shooting curious glances at the two strangers in their midst. As in the government building, Mike felt that the fashion sense of the people here seemed to consist of wanting to dress in featureless, dowdy, one-piece overalls, or otherwise, like bundles of rags. The citizens of Oceanus really had none of the fashions or sense of fun and the exotic which characterised the sartorial tastes of most people on Earth's continents. Like their tek, there seemed something vaguely familiar about all this but also very strange.

Ah, yes, he thought, the tek. He'd seen, first-hand, the nature of Oceanus computer tek in Arbella's office. Like her, his understanding was that some locals had use of ancient, bulky "personal computers" similar to those used on Earth back in the last quarter of the 20th century. But he knew there was nothing on Oceanus like the SolNet or SocioNet, or any of the others, back home. And he'd already had some experience of the "telephone" tek here. He'd also heard that some people even had cellphones, rarely used on Earth now. Here, the cellphones were primitive and extremely bulky. Tenak had also told him that some people, many of them working out on the land, had neither computers or cellphones. But Tenak had also made him aware that all of this was the result of a set of community decisions; the deliberate adoption by this society, long ago, of a "tek lag".

Of course, the original pioneers had brought with them all the latest technology available to them at that time, now long out of date in the Home System but still vastly in advance of anything on Oceanus now. Here, successive governments had discouraged the spread of the personal use tek paraphernalia ubiquitous throughout the Solar System, except in some limited places. Even private companies on Oceanus had eschewed such things, refusing to produce generations of "devices" for personal use, despite the obvious commercial gain made by those organisations who had done so on Earth, for a couple of hundred years now. Back home many felt that this had come at a cost to the environment and to people's psychological health. Mike didn't really accept this view but he grudgingly admired the Oceanus people for avoiding this sort of "game" and felt it was remarkable, Mike that the vast majority here had co-operated with and perpetuated the very different tek regime on Oceanus. Even so, he felt that in total, this place seemed utterly alien.

He would eventually find out how alien.

*

Mike had decided it best to blend in, having cast off his work tunic and trousers, and replacing them, begrudgingly, with a thin utilitarian one-piece jump suit, from the ship's stores. True Devian style, he told himself. Yet he still felt self-conscious and still seemed to be drawing stares. Was it something about the way he walked? Tenak had said these people were ultra-polite and not generally prone to staring at strangers but then, the Admiral hadn't seemed to waste a chance in defending them and their culture, Mike noted. But he had agreed that most Devians so far encountered seemed to be polite, almost to the point of being irritating. Even so, he was still getting the wide-eyed stares. Well, so be it. He really was the stranger here, after all.

Striding alongside him Tenak didn't seem to notice anything except the scenery. He still wore the dubiously spotted short sleeve shirt he had donned at the hotel and Mike felt almost embarrassed by him. He looked like a tourist in the subtropics on Earth of a bygone era, from before the dark ages.

As they strolled along the rapidly emptying streets they witnessed the beginning of one of the legendary sunsets of Oceanus. Ra was sinking quite quickly in the west, setting in the same direction as on Earth, because Oceanus also rotated from west to east. Mike knew well that Janitra was close to the eastern seaboard of Bhumi Devi and between the coast and the Capital was farmland, but cultivated land extended around sixty-five kilometres to the west of the Capital too. Beyond that lay the deep interior. So, to look toward the west was to gaze in the direction of the vast, almost uninhabited and, to a large extent, still mysterious, interior of the continent. At its greatest width the singular continent stretched, from the edge of the farmland, nearly more than eight thousand kilometres, to its western shores. North to south the continent was larger, extending nearly nine thousand klicks.

To the east of his Mike's position in Janitra, beyond the coast, which lay around 250 klicks to the north-east, was the vast, "Great Ocean". Like most geographical features on Oceanus the name had been given by the original settlers and they had wanted, symbolically, to divide the planet girdling ocean into more manageable subunits. The Great Ocean was the huge portion nearest Janitra, a titanic expanse whose wild waves crashed against the equally wild shores of Bhumi-Devi all along the eastern coast.

Ra was sinking now into a bed of thick cloud lying on the Western horizon appearing to Mike like a sea in the sky. It flamed with deep hues of carmine, orange, yellow and crimson. Tenak had been unable to stop gazing at it for several minutes while they walked. Not removing his eyes from the vision, he spoke to Mike in awed, hushed tones.

'No matter how many times you see the great things; you know – the things that surprise you by their awesome beauty, like ring planets gas out there ... and the gas giants,' he said, smiling, 'but there's something uniquely beautiful about a sunset on a planet with an atmosphere. And it doesn't matter whether that's on the Earth, here, on Prithvi, or Saturn's Titan. But I reckon the sunsets here are the best of all. Even more beautiful than on Earth, don't you think?'

'Well, they're certainly colourful, Arkas.'

'Still, you don't seem very impressed. That's too bad.'

'I am, Arkas. It's great but I also can't help looking at that ... that dark mass of ... landscape over there – below the cloud. There's no lights over there – artificial lights

I mean, not anywhere over there. No hover transports, no traces of super-maglevs. Nothing. It just seems very … kind of big. That's all.'

'There's nothing out there you need to worry about, Mike,' said his companion, 'at least not in these parts,'

He's just trying to be annoyingly reassuring, Mike thought. Tenak was very aware of Mike's form of agoraphobia. A more cynical person might think he was mocking him but Mike dismissed that idea straight away.

'What do you mean?' Mike retorted, deciding to needle Tenak a little. 'Perhaps you're trying to imply there's huge predators or other horrifying creatures *somewhere else* on this continent? Is that it? Well, there aren't any on Bhumi Devi, my friend. Do you think I didn't take the trouble to look it up on the shipNet?

'Okay, relax. You're right Mike, but your research was incomplete. There are one or two types of critters, way out there, that might put the "hyper-jets" *up your exit pipe.* Small ones maybe, but still fiercey-feist. Still, I think I'll let you complete your research to find out more. And there's not as much on the shipNet anyway.'

'Oh, I know that, but we know enough to be sure there aren't any large mammals here, no elephants, or big cats or dogs, or the like. Not on the continent. Odd that. I know these people like being a bit mysterious about their planet but even they wouldn't manage to keep quiet about things like that. No, my understanding is that the continent is mostly empty of large beasts, but I do know that there are some large sea-going reptiles out there – in the oceans. Mike glanced toward the eastern horizon, which was darkening rapidly, like an indigo cloak spreading toward the zenith. There was silence for a few moments, then Tenak said,

'Okay, but there's many species of large birds here. Just look up there.' He pointed toward the southern sky where it was still possible to spot a small flock of birds. And they had to be large, given their likely distance. Mike had seen some of the birdles earlier, but these things seemed as though they might be even larger. Their sharply angular, black shapes hardly seemed to move in the still air, far above.

'Those birdles have got to be about three metres across,' said Tenak. 'They're also more like reptiles.'

'More like a cross between bats and reptiles, surely?' said Mike. 'And they're called ... um, yeah, Arcingbirds? Ain't that it? And they're not dangerous to humans, Arkas. There aren't any dangerous birds on the continent anymore. In fact, I think the only ones known to be dangerous to humans are now on an island called Simurgh and ... I believe they were moved there by the early pioneers. Another mystery – like you said.'

'True enough, I suppose.'

'No "suppose," about it, Arkas. It strikes me as real odd that a lot of the explorations, and the studies done by the early explorers seem to have been ...sort of ... forgotten. Overlooked maybe. But mysteries there are, still. For example, why should a planet like this not give rise to any sentient species? It's so much like the Earth after all. A bit smaller, sure. Quite a bit younger, I suppose, but still over four billion years, I think. It's weirdly like the Earth. And yet, where are the large land animals? Even the planet's atmosphere is a close replica of Earth's, and I saw a note that said even the geology is very similar, right down to the presence of tectonic plates, volcanism, the lot. Didn't get into the geology stuff in a lot of detail, though. No point really.'

'Hold on, Mer Secretary, there's nothing to say that a planet like this *must* ever have large land animals,' said Tenak, evidently trying to slip a few words of his own into the conversation. 'And besides, maybe they were all made extinct millions of years ago,' he continued. 'There are theories about that, you know. Maybe there was sentient life here, once, but perhaps it was wiped out by something. Or maybe they wiped themselves out and most else along with them. Maker knows, Mike, we humans have come close to doing it to ourselves – and to the rest of life on the Earth. More than once. Maybe it's a deep-seated consequence of self-awareness. And that idea's been around for centuries.'

'Well, I did look up enough to know that there's never been a sign of any sentient species ever having lived on Oceanus, at any stage, Arkas. No fossils. And where are the roads, the buildings, the bridges, ruins of some sort, or ... manufactured things or something? No-one's ever found anything.'

'Because they haven't found anything yet doesn't mean there isn't anything to be found. Maybe some day.'

Mike snorted but he felt very talkative tonight, so he continued, in amiable mood, 'You mean the fact nothing's been found during the, what …? Oh yeah, the 130 years that humans have been here? That doesn't count for anything? Tug my wrist again, Arkas. This is the 25th Century, not the 17th.' Mike tried to keep from laughing out loud. He enjoyed this baiting.

Tenak was persistent too. Mike could tell his friend was enjoying this as much as he.

'Still, there's a different sort of mentality at work here, my friend,' said the Admiral, 'and I thought you'd realised that by now. Maybe the locals are more concerned with preserving what's right here, right now, in front of them. Maybe scraping some sort of living from the bare rocks of this planet and preserving as much of its wilderness as possible at the same time. That's always been my over-impression, Mike.'

Tenak wiped the sweat from his face with a kerchief. It was starting to get very sticky again, the breeze having died.

'I'm thinking that maybe, "maybe", is your favourite word this evening, Arkas,' Mike teased, 'Anyway, enough okay? Is this the place you were talking about?' he asked, as they turned a sharp corner and stopped next to a glass fronted portico. The sign above the window read, "The Argonautica". Mike was just able to make out the faded words underneath, which something like, "The Best Fishreum in Town". What's that mean, he wondered?

Tenak nodded, so in they strode. Mike was immediately amazed. This place still had people serving meals. They were called waiters, weren't they? A man wearing a white cloth thing, an apron maybe, walked toward them. Mike noticed the "apron" had some brown stains on it.

The man fussed over them as if he'd known them for years and, smiling broadly, showed them to a table, all the while making grand sweeping gestures with his arms. A stained uniform like that wouldn't have gone down well on the ship, even if they'd had waiters. Still, you had to make allowances, thought Mike.

The interior was quite spacious and there were few other customers. Strangely, the place seemed to be only half lit – by primitive looking light fitment things high up along the walls. A regular hive of activity, Mike thought sardonically. The tables were laid in a manner reminiscent of pictures he'd seen depicting restaurants in the 19th and 20th centuries, in olden Europe; the kind with chintz like cloths and small glass vases filled with exotic looking blooms. In this case, the flowers were mostly withered and brown. Must be locally grown, he thought. The chairs weren't sprung and were hard on the backside. As he settled in Mike saw a sheet of floppy greyish white material, like flimsy-plex, with an outdated form of Anglo-span printed on its surface. He picked it up and spoke to it.

'Please give me a full resume of the available meals and a breakdown of the nutritional … What's the matter?'

Tenak, who had been watching with a smirk on his face said, 'Don't be a flick-wit, Mike. You can't talk to it. There's no tek like that down here. It's a paper menu – made from plant fibres. Paper? Remember that stuff?'

Mike suddenly felt a fool and mumbled in embarrassment but as Tenak spoke again his smile was broad and genuine.

'Don't worry,' he said, 'an easy mistake to make. Just got to get used to this place, I guess.'

Mike then followed Tenak's example and tried to read the faded words on the printed sheet, but they didn't make much sense to him. Tenak had scanned through it already and recommended something called "Thragglefish", as the main course. He'd been here before after all, so Mike trusted his choice and agreed to have the same.

Within ten minutes or so the order had arrived. Each man was confronted with an enormous plate of steaming fish and vegetables. At least it looks the part, thought Mike but he wasn't entirely convinced by the smell, which reminded him of old-fashioned beef stew, rather than fish. Each dish came with "plotties"; a kind of potato but shaped like a carrot. Tenak waded into his Thragglefish with gusto. Mike was hungry but still suspicious. He put a small amount of the fish in his mouth and chewed carefully. As expected, it was a strange taste compared to the frozen sea food available on The Monsoon. Still, it wasn't unpleasant. But it wasn't long before he got bogged down in so many small bones they threatened to stick in his gullet. He grimaced at Tenak for, probably, the fifth time.

'Here am I, showing you the best place in town,' said the Admiral, 'and pointing you at the local delicacies, even paying for it with my own credits. And all you can do is look miserable and grunt. You're just a fussi-wigg, that's all.'

Mike feigned a look of shock, then said, 'Don't give me all that. You're leaving half of it yourself.'

Tenak's bluff face broke into a grin, 'That's what this stuff is like, my friend, so it's no good sending it back.'

It was Mike's turn to grin, 'Okay, but don't think I won't keep you to the promise about paying. I might just order something else – and treat it as "on the ship".'

Whilst they ate or, in Mike's case, picked at the fare, they began to discuss ordinary life for people on Oceanus. Tenak surprised Mike by mentioning something he himself had obviously missed on the shipNet. He said that transport of food around the eastern lowlands was done mainly with helium filled air ships, pushed by solar powered propellers. But items like Thragglefish would have been layed on ice and sent up from the coast by electric car, as fast as possible. For destinations further inland it would have to be frozen.

Mike was fascinated by the idea of air ships and as their discussion continued he found his interest building.

Tenak said that he felt the people on this planet were, 'closer to the world they lived in – the way the world really is. Much more than we are.'

'So, they're hickbits,' said Mike, 'or "back to the caves" characters.'

'Not at all, Mike, as somehow, they've managed to combine a simple life with an elegant civilisation of remarkable sophistication.'

Mike just gazed at him. He felt unconvinced.

After they had discussed Oceanus life for a few more minutes Mike said, 'It's a penging shame that there isn't quicker communications between the HS and this place. It might help to bring them up to date a bit more.'

'Don't let any of the locals hear you say that, Mike. They value their independence too much. Wouldn't want us or still less, the HS government hovering round them too much.'

'Yeah, I get that, but they *really are* isolated – big time, aren't they? Let's face it, the journey here through the conduit took about, what, a bit over 25 minutes? But it took our ship – and it's one of the fastest – five weeks to get from Earth orbit out to a suitable conduit transit zone. Then another four weeks from the other end of the conduit, in this system, to insert into Oceanus orbit.'

Tenak smiled lightly and said, 'That's because all conduit zones are billions of klicks into the outermost parts of system. That's the only place they can form, as you well know, Mike. And I know this system's the furthest you've come so far but you should be used to long journeys on the ship by now. Still, I take your point about the isolation.' Turning more serious he added, 'After all, that's what's going to scupper evacuation efforts if they don't change their ideas here. With those journey times it might start getting a bit close for comfort. But I'm confident we'll get there in the end. Faster remote comms would be a help, of course. Help with getting data back and fore but the conduits don't seem to allow for it at all. Weren't there supposed to be experiments with a new type of collimated beams or something?'

'Yeah, I know about that, but I don't rate their chances. Too many variables. Too little known about overall conduit physics. But I hear that the Kalahari is slated to be able to cut journey times by a fifth. New fusion engines.'

'Let's hope the efforts to bring that one online are successful, eh?'

With that the two men fel, quiet. After a rather strange dessert of locally made ice cream, flavoured with some sort of berry, and a cup of what was supposed to be kaffee, but was definitely not, Tenak said he intended retiring to the Hotel.

'I'm sure you'll want to stay around here and take in the nightlife, Mike,' he said, half smiling.

'What night life, Arkas? I thought you said they don't go in for that sort of thing in these parts.'

'That's not what I said. I just said you won't find the variety of nightlife, or as much of it as you'd get back on Earth. But there's still plenty of bars open till the small hours, if that's what you want. There's also local theatre shows and the like, open till about 12.00 pm, local. Don't forget that the day is slightly longer than on Earth and by shiptime. Anyway, did you know they have people who actually stand on a stage and sing or act or whatnot-much. They were called theatre shows at home – long time back. I thoroughly recommend them.'

'Wow, all that!' said Mike, the sarcasm ringing in his voice. 'To think they still have *theatre* shows here. Yeah, I've read my history. Nah, sorry Arkas, I think I'll just go for a couple of drinks.'

'Okay, your loss,' said Tenak and got up. 'I'll settle up here with my credit notes. What you spend afterwards is down to you. By the way, whatever you do, don't drink so much you get kruddoed because I need you to be in good form for tomorrow's meetings.' Tenak flashed a deadly serious look before turning and paying their waiter, who was standing at some form of ancient machine. Then he was gone.

Mike thought about the last time he'd been kruddoed, which was on his 22nd birthday. He had drunk enough non-synth alcohol to fill a Sol Class cruiser – and then paid the penalty for the next four days. Luckily it had been during an extended shore leave. That had been 18 months ago, back on good old Mars, and he'd hardly touched anything since so it seemed a bit unfair for Tenak to lecture him.

Realising that his stomach was churning slightly he contemplated the folly of having Devian ice cream after Thragglefish, so he got up and, trying to ignore his aching guts, he wandered over to a bar at the far end of the restaurant. At least the bars were recognisable here. He reckoned a warming drink might help his insides and, deciding to break his self-imposed, temporary only, ban on alcohol, he ordered something that was listed above the bar as a "stellar whirski".

'No stellars here, fren-manry,' said the barman, curiously. 'Not such tonight,' he added, staring at Mike as if he'd just come from a different world – which of course, he had. Mike thought it odd, but he didn't say anything. He decided to have a shot of Devian "rummer", which was, apparently, available.

The amount he got was tiny yet it came in a massive tumbler. But it tasted good and he was pleased with its stimulating effect. Still, he decided not to stay here. It was far too quiet and he wanted to some female company. He wanted that very badly. Abena, back on the ship, had been the last woman with whom he'd had sexual contact – until she started harassing him about developing their relationship ever further; a step he found as appetising as putting a hand in a fusion welder. She had even talked about monogamist marriage, when most people of her age were practising polygamy back in the Home System.

Mike wanted the multiple partner bit but without the bonding commitment; a tradition formerly known as marriage, but now called "merrie-bonding". He reflected on the fact that Tenak had been merrie-bonded and became one of his wife's three husbands, or "bond-masclas". Imagine that. An unlucky mascla, thought Mike. Apparently, it had seemed to suit Tenak at first. The three men had kept out of each-other's way as much as possible but there were inevitable conflicts between them and with the "bonder-fem"; the wife, in old parlance. But, thought Mike, it had to be just as bad for femnas, in the case of men who had several bond-fems. Not good for anyone, thought Mike.

He recalled Tenak telling him how he and his bond-fem had split up some years ago and he now saw little of the child who had been the result of the Bonding. The bond-fem had abandoned one of the other men and then kept moving home around the Home System with the remaining one, always staying just out of touch, without breaking the law. Tenak didn't talk much about it and Mike wasn't inclined to intrude but he understood that these days he was in communication with the son, now aged about 18, via Solnet only. Since then the Admiral seemed to have decided to be practically celibate. That fate wouldn't suit Mike at all.

He suddenly decided he would try his hand at "bouncing off", a local woman; in Navy talk that meant trying to get a quick sexual liaison with a mascla or femna. He wondered what the local women – femna, were like. He had read that the Oceanus culture was entirely monogamous. Polygamy was strictly banned by law. Mike had no time for the nonsense Tenak had gotten into, but banning polygamy seemed positively archaic. The overriding rule which governed polygamy back home was that you had to be open and completely transparent about all the relationships. So, having multiple partners, before or within marriage, was permissible but it was based on mutual consent. It was considered extremely immoral, indeed totally unacceptable, for anything to be kept back from all involved. Many groups had the rule written up in formal, legally binding, agreements. Mike understood these things but he felt it all introduced a significant inconvenience factor, and he'd always tried to find ways around it. Always.

After leaving the "Argonautica" he turned the corner and wandered down some dark backstreets, searching for a suitable bar where he might find some local women. The sky was now dark purple and the stars getting brighter. The evening was sweet and warm and the narrow paths he trod were lined with fragrant smelling bushes of some kind. Hardly anything stirred in the lowering light, as he continued to wander, paying no attention to where he headed.

Reaching a tiny footbridge spanning a babbling brook he crossed and entered a maze of tiny streets lined with some very old looking cottages. These were much smaller than anything in the main part of town and he realised he'd strayed into an outlying suburb. The old buildings seemed to get more and more ramshackle as he wandered on and sometimes he passed dark clothed individuals, whose faces he could not see, often just standing around. Or he was passed by small knots of people hurrying on their way. No-one seemed to be "living it up" or enjoying Tenak's "nightlife". No one said a word to him but he felt he was still drawing stares, though it wasn't always easy to tell in the gloom.

Street lighting was scarce but, in some areas there were small lamps which seemed to be the bell like flowers of tall, living, plants. How weird. They cast a soft bluish-white glow which threw down little pools of illumination in the darkness, every few metres. It wasn't like back home, he thought. Hardly enough light here, but it was pretty, he supposed. A group of rowdy locals careened past him, bouncing roughly off one of his elbows. That was the first time he had encountered anything less than absolute politeness amongst the local populace. But he knew what they'd been doing. He could smell alcohol in the air a klick off, long before they'd swaggered past. He tried to make out what they were saying but the thickness of their accents and the nature of the dialect mostly defeated him. Probably just as well, he thought. Much of it seemed to be directed his way and he reckoned it didn't sound too complimentary.

He saw a sign at the next corner proclaiming, "Bukkaneers Retreat: Best Shotties in Janitra." A cartoon hand on a wooden stick pointed toward some strange looking nearby bushes. But why bushes? If that's what they were. As he neared them he saw that they had been concealing a long, leafy, path that led to a low building which looked like a large, grey, shabby, shack. He walked some way along the path, whilst a little voice in thr back of his mind said this might not be a good idea. But then he spotted a young woman emerge from the shack's doorway and lean against the wall. She was wearing scant clothing – perhaps not surprising, in the still, warm, evening air – and then she saw him. She smiled broadly at his tentative approach. A good start, he thought, with rising anticipation and a very slight tingling in his loins. He must be desperate, he mused unhappily. Stilll, he warned himself, he must be careful. Calm down!

His doubts made him pause, just for a moment, but he overcame them and, as he neared the femna he smiled and voiced a greeting. She grinned and spoke with the kind of liquid, husky voice that many men, including Mike, found compelling, 'Haya stranger thar. You looking a bit lost yet. Comen in, comen in. Cooling comfort in here now,' and with that she opened the door for him, a sly smile on her face. He peeped in first, his eyes taking a while to adjust to the dark interior. He saw a bar area illuminated by small lights but not much else. There was clamorous music he didn't recognise and hardly anyone drinking; just one or two older men.

As his eyes adjusted, he could see there were several girls who seemed to be hanging around. He found all of them quite attractive and a sense of exoticism struck him. He thought for a moment and said, 'Maybe not,' then started to turn but the woman at the door looked sorely disappointed, and said, 'Don an be like that stranger-manry. Listen here, the drinks are half cost in a few minutes. It's bunkerie evening and all. Say, you not being from round here, are yer, stranger?'

'Well, no. What's a "bunkerie evening", anyways?'

'You stand out like a sore dingdoo, manry. Not that there's anything wrong with you like that. T'would make a great change from the usual manry we get. Come in. My friends and me will be making you have a great time. Soon see.' When she saw him start to relent she encouraged him further by saying, 'Awe, com'on – please. For me, just?' He thought her smile was glorious and sensual.

That was it. He entered, almost in a hurry, and she showed him to a high stool next to the bar, 'What shall I be gettin you?' she said, as he peered around the gloomy room. Once the door had closed it had become even darker, despite the rows of tiny, multi-coloured lights over the bar and a large rotating light in the far corner, where a large box sat, issuing the strange, all pervading, rhythmic, music.

'You didn't tell me what "bunkerie evening" was,' he persisted, smiling back at the girl.

'Oh, you be seeing later. Hope you like good times though. My name is Anina, yet what is yours?'

'The name's, Mike.' he said, then turned towards the bar when he heard a man's voice ask him what he wanted. At least, he thought that's what he asked. Who could tell in this place? He glanced at the tall, gaunt figure of the bar tend standing in the shadows behind the bar. The man sported a thin grey moustache which drooped, either side of his thin mouth, almost as far as his collar bones. Mike felt a momentary prickly feeling in the hairs on the back of his neck. Brushing the feeling aside he ordered one of the local rums and the gaunt figure grunted as he wandered off to to get his drink.

A board above the bar had a price list, written in incredibly old-fashioned chalk, or paint, script. After taking a few seconds to decipher it Mike was eventually worked out that the rum would cost him twice as much here as in the Argonautica. That's going to limit my intake, he thought, but, remembering his female companion he offered her a drink as well. He was nothing if not generous, when it came to female friends, he allowed himself. She obliged his generosity and asked the bar tend for a triple "Gemmar", as she called it. Mike looked down the list for the drink and sucked his breath in, as silently as possible. What was in it? Triple density mangar grain?

Anina asked him where he came from and as he replied he spotted another young woman approaching, smiling affably. The newcomer said, 'Haya.' As Mike acknowledged her, with a wide grin on his face, the new woman spoke to Anina, grinning.

'Where all did you get this one, kiddo? He is in such a great looker manry.' She sat on a stool the other side of Mike from Anina. Things are looking interesting, he thought, the familiar feeling stirring in his loins once more. Some distance behind this newcomer Mike could see a couple of stocky men sitting by the wall. Their large heads appeared to turn on virtually non-existent necks and they both stared at him with sullen expressions, on faces like sides of beef. They were, he decided, definitely unfriendly stares. Well, I'm not breaking any local laws, he thought, or even local customs – as far as he knew.

He was wrong, of course.

'This is Mike,' said Anina, 'and Mike, this is Katrana.' Anina turned to her friend. 'Mike was saying now, he is from the Home System.'

'Goodtime to meet you Mike,' said Katrana, in a light, fruity, voice. 'Hey, that is looking like a goodly choice o' drink,' she continued and began to stare at Mike with a look of expectation on her face, until he got the message and offered to buy her a gemmar, too. He wondered how many other women were going to approach him for gemmars in this place.

Still, these were nice femnas, so he just tried to relax but somehow, he couldn't quite push away the thought of the tough looking characters, seated nearby. They never seemed to take their hard little eyes off him. He definitely didn't want to offend them but he didn't feel he was doing anything he shouldn't. He decided to ask the girls about them, 'Are they ... your friends?' he said, pointing to them with his eyes rather than daring to point in their direction, 'cos I don't want to step on anyone's feet. I'm just here for a quiet drink.'

'Oh, don't be a-worry 'bout them,' Anina oozed, 'They are only yet looking out for our safeness. You get all sorta krummies coming in here, Mike.'

'But we don't mean you, sweedy,' said Katrana, quickly.

'They probably want to know if you-ar a goin' to want some of the bunkerie cells,' Anina added.

'Ahya,' one of the men called out. It was a curiously high pitch for someone of his size, looking as though he was carved out of a block of granite. He suddenly rose and approached, holding out both his hands in anticipation of an Oceanus style double handshake. Mike greeted him and shook both his hands, as was expected of him. This mascla looked extremely fit and positively bulged with muscles, even though he was probably about 20 centimetres shorter than Mike. He felt the man's fierce strength in his handshake and was relieved when it ended. Mike pulled back from it a little and the man gazed at him, knowingly.

'I'm Darianus,' said the man, 'and now, I see you yet been getting to know the girils here. Hoping you enjoying yoursev?' but as Mike started to answer, he continued, ''tis just kind of traditional for strangers to buy everyone here a drink, or praps, pay to go into the bunkerie cells. You be knowing? Get some shots? 'Twill only cost you 40 credits a go. That be good deal, yet, you know.' He looked expectant, his broad face beaming. Behind the façade Mike could see, what? Menace? Yes, definitely. In the background but still there, he thought.

Mike tried to push aside his anxiety and with genuine curiosity said, 'I'm afraid I don't know what a bunkerie cell is – but I'd like to. And I thought that drinks were "shots". They are back home, anyway, I guess.'

Mike heard a new voice. 'Ahya, you really arint from around here, are you?' This time it was Darianus's friend, the other large man, who also arrived beside him. He introduced himself as "Adriano", and although he looked younger than Darianus he seemed even more muscle-bound. 'Have yer not heard of bunkrie cells?' he said, through a sort of twisted mouth. Turning to the girls he said, 'So now, where's this jizzer yet from?'

Mike looked these guys over. Each sported leathery looking skin, redolent of spending all day, every day, out in the gleaming rays of Ra. They probably worked their muscles in the open air by day, then spent their nights in this gloomy place. There was a definite feeling of tension in this place now and it was starting to get to Mike. He had paid fully for his drinks and didn't see why he should have to pay more for the mysterious bunkerie or bunkrie cells, or whatever. He thought about leaving but didn't see why he should. Still, he felt he would have to keep it under close review.

'Coursry now, he is being from the Home System', said Katrana to Adriano, a humourless smirk spreading unexpectedly across her features, 'but will he pay for the bunkrie cells? No, he will not. Probably don' want paying for you kin neither.'

'Oh, I am seeing,' said Adriano, loudly, 'that do say a lot. Carnt expect much from this jizzer then.'

'Yeah, cos the jizzer is from the Home System. Don' you listen?' said Darianus. He turned to Mike, 'Came in on the Navy ship did you?' he said in sharp tones. When Mike nodded, as amiably as he could, he continued, 'You arint a rating though, I will be a-guessin.'

'Nar, he's too thin an' too much like a stringy Dirke plant,' said Adriano, 'an' he certainly arint an officer!'

'Look, is there a problem here?' Mike said, feeling aggrieved and a little insulted. Yet a sense of self preservation forced him to say it as calmly and in as non-threatening way as possible. He knew it came out sounding weak and pathetic. He felt very hot and could feel droplets of sweat running down his back. 'I don't see what I'm supposed to have done wrong,' he said, I'm just looking for a quiet drink. That's all.'

Darianus moved closer to him – uncomfortably close. Mike could smell strong alcohol on the man's breath and his body stank of stale sweat. He probably wasn't kruddoed, but still full of booze. But there was no doubting that he meant business, whatever was eating him. Mike wondered if the men's behaviour was an extreme reaction to his reluctance to pay for bunkrie cells. As if reading his thoughts, Darianus explained in agitated tones, 'Since you don' know, let me tell you the bunkerie cells is for them that want to get "cool-toned," my man-mate.'

'Yeah, holo-graphie "relief", you might say,' said Adriano, rather too enthusiastically for Mike's liking.

'Be shut'n up!' snarled his friend and stared again at Mike, 'Any decent Navy rating would know that, man-mate. Not that we get too many of 'em in here yet. Navy-like is too posh for us little folkie down here.'

'Too posh they are. Arfing Navy', spat Adriano, 'Arfing Home System. Think they know what's best for us on this world.'

'Yeah, who wants them anywayar?' said Anina now, a suddenly spiteful tone taking Mike by surprise. He was genuinely dismayed to see her fine features become contorted with emotion so hostile it had to be hatred. In a flash of insight, he realised what they'd meant by "bunkerie cells". It was the use of holograms for sexual relief. Really? That's probably how they got most of their income in here. He couldn't help but utter a nervous chuckle and then instantly realised that this was not a good idea. The looks on the faces around him seemed to harden even more.

Mike turned to Katrana, and somehow hoping for something sensible, he said, 'Why holograms? They can't *do* anything. Back home, if I was interested in paying, which I'm not, I could do it with a synthetic, "full flesh-feel" robot – completely realistic. They don't say a lot but they've got good movement programs, or so I understand. You've got to be … desperate though.' Mike chuckled, which, unfortunately, came out as a mirthless, anxiety ridden cackle. He knew he was starting to gabble, and his head was throbbing with the persistent, clanging, background music. And he quickly realised he had continued to make mistakes.

Darianus glowered at him, 'Not blegging good enough are we, man-mate? Not for the Home System. 'Arfing hypocrito-pops. You know we carnt do no robots. Wouldnar do 'em anywayins. You stupidy blizzer blegger? They're damnatious things – them robots.'

Katrana now joined the invective aimed at their hapless guest, 'Yeah, damnatious things. Why don't you just go back home - space boy,' she snarled, her features twisting with rage.

'If you arint a rating or an officer-man, then what are you, man-mate?' asked Adriano, his bushy eyebrows knitting together, 'Being a spy, or somethin'?'

'No, a pervershiary,' said Anina. Not the right word, thought Mike, at least not back home, but he knew exactly what she meant. It was time to leave. Unfortunately, it wasn't going to be easy to withdraw. He was surrounded.

Standing slowly, Mike began to sidle around his stool so it was between him and Darianus, who was practically on top of him. He didn't want to get closer to either of these masclas and he didn't want them to think he was challenging them.

Mike began moving toward the bar door, his legs starting to feel a bit shaky. He probably would have been able to hold his own against an opponent of equal height and mass. Well, maybe, he thought, just about. But not with either one of these bulging guys and certainly not two of them. Darianus alone probably weighed 50 kilos more than Mike and it was sinew. Bizarrely, he found himself making a mental note to do more weight training on board the ship. Then he reminded himself that he had to get out of this place in one piece first.

'Look, guys, I don't want any trouble?' he said in a voice that betrayed his anxiety. He started to move toward the door, very slowly, but the two men began to move with him.

'Too 'arfing late for that,' mocked Adriano, with an inane grin.

'I said yet, shut up!' breathed Darianus and he began to follow Mike's movements toward the door but he didn't launch the attack Mike expected, and that was because all the lights in the bar room flickered and just died at that moment. In the near darkness Mike heard the strange music machine squawk and groan, and its rhythms slowed to a grinding halt. There were exclamations of surprise from all around. Everyone was mystified – except Mike. It was Ra's outburst: the electrojet. And just at the right time, like the proverbial "cavalry to the rescue", except the electrical outburst was also potentially dangerous. As if to prove the point, the cables connected to the music box suddenly exploded with sparks and jumped out of their connecting mains supply, sending brilliant showers of tiny embers into the air. Then the cables sputtered out. Mike heard Adriano shout, 'Arfing 'ell.' There was a smell of burning rubber in the air.

At that point Mike decided to make his move, but in a moment of alarm he thought he might not be able to find the door in the darkness. He searched the area where he thought the door might be and saw a tiny crack of light. That was it. Lunging for it he grabbed the door handle, hauled it open and rushed through. At first, he slammed the door shut behind him, then hesitated. Even he was not that unheroic; that selfish. People would need to get out if a fire started in there. There'd been an acrid stench inside and flashing embers. He yanked the door open wide again but didn't wait to see who came out of it. Then he was away down the leafy path.

A glance back reassured him that the whole building had not caught fire. People were pouring out of the doorway. A further 20 metres and he looked back again to see Darianus outside the doorway, shouting to those still inside, 'All out now! My place is done. Mayst burn. Out, now!' The man then turned and spotted Mike.

Grimacing at him he shouted, 'Arfing blegger. Thress off.'

Mike needed no encouragement and hurried on his way but as he gave one final backward glance he saw what he hoped was a final rush of people out of the premises, including the girls. He assumed that Darianus and Adriano had more things to worry about than him and would not pursue him. Maybe Darianus ran the place – and Mike felt he had to give the brute some credit for not abandoning his friends; for taking responsibility for the safety of his "guests". He was still a brute, though.

He put on a spurt of speed and hoped he wouldn't have to meet any of that lot again as he started back toward the hotel. He felt as if he was sweating from every pore. The hotel, he thought. Where was it? His heart skipped again when he realised how lost he'd become. In his haste to escape the Bukkaneers Retreat he thought he had taken a wrong turn, for he didn't recall any of the little streets he now hurried along. He didn't want to go back so he took a left turn at the next crossing of paths, to try to work his way back toward where he needed to be. The tiny streets suddenly all seemed the same and he stared up at the stars. Maybe he could navigate. Difficult though, as he hadn't yet become familiar with the star patterns in this alien sky, but he would have to try.

Cursing himself he suddenly remembered – his wristcom. What had he been thinking? Must be real tired, he thought and – whatever was in the drinks. Alarm subsiding, he spoke to the device tightly wrapped around his thin wrist and it lit up instantly, showing him a route map culled from The Monsoon's databanks and from observations the ship had automatically made of the city as it had passed overhead. A few shadowy figures sauntered past as he looked at the small screen. They made rude sounding remarks in the local lingo and he decided not to ask his device to project its maps into the air in front of him. That could really freak people out.

That's when he heard the tinkling, spattering, sound of the little brook he'd crossed before, now just a few metres away to his right, and he made for it. He asked the device to talk him directly to the Argonautica, where he knew he could shut it off and find his own way home. Twenty minutes later he was hurrying past the restaurant.

As he passed the Argonautica he saw a stream of people issuing from its doors, the lights having gone off in there too. Mike knew that virtually all the electrics in town would have died. Curiously, the small, ancient looking streetlights were still lit. Different form of energy, he surmised. Probably biological. Otherwise, there was a blanket of darkness everywhere, but for the wan ivory light from the two small moons of Oceanus, almost directly overhead.

Ra was having fun and, of course, the OA government hadn't issued any warnings. In the light which was available he saw people spilling out of bars and restaurants. To the extent he could see their faces Mike didn't feel that they looked particularly inconvenienced by the experience. Back on Earth there would have been much gnashing of teeth if their precious way-lights had gone out.

He also felt, again, as though everyone was staring at him but he couldn't see enough to be sure of that, and deep down he knew it was only the stress of his experiences that evening. It took him 10 minutes to get back to the hotel and when he arrived he decided to look into the bar, to see if Tenak was there. Like everywhere else, the hotel and its bar were in darkness, yet still full of customers. But no sign of Tenak.

Mike flopped onto one of the plush seats near to the bar. His heart wasn't beating fast anymore but his nerves still felt frayed. He had been insulted and felt aggrieved but managed to feel guilty at the same time. Looking around he could see this place was as different as it could possibly be to "The Bukkaneers' Retreat". It was full of people who looked amiable enough and everyone continued to chatter pleasantly, despite sitting in the dark. A barman suddenly appeared and announced, 'I am yet glad to tell you, gentilhomms, that the hotel's privato generator will be coming back online very soon-so. Meanwhile, there shall be no reason we carnt continue to take orders. Drinks are served without lectric.'

Sounds good, thought Mike. I need something stimulating. He stood at the bar, still feeling slightly shaky, and ordered an "Oceanus Special kaffee" and a malt "whirsky". As he sipped the drink he turned to sit again but a very attractive woman caught his eye. Do I ever stop, he thought? No, and why should I? He hesitated for a moment, thinking of recent events but decided to push the memory of Anina and Katrana out of his mind. This femna was a more mature woman, certainly older than him. She was on her own but was she waiting for someone? She had a gentle looking, round face and despite the low light he could see enough to feel attracted to her. Should he try a chat line with her? His experiences this evening had started to get to him, he realised with chagrin. Otherwise, he wouldn't have hesitated.

The woman sat on her own, only 2 metres away and her glass was nearly empty. He leaned toward her very slightly and, smiling broadly, he asked, 'Excuse me Madama. Can I get you another one?' He pointed at her glass. Not exactly original – but never mind. She smiled warmly and said, with fairly mild Devian accent, 'No, thanking you, young manry. Waiting for my friend, I am. She's in the washment.'

Washment? Oh yes, he thought. She means the freshment room. 'Doesn't she let you have drinks when she's in the … washment?' he said, smiling broadly. A weak joke he knew, but she actually chuckled, briefly, more with embarrassment, he thought.

The room lights flickered just then and suddenly came on fully. A few people cheered half-heartedly. At last he could see the woman properly now. Yes, lovely, he thought. Her face was refined, and her eyes had a kind look about them. She smiled again for a moment, then said, 'Tis just that we were thinking of moving on yet. We were still to meet another giriling-friend but she did not turn up round here.'

In fact, the lights coming on seemed somehow to have made Mike pause in his drive to chat up this femna. She was on her own and might not want this sort of attention from a male stranger. Where were his manners, he thought? Back on Earth such concepts were rarely valid any more as many women there now took on an active role in searching out males, or women they were interested in, if that's what they wanted. It was very different from the past, with little of the emotional and psychological baggage it once had. But it might not be the same everywhere, he reminded himself. Putting Katrana and Anina aside, on Oceanus it might still be seen as improper to chat up a woman sitting alone at a bar.

This femna had not shown any signs of distressabout his attentions and he wanted to try again, though, given his experiences of this different culture so far, he decided to let things lie. He would just go back to his room. The Oceanus woman then surprised him by reopening their conversation herself.

'Young manry, I did not tell you my name. I am Aurenia. I have seen that you arint from this world, are you?'

'No, I'm not … I mean, my name is Mike. You're right. I'm new to your … your lovely world. Did you see the beautiful sunset earlier?' Ouch, he remembered, she's a local. She probably sees them every day.

'Ah, you are yet from the Home Systemry,' she said, 'and so, yes, I didst see evensink. But you should see the morningtons,' she replied gently and very warmly, 'I think you would probably say – dawnings – in your Home Systemry. I am most pleased to meet you gentle-manry. You did not say where you do come from, Mike.' Her eyes sparkled as she spoke. Mike thought her accent simply charming. The speech patterns of Anina and Katrana seemed harsh, uncouth, by comparison.

'From Earth originally,' he said. 'Came down yesterday, from The Monsoon. You know, the ship in orbit? I don't know if you heard about that?' Then Mike realised his mistake and cursed himself for mentioning the Navy ship, concerned she might react negatively, like the girls in the Bukkaneer's Retreat. He needn't have worried. In fact, her eyes sparkled with genuine interest. What was that? Curiosity, he thought?

'Ah, a new ship in orbit,' she said. 'No, I didst not hear of that. Does not happen yet often – ships coming here so. Does sound exciting as such – to come from Earth. I carnt e'en imagine space travelling.' She seemed to blush scarlet as she spoke.

'Well, I …' Mike started to say but Aurenia suddenly looked away, her attention drawn elsewhere.

A very tall woman had appeared from a corridor the other side of the room and she walked straight up to Aurenia, sat down between her and Mike, completely ignoring him, and said to her friend,

'Auri' let us be going. Jaena is not going to be turning up round now.' She looked at an old- fashioned wristwatch through narrow, suspicious eyes and glancing at Mike, gave him a cold, cheerless smile. Aurenia shot at Mike an embarrassed, helpless expression and mouthed a silent apology at him. Then she got up and followed her friend as she marched off toward the door, but she gave Mike one more glance as she left. The sparkle was there for a mere instant, then she was gone.

Just when he had thought the day couldn't get much worse, he noted, glumly, now it had. He thought he might as well just go to bed. It was 2.00 am, local time and was getting finally starting to feel refreshingly cool he rose. Walking wearily up the two flights of steps to his floor, he touched the infochip to the door entry pad and waited for the light to turn green. It didn't. Repeatedly. The electrical interference from the star, of course. Damnatious!

He thought he remembered seeing a large reception lounge on the first floor, so he set about finding it. He quickly found the lounge. It was full of people, lying on the floor or lolling over sagging, dishevelled looking, sofas, and a threadbare chair. They looked at him sympathetically and an officious male voice said something about all services being restored by "4.00 mornington". Or so they hoped. Mike just sat on a tiny bit of space at the end of one of the sofas, next to an older man reading a magazine. Another thing made of paper. Remarkable. But Mike wasn't in a curious mood and he was dog-tired. The stranger didn't look up. Good. Mike couldn't be bothered with more chatter. He sat back, closed his eyes – and woke up three hours later. Everyone had gone. No-one had told him the rooms were back in service. Typical, he thought. Tonight had been depressing and he had a feeling this world was not finished with him yet. Not by a damn and blast light year.

And he was right in more ways than he could guess.

Chapter 5

EVAPORATING HOPES

A figure wearing an immaculate, purple Navy officer's uniform, minus the peaked hat, exited the breakfast hall of the Janitra Central Hotel and strode confidently toward the Central Government Building. Despite his senior years, the figure had something of an athletic, loping, gait which covered the ground with smooth, easy, agility. Ra had been up an hour and was beaming its orange-yellow radiance from just above some low office blocks to the figure's right-hand side. The heat was building already but the humidity was not yet oppressive.

A slimmer, seemingly hesitant, figure, wearing loose black top and grey trousers, appeared in the hotel doorway and called loudly after the retreating figure. The purple uniform stopped, turned and bellowed back,

'There you are. I wondered if you'd forgotten my advice. Didn't see you at breakfast -   when we agreed.' A pause, then, 'You okay? You look like a fraggo-bod.'

'Thanks. Yeah, I'm okay, Arkas,' Mike shot back at him. 'Bad night. Got locked out of the room by the magneto' storm. You probably didn't even notice it. Hope you don't mind but I'm going to get something from the breakfast hall. Fast as poss', yeah? I'll catch you up. Okay?'

Tenak acknowledged and strode off powerfully around the street corner as Mike slipped back into the hotel, picked up a couple of bread rolls and a piece of local fruit called, curiously, a "pomriet". After hurrying back up to his room to grab his white tunic jacket, he set off after Tenak.

Mike reckoned the Admiral was a peeved about his absence from breakfast. Too bad. It wasn't that he didn't care about Tenak's feelings, he mused, but the guy seemed to fuss too much sometimes. Still, he felt it would be wise to avoid being late for the planned meeting. He hurried to catch up with the Admiral and reached him, just as he was about to enter the grand portico'd entranceway to the government building.

After what he felt was a half-hearted security check at the entranceway, or "Officio" booth, they walked into the large atrium, once again. The place had a lighter and airier feel today. Even Mike appreciated this, though the sheer size of the hall still intimidated him. This place might even be slightly bigger than one of the hangar decks on the ship. He was pleased that the effect on him seemed less than previously. It just made him feel a little on edge.

They walked to a large, ornate, wooden desk, with its curious "Ask ye Here", sign, situated near the centre of the atrium. A minor official looked up wearily from his papers. He reminded Mike of a type of dog called a bloodhound, on old Earth; an animal he'd only seen in holo-vids.

As the official opened his mouth to speak a large, somewhat imperious looking figure swept toward them. This was a haughty looking man, wearing a deep blue frock coat of a type Mike had seen in pictures of "gentlemen", back in the early Victorian era of old Britain.

'Mornimbrite gentilhomms,' said the stranger, smiling broadly now.

'Uh, Mornimbrite,' said Mike. Tenak flashed him a bemused glance but repeated the greeting, after which the official introduced himself as "Dariat", Private Assistant to Mes Danielsa Darba Trebruchet, Leader of the Oceanus United Democratic Congress Party. He announced that Mes Trebuchet would meet them soon, when she would be accompanied by Deputy Leader Gyorgy Nimius Pacolovic.

This was more like it, thought Mike and, with the Admiral he followed Dariat across the atrium, then up a set of wide marble steps to a large, wood panelled room like the one where they'd met the President. Again, the two leaders were not there to greet them. Tenak turned to Mike and raised his eyebrows but within a few minutes a gaunt looking woman entered with a squat man in trail. The woman, even taller than

Mike, had a pale, pinched, face and wore a long, tube-like black dress, from head to toe. She made for a slight, yet still imposing figure. Her stocky companion was dressed in a dark, one-piece suit only slightly smarter than the majority of the populace seemed to wear. His massive head reminded Mike of a hairy baked potato. He held some sort of old-fashioned board, with a sheaf of paper affixed to it.

Mike also noticed something unusual about the woman's left wrist, where it dangled below her veil like, sleeve. The arm was clearly artificial, and it appeared to be made of some sort of wood. Nothing strange about a prosthetic limb, he thought, but, in the Home System, this woman's arm could have been made of layers of composite material with full flesh-feel, and, possibly, electro-chemically connected to her brain; a fully functioning synthetic arm. And with it she would be enabled, to a large extent, to *feel* the world around her as well as being able to hold and grip things with dexterity. It could even have been a cybernetically enhanced arm but those were only available by way of multiple, hard to get, permits. And the penalties for illegal cyber-enhancements were severe.

In Trebuchet's case he doubted her own false limb provided much in the way of facilities. Mike had to remind himself, once again, of how different things were out here and how people seemed to prefer it that way. In any case, the woman seemed quite unperturbed by the stiffness of the false limb. Good for her, he thought. He wasn't going to feel sorry for her.

Dariat introduced her as and her companion formally, then left and the politicians sat on chairs opposite a kind of sofa where Mike and Tenak were invited to sit. It was much too small for them both but they squeezed in.

Trebuchet spoke first, a deep contralto voice, rich and warm,

'Tis deedly mornimbrite, with such distinguished guestso as you. Please call me Danielsa, by the way. I understand you did-nart get very far with my … illustrious colleague, Madama President, yester-morn.'

Ever the diplomat, Tenak said, 'Well, I'm not sure I'd describe it quite that way but we had an … interesting discussion.'

'Come now, sirra,' said Trebuchet, 'you can speak yet freesuch with us, Admiral, but praps you would not mind me saying that you should yet have been a politician. Ah now, you're so wasted on the Navy, my manry.'

Tenak's smile was very slightly uneven as he replied, 'Thank you Madama– but I don't think so though I do have to agree that even an Admiral sometimes has to be a politician of kinds.'

'Deedly, Admiral. I also say that I am surprised you are risking the ire-making of the Metateleosophists, by meeting us, the *third* largest party in this societiea, before them, sirra?'

'Perhaps,' said Tenak, 'but you see, we already asked them if we could meet them here this morning. They insisted we meet them at their temple in Ramnisos. We agreed but they advised they weren't ready for us until this afternoon.'

'Ah. That does not surprise me, such. Very well but yet, to get to business,' said Trebuchet, suddenly speaking quietly, almost conspiratorially. She told them they had seen the Home System science reports about Ra and that her party was broadly sympathetic to the findings, although they still had some genuine doubts. Tenak and Mike began to brighten, until Pacolovic, in a gruff voice, revealed that although their party would like to help them dissuade the government from its position their party was, unfortunately in a very difficult position right now. In recent times they had been shaken by several corruption scandals. These were, he said, all completely fictitious, of course. 'Of course,' echoed their guests.

Pacolovic began to say something about them losing more and more ground to the other parties but Trebuchet spoke over his words and left them hanging, as she said,

'Thank you Gyorgy. I think what you gentilhomms should yet know, if you have not already been a-guessing, is we simply carnt be seen to be supporting the Home System openly, Not at this momenti.'

'But, with respect, Mes, that surely isn't the point?' said Tenak, his face betraying some astonishment at this apparent new setback. He continued, somewhat bullishly, 'Wouldn't you agree that the lives of your citizens are at stake here. The safety of the population comes first, surely?'

'We are most sympathi-so with your sentiment, Admiral, as I didst say, but I did not say that even we believe your scientists … explicitly,' said Trebuchet, 'and our own society of natural philosophers … what you call scientists, have no real standing with the government, even if they did whole-so agree. Madama President's government has a strong think-team who are much opposed to the Home System's findings, as you are probably so aware.'

'And, tis true, ist not,' Trebuchet continued her monologue, 'that your Home System science has pointed to this suggested disaster, e'en though there have been several instances of such government and their predecessors, on Earth, promoting the wrong science, to a too-credible public?'

Mike wondered what in the galaxies she was talking about but then suddenly, it clicked. Tenak just looked puzzled. He began to speak but Trebuchet anticipated him. 'I am deedly sorry Admiral. You are confused I see. I merely refer to well known, so I thought, incidents, such as when a group of Earth *scientists* claimed their studies showed the water channelled through new networks of pipes and treatment plants were supplying tainted water to the new cities, so making people very ill.'

Tenak looked at his companion and said, 'Mike?'

'She's talking about the Atlantica area, way back. A well-known scientist said his group had found a chemical imbalance in the water being fed to the new city state. Lots of people, thousands, had a range of serious illnesses, including children born with birth defects. It was much later when the problems were found to be due to something else in the environment. Contaminated food brought in from elsewhwere, I think. Not the water system. By then the treatment system had been completely rebuilt at massive public cost.'

'Just a mistake, surely? said Tenak. 'A deeply unfortunate one but these things can happen, even in science.'

Mike shook his head as Trebuchet spoke again, 'But yet no, sirra. Twas found, wast not, that the scientist in question had falsify-ed his data as did all his team and because of his influence in the government, all attempts to bring to light failed – for years?' She looked pointedly at Mike.

'Yep,' said Mike, looking squarely at Tenak. 'She's right. There was some sort of …thing going on there. For a few years. Turned out the area government had ulterior reasons for covering up the errors – which they knew about. But Madama Trebuchet, that was a long time ago. Well over two hundred years, I think. In a way we'd barely emerged from the New Dark Age.'

'Ah yes,' she said, 'but didst not something alike happen some time after the deep space conduits started to be used? A HS scientist team claimed illnesses and possible damage to the *cosmos itself* were yet happening because of solid objects, like spacecraft, passing through them?'

Tenak no longer looked confused and said, 'Yes but those findings were overturned as well, I'm glad to say.'

'Yes,' she said, 'for otherwise you would not be sitting here now. All travel through the conduits was, I so believe, stopped, for near twenty years, afore the findings were "overturned". And, in these incidents, we are not talking about honest mistakes, are we? That time it was also a case of falsified and unverifiable findings, which was backed yet by large numbers of people in command of power and the media. Not true?'

'Yes, said Tenak. You're right. It was not a basic error. More a series of errors which were covered up so that the scientists concerned coud retain their influence in society. And I know it was backed up by those with political power who had some sort of axe to grind, I'm sorry to say. But Madama, those incidents are rare. The findings we're talking about have not been arrived at that way and …'

'Forgive me so,' Trebuchet said, 'but *I do not* mean to say I believe these new findings are falsified, even though they may be wrong. I merely do point out that the findings of *big science* can be so big that they take on momentum of their own and can deceive when, dare I say it, politicians, or the wrong sort of political parties, do become involve-ed. No? And the interference from governmental bodies and media did this e'en years before the Toba destruction, so long ago.'

Tenak flushed and reluctantly agreed. I see the point you're making.'

'Thanking you, Admiral. The point is, I think you see, that the people of Oceanus may have good reason to doubt findings made, so far away, without any contribution by them, especial-so when there are forces here ready to use that doubt for themselves.'

Mike sighed inwardly. It was going to be another long day on this strange world. As he sat, trying to look patient, mainly for Tenak's benefit, he listened to Trebuchet explain that she felt Arbella was altogether too strongly influenced by the Meta-teleos, mostly because the latter had recently won several key, district bielections. Most in her party believed Arbella's influence over Devi was fading and she might even lose to a vote of "no confidence" if she pushed too hard against the 'Teleos'. She also suggested that some in her own party were too scared to defy the Meta teleos. And she warned that if the Metas were able to force a general election they could well win, and then there would be little chance of any evacuation of Oceanus. Their world would reject the proposals of the Home System government.

Mike heard Tenak trying his best to suppress expasperated exhalations but, to his huge credit, the guy continued to keep his diplomatic "hat" firmly in place. He said they were hoping to explain their position more fully when they met the two chief representatives of the Meta- teleos later that day. Trebuchet tried to say, though she was very diplomatic about it, that she thought this was a waste of time, but she didn't wish to deter them from trying.

'You are best to try speaking to Professier Muggredge and his team, as soon as you mayst,' she said. 'For he is a very great-so respected, deedly venerated, intellect on Oceanus. He might still have some influence on Arbella's natural philosophers.'

'We mentioned that, yesterday,' said Mike, 'and the President seemed to dismiss any influence the Professier might have.' Tenak nodded.

'Ah, but she would,' said Trebuchet, 'for he is her brother and they have not spoken together yet for years. Split asunder they are.'

Mike and Tenak looked at each-other in amazement. Great, thought Mike. This was just getting easier all the time!

Pacolovic said, 'There is talk also that even he is not so necessary-like convinced of the Home System position.'

'And after all,' added Trebuchet, 'putting aside the ... I do accept, falsifyings, many scientific findings have been disputed over the centuries, for entirely reasonable grounds, no? Special so if there is contradicting and disputed evidence. I do yet think it best for you to contact the Professier soonest. But not now for we do understand that he is away from Janitra University, on business.'

'And we do not still know when he is to be back, sorry.' Said Pacolovic, for good measure.

Mike was starting to feel drowsy with boredom, though he tried to keep it from Tenak. The two guests from the solar system fell silent and at that point Trebuchet politely drew the meeting to a close, thanked her guests for coming, then she and her colleague rose. As they left Trebuchet uttered a parting comment which resounded in Mike's mind for a long time.

'I am yet sorry for not being able to advance your cause, gentilhomms,' she said, 'but I think I should be warning you about something. And that is the very basic truth here, sirra. Tis that the people of Oceanus just do not *want* to leave. They do love their world so and do not wish to believe tis doomed – if indeed you and your compadros are correct. Call it strange or worse, but tis the truth. It might be best if you recall this to mind in all your discussions. Good morrowbrite Admiral, Mer Secretary.'

And with that they went, leaving Mike and Tenak reeling.

****

On their way out Tenak paid a visit to some "washment" rooms on the mezzanine floor of the building. Out of politeness Mike said he would wait and, as he paced along the balcony of the mezzanine, he peered over at the hubbub of activity on the ground floor. After a few minutes he began to wonder what Tenak was doing in there and, turning away from the balcony view his eyes alighted on a young woman approaching along the mezzanine. She was a little shorter than Tenak but he was astounded by her natural poise and ease of movement. They were, he felt, electrifying, especially compared with most femnas of her age back home. Disappointingly, she wore the same sort of shapeless, baggy brown and grey things, which passed fro clothing here, and nicknamed by his crewmates as, "utils".

His eyes, magnetically drawn to her, followed the young woman as she passed within a couple of metres of him and she suddenly noticed him looking. His heart gave a tiny jump. But she continued on her way. Not being a man to let an opportunity pass by, he called after her, 'Excuse me, Madama. Sorry, I meant, Mes. I wondered if you could help us?'

She turned and hesitated for a moment, then walked slowly back toward him but stayed a couple of metres distant. Yes, he thought, she's certainly – special. She fixed him with an expression at once amenable and firm, with alert, startlingly violet eyes. They were eyes which seemed to miss nothing, gazing out from a smooth, round, face with a high forehead. Her demeanour suggested a certain seriousness, or rather studiousness, but her complexion spoke of significant exposure to Ra's rays. A splash of freckles ran liberally across her nose and cheeks, which complimented her wavy, shoulder length, auburn hair.

'How mayst I help you?' she said, in a light but slightly husky voice, raising one eyebrow in evident suspicion, yet not hostility. There was a note of curiosity there.

Mike thought she must have spotted the enthusiastic look he had given her. He focused his attention on her benign face and felt almost lost in it. There was something about her. Something unusual. She certainly seemed to exude an air of freshness and openness. She was loveliest femna he'd seen since he got here. His heart positively pounded.

'I'm so sorry,' he said, as innocently as he could muster, 'but, ah, I'm waiting for my friend, but he and I are trying to get to a meeting at Ramnisos. I don't suppose you'd know … the best way we could get there, do you?'

'Certaint, Mer,' she said.

That delectable voice again.

She tried to give directions, using her arms to amplify her meanings, waving in mid-air,

'Be yet turning left out of here, onto Demry Street, and still two blocks down the road, take the right-hand turn onto Polten Street, and still walk down all four blocks. You will yet find the nearest monorail station theresuch. It shall cost you near 25 credits, by the way.'

'Thank you so much,' said Mike, 'you've been … very helpful.' He looked at his wristcom, 'Ah, I see it's only 08.30. I don't have to get there until 14.30, so I wondered if you'd like to join me for a cup of kaffee? I thought you could help me to familiarise myself with this place. I'm struggling to find my way around the city.'

She chuckled and said, 'What about your friend? The one-such you are waiting for?'

Mike had forgotten he'd mentioned Tenak. 'Oh, he'll find a way to occupy himself,' he said, 'and, by the way, please call me Mike. Mike Tanniss.'

She still looked amused and said, 'I am so sorry as I will be on my way to see someone myself. My Auntine won't appreciate me being late. You are from the Home System arint you, … Mike, did you yet say? I suggest that if you are lost, sirra, you might so consult your ship's database - or be getting a goodly map.'

She was very perspicacious, thought Mike, so he decided to be cheeky, though he was starting to think he might have "lost this one.". He reckoned she was much too astute to fall for any of his garbling, or even his good looks. Her presence almost shouted out "blazing intellect". Trying to rescue the conversation he blurted, 'Do you mind if I ask whether your Aunt, I mean, Auntine, works here?'

'Actually, I do "mind" but since you are not from here-round - and still you seem desperate to find out all, someways, I shall tell you. Deedly, my Auntine does work here. At least for part of her time. Her name is Arbella Nefer-Masterton. You might yet have heard of her. Now, I wish you luck my lost friend and bid you morrowbrite.'

Blazing meteor storms! Here he was, quite obviously trying to bounce off a local femna, who just happened to be related to the President herself. Such was his embarrassment and concern about what Tenak would think that he decided not to tell this femna that he had already met her "Auntine". His sense of surprise was so acute he almost failed to notice that the woman had turned and was starting to walk away.

He called out to her, 'Aren't you going to tell me your name?' She looked back, shook her head and continued walking. Well, that's sad, thought Mike, and he also began to turn away, but then something seemed to change her mind. To his surprise and delight he saw her turn, smile, then call out to him, 'Alrighting. My name is Eleri. Eleri Tharnton Nefer- Ambrell. Morrowbrite to you, Mike.' The young woman quickly turned away and continued along the mezzanine floor. Away from him. Despite her confident and breezy manner, he thought he had detected a slight note of sadness in her voice. But that could have been anything he reasoned. He would definitely not go after ... Eleri, was it? She seemed the sort who would not tolerate that sort of thing. When she said goodbye, she meant it.

Arkas Tenak burst in on Mike's thoughts.

'You okay?' the Admiral asked. 'You eyeing up the femnas again?'

'I'll tell you later,' said Mike and he set off toward the stairs, lost in thought, trailing a grinning Tenak.

Passing the atrium desk Mike glanced behind and saw Tenak stop to speak to the desk official. He was curious and walked back to join him.

'Everything okay, Arkas?' he asked.

'I think I asked *you* that question a minute ago. I didn't get a proper answer,' came a surprisingly sharp retort. Mike had the wisdom to apologise; a rather unusual thing for him to do. Tenak continued, 'I just thought we should repeat our warning about the full magnetic storm. It doesn't look as if any of these people know what's going on.'

'That was Monzonite's job wasn't it?' said Mike.

'Maybe, but I reckon that after last night's little disturbance, they might think it's all done with. I just asked the official to put out an E-message to everyone in the building. Well, they call it "L-messages".'

'I can guess thye mean, "Lectronic?" I'm surprised they even have those on this planet,' said Mike, 'but maybe we should have mentioned it to Trebuchet. Have you got any more detail from Ebazza?'

'Yeah, I spoke to her before breakfast. Seems the main coronal outburst will reach here by around 20.00 or 21.00, this evening. It'll make last night's problems seem like the tantrums of a mouse. They think they know what it's all about, down here, but they have no idea, Mike.'

Mike nodded, 'Okay. I hope they take notice. If Ra's mass ejection event is coming that soon we'd better get over to Ramnisos – like yesterday.'

'True. We also need to be back in Janitra before the storm. The monorail and everything that's electro-mechanical is likely to go bust when that thing hits.'

And so the two of them hurried off to the monorail station and within seconds of arriving an old, tired looking, maglev train running on a single, ground level mag' track had just reached the platform. There were about six long carriages. Hurriedly, Tenak bought two tickets; Mike was once again astonished at the antique nature of such a procedure. They bounded up to the platform, and onto the mag', and settled into two seats in the first carriage, positioned facing each-other. A small table was, quaintly, fixed between them. The fittings of the train seemed antique, with chintzy, faded upholstery.

'The journey should take about 245 minutes,' said Mike, 'I understand there aren't usually delays.'

The maglev stopped for more passengers at the outskirts of Janitra, and then, despite its evident age, it set off at a cracking pace for Ramnisos, some 600 kilometres north-west of the Capital. After the one stop Mike noticed there were barely a dozen passengers left on their car. But still, it was a pretty comfortable ride, he thought, as he watched Tenak settle down to peer at the beautiful Devian countryside speeding by. After Janitra they did indeed pass through some beautiful countryside, though he couldn't bring himself to look at much of it for long. They passed great forests of massive blue-green trees, then later, by expansive open landscapes of rolling hills very occasionally dotted with small buildings. Tenak identified them as farms.

Most of the countryside seemed practically devoid of human habitation. Mike soon became leery of the increasingly open vistas rolling by, and much of the time he just had to look away. From his point of view, it just got worse. The view eventually changed to more dramatic landscapes as the train crossed bridges spanning deep gorges. One after another came deep clefts in the land, revealing frothing torrents plummeting over craggy ledges, tumbling into wooded depths below. The scene soon began to torment Mike, who started to feel a little queasy and decided to try to block it out by concentrating exclusively on the view within the car, such as the other passengers walking up and down the carriage.

A vast pale, aqua coloured, plain of sedge-like plants, dotted with the odd copse of purple-coloured trees, took over the view after half an hour or so. Tenak seemed to be raptly engaged with the vistas as they passed landscapes offering wide rivers, glinting in the late morning Ra-shine, meandering across pancake flat river estuaries. Tenak sucked it all in but, fed up with people watching, Mike decided to switch to a holo-movie projected by his wristcom into the space above his lap. He had two earpieces which meant no-one else could hear it, but he got some stares of astonishment from people as they walked past to the washment rooms or took exercise strolls. Occasionally a passer-by would stop for a few moments to watch but then quickly seemed to lose interest and went on their way. Mike was amused.

'I don't think they approve of me, Arkas,' he announced, smiling.

'I'm not surprised,' said his companion grinning. 'They're probably wondering why you're not taking in the views.'

'Yeah, rightso. They've got to be used to it anyways, don't they?' Mike retorted.

'Maybe not. You know what it's like when you're working all sorts of hours. You don't always manage to get to see what's right on your doorstep.' Tenak paused while Mike tapped his wristcom to switch it off. Exhaling with some impatience he sensed Tenak wanted to talk.

'Are you going to tell me what happened last night?' asked Tenak, straight to the point.

Mike felt a momentary flash of indignation. But it was also clear Tenak had sensed a problem. Was it that obvious?

'Oh, nothing, Arkas, I suppose. I don't know. I guess I just got into … a bit of … bother.' There was silence for several moments, then Tenak said,

'If you don't want to tell me, that's fine but it might be best if you do. Is it anything I can help with?'

'No, no. Listen, it was nothing. I just got a bit lost in the city. Fell into a spot of hassle with a couple of local goonie-guys. Managed to extract myself without losing all my dignity, I suppose. They were just flexing their muscles, that's all – and boy, their muscles were pretty impressive.' After a second, he added, 'I was thinking maybe I should start visiting the ship's gymnasium. You know, get to doing some work-outs.'

'Not a bad idea Mike, but generally, it's probably more about how you hold yourself. Your bearing. Self confidence, and all that.'

Mike sighed and looked around the carriage again. He hoped Tenak would not pursue this line but he had the good sense to realise the man was just concerned. To his relief, the Admiral asked no more about the incident but then, curiously, he noticed him carefully looking all around them. He was clearly checking for onlookers, known as, "wag-ears". Then he spoke to Mike in hushed tones, leaning closer over the small table.

'I wouldn't do this favour for anyone else, Mike, so I hope you'll treat this with the respect it deserves.'

'What in name of "Harlieman" are you talking about, Arkas?'

The Admiral took his wristcom off his left wrist and removed it from its wrist strap. Mike noticed the strap had a full backing strip so that the comm unit would not lay against his skin. Tenak laid the bare unit on the table. There seemed something odd about the thing, but so what, Mike wondered? It was a little larger than his own and was tinted red on top, and blue underneath. Non-standard issue, obviously, but probably reserved for senior officers. Puzzled, Mike was about to tell his friend he was being rather melodramatic, when Tenak contined,

'Look at the rim, Mike. Notice anything different?'

Mike picked it up and peered closely, 'Looks like the there's four micro-aerials instead of the usual two.'

'Correct, and the two middle ones are about twice the size of the other two.'

'So?' said Mike. 'Look, where's all this leading?

'Okay, I guess you've never heard of E-S com-units? Electro-shock units? You've led a sheltered life haven't you, me laddo?' he chuckled and added, 'This unit can render an assailant unconscious, Mike. The two larger aerials can transmit an electrical shock to any target within 2 metres.'

Mike's curiosity was piqued now, 'But those aerials are only about 4 mills long, Arkas. I'm smoked out, man. Sounds dangerous though. What are you doing with one down here?'

'An admiral needs to be prepared, Mike. You know that. The Service has lots of tricks up its sleeves. This is just one. But listen, this needs to be handled with care, with … great discretion. Judgement is needed. You must respect it. It's only deployed it in an absolute emergency.' Tenak sat back and contined, 'It's standard issue to all Admirals and Captains but no-one else is meant to have them. I'm breaking Navy law in giving this to you. You got that?'

'Giving it? *To me*? I … well, that's … great, I guess. Thank you Arkas, … I think. I can well imagine only top ranks getting stuff like this. You slipped that one under the nav-beams, didn't you?' Now it was Mike's turn to sound covert, as he lowered his voice to a barely audible whisper, 'Excuse me but isn't there a rule of – "no weapons to be brought onto the surface of the planet?"'

'The rule doesn't say, "no weapons". And anything can be used as a weapon, Mike. After all, it isn't a projectile gun, or sonic weapon. Those are the things *specifically* mentioned in the rules, but no, I don't talk about it openly. Why do you think I was being careful just now?'

Mike said nothing and looked the way he felt – confused.

'Listen,' Tenak continued, 'if you tap it twice quickly, pause and tap twice again- quickly - the unit becomes armed and starts using its holo-cam to observe whoever is within a wedge angle of 170° in front of you. Bend your arm around your back and it covers your arse, of course. You can, if you want, tell it where to strike, using standard Navy tactical-speak.' Tenak looked at Mike quizzically, 'Navy Tactics? You have done a course, haven't you? Tell me you have.'

'Yeah, I have. Yeah, don't worry. But I haven't said I want the unit yet, Arkas.'

'I noticed. Point is, if you're in a tight spot here, or anywhere else… well, you have an alternative. Now listen. It's use with care for a reason. The shock renders the subject incapacitated for a just a few minutes. That's all. Enough to make a getaway or to deter further attack, but you'd better remember that some people are susceptible to serious injury when shocked. You haven't had full training in how to use this, Mike, so I'm taking a trasking-great risk here. It's a last resort only. Don't let me down.' Tenak spoke those last words a little louder than perhaps he intended, and he looked around again, self-consciously. A local man suddenly approached from behind, walking up the aisle-way. He didn't even look in their direction as he went on his way.

'Okay, I'll accept it, Arkas,' said Mike quietly, 'And thank you. I know I don't always come across as too serious 'bout things but I do actually appreciate the risk you're taking. I just hope I don't have to use it. I prefer not to be in those situations to start with.'

Mike considered the unit for a second and smiled at his friend, 'I guess you need my com unit, in return?' Without waiting for an answer he took his unit off, ready to give to Tenak, but before exchanging properly each man spoke first to their own unit, again watching for listening ears. They used personal codewords, and specifically mandated instructions which enabled the units to be used by the "new" user. Otherwise, they would not obey that person and would shut down.

'By the way,' said Tenak, 'don't glue it to your skin – anywhere. It's not to be used near your chest, or whatever. And keep it attached to the backed-on wrist strap that goes with it. Otherwise, it'll burn your wrist and hurt a lot, believe me. Using it in very confined spaces is not advisable, either.' Mike nodded and said, 'Yeah, okay, I've got it.'

He fixed the unitinto its grip strap and fixed it around his wrist. He had never liked the habit adopted by some, of attaching com units to the skin with nanno-glue. No matter what anyone said, it wasn't as safe as a security strap.

They spoke no more about the matter the rest of the journey but Mike continued to wonder why Tenak had decided to trust him in this way. Was it a test? Should Tenak trust him? Did he deserve it? He decided to forget about it and let the tiredness from the previous night's adventures overtake him, until he slumbered.

Mike felt someone tapping his shoulder roughly and awoke with a start. It was Tenak. 'We've arrived,' he said. 'Come on.'

Chapter 6

TEMPLE OF MYSTERY

The town of Ramnisos proved to be even less urbanised than Janitra, with a centre composed mainly of low level, strangely organic looking wooden buildings. They appeared almost as though grown straight out of the ground. But there were other houses, built of a beautiful marble-like stone, sporting verandas with neat wooden fences. The streets were quiet but generally wider than those in the Capital and criss-crossed by embedded rails along which ran the occasional, small, tram-like buggies, carrying passengers. As Mike and Tenak had discovered in Janitra, all transport seemed to be small scale on this world and, here, whole trams could probably only take a dozen or so passengers at a time as they slowly traversed the streets.

Ra was riding high in the sky now and the heat was building, yet the place seemed to be a somewhat cooler place than Janitra. It was, of course, much further north and more than two hundred kilometres inland from the coast, so, to Mike's relief, it was less humid.

Mike recalled the ShipNet's encyclopaedia commentary on the general features of the Oceanus climate, which it said, "shared many characteristics with the Earth's climate during the early Cretaceous period," referring to the last part of Earth's great Mesozoic Era; the age of the great reptiles, which included, most famously, the dinosaurs. That period had ended, spectacularly, on Earth, over 65 million years ago.

Mike remembered reading that there had also been an age of reptile like animals on Oceanus, much longer than the one on Earth and it had ended relatively recently, fizzling out only a few million years ago, for reasons no-one understood. And, as far as he was aware, the only remaining similarity with the animals of the relevant periods on Earth seemed to be the continued existence of enormous sea-going reptilian creatures. These were impressive beasts which plied the deepest oceans – but, by all accounts, stayed far away from any coasts. Even far out, they were rarely seen; sometimes glimpsed by the crews of research vessels, themselves only occasionally given permits to sail, for conservation reasons. Mike understood that the sea reptiles *might* only be dangerous if you fell in, many kilometres out.

The physical similarity of Oceanus to the Earth – as the latter was more than sixty or seventy million years ago, meant that the climate across this planet showed relatively little variation in temperature across most latitudes. Only the poles were very cold, but the ice cover was still less than half that of the Earth's, despite climate changes on the Home Planet. Any controversy about human induced climate change had been wiped out by the human suffering caused by rapid cooling as a result of the ejecta from the super-volcano, followed by massive crop failure worldwide. The inhabitants of the Earth had entered a "New Dark Age," of human civilisation. Once again it was ironic, thought Mike, that the climate of Oceanus was threatened by an entirely different source, beyond anyone's control and despite the supreme efforts of its population to conserve resources and live in harmony with their planet.

As he and the Admiral began to emerge from the maglev station Mike marvelled at the many similarities between Earth and Oceanus; a mind-boggling thing. This planet had initially been the wish fulfilment of so many back home; dreams held for so long, to find a "second Earth", where humanity could live and breath and "start again". It was for so long held to be a ridiculous pipe dream and yet, here they were. Even so, despite its great similarities Oceanus still showed itself to be remarkably different in many respects.

Its slightly smaller size made its gravitational pull less than that of Earth's, but by a small percentage; hardly noticeable, but it was there. The much smaller total land mass also meant that the atmosphere worked differently but with no serious harm with respect to organic life. And that was partly because, so Mike understood, the land mass was somewhat larger in the distant past; much of the low-lying margins of the continent having been drowned by rising sea levels over the last few million years. It was thought that Oceanus once had several, small, separated continents many millions of years ago and tectonic forces had moved them together into their present configuration – before the land margins became "shelf seas", as the climate had warmed.

Now in the centre of the town and despite this place being cooler than the Capital, Mike felt the full force of the sun against his skin and absent mindedly wiped his brow with the back of his hand. He'd long ago learned that Ra was slightly smaller and cooler than the Sun, its light slightly shifted toward the redder side of the spectrum. That had caused the plant life of the planet to evolve a different version of chlorophyll to that on Earth. That was why the plants here were mainly blue-green or even purple in colour. And, almost as if to compensate for its cooler temperature the star held Oceanus closer to itself; its orbital distance was less than that of the Earth from the Sun. The same went for the rest of Ra's planetary retinue. And so, the Oceanus year was shorter than the home world's, a noticeable difference but, again, not excessive. Of course, that made the Devian calendar different too.

There were other, less obvious, differences, such as the fact that Oceanus didn't have quite so much of an axial tilt compared to the Earth. On the other hand, the density of the planet was a little higher than the Earth's, and so on. In the finer details the differences mounted. "Micro-differences" was how he thought of them.

*

He didn't know it, yet, but Mike would soon discover the effect of some of those micro-differences, in person.

*

'According to the database directions,' said Tenak loudly, catapulting Mike out of his reverie, 'the temple of the Metas is about 8 klicks out of town. We'll get an automated tram, to save time. Did you hear what I said?'

Mike grumbled affirmatively and glanced at the holographic map being projected by his old wristcom, now on Tenak's wrist. Once again, the sight of two people from off-world, and their unfamiliar technology, drew wide eyed stares from many inhabitants as they went about their daily business. Most seemed friendly and many smiled at them. Nice place, thought Mike, nicer than Janitra, maybe. His mind drifted back to the Bukkaneers Retreat. Hopefully that was just an anomaly. Wrong side of town. All towns and all cities had that kind of thing, didn't they? Still, this planet couldn't be all that bad if it produced people like Eleri. His mind had kept returning to her ever since they'd met. He wondered if he'd meet her again. He'd do his best to arrange it. But how?

The streets of Raminisos seemed strangely empty and, thought Mike, much too "open plan". This was not improving his general disposition. He was beginning to resent Tenak again, for bringing him to this particular, crazy, place.

The two men marched to a tram stop on the main boulevard and consulted a timetable – which, very surprisingly – was an actual *digital* display, albeit in 2D, displayed on a flat screen. The next tram to the location they wanted was due in about 8 minutes. There was nowhere to sit so they just had to wait, sweating, in the open glare of Ra, until a small van-like vehicle, carrying about 3 other people, turned a corner onto their road. The wait had been more like 20 minutes, and now the vehicle trundled slowly toward them, grumbling along on its small gauge metal track. It looked run-down and ramshackle.

After boarding it the tram seemed to leave the city precincts remarkably soon, rumbling out along flat, fertile, farmland to the west, travelling about 11 klicks, taking an achingly long time, until it reached a small cluster of houses, where it ground to a halt. Large flocks of tiny bird-like creatures flitted from one copse of trees to another, making peculiar, sharp, noises which seemed to Mike more like a cracking sound, than bird chirruping.

All the passengers stepped off after an automated announcement said, 'You have reached Sargonar village. This is the last stop. Please to debark unless returning to Ramnisos.' He had no idea where he was, but Mike knew their wristcoms would direct them from here and indeed the Admiral took the lead, "his" unit directing them directly into the countryside to the north west. Setting off along a narrow path they found it winding up a steep hill densely covered with towering tree-plants draped with hanging blue-green foliage. These trees were the largest Mike had seen since landing on Oceanus and, as he ascended he was grateful for the shade they gave from Ra's heat. And this sort of country made him feel more secure than the open stuff.

As they got higher Mike heard loud grunting and grumbling noises, off to his right. He stared at Tenak. It's not me, the man's eyes seemed to say. They came from somewhere in the bushes, quite close. At one point the noises rose to a sort of shrieking crescendo which, Mike felt, was starting to become a bit alarming. But they quickly died away. Tenak caught his companion's wide-eyed expression and said, 'Just the "borals". I think. Sort of cross between a mountain sheep and a wild pig. Nothing to be concerned about. Don't think they normally come near humans, but I'm not certain.'

'Thank you, Arkas. I'm glad you sound so sure,' said Mike, 'but I did say I'd done some research, remember? So, I knew that. Just sort of creepso, hearing them like that.'

At the top of the hill they emerged onto a ridge, where they paused for breath and gazed out through the gaps between the trees to a wide valley stretching into the distance. Mike felt a bit dizzy at the view and closed his eyes for a minute. When he opened them he saw, there, in the middle distance, still half a kilometre or so distant, the temple of the Meta-teleosophists; a structure occupying a larger area, by far, than the Central Government Building at Janitra but without its high vaulted roof. Their path could be seen to continue the other side of the ridge, becoming ever narrower as it wound down the other side of the wooded hill and out through a treeless area toward the temple.

The temple itself was rectangular in shape, and three storeys high, each one significantly smaller in area than the underlying one, almost as if going up in steps. Each level was surrounded by gleaming terraces and large plants in narrow gardens. The wide roof of the top storey was tiled with a brilliant red slate-like material and the ground floor sprouted several angular wings, jutting out from the main building. The whole edifice was surrounded by more gardens and enclosed by a tall perimeter wall.

Mike asked his wristcom to film the view and then to magnify the image. From this they could see that the grounds were beautifully tended and had many enclosures separated by small, glittering, white walls. The wristcom also showed a small number of people who all appeared to be dressed in dark robes and who seemed to be patrolling the terraces and the walls. If Mike felt he didn't know better, he'd have considered it an impressive show of strength. This place was more like a medieval fortress but was also redolent of a monastery.

'Better put that thing away,' said Tenak, 'cos they might not appreciate being spied on with HS tek.'

The two men picked their way down the path which led toward the temple on its plain. The route down was punctuated with large pools of muddy water, evidently left by recent heavy rains. Mike was wearing light grey trousers but the bottom halves of them gradually became painted a reddish-brown hue. Mike detested dirt or untidiness so this sort of thing bugged him but – it couldn't be helped.

Tenak's com unit told them there was a gate in the six-metre-high wall, about 300 metres off to the right, so they had to follow a right fork in the path, which became very narrow and difficult to navigate. Mike and Tenak walked single file. Although itself dry, each side of the path there was treacherous looking boggy ground, filled with shoulder high sedge-like plants. Their long leaves sported razor sharp edges. It was fortunate that their com units could advise them on a safe route, by using reflective spectral analysis of the surrounding landscape. The units suggested that the bogs were very deep.

'This is not good. And I was wondering,' said Tenak, 'about the siting of this place. The building looks kind of fortified. So, I wondered why they hadn't sited it *on* the hill, at the top, rather than on the plain. But these bogs give us the answer. The path is too narrow for a large group of people – unless they were all in single file.'

'I know and I don't like this Arkas. There's no clear safe approach is there, I guess. Unless you know the area. Weird, though,' said Mike.

They walked slowly and carefully. The data from their wristcoms did not mean they could afford to relax and enjoy the scenery. They had to concentrate and every so often proceed by testing the ground before them with their shoes. They both got muddier but they managed, eventually, to reach the gate; a wide, heavy metal door. An imposing black box was attached to the apex of the wall very close to the gate and they deduced it was some sort of security vid-cam. The entire portal looked as though it were automated. Not so primitive in their technology after all, mused Mike.

A tinny sounding masculine voice suddenly issued from a speaker somewhere above the gate, 'Please be identifying yourselves.'

So, their approach *had* been observed, thought Mike. Tenak loudly announced that they had an appointment with the Meta' leaders at 1.00 mid-tidings. After a short delay the gate slowly swung open and they were able to peer into an expansive interior courtyard paved with wide stone tiles so clean they gleamed. Aqua coloured shrubs and small trees, planted in humongous pots, dotted the whole area. Several sets of stone steps rose from the far end of the courtyard to a balcony on the second floor, and there stood two figures silhouetted against the sky.

The figures paused for long moments before climbing down the nearest steps. As they descended Mike could see they were garbed in long, deep blue robes which had more than a hint of the medieval monk about them. Again, redolent of monks, the figures also wore what appeared to be homemade sandals on their feet. To Mike's mind, the stately descent of these people smacked of an imperious attitude. Imperious? Really? As their hosts reached the courtyard Mike could see that one was male, the other female. The male raised a brown, hirsuit arm from under his cloak and motioned for Tenak and Mike to approach.

Once inside the compound Mike could see them more clearly. Neither was particularly young, and their skin was very weathered, probably because of long exposure to Ra's rays. Their "hosts" smiled broadly as they approached, and Mike thought he caught a gleam in the woman's eyes. She had an elliptical face and her deeply tanned skin had an attractive open-air look to it. Her overall appearance and demeanour reminded him of artists renditions he'd seen of historical figures, like queens Cleopatra, or Nefertiti, but without the jewellery or any other obvious trappings of wealth. These two, he thought, were anything but noble, though he suspected they might have thought that of themselves, despite an appearance of penury and privation. It all seemed very contrived.

The woman spoke first, introducing herself, in languid tones, as "Arva Clytemria Pendocris". Mike reckoned she was around 50 years of age, in Oceanus terms. Her strong, characterful face was framed by a mane of long black hair fixed in braids. She introduced her partner as her husband, "Patchalk Gradivus Remiro". He was a head height taller than Pendocris and his nose protruded, hook-like, from an oblong and rugged face. Given his weather-beaten face and thinning brown hair Mike placed him as being around 65 Oceanus years old. On Earth that would equate to about 56. To Mike, he seemed to wear a disingenuous, plastic smile.

Tenak introduced himself and Mike, and Remiro invited them to follow them back up one set of steps to the terrace of the first floor; a wide, sunlit area; a veritable piazetta, where they were invited to sit at a large circular table cooling under a huge, white, cooling parasol. A young man with a face like a chunk of granite, wearing long red and white robes, slithered into view from around a corner. He carried a tray with 4 slender glasses, each of which contained a frothy, purple, sweet smelling liquid. Pendocris invited the two Earth men to drink the perfumed beverage, as the glasses were set before them.

'Tis made from the local "Inventrius" plant. I think yet you'll find it refreshing after your long, hot walk,' Remiro said.

Arva added quickly, 'Do not a-worry. Tis juice alone, so does not contain alcohol. I yet expect you are not allowed to drink while on duty.'

'Generally, no, but there are exceptions,' said Tenak, smiling, 'but we're grateful for your hospitality. I, for one certainly need some refreshment,' He chuckled as he glanced at his companion. Mike, though thirsty, felt sceptical but Tenak's body language seemed to be telling him he must drink. Mike took the hint, but one sip of the liquid was enough to confirm his suspicion that it was distinctly unpleasant. It tasted like some "nettle" extract he'd once been persuaded to try. And, he thought, in a place like this, it might even be drugged. But then, that would be rather foolish of their hosts. Or, would it?

'It's a … nice … place you have here,' said Tenak. Was he being honest, wondered Mike? He went on, 'but it's a bit tricky to get to. On foot. A lot of boggy ground out there. Could be dangerous, especially for the unwary.'

Good man, thought Mike.

'Ah yes,' said Remiro, 'but unfortunate-so, the bogginess seems to have yet develop-ed since the temple was built. This is an olding structure, you must be realising. Even though it does look like something new.'

'Yes, we do take pride in such an place,' said Pendocris, with edgy voice.

Although she and Remiro did their best to play the amiable hosts, Mike felt they were trying rather too hard. The next few minutes were spent exchanging pleasantries, with Pendocris waxing lyrically about the beauty of Bhumi-Devi at this time of the year; the northern Spring, which Devians called 'New-frond'. They asked about the journey from the Home System and what was involved in adjusting to a new world like Oceanus Alpha. Tenak expressed pleasure about coming to such a wonderful planet but Mike just smiled.

He broke his silence and said, 'Yeah, it's a geat place, so it's a kind of tragedy that the beauty you're talking about will be destroyed ...' – before he realised his mistake. Too early. Tenak gave him a swift kick under the table. He winced but managed to avoid making it obvious.

'It seems you would yet like to plunge in with serious-such talking, gentilhomms,' said Remiro, his smile fading, 'and I am fully with that way forward. Why do run all around the Treminius bush, after all?'

'Yes, we are fully aware why you are here, gentilhomms,' said Pendocris, 'but, if you do not mind, we would like it so we could be speaking to each of you, yet one at a time and separately in this matter.'

Tenak's brows knitted, 'Is that really necessary? We've got nothing to hide.'

'Perhaps not. Perhaps yes,' said Remiro, 'but tis simple-like, we feel, that is – our teachings say, the truth is most readily revealed when a supplicant, you might be saying, comes with open heart. And with no-one to "rescue" them from their own words. I am sorry, but those be our terms for talking to you.'

They were hardly *supplicants* thought Mike. Cheeky bleggers.

Tenak paused for a while, searching Mike's face for signs of agreement. He wanted to refuse but Tenak went ahead anyway and agreed. It felt to him as though they were being put on trial but then, perhaps they were. And perhaps they might have expected something like this. Anyone making and – enjoying – drinks like that purple stuff had to be dodgy.

Another surprise came when Remiro clapped his hands loudly and two young, burly men, also garbed in red and white robes, appeared from one of the rooms on their floor, almost springing onto the balcony. Mike guessed they might have been heavy weight wrestlers in their spare time. It was also clear that they were wearing something bulky around their waists, under their robes. Weapons? Possibly, projectile guns, thought Mike. Either that or these guys were way too pleased to see them.

Mike immediately thought of these characters as "gimbos" and he watched them take up station a couple of metres from the table, while Pendocris, still all smiles, said,

'Gentilhomms, please be not alarmed, but yet in the name of our sanctuary's rules concerning outsiders, I must be asking you to hand over any weaponry you mayst have, as well as any lectronic communicators. I am sure you both yet have the wristcom unities. Am I yet right? I assure you they will yet be returned after our discussions.'

So, they knew about those things, thought Mike. He and Tenak glanced at each-other in resignation, then took off their wristcoms and placed them on the table. 'This is all we have,' said Tenak. Mike hoped these bozos wouldn't mess with the units. Wouldn't know how to operate them anyway. Still …

'Thankles. We now do invite you, Admiral Tenak,' said Remiro, 'to join us first-most for private discussions in our office. We shall speak to you in separation, Mer Secretary, and after the Admiral.'

It was not a request. Remiro, Pendocris and the two guard-accolytes, led a compliant but confident looking Tenak along the balcony to their office. As he went the Admiral gave his companion a reassuring smile but said nothing. Remiro told Mike he was welcome to wander around the grounds and enjoy the views but he would have one of his guards accompany him at all times. He said that security must always be respected. As they left with Tenak, his own guard appeared out of nowhere; a veritable giant of a man, with a head like a coconut and a hairy face which seemed deliberately modelled on the appearance of the mad monk, Rasputin. This was a character Mike had seen in holographic histories of the antique era of the early 20th Century. This guy had a particularly unpleasant sneer to go with his otherwise stone-like features. He grunted at Mike and motioned for him to go down the stairs. They obviously didn't want him being anywhere near the place where they were "talking" to Tenak. Talking, wondered Mike. Or was it interrogation, or something else? He was starting to get alarmed. He made himself calm down. His ideas were getting way ahead of him.

****

Everywhere he walked in the courtyard Mike felt the unsmiling gaze of the lumpen guard alighting on him. He was never more than one or two metres distant. Mike spotted a wide stone path leading from the courtyard and running alongside one of the large gardens they'd seen from the hillside. He glanced behind at the guard and said,

'Is it okay to go down there?'

No answer. Just a sullen look. Well, thought Mike, he didn't say no, so he started walking slowly along the path, the giant following in silence. At the top of a parapet running along the temple's enclosure wall, over on the far side of the garden, several other guards walked slowly back and fore, like prison orderlies. They were dressed like monks of old, but they certainly behaved more like armed sentinels. Where was the need for that? The men and women on the parapet were also watching him, the stranger in their midst. It felt as though his every step, every muscle movement, every facial tick, was being scrutinized.

He wondered if it was worth trying to talk to his guard again. Establish commlinks? Lighten the mood, somehow.

'Listen, Mer …., sorry, I didn't get your name?' he said. 'Where are you from, mascla?'

Silence.

'No answer? Listen, I'm not going to do anything I shouldn't. Couldn't you just let me have a walk round here … sort of on my own, especially if you're not going to talk to me?'

The man just stopped dead and gave him a glare blazing with contempt, but still he said nothing. 'Okay, sorry,' said Mike, 'I don't mean to upset anyone. Guess we'll … just keep walking.'

He'd had enough of this planet and what he considered to be its odd, and in many ways, hostile culture. He was also becoming slightly anxious about what was happening to Tenak – and what sort of interrogation he would get himself. He saw no point in belabouring the arguments he and Tenak had already tried to put forward. He might have felt it worth staying on Oceanus if he could have met Eleri again. At this moment the memory of her seemed, strangely, like a thing of the distant past, yet it was just a few hours. Would he ever see her again? He knew it was unlikely he would meet her again by chance and his wish to leave this world worked against the notion of seeking her out.

The day had become incredibly hot again, despite what he'd been thinking about the climate this far north. There was little shade around here and the sweat seemed to pop from his skin in bubbles and stand proud. After a while he arrived at a large pool near the end of one of the enclosed gardens and, noticing there was a rail around it, leaned on it and peered over at its sparkling surface. Very soon he saw movement. At least he thought it was movement, but he wasn't sure. Yes, there it was again – a dark shape under the water. It disappeared again. He leaned over the rail and then glanced behind him at the guard.

The guy was watching him intently, an inane smirk on his face. Mike thought he'd best humour him and was about to give him a stupid grin in return when a blast of shockingly cold water crashed against his chest and face. He recoiled instinctively and when he opened his eyes again he looked down just in time to see the head of an enormous fish, maybe two or three metres long, staring up at him; a bulbous thing with three eyes, the third sitting on the top of its hump like head. It immediately plunged back under.

The guard stood back and guffawed. Very funny, thought Mike as he pulled a large wad of tissues from his uniform trousers and wiped the side of his face. He felt fortunate that his mouth had been closed and his head turned away when the fish had squirted him. Maker- knew what kind of infection he might have got. His white tunic now had a huge brown tide mark across it. It was a while before he saw the funny side of it and even though he begrudged the injury to his uniform, it was only his pride which had been hurt. He grinned genuinely at the guard this time, but by then the man's usual sour look had returned.

Mike was still trying, unsuccessfully, to wipe off the mark when a female guard, also dressed in the standard red robes, approached from the far end of the walkway. She wore her hood over her head but although evidently young, Mike could see a severe look and manner about her. She asked him to accompany her back to the Meta leaders and nodded at the male guard, who promptly turned and walked back the way they'd come. She gestured for him to walk in front of her and pointed along the path to a door set in a building at its far end. It looked like the front of one of the main building's side extensions.

'Please be going through that door, Home System charmer,' she said.

Home System charmer? thought Mike. That's a new one, but at least she was communicating.

'You are to be questioned by our blessed leaders,' she added.

Finally, he thought. Let's get it over with. A minute later, after he'd been prompted to go through a long corridor that twisted through the building, then up several sets of stairs, he found himself in a cool and fragrant smelling room on the same balcony floor into which he had seen Tenak disappear.

Remiro and Pendocris entered by another door and his guard vanished behind him. The temple leaders motioned for him to sit the other side of a very ancient looking desk. Mike's eyes took a few moments to adjust to the relative darkness in the room.

'I am hoping the initiate who accompanied you on your little … walk, was the prime-most of courtesy?' said Remiro, trying to stifle a grin.

'Suppose so,' said Mike, 'but, you know, he talks too much.'

Remiro chuckled and said, 'Oh, and I yet see you were caught out by a Traiko fish. I think you shall find your uniform needs some deepso cleanie. I am supposing we should have warned you, but we did not. Such bad luck.'

Pendocris suddenly gave her husband a sharp look.

'That's okay,' said Mike, 'it's not important.'

'Tis good then. Anywayin, I would like to start our discussion by ...' began Remiro.

'Excuse me,' interjected Mike, 'but where is the Admiral?'

'Ah, but he is outso the back yard,' said Pendocris, looking impatient, 'yet you need not be concerned, sirra.'

Mike's face clouded over with suspicion.

'There is yet a set of stairs outside the back of this office,' she added, 'which will lead to another exit from this learn-ed Sanctuary. When we have finished our interview we wouldst be grateful if you could both leave by that route.'

Remiro huffed and began again, 'As I was to say, I would want to start so by asking you what extra evidence you can offer to be upstanding in your claim that our great sun and life-giver, wondrous, Ra, is going to become so violent and unstable – and so un-life giving?' He said those last words with a sense of shocked indignation. 'And before you be saying it,' he continued, 'and as I yet told the Admiral, I am aware of the recent lectrical problems in some parts of Devi. They are, in our view, nothing more than, how you say – transitory.'

'Those "transitory" problems are going to get much worse, I'm afraid,' said Mike. 'In fact, I think you'll find there's a lot more of them on their way right now.'

'Ah yes, you are referring to Ra's coronal outburst of some weeks ago. We, ourselves, predicted something like it. You need not look so surprised, young manry. We can and we do carry out our own observations of Ra – all through time. We are not so the ignorant savages you Navy people do think,' said Remiro.

'I never said ...' began Mike.

'We know that Ra has given us many outbursts in the past,' blurted Remiro, 'and this such is a mere 'nother. You may be aware that our society does not rely on lectronics so heavily as yours. I believe that seemingly *all* your Home System citizenry have various personal-such devices that do rely on lectronics and satellite signals of some sort. And yet the more such devices you have, the more problems you will encounter – in your socio-culture. As for Ra, we are confident that it will remain, in general, stable, for many millions of years. Even your own Sun occasionally graces you with mass coronal outbursts and flares, does it not?'

'I wouldn't say "grace", but, yes, though they're generally not as large or energetic as Ra's have been in recent months,' said Mike. He was fast losing the will to live. What was the point of arguing? Their minds were made up, like everyone on this blasted rock.

Remiro's brows knitted together, 'I am aware of that, as well, Mer Secretary, but Ra is a different sort of star - at yet a different stage of evolution, ist not? Tis yet younger than the Sun and I think you will find that your own star was significantly more active in the cosmic past than now.' He paused for a moment, then continued, much to Mike's chagrin, 'Look now young manry, I understand that you have a "Higher Doctrate" in Physic, so you will presumably be understanding these figures.'

To Mike's surprise he hauled a tablet sized screen from a drawer in the table, switched it on and set it on the tabletop, facing Mike. This was getting weirder all the time, thought Mike. Oceanus people with midi-comps. *Old fashioned* midi-comps but, still, impressive for this lot. Whatever next? Holo-vids?

Mike guessed that the two people the other side of the table caught his surprised look. They gave each-other smug grins. Remiro pressed a button on the midi keyboard and the screen flashed into life, showing lists of numerals, symbols and graphs which Mike recognised as representations of a star's physical characteristics. He thought he recognised the physical and chemical characteristics of Ra. Remiro pressed another button and the screen split in half, the previous data shrinking to one side and a new set of data flashing up on the other side.

'The data on the left side, are our own,' said Remiro, 'all such carried out over the last four years. You will yet see what they do say. On the right side are the data from the so-called "Omega 10" auto-probe your HS people left in our system. See how the figuries differ?' He waited for some comment from Mike and when he got none, looked astonished, and said,

'Our figuries show a very so different Ra, do they not? They show a much more settled and contented Ra. Benign, we would say. Your probe's do not.'

'Alright,' said Mike, 'so they differ. I might have expected that, because of the reluctance of you, Oceanus people, to accept our views. So what? I have no idea of things like the sensitivity of your instruments, so I know which figures *I would* place reliance on.'

Remiro looked like the cat who got the cream and he smiled smugly as he said, 'And now for the blunt truth, Mer Secretary. I will tell you now-time that your own people's probe stopped working 10 of our years ago!'

Internally, Mike felt a bit floored, but he tried not to show it. A nagging voice told him not to bother. At least they weren't trotting out the line that Trebuchet had mentioned, about deliberate falsification of data. At least not yet. Or were they?

'And so, young manry. How could you say your figures are so much better than ours? Yours are so-yet out of date, such that they are not worth bothering us with.'

Whilst Remiro wore a ridiculous grin of self-satisfaction Mike thought about what he might say now. He could think of a few things. In fact, his agile mind came up with several reasons why Remiro's figures were likely to be unreliable – apart from the fact that he simply did not think these people could be trusted. Okay, he didn't know the probe had stopped working. Tenak probably didn't either. He didn't think Remiro would have anything to gain by lying about *that*. It could easily be disproved.

But, the fact was that giant Home System telescopes, including the Far Edge instrument, had observed throughout the cosmos a certain set of stars of the same type as Ra, which had displayed different stages of unsettled, disruptive behaviour, in a cycle which ended with huge, disruptive surface storms of cataclysmic violence. All but about three were very distant stars and none were thought to have life bearing planets. Another thing was that current observations of Ra showed exactly the same characteristics, at an early stage, and the tell-tale signs dated to no less than 132 years ago. Stellar evolution usually took millions of years but the changes observed elsewhere indicated a super-fast rate of decay in this type of star.

At the time the pioneers first landed on Oceanus – and until very recently, astro-science had not made these alarming discoveries; stellar science having developed very rapidly in the interim, particularly an understanding of the changes which occur in the deep, middle layers of a star's body. This was where the virulent and potentially damaging changes had been found to occur in Ra-types. So, the science was pretty new but no less potent for that.

Also, a probe to Ra, *had* been dispatched some months before The Monsoon had set off, to report back with new, close-up observations. However, the data-pod it had sent back through a conduit had disappeared, mysteriously, within minutes of it showing up in the Solar System. The data sets it had begun transmitting had been cut short, but not before they had given a preliminary confirmation of the remote observations.

Then, finally, of course, there were the observations carried out by The Monsoon itself, meticulously made during the giant ship's three-and-a-half-week journey from entry into the system, up to orbital insertion around Oceanus – and continuing. Everything confirmed the science.

Trying to sound droll, Mike said, 'There are other data sets. Very much up to date … and a lot more …'

'So then, young manry, where are they?' said Remiro.

'I don't have them,' said Mike, though he was sure he could summon them up via his wrist-com. He could ask them to return the device but … why bother? If an elephant from the old days had been standing in the room with them, these people wouldn't accept it if they chose not to. And, in a funny way, *there was*. Momentarily distracted, he wondered what had happened to those wonderful creatures. Whatever it was, these people were going the same way, but this was *their* own fault, not someone else's.

Now look at these results,' said Remiro. 'These yet are our own observations over the same period. And now will you see that they show a similar trend but the graphs do so indicate a much slower growth rate in instability. Much slower – by a factor of at least 3 millions of magnitudes.'

'So what?' said Mike, tired of this charade. He began to explore another tack. He got no further than, 'Look, I'm probably not really qualified to talk about this but …'

'Not qualified?' blurted Remiro, staring at Mike with mock horror, then turning to Pendocris, said, 'so, yet he says he is not qualified. Never would I have guessed.'

'I was going to say that I'm not qualified to comment on your own data ...,' said Mike in protest.

But Remiro persisted, 'If that is so I wonder why you are e'en here at all. Your own Tenak was not able to fully understand our figuries but at least he tried. He showed us your own ship- made figuries, at least.'

Mike had simply meant to say that he wasn't qualified to comment on the veracity of their data because he didn't know how they had been obtained. He was becoming more and more exasperated and just wanted out of there. He responded to Remiro's comment about Tenak, by saying, 'And did you accept his figures?'

'Yet why should we? You are part of a conspiracy, after all,' argued Remiro, becoming suddenly irate.

'What does that mean?' Here we go, he thought. This is the falsification and cover up thing, after all.

'It has been made clear to us, Home System manry, that your very government wants Oceanus back. You need not look like that in your face. They do not want our independence to succeed, no? It would please them if we did all leave, since once tis done, and once our popularia are settled in some backside-water, some arse-place on Earth, or praps e'en shitehawk Mars, they would find it such difficult to return - ever.'

'Why in the galaxies would ...' started Mike.

'Because your government would want to emplace militaria centres on this planet – and yet to plunder its reserves of rare metals. You know, the ones which your lectronics people do use in those devices I mentioned soon-before.'

Oh, Maker, thought Mike. This is worse than anything Trebuchet suggested they'd say. These people really are paranoid.

'Look,' said Mike, 'we don't need to take those metals from the ground. They can now be synthesised.'

'Really so? I do not think so and yet, you just now said, "I am not qualified ..."'

Pendocris suddenly launched in and interrupted her husband, who blinked and stared blankly at her.

'Ah, yes,' she said to Mike, in a voice, soft, though in deadly earnest, 'but the synthesising of the MX metal crystals is often extremely expensive, is it not?'

'Well, I suppose so,' rejoined Mike, 'but ... well, it isn't really my area ...'

Remiro chuckled and Pendocris pushed her attack, 'So it's probably just as easy to take advantage of ready supplies of the raw material from here? It's one of many things that Oceanus has to offer in the way of material resources, surely?'

'Of course not. We could get loads of materials elsewhere, if needed,' said Mike forcefully, but he suddenly realised he might be getting onto dangerous ground here, vis-a- vis his employers: the government. What might get back to them from Oceanus, if he overstepped the mark on matters not in his purview? Well, they shouldn't have placed him and Tenak in this invidious position, should they? He was astounded by Remiro's accusation; a very serious one, in all truth. Mike couldn't believe these guys were so delusional.

Even supposing, for a moment, they were right, he wasn't at all convinced about the economics of what they were suggesting. He wondered how these people thought that politics in the Home System would, or could, allow such a thing in this day and age. It was the largest democracy in history, even though probably capable, like all democracies, of relatively infrequent but still potentially shocking breaches of human rights. But they just wouldn't *be allowed* to get away with something like this. Not with the heavy monitoring by the various citizen pressure groups on SolNet and the hundreds of smaller networks. But the New Rebels? Now that was different. Still, everyone knew that they'd proabably sunk into oblivion, didn't they?

'You have gone so quiet-est, youngry,' said Remiro, 'yet my wife be right, ist not?'

Mike just shrugged. He was at the point of just saying no more. Why should he play their little game? He pondered Pendocris, though. There was something odd about that one. She kept lapsing into perfect Anglo-Span when she talked animatedly. Her mannerisms were somehow different to those of most Oceanus people he'd encountered so far. He dismissed the thought. So what?

'Now, young manry, what is your answer to our figures for our star? Your Tenak had no such answer yet,' said Remiro, calmer now.

Mike wasn't surprised that Tenak had also failed to get through to them. The Meta's figures were probably nonsense.

'*Admiral* Tenak is not a physics or electronics specialist,' he said, 'but we have people on the ship who are. Why don't you talk to them?' Mike knew he was more than capable of pointing out the error of their ways, but he felt this a pointless game; an unwinnable one. This whole planet was a charade, a travesty of rational thought.

Pendocris took over again, her voice more conciliatory than her husband's. Those liquid tones again, like smooth velvet,

'You're quite right Mer Secretary. By the way, I think my husband meant to refer to your colleagry by his correct title – Admiral Tenak. Please accept our apologia.' Remiro looked at her sideways but said nothing. 'Please understand,' she continued, 'that we have every respect for both you and the Admiral.' She paused for effect, then said, 'Perhaps I should explain that we, meaning all the Meta-teleosophists, believe that humans were, in effect, meant to come here, to Oceanus. Tis Earth's sister planet, is it not?' She smiled, very charmingly. She might have the eye for him, Mike mused, then caught himself. What the fezzer was he thinking? She was a flick-wit, like her husband, just cannier.

Pendocris continued to smile and said, 'You might have heard of the teleological position on philosophy?'

'Yeah, yeah,' said Mike, his voice betraying his boredom, 'Teleologists believe in science but think that there is a greater purposefulness in nature. When applied to cosmology this philosophy translates as the "Anthropic Principle". That is to say, the Universe bears life, despite all the strange coincidences that are needed for it to exist, because it's designed to produce that result.' He paused. They seemed to be enjoying this. He continued, though he had no idea why he was bothering, 'The idea is that the purposefulness of nature is evidenced by the fact that if any one of the Universe's physical constants was very slightly different, then life would not have been possible, still less intelligent life. And so it goes onwards from there ... da de da de da... Don't tell me, but I guess the name of your group means you hold to the strong version of the anthropic principle? The Universe was meant to give rise to sentient life. Ours, in fact. Right?' He gave them his best sardonic smile.

'*Very s*trong version of the Anthropic Principle, yes,' said Pendocris, 'but there is no need of cynicism tones. You must understand that ours is not a belief in God, as such. It's easy for others to think this. No, rather, tis the concept that our Universe is exquisitely designed to be nominal for the development of life, particularly sentient life, as you didst mention. We say the Universe *is itself* alive and so gives rise to life most naturally and – inevitably. We believe we humans *had to come here*, to Oceanus, all those years ago, to make a human paradise – on Earth's twin. Our destiny, if you so wish, on a new Earth.'

'But better than Earth – as tis now,' Remiro chimed in, 'since humans have desecrated the original world. We must not do the same to this planet. That is why we have to ensure that the culture-trends and habituas of the Home System popularia are not allowed to contaminate our world. That is also why we need yet to limit the pace of the technological change that has enslaved the peoples of your worlds.'

Mike sighed and said, 'But then, I guess technology is what got you here in the first place, wouldn't you say?' He still wondered why he seemed to be playing their silly game.

'Well yes, we cannot be denying that,' said Pendocris. She leaned toward him, 'But don't you see? That was a golden opportunity for us to start again - as long as we do things the right way this time. Now we are here, we have a duty to protect the planet from the worst ravages of humankind. There's yet bound to be some small spoiling of the environment but we can and must limit it. Still, while we keep to that philosophy we know that the Cosmos won't destroy us, at least not by such a random thing as you and your people are suggesting.'

'No indeed,' said Remiro, 'for Ra will take care of us if we take care of its children – its planetary family.'

'And young manry,' said Pendocris, emphatically, 'please know that we are gaining new adherents across Devi, every day.'

'Why am I not surprised?' said Mike.

'Our people, the people of this world are just starting to see that they cannot trust the Home System. And we have the figures to prove it. Think upon that, you and your Admiral,' she announced.

Mike said nothing for long moments. They seemed to be expecting some sort of response from him. Okay, he'd go along with it, for just a few seconds more.

'You really do have it bad, don't you?'

'That is not an answer, youngry,' said Pendocris.

'Okay, try this. What you're saying goes a hell of a lot further than the anthropic principle, or teleology. All that stuff about "meanings".'

'It's certainly different. That is why we are called the Meta-teleosophists, Mer Secretary,' said Pendocris, 'That means - a modified form of teleosophy.'

'Yeah, yeah, I know, thanks,'

'And indeed,' said Remiro, 'we know there are those in your Home System who yet agree with our stance and …'

Pendocris looked momentarily alarmed and interrupted him with, 'Rather, what my husband means is that we indeed hope there are people in your system who will understand us and will also be supporting our position.' She looked acidly at her husband and continued, 'but t'will make no real difference to us, upon this world. We are independent in all important things.'

'Well, if that's it,' said Mike, stifling a yawn, 'I think I'd better be going.'

'Yes, I am pleased to agree with you so, for once,' said Remiro, sighing heavily and raising a hand in resignation. He indicated a door in the darker recesses of the room behind Mike, and said, 'Brother Dravak will show you out. I am supposing I should thank you for coming. It has been – flash-up. I mean – enlightening.' He looked at Pendocris, with an expression Mike couldn't see but could guess. But he couldn't care less.

He got up to leave. Brother Dravak was the very same brute of an "initiate" who had shadowed Mike earlier. This time the man held a weapon, quite openly, above his cassock. Mike thought it looked like some sort of electric stun stick. These guys probably think this weapon is advanced, he mused. Even so, Mike knew well enough that it could hurt him badly. Could even be lethal. He wished he still had the weaponised wristcom Tenak had given him. He could only hope he'd get it back.

Dravak ushered Mike through the door. No nice good-byes then, thought Mike acidly, as he entered a long, hardly lit, windowless, corridor. After about 10 metres it turned to the right at a sharp angle and continued straight ahead for what could have been many metres. The way became increasingly dark and dingy and Mike listened to the heavy footfalls of the Meta' acolyte behind him. He began to feel anxious about that guy. What had Remiro and Pendocris have planned for him?

*

Back in their office Pendocris spoke to Remiro with anger, 'I thought you had cordon-ed off the fish pool? You didst realise what would have happened if any of the thing's squirt had got in his mouth? Been such ingested by him? He could have died.'

'Well,' said Remiro nonchalantly, 'didst not happen. And yet, if had happened then we could so say t'was a mere accident. We didst warn the manry didst we not, we would say, but yet he still went too near? True? Coursry true.

'That's too risky, husband. Much too risky. No more of that such behaviour, Remiro. And I do not want to see anything like attempts on the lives of those gentilhomms. Nothing of that sort. We could bring the *whole Home System Navy*, praps e'en their government, on our heads – too soon, too quick-so by far. Also, it wouldst endanger the activities of our friends on the ship. You do not want that, do you, husband?'

'No Arva,' he said resignedly, 'and do not be a-worry. I will not try anything like such.'

She screwed up her eyes as she looked at him and said, 'Best not, husband. Best not.'

*

They reached another right-angled turn in the tunnel, this time to the left, and the way ahead was now pitch black. A light suddenly switched on behind him – a directed light of some sort. Glancing over his shoulder, he saw that Dravak's stun weapon had some kind of torch attached to it. And the beam looked more like it was trained on the centre of Mike's back, rather than being used for illumination. His heart started to race. Was he really going to be released? What had happened to Tenak? He kept trying to tell himself he was letting his imagination run riot. These people would surely not do anything that stupid? The dark corridor ran on and on. He tried to think clearly and analyse ways he might be able to overpower Dravak. It would be difficult bu he might have to try. He might get badly hurt but he remembered HS marines aboard The Monsoon once said that in a potentially fatal situation it was better to take someone down with you, rather than be slaughtered meekly. Easy for them to say, he thought – but he might have to try. It was getting hotter in this place. What fate awaited him at the end of the corridor?

Chapter 7

APPROACHING PERIL

Just over six million kilometres from Oceanus Alpha, a massive cloud, over seven million kilometres across, composed of subatomic particles, sped silently toward the planet. A vast globule of protons; atoms stripped of their electrons, in untold numbers, the cloud was the nuclear debris from an explosion, a flare, that had taken place on Ra's surface. Its power had been the equivalent of millions of human made nuclear fusion bombs. The particles, most of them mere trillionths of a metre in diameter, were detectable by the ultraviolet and X-ray radiation they generated as they swept through space.

And now the cloud rushed toward Oceanus at around three million kilometres per hour, atomic slurry slung out from the surface of the star by the tortured magnetic and subatomic quantum storms raging deep within it. Even in an age when humans knew so much more about star evolution, and behaviour, than ever before in human history, the mechanism of the birth of these storms, the so-called "Karabrandon Waves", were still only vaguely understood by Home System scientists. But the behaviour of such clouds, once born, were thought to be more predictable. The Home System physicists were to be proved wrong about that too.

In fact, no-one had ever observed an altogether different effect, which, crucially, had also never been predicted, that through a series of complex interactions with the magnetic field of Oceanus itself, and the galaxy's own magnetic flux, and the precise geometry of the cloud's approach, the particle storm was caused to *accelerate* as it neared the planet. It was to be a little while before *that* was understood by humans.

****

Staring at what was, evidently, an ancient but still functioning, computer screen, President Nefer-Masterton sat at her desk in her spacious office suite in Janitra. On the screen was a report from the Minister for the Interior, detailing surveys which showed a rise in the number of seriously addicted people in Bhumi-Devi. These people were addicted not to chemical drugs, nor even to alcohol, though the latter was just starting to become a social issue. In fact, this addiction was to *brain* stimulation, a habit that was rife in the Home System and which looked as if it had spread to Oceanus. Those affected used wire nets with electrodes, which they placed over the head, and which were connected to batteries and modulators that fed charges of varying strengths through the skull, directly to the brain.

The "brainstimo" electrical signals were of a type and intensity that tickled the pleasure centres of the brain; harmless if used but little and infrequently. Addictive, when used too often. In many cases usage increased to the point where there came a desire for constant use, to the exclusion of anything else, including eating, and eventually even drinking, in favour of the brainstimo. After that, death could, and often did happen.

In the Home System methods of neutralisation had been developed which involved permanently attaching tiny electrodes to the cranium, after which wire threads, a few nanometres thick; mere billionths of a metre, ran through the skull to the outer membrane of the brain. These produced a counter current which neutralised the stim effects. The downside was that users normally had to keep the implants in place for the rest of their lives. There were often psychological and sometimes physiological consequences.

Nefer-Masterton's concentration was interrupted by the buzzing of her desk intercom, followed by the gentle tones of her secretary, 'Sorry Madama President, yet I have Arva Pendocris on the phone for you.'

'Patch her through, Mandira,' said Masterton, sighing.

'Happy mid-tidings Arbella,' came the liquid tones of Pendocris, pouring like oil, out of Arbella's speaker, 'I am hoping I am not interrupting a thing un-so-important.'

'Unlike you, Arva, I am always doing still-important things. But go ahead, anywayins. What be you needing now?'

'We just had a visit from the Admiral Tenak of the Home System Navy, as well as his flunky-man, this afternoon. They said they had yet spoken to you early-time.'

'Yes, I have seen them. What are you wanting, Arva?'

'Nothing really. I just want to know when they shall likely be going home. They struck me as being rare naïve, or at least one of them did.'

'Then what is your problem?'

'The Admiral did ask some awkward questions, that is all. I don't know if he thought he could impress me but Remiro and I kept him off. His Mer-secretary didn't make any difference one way or t'other, but yet, the Admiral looks like trouble to us.'

'How strange that anyone should give you trouble, Arva. You surprise even me, and I am used to your shankle-tricks. I am also surprised at what you say about Secretary Tanniss. Both he and the Admiral seemed most astute-like to me. But then, I should not be surprised that your prandling would make someone give up the will to live.'

'Oh, nonsense Arbella. Do not forget, you are in some awkward position, now that Jezemiah Ptah-Feldickson has come over to our great cause. You carnt take many more defections, Arbella. You be knowing that. Anywayins, what are you going to do about these here, H. S. people? Carnt you send them packing off? I am suggesting you seriously do consider that option.'

'I have many options Arva, including ending this such ridiculous conversation. I shall not be sending them home just now. They have made some very good points and may still have something to contribute. I also do want to avoid the rest of the Home System breathing down our necks, present time. "Sending them packing off," right now, might precipitate that exact-so thing. Besides, please be noting carefully that *these two have my government's protection,* and their ship has governmento permission to stay, for times being. Please bear that in mind Arva – strongly.'

'Oh, I think they're a spent force anywayins, from what I could tell. I just want to see them off the planet and on their far-way, is all.'

'If what you say is true it should not matter if they stay a bit longer, should it? And you know we carnt always have what we want, can we? That is why I've got to draw this conversation to an end. Thank you and good even-tide, Arva.'

Arbella pressed a button on the intercom and Pendocris's voice vanished. She sighed again and, wearing a concerned look, rose to fix a cup of Devian kaffee, when the intercom machine buzzed again. 'And what now?' she said.

'Sorry again, Madama President, but your niecing, Mes Ambrell has just arrived, hoping to speak to you. Shall I ask her to make an appointment?'

'No, no, I shall yet see her. I could do with this sort of distraction, exactly now. Be sending her in, please.'

Seconds later Eleri Nefer-Ambrell breezed into the President's inner office as gracefully as though she were dancing across a stage. Arbella embraced her and showed her to a comfy seat and said, 'Tis good to see you Eleri, as is always. Can I get you some kaffee? I was yet about to fix some up.'

'No, thanking you, Auntine,' said Eleri, 'and I hope I am not interrupting too much. I know I should be making an appointment really, but I was in the Curia anyway, so you know...'

'That is fine,' said Arbella as she walked to a table and poured herself a mug of steaming beverage. 'Is there much I can do for you, loveliest?'

'Well, I am wondering if you were going to Unkling Muggredge's 71st birthingday next week? Tis Thasingday, but I am sure you know that.' Eleri appeared to hold her breath.

'Oh, I wondered if it might be something such like, young femna. I think you knew the answer, which is, no.'

'Oh, go on Auntine. You know he misses you. It would not yet hurt, wouldst? My meather and feether will be there. I do not think you have e'en seen them for around a year. Why do you cut yoursev off like you do?'

'I am not cutting off from anyone, Eleri. You know I have no argument with your parenti, but they do seem to spend so much time in your Unkling's company and ... well, you know he and I just do nerie get on. Never have.'

'I know, but yet I am still sorry to hear this, Auntine. Really am. I hope that Unkling's position on the Home System's findings has not anything to do with it? You know I have some sympathy with such, as well, do you not?'

'Eleri! I am surprised at you. How canst say that?'

'I am sorry Auntine, and true. I do not know a lot about this subject, but many people I know, specially in the teaching world, have much knowledge therein. They are saying the Meta-teleos are wrong to take their stance.'

'I'm still surprised you should e'en entertain any notion of it.'

Eleri looked dejected as she said, 'I am sorry for upsetting you and I accept that, at this moment, I am uncertain-yet, but I am vera-worried for this world, and you know how I love the wild things of this planet. We can leave but they can not. Yet, I accept that praps no-one knows all the truth in this matter.'

'Oh, tis fair comment. Let us say no more of it. And I am sorry too – about not seeing your meather and feether more oft.'

'Then I shall let them know you are coming – next week?' Eleri grinned then.

Arbella sighed and said, 'Okay. I guess so. I shall be there.'

Eleri smiled broadly and jumping forward gave Arbella a huge hug, almost knocking the kaffee out of her hand.

Sitting again she said, 'By the way Auntine, I hope you will consider again those scientific reports – the H. S. ones? T'would not be right to close ourselves off from them. Not this time. Tis too damnatious important.'

'Watch your language in here, Eleri.'

'Sorry Auntine, but you know what I mean.'

'Yes, of course but you also know I carnt just ignore our own people's findings. There are big differences of opinion out there. As a natural philosopher, you too should know that oft different conclusions can be forged out of the same set of data. True? Look at how many different theories, yet different interpretations, came out of the findings of quantum theory and relativity, in the 20th and 21st centuries. T'was only after the Earth's recovery and redevelopment – after the super-volcano explosion - that these theories were brought together and settled. Look at the science of weather, too. That is yet chaotic, and no-one has ever really understood it in fine detail. Same thing with the various ideas about negative energy activity in the interstellar conduits – so I do gather anywayins.'

'By the moons, you're very well informed, Auntine,' said Eleri. 'As always,' she added.

'You should yet do well to remember that, femna. And besides, I shouldn't e'en be discussing matters of government policy with you. You know this. You can be manipulative, youngry.'

Nefer-Masterton laughed lightly then. Eleri grinned, but said, 'I did wonder what happened when you met the men from the ship in orbit?'

'It seems you are also well informed, young Mes. Yet you also know that is confidential.'

'Sorry – again. I just wondered because I think I did meet them yesterday. Was the youngry called Mike, or something?'

'Not "something" Eleri but yes, he was called Mike. Mike Tanniss, I so believe. The government Secretary on the ship. Where in the oceans did you meet them? Oh, of course, you came in here yestermorn, did you not? I expect they were here to see the Oceanus Udec D C. Is that it?'

Eleri said nothing. After a short pause, she said, 'What did you think of the Secretary manry?'

'He seemed quite so charming I suppose. Fair astute, though I have recently heard comments to the contrary,' she said, rolling her eyes, 'but I would nar so take those seriously. Why are you asking?'

'Did you think he was good looking?' Eleri asked.

'Eleri? You know full well I don't think of any manry like that. You know well enough I do share my life with another femna,'

'Yes, course I am knowing, but he *was* good looking, was he not?'

There was a tiny twinkle in Eleri's eyes.

'I dare not think you should get involved there, dear-so. He is younger than you by a fair margin yet – and will be going home soon. Looks also, to my eye, like he might be a bit of a heart breaker too.'

'So, you do think he's a fair-looker, do you not?'

'I suppose so,' she laughed. 'Now, youngry, leave me in peace. I have work to do,' said the President amiably but firmly.

Chapter 8

DESPERATION

In the dark, stuffy corridor in the Meta-teleo temple Mike reached another turn, lit only by the guard's stunner torch, an inadequate source. Mike felt an increasing sense of apprehension.

'To the left, manry,' said Dravak, with a deep throated grumble. He motioned toward a large metal door to the left, just a metre or two further on.

'Turn such big handle in the middle and go through – and away now,' said Dravak. Mike gingerly grabbed the handle. What was beyond? Freedom – hopefully, freedom from undiluted bullshit. It was hard to move the mechanism, but it eventually gave a metallic shriek and grudgingly moved clockwise. The guard nudged him from behind and Mike pushed hard at the door. With difficulty he began to open it. Blindingly bright sunlight pierced the corridor. To his alarm Mike felt a hard-metallic object pushed into the small of his back and a large boot on his bum, as he was propelled through the door – and out into the open air. It felt like he'd been released from a long prison sentence. Wincing from the sharp pain in his back, he turned, concerned about what Dravak might do next, only to see the man vanish as he pulled the door closed. Seconds after it clanged shut Mike could hear multiple internal locking devices slotting into place behind it. He uttered some choice Home System expletives and gesticulated toward the closed door.

As he rubbed at the spot where Dravak had shoved his stun stick his eyes gradually adapted to the brilliance of late afternoon sunshine from Ra, and then he saw him; Tenak stood just a few metres away, at the top of a set of concrete steps. These led down to a part of the sanctuary's compound on the opposite side to the one they had originally entered. A single, armed guard stood at the bottom, waiting to open a massive set of wrought iron gates.

'You okay? You look like you've seen a ghost,' said Tenak.

Mike breathed a sigh of relief as he approached his colleague, 'I thought they'd done you in', he said.

'Nah. What the hell happened to you?' said the Admiral, smiling, as he pointed to Mike's soiled uniform.

'Oh, some sort of fish thing,' came the reply, 'but I'll tell you later. Let's just get out of here.'

'Here's yours,' said Tenak as he handed Mike a wristcom, the one which had originally been Tenak's.

'The guard who threw me out slung them back at me,' said the Admiral, 'I've checked 'em. They're okay. Come on, let's go.'

'I'll bet they didn't boot you out that door,' said Mike.

'No, they didn't.'

They started down the steps. The guard below said nothing, simply opening the metal gate, clanging it shut after them, then locking it with a massive, rusty, key.

On the long trek back to the automated car station Tenak asked Mike about his meeting with Remiro and Pendocris; the "terrible duo" as Mike dubbed them. The Admiral didn't seem very happy with the tale that Mike told.

'Didn't you try to convince them?' said Tenak.

'Convince them about what, exactly? Did they show you their "figuries"?'

Tenak nodded, as Mike continued, 'I don't know about you, but I certainly couldn't understand what those flick-wits were trying to say. I just said they should talk to our scientists.'

'You know they're not going to do that, Mike. Listen, I couldn't completely understand their figures, but *you?* You're supposed to be an astrophysics expert. At least, so I understood. I realise you're a ship's Secretary, but you knew I was relying on you for support, Mike.'

'What did you expect me to do, *Admiral?* Point out that their data was skewed. Obtained with outdated equipment. That our people back home have obtained reliable measurements by better means? Or something? No man, what the hell is the point?'

Tenak sighed, 'That's what we're here to do, isn't it? Because someone doesn't seem to want to listen, doesn't mean we shouldn't at least try to sound ... competent. Hell, don't you even ...?'

'Listen, man, they just blanked me out anyway. They went on about their teleological views, to the nth degree. They're motivated by ... well, what amounts to a religious *thing*. They reckon they're convincing the populace more and more down here. They just don't want people to leave and they're duping them into believing that the Home System has got ulterior motives.'

'Yeah, they gave me all that stuff too.'

'So, *what did you say*?'

'I just pointed out that even if they're right they have nothing to lose by allowing people to leave Oceanus. They could always return if Ra settles down.'

'And, they said...?'

'Didn't know what to say. It stumped them for a moment, till Pendocris said they aren't stopping anyone from leaving. Admitted they don't have the power. Said this is a democracy, and so on. And they're right, but they know full well that most of the population actually believe these ... hump-jammers. These guys are fully aware of how much influence they really have.'

'So, you didn't get through to them any more than I did?' said Mike broadly. A smile began to play on his lips.

'At least I tried.' Tenak flashed an irritated look at Mike, who decided to say no more for the moment.

WHEN THEY reached the auto-car station, sweating in the mid day sun, the illuminated timetable told them that there was a long delay because of some technical difficulties further down the line. They stood for half an hour and as they did so they could see swathes of cloud appear on the horizon and start to spread. They watched billowing clouds accumulate above, gathering like angry giants, changing from fluffy white to dark grey, then to black, and finally electric purple. Tenak suggested they start walking back to the monorail station and they set off in silence. Mike ruminated about Tenak's obvious displeasure at the way the meeting had gone and how Mike, in particular, had behaved. Too bad, he thought.

Ten minutes later it started to rain, lightly at first, then more heavily, as though the downpour was being cranked up by some huge sadist high above. Then it began to get cool, the coolest Mike had experienced since landing on the planet. Sod this shit, he thought. He was not used to rain.

'Let's jog,' Tenak said, more like a command than a suggestion, and immediately set off at a cracking pace. Despite his youth Mike struggled to keep up. He was relatively unfit for a young man but he felt obliged to try and keep up. And so, he did manage, for the first 10 minutes, but then it started to hurt his chest. He kept reminding himself it would keep him warm and feeling positive. But after another 10 minutes he thought his lungs were going to burst.

'This is running, Arkas, not jogging,' Mike complained as loudly as his lungs would let him. It came out more like a wheeze.

'Do you some good,' came Tenak's barked reply.

The "jog" seemed to go on and on but eventually Mike could see the monorail station in the distance as they rounded a bend, the path awash with rapidly deepening rainwater. Their trousers were soaked up to the crotch. Tenak's sturdy navy boots held fast but Mike wore only light Secretariat-issue shoes, and they were starting to squelch as he ran. He thought he could feel blisters popping into sore existence on his soles and he began to slow down. Tenak way ahead of him, stopped, turned, and looked at him quizzically.

Mike felt as though this rain was being vindictive. It was getting ever heavier, to the point of stinging as it hit his skin. The roadway had become a small river and it was getting hard to see more than a few metres ahead. He tried not to look too miserable as Tenak approached him.

'It's just a little rain, Mike. Nothing. Get used to it.'

Mike just gave him a sour look.

'Just what's getting at you, Mike?' demanded Tenak, 'you can't seem to be bothered with anything these days.'

'What are you talking about, man?'

'You know what I mean. I don't think you even tried with the teleos' back there. Hell, you only seem to want to chase femnas in this place. But maybe I shouldn't be surprised.'

Mike watched the rain running down the older man's face, collecting under his square chin before dropping like the run-off from an overflow pipe.

'You know I only do this sort of thing to try to help you,' Mike said, 'but the Maker knows why! I don't even know what I'm doing on this rock. There's no point trying to "convince" anyone here, Arkas. No-one wants to know. Can't you get that through your thick skull?'

At that point a little voice told him he was going too far but he felt he couldn't stop. Not now.

'And don't tell me you believe anything else, man,' Mike continued, 'I've just had it with these people. They're not normal. They're not reasonable. They ain't open to persuasion or science or anything, man. I just want to get off this shit hole.'

'Have you finished whining?' said Tenak. He pointed a forefinger at Mike and jabbed the air with it.

'You know something Mike? You give up too easy!'

With an abject look of disappointment, he turned and jogged on toward the station but stopped suddenly. He turned back to Mike and, to be heard above the roar of the rain, shouted,

'Okay Mike. If you want back to the ship, just go! I'll carry on here. I don't need your help. But listen to this. We're *not* going home till our mission here is done – or I'm satisfied we've tried everything we can. And I mean, everything. Got it?'

Mike felt a pang of guilt rise over his anger; an unusual sentiment for him, as he watched Tenak's back disappear into the spray kicked up by the rain. He wondered what had happened. Probably destroyed a good friendship? No, that wasn't true. He and Tenak had been through quite a lot together. Well, maybe not that much. He'd come around. Sure he would. But why was he so upset?

As he started to move again it came to him, as if out of the mist in front of him; a flash of insight into his friend, and a not altogether welcome one. Tenak was mainly worried that they had appeared *incompetent*. Yes, that was it, he realised. Well, it was true that the ship's small science team had not been granted access to the planet or its politicians, or "natural philosophers". As the Admiral had said, he and Mike were the ones on the grinding face right now. But did it really matter, if the people here, the *popularia,* sometimes called by the slang term, "womana-manry", didn't believe their news, their science? If they didn't trust the Home System, then that was their problem. Then, another flash of insight came to him, as Mike realised that if he and Tenak did appear as incompetent then the popularia and their politicians would be even less likely to believe them – or the rest of the ship's team. What a mess. Still, he still found it hard to get too excited about it, given the nature of the population here. This was surely the lost cause of all lost causes.

His discomfort had started to dissipate so Mike started running again. He wasn't certain he wanted to really catch up with Tenak right now, but he knew there was shelter on the monorail platform. The station had temporarily vanished from view but as he rounded another corner it was suddenly there, like a huge grey, angular mass, sticking out of the mist, only about fifty metres away. As he carried on jogging the rain simply stopped. Just stopped, as though some omnipotent being had thrown a huge switch. The sun burst out as he neared his goal and within seconds everything started steaming, the roadway, the plant life and Mike's own clothing. Weird place, he thought.

He still felt sodden as he walked into the station and showed his limp, wet ticket to the guard. At the top of the stairs he tried to locate Tenak but the man was lost somewhere in the pressing crowd. Astonishing, he thought, after the scarcity of people earlier, that now there should be so many locals all collected in this one place. But he imagined it had something to do with finishing work for the day. And the weather.

A droll announcement came over some sort of speaker system, a disembodied male voice, loud, dour and muffled, saying that all trains were delayed due to technical problems. The next one to Janitra would be an hour late. Just great, thought Mike. Easing his way through the crowds, he aimed for the edge of the platform where there were fewer people. Maybe he could see Tenak from there. Hey, why bother? The man was insufferable today.

Standing near the edge he noticed a series of tall wooden poles on the far side of the track, running parallel to it, lined up behind a low wire fence. Each pole was about 10 metres high and they were all linked by a set of thick, heavy looking cables. Some of the poles were standing at an odd angle, out from the vertical. They looked very old and in poor condition; a blue growth, like algae, or something similar, grew right the way up most of them. What the frizzer were these pole things for, he wondered? A couple of minutes later it dawned on him. Of course. He remembered, again, the days when he and his family had gone to City State museums back home. These things were called telephone poles and the Devians still used telephones, didn't they?

Tenak was suddenly visible, about 60 metres down the platform, stuck in an even larger knot of people than he was. Mike now felt bad about their argument. The guy could be kind of difficult sometimes, but, when he thought about it, which was rare, he had nothing but affection for the old space dog. But he didn't like to show it.

The late afternoon sunlight burned onto the steaming platform and Mike's clothes soon began to dry on him. That was one good thing about this crazy world. The massive influence of the planet's huge oceans produced a long tropical storm season, a *real* monsoon, every year. He guessed this might be the beginning of it. He'd have to refresh his memory with the wristcom's access to the ship's database.

After an hour and half of waiting, which began to irk him hugely, his legs were sore and there was still no monorail train. Another announcement gave an apology and said that the next train to Janitra would be at least another hour. A collective moan went up from the crowd. Some cursed loudly, in their Devian dialect.

Mike looked up and again spotted Tenak, many metres away, signalling to him by pointing to his own com unit. Mike glanced at it. He had no wish to use its holography facility right here, but he could see a tiny graphic and some numbers on its small screen, which advised that the plasma storm would be upon them in about three hours. They might not make back it to Janitra today.

As Ra sank deeply into a bed of oranges, reds, and carmine hues on the horizon, pale lamps lit up along the platform's ceiling canopy and Mike started to wind his way through the crowd, which seemed to be thinning in his area. He went to the platform refresher unit again and re-emerged onto the platform to see that some people had left the place in frustration – but it was still crowded. He would suggest to Tenak that they call it a day and seek accommodation in Ramnisos.

Events intervened.

The first thing was a call from Captain Ebazza. His wristcom chimed and he recognised it was a call from the ship. He set the unit on audio only and attached to his right ear a tiny button sized "audio-flake", which looked like natural flesh. The tiny device adhered itself to his pinna by a temporary glue-spot.

'Hello Captain,' said Mike, the wristcom's supersensitive microphone, identifying his voice and isolating it from all the voices around him.

'Secretary Tanniss?' she said, sounding slightly confused.

'Yeah. Don't worry. The Admiral's around here. You'll need to switch frequencies to reach him. We've swapped units,' and then he remembered to add, 'just for the moment, that's all.' He wasn't sure if Tenak would have wanted Ebazza to know he'd given Mike his unit.

'Why have …,' she started, 'but well, I guess it doesn't matter right now. It's about the CME, Mer Secretary,' she said, in dark tones.

She's being very formal, he thought.

She continued, 'The coronal plasma stream is accelerating. Yes, you heard me – *accelerating*. Cause unknown at the moment. We now think it will reach the planet's atmosphere within 20 minutes. Maybe less. It's hard to tell in the circ's. I note you're in Ramnisos. My advice is – stay there.'

'Roger that. I'll tell the Admiral straight. Out,'

Mike noticed that the com unit had been set by Tenak to auto-record, which meant the entire conversation with Ebazza could be forwarded to the Admiral in an instant. Mike spoke, under his breath, and told it to relay the message. He looked in Tenak's direction, saw the Admiral glance at his unit, then tap it, and he could tell he was now listening to the conversation. His companion gazed across at him and motioned for him to follow but then started walking in the direction of a station attendant, about 50 metres away. Mike assumed he was going to ask the woman to make an announcement to warn everyone.

A minute later a piercing bang issued from the opposite direction, further down the platform, behind Mike. Everyone ducked, in involuntary reflex, as though one person. Smoke started pouring out of a small building on the platform, possibly a café. People ran out of it, some shouting warnings, others screaming. The people standing around Mike looked at each-other with expressions of horror as a male guard appeared from nowhere and ran toward the café, brandishing a heavy red cylinder – an old-fashioned fire extinguisher. As he shouted for people to keep out away, a female guard joined him and they soon appeared to be getting things under control. The cause had to be the plasma stream, thought Mike, didn't it? It had started already. Even faster than Ebazza had predicted. How could that be?

At the opposite end of the platform he could see Tenak, apparently trying to calm people but an announcement boomed again over the tannoy, saying, 'There has been a minor incident, populari. There is no need of panic. The situation is yet under control. There is some such lectrical interference in our equipment but tis being controlled.'

Oh, no it isn't, thought Mike, as a series of flashes and sparks lit up the café end of the platform, further down. Several small fires seemed to be breaking out and the attendants didn't seem to know which way to turn. Suddenly, the crowd surged toward where Mike stood and, suddenly alarmed, he instinctively braced for impact, but at the last moment remembered his basic Navy training. He simply stiffened his upper torso and relaxed his lower body, preparing to be taken along with the flow.

There was nothing else he could do but he still felt a wave of anxiety wash over him, his heart pounding violently. Many rushing bodies collided with each side of him and he had to keep telling himself to relax as he prepared to draw his feet off the ground and be moved bodily backward.

But the expected didn't happen. Fortunately, the mass of people seemed, mostly, to brush past, though he was severely jostled and found himself ricocheting to the very edge of the platform. To his jolting alarm Mike remembered that the track was electrified but the next moment he was able to stand again properly. He wasn't being pushed over the edge.

There were more flashes nearby and electrical discharges arced along the trackway, like miniature, rippling, lightning. It hit what appeared to be a number of small electricity sub-stations the other side of the track, but they were situated near the base of several of the rotting telephone poles.

The surging crowd had reached the gateway to the stairs leading down from the platform and, to their anger, found it locked by large metal gates. Frantic shouts went up, crying for the gates to be opened, and there was more screaming. Mike had never witnessed anything like this before and his heart began pounding even more heavily. His legs seemed to turn to jello, and he felt physically unable to move, as if nailed to the concrete floor.

Another announcement barked, 'Please do not be a-panic, womana-manry. We have locked the gate to the stairs because we yet fear there will be an accident with so many going down them. We are making other ways to get out of the station soon as possly, but safely. I repeat, safely. Please be so patient. You will be safest if you do stand on the open platform and not enter any buildings. Be staying away from lectrical apparatus and do not get on the track. I repeat still, do not get on the track.'

Something remarkable then happened and no-one was more surprised than Mike. Over the next minute or so most people in the crowd actually seemed to take heed of the announcements, beginning to calm down. Much of the energy of the panick seemed to have dissipated. Mike was struck by the fortitude of this lot. They're made of strong stuff, he thought. A few people, a minority, continued to bang on the stairway gates but most started dispersing, though expressions of fear remained plastered on them.

No sooner had calm begun to descend when there was another frightening detonation, followed by an incredibly loud splintering noise issuing from the direction of the leaning telephone poles the other side of the monorail. Everyone, including Mike, gazed in that direction, only to see that most of the poles were already burning at their bases. A sense of fear reasserted itself as the flames spread up each pole. Someone shouted that they should not worry because the poles were the other side of the track, so they weren't a danger to people on the platform. But as Mike considered them with his physicist's brain, he immediately gauged that this was a misperception of distance.

He saw that two of the poles had almost burned through at the base, as surely as if one of the ship's defensive laser bundles had been trained on them. Flames crackled loudly and they started to lean over, tipping toward the track – and the platform. His heart racing, Mike shouted to everyone, as hard as his lungs would allow, screaming at them to get away from the edge of the platform opposite the poles. There was an ocean of noise and he wondered if any would be able to hear him. But people were starting to move again, flowing toward the other side of the platform, away from the danger. This time Mike willingly went with them.

But where was Tenak? Peering toward the Admiral's end of the platform Mike's saw him, but his heart leaped into his mouth. Poles were burning badly further along the track and one of them was starting to fall now, totally freed of its mooring. It arced down over the monorail track, as if in slow motion, and he could see that the top couple of metres of the thing would hit the platform. His hair stood on end as he noticed a very old man, just a short distance in front of Tenak, shambling along with some sort of walking frame in front of him.

Again, Mike seemed to be watching a slow motion holo-vid. The pole would surely hit the older man and squash him flat but the next thing he saw was Admiral Tenak launching himself forward, in a leap worthy of an inter-city state athlete. Tenak landed just behind the old man and, throwing out his hands, he shoved him bodily along the platform, just as the top part of the pole crashed behind him, chunks of wood and splintering everwhere. No, not behind him. Damnatious! It had hit the Admiral. Or had it? It was hard to see in the jostling press of people. *Fallen onto*

Tenak? he thought. Mike insides seemed to freeze, and his heart felt as though it was stopping.

In the moments after that he felt an emotional reaction of unexpected intensity. He still couldn't be sure if Tenak had really been hit. The scene seemed suspended in space and time; the unthinkable become real. Then, as the smoke cleared, he saw, with a start, that indeed, Tenak, and a few other people were lying, prone, on the hard concrete platform. A couple of locals were trying to get up, calling out in pain and distress – but Tenak lay motionless. Two cables from the telephone poles were lying across his legs, coiled and steaming, like huge, freshly boiled snakes.

Interlude

THE CONJOINING

In the time-space of five hundred cycles of our far distant sun have I slept, while the Super-Adjunct continued its ages long search for our goal. Before I am bereft of closeness I have need of full fusion of our thoughts, flowed Percepticon to Hermoptica, *so now let us fully conjoin, if you will consent.*

I agree with all my hearts, flowed Hermoptica, for it was the chosen one of Percepticon. It unrolled three of its metal tentacles and moved them toward Percepticon, and as it did so, thick metal joints in Percepticon's tentacles split open and protuberances of flesh immediately issued forth from the organic material exposed within. The fleshy tissue touched the middle of Hermoptica's small ovoid body – just below the left member of its two tiny, six-digit, vestigial claws, now useless remnants from a bygone era, millions of years past.

The long protuberances from Percepticon, three thick bundles of neurons and their axon stems, appeared to melt into her chosen one's body. They quickly *grew into* Hermoptica's body and within moments the full thoughts and feelings flowed, unimpeded, between the two beings, enhanced by additional connections between their respective cybernetic tentacles. The powers of thought of the two beings were thus amplified. It meant that their ability to understand and to share one anothers' emotions and thoughts was now magnified thousands of times. Every one of their organic brains was now connected fully with the others for here, organic connections remained dominant, even over the cybernetic.

Then, tiny clouds containing billions of nano-machines, purposeful things, each no more than a few billionths of a metre across, issued from the floor of the chamber below the two beings. Like a faint cloud of almost invisible soot, rising through pores in the floor, the nanites began to construct fresh metallic casing; their purpose, to protect and strengthen the exposed protuberances between the bodies of the beings. Within a few seconds the casings were complete, and the connection insulated.

****

Another of the super-sentient beings, one naming himself Demetia, approached silently on a sliding floor panel, slithering from a considerable distance across the sentience chamber, gliding then into close proximity, to settle beside Percepticon and Hermoptica. His cyber-tentacles joined with theirs, *I have news of great joy, issuing from the Super-Adjunct,* he flowed. *The Others cannot be aware of our presence. As expected, they are also constrained by the Universal law of light speed. All Adjuncts report that multi-frequency electromagnetic emissions from the Others are now being translated and interpreted but the full situation may not be known for some time.*

This is satisfying beyond measure, flowed Hermoptica.

Percepticon introduced a note of caution, *The Others may become aware of us as we orbit the star which has been our goal these many hundred cycles. They may yet interfere. They are life; they are complex. They are here but we know they have not originated here, and so, they may still upset the balance.*

No more than a Glargfly, thought Demetia.

Even flies can upset the balance, came Percepticon's returning thought.

Hermoptica flowed, *We must take all necessary precautions. We cannot risk accidental contact. When last this happened it resulted, for all of us, in a ten thousand cycle period of guilt and fear-loathing of further contact. For lo, the civilisation we encountered destroyed itself completely, soon thereafter.*

They were unable to withstand the culture shock and to our eternal shame they proved unworthy of the new knowledge gained from us, thought Percepticon.

Perhaps they were simply unworthy, flowed Demetia. *We beseech you: recall that the encounter happened more than five thousand cycles ago. Since we resumed our long journeying among the stars, we have seen no further examples of sentient species. We have also grown in maturity. We will seek to avoid contact. But consider that although one of our goals is now denied to us, there is another more important one within reach.* After a pause of barely a millisecond, a long time for such beings as these, he continued, *We all are aware that we must deal with this star, as we have so many others, especially as it is the great goal of our travel.*

The other two beings flowed their assent.

To control our forces adequately the Super-Adjunct advises that all those in the sentience chamber must conjoin by means of all cybernetic super-enhancements. Do you consent?

Our consent is given, with great gladness, thought both the others.

Chapter 9

NEW PLANS

'Yes, I understand what you're saying Indry,' began Yorvelt, 'but I just think it's time we took further action. I still think Tenak should have sent a message probe back by now but since he hasn't it's as good as a laser signal that something's gone badly wrong. With that, and what our advisors have said, I think we can be reasonably sure the Oceanus government is fighting off the science. Doesn't that mean we should send a Research Vessel to help establish the facts? I believe the Antarctica's got a free schedule at the moment.'

The General Secretary of the Allied Home System Government sat at a hyper-comp station in an office situated in the old Vancouver zone of the "Westa-Canadian City State". The office, one of five he used regularly when on Earth, overlooked ancient Stanley Park, still an area of outstanding beauty. Outside, dull grey cloud was replacing bright spring sunshine, this area being far outside the weather-controlled dome of central Westa-Can. Yorvelt glanced out at tall conifers swaying in the strong breeze, then returned his attention to the holo-vid image of his deputy, who appeared to stand right in front of him. Brocke seemed real enough to touch, but there was unfortunate interference today. The Deputy's image kept phasing in and out roughly every 10 seconds.

Indrius Brocke, himself, stood in a spartanly furnished room in government buildings in the "Amalgamous City State of Amazonias", part of the ancient "Rio'Zone". The man looked tired and it was obviously hot in there. Yorvelt watched tiny rivulets of sweat run down Brocke's face, which glistened under some sort of artificial light shining above him, just out of view. His clothes sagged on him like bags.

'I know that, Dar,' said Brocke after a slight signal delay, 'and I fully appreciate your position. We all want to see progress. It's just that I don't agree with the need to storm in on whatever Admiral Tenak's doing. We risk sending the wrong signal to the people of Oceanus. They might see the arrival of another ship as a threat to their independence – even if it isn't a Navy vessel.'

After a moment of interference Yorvelt said, 'Perhaps, but you know what Xander said. I don't want to talk too much about that over holo-con. You know I don't entirely trust holo-cons for security.'

'It's fine, Dar. Please let *me* worry about that. Besides, since the last inner committee meeting, I've taken the opportunity to beef up the holo channels we use.'

'Thank you for that. That will help, I'm sure. I hoped that our fleet of ferries would be able to amplify the evacuation many-fold. After all, The Monsoon could probably take about 1000, when fully refitted. The 10 Cruisers we can bend to the task can take about 500 each and we've got a few smaller vessels capable of taking smaller numbers. The ferries could have taken about 500 each, but they're fairly slow and after the supply problems, who knows? The Monsoon's all we've got at the moment.'

'Please, Dar. We won't have *just* The Monsoon, and that accident, or whatever it was, won't stop us, nor will the strike. We're working toward switching production facilities right now. And we'll just have to pull out all the stoppers, and lots more, but we will get the ferries completed, Dar. Believe me.'

'Well, perhaps, but I still think we need to send another ship to reinforce the science message, right now, and the Antarctica's the best option. Damnatious, I'd make the journey out there myself if I could.'

'I would too, Dar, but you know the Treaty of Algarion forbids it, without …'

'I know, Indry. I know. "Without the specific invitation by the Oceanus ruling party". And we don't have that. It's damnatiously galling. But the next best thing's a full Ambassador and that we can do. We've got to send one, Indry. Reassure the people. Why didn't this happen in the first place?'

'There was no agreement to do it, as such, Dar,' said Brocke, sounding rather dry, and continued, 'but it was briefly considered.'

'There was a vote, I recall. I also recall I was outvoted by five to one, including by you. I hope that doesn't return to haunt us, Indry. I feel I have to invoke my "pre-eminance" vote now.'

This time there was a longer delay, not aided by more momentary break-ups in transmission, before Brocke said, 'I understand your great concern. I am concerned too, Dar. Very concerned. But I think a softly, softly approach is best, and that's what Tenak is good at. If there is resistance to our plan, then that'll just get worse if we keep hammering at them. Besides, Dar, there are always going to be a certain number of people who will deny the truth and hang on till the bitter end. We know that's the case, from some of the natural disasters on Earth, and even one in the case of Mars, recently.'

'But those numbers, Indry? And we're not talking about people who *decide to* stay. We can't afford to sit on this.'

'That's' a good point Dar. I still believe in Tenak and he's got a good Secretary in Mike Tanniss. I know those two are a strong combination.'

'I don't know anything about Tanniss, Indry. I can look him up but it's not like knowing him. Still, I'll accept your faith in him. Regardless of that, it's unsettling not to have received a message from Tenak.'

'You could send an automated message bouy out to Ra. Remember, Tenak's not aware of what's happened this end. You could enlighten him. It might chivy things along – depending on what's happening there – on a political level.'

'I know. I could do that, I know, but I think it's more important to get the Antarctica out there – with an Ambassador onboard.'

'I agree but… look, Dar, I know our contract with the Antarctica's owners means you can commission the ship at short notice, but the Antarctica's not in suitable position yet. My understanding's that it's on its way from Lagrange Point 3, to high Earth orbit, for extensive repairs.'

'What in the skies happened to it, indry?' Yorvelt looked horrified.

Major fusion engine malfunction, so I understand … limping home right now. It's about 5 days out and I believe the repairs are expected to take around three weeks. Sorry, Dar.'

'What in beelzibub's name's going on? It's like some tragi-comedy holo-show from the 21st century.'

'They'll get it sorted as fast as poss. I'll see to it, Dar. But you know it's going to take a little time to get a suitable Ambassador, don't you? Yet more bad news, I'm afraid. I know you're only too aware of the political problems in *twelve* of the City States on Earth, as well as the renewed outbreak of hostile feelings towards us, on Mars. Yesterday, there were even threats to secede from the Greater Lunar Hegemony. Probably just local rabble rousing, but I can't risk pulling the ambassadors from those jobs, Dar. I need time to find someone who isn't working flat out on other things. After all, we can't be sure an Ambassador will make any real difference on Oceanus and, like I said, it could make the OA people more lairy. You also know how long the Oceanus parliament, their "Curia", takes to deliberate things. That's what might be delaying things, not a denial of the science.'

Yorvelt sighed. He sounded – and looked - worn out. 'I know,' he said, 'and I wouldn't dream of interfering in the field you've got delegated control of. But I can't give you long. I'm itching about this. You know that. If something happens to any significant fraction of the population of Oceanus there's going to be hell to pay and I, for one, won't be able to live with myself.'

'The media will never let any of us off the hook either,' said Brocke, 'but I don't believe it'll come to that.'

'I, for one, am very glad we put the entire General Committee on a media lock-down, Indry. If this gets out, we'll all be in trouble. But, in final analysis I'm not so much concerned about the media, as the stain this will leave in history – not to mention my own conscience. Alright, let me know as soon as you have someone we can send on the Antarctica – when it's ready to go! Yorvelt out.' The S-G hovered one hand over a small panel set into the arm of his chair, whereupon the Deputy Secretary General vanished abruptly.

****

A tall figure stepped out from the shadows in Brocke's poorly lit basement room in downtown Rio'Zone. 'That was interesting, sir,' said the figure. Brocke was staring at a hyper-comp display set into his desk.

'What was interesting, Dervello? Hm?' said Brocke absently, without looking up.

'Sorry sir. I just thought he looked very tired. He seemed to be distracted from his purpose very easily,' said Brandlis Barnstrorn Dervello, one of Brocke's two senior aides. Dervello, a chunky looking man with shoulders seemingly twice as wide as his hips, observed Brocke with piercing, intelligent eyes set in a pale oval face, undermining any notion that he was simply a dumb hunk of meat.

Still not looking up, Brocke allowed the merest hint of a smile to touch the corners of his mouth, 'You should have more respect Dervello. I'm surprised at you. By the way, have you actually looked for an Ambassador who will suit the purpose? I mean, someone who will really do the job? We don't want to disappoint the S G, after all.'

'Um, no. Sir, I only heard you and the S G discuss this now. I'll have to see to it, ...'

'Indeed. There's no time like the present, is there? So, what are you waiting for?' said Brocke, almost gently but with a hint of menace in his glare as he finally looked up at the man before him. Dervello turned sharply on his heels and left the room immediately.

Once in his own office the aide consulted a screen set into his desk and asked his holo-comp to establish communication with a person whose name he selected from a list on screen. After half a minute of trying to make contact the machine spoke to Dervello, saying that the man wasn't responding to any of his usual channels. Dervello then asked it to contact his own colleague instead; Brocke's assistant senior aide, Conjecta Dra' Proctinian. A perfect, full size holo image of an athletic looking young black woman appeared a couple of feet from him.

'Conjecta, there you are. Greetings. I'm trying to get hold of Ambassador Sliverlight. He's not answering any of his devices, on *any* channel. Can you help?'

'Sliverlight? What in Venusian purgatory do you want with him, Bradlis? Is this one of your practical jokes?' said the lithe figure in the hologram.

'How droll, Conjecta. Not at all. The Deputy wants me to find someone he can trust. Someone we can send *to Oceanus*. I can't find anything on the government manifest about his whereabouts. Seems he does a lot of work which you might call, "freelance". Maybe you know what he's doing, or perhaps I'm presuming too much of my colleague?'

'You always presume too much Bradlis,' she laughed, a dry, throaty sound which lacked genuine mirth, 'Alright. Leave it with me. I think he might be in the asteroid belt, conducting some sort of negotiations. It might be better if I locate one of his associates in the local part of the HS. You need to know that any direct comms with Sliverlight, out where he is, is going to involve a time lag of about an hour each way.'

'Of course,' said Dervello, 'Thanks for reminding me. Yes, please get hold of one of his associates. Perhaps they can enlighten me about his activities and maybe pass on our instructions.'

Around 40 minutes later, a chime sounded on Dervello's wristcom. Proctinian had located one of the Ambassador's closest associates, a man called Debrens, based in the "North France Urban Platform". She patched the man through to Dervello's desk unit and a holo of Debrens appeared in front of him. The man's shape appeared hazy and undulating, static interference dancing across the image, making it a wavy mirage. Even across the interference Debrens appeared a dishevelled looking individual, slouching in a type of threadbare armchair. And he looked irritated.

'Aide Dervello?' Debrens said, his words punctuated by bursts of rushing static. 'I can't see ………. image very well. I'm not sure what's …. the interference.'

'I have the same problem Mer Associate. It's probably a comsat malfunction. Can you tell me what Sliver …, I mean Ambassador Sliverlight, is doing?

'He's … the inner asteroid belt … some sort of negotiations with …. miners.'

'That's what I was told. Why wasn't this on the government assignment list or the … oh, forget it. I'll ask him when I see him. Mer Associate, I want you to get a message to your employer.'

'Do you indeed?' said the dishevelled man. He exhaled loudly, a noise pregnant with impatience, 'I suppose I'm prepared to oblige, but if that's all you .... I wonder why you don't just send ... a message. By the way, I'm not employed by the Ambassador. I just get paid to ... the odd job for him.'

'I'm happy we've sorted out your exact status,' said Dervello, glaring at Debrens, 'I'm aware that I could have sent a message, but I need to know when *Ambassador* Sliverlight is likely to be finished with his present work. And, when he could get back to the inner system. That in turn depends on how fast his transport is. I was hoping you could answer these questions, but I now expect you're going to say you don't know.'

Debrens replied, through continuing bursts of white noise, 'The negotiations he's conducting are delicate, I ...., but I think they should be nearing completion, probably within the next two Earth d.... He chartered a deep space shuttle, Rigel class, mark .... It's small but fast. Shouldn't take more than about 35 days. I also know ...... happy to get away from the microgravity environment out there .... the belt. If you have special instructions for him, I suppose I can send ......him for you.'

'Good. Please ask him to get his shuttle pilots to program their AI to inject into Lunar orbit when they bring him in. He must, I repeat, *must*, dock with the Collins Lunar station. Tell him to let me know when he's en-route and I'll meet him at the station.'

'Oh?' said Debrens, sounding perplexed, 'but is that really necessary?'

'Yes! I need to give him the mission specifics in person. They are sensitive.'

'Still don't know why .... can't send the message yourself. .... told you where he is.'

'I think it will sound better coming from you, as his colleague. I would be, that is, the government – would be grateful for your co-operation in this matter. Besides, my kewser has just let me know that you have certain Inner System tax matters which might be of interest to some of my colleagues, so perhaps I should ...'

'Alright, alright ... Aide ...vello. I'll comply with your request. Can you tell me where you're plan ... to send him this time?'

'Yes, certainly. He's to go to Oceanus Alpha. Is that going to be a problem for him?'

'You'll have to ask him that. I just know that … never done a conduit journey.'

'Well, it will be a new experience for him. Kindly remind him that his orders come from Deputy Secretary General Indrius Brocke, himself. Out.'

The image of Debrens vanished.

'That should suitably place our friend, the *ambassador,* off guard,' said Dervello to the holo of Proctinian, hovering well outside the deliberately limited holo cone that had been allowed with Debrens. She had been able to watch the conversation unseen.

Chapter 10

RESCUERS

Massive accumulations of cloud, glowering, angry looking, layers of purple grey, swept above the monorail station in Ramnisos. Smoke rose from the wreckage of the telephone pole where it had crashed onto the platform. There were still shrieks and the sound of sobbing issued from some of those huddling around a small group of people lying near the pole's remains near the platform edge. One of that group was Arkas Tenak.

How could this have happened? Mike asked himself. People near him started running over to where the wounded lay and suddenly Mike found his feet gradually becoming 'unglued'. His insides were still like ice but now he wanted, more than anything, to get over to where Tenak lay. Was he badly wounded? Could he be dead? Mike wondered how he would handle it if the man was dead. He simply refused to believe it, but severe doubt remained.

He raced to join the throng of onlookers and tried to shove his way through the tight knot of people. 'My friend's hurt,' he kept saying, 'the Admiral's there,' as if anyone heard, or was even interested. Their own friends and loved ones were probably there as well.

One or two victims lay between him and the Admiral and Mike rejected the apparently easy option of just climbing over them. People surrounding the group just looked on uselessly, as people everywhere are wont to do. Then a few others managed to part the throng and one woman in particular, got through the press and crouched over the injured.

'Auntin' Maybell!' said the woman and gently touched the head of a middle-aged woman who lay prone. An older man pushed forward too and threw his arms out aggressively in front of the crowd, saying, 'Give them some dammly roomspace, will you? Be giving roomspace!' He glared at Mike and smartly pushed him back. Mike, taken by surprise, started to push back and protested, 'My shipmate's over there. He saved that old man in front of him.'

'Well, bleggin' get over there then!' said the stranger, looming in his face, flecks of saliva flying. Mike grimaced and pushed past the rest of the crowd, then saw one or two others bending over Tenak. With huge relief he noticed the Admiral was trying to sit up. At least he was still alive.

'Whoa, Arkas,' Mike said loudly. 'Just stay still. Are you okay?' A stupid question, he thought. Why does everybody ask that of people who've just suffered obvious trauma?

Tenak didn't reply. Most of the downed telephone pole lay on the track, still smouldering, and in the ruddy illumination Mike saw Tenak's face contort in pain. A young woman squatting close to Tenak was talking to him and as Mike got closer he heard her ask Tenak, calmly and gently, 'Please sirra, do not try to move. I think you have yet hurt your back and legs.'

'Is he okay. I mean, will he live?' asked Mike.

'Yes, manry,' she said, with a look of relief, 'I think he shall be good. Who are you, sirra? I see you both wear outsider's uniforms.'

Mike quickly filled her in and she said, 'I am such grateful to your friend. He saved my grandling-feeth, who did stumble. He has just bruising, I think. My sishtra yet takes care of him – over there.' She pointed at a small knot of people a couple of metres away who surrounded the old man Tenak had saved. Against all expectation, and to Mike's utter astonishment the old man slowly but surely got to his feet, assisted by those surrounding him.

'I'm glad about that,' said Mike to the femna tending to Tenak, 'Are you a medic or something?'

'No, I am ….'

'No, she is not, but *I am a medicus*,' said a strident female voice from behind Mike. Turning he saw a thick set woman standing there. 'Please so move - if you would yet like me look at your friend,' she added.

'Yet tell me, what about my own bruthly,' said a man to Mike's right. A couple of others protested about their friends or relatives, also lying on the platform.

'I shall see to them in justmo,' she said, 'I carnt deal with everyone straight-ways. I yet know this manry saved another's life and is now downed. I will try to get to everyone as quick as possly.'

To a little chorus of approval someone added loudly, 'Yes, certant she's right. That Navy-manry saved the grandling fellachap. Or he would have died.'

A station employee came up behind the crowd, barking through some sort of cone shaped instrument. Whatever it was it certainly noisy, and harsh, at that distance.

'Please, womana-manry, please to vacating the platform,' blared the attendent, 'Now have we opened the gates to the stairs,' he continued, 'yet please move out 'less you are related to those injured or can help. I shall say again, please vacate the platform.'

Someone demanded to know if the man had called the emergency medical services. Yes, he said, but because the telephones were down they had sent a messenger *running* to the local hospital. It was only seven kilometres away! He would bring back help.

The "medicus" lady had now examined Tenak and, leaning in close to Mike, said, almost conspiratorially, 'So shall he live young manry, still he has lost very much blood from his left leg. I have such tied it off with striplets of bandars in hope t'will do for now. It looks that a part of the pole's metalwork praps hit the leg. There is yet something wrong with his spine-bones, but I am not sure what. I think we may have to move him, but I would advise against it at this moment. Now must I see to the others.'

Mike thanked her as she left him. Remarkably, some casualties were already sitting, or trying to stand. Lengths of cable, like glistening eels, were coiled across the whole area and Mike was amazed more had not been seriously injured. He wondered if some of the cable had hit Tenak's back, and he noticed that the pole's metal supports lay in ruin close to Tenak. He thanked the stars that they had missed his head.

Glancing around him he suddenly realised that relative calm now prevailed. Many more of the injured were getting up, including a very ancient looking lady, who just brushed herself off, gathered up her stick and hobbled off, one of her legs trailing a little trickle of blood. He felt huge empathy for her and realised that these people were extraordinarily resilient, displaying a degree of fortitude probably now rare in the Home System. And he included himself in that assessment. He felt humbled. No sooner had he turned back toward Tenak when, unexpectedly, the heavens opened again. Rain sheeted down, starting to drench the remaining wounded. It was as though a gigantic, dark, hand had closed over them, made more intense by of the lack of lighting on the platform.

A soft moan emanated from some of those present. Some of those still prone may have been badly injured and there was no shelter on that part of the platform. The "medicus" shouted that they needed to move the wounded and pointed out a section of the platform which was covered by a canopy, but it was many metres away.

'We shall be needing a stretcher for your friend, if we are yet to move him,' she shouted to Mike, 'but there is none here. Be going down the platform to see if you can find something we can use. We have to get him away from here or he shall chill. Already in shock he is.'

Mike unquestioningly did as she bid, racing around searching for something, trying not to collide with other people or objects hidden in the darkness, but often failing, painfully. There were three buildings on the platform, but all were fire damaged and inaccessible. He found a station employee, but she just shrugged her shoulders uselessly. 'Best yet wait when the emergency services get here,' she said. He chose to ignore her and rushed on but was getting very frustrated. His heart still beat fast, but he kept telling himself to keep calm. Tenak was a regular hero, but *he* was most certainly not. If he hadn't argued with his friend, he might not have rushed off as he did. Then he wouldn't have …. He knew he had to stop this.

The attendent encountered earlier suddenly reappeared behind him. Breathlessly, she said, 'The emergency servitia are trying to deal with several many emergencies in town. They have no power still. They arint coping at all. I am sorry, Mer.'

Mike was just about to give up looking when he found some sort of tarpaulin. Maybe not something which could be used as a stretcher, perhaps, but it could be used to cover the wounded. It was massive, soaking, and dirty but he pulled at it, rolled it into a bundle as best he could, then dragged it back toward his friend, as fast as he could. By now the group were huddled on a slightly drier part of the platform, still eerily half-lit by the dying remains of the fires across the trackway.

The Medic went to Mike, 'I be sorry,' she said, with a look of dread, 'but I am thinking your friend is the worst-so injured here. We must yet get him under cover.' She was about to speak again when the sound of a commotion burst from far over, beyond the trackway. In the glow of the dying fires they saw a small group of people running across the monorail itself, carrying a variety of objects, clattering noisily, and mounting the furthest end of the platform. In the lead was a middle-aged woman who shouted out as she approached, 'Hello to all. My name is Destrin. My family are with me, so to give help. Let us have these people over to my house. Tis just across the tracks. We've yet riggo'd some stretchers with sheets and poles. Come along, we must move.'

Six young men and women ran up behind her, carrying make-shift stretchers and began laying them next to the wounded.

'What about the track? Tis lectrical,' shouted someone, above the sound of the increasingly intense rain.

'Lectricity has been knock-ed out. Tis safe,' boomed a member of Destrin's family, a large and burly man. 'Come now. Be helping, please,' he added.

All the able bodied rushed to help lift the injured onto stretchers, under the supervision of the medic. The burning telephone poles had been effectively extinguished by the heavy rain. They steamed and hissed like vanquished, but still angry beasts. Mike threw down his tarp and rushed toward the group.

Within minutes the gang had lifted the injured and were carrying them over the tracks toward a large house with three storeys. All the lights were on in the house and they illuminated the tracks where the group crossed. Curious, thought Mike; they must have fixed up their own generator – and quickly. How resourceful.

Once they were through the front door the patients were taken into a huge reception room. It was warm. It felt good to be out of the pelting rain. The rug-like floor coverings soon became sodden as the group trudged in and laid the injured down. Mes Destrin got her family to fetch water, household medicaments, bandages, blankets and again, the medically qualified woman got to work. Calm had been restored and Mike was eternally grateful for it. He felt as if he could breathe again, as he watched two of Destrin's family, and the medic, tend to the Admiral.

Somebody asked how the house still had power and Mes Destrin explained that although most houses have their own solar power cells, the electrics had been burned out when the power failed, but she was fortunate to have had a backup wind generation system, not in use when the rest blew. She said one of her children, looking out of an upper floor window, had witnessed what had happened on the station and gave the alert. The family had hesitated before crossing the tracks, lest the still sparking monorail generate an electrical arc. Then they'd just decided to risk it anyway. Mike and the others thanked them profusely. 'No such need,' said Mes Destrin.

Members of her family entered the room carrying steaming hot mugs of soup, which they handed out to all, including any patients who could drink safely. Tenak wasn't considered to be one of them. Mike squatted by his friend. He could tell he was unconscious now. He hated seeing him like this but could do nothing, so he slumped in a corner and closed his eyes, still feeling cold. A gnawing tiredness pulled at his eyelids, as if they were made of leaden sheets.

Sitting forward he hung his head in his hands, feeling numb. This was ridiculous. *He* wasn't injured, after all. He felt someone drape a warm blanket over his shoulders and he was handed a mug. Thanking the person, he tried to drink but immediately retched, though did not actually vomit. He struggled to avoid that, in all the circumstances. He was sure there was nothing wrong with the beverage, but he felt peculiar inside. How stupid, he thought. He should be helping these people tend those who really needed assistance. He put the mug down but something inside him told him to drink it, or to at least try again. He did so, in small sips, and this time it went down well. He soon noticed it didn't taste too bad, but he had no idea what it was. Hanging his head in his hands again he once more chastised himself and decided he had to stay awake...

He woke up when he felt someone gently shaking his right arm. 'Mer Mike,' said a very young voice, 'Please be a-waking.'

Pulling his head out of his hands he said, 'Wha...?' as if drunk.

'A young woman sat on her haunches next to him. A kind face. She reminded him of someone else. Someone he'd met here or ... Where was here, anyway?

'Please wake up, Mer Mike,' she repeated.

'What is?' he heard himself mumble. 'Tenak ... is he...?'

The youngster pointed at the opposite corner of the room and said, 'Do not yet worry. See? The Admiral is awake. He asks for you.'

Mike forced himself to get up and, still feeling numb, walked shakily over to Tenak. He was hugely relieved to see the man awake but his face was ashen, with dark blue and black rings around his eyes. By his side was Mes Destrin and one of her sons, a lad of about 14 years. The boy said, 'Ist a lot better now, Mer Mike. So has he been telling us why you are here. You come from the big spaceship up above, do you not? You have been in space. I wish I could go into space.'

'Hush yoursev now, boy,' said Mes Destrin. 'Leave the manry to talk to his friend, alone like.' The two of them moved away and Mike crouched by Tenak,

'How are you, you old codgerman?' said Mike, softly. 'You had me worried back there. Wondered what I'd do without your nagging.'

Tenak looked at Mike through bloodshot eyes.

'You don't get rid of me that easy, Mike,' he said through dry lips. 'Listen, I know I need some specialised treatment. Can't feel my left leg, and my back hurts like bleggery, but listen up, Mike. There's other people here that need treatment more than me. You need to com the ship and get Ebazza to send a landing boat. Get her to send a med team down with it and ... take as many people from here up to the ship … as many as willing to go.' Tenak's voice started to rasp and he gulped his breaths.

'Will do,' Mike said, 'take it easy now.' Tenak's eyes seemed to swim around in their sockets and Mike felt that he might be starting to go downhill, right in front of him. He tried to keep the sound of anxiety out of his voice as he said, 'I'll go outside to get a better signal, what with the magnetic interference and all. I won't be long. Stay here.'

He started to dash toward the door but heard Tenak grunt.

'No, wait,' breathed Tenak, 'Ask Ebazza to send a second boat. Get an engineering team down here. As many as it can take. They … might be able to help … sort the systems in this town. The med team can help out at the hospital as well. See, … see if there's anything they can do there. Tell the authorities what you're doing.'

'Sure, sure, Arkas. Just try to get some rest now,' said Mike, gently gripping Tenak's shoulder but as he started to walk out Tenak, weakly, called him back yet again, 'Mike, Mike. Listen. The ship might not be able to send the boats yet, if the storm hasn't passed. Ebazza will know when. Meantime … get these people organised. Tell them … what we're doing … find out how many want to go up to the ship for treatment. I'm counting on you to sort this, Mike.'

Mike nodded and strode outside, fretting about Tenak but feeling better to be doing something constructive. He was starting to feel better in himself too. Was it the beverage that revived him, or his blackout? Did it matter? The air outside was surprisingly cold but it had stopped raining. It was probably the first time he had encountered such cold weather on Oceanus. He shivered but at least his clothes had dried.

The clouds had virtually cleared, and it was now quite dark except for the lights of the house and one or two others nearby and, as he looked up, he saw great luminous sheets of aurorae overhead. They formed curtains of soft undulating colour, sparkling with occasional bursts of more brilliant chromaticism, dancing all the way from the horizon up to the zenith. Sharp points of starlight poked through in the areas in between them.

Mike first asked his wristcom to make contact with the government in Janitra, but it told him there was currently no response. It would keep trying. Then he asked it to try audio contact with the ship; holo probably wouldn't work. After a minute and a half of miserable static Captain Ebazza's voice finally burst through, distorted by the crackling interference. He summarised what had happened. She was shocked but acknowledged Tenak's orders. As expected, she said it wasn't safe to send out the LBs but estimated the ion storm should end in about 30 minutes. She would then send the boats but warned they would take a further 20 minutes to get down to his co-ordinates. And they would then have to find the nearest safe landing spot. He mused that she didn't really need to tell *him* that. He told her he'd spied some flat, open land nearby. It was probably enough for only one LB, but the crew would need to use full ground scanning sensors. The other ship was destined for downtown Ramnisos anyway.

Mike returned indoors and, asking everyone for their attention, announced what would be happening. He said the boat would have enough room to take every injured person and one other person to accompany them. There was murmering and muted discussion in the room, and then all, except for two, said they would be happy to go up to the ship. The two who refused muttered that they would take their chances with the hospital. They didn't feel they were particularly badly injured, anyway. Mike thought that one of them, a woman, looked extremely unwell but he reckoned it was her choice anyway.

It's a pity I can't raise the government, he thought, but I'm still getting those boats down here *whether the lousy OA Government likes it or not.*

***

A noise like distant thunder rumbled across the now quiet sky high above the ruined maglev station at Ramnisos. Mike heard it and realised what it was – and only 40 minutes after he'd spoken to Ebazza. Begrudgingly, he accepted she'd done well. Mike went back outside and saw that many locals had come out of their houses and were staring into the heavens. Some pointed upwards and chattered loudly, nervously. Mike was pretty sure most had never witnessed the arrival of a spaceship.

For some decades any such arrivals had been restricted to the airports in Janitra, and in Demnisos, much further south.

The clouds had gathered again but it was not raining. Then he saw the higher levels of cloud, far off to the west, become live things, exploding with white tendrils of illumination, and flashing with bright red and blue light beams. Within seconds a dark, streamlined shape with wide, quite obviously swept back "delta V" wings, broke through the cloud deck to become dramatically silhouetted against the illuminated cloud mass.

A high-pitched engine noise reached him, rising against the background rumbling which had heralded the ship's arrival. But Mike felt sure that the overall noise level was not over-intrusive or alarming. Of course, he realised, *he* was used to it. Most people around here were not, and he noticed that a few onlookers had put their hands to their ears and were going indoors. It dawned on him, then, that this place was well outside the air routes to and from Janitra, as they might otherwise have been used to the sound of propeller aircraft engines, though that was somewhat *different* to what was happening now. Even so, he also noted, with some satisfaction, that most of the local people remained outside, looking up with a degree of wonderment. It was exciting, after all. And for Mike himself, after the days he'd spent on this planet, the sounds and sights were like sweet music.

Despite the aversion of many locals to modern HS tek, he felt incredibly proud of what these shuttles, the so-called landing boats, represented. Their engines did indeed produce *some* high-pitched sound, but, in accordance with environmental accords, it was well damped down by long established technology. The sound came from the boat's two air breathing engines, known as "SCAA-jets": super-conducting airflow acceleration jets. These were the descendants of the ramjets of old. These babies sucked air in at anything up to supersonic speed, from a *standstill*, and they could be rotated through any angle to provide directional thrust. One engine was buried in each wing root of a boat and they could kick the shuttle, inside an atmosphere, from subsonic speeds, up as far as Mach 15, on occasion. They could also safely propel the vessel from very low altitude up to about 75 kilometres.

Above that atlitude there was insufficient air even for them to "breathe", so to get into orbit the boats used the four "UECRE" engines each one was equipped with.

The name stood for "ultralow emission condensing rocket engines" and they represented two hundred years of rocket development. They utilised the air they sucked in and stored, from the SCAA jets, and converted it to rocket fuel, which, when added to the small amount of propellant they carried, enabled the boat to accelerate to orbit. They could carry out many days'worth of manoeuvres in high or low orbit, as required but, ordinarily, that length of time in orbit, on their own, was completely unnecessary.

On planets like the Earth and Oceanus, with atmospheres, the boats neither needed, nor were allowed, to have fusion engines, like the giant one the mother ship had, and which were so much more efficient and powerful than the primitive chemical rockets of old that they had replaced. As he watched the shuttle approach Mike was only too well aware that fusion engines were banned from worlds with atmospheres for very good reasons; for although modern fusion power plants were several million times safer, and more efficient, than the early ones, there was still a risk to health if a vehicle with such an engine crashed on the surface. The Monsoon used aneutronic fusion, meaning that the huge engine was designed not to shed free neutrons – highly damaging to organic tissue. But though it rarely happened, there was still a very small risk that, even with an aneutronic power plant, some neutrons could be emitted. That was why The Monsoon had a giant parasol shaped shield between its engine and everything in the forward end of the ship, meaning the crewed hub and the landing boat hangars.

The boat was almost overhead now and as it slowed, very noticeably, Mike ruminated on the fact that the lack of a fusion engine meant that none of the landing boats were able to leave planetary orbit and travel interplanetary space; so completely unlike The Monsoon, which could *only* travel in interplanetary – and interstellar space.

Ironically, for Mike, depite his deep interest in this tek, the thing he was most proud of, here and now, were the ultralow levels of pollution the shuttles produced in an atmosphere. The SCAA's generated hardly anything; storing and recirculating most chemicals regarded as pollutants, emitting small trace amounts of some hydrogen compounds, and water vapour. The rocket engines produced marginally more pollution, though it was mostly small amounts of derivatives of nitrogen, oxygen, carbon, and water. And those emissions were mixed with compounds which caused most of these derivatives to break down in an atmosphere, completely harmlessly, within weeks or months.

Mike remembered Tenak telling one of Arbella's "minions", when challenged about HS tek, that the LBs produced no more pollution than the propeller planes they still used here on Oceanus. That wasn't true, he thought. They produced *less.* Even so, the first government of the newly independent Oceanus Alpha had demanded that the Home System carry out yet further modifications on the landing boats, before they would be allowed to land on Bhumi-Devi. Madness, thought Mike, and so intensely ironic, given that their whole world would soon be overwhelmed by a natural disaster from which they could not hope to recover.

Mike's wristcom suddenly bleeped; a call from the government. The unit told him the call was from someone calling himself Edlin E. Monzonite. Oh no, *him* again, thought Mike, with dismay. The minister said little but actually gave Mike the necessary permissions he'd been awaiting. In fact, Monzonite sounded embarrassed, but Mike didn't give a monkey's arse about the guy's "permissions". Too late for that. The landing boats were here and, he mused, there was probably nothing on this world that could stop them now. Delicious idea, he thought, slyly. But why in the worlds would anyone want to stop them? They were now providing a vital, timely, service on this particular world.

**

The boat was above him now, its 38-metre length more obvious. When its V wings were fully extended it was almost as wide as its length. Mike guessed this one could be the "Agamemnon". Strangely, it was the usual choice of the ship's pilots, for some reason. Just then he caught sight of another bright light, again off to the west. That must be the other boat, presumably on its way towards the Ramnisos central hospital. Good. Now things were moving, he thought.

Drafts of air began to pick up around him as the the Agamemnon moved past his position, still several hundred feet high. On this trip The Monsoon had three of these boats for use at Oceanus, unarmed, as required by Treaty, but the mother ship also had two other, larger shuttles. These were armed and capable of carrying a small contingent of HS marines. There were, of course, no marines on this trip and those vessels would definitely not be making an appearance on this planet - yet. Modified, these boats could be used for evac', should the planetary authority agree to this, but he knew Tenak envisaged taking only a few hundred people back home to start with. There had not been time to modify the mother ship sufficiently so that it could safely take larger numbers through a conduit.

And he was aware that the Navy first wanted to test out the evac' system, with relatively modest numbers, especially as plans continued to develop the smooth repatriation of evacuees back in the Solar System itself. After all, Mike thought, the science which predicted the coming disaster was very new – but no less forceful for that!

As the Agamemnon slowed to a halt at about 100 metres altitude, the constellation of nav' lights and ID beacons just about enabled him to see that the ship's SCAA jets had rotated from horizontal to vertical orientation, which would allow the ship to descend vertically to a landing.

The boat was now dropping slowly over the spare ground near the house, the blast of the engines inevitably causing amplification of their noise. Still, more local people scurried away in fear. Understandable, thought Mike, and it was a shame, but it was interesting that more locals stayed than fled. In any case, this operation was vital. And these people would, he knew, have to get used to this sort of thing; more in fact, if they wanted themselves and their families to survive the coming onslaught from Ra.

Despite the award-winning eco-friendly engines, the downdraft from them meant that the boat inevitably kicked up a significant outblast of mud, grit and water from the recent rain. No-one was close enough to be affected, and Mike was at least grateful for that. He had been prepared to rush over and warn anyone.

And then the ship was suddenly down, settling softly onto its nose and main gear. With its engines winding down the main hatch door was already starting to open. A ramp with a set of steps incorporated into it arced very quickly out of the ship's front port side and telescoped down toward the ground, 9 metres below.

Within seconds, it seemed, half a dozen men and women were out of the hatch and hurrying down to Oceanus soil, all wearing orange, fluorescent, jump suits and carrying boxes of equipment and supplies, undoubtedly including various types of medical gear and medicines. Mike watched them come and he smiled. He'd never been so glad to see his mates from The Monsoon. But in the relatively near future, he'd have reason to regret the arrival of at least one crew from a landing boat.

Chapter 11

REACTION

The Bhumi Devi Times (newspaper): Verningsday, 22nd Mid Tertiary month.

Editorial

Yester-eve the usual serenissma of towns and cities across Bhumi Devi was rocked by chaos caused by a Mass Coronal Ejection from the surface of Ra. Clouds of plasma wrought blows upon our atmosphere, knocking out satellites and communicatry across the globe. Well-near all lectric apparatus was affected such by the magnetic storms which came alongside plasmaforce, the ferocity of such, no-one has seen in generations.

Fires, started by lectric short-outs and surging, broke across the inhabited areas of our continent, particularly in Janitra, Demnisos and Ramnisos, but no-where was yet free of problems. Tragically, tis confirm-ed that three people died in Janitra, from fires in private houses, and one person was killed by lectric arcing at an autocar repair works in the western plateau town of Bandastera. Ordinary lives became most-yet affected by extra-dangerous events. Many rescues were carried out by valiant citizens right across the continent. A light aircraft was brought down over the southern swamplands and local rescue workers searched afar for the pilot and passenger lasting long into the night. Sad such, the aircraft has not been found so far. Searches continue.

Danillsa D. Trebuchet, of the Democratic Congress Party saith, 'Tis a terrible night for those living in Devi and I think the Government must yet take its share of the blame. For we do so believe that warnings were given to the Government but were not so acted upon yet quick enough. We have put this said thing to the government, but they remain tight-lipp-ed as such. E'en so, I do believe that the Minister for

Interior has been dismisso'd. Praps this be enough but more needs to be learn-ed. And still I believe we can all grow stronger as a result of these events. We can and must learn from this. Though most homes and, still businesses are powered by their own solar generators there is yet a clear need to introduce more effective means of protecting and insulating them from events such as this. Hospitals and emergo-services also need to develop more back-up capacity.' _ So said the DC Party.

Tis also reported, in Ramnisos, that an Admiral of the Home System Navy was seriously injured when he did try to save an elder-citizen, at a mono-station afflicted by fire. We are yet told the Government gave permission for several shuttle-ships to descend from the Admiral's orbiting vessel, to pick up him, and other injured citizenry, for advanced medical treatment on said ship. Local hospitals could not help still, as they were said to have been overwhelmed by an vast inflow of injured people, and by their own lectrical breakdowns. It is so said the Navy ships are helping restore the hospital services.

Blue Planet Chronicle

Editorial

Ra didst surprise us all yester-eve and has now caused many citizenry to doubt that there is yet a future to living on Oceanus Alpha. Despite all such things said, we do not believe there is reason to panic. That is simply not our fore-way. To all outsiders we say – we do not so frighten yet easily. Our ancestors fought hard-long to establish a working colony and that colony prospered and didst grow until a new Nation, e'en a One-World Nation, was so formed. And we say, we rightfully claimed and won independence. One people, one nation: the nation of Oceanus, our Worldheam. Difficult living-times were second nature to our ancestors who suffered with more privations than we can now ever imagine, 132 years on-time. They too had their full share of disasters, natural and artificio. They had studied our star and declared it to be benign and they believed such in Oceanus. We have yet now seen little e'en to make us change our minds about that.

Some would have us believe that "new evidence" from roboti-craft the Home System left in our star system long ago, shows us Ra is developing into, and, to use their words, an "ultra-long variable star", set so to flare-so out of control and "kill us all". And so this, remember, from probes that are now 20 years old. The navy ship in orbit above us claims to have verified these findings. We say that this ship is a military vessel, not a research vessel. So, tis not something that we must trust of necessity, though we do not deny that the navy people have, this week, shown they mayst be helpful.

And we are grateful, but there are limits to our gratudinry and to our belief in the science of the Solar System, that so-called "Home System". That system of mani-worlds has shown itself to be at odds with its own identity and be ready to go to war within itself, and yes, within living memorie. Very many in such "Home System" have ulterior motives and so we say: <u>we must be wary of such populari and guard against rash judgement bas-ed on what they do advise.</u>

Chapter 12

SEARCH

The tiny blue autocar wound around the streets of Janitra, heading toward the University building where Mike Tanniss was due to meet Professor Muggredge. The streets had almost vanished in a thick grey-white veil of fog this morning, and Mike, sitting in the front of the car, felt a bit like a fish in some sort of bowl. Peering out he spotted the occasional passer-by, distorted into fuzzy blobs by the fog, as they walked past the autocar track. The vehicle travelled no faster than 10 klicks per hour, so he had a lot of time to ruminate.

He still worried about Tenak. Ebazza had told him the Admiral was recovering but he had undergone a complex operation on his back, involving the repair of several fractured lumbar and thoracic vertebrae, and, of greater concern, damage to part of his spinal nerve. He had also suffered a compound fracture of his right femur, and tears to any number of ligaments. On the whole, he supposed the guy had been lucky. The operation had gone well. Bone repair, using specialised synthetic tissue was now a fine art, and more recently, even nerve reconstruction had been fully developed. And, although things could still go wrong, Mike felt that Tenak would probably be fully on his feet within three or four weeks. He knew the man would not want to be out of the loop for long – but he was still laid up for the present.

As the autocar clunked along on its miniature rail, only functioning thanks to repair work done by engineers from The Monsoon, Mike reflected on what Tenak had somehow managed to tell him as the medics had conveyed him to the Agamemnon. Lying on the automated gurney he'd suddenly revived enough to wag a finger at Mike as he'd walked alongside.

'It's down to you Mike,' he had said, through gritted teeth, 'but listen … I guess I'm sorry I pulled you into all this, but I've got to load it on you now. See what you can do. Talk to Muggredge. Persuade him to do something. I'll get Ebazza to give you whatever you need.'

Despite feeling daunted Mike hadn't argued.

When they'd loaded Tenak onto the shuttle he'd called out, yet again, 'I know you can do it Mike. I know you can.'

Mike's sinking feeling had not gone away. The sense of a huge responsibility thrust onto him was unnerving but, somehow, he also felt a determination to try to help his friend. Tenak's mission was now his alone, at least for the time being. No-one down here was talking to the ship's science team, were they? But at least he felt some of the locals "knew him" already. Perhaps? So, who else that was planetside, could be "on the spot"? What if Muggredge wouldn't listen? What then? He had no idea – but he knew one thing for sure. He was determined he wasn't going to be the "patsy" for the coming disaster. It wasn't his fault. Even so, unbidden thoughts assailed him now. What would history have to say – about him – about Tenak – about the capital ship?

Mike had signed into one of the few hotels in Ramnisos for the time being, while The Monsoon's teams of teks and engineers had worked with local people – to get electro-mechanical systems working again. Mike's first couple of evenings had been spent mostly without power but he was getting used to that. Those evenings and the nights had also been filled with violent storms and most days awash with torrential rain, often hampering repair work. The bad weather eventually eased, and the repair teams were able to get going properly, but long before then Mike had summoned a landing boat to take him to Janitra. He called Professier Muggredge's secretary and arranged a meeting with the academic but he had no idea what to expect.

On the day of the meeting he set off for the University and on reaching the main building, about 4 kilometres out of town, Mike found himself walking into what seemed to be a large, ornately porched main entrance, tall pillars either side of it. There was a man in a booth just inside, asking him where he wanted to go. Once again, he noted that, apart from the official himself, there were no real security checks or automated scans. He guessed they probably didn't even have scanners.

He was directed to the building next door, to the "Natural Historie Society – Scienti- Mangament" block. There was nobody on that door, so he just wandered in. It was very cool and quiet inside, and he could smell the natural wood panelling lining the walls. His hard shoes made a loud squeaking sound as he trod the polished wooden floor. Then he noticed that the walls further in were awash with pieces of old-fashioned paper. That stuff again? Peering at some the pictures on some of them he could see they were photomicrographs of cells and tissue samples. There were still photographs all around, showing curious looking animals and plants, and fading academic notices were everywhere.

The physical "flatness" of the pictures appalled his sense of taste, for there were no holos anywhere. But then, suddenly, one particular picture drew his immediate attention. He could tell that it had been removed from a news bulletin; one of the "newspaper dailies"in vogue down here. The magnetic appeal of the picture was simply that it was a photograph, now faded, but quite obviously, of the young woman he'd met, frustratingly briefly, in the Government Building. It was Eleri, the niece of Arbella Nefer-Masterton.

In the picture, Eleri was standing on a blindingly bright, sandy beach, next to the body of a truly enormous fish, or at least it looked like it might have been a fish. There was some text underneath which trumpeted, "Eleri T N-Ambrell, being 25 years old, and Doctoratian student of biolry, yet with the Natural Historie department at Central University, poses next to a Prolixamorph, washed up on such wild shoreline of the Armstrong Sea. Eleri has yet been studying this genus of fishrine since …."

So, she was not only the President's niece, but also, more importantly, an accomplished academic, a scientist or – a natural historian – as they called them here. He saw that the article was dated three Oceanus years ago.

He was elated at finding this info', this tidbit about the lovely femna and he searched amongst the notices for anything else about her, but some minutes later, finding nothing, he continued wandering along the empty corridor, reminding himself of his promise to Tenak. He wondered where the students were right now, but then realised this was the admin' department, not the teaching building. It still seemed odd. Finally, he saw a sign which said, "Senior Academry Staff," pointing down a corridor to the right. The professor must be along there, surely? He followed the sign and duly arrived at a closed door bearing the Professor's name plaque: Professier D. Therplie Muggredge.

He knocked. Silence. He knocked again and a female voice issued from inside. There was something familiar about that voice, even though muffled by the interposing door. The female tones bid him enter and as he did so, he saw an older man sitting in an armchair opposite him, on the right hand side of a quaint little office which smelled of something like pinewood, with overtones of musty books and paperwork. And on the left-hand side of the office a young woman sat on the edge of a large, ancient looking desk. Of course – the voice. It was her, the femna in the Central Government Building, the one whose photograph he'd just seen. The one who'd been regularly popping into his thoughts ever since they'd met.

'Eleri!' he said, 'I didn't expect…, I mean…' His cheeks suddenly felt as if they were burning. Burning? Really? Mike Tanniss didn't blush, did he? Never, and yet ….

'Tis nice to see you too, Mike,' said Eleri, smiling broadly. Was that a deepening of the already rosy hue of her cheeks, he wondered? Mike's heart leaped high. Get control, he thought, annoyed at his over-the top reaction. Yes, he usually felt elated when meeting young attractive femnas but this reaction, right now, was in a much higher spatial grid.

The older man spoke then, genuine warmth glowing in his voice, 'Hello, Mer Mike. Thanking you for stopping by-now.' The "Professier" was a thick set man, with a paunch and a skim of surprisingly dark but steadily thinning brown hair, framing a square shaped face, a lined face, full of character. He looked as though he laughed a lot. His eyes shone. Wearing a cool looking powder blue jacket and black slacks he appeared very relaxed and amenable. Mike could only hope.

'Hello Professier. Glad to meet you,' said Mike.

'Please call me Draco. My real name is Dracus, but no-one calls me such. Come in yet. Sit down young manry. I should introduce you two but, I am thinking you look like you mightst have met already,' he said, glancing at Eleri. He continued, 'Would you be liking something to drink, Mike? I only offer you kaffee or fruit juice, fraid. Alcool is not allowed on such an premises.'

'No, thank you. I'm fine,' said Mike as Muggredge waved him toward a wooden chair near the desk. Eleri promptly hopped off the desk and sat on a large chair next to Muggredge. She wore a maroon-coloured one-piece suit and she also looked cool, despite the evident heat of the day. She and Mike gazed at each-other, a slightly embarrassed silence ensuing, till Muggredge broke in with, 'I was so much sorry to learn of your Admiral's accident Mike, but I believe we owe him a debt of gratudry. Our *lord and master*, the great Arbella, herself, has yet said so. I see you are surpised so. Yes, she didst appear on our television system but last night, praising such the Navy and your admiral-mer. And so she should, tiddly bit silliest that she be.'

He chuckled as Eleri said, 'Come on Unkling. Less of that. Let us not be too unkind.'

'Okay, just a bit then,' said Muggredge grinning. Eleri laughed again and flashed another smile at Mike.

'You're the Professier's niece, as well as…?' Mike said to her.

''Fraid so,' she said quickly and continued, 'yet praps tis hard to believe but Unkling Draco and Arbella are bruthly and sishtra. Am sorry Mike, I mean brother and sister. I must try to talk in Home System dialect.'

'That's okay,' said Mike, 'I was thinking just the opposite. I need to start practising *your* dialect.'

'That can be arranged,' said Eleri, smiling coyly, her fresh air complexion reddening still further. The freckles on her face seemed to deepen. Mike was transfixed.

'Um, I am a hating to break this up,' said Muggredge, 'but I shall suppose we need to talk business, Mike? I appreciate you have come yet a long way. Actual an understatement.'

'I shall yet go,' said Eleri and stood. Mike protested, as did Muggredge, but she insisted it was more appropriate that Mike have the undivided attention of her unkling. Besides, she said, she had some important material to research before she gave a lecture to her out-of-term special students. Smiling broadly at Mike, she swept out of the room but before leaving turned and said, 'I am hoping I will yet see you again Mike Tanniss, Secretary to an Navy ship, Monsoon.'

Mike nodded enthusiastically and gave her a huge smile as she went through the door. He almost felt a sense of loss as she went. That's strange, he thought.

'Ah, such a nice giril,' said Muggredge, 'and I am thinking … she likes you yet. And there was no need of her to go, but she is best-keen on her research,' said Muggredge.

'She said she lectures to students,' said Mike, 'but I haven't seen any students. I assume it can't be term time?'

'Ah, not such,' said Muggredge, 'but still there is a group with special-so needs who rely on her tutoring at such out-term times. Yet, that work will come to an end very soon as e'en they go home. Now, before you yet say anything more, young manry, I know why you are here and I know something of the travailies of you and your Admiral, in so trying to persuade our political oafers. Sorry, I should be saying, political parties.'

'Maybe you were right the first time, sir. I'm glad you know about that, but I hope this means you might be prepared to … let's say, "push" from your end?'

'Really, Mike? Push? Do you think I am yet so powerful? So persuasive? Ah, young manry, if t'were that simple. You know of course, that sishtra and I do not walk hand in hand? Sorry, I mean we …'

'Yeah, I know what you meant.' Mike smiled.

'I know such things should not be important, but we are talking about human nature, arint we? Tis also human nature that means the majority of the population arint prepared to listen to scientists, like us. Not when their homes and livelihoods are at stake. When a whole way of life could end – simply so because of some Home System observations…'

Mike began to interject but Muggredge continued, determined to make a point.

'I shall say that observations are genuinely disputed, Mike. Mysem, I have looked into this. Please do not look at me like that, young manry. I have studied it all, much – and can see areas where the findings can be disputed. There is no up to date information or data – because the probe your Home System left in orbit, round yon Ra, stopped working years ago.'

Mike gave a sour smile, full of irony. 'So, I understand,' he said.

'Oh, so you knew?' Muggredge was wide eyed.

Mike explained about his "interview" with the Metateleos. The professor huffed at the mention of them.

'What I didn't say, at the time,' Mike recounted, 'was that there are more up to date observations. Well, if that isn't a contradiction in terms. They were made back home. They've captured a sequence of changes in the deeper parts of other stars. Super-hurricanes of gas, if you like, inside stars just like Ra. They show a definite pattern which point to serious problems with your own sun. Well, … there's more.'

'Please do be carrying on.'

'There's also the observations we made, or I should say, that my colleagues made, as our ship came into this system.'

'Your colleagry?'

'Yes, Professier,' and Mike explained his real job on board the ship.

'And they slump-heaped upon and your Admiral, with this job?' The Professor looked surprised.

'Well, I suppose, but we did bring a team of scientists with us. They've been refused meetings with President Masterton – and the Teleosophists.'

'Those moggitheads! Still, does not surprise me. I think you already know about the terribleous hold the teleos have here. That makes for a difficult scene for the government. They do not want to risk the teleos getting more power but still do not want to close the door on the Home System advice, either. I see from your expression, that you have become familiar with this picture.'

There was a long pause. Then Mike said, 'So, may I ask what position you take, though, from what you said earlier it doesn't sound too promising?'

'Do not be prejudging me, Mike,' retorted the Professor, with an unexpected hardness of tone. 'All I said was, I can see gaps in the data-info. Gaps that are now being filled with anthropic nonsense from the teleos! Actually, I do yet sympathise with some of the Home system findings, Mike. But you are wrong if you think I can change all-things around, just like that.' He waved his arms about as if rearranging invisible play tiles on a board. 'But there is yet something else that could be working for us all. What is needed here, fren-manry, sorry, "my friend", is a diffy-angle approach and I think I might have the same.' He signalled Mike to move closer, as if afraid the walls had ears. Mike thought it was probable almost nothing could be further from the truth on this planet.

Drawing slightly closer, Mike listened intently as Muggredge explained, in almost conspiratorial manner,

'Do you know anything about this planet's geolry? I mean – geology. No? Well, it so happens that I have been looking into it. Very much so, recent-times. Extreme interesting, too. Not a lot of work done on it throughout our history – not enough, by Nadder. Most was done by the early pioneers but there was no need to find coal, say, or all-forbid, oil, because thanking-full, we had moved on away from fossil fuels. Lots of minerals there are - and some, are used in industry, true enough.'

'But there's not a lot of industry on Oceanus, right?' said Mike.

'True so. We use, most of all, renewables. More than 90 percent of times, and we do mabber-loads, up to 98 percent of recycling and re-use. Much of the plant life of this planet has evolved in surprising ways, you know. A lot of the buildings in the older town places, are being converted, and all places in new towns, are being made of "Larpett wood", which can actually be *grown* into a shell for building homes. This surprises you, yes? There is also another species which can be grown into many more shapes, for more functions, but tis difficult to grow just anywheres. Many species of plant provide oil substitutes and of course we can synthesise oil – like the Home System does now, but that is less common here.' The Professor almost sounded as though he were giving some kind of private tutorial to his students. But Mike was enjoying this, even though Muggredge seemed very much to have strayed far from his original point. Just then the Professor shook his head as if to mentally pull himself back to the point he wanted to make originally.

'Anywayins, the point I am making,' said Muggredge, 'in round-abouts way I suppose, is that there's been little geolry research in generations. My main interest now is in the deep past of Oceanus. As in Earth's continents, Bhumi-Devi is made from all the same types of rock you have on your world. That is, igneous rocks, formed by volcanic activity; metamorphic, formed by pressure on pre-existing rock, and yet sedimentary – those formed by deposition in rivers, seas and so. On this continent, rocks as old as 3 billions of years have been found, all the way up to rocks just three and a half million years ago. And then – they do *stop*. They do stop – until we are finding rocks more like 8 to 9 millions of years old.'

'They stop, Professier?' said Mike, his brow furrowing.

'Yes, well, you see, there is yet, you would say, an unconformity in the strata, at 8.3 million years. A huge one.'

'A what? I'm sorry, Professier, but geolry is not my area.'

'Well now, put simply, an unconformity is where there is a gap in the geolry record. Tis usually because material laid down on top has been eroded away. The surface might have been raised up above the sea and become, you might say, a desert, so sand or soil gets blown away by winds, or carried to sea. I see you are wondering what has this to do with the problem at our hand, yes? Surely, yes. But listen again, for I shall tell you, since you didst not list. There arint any rocks between the ages of 8.5 and 8.0 million years, anywhere on the continent. Much rock that is younger there, but none in that age range. Now do you yet hear?'

'I'm sorry, Professier. Now, I really am confused. How exactly does any of this help us?'

'So sorry, Mike. I had thought you might be knowing about the fossil content of our sedimentary rocks – from your ship's own datanet thing. For, yes, I know such an thing exists. But I do not blame you. Why would you consider geolry? True.

Forgive me. Well so now, there are fossil-rich rocks leading right up to the unconformity. Many masses of different creatures have been found. Life was flourishing on Oceanus. But *after* the unconformity, in much more recent rocks – very few fossils of animals. What does that suggest to yoursev, Mike?'

'I suppose … something happened to most of the life … during the period of the … unconformity, did you say? Did it die out or something?'

'Exacto-so right Mike. Yes, yes. We think there was yet a massive *extinction event* somewhere bit more than 8 millions year-time ago. What might cause such? Well, there do not seem to be any meteoritie craters that would be fitting such requirement. There could have been a super-volcano, like affected poor Earth recent-times. But then we think there would be other evidence to show this, but, no, there is nothing big enough in more than 5 million years. Plenty volcanoes, but none such big as that. Something else happened. Praps something to do with another outside influence? Outside the planet? Getting my drift-move, Mike? Now, tis the important bit - for you. The geolistas in my team think there are some records, old records, that might point to beds of rock of the right age – on Simurgh. You know, tis also known as the Great Southern Island.'

Mike nodded.

'So, indeed,' continued Muggredge, there may be records that indicate the location of rocks aged between 8.5 and 8.0 million years. A whole series – on that island. At this moment our hands do not have those records.'

'Well, why don't you just go there and…' Mike began.

'Just "hold to the telephone", young manry,' said Muggredge, raising up a silencing hand, 'Before you nadder on. That island is a sanctuary. A park, you will say. And has been, for generations. Tis meant to preserve the environment exactly – before humans first came here. That means no development and no visiting, even for research – at least without a hard-to-get permit.'

'Surely, that's… Oh, I suppose I can see why,' said Mike, his sense of frustration building once again.

'Do not get resign-ed, Mike. There is yet a way to get all-round most things that so obstruct us. I just meant we carnt go shooting off there this minute. We have to get a permit and that is the government, again. To get the permit we need some solid evidence that there is a *need* to go there. E'en then, t'will only be a small team of trusted people allowed. A search is being made for the records I mentioned, right now. Eleri is part of that effort, so am I thinking you might want to help her?'

Mike nodded, with more than enthusiasm than he'd wanted to reveal. Muggredge continued, a smile playing on his lips, 'If we can yet produce the records and if they really do show what we think they do ... well, we might just get a permit after all.

'Sounds great. But it seems a long shot, as we say. I've been thinking about life on this planet since we got here. What if most of it died out because of disease or something? And what makes you so sure that something happened back then which is going to help us prove our point?'

'Please be forgiving friendling, but I was yet economical with the truth when I said that there arint any rocks of the required age on the continent. Actually, some rocks from such time, around 8.2 to 8.4 million years old, were so found in one tiny-small location deep in the central deserts.'

'And?'

'And, they show some evidence of a mysterioso layer of *carbon deposits*. Carbon deposits, yes, Mike-friend. It does show only that there was some big burning event – at that time – at that place. But now is the crunch. There was also yet a suggestion of isotopes of Beryllium 10. Ah, I see your face shows some recognition, Mike. It does show - no suggest - only suggest – that there was some sort of gigantus-burning of vegetation, massive wide-scale, brought on by something of cosmic origin. The small amount of deposit is not yet sufficient to so prove this. The trace elements were never still confirmed. But that is why we need to look yet at Simurgh. If there is more abundant evidence of widespread burning and more confirmable deposits of Beryllium 10 isotopes, we might be able to… Well, praps you can tell me, Mike?'

Mike almost felt like he was at school again, but he was getting to really like this older man. He knew that the element Beryllium 10 was a characteristic component of the Sun's atmosphere, back home, and he was pretty sure this was the case with Ra too. Mike quickly realised that as the element in question was a relatively heavy radioisotope its presence in deposits on Oceanus could only mean one thing: significant amounts of material from Ra, undoubtedly in the form of gases, must have hit the surface long ago. If Muggredge was right.

'You're suggesting we could show there was a huge catastrophic event that involved the scorching of the whole land surface,' said Mike, 'caused, maybe, by a massive surface eruption on Ra? A previous Karabrandon upheaval,' he said, his eyes lighting up with the possibilities.'

'Exact-so. And none of the Beryllium 10 does occur, methinks, on this world, in a natural state. And tis not just about the isotope containing deposits, Mike. Remember the lack of animal species for long after the time we talk of? From fossils we found we see plants do come back early after, but not large animalia. Only small ones – on land yet. Without super-volcano or asteroidy impact the only other way a conflagration on that scale – capable of making so many species of animals and plants extinct, would be something to do with Ra. Do not be forgetting. I say – praps. And you mayst recall, from your own studies, that expecting to find evidence to prove your theory does not necessarily make good for the best science. We carnt be sure that this carbonised deposit exists in any large amount – or if does so, what it yet really proves.'

'I know Professier. You're saying evidence should be viewed objectively, with the possibility that something might disprove the theory, rather than prove it. But there's rather more at stake here than the reputation of science.'

'Oh, no, no. I should say that this is *exacto-so* what is at stake here, Mike.'

Looking at his wristcom Mike had a flash of inspiration and he said to Muggredge,

'Professier, do you mind if I show you some of the data my coleagues picked up when The Monsoon came into this system – the long journey in. This is up to date info. I'm not saying you must accept it all … But, if there's something you're not happy about, maybe we can just … talk about it?

'Coursery, friending. Coursery.'

As he showed holograms of the data, projected into a small space above Muggredge's desk, he realised no-one, not even Tenak, would have been more surprised by the change in him.

**

After about 35 minutes Mike switched off the wristcom. Muggredge sat back in contemplation.

'That is all and good young manry,' he said, 'but t'will not of its own satisfy the authoritaries here. And you do know that. I yet think that our best chance of convincing every person – lies with the records I didst mention.'

'Okay,' said Mike, 'so, what now?'

'We get to finding those records quickso. I am yet expected to do much admino work over next weeks so t'will be you and Eleri to find the records. Praps with some help from another student. I so hope this will be to your happiness?'

'Yes, okay Professier. It's what I'm here for,' said Mike and rose to leave. He felt that the Professor might just be onto something here, and he was more than happy about the chance to spend time with Eleri. And he might get to go to other parts of this world, like Simurgh. Finally, this should be interesting, he thought.

*

He had no idea what the significance of Simurgh would be, for him, for Tenak, and for the *whole* of humanity.

In the meantime, the tortuous path to Simurgh would turn his own personal world upside down – more than once.

Chapter 13

TWIN

He found Eleri in the Building's library. When Mike entered the large reading room he found her squatting near a low cupboard, below a long, scenic window. She had changed into a thin white tee shirt and dark blue slacks and she looked completely at home in this academic environment. He drank in the sight of her there, her bare, lithely muscled and tanned arms sporting shoulder freckles deeper than those on her face. He felt confirmed in his view upon first seeing her that, although quite a bit shorter than him, she was much fitter and obviously athletic.

She had both hands buried in the cupboard and was rifling through piles of paper. Paper – again. Still, he was getting used to this now.

'Is that old fashioned wood pulp?' he asked, and she looked up. Her eyes betrayed no surprise at his presence. She must have heard him come in.

'So, greets again, Mike. Tis a sort of wood,' she said, in that slightly husky voice of hers. 'and tis deedly made from the flesh of a native plant and is renewable, of course. We cultivate the plants all over.'

I was told you made paper from a material which decays and dissolves within about a month?' Mike said.

Speaking in the unique Oceanus idiom she said, 'Only if we do not want the stuff to stick around for too long. Things like newspapers. And before you spring a mind-leak, yes, we still do make newspapers, but they are meant to decay quickly. Papers like these are academic stuff. We normally want them to remain around, so they're made of the ordinary pulp.'

Eleri rose and invited Mike to sit at a long wooden desk along one wall.

'Have you been sent to help me?' she asked, a smile playing on her generous lips.

'Well, the Professier seems to expect me to do this job with "help from a student," he said. But I'm very glad it turns out to be you.'

'Cheekie manry. For I am not a student, you see. I am ...'

'I know. A researcher – and a lecturer. He told me, and I saw some articles on the walls back there. I'm still grateful for your help.'

'Well, I am supposing this thing could be done better with two – as long as you are not distracting me too much,' she said with mock sternness.

'As you wish Madama,' he said, smiling broadly, and asked, 'Just what is it we're looking for?'

Eleri then told him the obscure but now, suddenly significant, story about how a colleague, Marcus Ra-Senestris, a rock specialist in Muggredge's team, had taught a graduate student, many years ago. Nothing strange there but the student had been doing a dissertation on Simurgh's rock strata. He hadn't actually visited the island himself but had analysed photographs and video film taken by aircraft which had overflown it, decades before. These survey craft had done extensive aerial filming of the island's surface features, including the vegetation cover – and the geology. The student believed he had seen extensive outcrops of rocks of roughly the age that would fill the gap left by the unconformity on the mainland. This tied in with a land survey done, on foot, by explorers amongst the pioneers who first landed on Oceanus, over 130 years ago.

A promising start, suggested Mike, but Eleri pointed out the problems, 'First,' she said, 'there are yet no known records of that pioneer survey done on foot. Second, we have not so found the student's dissertation and third, Marcus carnt remember much detail about the dissertation, or what it said.'

'Surely,' said Mike, his voice full of surprise, 'there are records of the dissertations done by all the students, aren't there?'

'This was done a long time ago, Mike. Marcus is in his fifties-years and his student, a man called Andriwnes Dar-Lisdon, did his work – mayhaps 20 years past. Do you think we still have all the work done by all the students, going back to such early-time?'

'It's not much to go on, then,' said Mike, realising that, on Oceanus, there weren't any of the hyperdensity data logs available in the Home System.

'Tis all we have,' she said, with a heavy sigh. 'Marcus just carnt remember any more, and even if he could, tis not reliable evidence. So, all we can do is yet work through the stored dissertations and other other papers. We can also look through the computer records from that time.' She saw his look of surprise and added, with humorously, 'Yes, you moggit-head, we do have computer records. I was wondering if you could like to make a start on those?'

Stifling his amusement, he nodded while she directed him to an old-fashioned computer monitor in the corner of the room. It was so old. He told her he wasn't sure he could handle a machine that ancient. In response to her quizzical expression, he said he was used to *talking* to computers or waving his fingers above screens. There were micro-keypads available back home, but they were seldom used. She seemed shocked when he told her that some hypercomp users, back home, had electrodes fitted into their heads, which allowed some thought control of computers, albeit limited. She recoiled in horror. And he had to admit to himself, that he was with her there.

He was relieved when she offered to do the comp work, if he was happy to look through the papers. He was hardly happier in the circumstances, but he could also tell she was becoming peeved at his excuses, so he decided to comply without further comment. He didn't want to spoil their developing relationship, despite it being purely a working relationship at the moment. He'd try to broaden that soon, he thought, but he could see she was intent on the work right now. Academically inclined she might be, but he had no doubt she was strong willed right across the board. There'd be no messing with this one. Okay, that was fine with him.

Over the next three hours Mike sifted papers and sorted through cardboard folders and capacious boxes filled with documents; work done by numerous students of geology over the years. Many were dissertations - but there were none by "Andriwnes Dar-Lisdon". He asked Eleri why they just couldn't look for Mer Lisdon himself. He might remember where his papers were, or even have a copy. She said that Lisdon had emigrated to the Home System many years ago – and hadn't been heard of since.

'Emigrated?' said Mike. He grinned and added, 'but … I shouldn't be surprised. Probably got fed up with pulp fibre and ancient flat screen computers.'

Eleri turned in her chair and flung a sheaf of papers at him. He picked up some of them, chuckling and then said, half seriously, 'I didn't see these. I guess I should check them.'

'Do not be a-worry. I already have. Listen manry, we've been at this long enough. We are yet needing a break. Well, I do. Am not used to the long hours you Navy people put in without a break.'

'Now you really are joking,' he said.

'But yet, Mike, you have not really said what you do in the Navy. For I know you are not a sailor.'

He chuckled amiably and said, 'No, I'm not and we don't call them "sailors". They're just crewmembers – either engineers, tek staff, security guards or scientists. And you're right. I'm not one of them – just a "ship's Secretary". A nobody really. Well, it feels like that sometimes.'

'Ah, but yet I think you mayst jest. I suspect that "Secretary" is important. No?'

'Well, we were, once, I guess. If you really want to know, I'm supposed to be a reminder to the crew, especially the officers, that the ship is under government control. I have a quasi-legal role, I suppose. But it's more complicated than that. I wouldn't bother getting into it more than that if I were you. Too boring.'

'I am yet sure there is more to it, youngry,' she said, grinning and carried on with her comp research.

Mike thought, in that moment about how he'd like to swap with the scientists aboard the ship, for that was where his real interests lay. Still, being ship's Secretary hadn't worked out too bad so far. And, thinking about Eelri's question, he tried to convince himself that secretaries were supposed to have quite a lot of influence, and yet, not really. He could, *in theory* even relieve a senior officer of command, if he knew an attack on the Earth or another Home System world was planned. But that would obviously require widespread support and co-operation with other officers. Mike mulled over the fact that different types of military action against a recognised enemy force could be *opposed*, if necessary, by the Secretary but they couldn't interfere with a military action once it had been ordered by the most senior officer present.

He wondered how he could ever manage to use powers like that when in an *extreme* situation and he thanked the fates for the stability of the Navy, in general, and the steadfastness of those in charge on The Monsoon, even including, begrudgingly, Ebazza.

As he sat and looked out the long window, he saw the sun was baking the soil and bushes outside, but it was cool in the room. Must have temp control, he thought approvingly. For a change, subtle and unusual, down here. Probably needed to preserve the books. And his brain must have been in "ship-mode" not to notice earlier. Either that or he was … distracted by present company.

Eleri stood up, yawned, stretched herself and walked toward him. His heart beat faster, as she said, 'I am thinking we could go to the local Kaffee House and take yet a nice long break. What say you, manry?'

Mike didn't need persuading. But he continued to be surprised at his own reactions to this young femna. He was behaving like some naïve person, ten years younger. Shy he was not. Overreacting to women he was not. This wasn't like him at all.

****

As he drank an unispiring, grey coloured mug of kaffee, which still tasted surprisingly authentic, Mike listened to Eleri wax lyrical about the wilderness and the wildlife of Oceanus. The kaffee shop was small but hardly intimate, being so busy it was packed full of chattering, bubbling locals. He guessed they were here for their mid-day break, if they had such a thing around these parts. Yet, when Eleri spoke he seemed to forget about everything else going on around him. Her enthusiasm for her subject radiated from her and he was transfixed.

'You know, Mike, when I was much younger yet, I was disappointed with this planet,' she said, in her sparkling Oceanus dialect.

'Really? How so?'

'I saw there were no really big animals and a lack of large ... herds, you would say, of animals, especially compared to the Earth, or at least what I had seen in films and books. Never have I been to Earth but still I watched history tele-visual images of vasty herds of things like ... wildebeest and ... elephanti. Then there were the great predators. The lions and so on.'

'That's doubly sad,' said Mike, sighing, 'because most of those creatures have gone – some time ago – in the wild.' He had not really ever been into biology or animal science but that didn't matter. Most people back home probably felt the sadness of the passing of the great beasts from the wild places, though there were still some in very small pockets, in very remote areas. Ironically, the "New Dark Ages", for humans, had seen a "come-back" for many species which had not already died out. But that didn't change the huge losses from earlier times.

'I know about *that*,' she said with some vehemence, and looked askance at him, as if, somehow, it was his fault.

'Hey, it's not *my generation's* doing. Most of them disappeared a long time ago and I don't like it either.'

'I know Mike. I am sorry. Tis just ... such a terrible, horrible, waste, though. No-one did anything – or not enough, when it mattered. And now tis all over – gone. A crime humans didst commit.'

'It's not completely over, Eleri,' he said and explained something he thought she might not have heard about. He said that he'd heard of breeding programmes launched some decades ago, designed to keep many species extant, albeit in limited areas. Then there were the massive gene banks which had been set up; carefully controlled stores of body tissue, and gametes; the sperm and eggs of thousands of species. Hundreds of DNA producing tissue and gamete pools, of both animal and plant species, had been preserved in huge tanks of liquid nitrogen, buried deep underground. Some of them, he understood, had been set up in the mid-21st century, before the disasters which beset humanity. He wasn't up to date on whether they had actually survived the depredations of the new "Dark Ages".

'I think the plan is to thaw them out and use the stores of gametes,' he said, 'either to repopulate the Earth with animals someday – or, less likely, to seed a suitable, uninhabited planet. Trouble is, we've run out of "suitable uninhabited planets", at least in the human explored zone.'

'Tis still just a dream then, like so many others.'

'Yeah, suppose so. There don't seem to be any other candidate planets within reach. Well, the plan's got the saving grace of having a lot of potential. Anyway, you were saying about your early feelings about *this* world. Please, tell me more.'

'Yes, ist right. I was yet very young, my frend. I just could not yet understand the lack of great animals or herds. After all, this planet is so much like the Earth.'

'Yeah, right,' he interjected, thinking back to his discussion with Tenak, 'I've heard all this before. This place being, "Earth's twin", and the rest.'

'Not quite sirra – but – in essence, yes true. There should be more mammalian types than do exist. More biologically complex species. I am a big believer in convergent evolution, Mike. Experience as a biolrist has made me feel there is a lot in that.'

At his puzzled expression she briefly explained the idea of convergent evolution – as applied to different planets: the theory that on different worlds with similar environmental conditions, similar evolutionary developments would likely occur. That could mean similar *types* of creatures, not the same creatures, but filling similar natural functions in similar environmental niches, and so on. She continued, 'Thing is, Mike, that as I got mature more, and actually investigated this world mysem, I came to see there is so much more to Oceanus than meeteth the eye.'

'I can believe that,' said Mike. There's certainly more to *the people* here than meets the eye, that's for sure, he thought.

'There is, in reality, Mike, a wide diversity of animal life on the land. Tis just small, sometimes very small, mammal-like creatures and slightly larger reptilians but there are many wonder varieties of insectoids, as well as a huge biota of microscopic creatures. The seas are even more diverse and that is where you get the largest living animals on the planet, and most numerous. Sorry, I am yet boring you.'

'No, not at all,' he reassured her. He liked listening to her voice. He loved it in fact. 'Please carry on.'

'I found long agos that there's really such a rich biosphere here. I had no right to be condemning it or yet be disappointed in my early days, just because it did not live up to expectation from Earth stories. At least – we humanry – have the chance to make a new start here or try to. Avoid the mistakes made on Earth, if we can such. Mayhap humans should not e'en have come here to settle in the first place.' She paused for a moment. The Kaffee shop was starting to get even more crowded and the heat of the Devian day was beginning to build to a peak. Mike was sweating profusely.

'I yet like your idea of an uninhabited world,' she continued, 'like one which could be seeded with animals from the past. A primo-dream though. And, trouble is, it probably would not work without human intervention.' She suddenly went silent and became wistful.

'Please go on,' Mike said, 'Tell me your thoughts.'

'No, another time, praps.'

'What's wrong Eleri?'

'Nothing. I just seem to be doing all the talking,' she said and then brightened. 'Tell me about yoursem, Mike, Mer Secretary to the Monsoon.'

'Nothing much to say really.'

'Oh, come so. A manry of the cosmos, like you? All the worlds and sights you must have seen. All the girils you must have swept from their feet.' She grinned.

His gaze fell into her eyes and he suddenly felt shivers go down his spine. He kind of liked that but it certainly wasn't his usual reaction. He looked away for a moment or two. What was going on here?

'Like I tried to say before, 'I'm just a glorified administrator. That's all.'

'I can see you like the Admiral,' she said.

'I suppose. He's a fuss-narda really but his intentions are okay.'

'Arint you concerned about him Mike? He did a marvellous thing – you know - over in Ramnisos?' Eleri's brows knitted.

'Yes, of course Eleri. I know that, but they're taking good care of him on the ship. The best. At least he's the lucky one to be back on the ship.'

Oops, he realised that that had probably come out the wrong way. He scanned her face and saw a slight change.

'Oh, I see. You are not liking us on this world, Mike?' She looked puzzled.

'No, I mean, yes. Look, don't get the wrong impression. It's just that … Well, my experiences here, so far, haven't been …great.' He hastened to add, emphatically, 'Except for meeting *you*, of course.'

'Don't soft-pandle me Mike. Listen me yet, I know what you did mean. You just spoke to all the wrong people before, tis all.' She chuckled and brightened again.

'Even your Auntine?' he teased.

'Especially Auntine. Hey, but do not be telling her that. She's alrighty really, you know. Just got to get to know her.'

Mike could think of lots of questions he could ask this wonderful femna, but his main concern was starting to be how he could hit the sack – with her. It wasn't going to be easy with this one. He was fascinated by her but strangely reluctant to make those sorts of overtures and yet, he didn't think he'd ever be visiting this planet again. So, he might as well make a start. Why was he so nervous about it? he mused.

'Eleri,' he said, 'I'd like to invite you out for dinner – say tomorrow evening?'

'I am sorry, Mike. I do not think so.'

His heart sank into the depths for a second and he quickly asked, 'Any particular reason?' His pulse raced. He desperately hoped she wouldn't fusion-blast his dream of getting to know her better.

'Yes. I am visiting my parentia. Sorry, I should say, my parents. I have not seen them in – oh, months.'

'I see. Where do your folks live?' He breathed a sigh of relief, inwardly. She wasn't cutting him loose completely. At least, not yet. What was matter with him, he wondered? He was usually much more confident than this. Was he losing his touch?

'Chantris,' she said, 'they live in Chantris, a very small town about 300 kloms inland from here. I will be gone for the whole day. So sorry.'

'No need for apologies. Maybe we can meet up when you get back?' he said, hoping he didn't sound desperate. In truth though, he really did feel a little desperate. But then, if it wasn't to be with this one, he reckoned he'd make it with some woman on this big rock. Then again, maybe not. He'd not seen much to impress him, until now. There was the woman in the Central Hotel, but she had disappeared. At last, he thought, he was getting back to his old self.

'Maybe we can,' she said.

'What about the research?' he said reluctantly. He realised, soberly, that he didn't really want to spend the next day rifling through more piles of dusty papers; a "wild fusion blast" to nothing.

'Oh, coursry. Sorry, Mike, I should have mentioned it before. Do you mind? I think another member of the team is yet coming down tomorrow anyways. I am sure he shall be big help.'

A man. Just great, thought Mike sardonically. Then an idea popped into his head and he whistled. 'What's wrong?' she said, her brow furrowing.

'I just realised. I'm sorry Eleri. I think I could have saved us a lot of time if I'd thought about it before.'

'Spill the treasure-trove, Mike.'

'Why don't *we* overfly the island? I mean – the Navy – using a landing boat? Your Aunt gave us permission to fly civilian missions, just as we wish.'

She nodded vigorously.

'Do you yet think we – I mean you – could do such an thing?' she said.

'Maybe. I'll have to put it to the Admiral of course.'

'And so, we must first ask Unkling Muggredge.'

They both grinned with satisfaction, got up and left, straight away.

****

'No, fraid not. Absoluto not,' said Muggredge, speaking to his niece and Mike over a University telephone set on loudspeaker mode. The Professor had left Janitra, on business.

'Why in Ra's beam not?' said Eleri, standing next to the desk phone. Mike stood opposite, with his arms folded. Here we go again, he thought.

'Neither of you have noticed what Arbella really did say,' replied Muggredge. 'She said the Navy could fly on missions *over Devi*. The continent. Not else-awheres.'

Mike grimaced. The guy was right. His enthusiasm had ejected that bit from his memory. He felt he'd misled Eleri.

'Sorry Professier. I forgot,' said Mike, out loud.

'Deeding,' continued Muggerdge, 'and Eleri, you know how difficult tis to get permits to fly over Simurgh, even with our own airplanes.'

'Yes, sorry Unkling,' she said.

Yes, they'd *both* forgotten about that, thought Mike.

Muggredge's voice, sounding tinny and faint on the mono-channel speaker, said, 'I am thinking we shall just have to look harder to find the evidence we need. E'en then, a permit is up to the government "Inner Committee". Not just Arbella. She does not rule by decree, even though we sometimes have reason to think such.' He sounded as though he might be chuckling. It was hard to tell.

'A permit could just be the start,' he continued, 'and we are unlikely to get a permit to overfly the whole island, even in a plane. There is an airstrip a few lints inland from the North West coast. Sorry, Mike, I should say, *a few kilometres* inland. If we have to go further in t'will have to be on foot. And you know about the wildlife, Eleri. The birds, I am meaning.'

'Just a second Professier,' said Mike, 'I'm told Simurgh is over 10,000 kilometres from the mainland, isn't it? So how can your planes reach that far? They'd have to refuel, wouldn't they?'

'Yes Mike,' he said, 'for our planes are not so big as to carry enough fuel, but believe it or not, we arint quite as backward as you might think. There is a refuelling station – on a very small island mid stage to Simurgh. That is just the detail, Mike. We first have to get that permit, so, if you are not minding, praps I can ask if you would like to continue the search of the papers? To help Eleri?'

'Yes, of course, Professier,' said Mike, smiling inwardly and feeling relieved, as well as elated, when he saw how Eleri suddenly beamed but he tried to keep the signs from her. That was how he was going to have to play this one. She was not like most women back home.

'Thankly so much Mike,' said Muggredge. 'Well, so sorry but I must go now, my childers. Be having fun – but not too much.'

Yeah, right, thought Mike.

****

Ssanyu Ebazza left her private quarters aboard The Monsoon, a large suite situated in a block on the inner surface of the ship's rotating torus, ready to begin the day's work. As she reached the door of the "secondary bridge", further along the torus, her com unit chimed.

'Statton here, Captain. I'm on the Observation deck. There's something I think you need to see. Where should I send it?'

'Patch it into my station on the bridge, Commander,' she said, 'I'm nearly there anyways.'

When she entered the bridge, the other officers stood to attention. 'At ease, gentilhoms,' she said and sat at her command seat, one of several dotted around the ship. She saw that the report from Statton was ready to roll up on the widescreen comp unit in front of her. She said to the unit, 'Proceed with Statton update,' whereupon a series of multi-coloured graphics and sets of data flashed onto the large screen, sliding across it in streams.

'Is that what I think it is, Commander? Another CME?' she said, as a holo' of the Executive Officer's head popped up from her station.

'Yes Captain. It's bigger than the last one but fortunately, it's coming off the surface of Ra that's pointed away from Oceanus. It won't hit the planet.'

'Fortunate indeed.'

'Shall I patch this through to the Admiral?'

'No, I don't think so. He's still recovering from the synthetic tissue graft into his back. Leave it for now, Lieutenant.'

'Aye, aye. But there's more, Captain.'

'Go ahead.'

'There was an unauthorised transmission from the planet – to *this ship*, at 02.10 hours ship-time. We know it was unauthorised because it used an unapproved encryption. It was a hyper-narrow wave burst. About a second long. We picked up some of it but not enough to enable full decryption. Just garbled nonsense.'

'Encrypted messages from the planet?' Ebazza said, her face creasing in surprised puzzlement, 'and carefully done it seems. So, where did it come from, Commander?'

'Somewhere in Ramnisos. Can't be more specific - and we don't know who it was intended for on the ship.'

'Really? It seems like we need to tighten up on all comms with the planet, Lieutenant, and keep a look out for anything else like this - but I'm sure you've got that in hand? Put out some feelers amongst the crew too. I'd like to know who's communicating with person or persons, unknown, in Ramnisos. Out.'

She looked up. There were eight other officers on the bridge. All ears were "flapping" at that moment.

'As you were, gentilhoms,' she said. She left the bridge and once outside, alone, she verbalised a private log entry on her wristcom, 'This is not good. I cannot bother the Admiral about it right now. Make a diary entry to speak to him in 48 hours. So, which crewmember wants to have secret comms with an unknown source on the planet? And why?'

Interlude

Signal Evaluations

The giant sphere of the alien ship swept along in its wide orbit of the orange-yellow star which lay closest to the exit point from which the vessel had materialised into "Real Space". The glow of that dwarf sun glinted off the ultra-smooth, glass-like, surface of the ship – but the star was still distant. At such a remote location and at its current, relatively low speed, the speed it needed to stay in orbit around that star and not fly loose, the vessel would take nearly ten thousand years, in human terms, to complete one elliptical orbit.

Inside the craft Demetia's thoughts flowed into the collective consciousness of all the beings in the sentience module,

The network extensions have been released successfully. We are grateful.

A chorus of the thoughts of many conjoined beings echoed the feeling,

Yes, the Super adjunct advises us the release was uneventful and the extensions are splitting into their multiple robotinoids. All that should be, is well. We may now unjoin – until union is needed again at the time of full interaction with the star we named Qardestriana-chonis-ektra, so many ages ago, when we were primal.

At that moment a massive, pancake shaped, organic being, flame-orange in colour, descended on a rope-like loop of body tissue, from a hollow in the centre of the domed ceiling far above. As it sank toward the beings below it expanded outwards by flattening itself into a wide, thin disc. Then it extended fourteen gossamer thin tentacles so that they came to hang above a similar number of metallic cones which rose upwards from the perimeter of the floor of the vast chamber. The orange being began to glow, its internal brains, nerves and vascular system, all becoming visible, in dark silhouette, through its outer membranes.

In an interval of time that humans would have measured in mere milliseconds, the mental connections of all the other beings, as a group, were separated from each-other, and the gigantic hovering being stopped glowing, then slowly receded back to its niche high above.

After a thousandth of a second; a very long time by the standards of these creatures, Percepticon's thoughts flowed back into Hermoptica, the multiple connections on the floor of the chamber having been restored, *Through the universal connection I glimpsed that which is known about the Others, here at Qardestriana, gleaned from ongoing translations of their electromagnetic emissions.*

I have glimpsed it too - but do not fully appreciate. They truly are primitive. They lack cohesion. They may be dangerous, flowed Hermoptica.

They appear to be bipedal, hairy, placentals. They have large complex brains and a tribal social system which is hierarchical, flowed Percepticon, *And they live in familial goups, which accumulate in still larger aglomerations. They co-operate through an economic system based on trade and exchange.*

Then they cannot be of consequence to us, intruded Demetia, his platform sliding to join them from afar, his cyber links connecting to theirs in microseconds.

All sentience is of consequence to us, came a gentle reproach from Percepticon, *but I feel your meaning is that they cannot harm our intent.*

We do not yet know how they arrived at this place, flowed Hermoptica, with a mere hint of alarm.

The Superadjunct has but now announced: it has located their origin. It is a yellow dwarf star, marginally more massive than Qardestriana… and its distance is but a short step for us. The Superadjunct assures us that they, like us, are not able to transcend the Universal electromagnetic speed limit in real space. So, it seems it is still not known how these beings arrived here, but it was not as we did, flowed Demetia's thoughts.

Then we are indeed grateful, flowed the other two, *for they evidently do not use the dimensional shift to Complex Space, as we do. But their propulsion technique and their presence here is still a mystery and so more observation is needed,* thought Percepticon and Hermoptica together.

Demetia warned again,

The individuals that comprise these beings and their social groupings, appear to be completely disconnected - each one from the other. They are singular biological units!

Minor but perceptible tremors of horror ran through the two other beings. Demetia continued, undeterred, *I too, am alarmed, for this implies they do not understand each-other. They are disparate and emotionally volatile. Some of the other emissions we have lately intercepted give rise to the interpretation that they are capable of exceptional aggression. There is a probability of 0.898 that they will try to intervene in our purpose here.*

They are lost and are to be pitied, flowed Percepticon.

Chapter 14

DEAD ENDS

Mike despaired of the fact that he was back in that damnatious library, this time on his own and engaged, yet again, in a boring and probably pointless exercise. It was the way he felt all of his endeavours had turned out down here; toiling on what he considered a mostly hopeless endeavour. He had been told he would be joined by someone called "Danile Senwosret Hermington", apparently a junior, but gifted, palaeontologist on Muggredge's team. At least it would help to have a geologist search for Lisdon's papers and comp records. But it was now 1.40, in so called "mid tidings", and no sign of him, or any other help.

Mike had contacted the ship to ask after Tenak, the good news being that the Admiral was making a speedy recovery from the second of two operations. He was still resting in one of the med bays. He also learned that all the injured locals who'd been taken up to the ship from Ramnisos, had recovered, were discharged and had been ferried back to the surface. That must surely have been the ride of a lifetime for most of them, he mused.

He had also asked the ship's secondary comp-nexus; the "minor AI", to make a search for the name Andriwnes Dar-Lisdon, through all accessible databases, including the latest updates from the Home System's Solarnet and the Navy Nexus. That meant, of course, that it could only include updates received just before the ship entered the interstellar conduit. The AI had taken as long as a half a second to analyse and report back, saying that a thorough search of every possible source had turned up – nothing. So much for that. With a sigh Mike had turned back to sifting through yet another large box stuffed to the rims with papers.

Thirty minutes later he was about to take a break when a tall young man breezed in through the door opposite him. The newcomer muttered something unintelligible and sat at a computer console, his back turned toward Mike.

'Sorry, I didn't hear you,' said Mike.

The man glanced over his shoulder, 'I said I 'm guessing yet I'm a taddli-bit late.'

'Danile Senwosret Hermington, I presume?' said Mike, amused at the man's flippancy, but also noting he'd used the contraction, to "I'm", an unusual thing down here.

The newcomer just nodded and continued to log onto the comp unit, but Mike persisted, 'We haven't been introduced. My name's, Mike Tanniss.'

Without turning to face him, Hermington said, 'Yeah manry, I know who you are. I was briefed by Eleri.'

'Well Mer Hermington, both Eleri and I have looked at the stuff on those units you're working on, and we couldn't find anything of significance.'

'I know you both looked, but still so there's nothing like some fresh eye pairs, is there?' came from Hermington, his back still to Mike.

'I admit I'm not used to these ancient systems, Mer Hermington,' Mike persisted, 'but I'm certain Eleri is. I don't know that there's any point to duplicating her work, is there?' He was starting to feel his patience ebbing from him. What was the point, he wondered?

'Mayhap she still missed something.'

Hermington continued to scan the comp screen and Mike thought it best not to bother with further conversation. Ten minutes later Hermington stopped and turned to face Mike, who was shuffling through his tenth full box of the day.

'Look, manry-matey, I'm sorry,' said Hermington, 'but I am now thinking we might have started off on a bad turning. My fluffry. I mean, fault. Sorry. And yet I'm sorry I was late, but I'm a member of the local Redara-Bungist sect and I was yet stuck at the local shrine much longer than had so-thought. I was annoy-ed.'

Mike gazed at him. What the feg was a "Redara Bungist sect"? He opted not to go there. Hermington was maybe a little older than him, probably around 24 or 25, and was a little shorter, but he was also slightly stockier. He looked very fit. Mike wondered why everyone on this world seemed so lithe, even brawny. Must be the outdoors life. Hermington's elliptical face didn't seem sharp or severe, but he sported a nose even longer than his own, something Mike was glad about at least. But the man's eyes seemed to glow with amiable humour. Not exactly the sort of person he had imagined, given the man's initial behaviour. Just waggishness, wondered Mike? Bad day?

'Okay Danile, I'm glad you said that,' Mike said, 'about the the bad start, I mean. And it's okay. I was wondering if you spoke to Eleri recently? I don't suppose you know when she might be back?'

'I rang her at her parentia's home last night. I think she is planning to be back at even-tides.

'So, she went to see them last night?' said Mike, his eyebrows lifting with surprise. 'She didn't let me have the phone number,' he continued. 'I would have liked to have spoken to her.'

'Yet, why would she, Mike? My understanding is she does not know you so well. Still and such, she and I have been colleagry for some years.'

Mike started to bristle again. So, what if this mascla had known Eleri a long time?

'Is that right?' Mike said. 'How can you and she have been *colleagues* for so long? You only look about … 22, or something?'

'I am 22 deedly. And I was one of her students, manry. Star student, in so-fact. T'was when she used to teach in junior college. I went there when I was 16. I was …let us be saying, an "early developo" in the studying of the natural histories.'

Given the way he spoke of her Mike wondered whether this man and Eleri had something else they shared now, beyond being just colleagues.

'Anyways, that's yet why I decided to go over these comp records,' Hermington continued, 'yet I quite often pick up things other people miss, including Eleri.'

What a whipper-snape, thought Mike. 'Oh, really? Sounds like a great talent,' he said, a degree of acid colouring his tone. Then he returned to his own papers, but he glimpsed the shade of a frown from Hermington.

After another half hour Hermington turned to him and said, 'I'm a-wondering if it might be possible for you to make a search for Lisdon in the Home System itself? That is where he went, ist not?'

'So I'm told,' replied Mike, smugly, 'but I already thought about that. The ship's AI drew a blank.'

'Oh, so I see,' said Hermington, 'but yetways I was thinking more of a *search* inside the Home System itself.'

Mike was going to enjoy this. His brows furrowed with mock severity.

'You aren't serious, are you? Have you any idea what would be involved? The only way to do *that* would be to send a probe all the way back through a conduit – at massive expense, by way. And then – since there are *billions* of people living in the Home System the only way would be to search the usable e-nets. Someone in the Home System would have to be engaged to oversee it … and because sensitive material is only accessible by a few, that might prove impossible.

'And Lisdon's whereabouts would not be on any of the main nets, anyway, otherwise the ship would know about it. And a lot of people, from the government *security services* by the way, would have to initiate searches through any separate covert, "underground" planetary databases in the Solar System. That would have to include any for the Earth, Mars, the Moon, the Titan base, plus those in the asteroid belt communities. Not to mention the floating habitats. They probably wouldn't be able to identify more than a few hundred. This Lisdon fella-chap could be anywhere. He might be dead in a ditch or whatever. And we still wouldn't be able to find out.'

'Okaiyo, okaiyo, I am supposing so,' said Hermington, his face registering surprise, like that of a small boy caught eating banned sweets. 'Yet sorry, manry,' he continued, 'I do accept I did not think it through nuff-much. I'm not very familiar with the Home System.'

Well, that was a more amenable reaction than he expected to his "lecture", thought Mike, who smiled and rejoined, this time as amiably as he could, 'Yeah, I suppose so and, by the way, you're not the only one on this planet who isn't familiar with the Home System.' Mike smiled. He would not rub this lesson in.

A few minutes later, when he caught Hermington staring into space, Mike said, 'Look, this task is "like a fusion sled to galaxy's edge".'

At Hermington's puzzled look Mike said, 'Forget it. Figure of speech. The point is, we need to find a different tack. This ship is doomed to founder.'

'What do you suggest - Mer Tanniss?'

'Don't know, but I do know we're not getting anywhere in this place – at conduit speed.'

'That is not very helpful, really. I wish Eleri was here now,' said Hermington. That provoked another sharp response from Mike.

'I thought you knew better than her?' he said, his brows knitting, then said, 'But she isn't here, so it's down to us.'

'I did not yet say I knew "better than her". Never would I suggest that. Eleri is a great scholastica and a very nice femna, in personry.'

'Yes, she is – whatever you said.' For a few seconds both men glared at each-other, as if each were sizing the other up, intellectually at least.

Mike wondered if Hermington, though younger than him, might have been had enough insight to tag onto what was going on in the background; Mike's attraction to Eleri and his nascent – incipient – relationship with her. He hoped not, but he soon realised that the guy had picked up the vibes because he suddenly asked, quite brazenly,

'Please be telling me if you are so-interested in Eleri, in romancio?'

Mike was quite clear as to what he meant, and he was taken aback. He said, defensively, 'I … maybe. I can't really … I don't think I should say.'

'Ah, manry. That yet does tell me the answer. It is alrighting. I shall not intrude more-so. It's just that she and I are quite-so open 'bout such things. We are, as you canst see, very close.'

Mike's heart seemed to drop through his stomach, as he said, 'So, you ... you're an item. I mean you're ...'

'I know what you didst mean. But no. No, Mike, we arint. She did make a pass at me some time past. She wouldst not admit so.'

What a cheeky gimbo, thought Mike, but Hermington jumped to clarify for him, saying, with a good-natured smile, 'I canst see what you do think. You mabberhead. I do not feel that way about *any* womanry, Mike. No femna at all. Ever.'

'Ah. I see,' said Mike. Inwardly he sighed with relief. He smiled then at Hermington but said, 'Okay, enough. I don't think we ought to be talking anymore about the femna in her absence.'

Hermington nodded his assent but said, 'You are right. I just thought I should be – clearing the airs. I think we did get off to a bad turning. What say, "we turn again"? And by the by, Mike, I shall not be mentioning this teensy discussion with her. If you are so interested to pursue, then I leave that to you to so deal with, yet. Correct?'

'Correct,' said Mike, 'but it doesn't alter the fact that we're getting nowhere with this job.' He chuckled awkwardly for a moment, then said, 'Danile, I noticed you seemed a bit dewy eyed when you spoke about the Home System, or am I being daft?'

'Daft? What ... Oh, I see. No, not really. I've been interested in going to the Home System for years. I applied to study on Earth but didnar get it.'

'That's news, coming from someone on this planet. No-one seems interested in the Home System at all. Why do you want to study there?'

'Better qualification, for a start and ... tis just, well, there's so much *more* to see there. What am I? I am yet a geolrist. More, I am interested in fossil life forms. The fossil assemblages so on Earth are ... huge. Incredible. Not anywhere near as much on Oceanus Mike, believe me.'

'So it seems. Professier Muggredge talked about life flourishing here – before something happened to wipe out most of it, but there must be plenty of fossils from before then, surely?'

'Well, yes, a lot, I'm guessing, but much of the fossil holding strata is inaccessible, Mike. A lot of the continental rock is relatively new and uplifted by the last set of tectonica, sorry, I mean tectonic movements. Much is under the water as well, down in rock of the continental shelves, but there are *very* few permits to study that. Conservation laws will not allow it. There is much on Simurgh but tis difficult to get permits for that too, as you do know. The stuff we have is fantastic, at least for outsiders who yet have not seen anything like it, but then, I have not *seen* the stuff on Earth. Just phots. Not for real. And more is always being discovered there, all the time.'

'I need to ask you this Danile, but do you accept what we … that is, the Home System, says is going to happen on this planet?'

Hermington looked deeply puzzled. 'But so I do, Mike. Didst not think so? Why else am I here? And yes, I know that I will get to see the fossil collections on Earth much sooner than I did think. And for wrong reasons. That does not fill me with glee, Mike.' Hermington cast his eyes down.

'No, of course not.' He felt sad that he'd reminded this young man about the coming destruction, but he was right. That was why they were both there, in that library.

**

After more exhaustive searches Hermington turned to Mike. 'I think we should look in the other library, Mike.'

'Other library?' cried Mike.

'Yepry. Did you not know? This is the geolry library – but the biolry library is down the hall. It has only 'bout 150 boxes of stuff,' said Hermington, grinning at Mike's obvious discomfit.

'But we've already searched about 200 boxes in this place.'

'I'm wizzlying you Mike. I am yet pleased to say, only about 50 of those box files canst possibly be relevant in the other library. I think I will make a start there, anyways. Up to you, manry, if you want to join me.' With that he stood and marched out of the room. Mike stayed put for a moment, trying to summon up more patience, then followed.

After four more hours of further searching, during which the two went for no fewer than three Kaffee breaks in the local shop, they heard a loud ringing noise from the hallway. Still unused to the telephones Mike sat unmoving, not fully realising what it was. Hermington waited a couple of seconds and said, 'Well, I am guessing I shall have to get that?' and marched out. Mike could hear him talking on the wallphone he remembered was situated in the hallway, but couldn't hear any detail. After a few minutes Hermington popped in and said, 'Tis for you, Mike Tanniss.'

Mike was genuinely surprised. He was even more surprised to hear Eleri's voice on the "other end" of the phone.

'How are you Mike?' she asked, in tones which filled him with pleasure. Mike's day suddenly seemed to brighten exponentially. It was as though someone had turned on a light in a huge, dark hangar.

'I'm fine, just fine. It's so good to hear from you Eleri. So good. Where are you?'

'In Janitra. I just got back. I hear your searches are going thorough-like, and, of obviousness, I see you have met Dani.'

'Very funny Eleri. Yes, I've met "Dani". When can I expect to see you again?'

'Strange-such you should be saying that.'

'Why?'

'Well, I wondered if that dinner invitation was still open – for tonight?'

At last, he thought. Thank the galaxies. He hoped she wouldn't invite Hermington as well.

Chapter 15

SURVEILLANCE

Within a week of Mike's dinner date with Eleri, which he shared exclusively with her, the two of them had joined up with Hermington and continued to search for the elusive papers written by the mysterious Lisdon. Tenak contacted Mike, by holo', to say he was finally up and about but still on med' leave.

*

Mike was alone in his room at the Central Hotel in Janitra, his domicile for the last two weeks, when Tenak buzzed him. The holo-vid showed the Admiral dressed, disquietingly, he thought, in full, gaudy nightclothes, sitting in his armchair in his large cabin.

'I've heard from Muggredge,' said Tenak's 3D image. The Admiral leaned forward in his chair, a glint in his eye. Mike thought that Tenak's bulky robes, with their long, ornately decorated, drooping sleeves, like some Victorian era nightgown, seemed as obviously unfashionable as the rest of the man's off duty apparel. He said nothing, smiled thinly and said, 'Well, we haven't been able to reach him recently. Even Eleri was surprised. What's he been up to?'

'Quite a lot, Mike. He's even started contacting me by *video* link. We set it up for him, of course. I think we'll set him up with some holo-link feeds, soon. Anyway, seems he has a friend in academic circles. Someone with close contacts in the government's "Central Policy Committee". He's persuaded this friend to talk to some of Arbella's ministers about a new initiative he's come up with. The idea here, is to try a political tack, given that you and your new colleagues have come up with zipp-null. No offence intended.'

'None taken. Go on, Arkas, though I can't say I get excited about any so-called political "wisdom" on this rock.'

'Yeah, I know what you mean, but I think this has promise. Might be the last chance, Mike. And it's worked already, up to a point. This friend of Muggredge has already persuaded a number of members of the Policy Committee to agree to a proposal to be put to the Devian Forum House, their *Curia*, as they call it. It's their Congress or Parliament or whatever. The proposal will be for an Interstellar Conference – an Inquiry into the issue of Ra's instability – and the current threat to life on Oceanus. Well, Mike? You don't look impressed. That's excellent news, isn't it?'

'It is?'

'Of course, it is. Of course. The whole Policy Committee hasn't agreed yet but Muggredge thinks they will. If they do and it goes to the Curia ... You don't look convinced.'

'Well, ... carry on Arkas, anyway.'

'As I said, if the Curia agrees to the proposal it'll mean a formal *interstellar* debate on the whole thing. That'd mean all interested parties, *including scientists from Earth* – and Oceanus, plus social philosophers, politicians, community leaders, whatever, will all have the chance to make submissions. Including the Meta-teleos of course. They'll have their full say,' Tenak stopped for a moment, a frown creasing his forehead, then said, 'You still don't look pleased Mike.'

'I suppose the operative word there, was – "if". If this ... if that. Listen, I'm sorry, Arkas. I don't mean to dampen your fusion-drives but like you said, this thing has to be approved by the whole Forum House, doesn't it? Didn't you say the Policy Committee hasn't agreed it yet?"

'Yeah, I know, I know, but it's still a step forward, Mike. Small but significant. Remember, *no-one* was listening to us just a short while ago. And this probably wouldn't have happened if *you* hadn't spoken to the Professier like you did. Now, you actually look surprised. Yes, that's down to you, Mike. Muggredge spoke very highly of you.'

'Wonders will never cease,' said Mike, almost to himself, chuckling, 'Glad to know you think I've been of assistance – for once.'

'I am too,' Tenak said with a sly chuckle and added, 'but, in fact, you have been. You – and that young woman you've been working with – have done very well. She seems a stellar treasure. You guys have put in a lot of work recently. That's commendable.'

'Stop it, Arkas. You're starting to embarrass me.'

'I mean it, Mike. Look, why don't you take a sabbatical or something? Take a few weeks. Go get a look around Oceanus. Use some of that downtime you wanted. The Policy Committee meets again in a few weeks and after that – who knows? The Forum House might not discuss it very quickly anyways.'

Mike's jaw nearly dropped, 'Um, thanks Arkas. Now that's what I call good news. Really good. But you'll need to transmit some funds to me. The Central Hotel is getting expensive.'

'Sure, sure. You don't need to stay there anyway. Start getting around that planet a bit more. Try taking that Eleri Nambrey with you. Muggredge says you two work well with each-other and ... I can guess how *you* might feel about her.'

'It's Eleri Nefer-Ambrell, Arkas. But she doesn't use the "Nefer" bit. And thanks for the suggestion but I think it'll be more like her taking *me* around the planet, don't you?'

'Sure thing, Mike,' chuckled Tenak. 'No problem. Just one thing. Make sure you treat her right, Mike.'

'Of course, Arkas.'

'Don't give me that sort of look. I mean it, Mike. She's the niece of Professier Muggredge *and* the President. If you mess her around, we'll both get thrown off this planet.'

Mike huffed but he knew Tenak was right. He'd not managed to get Eleri into bed as yet, but, strangely, he had never really felt the time was right. After their dinner date he had walked her to the autocar station, in an extremely old-fashioned way. It seemed to be what people still did here. He'd simply kissed her hand and bid her goodnight. This was seriously not like him! Perhaps he was turning a new page? Maybe, but probably not.

'Stop worrying Arkas,' he said. 'You don't change, do you?'

'I'm worried you won't, said the Admiral. 'Tenak out.'

****

Darik Yorvelt watched Indrius Brocke, on a monitor, as his colleague entered the vestibule to his office suite set three hundred floors above ground level, deep in the maw of the "New-York and Easternboard City State". He went out to greet him, his face heavy with concern.

'See that we're not disturbed, please,' he muttered to his aide. He waved his friend into his spacious inner office, a light and airy space with a domed, blast proof, alumino-glass alloy roof, giving unimpeded views of a sky of steel blue.

'Good to see you again, Indry,' said the secretary General.

'And you, Dar. And you,' said Brocke, a grin of smug satisfaction spreading across his face.

'You look happy, Indry.'

'Of course, Dar. I have some great news,' said Brocke, as he thrust out his arms and gently clasped his superior's shoulders. He continued, 'I wanted this meeting in person because I know you're lairy of holo-coms. And I'm so glad to give you the news now, Dar. The truth is, I've managed to pull together the resources needed to get the fleet of ferries built. Well, to make a start anyway. In fact, construction should get underway within a couple of weeks.'

'That's marvellous news, Indry. Is this something to do with your special "action group"?'

'Absolutely. The action group sub-committee I formed – after the Exec' Committee gave their blessing. Yes, I've secured a ready supply of duralamium alloys from some of the colonies on the Moon – and a couple of the City States on Earth, that are super-loyal to us. We've also got a large contingent of skilled people and a whole tranch of auto-bots, from – believe it or not, Mars. They're all starting shipments – within days.'

'Would that be to Lagrange Point five in the Earth's orbit?'

'You're well informed, Dar.'

'Of course. You can't keep me completely in the dark, Indry. And I'm aware you've already sequestered the use of the rigging for the proposed Floating Habitat number 4. It's been moved into position, hasn't it? That was quick work.'

'Sort of, Dar. It's certainly on its way. I was glad of your support on that one. Without it the Exec Committee might not have gone with the idea. At least now, there'll be a framework for the space dock to take shape. There've been a few objections, but we have to do this. By the way, I think you've stolen my thunder, Dar. Never mind.' He laughed.

'Sorry about that Indry but, as for objections, I suppose we might have guessed Jonsuh Jai would have to say something about it. She's also not happy about the circumvention of the strikes, on Earth.'

'I know. You didn't want to break the strikes, Dar, so this was the only alternative. I'm also glad we're allowed to go forward with making all this a covert op.'

'How are you dealing with that, Indry?'

'I've had my aides – and the action group, promulgate the story that we're going ahead with the contruction of new Navy cruisers, mainly for peace keeping duties *within* the Home System. I know there are questions being asked about *why* we need to do that, etcetera. But we just have to go with it for now.'

'I've got the feeling that, even with security drones and bouys around the construction platform – and putting working crews on lockdown, we won't be able to keep this secret for long, Indry.'

'Agreed. But we'll have to cross that star-bridge when we come to it. At least we're making a start on the ferries. And the refitting of most of the Navy ships is well underway.'

'I'm sorry to drown your hopes in sour wine, Dar, but Xander has given us more details of his analysis.'

'And?'

'And, he says that he *already* considered some emergency measures we might institute – like building the ferries in double-quick time, refitting the Navy super-fast, and so on. He still says he thinks we'll fail to get the whole population off Oceanus.'

Yorvelt looked downcast as he spoke. Brocke continued,

'I suppose I'm not surprised, Dar. But what other choice do we have? We can't let artificial intelligence machines distract us. I think it's one of those occasions we'll have to adjust and react to changing circ's. Amend our plans as we go along.'

'I suppose you're right, Indry. Of course. By the way, how's the situation with the Antarctica?'

'That's good too, Dar. I'm very pleased to say the ship is repaired and on its way to rendezvous with the Earth. Shouldn't be more than a week. But she'll need another week or so to restock, refuel, and so on.'

'And what about an Ambassador?'

'Well, I tried for the best …but, well …'

'What's the matter? Why that look on your face? Spit it out Indry. It's not like you to buzz round in orbit.' Yorvelt's eyes narrowed.

'Don't worry, Dar. I have indeed found an Ambassador to go to Oceanus. My aides had a hard time tracking down anyone who was actually … available, but they managed to contact this one. It's … Sliverlight,' Brocke winced slightly as he spoke the name.

'Oh no! Not Sliverlight, Indry? But why? Why him?'

'He's the best we've got, who's actually free, Dar. All of the others are fully engaged and far out in the boondocks. Even Bradfield, and Durbham. They're both much too deep in the system to get them back soon enough. As I said, Sliverlight is available and he is eighth in seniority in the Diplomatic ranks, after all.'

Yorvelt exhaled heavily, 'Yes, I know Bradfield is in the middle of conducting negotiations on the Titan base, but where's Mes Durbham?'

'She's on a research base on some rock out near Neptune.'

'Neptune?' said Yorvelt, sounding disbelieving, 'so what's she doing out there?'

'She's an astrophysicist in her spare time – and she is entitled to spare time, Dar.'

'We have the power to order her back to duty, Indry,' grumbled Yorvelt.

'I know. We tried to raise her, but we couldn't and she's about eight weeks away from us right now. At least Sliverlight is nearly here. I'm sorry Dar. I know you and Sliverlight don't get on with each-other.'

'That's not really the point, Indry. That mascla nearly ruined our negotiations with the Lunar Breakaway Coalition – when they threatened to leave the Alliance. As I recall, *you* were the one who had to take over. And he left negotiations with the Hindu Floating Habitat in a poor state. And I understand the asteroid miners weren't too impressed with him either. He's not called "Sliverlight the Obfuscator" for nothing, Indry.'

'I know but let's not be unfair, Dar. He did help – a lot – in our negotiations with Lunar Prime, five years ago – and with the Mars colonies a few years before that. Give him a chance, Dar. If he was as bad as you suggest then we should have had him stripped him of his status long ago. But we didn't. There was a reason for that. Besides, he's all we've got at the moment and he'll be ready to go to Oceanus within … a few days. You've been itching to send the Antarctica. It can go very soon.'

'Alright Indry. Alright,' said Yorvelt, sighing heavily, 'and I suppose we must be "fair" to him. Alright, send the Antarctica with – the galaxies help us – Yardis Octavian Sliverlight.

****

The twin barrel shaped deep space shuttle, with its relatively small torus held out on spindly stanchions from its mid-section, docked slowly and carefully with the number 5 docking bay on Collins Station, itself flying in permanent lunar orbit, 400km above the Moon's pumice grey surface. Although a deep space vehicle, the shuttle was small, with capacity for only five fare-paying occupants and three crew but, on this flight there had been only one passenger: Yardis O. Sliverlight.

Sliverlight, a towering individual, aged in his 50s, but looking much older than his years, now floated in a twisted, almost foetal, position, as he moved through the narrow transfer tunnel connecting the ship to the station. An inherently clumsy, ungainly person, he had been advised to keep his body, wearing his baggy grey coveralls, as straight as possible, and to point himself forward so he could enter the station comfortably and safely. But he had evidently failed to listen to any of this and, as a result, collided with various tunnel collars and rings along the way through. But the foresight of the station's original designers meant that these items had been clad long ago with substantial padding. That didn't mean unwary or awkward passengers couldn't be bruised debarking from or boarding shuttles, as evidenced by the painful grunting sounds frequently issued by Sliverlight, throughout the process.

He clambered out of the tunnel into a large reception chamber where a station worker, wearing standard smart blue single-suit, welcomed him. The man tried to help Sliverlight to orientate himself.

'Please remove your hands from my waist, young man,' said Sliverlight and, grumbling loudly, continued, 'I hate microgravity. I've been stuck in this state for hours now. I'd just like to get into the rotating part of this station, so I can get back to some semblance ... of normality.'

'Yes, of course sir,' said the station worker, grimacing at some of Sliverlight's erratic movements. 'Please enter the elevator tube behind me,' he said, 'and it will take you straight to the torus. At the bottom you will be asked to produce your credentials, all necessary I D, and submit to the usual scans and searches before you can enter the main torus ring. It shouldn't take more than a few minutes, sir.'

The Ambassador glared at the man from narrow, red rimmed eyes which appeared like bleary slots in his long, unshaven face, puffy from the trials of his journey.

'I know that, you idiot,' said Sliverlight. 'Do you think I've never done this sort of thing before?' He brushed past the man and floated, awkwardly, forward into the empty elevator capsule waiting for him, although he did remember to point his long, flipper-like feet in the direction of travel of the capsule. As the solid door of the capsule closed behind him the station worker gazed at a nearby colleague and made an obscene gesture at the closed door; his assessement of Sliverlight, made crystal clear. With an incredulous look on his face, he mouthed silently to a colleague, 'Is that supposed to be an *Ambassador*?'

Sliverlight sat in what was, for him, cramped conditions, inside the elevator capsule, which moved very sedately, down, or, according to your point of view, up, toward the torus. The slow speed was deliberately meant to avoid problems adjusting to the centripetal forces transmitted from the rotating torus to which it was attached. It also allowed an occupant to get used to the gradually returning sensation of gravity. The capsule slowed more in its tube, as it neared its destination, eventually coming to a gentle stop, at which time Sliverlight's feet were planted firmly on the "floor" of the torus.

On exiting the elevator, Sliverlight tried to stand and walk - but collapsed almost immediately. A senior security guard was on hand to grab him, 'Whoa, sir,' said the guard. 'Steady there. Your body is used to microgravity. Didn't they warn you about this in the hub? You were supposed to sit inside for at least 10 minutes.' He smiled a greeting at Sliverlight. It was not returned. He continued, 'We also have magneto-sleds here to help you walk, if you wish, at least for the next couple of hours. You're looking very pale, sir. Do you need some med help?'

'No, I'm fine. Just fine. I just need some rest, that's all,' said Sliverlight, ashen and stony faced.

'Please just sit in the security booth over there, sir. Just for a few minutes,' said the security man, gesturing toward an alumina-glass booth a few metres away, 'so we can scan you properly. Your total luggage is one large bag, I understand? That's being scanned in the docking module, so it will be with you shortly.'

'Very well, Lieutenant. Is there a refresher I can use up here?'

'I'm sorry sir. We need to get security checks done first but there's a toilet refresher unit, just the other side, after we clear you.'

'Lieutenant, I'm sorry if I sound like a bit of a grumbleton but it's just that I'm getting a little old for shooting around the solar system. I hope you can understand.'

'Yes sir, of course. My father is in his hundred and twenties. I know microgravity plays havoc with his bones. Still travels though. We're nearly done now sir. Just need to carry out a light body search.'

'Is that really necessary, Lieutenant? I am a *senior* Home System Ambassador. I'm hardly likely to be smuggling drugs or something. I have the confidence of both the Secretary General and the Deputy.'

'I'm sorry sir. We aren't allowed to make exceptions.'

A deep and commanding voice, then,

'That's alright Lieutenant. You can dispense with protocol on this one occasion.'

'Oh, sorry, I didn't know you were there, Mer Dervello, sir,' said the security man, turning to face the Deputy Secretary General's chief aide, 'Even so, I'm not sure about this, sir.'

'I said it's okay,' said Dervello, very firmly. The tone of voice said that its owner was not used to being thwarted. 'Don't worry,' he continued, 'I'll take full responsibility. You can see he's come through all the scans. There's the "Full and Safe Clearance" sign.' Dervello grinned at the Lieutenant, who, with reluctance written all over his face, waved Sliverlight through to the other side of the barriers. Dervello followed him, smoothly and silently.

'Thank you, Mer Dervello,' said Sliverlight, turning to glance at his companion, when they had reached a turn in the corridor beyond security, 'Thank you for your intervention.'

'Why?' said Dervello, the smile completely gone from his face, a muscular jaw set as though it was made of concrete. 'You're not trying to hide something are you? I can always put you back through security,' said Dervello.

'Of course not, Mer Dervello. Of course not. I just meant you saved me the embarrassment of a body search. No-one likes those, do they?' The Ambassador continued, with strain evident in his voice, 'When do I have to board the Antarctica? Not for at least 24 hours, I hope?'

'It's 21 hours in fact,' said Dervello, 'but I'd like to have a moment with you first, to debrief you fully. If that is alright with you.' Dervello's demeanour suggested this was a command rather than a polite request.

'Really? Is that necessary? I did read the docs you transmitted to the shuttle and believe me when I say I'm conversant with all the necessary …'

Dervello gave him a look that could melt lead set in concrete and said, tersely, 'I said I have to debrief you - *fully*. Meet me in conference room B, just down the corridor, in 15 minutes, please, Mer Ambassador. That should give you plenty of time to freshen up. By the way, please address me as Mr, not Mer. I despise these "new era" phrases.'

'Of course. If you wish. Looking forward to our meeting,' said Sliverlight, his voice catching in his throat.

****

A few minutes after his encounter with Dervello, the Ambassador stood in a very small toilet facility, sited a long way from the security area and any other busy areas of the station. As advised by his aides, he had gone straight to male refresher number 3, Hydroponics zone, and hoped that it wasn't occupied. The toilet had been chosen precisely because of its capacity to take only one person at a time.

There was no-one inside when he arrived, so he entered, locked the door behind him, then checked for any hidden cameras or other surveillance devices. Satisfied, he groped underneath the washhand basin for a tiny package he'd been told would be there. It wasn't. His eyes widened with alarm.

He bent over in the cramped space, as best he could, and tried to search visually but the poor light in the room wouldn't allow him to see into the shadows. Finally, his groping fingers alighted on a minuscule, plastic-like, wallet taped to underneath the furthest reaches of the back of the basin, next to the wall. He pulled it off, examined it, then reached into a concealed pocket inside his flight coveralls, from which he produced a pair of synthetic gloves. He paused and looked at his reflection in the mirror above the wash basin.

'Well, this is it, you old dog,' he said, staring, smiling at his own image, 'let's hope he doesn't detect anything, cos if he does …. you've had it.'

He slipped on the gloves, squinted at the tiny package and tried to rip it open. It resisted at first but finally yielded. In the mirror he could see his face register palpable relief. Tipping the contents into his palm he stared at a tiny rectangle of aluminoplast. It was no more than two millimetres across; a wafer which carried several sets of sophisticated microprocessors and masses of circuitry, designed to record and transmit encrypted video and audio data to the station's own powerful antennae. This would then be re-transmitted several million kilometres, to a secure installation crewed by his associates.

This device was Sliverlight's insurance, planned with the knowledge he would be interviewed by Dervello. One of Sliverlight's associates was a station employee, with full security clearance. He'd also been the one to plant the device.

Sliverlight had never used this equipment before and he was taking a big risk on it functioning properly; to send a covert signal, via the station, by 'piggybacking' on some ordinary, innocent, com signal. After passing via several other stations it would be picked up by Polydorus Debrens, somewhere in the "Free South Eastern France City State", back on Earth. Sliverlight probably wouldn't know whether the subterfuge had been successful until he returned to the Home System, but any recording picked up successfully could be extremely useful.

'I can't erase your recording, so I'm afraid I'll have to abandon you soon, my little friend,' he said to the package, 'somewhere it's safe to do so.'

After squeezing the wafer very gently, as he was required, he waited for the slight vibration he'd been told to expect; a sign that it was activating. He started to bring his palm close to his face, as if he thought he might see something actually working, but before he had completed the action the device buzzed, showing it had activated fully.

Sliverlight looked in the mirror again, held the wafer in his left hand and brought his right hand up to his left eye. He grasped the front of his eye, as gently but as firmly as possible, and turned it. It was wet and his fingers slipped at first, but he was eventually able to unscrew the whole front part of the eye; the part visible to others. He placed it in his right hand. Then he picked up the wafer and inserted it into the back of the artificial organ, using his left thumb and forefinger. The wafer automatically adhered to the sticky, composite, back surface, of the false eye.

Breathing heavily, Sliverlight gazed, with his one real eye, at the gaping cavity of the synthetic organ and muttered to himself, again, 'Good job I decided not to have you replaced with a specially grown eye. I guess I've missed the stereo vision … but you've been of great service to me.' The eye had been made especially for him, at enormous expense and secrecy, designed, as it was, to move exactly as a normal eye would, using modified muscle attachments. The special layers that formed the eyeball were excellent at foiling security sensors, as indeed they had this afternoon. The video wafer on its own was, however, detectable, which was why it had had to be brought in separately, by other means, then stashed in this hiding place. There were a great many very serious risks involved with this gambit, but it was done now. No going back.

****

Dervello sat in his debriefing room and started to rap his knuckles on his low desk, a sure sign, to anyone who knew him, that he was getting impatient. He looked at the guard standing near the metal door and began to say something when a buzzer sounded. The guard operated the door and in walked Sliverlight, looking anxious.

'You're late,' said Dervello and motioned for the Ambassador to sit opposite him. He motioned for the guard to leave. 'See that we're not disturbed,' he barked.

Dervello turned back to Sliverlight, 'I assume you've been told about what we really want you to do at Oceanus?' said the aide.

'I have but …' Sliverlight began.

'I also assume there are no problems? After all, you agreed to do this after my associate primed you, back on the asteroid base. You signed up to it. Remember?'

'Yes,' said the Ambassador. 'Look, I'll tell you what I told her. I'm happy to speak to the Meta-teleos, as you ask. I'm fully aware of the divide between them and the Oceanus government. I'm just not happy to lie about the Home System's data. I'm not a scientist. *They'll see through it.*'

'You dolt!' said Dervello, explosively, flecks of saliva flying. 'We're not asking you to argue about data. You just need to spread a meme, the meme that the Home System has been lying to *them* about the data – purporting to show problems with Ra. You know what I mean by "meme", I take it?'

'Of course I do. A meme is ... the information equivalent of a gene. Like genes, they spread laterally, as well as to succeeding generations. A rumour, I suppose, in old fashioned talk. But I think it's going to take more than a couple of memes to do this job. I don't ...'

'Stop there. I don't believe you're being paid to have opinions, are you?' Dervello slammed his hands flat on his desk and glared fiercely at the man opposite him. 'You're just supposed to do the fegging job – and any other tasks we want you to do while you're out there. Got that ... *sir?*'

'I didn't agree to any more than you've just outlined,' Sliverlight said, almost under his breath, with an expression of alarm plastering his pasty face. Then, more loudly, he said, 'At this rate *I'm* going to be the one who's landed with responsibility for something that could very well be called – an act of terrorism. You do realise it's terrorism, don't you, Mer ... Mr Dervello? There don't have to be bombs or whatever. If we dupe the people of Oceanus into abandoning evacuation – and Ra blows ....' He left the sentence hanging.

There was silence for a few seconds whilst Dervello looked to be deep in thought. The man stroked his smoothly shaven, square, chin thoughtfully, then stood up and paced around slowly, as if considering Sliverlight's words carefully. Without warning, when he was behind Sliverlight, he lunged, grabbing the back of the ambassador's chair and pulling fiercely, tipping the man onto the floor, like a pile of loose clothes. At the top of his voice he screamed at the crumpled figure on the floor, 'I thought I just told you not to analyse the situation! You – have – made – an – agreement! That's all you need to know.'

He walked around to face Sliverlight, who was slowly picking himself up. The Ambassasor looked down at Dervello's feet, rather than up at him, but, reaching down, the aide grasped his victim's jaw, vice-like firmly – and pulled it up sharply, so Sliverlight had to look up at him. 'It sounds to me like you're getting cold feet, *Mer Ambassador*. It's too late for that, I'm afraid. My colleague, Mes Proctinian, obviously didn't make it crystal clear just what's at stake here. So, I will. We're going to take this damnatious Home System Government and throw it out with the trash. The destruction of human civilisation on Oceanus will push us a long way toward that goal - through political and moral destabilisation. Do you understand, you damnatious oaf?'

Sliverlight tried to nod but Dervello was still holding his jaw tightly, and now he squeezed harder. Sliverlight winced with pain as his tormentor continued, 'Now, before you analyse this any further, just remember what we know about you – and your family.'

Sliverlight's eyes widened yet further. He tried to speak through lips hardly able to move, but Dervello just shushed him, the way a parent might a small child, saying with a soft, almost gentle voice, 'No need to panic Mr Ambassador. Calm down. Calm down.' He moved his face still closer to Sliverlight's and spoke in a whisper, 'You see, we know about your arms trafficking to the old Rebel Alliance, all those years ago. We know about the profits you've been creaming off the deals between the asteroid belters. Well, of course you realise this, otherwise you wouldn't have agreed to do any of this in the first place, would you?'

Sliverlight stared, seemingly terrified and silent, as Dervello continued, 'What you might not know is that we've also been keeping track of your son's indiscretions at College. Yes, my dear. We know you got him in there under false pretences, and we know what he's been doing there. All the brain stimulator sales and the drugs. Tut, tut. The morals of the younger generation. What's the Home System coming to? We also know about the scams your two wives have been practicing in their law firms. Yes, those as well. Ah, I see you're beginning to understand. We also know about all the political tricks you've played. All of them, even the ones you've forgotten about.' He released his pressure on Sliverlight's jaw. The Ambassador slumped back and just sat there, rubbing his face.

'I'm sure you can see that withdrawing is not really an option, *Mister* Ambassador, sir,' said Dervello. 'We've got enough on you and your family - and your associates - to sink you all in "drak mud" up to your necks, in the Mars penal colony – for the rest of your miserable lives. And, if that doesn't scare you enough, … well, things might just have to get a lot messier, much sooner. I hope I don't need to elaborate?'

Dervello moved even closer to his victim and thrust both his arms toward him. Sliverlight shut his eyes tightly but Dervello merely grasped his upper arms and shook him, surprisingly mildly, 'Belive it or not, I'm sorry to be like this. I just wish it wasn't necessary.' He released his captive and started to walk away, then turned and said, 'This is all for the greater good of the Solar System and its people. You do know that don't you?'

Sliverlight nodded, 'I understand,' he said, 'but perhaps it's also for the greater good of your boss.' He winced as though expecting more punishment to follow, as Dervello turned and advanced toward him again, but the man suddenly stopped, and stared at him agog.

'What? Are you being serious?' said Dervello, almost laughing. 'He's a fool. He has no idea what's coming – to him and any Allied Government lapdogs who stand in our way. It's time for them all to go and a new Order to take over. A new hand is needed on the rudder. One that's identiment but also libertarian, just like me. But also one that'll take a firm hand and steer a sensible new direction forwards. Anyway, as I said, it's not your place to enquire about things you don't understand, nor ever will.'

Then Dervello glared at Sliverlight and using a shooing motion of his hands, said, 'Time for you to go too, *Mister Ambassador* - and do your job. Our crewmember on the Antarctica awaits you. She'll be keeping an eye on you, remember, and don't forget that we have operatives on the Navy ship out there. And they're in touch with the Meta-teleos. You and they have to convince those zealous fools that Ultima is on their side.'

Sliverlight rose and hurried toward the door but Dervello called him to stop. The Ambassador turned, with a look of dread on his face.

'You will remember what I said won't you… *sir*?'

Sliverlight nodded quickly, turned and exited the room as fast as his spindly and shaking legs could carry him.

Chapter 16

THE STRANGELY OVERLOOKED

A wide expanse of water sparkled sharply beneath an orange-yellow sun travelling almost imperceptibly toward its zenith in a steel blue Oceanus sky. Dozens of four-tusked boar-like animals, the ones humans called "Borals", stood in water up to their shaggy bellies, at the edge of a broad fresh water lake. They lapped cat-like at the water, grunting and grumbling as they stood nervously beneath the silent, wispy traces of white cumulus, drifting high above. Clumps of thin stemmed plants grew out of the water all arouns them, the way fresh-water reeds would on Earth, but these plants were topped by blue and orange blooms, each shaped like neat icosahedrons.

Stands of tall, curving, trees, known to the Devians, as "Foople trees", lined the shore of the lake, their wide, pink-hued, trunks forming graceful arcs and, at their extremities, dangling masses of long blue-green, ribbon shaped leaves into the water's edge, like humans trepidatiously dipping their toes in the water. Behind the Fooples stood a dense forest of even taller trees; mixed masses of purple leaved species', which formed a sort of hazy cloud sprouting out of the deep grey soil. Before this world's fate had became known to humans, almost any visitor from Earth would surely have considered themselves fortunate to have witnessed this scene, or the beauty, and strangeness, of the hundreds of thousands of other wild scenes on this world. Many might even feel some degree of envy, perhaps. Until very recently.

The bushy coated Borals represented only one of about twenty species on Oceanus which could genuinely be called mammalian. Here, now, they twitched skittishly, swinging their angular, knobbled, heads at each-other, their snouts glistening with splashes and drips.

Near the Borals a different creature, another mammalian type; this one known as a "Gapotie", sat on the curving trunk of a Foople tree, watching everything around it. The size of a small dog, but looking more like a large rat, its long wiry whiskers twitched constantly on a shrew-like nose. After spying on the Borals it scanned the green-blue horizon for signs of danger, its nervous gaze settling on a lizard, known as an "Argaran", stretched out on a flat lakeside rock, almost a hundred metres away. By far the largest animal at the water's edge, the Argaran was the size of a human and, though unmistakeably like an Earth reptile in general appearance, this one, like all its kind on Oceanus, sported not two, but *three* pairs of legs. These were spread out flat, almost lethargically, from its sides as it sunned itself, the prodigious head of the creature resting on the rocky platform. It seemed unconcerned with its surroundings. It almost certainly was not.

Neither the Borals nor the Gapotie were in danger from the Argaran, for its prey lived in the water; a species of large, three eyed, fish-like animals that swam in the murk below. Even so, all the other creatures at the water hole kept a wary eye on the lazing lizard.

In an instant, as though upon a universal signal for panic, the Borals raised their heads, in unsison, as a flock of tiny blue and red bird-like creatures flew out of their hiding places amongst the reedy plants. The other species craned their necks – as far as nature would allow them – as a strange, lazy buzzing sound drifted down to them from high above. Was it a plague of the Stingflies that too often made life so difficult? No, this was different and came from high above, but it might still be dangerous. As the noise got louder the Borals bolted for cover, raising explosive splashes of water, as they thundered through the lake margin toward safety. Then a small shadow sped across the ground at alarming speed, so that even the Argaran now moved, slipping silently into the water below, hardly disturbing the water's surface at all.

The buzzing quickly reached a peak, very distant and not especially loud, at least not to a human, then diminished, just as speedily, as the shadow raced out and over the lake. The creatures began to venture back. It wasn't, after all, one of the bat-like raptor birds looking for prey. In fact, the resilient lakeside animals all quickly returned to the water hole. They were safe once again as peace returned – for the moment.

****

A single, piston engined, propeller aircraft sailed above the verdant terrain of Oceanus, as it approached the coast of the continent, passing above the countryside known locally as the "wilda-bushlands", with all its myriad of small and medium sized animal life forms, down amongst the forests and lakes.

The aircraft would have been considered archaic on Earth for it was a high wing, four-seater craft and sitting in the front, right hand, seat, Mike Tanniss tried hard to concentrate on the instrument panel in front of him. The pilot, Eleri, in the left-hand seat, sat confidently keeping the plane in straight and level flight. Mike was doing his best to ignore the wide-open vistas of the landscape slipping below. Both he and Eleri each wore a standard communications headset.

'Eleri glanced at him and through his headset he heard her say, 'You do not seem to be enjoying the scenery so? I thought you were interested in really *seeing* Oceanus.'

'Sorry, El,' he said into the microphone. His voice sounded fuzzy in his headset. He'd have to get used to that on this flight.

'Well, I'm not afraid of heights, if that's what you're thinking,' he said.

'T'would be strange if you were. You being a starship manry. But, then what ist?'

'Hard to explain. Later, maybe.' He didn't particularly want to make an admission of his particular form of agoraphobia to Eleri. Not just yet.

'Okay now,' she said, 'so sorry you carnt enjoy the view. Tis really something.'

'You enjoy flying don't you. Eleri? How long have you had this plane?'

'Oh, some two of years only. My feether has been qualified as a private pilot for many years. Used to fly for the Planetary Survey Union, he did. Stopped doing that years long-past. He encouraged me to learn. It cost a lot yet, but I eventually did it and so I qualified three years ago and have not looked back.'

'Sounds great. I thought it would cost too much to run something like this. Privately, I mean.'

'Sure and you are right, for I do not own this ship. The University does. More correctly, the science and natural history department do own it.'

'I thought Oceanus frowned on machines. They produce pollution, don't they? Almost everything that moves down here, is electrically powered – by solar cells, wind or whatever.'

Eleri chuckled. 'You are right, I am supposing. We have solar powered aircraft as well but they arint very efficient or powerful, fraid. Still, this aircraft uses organic oil from "Strapweed" plants. They produce a high-octane fluid that makes an excellent fuel, so the bonus is that it produces a tiny fraction of the waste gases. I have to admit yet, we've also used some engineering techniques that were borrowed from your Home System, so to increase efficiency.'

'I'm shocked,' he said, with mock indignation, 'Using Earth technology? What next?' Mike watched her delectable mouth break into a grin. He thought again about how beautiful she was and once more he longed for more intimate contact.

Mike also looked forward to landing on "Fire Island", their destination, about 400 kilometres, or 'lints' as the Oceanus people often called them, east of the coast of Bhumi Devi. He risked one quick look down out of the canopy. She was right. The views of the wild countryside were spectacular, but still disturbing to him. He noticed that they were nearing the coastline, an incredibly bright wedge of deep blue spread out some klicks ahead. The scene made him feel a little queasy. The altimeter showed they were flying at 3,000 feet and their airspeed was 120 knots. Old fashioned forms of measurement, he thought, but they still had their uses, given that a "knot" was one nautical mile per hour – a measurement which tied very conveniently into angular measure on the surface of the planet: useful for navigation.

After mere seconds he was happy to yank his eyes from the vista, though he realised with surprise that he had not become as disorientated as expected. Maybe it was because he was enclosed in the relative confines of the cockpit and its protective canopy.

The aircraft suddenly and unexpectedly dropped, maybe only 50 or 60 feet, rose just as suddenly, after a few seconds, then dropped a little again. The wings wobbled, but only slightly, as Eleri brought the ship back into straight and level flight.

'Sorry Mike,' she said, 'tis only turbulence. There is yet a big forest below. Must be putting out much thermal current, upward so. We shall be over the sea in a moment. Should so calm down then.'

She looked at him and saw he wasn't perturbed at all. 'That's' fine Eleri,' he said, 'you should see, or, I should say, *feel*, the turbulence you get when a starship goes through a negative energy conduit. Now, that really isn't nice, even in something as big as The Monsoon.'

'Wowter!', was all she said.

'There's other aircraft, larger than this one, operating on this planet, aren't there?' he asked.

'Yeah, so sure. There is a big commercial set-up that has a whole fleet of big two *and* four engine planes, Mike. Mostly they take passengers 'tween Janitra and Tharsington. One flight per day. Another set-up takes passengers between New Cardigan, way to the south, up to Thunder Bay on the north east coast. They do go up around the coast route, so to avoid crossing the deep interior, and they refuel at airports along ways. Still, there is a large gap between some of the northernmost refuel stations. Tis cheaper in fuel, to use helium airships. Many such are used, such for cargo transport and for people who like slow travel. But, yet tis sometimes difficult to manufacturie enough gas for them to be used.'

'I thought there were some towns way up on the north west corner of the continent as well. Anyone go there, or do you have to reach them by sail ship?'

She glared at him but smiled broadly, 'Now Mike manry, do not be teasing about our tekno.'

He thought it was like the sun coming out from behind a cloud bank when she smiled.

'As yet so happens,' she said, pride inflecting her voice, 'there *are* deedly flights, to "Innovation", a town furthest way up, on the tipmost of the north west. But only one such per month.'

'How do they get all the way over there?'

'They do go up around the coast route, like I said. We do not fly over the deep interior because there is but little chance of quick rescue if any such thing goes wrong. Pure-so commercial flights do go over but tis not deemed safe for ordinary poulari.'

'Your towns are certainly isolated from each-other,' he mused.

'Similar so, to the way that Oceanus is isolated from your Home System. We are used to it. How long do you have to be sailing space to get here?'

'Many weeks, El. Even The ship I came on is the fastest crewed ship in the Navy. Still takes about 5 weeks, sometimes more, just to get from the inner Solar System out to the transit zones. You know, the volume of space out in the boondocks of the system, where the conduits form? And the ship travels at virtually constant acceleration most of the way. Can get up to 4,000 kilometres per second.'

'So, I think I had read that the conduit part of the journey takes yet the smallest time. True?'

'Yeah, that's really something ain't it? Yeah, the transit through the conduit, to get to the Ra system, for example, just took over 25 minutes. But then, we took about another 3 weeks to get from the outermost part of *your star* system to Oceanus, decelerating hard all the way. Most of the Navy's cruiser class vessels are much older, so they can take up to ten weeks for a one-way journey.'

'Ooh, no to all. Tis so long time to be cooplied up on a spaceship,' she said, her nose wrinkling with distaste.

'Well, it's not too bad. Lots of activities on board – and there's work of course. And maybe you don't realise how big the ship is. The Monsoon is a carrier, El. It's the largest ship in the Navy. More than a kilometre long, it's got entertainment halls, restaurants and cafes, mess rooms, sports complexes and holo suites. The ship's complement of corvettes and landing boats are housed in massive hangars. You should see 'em.'

'Still, such life would not suit me, Mike. I would yet miss the outdoors too much – regardless yet of how big the ship is.'

'I think you're forgetting something El,' Mike said, suddenly serious, 'I'm sorry to mention this, but you and your family – and just about everyone you know – is probably going to have to leave here in ships a … bit like The Monsoon.' He decided not to tell her – yet, that the standard cruisers were less than half the size of The Monsoon.

Eleri's smile vanished and he wished he hadn't said anything. She glanced at him and said softly, 'Tis hard to think of a thing like that, Mike.'

Mike's face dropped and he could only glance regretfully at her suddenly dewy eyes. There was silence for a while until she broke the spell, 'Anywayins, in such meantime we have Unkling Draco's mission to accomplish.'

'He was really inspiring at that meeting he set up with the university committee.' It was a relief to change the subject.

'Glad you think so. Tis a pity that neither me, nor any of the scienctia teams themselves, were there. The "Maheshtras" could not a go anywayins but we shall tell them all about it soon, and in person yet. And we can start our part of the mission on Fire Island too. Oh, and Mike, I should warn you that our science camp at Fire Island is also bit isolated too, but I hope you do like it.'

She had mentioned isolation. Given what he'd been telling her he thought it strange that even though humanity had finally reached the stars – well, some of them – travelling in person to other star systems made for a very isolated activity. The travel times he'd been talking about had come as a shock to most people. The distances that had to be traversed *within* star systems and lack of an ability to even send *signals* between systems – without sending physical autoprobes through the conduits, made isolation writ large for far flung communities like Oceanus and Prithvi. Mike likened it to travel in the ancient days, long before spacecraft or even aircraft, or even steam powered vessels, more like the days of sailing ships, when travel times across the Earth's oceans, back then, could take many weeks, even months. How ironic, he thought, that, in some ways, such times had returned. Perhaps a totally new means of transport was needed, he mused, but for now, advanced nuclear fusion power was the fastest, best means of propulsion ever devised. New designs of fusion engines were being regularly tested, to speed up journey times *within* star systems but the only means of interstellar travel were the mysterious conduits. Without them any currently envisaged form of human travel between stars would take thousands of years –just between the closest ones. And Oceanus was over a hundred light years out.

'I'm sure I'll like the camp,' he said and after a short pause, 'By the way, I was wondering why it's called Fire Island?'

'There is yet an abundance of bushy vegetation that is coloured yet flame red, right across the island. Probably did co-evolve with the "Tandy" birdles that nest in huge-big colonies on coast rocks. We know the birdles drink nectar from the Fire Plant vegetation, but most of their diet is fishlings. We are thinking the plants have somehow conditioned the birds into drinking the nectar and so, proliferating the Fire Plants, by spreading their seed-pollen.'

'If that's right, doesn't that mean there would be Fire Plants on the nesting rocks as well?'

'Not likely still, because the birdles travel, as do bees, say, on Earth, from plant to plant, but then they normally fish in the sea before roosting. Besides yet, there is practically no soil on the rocks for them to grow. So, we would have expected a few plants, mayhap, but there arint any. There is a lot more to understand, like with so much of the wildlife on Oceanus. You have made a good point Mike. Well done to you. Not bad for a physicsman. You are really getting into biolry, arint you?'

'Thanks for the compliment,' said Mike, but he thought it was more a matter of common sense than any significant observation. Was she humouring him?

'I guess I've specialised so much in physics throughout my life,' he said, 'at least until I joined the Secretariat, so it's good to look at a different subject for a change.'

Glancing at the air speed indicator and remembering some of the ground features Eleri said they'd crossed, he looked at the paper map next to her, and said, 'Looks like about three hundred klicks to go, so, at our present airspeed, I reckon that means we should get there in about one and a half hours, yeah?'

She nodded and the smile came back.

****

The long approach to the airstrip on Fire Island took them over deep blue bays edged with high, pale, limestone, cliffs. Massive white breakers could be seen making their way in rows toward the cliffs, crashing and swirling around tall pillars of rock standing in isolation of the coast. Gently rolling country carpeted with blue green vegetation lay inland from there.

Mike tried not to look at the view too often but could hardly help being awed by the wildness of this place. His perusal of Eleri's maps had shown that the tear drop shaped island was only about 20 kilometres long by about 15, wide. No more than ten minutes after crossing the coast they reached their goal; a tiny brown dirt airstrip, marked out with what looked like drums, lying on a broad flat plain. Despite his sketchy idea of history Mike was able to guess that the drums probably contained something flammable, so they could be lit, to enable night landings.

As they approached the narrow, rough, airstrip Eleri made the aircraft lose height and speed, then activated flaps to give her better control. Mike could see a few small buildings, like shacks, standing near the airstrip and a wide, rough track leading away into a scrubby countryside covered with bushy plants. Further inland he could see large areas vividly carpeted with brilliant reds and oranges. They were the so-called, "Fire Plants".

Eleri brought the craft into final approach then expertly landed it on the dusty airstrip, and as she did so, Mike spotted two figures standing some distance beyond its far end. They must be the people El had called, "Chanda Sobeck Maheshtra" and "Gajana Selket Sar Maheshtra"; the meri-bonded scientists who had been working out here for some time. They'd been the only humans on the island – until now.

Mike wouldn't admit it to Eleri, but he'd been a bit apprehensive about the trip as he had never flown in a ship as ancient or as small as this before. But he'd been impressed by the sheer quality of Eleri's flying skills and by the quality of the aircraft itself. At least he had been prepared for the turbulence. The shuttles could, despite their advanced structure, still be affected badly by turbulence, like all craft which flew through planetary atmospheres. And that was quite apart from the issue of the interstellar conduits.

After the front wheel touched down the plane rumbled noisily along the strip, rolling over the gravelly soil, clouds of grey-brown dust billowing behind it. After the plane had rolled to a final halt they unbuckled their seat belts and prepared to debark, their hosts jogging swiftly to greet them. Their broad, open faces wore generous, and genuine, smiles. As he climbed out Mike felt glad to be rid of the aerial vistas, but he reflected on the fact that, on the whole, he'd actually enjoyed the ride.

Gajana Sobeck was a willowy but athletic looking man, taller even than Mike, with quick bright eyes which beamed warmth. Chanda Selket Sar, his wife, was shorter than Eleri and of a more rounded build. Her radiant smile made Mike glad to be out there. He was sure he and Eleri were going to have a great time.

After the necessary introductions the Maheshtras invited them to board their nearby electric car. The science encampment was only about 20 minutes' drive away. As he came out from the shadow of the plane's wings Mike suddenly felt the fierce heat of the place, fiercer yet than in Janitra. Various crackling and clicking sounds seemed to leap out at him from all around. He wondered if they were possibly some kind of insect thing, crouching in the tall bush-like plants. He noticed little shadows race over and, looking up, saw a flock of tiny bird like creatures shoot by over their heads. They could only have been a few centimetres long, flying so fast they vanished in far less than a second. He had no time to even register their appearance in his mind but Eleri, who knew of their kind, said they were like a cross between a horseshoe bat and a swallow. As they stood transfixed, he reflected on his growing interest in biology. Perhaps this world was starting to weave some sort of spell on him. He quickly dismissed the thought.

He and Eleri fetched their large holdall bags out of the plane and insisted on carrying them, despite Gajana's generous offer to take them. They reached the car, another of the small, stumpy vehicles of the type he'd seen in Janitra, but this one was open to the elements, and not an auto-car. This thing had to be driven, on tyres. Mike had to admit it seemed well suited to the terrain, with extra-large wheels and deep, dusty treads.

Vaulting into the back-seat Mike felt that this island was the perhaps the wildest place he'd ever visited in his whole life.

It was to prove wild beyond his imagining – or his liking.

*

Though surrounded by bushes and a few trees, with little in the way of open vistas in sight, Mike once again began to feel queasy. He sat still and closed his eyes as Eleri took the seat next to him. He tried to hide his discomfort from her, but he knew it would be no good. Why was he trying to hide it, anyway? Gajana and Chanda got in the front seats and they started off along the track at a cracking pace.

Eleri, caught sight of Mike holding his head in his hands and said quietly, 'You okay yet, Mike? Ist the plane ride?'

'No, I'm fine,' he said after a few seconds.

'Would you be wishing us to stop? Get your breath?' she said.

Gajana, in the front passenger seat, turned and said, 'Is it yet motion sickness?' He frowned with concern at Eleri when Mike failed to answer.

Eleri shook her head but said nothing. Mike was glad. He was very embarrassed by the whole thing. 'I'm just a bit tired,' he said, sounding groggy but still trying to pretend there was nothing really wrong. Chanda shouted over her shoulder to him, 'Tis now only a few minutes. I am guessing you two would like to freshen up when we get there? We are having eventides meal at the six-thirty, if you should like to join us. Still, we will understand if you cannot, Mike.'

Mike grimaced. Others usually mistook his agoraphobia for motion sickness. He knew that once he was in a more enclosed place, he would be able to recover his appetite. Still, he appreciated Chanda's warm concern.

After they reached the camp Mike realised the place was surprisingly sophisticated for such a remote outpost. Three very large, cream coloured, marquees, shaped like the top halves of massive teepees, sat in a broad clearing in the vegetation. The marquees appeared to be made of some sort of tough, thick, canvass material and were pinned down tautly by substantial ropes, cleated to large steel pegs, robustly planted in the ground. A sizeable radio dish antenna rose from beside one of the marquees. This was the highest tek Mike had seen since planetfall here.

Clumps of tall purple trees surrounded the entire encampment, which was, itself, thickly dotted with dark bushes. A rough track wound its way between them and out the other side of the camp. Mike thought he could see some green coloured machinery – quite heavy plant, some way off into the bushes. Since he didn't reckon Gajana and Chanda would have erected this entire site by themselves, Mike supposed that a previous expedition must have used that machinery. How did they get that gear all the way over to this island, he wondered? But then, he remembered – the helium airships Eleri had mentioned.

'Such camp is designed to be semi-permanent,' said Gajana, as if reading Mike's mind, 'but t'will be taken down in time's fullness. We will be leaving for the next assignment in a few months and another team will yet come here.'

'You might still need to change your mind when you hear about Professier Muggredge's speech,' said Eleri, as Gajana took their bags out of the car, despite protests from his guests, and carried them into the nearest tent. The structure was very roomy inside and subdivided into different sections. It felt comfortably cool, a great relief for Mike, whose sweat was standing in beads on his skin. Gajana led them into a separate dining area. He explained that this "markrie", as he called it, was the "living and relaxation zone" and the one next to it held the bedrooms, showers and freshment rooms. There were six bedrooms, so Mike and Eleri could each have a choice of any. The marquee next to it was the laboratory and "tekno area".

Eleri said she wanted to shower straight away, so Chanda led her to those facilities and to choose her bedroom, leaving Mike with Gajana.

'Tis so much good to have someone from the outside world with us,' Gajana said, 'yet in your case I should be saying, far waysome, outside.' He laughed then; a joyous, booming sound. 'I hope you do enjoy your stay. Are you here to observe only, manry-frend?'

'Thank you,' said Mike. 'No, not just observe. I'm hoping to do some useful stuff – under El's supervision, of course. Or I'd be hopelessly out of my depth. I wonder if you know about Professier's talk to the University staff, back in Janitra?'

'We did hear about it, yes, and Eleri did so mention it just now. I so understand yet that he didst set out some new plans. I do yet look forward to hearing it.'

I can do better than that, thought Mike.

****

He couldn't take his eyes off Eleri. Mike sat almost opposite her at a wide table in the capacious living quarters, where the Maheshtras had set out a meal consisting of the Oceanus version of ancient Indian curry. It included all sorts of local fruits and vegetables in rich, spicy, sauce. There were all sorts of side dishes, though he couldn't identify most of them. It was a wonderful spread. The curry smelled delicious and even he could recognise that it had large pieces of pomriet in it. After the delicious meal, the group settled down to chat.

Eleri had changed into clothes of a sort Mike had hardly ever seen on a woman before. He didn't know femnas still wore such things – maybe it was only on Oceanus. She wore a *skirt* and a short one at that, with a hemline above the knee. Things like this were an almost completely extinct sight on old Earth. He tried to think about something other than Eleri but found himself drawn back to the same thing, his desire beginning to flare in his mind, a palpable, longing. But he had to resist it. His relationship with her was still too fragile for him to suggest anything intimate, at the moment. He watched how she laughed and joked but, besides the lust, he felt something else, something more sobering and deeper. Something he couldn't have put into words just yet. This was discomfiting indeed. Sure, he had cared about other femnas but nothing like this.

He wasn't sure he should be feeling this way, so he decided to try to forget about it by launching into deep conversation with Gajana about his biology work here, with Chanda. He caught Eleri staring at him with an expression of surprise on her face.

'Mike,' she said, 'I didnar know you were so keenlie on this stuff. Just let your keenlies go for tonight, Mer Secretary. Sorry, I mean "let your hair down" – if you want old Anglo. Plenty of time for this on the morrow.'

Mike actually felt a little hurt by that, but playing it cool he just said, 'Sorry El. Of all people, I thought you would know how much catching up I've got to do.'

She simply shrugged and turned back toward Chanda.

For her part, Chanda turned to Mike and said, smiling broadly, 'Praps Mike is right, you know. I understand you have some sort of recording of Professier Muggredge's talk to the team? You have some sort of disker recording of it, do you not? May we so hear it?' Mike returned her smile and nodded with enthusiasm but Eleri looked disappointed.

'I hope I can do better than that,' said Mike. 'Would you like to actually *see* the Professier's speech, exactly as it was at the time?'

The Maheshtras looked puzzled but Eleri shook her head and said, none too sweetly, 'Oh no, look out, yet. He's going to do his party trick now,' but she then chuckled and gestured for Mike to get on with it. 'Manry toys,' she said with mock impatience.

'I'll have you know this is a useful bit of kit,' countered Mike and removed the com unit from his wrist. He tapped it twice, placed it on the table, and said to it, 'Replay recording of University Admin' meeting, 23rd of the month, Janitra University. Appropriate magnitude and full spread please.'

A few metres from the table, in a large open space, suitable for the viewing, a duplication of the meeting called by Muggredge, burst into 3-dimensional life.

As the vid began Mike recalled how Muggredge had dreamed of an idea, new for Oceanus, but said that Mike had inspired it, and, after at least two weeks of trying to persuade the university authorities, they had finally given him the go ahead – and the necessary funding. After that he had cleverly gained approval for a meeting with all the other departmental heads, which enabled him to extract some publicity from the venture, albeit only within the university community. The director and sub-director of the University were present, together with the "Professieri" of the departments of Arts, Literature, Mathematics and "Socio-scientium". The Science department wan't there as Muggredge had already appraised them, on an oath to keep it secret until after the meeting.

Muggredge had invited Mike to attend, as an "outsider", an unusual move, simply because of the notion that it was his idea which sparked it off. And, although Mike knew he shouldn't be self-congratulatory about it, he nevertheless felt he had a right to be proud, in a way he hadn't felt since before he'd joined the Secretariat. He'd asked if he could record the meeting on his wristcom. That was agreed provided he did not broadcast it to the general "popularia", mostly because the Professier didn't yet know how things would work out. And because the reasons were still very controversial. It had also been a condition of funding.

Each person in the hol-vid appeared around half life size. The Maheshtras' jaws dropped at the sight of the vid, and their delight registered in their faces. Mike allowed that it was his "party piece", and his hosts now looked like children about to open their birthday presents. He caught a slightly jaded expression on Eleri's face. She had seen it all before, of course, when he'd transmitted it to Tenak aboard The Monsoon. Still, he was a little mystified by her behaviour. Perhaps later he would find out why, maybe?

In the holo movie, the assembled University staff, sitting around a large table in an ornately carved room, could be seen to be talking together in a huddle – until Dracus Muggredge rose to speak. Mike had been surprised that the academic authorities had given in to the Professier's request in the first place, especially as the controversy about the Home System's findings had riven the Oceanus community so thoroughly. But then, he surmised, they probably thought that if he was justified in his renewed belief in the outsiders' findings, their own prescient action in approving his "Project" would pay off. And if he turned out to be wrong, they could blame it all on him. Mike wondered if he was being cynical. But, so what?

Muggredge had begun by summarising the schism between the HS data and those gathered by the Metateleos. He knew that the Professier had agonised about how much detail he should go into when referring to the controversy.

And so, the small group in the marquee on Fire Island watched the meeting play out in front of them, in authentic detail. They saw the confusion on the parts of some delegates as to which set of data to believe; the Home System's or the government's and metateleo's. Feelings seemed to swing back and fore, with some heads of department criticising Nefer-Masterton's handling of the whole affair and others casting aspersions on the motives of the Home System. But then Muggredge had stood and spoken at length about the importance of the "more recent" findings by the "Far Edge" telescope in the Home System and had actually invited Mike to talk about them. Mike had been almost embarrassed to have been brought in like this but he was at least used to speaking to groups of people, mainly crewmembers and officers aboard The Monsoon.

Mike had backed up what the Professor had said about the telescope findings but, so as not to give anyone else at the meeting the idea that he was the Professor's "yesman" or stooge, he said he personally wanted to place more emphasis on the observations and measurements made by The Monsoon on its way into the Ra system. This seemed, genuinely, to take the Professor by surprise, so it gave the needed impression that Mike had wanted to achieve, though the Professor had only been slightly bemused. Although he may not have been so familiar with the ship's findings he had nonetheless endorsed Mike's points. Mike, himself, had said but little anyway and quickly fell silent, Muggredge having warned him that he was not there as a delegate but mainly as an observer.

Muggredge had also used Mike's comments, not as some sort of statement of absolute truth but had, cleverly, thought Mike, used it as an example of the commitment of the Home System to a continuance of a program of study, of Ra and other similar stars. In that context he'd also mentioned the sacrifice made by Tenak in the maglev station at Ramnisos. The murmurings of disquiet that had punctuated the proceedings until now suddenly stopped.

Then had come the time for Muggredge to announce his grand new "plan" and the group in the marquee watched as he said to his colleagues in the university, 'My friends, I do not see subterfuge in the efforts of the Home System scientists, nor e'en their politicians – leastways on this one only matter. I carnt vouch for anything else they do over there,' Muggredge said, with an ironic smile. There was very subdued mirth in the conference room. He continued, 'Having said this, I now want you, esteemed colleagry, from this moment on, to put aside any misgives about evacuation from our beloved world. For the moment the answer to further political debate does depend on whether our government will decide for a debate on the issue in the curia forum. For the meaningtime I want a change of direction, to do something now and continuing, that I hope we canst all agree upon.

'My friends, while human life here seems so to hinge upon deliberations of natural philosophy, politicians and religious communities, no-one has thought to speak up for the wildlife. For the flora and fauna of this wondersome planet. No matter what is decided about the human future on Oceanus, I feel we are duty-fixed to try to protect and preserve as much of the Oceanus biome as possibly we can. It was Mike here, who inspired me yet to this idea when he told my colleagry – Eleri, about the animal tissue, about the sperm and the egg banks, which are kept on Earth.'

He'd gone on to explain the concept in slightly more depth, to a background of surprised murmuring amongst the delegates around him, before continuing, with, 'Yes, on Earth they have tried to preserve many species also threatened with extinction – for totally different reasons. I so believe they also do have massive seed banks, for to preserve as much of the plant life as possible. Those have been in existence many longso years.

'I have asked all in my own team of natural philosophers, nay I rename it, our *science* team, to now-for bend ourselves to a new task, to investigate as many areas of the biosphere as we can, to build on what we already know. To extend our knowledge, and yet embark on a program to investimagate and catalogue as many species and their habits, as we have the time to cover. We shall take such-many steps to preserve tissue samples, for DNA, and yet gametes, for possible resurrection of species – praps on another world - or still on this one, whether Ra has wreak-ed destruction or not. It would be a noble and great purpose e'en if this world was not in danger. We owe this to the biosphere of this world and to ourselves and the generations before us who were nurtured here. Let this be our legacy, my friends, for the good of this world. To show all humanry, where'ere they be, that *we were the ones* who decided to take this step, now, to guard against extinction that the biota has *no say about*. To safeguard the future wilder-life of an entire world!'

Mike had been surprised when a chorus of applause, albeit somewhat subdued, broke out in the meeting room - and at that point Mike's recording stopped.

The Maheshtras also applauded, then Chanda said, 'That was yet amazery. At last, have we something we can all work towards.'

'Tis a relief,' said Gajana, 'but yet what did happen after that recordio stopped, Mike?'

'Not much,' said Mike, 'cos the directors just thanked the Professier and, kind of quickly, repeated that they had given the go ahead. Then they called an end to the meeting. Although the matter had been decided, sort of, I think they and Draco felt it was necessary to bring the other academic departments into the fold, as it were. Get them on side. And I think they did succeed.'

'Praps, but I am thinking there was some continuing disapproval,' said Gajana.

'Yeah, there were some miserable faces as they left but I reckon they were in the minority. And now "the fusion engines have been lit". I mean, well, I mean ...'

'I understand so, Mike,' said Gajana.

There's only one other thing the Professier thought we should commit to doing,' said Mike, 'and it was something he mentioned to El and me, before we came out here. He wants all of us to devote as much of our time as we can to look for "geolry" evidence of the extinction event we believe happened three and a half million years ago. We need some prima facie evidence, so we can get the necessary permits to go to Simurgh.'

'I am supposing we all have some geolry knowledge, Mike, but tis hard to see we shall get enough time still, said Gajana.

'Also, tis hard to know how we could get such an evidence without going directly to Simurgh anywayins,' said Chanda.

'I think he was talking about looking for any comp-data or other evidence,' said Eleri, finally deciding to speak, 'and I am suggesting we keep this goal in mind but, meaningtime, go on with the work of further investagation – and recording of the life cycles of this world's wildlife. And collecting tissue and gametes. That is why Mike has come here, at the Professier's bidding – and my invitation. Hopefully yet, he can help us with the necessary computer logging and admin' work, and who knows, maybe he shall even get to be a biolrist,' she chuckled amiably. It was good to see her smile at last.

The group sat together chatting and Mike noticed that Eleri seemed to relax more, catching up with news from the Maheshtras. Also noted Mike, no alcohol, not even synthalc, was available to drink here; something that Mike regretted. But, although he wouldn't admit it openly, he inwardly admired these people for it.

After a couple of hours Eleri rose and said she was retiring for the night. She turned to Mike and said, 'Thanking you for yet giving up your holiday leave, Mike. I know the Admiral still wanted you to just take it easy and all things, so you didnar have to get involved in all this.'

'That's okay,' he said, 'cos what else would I have done? And this way I get to be … around you, too. You know I like being with you and, besides, I think this biology thing is just getting too interesting to ignore.'

She chuckled and said, 'See you on morrow then, at 07.00 hours. Bright and early?' She kissed him lightly on the cheek before walking off. Mike watched her go, entranced by her elegant, yet down to earth, stride. But how chaste was that peck? Another opportunity missed? He was too tired to pursue her now, and he was sure she was exhausted. Besides, he was not at all certain how, or even whether he should try to invite intimacy. One false move might destroy their relationship. Relationship? Now, that was a loaded term. No, he could see she wasn't ready for such an approach yet. He would have to continue to wait for the right time to talk to her of such things.

Chapter 17

TRANSFORMATION

On board the research vessel, H S Antarctica, a billion and a half kilometres out from the Earth, deep into the outer Solar System, Yardis Octavian Sliverlight sat in his bijou cabin situated in the central hub section of the vessel. Arrival at Oceanus wasn't expected for another nine to eleven weeks. They had been en-route for just about 23 days, and for most of that time he had stayed in his cabin, rarely mixing with the crew or the scientists on board.

The vessel had already reached the equivalent of the distance of Saturn from the Sun, and was still accelerating, at nearly one gee, toward the outermost parts of the Solar System, there to rendezvous with a so called "transit zone". Just as on Navy ships the Antarctica's quantum computers, working with hundreds of sensor aerials projecting from the prow of the vessel, would seek the presence of a negative energy conduit. When one was found, giant superconducting rings on the ship's forward module would effectively guide the ship toward what was euphemistically called "the mouth" of the conduit. Einstein's theory of relativity still held sway over travel in "ordinary" space-time and therefore the ship couldn't travel faster than light, but it was the negative energy of the conduit which would pull the ship, once it entered the thing, through a distortion of space-time itself and out on the far side of the conduit. At that point it would finally be ejected into the ra system, at a greatly accelerated velocity. Then, an extended period of deceleration would bring the ship into the innermost part of that system.

In his cabin's bathroom Sliverlight again stood in front of a mirror.

'How am I going to get rid of you, you little rascal?' he said as he once more unscrewed the front section of his synthetic eye, wearing a pair of bright blue, sterilised gloves. He again removed the tiny tranceiver from his synthetic eye and placed it in its packet. He nearly flushed it down his toilet, then stopped mid-action and walked to the com station in his lounge, pressing a key on the fist sized hypercomputer. He asked it to put him in contact with someone on the "Command Deck". After he had presented his I D credentials to the machine it told him to place a finger flat against a small screen and a few seconds later announced he'd been recognised. It then called the Command Deck for him. Shortly afterwards the voice of one of the ship's bridge officers came ringing through.

In a charming voice Sliverlight said he simply wanted to ask some questions about the journey and that, as an Ambassador for the Home System he would appreciate their indulgence – when they had the time, of course. The officer asked him to wait and after a while returned, saying the Captain and senior officers would be delighted to speak to him – if he would like to make his way forward. Donning a smart evening jacket, he left his cabin and made his way toward the Command Centre.

Like every interstellar vessel the ship's hub decks, from the prow end to the stern, were arranged one above the other, like stacked plates, all at right angles to the direction of acceleration. That direction was therefore directly "above" the heads of the ship's occupants. Elevators and stairways connected each deck and as the ship travelled the inertial effect "pressed" the occupants toward the decks on which they stood, creating a "force of gravity". It was a very realistic effect, and it promoted health and comfort, but the "gravity" was illusory.

The problem was, for all interstellar vessels, that the one gee acceleration could only be maintained for a few weeks, until an optimum, and, in fact, a limiting velocity was attained. After that the journey to the nearest conduit was a smooth, unaccelerated coast. But, as the vessel was no longer under constant acceleration, its rotating torus could start turning and the majority of crew could decant into it, leaving the hub as a microgravity environment.

Once through a conduit, taking mere tens of minutes, such a ship had to decelerate hard, to be captured by the gravity well of the new star system, meaning it had to turn through 180°, to point the engines in the direction of travel. The ship then travelled *stern* forwards and, this time, *decelerating* meant inertia once again pushed the crew toward the deck plates, replicating the gravitational effect. Turning at high velocity after exiting a conduit brought its own problems, often causing motion sickness so that, in the early days, small ships had engine modules each end of the vessel, to avoid any need to turn. However, that had necessitated the crew switching to living in duplicate living quarters which were, in effect, on the *ceilings* of their decks.

The fact that the corridors Sliverlight now trudged, in his awkward manner, were subject to that illusory gravitational force, meant he didn't have to struggle with the effects of floating, as he had on Collins Station. The Antractica, being a research ship only, was not exactly thronged with people. Sliverlight only passed a bare handful of others, mostly scientists, wearing light blue tunics. They all wore some sort of odd-looking bandana or headband, with a knob at the front. And they all seemed preoccupied.

Being a government leased, civilian ship, dedicated to scientific research and exploration, the Antarctica was small, compared to most Navy vessels. In particular, the Antarctica was less than a quarter of the size of The Monsoon and was completely unarmed. As it was often required to spend even more time in deep space than most Navy ships, it had a full- size torus, even bigger than in most Navy vessels, including The Monsoon. It thereby assured a healthy and comfortable zone for the scientists to work in. Since the Antarctica was small compared to military ships, it looked as though it was almost *all* torus, with a tiny hub. And although the ship's engines were powerful, their relatively small size meant they had to propel a comparatively large mass. This, in turn, meant that members of this type of vessel were much slower than The Monsoon in travelling from one system to another.

Despite the relative comfort of walking on the ship's decks Sliverlight still had to negotiate dozens of metres of corridors, elevators and flights of stairs, as he followed signs to the Command Centre. And he sometimes had to ask for directions. He was eventually directed to an elevator, beyond which there was "No Unauthorised Admittance". He'd been told to touch a com screen outside the elevator, and after that the image of a bridge officer, a ruddy faced man in cream uniform, replete with peaked hat, appeared on-screen. He asked Sliverlight to enter his credentials again and this time he had to peer into a large red coloured disc on a panel: a retinal scanner. Sliverlight made sure he presented his *righ*t eye and seconds later the elevator door opened. It took him up one deck and when the door opened he was met by two burly security guards, each holding a stun pistol. He had to show his ID card again and was then allowed full entry onto the bridge proper.

First Officer "Marlon Vergil Florian", a sturdy looking individual, with severely short grey hair and weathered face, greeted Sliverlight near the elevator, waved away the guards and escorted him to the main control room. There he saw a bewildering array of screen banks and hyper-comp interfaces. Three officers turned and smiled at him, including the man who'd appeared on the screen. Then the Captain, "Jennifer Livia Amily Providius", stepped forward amd greeted him, introducing him to her fellow officers. Providius was shorter than most of her colleagues, pleasantly round faced, with short, bobbed blue-black hair, and she exuded an almost palpable gravitas. She wore an impressive, all white uniform, emblazoned with gold braided cuffs and collar, the gleaming whole matched by her genuine smile.

'What can we do for you, Ambassador?' she asked, 'for I trust your accommodations are suitable?' She gave him a penetrating, yet friendly gaze.

'Oh, yes,' he said, 'I'm sure everything's fine. I just wanted to ask you a few things, that's all.'

'Fire away sir,' she replied as her fellow officers regarded Sliverlight with silent curiosity.

'Well, I've never been on an interstellar flight before,' he admitted, 'and I was just wondering what to expect. I've had a look at the manuals of course but I understand there is a degree of ... of pain involved.' He looked at them, apprehensively.

The square jawed Florian stepped forward and invited Sliverlight to sit, while the Captain tried to reassure him, 'There's no reason to be alarmed, sir. It's nothing a normally healthy adult cannot tolerate, and I believe you've already been examined and passed as fit, haven't you?'

Sliverlight nodded but still looked apprehensive.

'I suppose,' he said, 'but I just wondered whether I should take some analgesics or something.'

'Probably unnecessary,' said Florian, 'though some people do, but it could actually cause more problems, mainly because it might result in disorientation. Your crash couch should suffice, sir, but, of course, it's up to you.'

Captain Providius said, 'Thank you Marlon,' and turning to Sliverlight, said, 'My First Officer is completely right, sir. Please make full use of the crash couch and remember to use it again, after the conduit, when we turn the ship through 180°.' The Ambassador nodded. Providius continued, 'The crash couches have been specially designed and perfected, over decades, to ease the pressures experienced during transit. Don't forget, travel through the conduit should only take about 25 minutes. The "pain" you've heard about is a little like the discomfort astronauts experienced in the old days. The so called, "G forces". You've probably entered orbit from the Earth's surface, sir and no doubt, travelled around the Solar System?'

Sliverlight nodded, but he continued to have a lame exprsssion on his gaunt features, so Florian spoke again, 'That means you've already experienced G forces, sir. When an interplanetary ship accelerates toward its destination, then decelerates again, you get mild G forces until one full force of gravity is achieved. That's how we can all move about normally, as if we're standing on a planet as big as the Earth. Well, almost normal. Getting into orbit around the Earth, from the surface, usually involves more than one G, but it's not as bad these days compared with the early times. That's probably because most shuttles fly into orbit rather than being launched straight upwards.'

'What my number one is trying to say, Ambassador, and maybe not too succinctly,' said Providius, winking at her First Officer, 'is that the pain can take different forms in different people, depending on their physiological makeup. In the conduit the G forces can act in several different directions at once and it's sometimes combined with a little disorientation – as when you've imbibed real-alcohol, say – except it's without the euphoria. Some people report feelings of "pins and needles" in various parts of their bodies, and some report more severe symptoms - but not often. As we've said, it lasts only a short while and as long as you stay in your crash couch the effects will be minimised.'

Another officer added, 'If you were to leave your crash couch, sir, the effects would be much more pronounced. Still not damaging or serious, just very … unpleasant.'

'Okay, thank you,' said Sliverlight, looking only slightly less concerned. He continued, 'I just thought a means to stop these effects happening might have been found by now.'

'Not until we fully understand what causes them, sir,' said Florian. 'People have been flying through conduits for well over a hundred years now, but we still don't really understand what actually happens to the ships themselves. We know there don't seem to be any long-lasting side effects on people, or on ships' structure. And thousands of experimental flights have been done. But the "Qewsers" – that's our slang term for quantum computers - can't seem to derive enough sensor info from the conduits themselves to determine their full characteristics, even as we fly through them.'

'We know what the conduits do – but not how,' added the Captain, with a degree of finality. She continued, 'Well, I hope that answers your questions sir, and I hope you've been reassured? At least to some extent. Just remember, we have a great medical team, an award-winning team, on hand, here on the Antarctica. They can be with you in minutes if needed, but I'm sure that won't be necessary.'

'Well, I think I feel a little happier,' said Sliverlight, none too convincingly, 'and I'm impressed that your medics would be prepared to face the consequences of not being in crash couches. So, I'll just go back to … Oh, there's just one more thing.'

Most of the officers' faces fell a little. Sliverlight continued, 'I just wondered, what with that ship, The Monsoon, already being at Oceanus, what happens if you meet a ship coming the other way? Through the conduit, I mean.'

'That's not a problem at all, sir,' said the Captain, seriously rather than jovially, the other officers glancing at each-other as if they'd heard this question a million times. Providius continued, 'A lot of people don't realise that the energy signature of a conduit changes in very defined and measurable ways before a ship enters it. We would pick up the other ship's signature instantly, well in advance of transit and would know that another vessel already "occupied" the precise energy level of *that* conduit. So, of course, the superconductors would "turn off" and we would not enter. But anyway, thousands of experiments have also indicated that the way conduits work, is that they would not actually allow another ship, or any other solid object, to occupy its energy level at one and the same time. It's a sort of "exclusion principle". Remember Pauli's exclusion principle concerning spin up and spin down electrons? Quantum physics?'

Sliverlight looked blank.

'Still,' she said, 'we're not taking any chances, so we keep full vigilance with our sensors.'

Florian added, 'The other thing to remember is that when a conduit mouth; that's the part we call the "Zeroth Power Expansion", projects a vessel through the conduit, the mouth often snaps out of existence almost immediately afterward. A vessel seeking to enter from "the other side" then needs to find a different conduit, and that's not normally a problem because there are conduits opening in the same transit zone all the time. The sensor arrays and Qewsers can normally find one within a few million kilometres.'

Providius and the other officers looked at Sliverlight expectantly, obviously hoping anxiety had been assuaged. He thanked them as they bid him a happy onward journey and reminded him not to hesitate to ask them if he had any further questions. He had a slightly sceptical look on his face as he walked away but he suddenly turned and, with a look of discomfort on his face, said, 'Oh, I'm so sorry. I'm afraid I've been taken a bit short in the "water-plumbing" zone, if you see what I mean? I wondered if I might use your refreshment rooms on this bridge. I take it you have some? Would that be permissible?'

'Yes, of course, sir,' said Florian, as the Captain and the others went back to their duties. 'It's down the corridor, then take a right before the elevator you came up in. It's about ten metres down that corridor.'

Sliverlight watched as Florian turned away, then walked to the refreshment unit and flushed his transceiver down the toilet belonging to the bridge crew. That meant it would surely be vented to space.

****

After spending two weeks with Eleri, Mike was starting to get used to the outdoors life on Fire Island. He had been with her when she had placed what she called "quadrats", or square frames, a metre on a side, in selected areas of countryside. They were used to count the numbers of different species. And he had finally "confessed" to her about his agoraphobia. She thought it odd that he hadn't mentioned it before but, otherwise reacted with understanding and a desire to help – as he had hoped, though he didn't really believe she could help.

However, he soon found that his form of phobia didn't mean Eleri would "let him off" going out into the Island countryside, or to wide open areas. In fact, she encouraged him strongly, sometimes almost forcing the issue. Naturally, he'd been unhappy about the openness of most of the places she took him to, and she had sometimes guided him into sitting in the occasional "hides" that had been constructed, to watch wildlife, unobserved. He had felt stupid doing it, but it seemed to relieve his symptoms for a while. He believed she thought his phobia was not very severe and she seemed determined to try to get him to overcome it. This always made him smile to himself. It was nice of her; very well meaning, he thought, but it was unlikely he'd just "snap out of it". He'd always had it and maybe he always would. But, then again, maybe a gradual exposure to open country was what was needed.

In any case, his burgeoning regard for Eleri meant he was neither inclined to leave the place, nor to admit defeat in front of her. His feelings had, in fact, reached a level where he hated being apart from her, yet he didn't want to follow her around like a puppy dog. Yet, of the two of them she was the only one who really knew what she was doing, after all. And he still hadn't figured out how to propose that they sleep together. This disturbed him. Was he was starting to get shy? Surely not? Was he tired of that sort of game, the pursuit? Perhaps he had pursued too much, over the last few years? Surely not? Time would tell. He did know he didn't want to ruin the mutually respectful relationship they'd developed by suggesting something too advanced, too soon. He wasn't yet sure how she felt about him and what she would later think if he rushed things. What was this? The way a woman felt about him after "the act" hadn't meant very much to him in the past. But this time, it did, even though the event hadn't happened yet.

Mike was sitting in the laboratory marquee, watching the antics of the larval stage of one of the insect-like species on the Island. The creature crawled up a full-size Fire Plant which grew in a pot of soil, placed in a large glass tank, under a large lamp. The creature was about 4 centimetres long and reminded him of a caterpillar, similar to those found on Earth. Striped all over with bright bands of black and white, it had 20 pairs of tiny, pin-like legs which it used in a type of wave motion, to slowly crawl up the plant stem. Eleri had said this was an unusual species, only found on Fire Island, and that it eventually underwent a sort of amazing transformation. He'd like to see that. El's enthusiasm for biology had started to infect him.

He had frequently watched Eleri at work, and occasionally assisted her, whilst she carried out careful experiments involving respiration in Fire Plants grown in large tanks. It involved test tubes to measure the take up of oxygen and production of carbon dioxide in bacteria found amongst the plants. He was intrigued by the intricacy of the experiments and Eleri's deft use of the mystifying single, ancient, computer in the lab. He thought It did little more than record the data she fed into it and produce graphs and charts for comparison with previous data. Amazingly, it didn't speculate or suggest improvements for her experiments. It didn't even *talk* to her! But it didn't seem to get in the way of her producing interesting results – or, what she described as "useful-such results".

The poor-quality equipment here grated on him, even though he didn't understand her work and it made him do something he then regretted. He asked why she bothered with such inefficient equipment and a very slow methodology. She was not impressed.

'Please be not interfering,' she said, 'because I am deedly aware that you and all your ship's personry have more *advanced* tekno.' She looked cross and he apologised.

'I'm sorry El. I didn't mean to go at you,' he said quietly, 'but I just thought that … Well, you could get through this work so much quicker and more efficiently if …' He stopped when he saw the look on her face.

'As I said, I am yet sure your people could do this much better and faster but that is not our way on Oceanus. I thought you had yet realised so, by now. We have our own pacing in life, and we are happy to do things the old way, even though it means some mistakes, praps. But it does not, usually. We are a methodical people.'

'I can see how methodical you are and I'm sure you get results, but ... oh, it doesn't matter,' he said.

'Yes, so it dost matter,' she said, 'and results are the most important thing. Not the way you get them, or the speed of it, yet. If you ask me, your Home System relies too much on your top-tekno. I have heard many things such about how people in your solar system, ordinesty, sorry ... ordinary people, use things to *spy on each-other*. They damage relationships and yet make all manner of indignities by speeding bad messages across all the Earth world and the many worlds.'

'Yes, I suppose that's true, but ...'

'Yes, and yet they use things like that watch-thing you wear on your wrist and other devices. Many others too, yes? Too many for me to grasp in my mind. In fact, and you may deny so, but are they not obsessed with tekno and have lives dominated by it? Does it not colour everything they do?'

There was a pause while he considered his reply carefully, an unusual thing for him to do, he mused, but she obviously expected a thoughtful response. Eventually he said, 'Yes, I suppose there's something in what you say, El. Thing is, it's all gone too far now to change – and you're right to some extent. I know most people on Earth probably obsess about hi-tek, but that's not true of the navy or the Secretariat. We use devices like these wristcoms, as tools. Tools we need. There can be disciplinary consequences if there's abuse. And I think what you say does apply to some societies back home, but not all. A couple of the orbiting habitats have chosen to live in some very ... unusual, very retro', ways. Old fashioned ways, if you prefer. And the inhabitants of Mars seem to want to go their own way too, for the most part. But don't forget many of these people can only live where they do, and how they do, by means of hi-tek. And your own ancestors wouldn't have got to this ...this amazing place, if they hadn't used the hi-tek of their day. But you're right, El. I shouldn't interfere. I am beginning to understand how your people live and their reasons for it. Really.'

'Good. Glad I am. The whole pace of life is different here, Mike. Also am I aware of the debt owed to my ancestows. Yet, they and their successors made decisions to start things going in a different way here, did they not? And we still observe that as far as we are able.' He nodded, trying to appear solemn, but she cast her eyes down and looked suddenly crest fallen.

'What is it?' he asked. 'I said I'm sorry, El.'

'No, tis not that, manry-friend mine,' she said, raising moist eyes to him. 'Tis just that I have long thought about our future. The future of my friends, my familia, my colleagry. Tis really true, is it not? The whole planet is doomed?'

He nodded slowly and said, utterly seriously, 'I wish I could say no, but I can't. And your Unkling certainly knows it's true, even if your Auntine doesn't. But listen, it's still a long way off yet.'

'E'en so, your very presence here is to convince us all to start moving to your Home System.'

'I guess …well, you know it is. And I'm sorry as hell about it.'

'No, … no need to feel yet sorry, Mike. Do not.' She smiled wanly at him, then returned to her work and, as she spoke no more about it, neither did he.

As the days passed, he began to realise that he'd learned a lot about biology from Eleri. He now knew that the insectoids, for example, were found everywhere, on all the land masses, just like insects on Earth, and occupied just about the same place in the ecosystem. But most insectoid species on the planet had ten legs, in five pairs, not six, in three pairs, as did most species on Earth. And their bodies were formed of *two* main parts, not three. That was why the technical name for them, here on Oceanus, was "bilobian". There was a head section, but it was mostly fused with the upper thorax. Then there was a lower thorax, separated from the upper one by a narrower section. The lower thorax was fused with the abdomen; the two parts separated by a "waist", much narrower than the one in the thorax.

Again, oddly, at least to human eyes, the front thorax had two pairs of legs but there were three on the rear thorax. A strange asymmetry, Eleri had said, and one which many of her fellow biologists had spent years trying to understand. She also said that most of the insectoids were harmless to humans, but some were very poisonous and to be avoided.

One day Mike walked into the lab tent to talk to Eleri but couldn't find her. He was walking around the various benches and equipment in the laboratory when she walked in, carrying a large tray of equipment. She smiled at him as she neared the "insectivarium", where the Fire Plant and caterpillar thing were kept. Her smile was exceptionally warm today, he thought. Very captivating. He greeted her with enthusiasm.

'What did you say this thing was?' he asked, pointing to the caterpillar.

'We call it a "glass-fly", Mike. Does belong to an order of insectoids similar yet to the Order Diptera, on Earth – the flies. But I think tis nearer in nature to the Butterflies and Moths on Earth. For it has similar-like wings. But on other hand, it does light up – photoluminescent, you would say?'

'Amazing. These creatures seem to defy classification, don't they?'

'But yes, for they are not Earth insects. They be similar in some aspects of structure. Hard external skeleton, articulatio-limbs, and so and so. But they are their own kind. Insects – but not insects. Like all animals on Oceanus, Mike.'

'I guess, so how do you guys classify them?'

'Well, Mike, what do you think?' At his puzzled expression, she continued, 'We still are using Latin, sometimes Greek, names for the species and genus, familia and so on, just like on Earth. Tis an old and well understood tradition. No use changing now, and it allows Earth scientists to compare their data with ours. Our names do vary with the ones used on Earth, to suit the animals here, but they are accepted-yet on your world. Or so I do understand.'

'So, you use some similar names, like *flies*,' said Mike, 'but I don't really see – oh, I get it. This is the larval stage we're seeing, yes? I'm guessing the adult is the fly?'

'Yes, young manry. The adult stage is the glass-fly, as tis entirely see-through, so you canst see its internal organs. The pupa stage does precede that. We should get to see both stages within the next day or so.'

'Really? Bit quick, aint it?'

'No. On this island, as in many places here, the insectoids develop muchly fast. Life cycles are most dependent on it. Do you want to know the story of this creature?'

Mike nodded affably, so she continued with her story. She told him that first, the adult flies laid their eggs on the Fire Plants. The soils of the island were deficient in the nitrogen needed by all Oceanus plants, as they were on Earth, because nitrogen provides a key stage in plant respiration. So, the female glass-flies provided this much needed element for the Fire Plants, which they did by laying their eggs *inside* the plants, injecting them through two sharp tubes projecting from their abdomens. The eggs were rich in extra nitrogen, obtained by concentrating the waste the flies produced from ingesting other plant life they fed on, and other insectoids which were part of their diet.

Once inside the plant the eggs secreted that spare nitrogen, but in return received nutritious sugars from the plant. It was a rich symbiotic relationship, not just between two completely different species, but between two different "kingdoms" of life. Similar relationships were found in many species of animal and plant on Earth, but this one, on Oceanus, was, said Eleri, quite unique.

She also told him that, when it was ready, each egg hatched into a larva which burrowed out of the plant carefully, so as not to harm its host. It then formed a pupa on the outside, still providing nitrogen and receiving sugars, and perhaps other biochemicals in return, until it hatched out into the adult stage; the whole process taking just a few days. The adults, when ready, flew above the plants, becoming luminescent at night; a 'wondrous sight to behold', she said. On these special occasions millions of them could be seen floating above the island in a blaze of bright purplish light. When Mike's face lit up with anticipation, she said that unfortunately, this was not the right time of year. Maybe another time – or maybe not.

Once airborne, the flies mated and settled onto the plants to begin the process all over again. A by-product of the whole process was that the Tandy birds, the ones she and Mike had discussed on the aircraft, got a feast whilst the flies did their aerial display. As there were so many flies the birds never had a significant effect on the welfare of the plants. And, the birds played a different part in the life cycle of the plants, as she had told him on the flight.

'Well and now, Mike,' she said after she had told him the story, 'yet you sit there without a word and I do not know if you are really so interested or not?'

'Of course, I'm interested,' he said, looking hurt, 'but I told you I'm a newcomer to biology, or biolry, or whatever. I've heard botanists and entomologists on The Monsoon's science team, referring to things on Earth – and Prithvi, but didn't take much notice. But somehow, it all seems so much more interesting when you talk about it.' He saw the dubious look on her face, thinly disguised by her quirky smile, and said, 'Well, maybe, but you have a great way of explaining things. And you are a teacher, aren't you? I wish I'd been one of your students.'

'And so you are, in a way,' she said, smiling brightly. She moved closer to him, where he sat, and he luxuriated in the sweet scent of her. He couldn't help but look at her with longing, but the moment was suddenly gone, and she moved away, walking over to her microscope bench. 'Could you bring me the tray of seed in agaria, from the next room, Mike,' she said lightly, and he obligingly set off for the item, feeling that an opportunity had been lost – again.

****

During the next two days, whilst he assisted her with experiments, Mike and Eleri became much closer, discussing their lives and their feelings, the Universe, and all the rest. Mike emphatically denied that there were any females aboard The Monsoon that he currently shared his life with, nor had he ever really got close to any of them. For her part she told him she'd had three or four "manry-pals" over the last few years but nothing serious had developed, except once. He had let her down very badly, signing on for a four-month stint as a scientist on a research ship in the Great Middle Ocean, without any warning. That was, in any event a very unusual posting. She never saw him again but heard that he had fallen for the female "deputy Captain", and the two of them had moved to the western seaboard of Bhumi-Devi.

'Best place for him to be so,' she had said, with something approaching sourness, but in answer to his gentle and poorly worded enquiry, which she saw through very quickly, she assured Mike she was well over him.

He couldn't help thinking that upsets like that were one reason, and only one, why he had avoided getting too emotionally entangled with any one single female, let alone two. It just got in the way of fun and everyone knew life was too short anyway. But was it a valid reason anymore? He couldn't go on like that, avoiding risks; well, that sort of risk anyway, could he? He just didn't know. Right now, he he knew he wanted Eleri more than he had ever wanted anyone or anything in his whole life and, to someone like him, there was a stark realisation this was starting to get serious. Even more unusually, he knew he just didn't want to withdraw from this nascent relationship. But a large part of him still couldn't understand it.

Late one very warm, lazy afternoon, some days after her story about the glassfly, she came to fetch him from the living-zone tent. He followed her to the lab tent where she sat by the tank containing the Fire Plants and the glassfly pupa. Amazingly, he saw that it was starting to hatch, to break open and produce an adult fly. Mike and Eleri sat on stools right next to the the tank and she dimmed the lights above the apparatus. Mike had seen holos of butterflies emerging from pupae on Earth and settled down to watch something similar. Those holovids had been speeded up, as it normally took several hours.

Watching this creature before him he gasped as the pupa swelled visibly into a tiny, fat ball and its skin began to undulate with the movements of the creature inside. There was a pause of a minute or two and suddenly the top end of the pupal case literally burst open and a silvery worm like creature, about four centimetres long, quickly hauled itself out into the dim light. It was soaking wet but appeared to dry in mere seconds. Then, long wing structures unfolded and spread with astonishing speed. Eleri turned to Mike and grinned. He returned the grin and, at that moment, he realised he didn't want to be anywhere else in the entire Universe. Not on Earth or anywhere else in the Home System, not even on The Monsoon. He knew he would feel utterly at home wherever she was.

He sensed her presence acutely as she sat next to him, and it seemed like an electric current feeding him energy and sustenance. It was like being on brain-stim but without its associated risks. Even now, a tiny warning buzzer sounded in his brain – and then he pushed the thought to the back of his mind, forcing it into the darkness from whence it came.

In the tank the insectoid had pumped its wings out fully. There were four pairs of them, and they were incredibly large for such a small life form, probably measuring about ten or twelve centimetres across. He was astonished – and his heart gladdened by this little creature. Without more ado, it climbed rapidly up the two-metre stalk of the Fire Plant and as it did so Mike found he could indeed see right through its body. He could see its internal organs pumping rapidly with blood, purple blood in this case. When the fly reached a point close to the flowers it launched itself into the air in the top part of the tank and that was when Eleri pressed a button to shut off the lab lights. Then, gloriously, the creature lit up like an old-fashioned light bulb, its abdomen a veritable blaze of bluish-purple. Mike watched with mouth agape at the incredibly beautiful glow which reflected off its huge, slowly flapping wings. It was mesmerising.

Mike turned then to Eleri and studied her features glowing with the light from the tank. She was smiling as she watched the creature, but she noticed his gaze and turned to face him, eyes probing his. There was something in that serious but somehow joyous look she gave him, he realised. Their faces were just a few centimetres apart and they peered longingly into each-other's eyes, the way lovers have done since the dawn of humanity. Nothing was said. There was no need of it. The flapping of the insectoid started to slow and the creature began to settle back onto the Fire Plant. Mike began to turn toward its hypnotic light but Eleri gently touched his face with warm, welcoming fingers and turned it slowly back toward hers. Then she drew even closer and brought her generous lips into contact with his. He felt a kind of electric bliss as her tongue sought his, and he reciprocated. They had kissed before, chaste kisses on the cheek, even once or twice, lightly, on the lips. But nothing like this. The passion became almost unbearable.

'Oh, my Maker,' he whispered, coming up for air, as he clasped his arms firmly but gently, tenderly, around her body. Things suddenly became more urgent and they almost fell off their stools as they moved to hug each other yet more tightly, a deeply sensuous hug, as they kissed again and again. It was urgent but not the kind of desperate clutching, grabbing and mouth clamping exercise that so often occurs when two people have fallen 'in lust'. Mike had done that often enough. He doubted Eleri had. No matter. This was altogether gentler, slower and more sensual. He resisted the urge to try to manoeuvre her toward somewhere where they could lie together, or even to suggest it to her, but suddenly, she was the one who tugged him, very lazily, away from the tank. She said, in a low, husky whisper, 'The Living Zone. My quarters.'

'What about … the Maheshtras?' he said, feeling a little drunk even though no alcohol had touched his lips.

'They're such going to be out till late. Still studying the birds. Anywayins, we shall be in my *own* quarters. Come on. You are yet wasting time.' She grinned as she led him by the hand, out of the lab tent. It was starting to get dark outside and Mike could smell the heady fragrance of the Fire Plants surrounding the camp. He felt as though he was on fire himself, burning with a painless but brilliant flame. No, perhaps he was glowing – just like the glassfly.

Once inside her private area of the Living-Zone tent, separated from all the others by stout tent walls, she pulled Mike toward the bed. For a fleeting moment Mike noticed how untidy her quarters were. Eleri was the epitome of organisation and tidiness in the lab zone and in all her work, but he noted how upside down her bedroom was. It didn't matter. Nothing else did now, as he sank onto her unmade bed and they fastened lips again.

They just kissed – for a very long time, before starting to remove any clothing and when that happened it was, once again, Eleri who took the lead. She pulled off Mike's shirt and began to wrestle his trousers from him, whilst he eagerly sought her breasts. For a moment he was flummoxed by the way her brassier thing was kept on. It was like nothing any Navy woman wore. She giggled and pulled it off by unclasping some sort of device between the cups. Curious, he thought, how clothes are used on this planet. Even brassiers were unusual amongst femnas back in the Home System. For those who wanted them some tops had stiffened "cups" built in.

Eleri had got his trousers off by then, whipping off his undergarment she placed her hands on his bottom, gently pulling his solidly erect penis toward her belly. He managed to undo her own trousers, much more easily than her bra', and as they came off, she giggled and clasped her legs around his waist. He felt her squeeze and realised the strength in her thighs – and winced. Then began an extended period of simply stroking and caressing each-other's bodies, kissing each other in all the right places; the nipples, the tummy and each-other's necks, as they lay side by side.

Eleri looked deeply into his eyes and almost whimpered with desire, and at that point he knew he should enter her. She tightened her legs around his waist and sucked in air, in a sensual gasp, as he tentatively pushed his hard penis tentatively into her vulva, gently exploring and teasing her. If he was nothing else, Mike was a good lover and he knew how to please a woman. He continued to caress her body, almost reticently, and to kiss her, without moving more fully into her.

Before going further, he placed a hand firmly but gently on Eleri's pubic mound and sought her moist clitoris with two of his fingers. Rubbing gently, he felt how wet she was deep inside. She opened her mouth in a silent gasp of pleasure. What she then uttered almost surprised Mike, as a kind of deep, animal like, guttural grunt emerged from deep in her throat. She had climaxed and as he began to push his penis inside her body, he felt he go rigid with another. There was a sort of slurping sound as he pushed into her and out again. Boy, was she wet, he thought. It pleased him no end.

They fastened mouths again, as if their lives depended on it, and she pulled herself up, so he was underneath her. That was a fast move, he thought, but was fine with him. He liked that, and as she mounted him, he revelled in her grinding away over him. They turned to lie on their sides again after she had climaxed once more – and then it was his turn to climax. He felt a slow and incredible build up, as his sperm started from somewhere deep inside and boiled up through his penis, and then the release and intensity of pleasure as he could feel it shooting deeply inside her.

They both lay exhausted after that, gasping and sweating profusely in the heat and humidity of the Oceanus evening. Though mostly silent, he broke the spell when he suddenly thought of something he'd not discussed with her. It had all happened so quickly and spontaneously! He had a moment of alarm until he realised that if the Oceanus medical authorities didn't have the means, The Monsoon could easily supply the meds that might be needed. He asked her, gingerly, if she had taken the one-off anti-pregnancy pill that nearly all women did in the Home System. It was taken in adolescence, and he'd read that they also did this on Oceanus. She laughed and berated him gently for thinking that she hadn't already thought of such a thing and, yes, she had taken the meds in her adolescence. They were not living in the stone ages on Oceanus, she said, chiding him again.

As they laughed they heard a noise outside; it was the E-car. The Maheshtras were returning. They listened in silence as their friends made bumping and clunking noises while they off-loaded cameras and equipment. Mike and Eleri chuckled softly, like naughty school kids.

'Hi-la,' came Chanda's voice, after just a few minutes, floating in from the main living area of the tent. 'Tis only us. El? Mike? Are you here?'

Eleri chuckled and said to Mike, 'I had better be going to her. I shall simple say we decided to go to bed early.' When he looked a little embarrassed, she said, 'Do not be a-worrying manry-mate. They will understand. I think Chanda has been guessing that I been falling for you some time since. But listen yet, don't be a-worry. She guessed – for I did not tell her such an thing.' She gave him a quirky smile again and pulling on her clothes hurried to the opening of her quarters, slipped through and closed it firmly behind her with its heavy press-studs. So, at least she doesn't want Chanda or Gajana to be able to see this far into her privacy, thought Mike. How touching.

He lay back on her bed and relaxed. He could smell her body odour and the pungent perfume of mingled and spent body fluids. He felt a flood of genuine and deep affection for this femna. Feelings, he realised, that he couldn't ever remember having for a single femna – before now. Before here. It was different but it was good. What had Oceanus done to him, he wondered, without any real apprehension, just curiosity. And what was yet to come?

The answer to the last question seemed to be answered quickly, at least as far as the rest of this night was concerned, when Eleri returned, having been absent for a mere minute or so. She bustled into the tent, walked swiftly to the bed, settled down next to him and smiled like the cat which had got its special meaty treats.

'I have told her we do not want to be disturbe'd. I am sorry yet, Mike, but I did tell her we are now together. Still and I know she will be discreet.' Eleri suddenly looked worried. 'I am so sorry, if you did not want them to know. I have been the one who is yet not discreet.'

He held her and peered into the depths of her bright violet eyes. 'It's okay,' he said, 'cos I'm sure they would have realised before too long. And if you trust them, so do I. They are my friends as well now.'

'Coursry,' she said, relaxing. Then her brow furrowed again, and she said, 'We are together now, Mike, are we not? I should say, I mean, you do feel strongly, do you not? Like I, about you?'

'Of course, El,' he said, and he meant it. It was an unfamiliar thing, but it was definite. He knew that things were not going to be the same ever again.

He didn't yet know how true that would be.

*

During the pauses in lovemaking which followed, Eleri said, 'Mike, I am not going to say I full love you. Really, really love. Nay, not such now. But soon it may come, if we should stay best of mateys and be understanding of each one's needs. And I will be loyal yet, to you. Will you be so to me, Mike?'

'Yes, I will, Eleri. I feel …. Well, when I'm with you I feel quite different from when I've been with anyone else. I mean it. As for love. Well, I don't know much about that kind of thing, yet. Not love that's romantic – like the ancient ones talked about, that is. But, if the way I feel now is anything to go by, then it may well be love.'

Eleri's face broke out in a blazing smile once more and she kissed him. This time it was he who gently pulled her to him and began to pull her clothes off. She quickly reciprocated and soon they were making sweet physical love again.

Breathlessly, she suddenly whispered into his ear, 'Please, we must be yet quieter this time. I am fraid Gajana and Chanda may still hear. They know now but ….'

'Come here,' he said as he hugged her still tighter, and chuckled.

**

A long time afterwards, as he half dozed in the depth of the night, he lay with Eleri snuggled up to him, and wondered sleepily about what this sweet woman would do when it came time to actually leave the doomed planet. Although she said, and he believed he, that she accepted the science of the Home System, he had also detected a marked reluctance to accept that she would really have to leave this place. Would she come with him? If so, where would they go? Would they even still be attached, emotionally? After the hours of unalloyed pleasure, for both of them, he was troubled by these and similar thoughts but his physical exhaustion at last pushed him deeply into the world of sleep.

Chapter 18

ENTRAPMENT

Admiral Tenak was watching an old-fashioned, dead flat, video image of Dracus Muggredge, displayed on a large, multi-function wall screen in his private cabin suite on board The Monsoon. 'So, how is Michaelsonn Tanniss, Draco?' said Tenak, 'cos I last spoke to him about a three weeks ago.'

'I think he's a bit busy Arkas. Too busy enjoying himself. I have not heard from him – or Eleri,' Muggredge chuckled.

'I thought he was supposed to be working on your grand project?'

'Sure now, but – well friendling, you do not have to be a genius yet to realise that he and my niece get on *very, very well*. I think he would be happy still, just about anywhere, as long as he was with her.'

'That might be just what he needs, Professier. Anyway, how can I help you today?'

'I have a request, friendling sirra, but firsting, let me say that I for one am enjoying our weekly chats over this video phonery thing.' Tenak nodded and the Professor continued, 'Actually, I do have some good news, Arkas. I am yet pleased to say that the University here has agreed to fund my new program to preserve as many seeds, nuts, fruit, animal sperm, eggs, and all such. This material is to be frozen in liquid nitrogen, and saved for future time, for either re-growing here or … some so-place else. Unfortunate yet, Arkas, they didnar agree to my request to ask the government for funding to place them in pressurised vessels and bury them underground, here on Oceanus.'

'Too expensive, I should think,' said the Admiral.

'Exact-so. Tis shame-most. Which brings me to my request. I am wondering if these gametes, and such, could be stored aboard your vessel, and yet other Navy ships? Then, to be taken to the Home System?'

Tenak was silent for a moment, then said, 'I would think so, but it depends on the overall sizes of the consignments. We've probably got enough room in unused hangars but, remember Draco, our primary mission is to carry as many passengers as possible. We're here to start an evac' process and we haven't got much room that's suitable right now.'

'Okay, Arkas. Coursry, but I do not think you have many takers for evacuation so far, do you? But if that changes, still I will understand. And I do not think this need preclude my idea? Praps you might be able to take them else-time? Anywayins, I will try to get more information about the likely size and volume of the containers as soon as poss'ly.'

'I'm happy to keep your request in mind, Draco. I think the material could be transported in modest quantities, whenever practical.' Tenak paused for a moment and continued, 'Leave it with me Professier. Now that there's been some positive developments here, I've sent a data probe back home, to explain what's been going on. I'm well behind with that task. I might have to send another, to ask authority for your proposition, but it's expensive to send probes, so I'll probably wait for an appropriate time. I will push for it, my friend, you can be sure. If necessary, they'll have to send some research ships to take them but don't forget, all such material will have to be screened for pathogens, security issues, and whatever, by HS Authorities, before it can be stored anywhere on planets back home. Meanwhile, I wish you luck with the program as planned.'

'Thank you, Admiral. You are yet so very generous. Morrow-times for now.'

****

The Antarctica was still accelerating, now five weeks out from the Earth and one week away from the transit zones situated beyond the Kuiper Belt, far into the outer reaches of the Solar System. This was a region was known generally as "the Classical Edge". On the ship's bridge a small instrument panel flashed on in a blaze of light in a room with otherwise subdued lighting. It was the "night watch" on board and there were few officers on deck, but First Officer Florian was there, on Watch. A tiny communications bud in his right ear bleeped softly in synchrony with the panel and made him tap his wristcom and summon Providius, 'Urgent com to the Captain. Forward the incoming message.'

The ship's Qewsers had picked up a message from an artificial object travelling in the opposite direction to them, at ten thousand klicks per second, on its way from the Classical Edge. Although the signals were massively shifted to the blue end of the spectrum, which confirmed that the object was indeed inbound, travelling in their general direction, other instruments showed that it was, in fact, several million kilometres wide of their position. The onboard AI confirmed no danger of collision. It was near enough for the hypercomp to be able to interrogate it, but the object only willingly released a minuscule part of its data cache. It turned out it was a dataprobe from Admiral Tenak. He and his ship were okay. The rest of the message was securely marked for Allied Government attention only.

****

In the unimagably distant Ra star system, the huge Navy capital ship continued in its high orbit above the equator of the massive, shining, blue bauble called Oceanus. Admiral Tenak stood at a guard rail at the front of bridge number one, a large chamber inside the outermost layer of the main hub fuselage of the vessel. The outermost wall of the bridge projected, bubble-like, from the hub here. Tenak gazed wistfully out of the wide windows set in that bubble, which, at the moment, happened to be overlooking the planet. Strictly speaking, windows were no longer necessary on crewed spacecraft, Naval, or otherwise. Instrumentation and comp screens were highly evolved technologies and more than adequate. Humans, though, still liked and *wanted* to look to look out of windows. It brought a psychological sense of well-being and stability, to be able to see outside; to be able to observe, in some way, where they, personally, fitted into the cosmos and to *feel* the connection. It was a sensation which was not, thus far, compensated for by computer simulations, or instrumentation. And, perhaps surprisingly, the presence of windows allowed the "larger picture" to be seen, by Navy personnel, in particular, enabling them to catch things sometimes missed when purely artificial methods were used.

The windows through which Tenak gazed in such silence, were expansive, 5-metre-high, "meta-glass" panels made of composite alloy, or "invisi-mesh", enhanced with modified diamond dust, called "Duralamium Gamma Four", in a thickness 9 layers deep. The windows could also be rapidly isolated behind massively thick composite bulkheads if the ship was raised to battle stations.

As it was not subject to the simulated gravitational effect of the rotating torus, this part of The Monsoon was, currently a microgravity environment. And yet, "normal" movement was made relatively easy, or nearly so, because both the floors and the shoes of the crew were coated with "Microloop", or "positive grip layer", a very advanced, mineral form of the fabric hook and eye material, first used in the 20th century, for fastening garments. The microloop was a microscopic version of that, with superb adhesion when walked upon. It had the flexibility of allowing very natural locomotion over floor surfaces. And yet, it still had its limitations, tending to try to "keep hold" of those who attempted to run over it if they attempted it at high speed, but letting go of them suddenly, sometimes propelling them into extended floating.

It also deadened the sound of anyone walking on it quietly, so that Tenak, who was in any case, lost in deep thought didn't hear the person joining him from behind, till he heard a warning cough.

'You're planning something, aren't you Admiral?' said a female voice over his shoulder. He knew the voice's owner, instantly.

'Just because I'm enjoying the view, Ssanyu? How insightful,' he said, smiling.

Captain Ebazza walked slowly to his side and joined him in staring out at the marbled planet floating in the void. 'Impressive, isn't it?' she offered.

'I never tire of it,' he said, 'You know, we've come so far - as a species, I mean. Yet, we're so far away from what we need to be – where we mean to be. What we have to become, I suppose, to … flourish in this Universe.'

'I agree, Admiral, but perhaps not everyone aspires to your ideals for the human species. Some are still just interested in … power, or wealth. Or both.'

'I know, I know,' he sighed, exhaling slowly, as if with impatience. 'Anyway, I reckon there's something strange going on down there, Ssanyu.' He nodded toward the planet and continued, 'and you're right, in fact. I have been planning something. Not sure if it's ethical. Wondering if it's just going to get us into more shit, big-time.'

He paused for a long time. She looked at him quizzically. 'Well, are you going to tell me, sir, or do I have to guess?' she chuckled.

He turned to her and in the subdued light he ran his eyes over her wide, smoothly moulded ebony face, which reflected the ethereal blue light from the glistening planet far beyond the window. 'I think you'll like it, Ssanyu,' he said. 'I want you to launch a probe. Send it through a series of orbits at varying angles to the equator – and no higher than, say 85 klicks. *We're* going to look for signs of the geology that Professor Muggredge was talking about. You know, that stuff about the strata bridging the gap around 8.5 million years ago. We've already searched for the rocks using the ship's long range intruments but came up blank. Must be very small amounts of it, if it's really there. We need to scan the continent, of course but we know we're probably looking to Simurgh for the best chance. So you know where to concentrate the probe's orbits. But don't neglect any of the larger islands, Ssanyu. There's a lot of ocean to cover down there.'

'I have to admit, I don't really understand much of this stuff, Admiral. I guess I didn't study geology very carefully at the Academy.'

'Neither did I, but maybe we need to get more familiar with it now. Muggredge needs to give me more information about what our instruments should look for. I'll get in touch with him now and ask him to upload as much data – that's specific to Oceanus – as poss'. The ship's own database on geology should suffice for the rest. We're going to compile a geological map of the planet, Ssanyu. If those rocks are there, we'll find them.'

'Very good Admiral, but won't the authorities, down there, notice this?'

'I trust not, Ssanyu. I don't think they'd pick it up visually. The probe could do, say, 30 orbits to try to find something. Then bring it in, before their old-fashioned sensors lock on.'

'That gives us about two days. And we can instruct it to maintain telemetric silence until it's due back in, so we avoid any radio frequency traffic being picked up, on the planet.'

'Exactly.'

'At once Admiral, and, by the way, you're right. I do like this.'

****

Mike and Eleri were enjoying the midday sun outside the laboratory tent. The Maheshtras were the other side of the island, observing the Tandy birds again, and Eleri was planning a field trip to Silbershell Cove, some kilometres distant. Her plan was to collect samples of a seaweed-like plant that grew in large quantities on one side of the cove, where it was usually in shade.

The plant grew so fast it could very nearly be watched spreading. No-one understood why it grew on that one side of the cove only, but some sort of biochemical reaction to shade was suspected. She needed to collect samples for analysis and carry out in- situ observations, for which purpose she'd already left slow speed video cameras, on site, for about 3 days. It was just part of her studies and though it didn't seem to quite fit the current mission, Mike said nothing. Were they really so concerned about seaweed? Well, it was a life-form on Oceanus, after all, he thought. He didn't want to display his ignorance.

The two of them sat outside the tent, holding hands and laughing about the various discussions they had had with the Maheshtras the evening before.

'Gajana's comment about the Tandy birds' webbed feet was yet so funny,' she said, 'By ways, Chanda suggested I take you along to Silbershell Cove today.'

Mike gave her a non-committal look. '

Don't fancy it?' she said.

'I fancy you,' he said, 'and I've got a better idea,' he continued. 'Why don't we take advantage of the fact that Gajana and Chanda are going to be out the rest of the day?' He winked at her. She was not amused.

'You're a doopi-shrak, Mike. Tis what we say here, when we talk of someone who carnt get enough sex. You are yet driven, young manry. Driven, so you are.' She laughed and swept away his hand that had suddenly started creeping along her left leg. 'I am sorry my manry, but the collection really does need to be done today. I didst mean it when I said you should come along. You know you have made muchly progress in overcoming your fears about open places. I have watched you do stuff you never would have done still a few weeks ago. Oh, come on. Why will you not come with me? You mayst want to take swim in the cove. Tis really protected from the elementsa. Tis almost completely enclosed too. You shall not be fraid there. You know how to swim, do you not?'

'Yeah, sure I know how to swim El. Believe it or not, I actually do swim in the smaller pools aboard The Monsoon. When I was a youngster I even won a speed-swim medal, once, in an indoor pool. Haven't done much for a couple of years, though.'

'Well, there you so go, my Mike. Do you like diving? I mean - diving to the bottom, under the water?'

'I never dived "to the bottom" of anything, El. I tried an aqualung set once and used it in a social pool, for practice. Never used it in the sea, though. Did a bit of snorkelling. Again, when I was but a kiddly.' Mike used the Devian word for child. He was suddenly starting to sound like Eleri, he mused. 'The breathing gear they use back home is a type of small mouthpiece that extracts oxygen directly from the water and feeds it to you,' he said. 'Sort of like fish gills, I suppose. I'll bet the gear you've got here is the old aqualung stuff. Air bottles and so on?'

'Scuse me, young manry of mine, but that is where you are wrong,' she said, 'Most people do use air cylindry, tis true.' Mike started to nod and laugh, but she continued, 'Listen here. We do have the air-breathers as well. I have yet used them. There arint many of them around but our team has a supply, so before you do criticise, just try out one of those and see if it yet compares with the gear on old Earth.'

'Oh, I believe you,' he replied, 'And I never said *I'd actually* used one of those things.'

'Then now shall be the time to try, youngry.'

He grimaced but she continued, 'Look now, I will help. I have some experience swimming in these waters, with and without apparatus. I am preferring to free-dive, but I can show you how to use the air-breather device. How about it, Mike? I know you shall enjoy. The sea water is warm here and, like I said, the cove is surely enclosed and mostly shallow and …'

'Okay!' he protested, 'I'll come along, okay?'

She jumped off her seat, bent over him and hugged him as he sighed in resignation.

'I can guarantee you shall love it,' she enthused, 'and, still you never know. If we get back here quickish, afterward, there might even be a bit of "doopi-doopi," before the Maheshtras are back.'

'Doopi-doopi?' he said, 'that's what you call it? Really?'

She nodded and winked, but he said, 'I thought this place is about 20 klicks away? Since the E cars travel *so fast,* that means we'll have to get a move on. We might get there by Ra-down.'

She just rolled her eyes.

They were soon on their way southwards to Silbershell cove, Eleri driving the one available electrocar. Mike thought she looked so elegant and beautiful in a white, one-piece swim costume. The journey took them along a plain which formed the southern half of the island but as they neared the cove Mike noticed they seemed to be climbing uphill. But the cove was on the coast, wasn't it? When he asked Eleri about it she told him that the cove had actually formed where the sea had partially broken into an old crater. There was a small rise to surmount the thing. The crater was thought to have been formed by a meteorite strike very close to the coast, no more than 8 thousand years ago, after which sea levels had risen. That got his interest. Such things were highly unusual, she said. So they were, he thought.

A grindingly slow 35 minutes later they arrived, and Mike's heart started beating hard with anxiety, but he tried to hide his nerves. The land had risen sharply the nearer they got to the coast and, parking the E car in a small defile which erosion had cut into the landward side of the crater, they walked up and through the gash, emerging some way up the landward wall. Given the view from here, it was certainly true that the area was extraordinarily beautiful, thought Mike, pausing for breath.

A classic crater bowl shape, about a half a kilometre wide, lay before them, with the peaceful cove nestled in the bottom, surrounded by the hillocky lip of the crater. Tufty Fire plants grew all around the crater edge and provided even more seclusion. And at the far end, directly ahead, lay a narrow gap, where the crater edge had collapsed. Beyond that Mike could see a wedge of deep blue sea.

They walked down a steep sandy track to a small white beach that curved around the cove in a nearly perfect arc. The sea water here was a greenish blue and lapped gently at the narrow strip of silvery sand. Mike was certainly impressed, and he could feel himself starting to calm a little. She had chosen an amazing place to come, because the cove was almost completely enclosed, though the broad sky above still lent it a very open feel. But he was beginning to feel he could cope.

In the distance the visible wedge of ocean was flecked with breakers. It looked raw and wild. He wouldn't have wanted to go through the gap into that. The open ocean struck fear into him but Eleri told him not to think about it.

'There are yet some reefs out there, just beyond the gap,' she said, 'so big they stop the wildermost waves from coming in the bay. That is why tis so sheltered in here - and good for observing the flora and fauna.' She fetched a small duffle bag out of the E-car and rejoined him.

'I can see the reefs, but I don't intend getting a close look at them,' he said as he took off his canvass style shoes. He wore shorts that doubled as bathing trunks and a Navy standard issue bathing top which protected his upper body from UV light. He was ashamed he still wasn't used to exposure to sunlight, despite his time on Oceanus.

To the left-hand side of the cove was what looked like a long wooden walkway a metre or so above the water. In about the middle of the walkway was a very small, padlocked shed, the only building in the whole area and a marvellously incongruous sight. Almost an eye sore, he thought, and, in the circumstances, it surprised him. Whilst he momentarily soaked up the mellow sunshine and mild sea breeze Eleri trotted off to the shed and opened it. He quickly joined her, and she handed him one air-breather device, taking another and stuffing it in her duffle bag.

The device was sleek, black and shaped like a muzzle, about the size of a fist. He was surprised by its lightness and, turning it over in his hands he studied it, perplexed, as though it were some sort of alien egg.

Eleri suggested he try it on. He was reticent but co-operated as she pointed out a couple of switches on one side of the device, used for regulating the amount of oxygen being extracted from the water, this being sucked in through vent-like grills, one either side of the central muzzle. The device was held on the head by metal strip reinforced elastic. Eleri took the device and briefly demonstrated its proper use, showing him how to adjust the oxygen level till he was comfortable with it and how to tighten the elasticated head strap. She also gave him a transparent mask for his eyes.

Eleri emphasised the simplicity of the device and said it was important to ensure it didn't come off without the wearer realising. She also warned him that it could operate continuously for 2 hours only, after which two internal filtration cartridges would need changing. If they were *not* changed toxic gases would build up in the mask very quickly. With that she shooed him off into the water.

Mike's heart beat faster. He couldn't turn back now. She was watching him. He waded in, pushing deeper against the force of the water. There was shock at the feel of the water; colder than he'd expected. The smell of the spume reminded him of the odd occasion he'd been near the sea, back on Earth. Pushing himself waste deep he realised, or hoped, he'd quickly get used to its coolness.

Eleri cried out from the shore that he hadn't put the device on yet, and he grinned at her, absent mindedly, but as he was about to don it he noticed the femna pull a long, slender tube like device out of the shed on shore. 'What's that?' he shouted to her.

'Tis a precaution, no more' she said, 'yet what we call a sting-tube. I suppose you mayst say – an harpoon - but this can fire a little metal bolt that explodes. Just a little explosion.'

'What do you need an exploding bolt for? You're not going to shoot me, are you?' He laughed nervously, anxious about the water of course, not her.

'I told you,' she shouted to him, 'tis just a precaution. I have been diving these seas all my life. I know you always have to take precautions. Do not be a-worrying. Carry on so.'

As Eleri was already wearing her costume she now began to join him, wading smoothly into the water, carrying the sting tube, looking more like a see-through rifle, by her side. 'Are you coming swimming with me now?' he asked, hopefully.

'Later, bronco boy. Later,' she said as she reached him. She showed him the sting tube and he held it uncertainly, looked it over, then gave it back to her. 'Here, you have it. You're the expert. I still don't know what you'd need that for. You said there aren't any carnivorous fishling things around here.

'I am sure there are not, Mike of mine. Tis true there have been some wilding storms in this area recent-times but I do not believe they should have pushed in any of the larger beasteries.'

That's alright then, he thought, acerbically. I'm glad you told me about *larger beasteries*, earlier, he mused.

'I do not think we've got anything to worry about,' she continued, 'but the waters in this cove get quite deep nearer the sea gap. Out there tis over 15 metres down. You have to respect nature Mike but be not too afraid. You shall be fine. I mean it. Now, get ye going. Let me see you swim a bit. Then switch on the breather and do little bits of diving – just yet in shallow water. Do *not* be going beyond 3 metres depth. I shall stay here, for I want you to be doing this on your own. You will feel better about it. Okay?'

Well, he thought, he'd give it a go. He was sure she was right. In fact, from the point of view of his agoraphobia, Eleri had chosen the location very well. And being underwater didn't normally generate his phobia if he was in a relatively enclosed area.

'Okay,' he said, after a short while. He waded in further, then took the plunge and launching in, using a good old-fashioned breaststroke. More shock of the cold and the bitter tang of salt-water splashes. After a while he stood, grinned at her and shook the water out of the breather which had been strapped around his right arm. He then donned it and switched it on. The device's sensors noticed that his face was still above water, so it just became porous to the air, which meant he didn't breathe in his own carbon dioxide. He immersed himself very slowly and as the water gradually covered the mask it bubbled briefly and started pouring cool oxygen into his mouth and nose. The water made a gurgling noise in his ears. It had been a very long time since he'd done anything like this and his first reaction was to stand up, immediately and almost pull off the device. He saw El, some way off, looking concerned. Then he submerged himself again nervously and slowly and stayed slightly under the surface, unmoving, while the device worked and gave him confidence to move.

He swam around uncertainly in circles, at first, about 30 metres out from the sand strip and occasionally diving below the surface, down to the sandy bottom, stirring up opaque clouds of yellow sand. He quickly adapted to the device. This is good, he thought. Then he decided to brave it and go further, keeping an eye on depth, which was being measured by his wristcom. About 60 metres out he could see the bed of the cove through the green murk and noticed it that was covered in grey rocks, except they weren't rocks. He remembered Eleri saying this was a calcium carbonate deposit made by microscopic creatures, just like corals back home.

Then he saw long, billowing, fronds of yellow seaweed-like plants anchored in the coral, waving to and fro' in the gentle current. There seemed to be clouds of tiny fish like creatures, mostly bright blue in colour, but some purple, and others yellow. Whilst the land animals, including the "birdles" were similar to those on Earth, he'd seen noticeable differences. But these small critters were much more like the fish everyone knew back on Earth.

The "fishlings" all swam easily away from him as he moved through the murk toward them, but still he gave playful chase, moving absent mindedly into the deeper water. He noticed strands of brightly coloured seaweed lying on the sea floor and decided to take a closer look. It was wonderful to be able do whatever you pleased, staying under the water. It felt so free. Why hadn't he done this before?

As he neared the white strands, they unexpectedly drew away from him, as though they sensed his presence, just like the fish. Could seaweed do that? he thought. Well, this was not Earth, after all. He swam onward, and as he tried to catch them he noticed they were covered with structures which looked like little blue bubble things and grey wart-like nodules. The strands kept evading him and it was then that he noticed large numbers of them close-by. But these weeds were thicker than the first ones he'd seen; some as thick as his legs. Their bubbles and nodules were correspondingly larger.

The mass of strands were stretched out along the sea floor like a colossal mat of thick white spaghetti, and he peered ahead into the murk, to see where they led, but a curtain of green gloom obscured his view. A sudden movement caught his eye and he turned to see a large red and white fish threshing about, apparently trapped in a mass of the smaller strands. As he watched the body of the fish started bleeding; a thick, darkly glutinous, red, stain spreading through the water. The creature was then whisked away into the green murk ahead and at that point he realised, with a cold numbing sensation in his stomach, that he might have fallen into a trap.

Turning, he tried to swim for the shore but began to feel confused. He couldn't tell which was the right direction. No matter, he needed to get away from there. His heart started to pound wildly as he felt something wrap itself around both his legs. It felt like a large rubber hose, so he looked back and, sure enough, it was one of the thicker white strands. Strands? No, they were tentacles, he realised, with rising alarm, and immediately tried to swim out of trouble. But at that point another thick tentacle caught him; this time wrapping itself around his waist.

He was starting to panic, threshing about madly, and he thought of the bleeding fish thing he'd seen just moments ago. He knew, then and there, that the same fate could engulf him. He hammered the tentacle round his legs with both fists but there was no give in it. There seemed to be no escape; the tentacles were immensely strong. He couldn't believe what was happening. Was he going to be eaten? Things like this didn't happen to Mike Tanniss. They didn't happen to any real person in the real world, did they? You just read stories about it.

His thoughts suddenly turned to anger; he had to fight it. He gulped in air through his breather, grasped the tentacle around his waist and yanked at it with as much strength as he could bring to bear. It seemed to work! It was starting to dislodge. Great, he thought. This might be easier than he'd imagined. The fish hadn't had arms and hands with which to *pull*. He did.

He suddenly went rigid with pain, as three spots of searing heat seemed to drill into him, two in his legs and one in his right hip. What was happening? The pain started to dull a little and he bent himself back to the task of pulling off the tentacles around his legs but as he did so, he saw four more massive tentacles whip from behind him and attach themselves to his waist. He was starting to tire now, and his feeling of utter disbelief returned.

Then, he remembered – the electro-shock wristcom that Tenak had given him. He fumbled for it on his left wrist. It wasn't there. Surely not? Must have dropped it, he realised, panic again starting to claw at his chest. His mind became filled with a ghastly certainty that the wristcom had been his last chance.

He felt incredibly tired but tried again to swim away, out of the engulfing strands, when he felt the jolt of half a dozen or more blasting stings, coming from different parts of his lower body. This creature, whatever it was, wanted him and it wasn't going to take no for an answer. A strange thing happened then. A sort of calmness seemed to descend on him. He began not to care, not feeling terror anymore. What was the point, he thought, lazily and he began to close his eyes and slowly, to dream.

He seemed to be drifting freely, but how could he be? Who cared anyway? For a moment he became dimly aware of his surroundings again and sensed that something large was hitting the water, very close to him. Then his mind began to drift again. He wondered if the splashing disturbance was another of these creatures, maybe closing in to take its share of him. He had an awful mental image of several of these things fighting over him, all trying to get the juiciest bits. In his fevered mind he imagined the tentacles as massed bundles of fibres springing, medusa-like, from gigantic faces which frowned with anger, their huge, dark mouths agape, seething with thousands of knife-like teeth. He thought that one of those mouths was very near now, but he didn't really care any more. He was just too tired to bother, and he started slipping into darkness. No fear, no love, no hate. Nothing but blackness.

PART TWO

THE PAST UNLOCKED

Chapter 19

ISOLATED

Admiral Tenak arrived at Prime Science Station, situated in Block 3 on The Monsoon's rotating torus. No Positive Grip Layer, or "PGL", was needed here, the torus producing a comfortable 0.92 Earth gravity. The Chief Science Officer had offered to send Tenak all his latest data, via his wristcom. But Tenak, from his position in the hub observation deck, had floated through more than 200 metres of corridors in the bowels of the ship, then jogged, carefully, across 350 metres of PGL covered decking in the same section. Then, rather than catch the elevator he'd climbed 170 metres, up through the number three "spoke", to the torus. The climb was by ladder, running through a tube no more than 1.5 metres wide, alongside, but separate from the elevator shaft used by most people. At the start of the climb, in the micro-gravity of the hub, where you could float, it was necessary to climb "up" *feet first*, because the gravity increased gradually as you got closer to the end of the climb, in the torus itself. By that time, you were "descending" quite naturally and safely; not coming down head-first.

'Admiral?' said Jennison, the ship's Chief Scientist; a position known as, "Doctrow", in the academic world of the 25th Century, but, in the ship's hierarchy, ranking as a Lieutenant. Orben Thietmar Heribert Jennison's long, thin, slightly haggard face showed surprise as he saw Tenak emerge, boots down through the hatch which exited the ladder tube in the ceiling. The tall, narrow framed Jennison clad in a baggy, ill-fitting blue one-piece, happened to be standing near the elevator door, patiently waiting for the Admiral's comment on his findings, via wristcom.

'I wondered what had happened after I sent the data, sir,' he said. A puzzled look fell over Jennison's face, a clouded visage, which spoke volumes of its owner's over-long hours of research and study, secreted away in this part of the ship.

'Oh no, lieutenant,' said Tenak, 'I'm surprised you aren't up to date with my preferences, these days, for getting around the ship, on foot. You are now. I wanted to talk to you and your team, face to face. Not just gawk at another holo-feed, and – I felt I needed the exercise. Anyway, please show me your findings. Oh, by the way, I also prefer the larger holo screens in your lab.'

'Of course, sir,' said Jennison, looking bemused. He turned and led Tenak through the Science Observatory Module, straight to the main lab', where he reported that astonishing data had come through just a few hours earlier. Tenak followed him past rows of automated equipment and the occasional blue coated scientist peering at graphics displays or poring over hand-held data-pads. There was a continuous background hum in the area.

Seconds later they emerged into a large rectangular room, the walls of which were covered by several rows of huge gel screens, rising from the floor up to the high ceiling of the chamber.

'Darken by 50%,' said Jennison, addressing the room itself, as they entered, and he invited Tenak to watch one particular wall screen. Then he spoke to the hypercomp AI

'Aleph Blue, run data stream Omega Two. Security clearance Beta One Eight.' The massive screen burst into life.

'Show graphic of Ra system,' said Jennison, and a semi-3 D animation of the Ra stellar system spread across the screen, an orange ball representing the star itself. Against that background the computer projected the "real time" video record of the event Tenak had come to see. On the image a sudden flash expanded outwards behind the disk of Ra, spreading a radiant blue light which washed out to the edge of the screen in a fraction of a second. 'The A I, has toned down the brightness for our benefit and the colour is false, of course,' said Jennison.

'A gamma ray burst,' said Tenak, 'but was it just gamma rays alone?'

'No, about 70 % was gamma, about 16 % was X rays and 14 % visual wavelength light. Let me slow the vid down for you. This is what makes it interesting, sir. This is it at one ten millionth real speed.'

As they watched again, the flash began from a kind of nucleus which simply popped into existence about 20 degrees to the left of Ra, as seen in the screen. It blossomed out like the petals of some brilliant blue flower, then swept outwards in all directions.

'The nucleus was certainly small. Maybe a disc shape? Can we see that nucleus in more detail?' asked Tenak.

'Your observation is spot on. I didn't notice it till the AI overlaid the nucleus with graphics.'

The AI obligingly overlaid the source of the light burst with a tiny contour map accompanied by sets of glowing red figures.

'That doesn't seem to show a lot more, lieutenant,' said the Admiral, 'just a flat disc.'

'I agree,' said Jennison. But, in fact, we shouldn't even be able to see that much. The point is, we would have expected a stellar object to be more like a point source, even using the ship's telescopes. Our instruments just aren't large enough to resolve distant stars into their proper spherical shapes if they're more than 10 light years outside of this system. We can resolve about 30 of the nearest stars into discs, which show quite a lot of features, but the position and characteristics of this thing doesn't fit any of those.'

Tenak folded his arms and held the tips of the fingers of one hand against his chin, seemingly lost in thought, as the scientist ordered the AI to run the video again; this time at one *billionth* of normal speed, and then, to freeze the image. The screen started with background black again, then the source of the flash appeared as a tiny, blazing, disc-like shape but with no detail. Columns of figures, produced by the AI, rolled along in strips both sides of the images. Jennison next asked the machine to magnify the view five million times and the disc immediately grew larger, but it was now simply a dimmer, blurry disk. Jennison said that neither the AI nor the ship's telescopes could achieve satisfactory resolution.

'There's another thing we've discovered, related to what I mentioned earlier, Admiral,' said the scientist, clearly relishing what he was about to say, 'which is that this object is not at the same distance as any other gamma ray burst ever seen.' Tenak's brows knitted at this, as Jennison continued, 'Gamma ray bursters have been observed for hundreds of years. They were discovered in the late 20th century. Since then, hundreds of thousands have been catalogued, but the vast majority were found to be billions of light years away, far outside our galaxy. Most of them were beyond the local cluster of galaxies, the group the Milky Way belongs to. They were theorized to be exploding hyper-giant stars, or the collisions of neutron stars or black holes. A few have been observed within the local galaxy group but they're unusual – and shockingly close for something that represents the largest explosions ever seen in Nature.'

Tenak pre-empted Jennison's next words, 'Clearly, this object is very close indeed, relatively speaking. How can that be?'

Jennison looked as though he was about to deliver the shock of a lifetime. And in some ways, he was.

'The ship's sensors have been able to triangulate this burst.'

Tenak's eyes widened as Jennison continued, 'Yes, sir, *triangulate*. And it looks as though it's no more than a light *month* away from this system.' Tenak's mouth opened but his jaw didn't quite drop.

'Yes,' said the scientist. '*That close.* So, it means the power of the burst must be relatively tiny. Minuscule in comparison with the usual ones. If it weren't, we would all be dead now, or at least irradiated to hell. And that would include everyone on Oceanus.'

'So, isn't there anything that indicates the real nature of this object? What about its gravity waves?' asked Tenak.

'We haven't got that far, yet, Admiral,' said Jennison, then addressed the AI again, 'If you've finished analysing the data, Aleph Blue, please now show us the gravity wave profile. Highest resolution, please.'

It took a small fraction of a second for the hypercomp to flash its analysis onto the screen, showing it as a contour map, with accompanying figures, again in rolling columns next to the image.

'Well,' said Jennison, 'it looks like the gravity waves show a relatively small body, as I expected, but the lack of resolution on the image data is frustrating. Looks like it might be, say, the mass of a moon? Probably a large moon, like Callisto, one of Jupiter's moons, back in the Solar System. Maybe bigger. But I don't ever remember seeing gravity waves from anything with features like *that*.'

'Explain please.'

'Very difficult to be precise – but look at this,' Jennison pointed to the way the graphics showed the gravity waves spreading out from the object, representing them as hundreds of overlapping, expanding, concentric shells. He said, 'This is … amazing. You can't see it very well here, but the graphics indicate they might originate from *multiple* points on the object – not from its gravitic centre. It doesn't look as if the AI has anything in its database remotely similar and it also can't resolve the image anymore. And look again. It's even more mysterious,' Jennison elaborated excitedly, 'because it looks like the graviton fields may have interfered with the last plasma cloud ejected from Ra.'

'Interfered with it?' said Tenak.

Continuing to interpret the figures and graphics which rolled up on the giant screen, Jennison explained, 'It may have … Well, it looks like it might have been what caused the ion storm to *accelerate* as it neared Oceanus. We know that the storm continued to accelerate well beyond the planet. If the waves did induce acceleration, it would mean … this object caused a lot of trouble down there. It nearly did you in.'

'Possibly, Doctrow. Possibly. Looks like it's too early to say. But then, Nature's kind of like that, isn't it? Has a way of surprising us when we least expect it? But, in case you're right, we'd better keep an extra special watch for the precise position of the next boil off from Ra's surface. Please see to it, Doctrow.'

'Of course, sir. The only thing we're sure of, right now, is that the waves first appeared when the object materialised. Anyway, there's one last thing I want to show you. We've analysed the light spectrum from the burst. Look at this.' Jennison pressed a button on his hand pad and the screen cut to a graphic showing spectral bands; multi-coloured stripes representing the light from the object split into its constituent colours. These were astronomical spectra, so they showed bright lines; the emission lines indicating which elements were being excited into emitting energy.

'As you know,' said Jennison, apparently loving this puzzle, 'these lines should tell us what the object is made of but, for some reason, the AI can't seem to resolve them. It's extremely odd, sir. We can see hints of iron, cobalt and molybdenum but it's a strange mixture which … ' Jennison suddenly stopped speaking.

'Which? …' said Tenak.

'Well, from these figures, it almost looks like the full spectrum is being … sort of, … masked in some way. Sorry, I don't understand it. Neither does the AI. I've asked it to keep working on it. Anyway, at least the emissions mean we can determine the movement of the thing. All the lines are shifted toward the blue end of the spectrum, which means….''

'The object is coming toward us,' interjected Tenak.

'Yes, but we actually find it's approaching at an oblique angle. Somewhere between 28 and 30 degrees to "the starboard" of Ra, as we see it from this point in our orbit. We calculate it will go into a very wide hyperbolic orbit around the star.' There was silence for a moment, Tenak, again, appearing deep in thought. Then Jennison said, 'I suppose that's about all I can tell you at the moment, apart from the fact that we're obviously monitoring the object continuously, and the entire sector of sky where it first appeared. But nothing else has been detected. No clue as to its origin.'

'Putting the possible acceleration of the ion storm aside, do you think it's a threat?'

'Not as far as we can tell. It's likely to go into a wide enough orbit so it's not a physical threat to the inner system. And the gravity waves seem to have settled into what you would expect from a relatively small, compact, object. So, it shouldn't cause more surprises with plasma storms. But who knows? The main emissions seem to have all happened at the instant the thing appeared.'

'Thank you, Jennison. Good work. I know you'll appraise me of any developments. But a hunch, or surmise, by you, your team, the AI, let me know. Anything at all. Understand?'

The scientist nodded, and as Tenak started back to the ladder tube he turned briefly and said, 'Oh, by the way, I intend asking Secretary Tanniss to have a look at this stuff when I next see him.'

'Secretary Tanniss?' said Jennison, looking confused, 'I'm sorry. I didn't know he was qualified in …'

'Yes, he achieved the Highest Distinction Level in his Doctorate Mentor and Research degrees in astrophysics. Level 12, in fact. Ship's Secretaries can hide surprising talents, Lieutenant,' said Tenak with a knowing smile, and continued, 'added to which, I've learned to trust his instincts about most things in physics.'

Jennison nodded but his lips seemed to curl into a barely concealed sneer of disapproval. Tenak ignored him and turned to resume his journey back to the bridge.

****

Deep inside the Collins Lunar Station, Bradlis Dervello heard his office door buzzer go, and operated his desk comp screen. The view outside showed three figures wearing smart purple coloured uniforms; Navy personnel. He sighed and pressed his intercom button. 'How can I help you gentilhomms?'

'We need to speak to you about station security sir. May we come in? Here's our ID.' The officer who had spoken lifted a card to a small panel on the outside of the door and the machine within read and analysed it, then instantly sent a report to Dervello's desk comp. The aide looked at it for a second, then pressed a button to unlock the door.

Once inside the spacious office, Dervello invited his official visitors to sit on chairs the other side of his broad desk. The youngest officer sat, removing his peaked hat. The other two, older and more seasoned looking officers, also removed their hats but remained standing behind their colleague, silent and grim faced.

The young one smiled lugubriously and spoke in a soft, amiable voice, 'My name is Trannit, Chief Security Officer Trannit. I'm sorry sir but there's been a breach of security. Not necessarily one of the highest seriousness, but a breach nevertheless.'

'Please explain,' said Dervello, 'It must be important for the Navy to get involved. As you know, I am also tasked with overseeing some aspects of security, by the Deputy Secretary General's Office. But I haven't heard anything ... unusual.'

'Yes, I know that, sir and I'm sorry to bother you but this concerns an area which you are not responsible for. That's external comms,' said Trannit,

'External comms?' said Dervello, 'alright but please get to the point, Chief. I think you'll understand I'm busy.'

'Certainly, sir. It's just that an unauthorised signal, an encrypted signal, was transmitted from *this* part of the station, about four weeks ago. It was piggybacked onto another signal. One that was received by an Allied Government facility.'

Dervello's eyes widened with surprise. 'Since you wouldn't be here if you hadn't double checked your facts, all I can suggest is that you investigate the facility concerned.'

'We have sir, and there's no problem there. We've been carrying out extensive enquiries but keep getting led back here. The real problem is that we can't decrypt the signal and it bears the hallmarks of an old Rebel wave-signature. One that goes back, oh, maybe forty years. I'm sorry, sir but I have to ask you...do you know anything about this?'

'No, of course not. I was not aware of any such signal, nor have I authorised anyone else on this station to transmit one.' Dervello looked indignant.

'That's' fine sir, so I take it you won't object if we ask you for all your data blocks concerning transmissions into, and out of, this part of the station, over the last few weeks?'

Dervello sighed but didn't object. He said he would get his assistant to dig out all the material and hand it over within the next hour. Trannit smiled amiably but insisted that the material be handed over within the next half hour, and despite Dervello's expression of fury he left his two security officers outside the Aide's office, whilst he continued with his duties.

Some while later, Dervello marched into his assistant's office. 'What the fezzer was all that about, Despinall? You better not know anything about that signal!'

Talus Brachta Despinall span around from where he was concentrating on a comp panel, wide eyed, then gave Dervello a shy smile. He said, with a calm voice, that of course he hadn't known anything. It had been a shock to him, too. Dervello's demeanour calmed almost immediately and he walked to Despinall's office chair and flopped into it. 'Yes, of course, Talus. I'm sorry. I shouldn't have said that. Please forgive me. I didn't mean to sound angry with you. You know how I feel about you. Please don't doubt that.'

Despinall stepped over to him, gently placed a hand on Dervello's shoulder, rubbing it smoothly, then bent over and kissed his on the cheek.

'I know, but I'm completely amazed by all this,' said Despinall. 'How the feg could there be a breach of our security that we didn't already get a handle on?'

Dervello caught Despinall's hand, kissed it and held it to his cheek tenderly, then stood, flexing his back and starting to walk out. 'Alright, my love,' he said, 'question everyone we've got. Find out exactly where they were and what they were doing at the time of the signal and …. Wait a minute.' He turned back to his companion, 'Sliverlight! He was here at that time. The exact time. Just before I briefed him for Oceanus. Damnatious! Yes, he was … I'll bet it was him. How in the shithouse did he do that? I checked on him myself. He went through security.' He paused for a moment, then said, 'Alright, we still need to question everyone else, Talus, but if they all check out, as I think they will, we'll be left with *Ambassador* Sliverlight.'

'If you're right about this, Brad, it'll be too late to do anything about him.' Despinall looked at his wristcom, 'I reckon he'll have gone through, or maybe is about to go through a conduit by now.'

'Yeah, guess you're right. You know what this means, Talus?'

Despinall nodded gravely and said, 'Guess this puts our plans for Oceanus in real shit. Shame.'

'Maybe,' said Dervello, with a sly look on his face, 'but … I have faith in our other operatives out there. And – if Sliverlight really is behind this, we'll have a nice surprise waiting for him when he gets back. *If he gets back.*'

****

A buzzer sounded in Yardis Octavian Sliverlight's cabin. It was late. He huffed to himself and reached for the intercom button next to his armchair. 'Yes, who is it?'

'It's Heracleonn. It's 23.10 exactly, isn't it?' said a female voice that seemed to imply, *who else did you expect right now?*

That got Sliverlight's attention. He told her to enter and released the door lock then stood and watched as a lithe, well-muscled, woman of, maybe 35, walk in. She had a round face with smooth, almost classical features but with a hard edge to them. Her hair was black, straight and cut very short and she sported a large skull and crossbones tattoo on the left side of her neck, just below her ear. Below it was the word, "Justice".

'Hello, … sir,' she said, with a complete lack of enthusiasm, 'Mer Dervello wanted me to make contact.'

'It's okay, Mes Heracleonn,' said Sliverlight, 'and yes he did but I'm glad we're far away from him now. Perhaps you are too? Well, maybe not. Please, why don't you sit down?' He motioned for the impassive young woman to take a chair opposite his. She sat, apparently with some reluctance but she perched on the edge of the seat, as stiff as though she had a broom rammed up the back of her cream-coloured ship's uniform.

'Do you know what you have to do?' he asked, looking into her deep green eyes.

'Yes, sir.'

'By the way, you are off duty right now, aren't you? You won't be missed somewhere, will you?'

'Of course not. I'm not stupid,' she said.

Sliverlight's eyes widened. 'No-one said you were, Mes. We just can't be too careful, can we? Do you have the access codes for the mainframe computer memory bank, or will you get them when we're closer to Oceanus? You'll have to humour me, Mes Heracleonn. I'm not au-fait with these things, myself.'

'Then perhaps they should have sent somebody more experienced,' she said, in a manner so cold her words could have frozen the air between them. 'I don't want to get caught because of a weak link in the system … sir,' she continued.

Sliverlight frowned, 'I hope you're not suggesting what I think you are, young Mes,' he said, 'I'll keep my end of the bargain, don't you worry. Now, perhaps you'd like to answer my question?'

At that, Heracleonn looked away momentarily and her tone softened slightly, 'Yeah, sorry. It's not your fault they sent you. It's just that I can't afford for anything to go wrong, that's all. I won't attempt to get the codes yet. It's too risky and we've got a long way to go. I'll get them after transit through the conduit. I have the confidence of the second in command in the data-unit, so I have pretty much unfettered access. But only at certain times. And the timing will be critical in this, but it's manageable.'

'And I'm assuming you can cover your tracks afterward?'

'Of course. Ultima has trained me for this sort of job for a long time, and I didn't get to work on a research ship for nothing. Don't worry, *Mer Ambassador*. As I said, I'll do my bit for the new Order. Make sure you do the same.'

'Yes, quite so, Mes Heracleonn. Thank you.'

She got up to leave and he stared at her back as she went.

'I assume we won't meet each-other again?' he said.

'I hope not,' she said sourly.

****

He woke up but, at first, his eyes couldn't seem to focus on anything. Then, very slowly, his vision began to resolve, and he saw a grey, slightly convex surface high above. It looked like some sort of tent roof. His mouth felt very dry and tasted as if some small animal had died in it. He gradually became aware of a burning pain in his back and both legs. What had happened? How did he get here? He struggled to remember if he'd been here before but just the effort of doing that seemed to exhaust him.

*

A loud bleeping noise rudely awoke Chanda Maheshtra, where she dozed at an equipment bench, in the lab' tent on Fire Island. She'd been working until late the previous evening, mainly treating the injuries to Mike Tanniss, whose condition had added much stress to the lives of the small team on the island.

At first, she didn't understand what was happening right now but, shaking the sleep from her mind she remembered the electronic connection to the video camera which had been placed to monitor Mike's movements, as he lay in the med-centre sick bay. It was just a few dozen metres from her lab. She rose to look at her monitor, saw that Mike was awake and trying to sit up in bed. At last. He'd been unconscious for two days. She hurried out.

The sick bay had 3 beds which could be used but none had ever been needed – till now. As she hurried in, she saw Mike gazing up at the video camera about two metres from his bed.

When he saw her Mike suddenly remembered her name but couldn't work out where he'd seen her before. He tried to smile.

'Well, hello young manry,' she said softly, 'so are you feeling yet better?' He tried to sit up but winced, and she encouraged him to lie back.

'How long have I been out?' he asked with weak voice.

'So far in, two days, fraidling.' She saw his shocked look and placed a hand on his arm. 'I am thinking you are yet over the worst of it now, but still you need to rest.'

He noticed than that there were metal bars positioned about forty centimetres above the length of each side of his bed.

'So sorry,' said Chanda, 'but we had to put the sides up. You were flet-threshing about so much. There was someone with you most times, Mike. After that you calmed down so much, we found we could leave you for long-times so switched on yet the monitor camera.'

Mike just felt glad to be alive, but he realised he couldn't remember what had laid him so low. Whatever it was, he did remember that it had been something horrible. 'Thank you,' he said, huskily, 'thank you so much, but where …? Where's Eleri? Is she okay?'

'She is not here right now. Do not be a-worry, though. She is fine but has flown over to Boulder Island. Tis about 150 lints to the east of here. Tis bigger island and has supplies she has to collect, such including medical stuff. Should be back soon. Oh, so happy she will be that you are back with us in consciousness. I carnt tell you how worried she has been. We have all been.'

Mike was starting to come round a little now and as he did so he could tell that both his burning legs were huge; they felt as big as tree trunks. There was a raging soreness in his left forearm too and upon touching it he found it was bandaged up, with the tube of an intravenous drip snaking out of it, leading up to a bag of fluid suspended above his bed. His right thumb had a thin metal strip wrapped around it tightly, attached by a wire to a machine with a small screen. Chanda watched him, 'The drip is saline fluid, tis all. Your thumb is yet attached to a heart monitor. Seriously, Mike, tell me how you feel now?'

'I suppose I've felt better, Chanda.'

'Ist all? Please enlarge, Mike. Do not be hiding stuff. Tis important. So, tell me how you real-so feel, please?'

'Sorry Chanda. Well, I've got sort of … burning spots, all over my back and my legs. Sort of aching through my whole body too, and … I'm dog tired. Otherwise, I'm fine. I've got some stuff wrapped round my body, Chanda. What is it?' Mike deliberately underplayed the pain he was experiencing. He didn't want to appear weak and pathetic in front of Chanda. He was deeply disappointed about Eleri's absence but accepted there were probably good reasons.

Chanda was busy writing notes on paper stuff. She was silent whilst doing that, so he said, 'Chanda, I feel stupid, but I can't really remember what happened. it's a blur. I remember swimming and there was a fish thing. A bleeding fish. Lots of deep red blood – but it might have been my own. I don't know. There was … something else, just out of reach.' He suddenly felt nauseous as he remembered more. 'There were white things, long things, like …. ropes.' He suddenly had a vivid image of a bundle of thick ribbon things and for a fraction of a second thought he was back in the water with them. He looked wildly around the room, as if expecting to see them in front of him.

'Don't be a-worry if you carnt remember, Mike. Yet it will come back. All too vivid-like praps. Mike, I should not tell, praps, but I think I will tell yet. You were attacked by a sea creature. A big one. T'was what we call a "grotachalik". Sort of cross between… let me see now, what do you have on Earth, that is similar? Ah, yes. Tis a bit like a huge jellyfish crossed with a squid, but tis neither. Yet it has a soft body – about 6 metres across, like gelatio, and a mass of tentacle streamers, about 20 of them, which dangle from the main body. They have suckers and sting pods all along them. When they sense prey – usually fish – and can be large ones, they sting it to death. Then the tentacles reel it back to the body. The prey is then absorbed but this can take long-times. Grotachalik's have no mouths, nor anything like that, so tis probably most like a jellyfish. Sorry to be so graphic, Mike. You were nearly finished for.'

'I think I know that, Chanda. Those things sound … so wonderful, don't they? How did I escape?'

'You really do not remember, do you? Tis shame yet,' she said.

He shook his head in bewilderment.

'Twas Eleri, Mike. She was so bravrie. Very bravrie. She jumped in and shot that thing with the sting gun. That did the trick, be praised. It released you. Actually, it shed the tentacles wrapped around you, then swam off. I think Eleri struggled to get you out of the water, but she managed, so then drove furios like back here. We had begun to worry 'bout you twos, so we started on our way. Tis good that Eleri left a note as to where you wanted to go but we could not do much until we didst get back her. Sept Gajana gave you some adrenalin injection.'

'Thank you, Chanda. I just wish she was here, so I could thank her in person. She's really .... amazing,' he said, 'I don't know what to say. I'm just so grateful. And I'm grateful for you and Gajana.'

Chanda grinned, 'Mayst you tell her these things yourself when she gets back.'

Mike looked away from Chanda, in embarrassment. He felt overwhelmed with feelings of affection and admiration for Eleri. He'd felt that way before she rescued him and he suddenly realised he had been trying to deny it, for some time. The sexual union they had shared was more than just the usual romp. And now, he owed her his life. That was a debt not easily repaid. He wondered if he was worthy of her. Chanda looked on as he just lay there but tears suddenly came to his eyes, unbidden but unstoppable. 'I'm sorry Chanda. I feel like a fool.'

'Why so?' she said, frowning.

'I put my own life in danger, as well as Eleri's. Being selfish again.'

'Not at all Mike. No fool you, manry. It could have happened to any. We did not expect the grotachalik to be in those waters. List, Mike, I must tell you. Eleri feels very bad. She feels she did let you down for getting you in the water and encouraged you to swim in the bay. Still the neck of the bay is protected by reefs, but we think the recent storms must have broken some of the reefs away. The creature must have got through, but still the waters of the bay are nearly too shallow for creatures from the wide sea. But the gotachalik has a squidgio body.'

'It wasn't Eleri's fault,' said Mike, emphatically, 'I can't accept that, Chanda.'

'Yet, she knew the risks more than you, Mike. Still, I do not think it best to be concerning yoursevs with all this now. Is it not true that you are both alive and that is all that counts? The outcome is a blessed one.' Mike suddenly started to feel worse and his head started to ache like someone was hammering away inside it.

'Please Mike, think no more about this now. You need to get rest. I can see you are tired.'

Mike nodded feebly and started to drift off to sleep but he had one more question. He turned to Chanda as she retreated from the room. 'Chanda. I was wondering ... could I have some water? My mouth's like the exhaust pipe of a fusion engine.'

'You mayst but only for wetting your mouth yet. You must not drink it. I am being so sorry. That is why you have got the saline drip. Tis alternated with glucose. Gajana said you are to take in nothing by mouth and I am not about to countermand that. Remember he has quite some medic qualification. Sorry, my friend. He is out right now but when he returns he shall want to have a look at you anyway. You can talk to him then. Okay? Now, try to get some rest.'

The world starting to turn grey, Mike ran his dry tongue around the salty, unpleasant interior of his mouth and looked up at the saline bag hanging above. Then a strange feeling overwhelmed him, and he passed out.

***

When he awoke again Mike had to fight hard to gain his bearings. This place didn't seem like the peaceful, quiet sort of place it was before. The curving roof of the med bay was rippling like the surface of the sea. He could hear a howling sound and a raucous metallic rattling noise came from outside. What in the galaxy was going on? He still felt awful and looked around for Chanda. Nowhere to be seen. His heart jumped as an ear-splitting crash came from outside. He tried to shout for help but his voice squawked out of his dry throat like some pitiful croak, 'Hello? Hello? Chanda? Where are you? What's happening?'

No sign of her. He tried to sit up but felt extremely dizzy and eased himself down again. The rippling in the roof continued and he suddenly realised that it was real, not something in his imagination. The whole of the marquee was starting to shake violently, and the howling wind rose more strongly outside. It was like the growl of some enormous beast and it sent shivers through him. There was another sinister crash from out there, as though the whole place was being torn apart from some huge demon. Or a creature. Perhaps a type of grotachalik that lives on land? Who could tell? His mind began to play tricks on him as he lay there, virtually powerless. Although the camp was meant to be a seasonal, it was, in fact, built very securely, anchored deeply in a sheltered bowl in the landscape. And it was well protected by trees. Well, maybe not so well protected, he thought sourly.

Chanda appeared then. She was soaked and had a horrified look on her face. 'You are okay yet, Mike?' she called out, breathlessly. 'Worst storm I have seen in years. Gajana is on his way here. He's trying to fix something outside. There's been some … damage. Fraid Eleri is not back either. I am hoping she has not even taken off from Boulder Island,' she continued. 'So sorry, Mike, we were warned about this storm, by radio, some time ago. I did not want to yet worry you. We do not normally get such storms so bad.'

Gajana also then appeared from around the corner, 'The recreation lounge has gone,' he said, panting, 'just gone in wind.' He too was soaked to the skin and had a raw gash on his right forearm. It dripped blood onto the already wet floor at his feet.

'You're hurt, my manry,' Chanda cried.

'Tis okay, for now. I will sort it out later,' said Gajana, 'yet right now I think we should try to rescue some of our stuff from the storage tent. The whole of the outer tent layer's been blown away. Come on.' He tugged at one of Chanda's arms and as she turned to go with him, he called to Mike, 'Just be staying where you are, Mike. Try to keep calm. This tent is strongest yet with the lounge one. We will be back soon as possly.' The two disappeared from view.

How he was supposed to keep calm in the circumstances? Where was Eleri? Had she been trying to fly back, in this? He tried to get up again, but his weakness pulled him back down. He felt frustrated and useless, but he was determined to try to help. Gritting his teeth and gathering all his strength he threw one massive leg out of the bed but then realised he was still linked up to that damnatious drip. He wondered whether it was really wise to try to take it out. Probably not, but even so … He could hear all sorts of bangs and tearing noises from outside, and above it all the increasing clamour of the storm.

Surely, he had to do something? He felt a wave of nausea come over him and he belched, suddenly bringing up a stream of brown fluid, burning its way through his mouth, splattering onto the floor. He felt dizzy and almost fell back against the bed.

At that moment a tear appeared in the tent roof high above. He looked up with horror as the tear widened, and then the rain slashed in. The whole roof's going to fly off, he thought. But, somehow, it seemed to hold. His heart was hammering, as the torn piece of roof material flapped crazily in the wind, like it had some bizarre life of its own. Mike could only lie back and stare at it, almost mesmerised.

The rain kept pouring in. His vision started to blur and he became insensitive, almost failing to feel the cold gusts raging through the roof. He couldn't tell what was happening outside, but he began to hear loud voices somewhere nearby. He thought he ought to know who they were, but he couldn't remember. Then he felt a jerking movement and slowly realised his bed was travelling somewhere, but he knew not where. Perhaps it was flying up into the sky, into the storm, to crash to the ground again in ruin. His mind ran riot. All he knew was that there was nothing he could do about it.

The next time he awoke he couldn't, at first, recognise his surroundings. Slowly, very slowly, he began to work out that he was in the living quarters marquee. The place had been very spacious and was probably the strongest structure in the entire camp, but it was now crammed full of clothing, bedding, medical equipment, food stocks; all sorts of things, all piled up hastily in mounds all over the place. He couldn't believe it but he also realised that he was now wearing different clothing; some sort of loose dungarees, but they were dry, and so was the bed. And there above him, still, was the drip feed.

Gajana and Chanda were there. They must have saved him again. He saw the Maheshtras sitting closeby, their backs to him, bending over an old-fashioned radio set. How did they manage to get him, and all that stuff in here, he wondered? Even Gajana's arm wound had been dressed. Mike tried to get their attention but the sound he made came out a crow's cry. Gajana looked over his shoulder and came over, asking him how he was feeling now.

He told Mike the full story, explaining that the laboratory and med tent had been damaged badly, but at least it hadn't disappeared completely, unlike the recreation centre and storage tents. The man looked haggard but managed a wan smile.

'We had to move out veraquick,' said Chanda, as she joined the two of them. 'Twas a bit of rush but it was impossible for you to stay in there. We have put the lectric heaters on in here. I think we shall be alright now.'

'Yes, I think the worst of the storm is over, thank Vishnu,' said Gajana.

'I don't know what to say to you two, except – thank you – both of you,' said Mike.

'Oh, there is something we thought we must yet tell you,' said Chanda, sounding apologetic.

'Tis not about Eleri, is it?' Mike asked. He began to feel alarm again.

'No, no,' said Gajana, 'Not so. What Chanda is trying to say, Mike, is that all the long-range aerials have gone down in the storm.'

Mike looked at them quizzically, then realised, 'You saying we can't communicate with the outside world.'

'Precise-yet,' said Gajana.

Mike looked, absent-mindedly, at his left wrist. Not there – nor on the other wrist,

'Oh shit. My wristcom's gone … I think it came off in the water.'

'Well, praps we can look for it – when the weather improves,' said Gajana.

'No, Gajana,' said Mike, 'it's too dangerous. Don't go down in that place.'

'T'will be okay, Mike. Do not be a-worry,' said Chanda. Mike tried to smile but started to feel pain again and his vision began to blur. Chanda looked at Gajana with alarm. Mike heard her say, 'He's slipping out again.' He heard nothing more.

Chapter 20

DESPERATION

'Hello? Hello, Admiral Tenak?' came weakly over Ebazza's video link aboard The Monsoon. The picture was full of impenetrable static noise. Hardly anyone would have recognised that behind the image was a real person. The audio link continued, also with static interference,

'This is Jennifer Providius, of the Research vessel Antarctica, out of the Denovian Sector Transit zone. Admiral, we exited …. conduit approximately 7 hours ago, standard time. We … through without incident. …. should be entering the inner planetary region within 3.8 weeks …. will enter orbit around O A, after braking to loop around Ra. Let us …. if you have any specific matter you wish us to investigate and we'll do our best. Otherwise, I'll contact you again … we get past the orbit of Kumudu. Providius out.'

Arkas Tenak and Ssanyu Ebazza stood in front of a large, flat, wall screen in the Captain's private office, in a hab module, out on The Monsoon's rotating torus. The light in the room was dimmed to help them see the transmission but the visual signal kept flickering on and off. Poor vid was common in transmissions from the conduit zones in the outer parts of any planetary system. Holo' would have fared even less well and wasn't worth transmitting.

'So, they sent the Antarctica to join us,' said Tenak. 'Do you know Jennifer Providius?'

'No, but I've heard the name, except I thought it was Livia Providius. I *still* don't know what she looks like, but I don't know many crews of research ships,' she replied. 'I'm guessing you know her?'

'Yeah. Met her at a Navy ball, on Mars. Long before my second marriage. She's a very competent officer, as well as a senior engineer. Got a lot of plaudits in the world of fusion engineering. Livia's her middle name, by the way.'

'Admiral, you look as though you have, shall we say, fond memories of her, judging by your face,' Ebazza said quietly, a sly smile on her face.

'How presumptuous of you, Ssanyu. And prescient. You're right. But it was nothing long lasting. Oh, I don't mind you knowing. She and I, kind of, hit it off for a while. Haven't seen her for about 15 years, though.'

'Sorry Admiral. I didn't mean to pry,' said Ebazza, with evident embarrassment.

Tenak just smiled, 'No need to feel uncomfortable, Ssanyu. It was, as they say, a long time ago. Lot of space under the bows since then.'

Ebazza paused for a moment, then said, 'So, the Allied Government felt they needed to send another ship?'

'Well, they couldn't help but realise we're in trouble with our "negotiations" I've only recently sent a message buoy back.'

'Yes, I know, sir, but I expected a skiff or something, with, maybe an ambassador. I don't know if the Devians are going to take *any* notice of more scientists. Surely, they must have worked out it's the science; *our* science, they don't trust?'

'Maybe, but I'm fairly certain the Antarctica must have been dispatched before my message pod could reach the inner Solar System. The pod will just confirm their suspicions, of course. And it's possible the Antarctica brought an ambassador, I guess.'

Tenak stood up to leave and Ebazza rose too.

He turned to her. 'Captain, please send a transmission to Captain Providius. Update her about our situation but advise her we'd be grateful if she could do something really special for us. Send her all the data we have on the gamma ray phenomenon. When the Antarctica brakes into its elliptical orbit she'll come around to the other side of Ra from us. That means she'll be in a perfect position to train all her instruments on the perimeter zone, approx' one light month from Ra and two light months from the "Arras Cometary Cloud", way beyond this system. That's where our mystery object has appeared. With the range of detectors at *her* disposal, she might just detect enough residual radiation to be able to track back to where that thing came from. Should be able to work out its current movements in a bit more detail, too. I'm fascinated by what might be out there, Ssanyu.'

'Or what *was* out there, Admiral. A light month ago.'

'Good point. But I've just got a feeling something's still going on out there. I just hope it's not another threat. We've got enough to deal with, here.'

****

'Hello Mike, can you hear me? It's Eleri. I'm back. I'm yet back now. Keep holding on Mike. Keep holding on, please.'

'I don't know if he can hear you, El,' said Chanda, watching Eleri as she gently stroked Mike's right arm, where he lay unconscious in the makeshift med bay.

'Praps not, but if he can it might help him to know I am back. How long since he was last conscious?'

'About 20 hours. I am a-worried El. This shouldnar be happening. I have every faith in Gajana but he carnt understand why he's like this, either. Mike was starting to make good progress, till the storm.'

At that point Gajana walked in, went to Mike and placed a hand on his forehead. 'Still a bit damp. Warm too. The thermo' stick indicates a high temperature. I have not been able to bring it down and I don't understand why. I treated him with the right anti-toxins for the stings, least the known anti-toxins, and my analysis of his blood does not show anything except the usual poisons from the grotachalik. I am yet missing something.' He frowned deeply.

'Do not be a-blaming yourself,' said Eleri, 'for you've done what you can. None of us did anticipate this. He had 12 stings. Might the sheer volume of toxin be doing this?'

'No, I don't think so,' said Gajana, inspecting the glucose drip feed into Mike's arm, 'I can only think he has yet been injected with a toxin we know nothing about.

'Mayhap. I do not think it can so be a native bacterium,' said Eleri, her brow wrinkling in thought, 'or a virus, because they have co-evolved with their hosts on this planet. We are the aliens on this world, so we are immune to them. So, if not a toxin, what else mayst it be?' Eleri's brow furrowed deeply with anxiety.

'You are right, surely,' said Gajana, 'but you are talking about native microbes. We humans have brought our own bugs, and yes, viruses, with us, and they have been evolving on this world, also – in us. Either way, I carnt do any more. He needs specialist attention and needs it now. His organs will yet start to fail if this fever dost not break. Even if he recovers due course, Vishnu knows what sort of health he shall have evermore, if the infection isn't treated proper-so.'

'We need to get him to the mainland,' said Eleri, 'I'll just have to take him, in Betty.'

'You carnt take him in your airplane, El. I do not think he should be moved such. Even if he could be got as far as the plane itself, the likely turbulence you could get would do him in. Too dangerous, friendling. I doubt so he would make it as far as the mainland.'

'Well, it's better to try – than let him die here, ist not? said Eleri, her eyes flashing with frustration and anger. Tears began to glisten in them and dribble out.

'Because of that storm we carnt contact the mainland to get them to send an airo-ambulance. What else can we do?' Chanda said to her husband. He sat and hung his head in his hands.

'I could fly back to the mainland on my own – and get auntine to contact the big ship and Admiral Tenak,' said Eleri.

Faces brightened all around until Gajana said, 'But that storm will for certain be raging over the mainland, El. You would be flying straight into it.'

Eleri's face dropped again. 'You are right, friendling. So, even if stronger, Mike could not be taken back anyways.'

There was silent for a while. Then Eleri brightened again and said, 'But e'en so, praps there is one last thing to try. We need to find his wristcom. If we can sue it to get in touch with his big ship they can send a smaller pick-up ship – a landing boat. That will surely save him.'

'How are we going to do that Eleri? Be yet sensible please,' said Chanda, her dark eyes pregnant with concern. 'Tis at the bottom of the bay and we've yet had a storm. That means the thing has probably been covered with strap-weed, also sand.'

'If we do go down in pairs,' said Eleri, 'one guarding the other with sting sticks, we can look for it. I doubt the grotachalik is still there anywayin. It will be feeding out in the ocean and trying to regrow its lost limbs. Besides yet, I do not think we have any choice. Look, both, I do not want to bully either of you. You have done so much for him already. I shall look for it on my own.'

'Absolute not,' said Gajana, 'I am not a-letting you go a down there on your own.'

'That makes three of us,' said Chanda, 'But still, someone should stay with Mike. We will have to take it in turns. And besides that. Have you forgotten yet? We have only two air-breathers.'

So it was, that Chanda and Eleri went back to the cove, the first time, leaving Gajana to look after Mike. They spent the two hours maximum they could, swimming up and down the area where Mike got into trouble. It was deep water, close to the western shore of the cove, near the wooden walkway running along the shore, close to the break in the crater wall. The walkway had been the structure from which Eleri had launched herself in to carry out her stunning rescue. She told Chanda she'd seen the jelly-like dorsal fin of the grotachalik when she had been standing the other side of the cove. She'd also had a very good idea where Mike had been swimming because of his air bubble trail. Then she'd raced break-neck, across to the walkway.

Now, the water was extremely murky where they were looking for the missing device. Chanda had been right. The storm had stirred up a green and amber nimbus of silt and weed, but at least the storm had dissipated. Eleri searched through the muddy bay bottom, carrying an electric lamp in one hand, while Chanda swam beside her with the biggest sting stick they had, her eyes searching all around for danger. They eventually drew a blank and returned to the camp empty handed.

A couple of hours later Eleri returned, this time with Gajana, but they came up empty handed, again. Eventually, someone had the idea of getting the metal detector they kept in store. But where was it? It had been amongst the items the Maheshtras had rescued from the storage tent. A long, nerve-wracking, time was spent searching for it and they began to fear that this device was also irretrievably lost, until Chanda risked taking some time out from watching over Mike, to join the search. They finally found it, but by that time it was getting dark and none of them wanted to risk going down into the bay. They would start again, next day, early as possible. Mike still hadn't regained consciousness.

But he woke the next day, finding Eleri sitting next to him, smiling wanly. He was overjoyed to see her, as she told him about the wristcom and said the others were still looking for it. He fussed about their safety but, even as they spoke, Mike slipped back into unconsciousness. Eleri hung her head and tears ran from the corners of her eyes.

'Oh Mike, what is the matter being with you?' she said to his supine body, but there was the sound of footsteps outside the tent. The Maheshtras marched in, their faces worn and miserable. The usual sunny sub-tropical weather had returned but still no sign of Mike's device. Still wet, they sat down around Mike's bed. Chanda looked at Eleri, 'I am not knowing what more we can do.'

Gajana looked up and said, 'Praps we are yet looking in the wrong place.'

'We've looked all over the bay,' said Eleri, 'everywhere yet.'

'I know – but we have looked *under* the water. We have ignored the strand above it. What about the shoreline? 'he said.

'Well and all, I have been keeping a look-out, in general,' said Eleri, 'but ... you may be right, yet. So, if we use the metal detector and trawl across the shoreline and the land margin ...'

The three rose as one but Gajana suggested Eleri to stay with Mike, while he and Chanda raced out of the tent to get the metal detector again.

Eleri sat alongside her lover again but gradually drifted off to sleep in the bedside chair, waking with a start when she heard ragged shouting from outside. But this time it was a joyous noise. Gajana burst into the tent and in his right hand he held a thick disc shaped device, like a large wristwatch. It was stained slightly green but, otherwise, seemed undamaged. They were jubilant.

Chanda appeared, whilst Gajana set the device down next to Mike's bed. 'We found it ways up on the shore, roughly in line with where Mike was attacked. The storms must yet have pushed it up the beach.' He beamed.

'T'was covered in seaweed,' said Chanda brightly, 'but we didnar need to use the detector. The rays of Ra did yet bounce off it, though stained. Didst flash like a beacon. I spotted such after we'd been looking for more than an hour.' She whistled with relief as Eleri picked the device up, wiped it and peered closely at it. Then she tapped it twice, as she'd seen Mike do many times. Nothing happened. Eleri tapped it *three* times. Nothing. 'Yet, I've seen Mike do this,' she said, as the Maheshtras looked on with puzzled expressions. She tapped it three times again, quicker than before. Still nothing. 'Praps tis damaged,' said Chanda, her mouth slumping with disappointment.

'Yes, praps ...' began Eleri, but the device suddenly buzzed., causing Eleri to jump. As the three stared with surprise a loud, sultry female voice issued from of the thing.

'Please tell me what you require?' it said.

'Mike Tanniss is injured,' said Eleri, looking bemused. 'And, we are needing to get in touch with The Monsoon spaceship. Admiral Tenak must need know about this. Tis vital that Mike is rescued.'

'You are not authorised to use this unit,' said voice, sounding stern now. 'This unit is now shutting down.' The wristcom buzzed again and went silent.

'No, no!' said Eleri and the Maheshtras darted forward, as if they could do something *physical* to stop the machine carrying out its threat. Eleri tapped the suddenly inert device three times, again and again. No response.

Gajana said, 'Try talking to it, still.'

Eleri did so. Nothing. All of them tried. It didn't respond in the slightest.

'Tis dead,' said Chanda. He looked mournful.

They stared at each-other and there was a long silence. Despondence had returned. Gajana shrugged his shoulders and sat on a lab chair. Chanda started pacing around near the tent entrance but Eleri continued to examine the unit, turning it over and over, as though she might find something like a hidden button she could press. Gajana spoke, his voice heavy with gloom, 'I think this is now over to you to make a decision Eleri, but I believe there is only one more thing we can try.'

The others gave him puzzled looks.

'We have to wake him up and get *him* to operate that thing,' he said.

Eleri brightened a little, 'You can wake him? Okays, let us get going yet.'

'You do not understand,' said Chanda, 'for what my husband suggests is vera-dangerous.'

Gajana went to Eleri and looking her straight in the eye, said, 'I am not sure this will work, but if I inject him with carboxinin, which is an adrenaline derivative, he may wake up and be lucid so as to help. But t'would be just temporary. He would clunck out again after a few minutes. The really bad news is that it could cause him much serious harm. There is a reason why his mind has shut itself off. If we override that - we may cause more problems than solve. Think now, we do not have backup here and I do not know exactly what is wrong with him, so tis possible that ... Well, Eleri, he might e'en die.'

The three of them stood in silence. Eleri spoke first, 'I think ... we have to do this, Gajana. If we carnt get him to the ship, he might die anywayin. Praps tis a risk we have got to take.'

'This is all guessing work, El. But I need to be very certain you agree to this action,' he said. She was silent for a long moment, then, with a deeply troubled expression on her face she nodded silently to him.

**

Mike swam back to consciousness like someone surfacing from the depths of a sunless sea. He opened his eyes and flinched with the brightness of the world, closing them again for many moments. Then, he opened them again, but couldn't focus well. He thought he could see Eleri but wasn't sure. He just sensed her presence more than anything. His throat felt so bad he tried to speak but nothing came out.

'Mike, Mike! You're back with us. How're you yet feeling? Can you speak?' she cried.

Mike just stared at her blurred image, then at two other people standing nearby. He licked his lips and grunted, 'Where am I? Where the ship?'

Eleri quickly told him that Gajana had given him a shot to try to wake him up. Gajana then took his pulse and Mike looked at everyone's faces with puzzlement, for in truth he could barely remember who was and why he was in this place – wherever *this* was. Most of what he could see was bright lights and blurred faces gathered around him, staring. All talking, asking questions. He felt a searing pain in his back and legs and more nausea in his gut.

'Ask him. Ask him now. Quick-so,' said Gajana, looking desperate. Eleri tried to explain to Mike that they had found his wristcom, but he needed to tell them how to use it. It kept saying they were not authorised.

Mike could hear Eleri but he suddenly felt confused. Images came and went in his brain. What were they talking about? Then, he felt searing pain in his back and legs, moving now to his chest, starting to bore into him like knives of molten lead.

Eleri and the Maheshtras watched Mike lie back and start to thrash about with evident pain. For his part he could still see Eleri, vaguely, through a sort of haze but he wasn't entirely sure who she was any more. She was asking him something. Something about the wristcom. He focussed on that, the wristcom. What about it? Somehow, he had a moment of clarity, a momentary flash of insight into what was happening. He felt galvanised with sudden energy and sat bolt upright up in his bed. He saw the wristcom and literally snatched it off Eleri. He knew he had to be quick.

Fighting to keep the dark haze from enveloping his mind he stared at the device. The haze was creeping up on him like a cold blanket. If it got to him he knew he would disappear into nothingness, again. Eleri held his hand, looked him in the eye and said quietly but clearly, 'Mike, I need you to tell me how to use the wristcom. If we do not call your ship and yet get them to send a landing boat, you mayst die. Do you understand me, Mike?'

In a moment of sudden brightness in his mind everything seemed to make sense. He knew who this femna was and what she wanted him to do but he couldn't really understand *why*. Still, he wanted to please her, so he had to concentrate all his energies to do her bidding. Then he felt he really didn't want to. Something was dragging him back. Numbness then, but a second later, another lucid moment. Even so, the dark haze was coming. He didn't have much time.

Mike looked at his lover. She was so beautiful, he thought. Then he nodded and tapped the wristcom. He tried to talk to it but, at first, the words came out in a jumble. Closing his eyes for a moment he concentrated and tried again.

'This is ... Mike Tanniss. Please take a reading of my voice and ......,' he swallowed hard, then said, 'and allow Ele ...? The next ... person who speaks to you to ... act ... on ... my behalf. Let her... let talk with ... whoever she ... wants.' He gazed at Eleri and calmly handed the unit to her. Just before he blacked out he felt a rush of emotion; a longing for this woman who had befriended him. A woman who had finally allowed sweet intimacy between them; something that now seemed a thousand years ago. Another age. Another lifetime. He would never forget her. He tried to squeeze something out of his aching larynx, but it didn't seem to be working anymore.

Eleri heard him say, 'I should ....,' He then blacked out, slumped back and hit the pillow hard. Eleri tried to grab him, 'Mike. No, don't ...'

Gajana bent over the patient and examined him. 'He has just passed out, El. We will yet have to keep a close eye on him. The heart monitor is still attached. I shall suggest you use the unit vera-kwik,' he said.

Eleri nodded, tears streaming down her face, 'We will try now,' and she gently took the unit from Mike's hand. Holding it in front of her, she said, 'Now, Mes machine. You heard your master. Please be contacting The Monsoon.' There was silence for a few seconds and it then spoke. The voice now sounded co-operative, 'Who do you wish to contact on The Monsoon?' it said.

Eleri hesitated, concentrating, for a few seconds, then remembered the Admiral, Mike's good friend, 'I wish to speak to Admiral Tenak vera – very quickly and ...'

Before she could finish, the unit beeped once and, to everyone's utter shock, a three-dimensional image of Tenak's head and shoulders, a few centimetres across, seemed to pop out of the wristcom and stare at her. The Maheshtras stepped back reflexively. They stared, wide eyed, as Eleri spoke to Tenak's image. His visage kept appearing and disappearing, flashing in and out of existence, staccato like.

Tenak asked Eleri what was happening, but his voice was broken by static interference. 'I'm sorry Eleri,' he said, 'but the ship is on the opposite side of the planet from where you are. We're having to use your own world's comm satellites as relays. Your government won't let us use our own ...'

Before he could finish, she said, 'Admiral, please be listening – now, please! Tis Mike. He has been hurt, Mer Admiral. Terrible accident. Dying he is. I will explain another-morn but tis vital you send a landing boat down for him. Now, please Admiral. *Now.*'

Admiral Tenak's expression changed immediately. 'Okay Eleri. I'm getting my wristcom to take a more precise location reading for you,' he said, through the electrical interference, 'We'll send a boat ... a medic team as soon as we can. The boat might take a little while to .... there, because we're at our most distant from your ..., in orbit. But please ... not worry. We'll get to you soon as ... can. Please tell me how critical he is. Can you hold the unit near him – if your circumstances allow?'

Eleri held the wristcom about a metre from Mike as he lay on his sick bed and she turned it slowly, as if to scan the scene. Tenak's image looked down, he grunted and said, 'Not good but he looks peaceful right now. Stand by, Eleri. I've got to give some orders and I'll keep you informed of progress. Out for now,' he said, and his head and shoulders seemed to be sucked straight back into the unit.

Eleri said to the wristcom, 'Thank you Mer machine. Please stay activated, as we will continue to need you.' She put the unit on her wrist, with a determined look on her face. 'Never shall I be losing this thing again,' she said to her friends.

'Let us be hoping this Admiral manry really can get his lander boat here in short while,' said Chanda, with a frightened expression.

Chapter 21

CONSPIRATORS

A pale faced, lean young man of medium height, with a square shaped jaw and crew-cut hairstyle, sat at a desk which would not have looked out of place in an advanced, cockpit, such as in a landing boat. He was dressed in a smartly cut, spotlessly white uniform and the desk which he "rode" curved tightly around his slim figure. Its smooth surface was covered with various flat, geometrical shapes, softly lit in pale pastel colours; the control surfaces over which the young man ran his hands with lightning speed.

He waved his hands a few centimetres above a subset of the lit panels and bright texts and sets of figures, glowing in oranges and blues, appeared in mid-air, a few centimetres above the desk. The man briefly perused each set and called up more from his desk-comp. Despite the appearance of his "desk" this man was not a pilot.

In fact, he and his desk occupied just one corner of a modestly sized room, a space which literally sparkled and shone with its cleanliness, from wall to wall and from ceiling to floor. Gleaming video screens of different sizes adorned the walls, but most were currently dark.

He stopped for a moment, looked pensive then sat back in his ergonomically shaped chair while a gentle, sexually neutral voice, as sterile as the room, issued from a blinking pink desk rectangle to his left. The voice said, in echoing tones, 'Michaelsonn D. Tanniss is now fully awake, hemi-med Lomanz.'

Then hemi-med Lomanz turned his clean-cut face to look to his left and a broad smile spreading across his face.

'Good. Thank you,' he said, 'give me a whole soma-scan, please.'

A life size, three-dimensional, fully "see-through" image of Mike Tanniss, appeared in mid-air, in supine position, about half a metre above the desk. Mike's transparent head appeared to be moving, as if he were trying to look around him. The patient began to haul himself up on one elbow, as he did so. The image showed Mike's skin, as an outline in pale blue, but the muscles below showed up in see-through pastel pink shades. Most of the major blood vessels showed up as a network of rich reds and blues, in the complex pattern in which they really existed. Deeper still, below the muscles, amongst and between the blood vessels, all the patient's organs could all be seen, transparent as gossamer. Further in, the bones appeared in shades of cream. It was as though Mike was entirely made of glass of different colours and hues.

Hemi-med Padrigg Metachion Lomanz stood and looked through the whole image, sometimes peering in closely, sometimes drawing further back. He then hovered one hand on the part of the patient's left thigh, in the image, and another over Mike's right arm, then turned the whole representation of the body, so that the patient's image was now facing downwards. Again, he peered closely.

'Delete everything except the blood vessels,' he said, and, in a millisecond, the intricate image of Mike's inner body changed to an interconnected, labyrinthine mass of arteries and veins, which now changed hue to bright, light, reds and blues. The walls of the blood vessels then changed so they became translucent, such that Lomanz was able to see the patient's blood itself coursing through them. With a wave of his hands and an action as though drawing something toward himself, Lomanz drew out of the image an entirely separate view of some tiny blood vessels from Mike's right thigh, in microscopic view.

This new image resolved itself into the form of a 3D block, hovering in front of Lomanz's face, showing the very smallest blood vessels and, within them, the flowing blood plasma and all the different types of blood cells, platelets, and anything else travelling in them.

The medic caught sight of something he'd evidently been looking for; a tiny cloud of smaller, dark, particles, which could be seen as vague shapes, flowing through the tube-like vessels. But they were elusive and easily missed. The computer made image seemed to have trouble pinning them down. Lomanz asked the med AI to generate an image of some isolated examples of the particles, which it had pinpointed in a physical sample earlier in the day. A separate hologram of the blood sample popped into existence next to the images Lomanz was already looking at. Whirling an index finger in a circle near them he caused a massively magnified image of the particles to appear in place of the previous image. The particles looked like tiny dark springs and they seemed to spin slowly as they moved along. The image then seemed to falter, fading in and out of focus and the older image of the sample, showing the particles as small dots, returned.

'Well, they're the things we're really interested in,' said Lomanz, 'so, can you enlarge them any further in that setting?'

'Unable to comply without using the E-ultra-viewer' said the hyper-comp.

'That'll mean isolating a smaller group of them. You're saying I won't be able to see them in situ then?' said Lomanz. 'But we've already used the E viewer four times. Okay, just show me the figures, for now.'

Two small "panels" flashed up before him, floating above the image of Mike's body – the patient now appearing to sit up fully in bed. Miniature, animated graphs and lines of data ran along the panels, figures occasionally jumping out and standing out in front of his eyes. 'At least they don't seem to be proliferating as much as they were 10 hours ago,' he said to the hypercomp.

'Their rate of reproduction does indeed seem to have been slowed,' said the machine, 'and, in fact, my current estimate is an expansion rate of e, to the power 0.0014.'

'Still too high, but it's going the right way,' said Lomanz and the desk parted in the middle allowing him to step out and walk through a door connecting his office to the individual wardroom where Mike Tanniss lay.

**

There was something strangely familiar about this place. But where the hell was it? Could it be in The Monsoon? No, surely not? For he'd been somewhere else, hadn't he? Try as he might Mike just couldn't wrench that memory out. If this was the ship he wasn't very familiar with *this* part of it and yet, it surely had to be the massive carrier vessel he had come to think of as "home". At least this place wasn't shaking all over the place. Although he couldn't remember where he'd been before, the one thing he could recall was the pain. He'd always remember the pain but, mercifully, that seemed to have mostly gone now. He breathed a sigh of relief and thanked his lucky stars. There was only a kind of dull ache left in the background but even his head seemed pretty clear now.

A man in a stiff white uniform, probably not much older than he was, suddenly entered the room and smiled at him. 'And how are you feeling today, Secretary Tanniss?' he said.

Something familiar about him. Mike struggled to remember the name but then it finally came to him. This was Padrigg ... something or other; one of five hemi-meds on the ship. Hemi-med was a medical grade which could be said to rank between a grade which was once called "senior nurse"; and that of a junior doctor. It was strange, he thought, that he couldn't remember how he got here, but he was able to recall all this abstruse stuff about medical staff. A smile of recognition spread across Mike's lips. He'd always found this guy amenable, but he didn't know him that well, not usually getting to socialise with him. Seemed quite shy, he recalled. Always seemed to be studying. Maybe *he* should have stuck to that, he thought, sullenly.

'Hello Lieutenant. I guess I'd say I feel a bit weird,' said Mike, listening to how croaky his own voice sounded.

'Are you in any pain right now?' asked the medic.

'No. Well, not like I was. If you're responsible for getting rid of that I can't really thank you enough, Padrigg. How long? I mean, how long have I been out, man? Did something happen to me on the ship? Weren't you supposed to be going to Oceanus, or was I dreaming?'

'I don't think you'd be in the med bay, if you'd just been dreaming, my friend,' said Lomanz, 'and *you* went down to Oceanus, not me. Don't you remember anything about the planet?'

'I don't know. I think… I remember seeing it, from orbit. Did I really go down there? Is that where …?' Mike screwed his face up as if trying to squeeze the memories out, like trying to wring water out of a face cloth.

Lomanz placed a hand on Mike's shoulder, 'Yeah, you did go down there, but don't worry about it right now. You've had a bit of trauma but you're on the mend, so you should be up and about in, oh, say, 3 or 4 days, ship-time. We need to keep observations going for at least that long. I'll ask Senior Med-Surgeon Atrowska to talk to you when she comes back on duty. She'll be pleased you've woken.'

'How long have I been out, for Maker's sake?' asked Mike, his mouth feeling as dry as the husk of a long-dead rat. 'And why? What happened down there, man? Or is it manry?'

Lomanz looked puzzled, then said, 'So many questions. All in good time, Mike. Don't get wrung-up about it. What I can tell you is that you contracted a disease down there. But we've got it under control now. Taken a while, but we're winning.'

'Disease? What disease? I didn't think that was … possible – on a planet with an … Sorry, I'm getting jumbled up.'

Yes, it's understandable, Mike. You're still very tired from fighting the infection. Like I said, it'll take a few more days. Give it time. Maybe you were trying to say … a planet with a completely different evolutionary pathway? Separate from the Earth's?'

'Yeah, right. Right. So … how…?'

'Sorry, Mike. We don't know right now. My lab team are working flat out on it, cos it's got implications for all of us, I guess. The med hypercomp's best guess is that this is a one-off. The agent of infection is smaller than a virus and this one's never been seen before. It's not likely to be present on the land, down there.'

'So, where did I … catch it? What …?'

'Sorry, Mike, but I've got to be tight about this. You *must* get some rest. Please don't look at me like that, man. If you try to take in too much info' right now it could harm your recovery – even more than not knowing – frustrating though it is. Give it time. Memories can be strange things, Mike. Can cause a lot of psychi-damage, if not handled properly. Besides, I don't really know the answers to all your questions, anyways.'

'Padrigg, is my brain ... damaged, or something?'

'No, not physiologically. There's nothing physically wrong with your brain but, as far as your psychoric-mind is concerned, we'll need to carry out some eval's in a couple of days. No rush. Just relax. Everything you need is here. You can start eating whenever you wish, and you must keep drinking. You need to flush out your system naturally.'

'Thanks, manry,' said Mike. Lomanz looked puzzled again.

'Okay, so don't worry,' said Lomanz, as he looked up at a small instrument panel about two metres above Mike's head, and said to it, 'Current aleph M, brain function please.' A bright blue beam of light shone from the panel, producing a set of figures hovering in front of Lomanz. He appeared reasonably happy with it and waved the machine off.

'Looks like you're making good progress, Mike, so as I said, don't push it. The memories will return in their own good time. Nature's time – not ours. And I don't want to have to give you a sedative. So, if you don't need anything else right now, I'll leave you get some rest.'

Mike simply asked for a drink of water, which Lomanz supplied, then left. His patient settled back onto his pillow and almost immediately fell asleep. As he started to drop off a very pleasant, round, instantly appealing, female, face floated into his head. She had violet eyes, freckles over her nose and auburn hair, and she seemed to be speaking to him, but he couldn't hear her clearly. He thought he knew her - but then again – no. Perhaps he'd seen her somewhere. Perhaps in a holo-novel? He wished he had met her, whoever she was.

****

Arva Pendocris stood on a balcony on the top floor of the Meta-teleo temple, near Ramnisos, in north eastern Bhumi Devi. She peered out at the late evening sky of deep blue steel, studded already with twinkling stars.

She spotted a particularly bright point of light, steadier than the rest, and it was moving fairly quickly, rising from the eastern horizon. She followed its progress as it moved up toward the zenith. A cool breeze blew from behind her, making the folds of her long robes flap and ruffle. She closed her eyes for a moment, appearing to enjoy the sensation. Picking up the bright dot again, she began to reach into the folds of clothing over her right breast. There was a rustling sound behind her, and she tensed slightly, withdrew the hand and relaxed her stance. It was Remiro. He came to her side and looked up, mimicking her pose. 'Is that what I think it is?' he said in his thick Devian accent.

'The Monsoon. Yes,' she replied. There was a sharpness in her voice.

'Is everything alright such? You seem a bit distracted recently, Arva.'

'You think so Patchalk?' She paused, then turned toward him, 'Oh, I'm alritey. Just wondering how long we're going to have to be yet tolerant of those people,' and she gestured toward the moving star in the sky.

'We are doing such we can, Arva. I understand that both of those meddlesome mabberheads, Tanniss and Tenak, have gone back to their piddelry ship. Our people are still working on Arbella Nefer. We are doing as much as we can to put pressure on the government. What else mayst you so suggest? Not *terrorismo*, surely, my love birdle?'

'Do not talk nonsense Patchalk. Of course not. The people of Devi would never forgive us if we stooped that low. No victory there. You know that. We have to do what we can by persuasion. There is no history of terrorismo here on Oceanus. I do not wish to start one now.'

'Agree, I do, but still, a little bit of pressure, praps, of a different kind, wouldnar go amiss?'

'Don't go over-so edge, Patchalk. Do not be doing anything to besmirch our good name. The popularia need to believe in us – not fear us.'

'Coursry, coursry, darlie. I am just thinking – maybe tis time our supporters demonstrated our strength of feeling. A little march in the capital, praps?'

Pendocris paused for a while, then said, 'Very well. If you so wish, husband. But, as I said, do not so overdo it. Besides now, you know how hard the Securi-pol can be when things get out of hand. We may not have terrorismo here, but things have gone out-mad sometimes, specially with violentia demonstrations. And the securi-pol have been extreme so-efficient in their enquiries. We do not want them still prying into us too much. Remember, Patchalk, that not even you have any real influence with *them*.'

'Yes, yes, Arva. Stop worrying. I know that even we arint big enough to be influencing everybody. Well, not yet.' He placed a hand on her arm, squeezed it lightly, then walked back inside.

She smiled slyly as she watched Remiro enter the room behind her. She waited for the door to close, then trepidatiously pulled out of her inner robes a small, square, metal device that was silently vibrating. She turned toward the balcony rail again and folded her robes around the device as it lay in her hand, so that any light from it would be cloaked from the rooms behind.

As she peered at the unit it lit up with a soft amber fluorescence and she was able to see the button she wanted to press. After pressing a video picture appeared on the tiny screen. A middle-aged man with a large mane of ginger hair stared at her, smiled and said, 'This is "darkling". You are my contact, I presume. Code please?' he said.

'Yes, alright. RXV08708 – VY - Rainbow,' she replied. She turned the volume of the device down and glanced furtively behind her.

'Very well,' said the man on the screen, 'I'm sure you'll be pleased to know that the Home System government is sending a second ship out here. Not a Navy ship, I'm glad to say. It has an Ambassador on board. Yardis Octavian Sliverlight.'

'Is that supposed to be good?' said Pendocris, in perfect Anglo-Span, but steeped deeply with sarcasm.

'Yes, so we believe. Sliverlight is indoctrinated. He's been ... persuaded to assist us. His ship is due in orbit within three weeks. Sliverlight must talk to the government first, of course, and then the opposition parties. I'll be doing my bit with the data transfer and after that, Sliverlight will feign indignity. That should add authority to his words.'

'" His words?" Don't you mean, *our words*?'

'If you wish. Please don't forget your origins and where your loyalties lie, "Rainbow".'

'I'm always loyal to the cause. You know that. But this has to be done *our* way.'

'Don't you mean – *your* way, Rainbow? Not ours? No matter. Tell me, is that husband of yours still under your ... influence? Perhaps I should say under your thumb, Rainbow?'

'Just take care of your side of things and I'll take care of mine.'

'Whatever you say. By the way, we have another operative on the Antarctica. I won't tell you any more than that. Anyway, I have to go now. I couldn't risk sending this directly from the ship, so it's reaching you via a science probe that Tenak sent out. The probe will be past your horizon in a few seconds. Darkling out.'

Pendocris shut the device off and glancing up at the sky again and there, not far above the horizon, she saw another bright speck, much dimmer than that of The Monsoon, but still visible. It was descending rapidly into the thick, darkening east.

****

In the med bay aboard The Monsoon, Mike Tanniss awoke and as he rubbed the sleep out of his eyes he turned to his right, glancing at the digi-screen embedded in his bedside cabinet. It was 0530 ship-time.

'Bed light,' he said and a small lamp above him lit. To his surprise, it illuminated a bi-convex metal shape lying on his table. The edge of the shape gleamed in the soft light and it immediately sparked off a recollection. He started to sit up, suddenly recognised the object and snatched it up. He had the distinct feeling it had been lost but where? How?

He admitted he felt a lot better this morning. A bit more energy, more motivation. He hadn't been able to remember why he was there in the first place, but med-surgeon Atrowska had told him his memories would return – but must not be forced. She was eschewing drugs unless it became absolutely necessary.

That had been about two days ago. Or was it longer? Every day seemed to melt into the next in this place, but he hadn't been able to get up and about much because of a deep, aching weakness and lack of motivation. He hated that but could do little to change it. Hemi-med Lomanz had told him that his body was far from having recovered but the med staff were still reasonably pleased with his progress. They said the infectious agent had declined to well below the value of e to the power of one. That sounded good, he thought.

Mike stared at the wristcom again and, although it was shiny and looked clean as new he thought he could see hints of blue-green slime on it. Surely not? Where was that from? He peered again, turning the unit's surfaces toward the lamp light. He suddenly felt queasy and a rush of images and sounds thrust, unbidden, into his mind. 'Oh Maker!' he said and slammed the device back on the cabinet.

He sat back in the bed, closed his eyes and held his hands to his face. His breathing got heavier and he was sweating from every pore. He was beginning to remember – something, and it wasn't good.

He could remember going down to the planet below, and who he had gone with - and why. Some of the details were still hazy but –! He suddenly recalled his first meeting with the woman he'd seen in his dreams. As he lay there in the med bay he was, in his mind's eye, flying in a strange, ancient, type of aircraft. That lovely femna he'd met was in control of the ship. Memories of the island they'd visited came back to him, but what was it called? Then, he remembered something lovely; wonderful sexual union with the femna; the gush of emotion, the ecstatic closeness, the feel of gently penetrating her and of blissful mutual release. It was a wonderful memory, and he began to relax. And yet, somehow, there was something different, something about he felt about her. Something that he'd felt was unfamiliar. She really had meant something to him. Had, or did still? Yet her name continued to elude him, even though he felt he had known her all his life. A further flood of memory then arrived.

'Eleri!' he shouted. That was her name. Suddenly acutely self-conscious, he looked around to see if someone had heard him. But why should he care? He could remember so much about her now. But, like a wet blanket being thrown over him a sort of mental fog dropped again very quickly, choking off his mind's eye view of what had happened after his lovemaking with Eleri. He knew she was central to what had occurred, but he still couldn't quite reach it.

On the spur of the moment he decided to get out of the bed and get out of this place, re-join the rest of humanity. There was no-one else in the place; a testament to the efficacy of 25th Century medicine, he wondered? He raised himself, threw his legs out of the bed and felt the floor beneath his feet; smooth, hard and surprisingly warm to the skin. He started walking, dressed only in a pair of shorts. He got to a set of sliding doors and as he put his hand toward its control panel he felt something give way inside him. There seemed no way to stop it. He sank to his knees, starting to feel indescribably, horrendously ill, and all his energy seemed to leave him. Full stop.

The main lights flashed on and hemi med Lomanz seemed to appear from nowhere.

'Mike. I'm here. I was alerted as soon as you woke but I didn't want to disturb you. You're not really well enough to start running round the ship, are you? Sorry, but it's back to bed – or maybe sit in your chair?' Mike nodded, reluctantly, whilst Lomanz helped him up, and over to the large, comfortable chair next to his bed.

Mike sat, breathing heavily, as Lomanz placed a cool hand on his forehead and fussed with some bedside equipment. After a few minutes the patient felt a little better and said so. At that moment a familiar person walked through the open door and Mike heard Lomanz say, 'Admiral. Good to see you.' The medic saluted.

'Is the patient strong enough to cope with a visit at the moment, Lieutenant?' asked Tenak.

'Well, he's had a nasty reminder that he can't just start running round the place, sir,' said Lomanz, glancing wryly at Mike, and continued, smiling, 'but I'd say he's up to one visitor. Looks like he's all yours, sir.' He promptly left.

Tenak gave Mike a warm smile and sat in an armchair close to him.

'The med-hypercomp just told me your memory seems to be returning, young man,' he said, 'which is good news, cos I was hoping you'd could get back to duty ... soon as. Lots of things to do on board right now. No time to lose.'

Mike was perplexed at first, then realised Tenak was baiting him.

'Okay, okay, manry ... oh, there I go again. Must have picked that word up down there,' said Mike, 'like this ... blegging infection. By the way, what happened ... I mean, how did I get back to the ship? Where ...'

'Take it easy, Mike. Take your time.'

'I know but ... at least tell me where Eleri is? Come on, you must know?'

'She's working with the Professier. You remember, Draco Muggredge? By the way, I guess you know we got the "special" wristcom back. I came to visit you last night but you were in deepsleep, so I just left it. So, use it. Get in touch with your beloved femna.'

Mike sat back. Various images of Eleri and things about Oceanus swam through his mind, almost as if he were dreaming but yet Tenak was sitting silently in front of him. He must have appeared almost catatonic for a minute because Tenak began staring with alarm and was on the point of summoning Lomanz, when Mike looked up at him, his eyes glistening. 'It's all coming back, Arkas,' he said, 'I just remembered. Just like that. I know what happened.'

'Don't push too hard,' said Tenak.

'So everyone keeps telling me,' said Mike, 'but it's come back, Arkas. I don't know how. I ... almost wish it hadn't.'

'Okay, Mike, what can you remember?'

'I ... could see Eleri next to me ... standing by some sort of lake. No, the sea. I went in the water – with some sort of air breathing device. Tasted foul. Lots of fish things in the sea. Multi-coloured things and …' He stopped talking and put a hand on his stomach. 'I was … sort of caught up in something like … white netting. Kind of streamers or … filaments, and … I remember some shit-almighty stinging and that huge, long thing.' He shuddered as he remembered the monstrous, tentacle thing. Tenak's face took on a serious look.

'Listen, Mike,' he said, 'we all know you've been through a trauma. But it's over now. You're okay. You've got to remember that. And you need to stay put here for a while till we know you've recovered. I'm sure that Lieutenant Commander Medic Atrowska can administer any necessary brain "recuperants". Though, I've always believed in the naturalist approach for emotional damage.'

'Yeah, I know, and I agree with you. Especially from what I've heard about those things.'

'Might take longer …'

'That's okay. Thanks.'

'You know you have the med team's support – any time you need it – and mine.'

After Mike had settled a little, he slowly told Tenak about how he'd woken back in the Fire Island camp. He spoke of the violent storm and a memory of Eleri, seemingly, thrusting the wristcom in his face. She was pleading with him to use it but he wasn't sure why. The rest was still a blank, till he woke up on the ship. At this point Mike started to feel anxious and confused again.

'Yeah, well, I sort of know most of that, Mike,' said Tenak, after encouraging Mike to settle again, then said, 'It's only for the good that you're remembering it for yourself. If it helps, I can fill in some of the missing bits. If you want?'

Mike nodded and Tenak continued, 'I sent an LB to pick you up – esept I went with it. Wanted to check you were okay, for myself. Stayed down there for a little while too. Wanted to get the whole story from Eleri … and the Maheshtras. Seems you owe that femna a lot, Mike. Do you recall being told that she dived into the water? When you were attacked by that sea creature? Well, she did, and she shot that thing too. Seems it scooted off. Then she physically pulled you out of the water, got you – somehow – on the electric car and started back. That's when the Maheshtras caught up with you.'

Mike felt guilty but he was beginning to remember that one of the Maheshtras had told him something like this. Feeling in awe he shook his head in wonderment, then said, 'You've no idea how I feel about that femna. But, Arkas, I felt like that before I got into trouble down there. You have to believe me … Please be believing me …'

Tenak waved his hand dismissively and said, 'Sure, it's okay. I believe you. I guessed as much anyway. You two have been inseparable for weeks. And you have to thank Gajana and Chanda – and Eleri – again – for finding your wristcom and bringing you round enough so you could give your authorisation. It nearly cost you your life, though. They had to gamble. Lucky for you, and us, it paid off.'

'I owe them all – you all – so much, manry. That Eleri's really something, aint she?'

Tenak smiled, nodded, then said, 'Another thing you didn't know … she wanted to come up here with you but at the last second decided against.'

'I wondered about that. Suppose I can't blame her, but …'

'She had a tough decision to make, Mike. Let me explain. That storm was a blegging big 'un. After it cleared your area, it hit the continent. Caused a lot of damage and … well, it hit pretty far inland. And it caused some real hassle for Eleri's folks. Smashed up some of their farm. But don't worry. Her parents are okay. They asked her if she could get back to them, to help, when she called them on your wristcom. I offered to help her out. Repairs and so on. So, I called down another boat and we took her over to her farm. Just dropped her off with a few engineers and teks, and some equipment. Enough to do the job. But you need to understand something Mike. It wasn't an easy decision for her. I explained that you'd be well looked after up here – which was really the best place for you to be, and she eventually decided to get over to her folks. Which, by the way, I think was the right decision – if my opinion counts for anything.'

Mike sat, moist eyed as he said, 'I don't blame her for that one, Arkas. I know she did the right thing.'

'They you are. I told you. I questioned the engineers when they got back here. They made sure she and her folks were okay.'

'How come I've still got the wristcom, Arkas? What's she doing now?'

'As to the last bit, I already told you. She's back working for Muggredge. I asked her for the wristcom back. Had to, Mike. You know it's a special, right? But I gave her an ordinary unit in its place. Not strictly adhering to Navy rules – giving civilians navy issue stuff? But I'm not saying anything, and neither is she.'

'Okay, Arkas, that's fair enough.' Mike leaned back in his chair and exhaled heavily. Just talking to Tenak seemed to have exhausted him.

'Okay, Mike. I'll go now. You look fazed up.' Tenak put a reassuring hand on Mike's shoulder, then rose to leave. 'Get some rest young man,' he said, then he was gone, and Mike suddenly felt a sense of loss. What was getting into him?

Getting up slowly he dragged himself into the bed and suddenly felt drained of all energy. He would try to sleep. He lay back and switched off the light but images of Eleri kept popping into his mind. Where was she now? On some other Maker-forbidden island? He'd like to see her family's farm some-day. How was he going to thank her for everything she'd done?

Unable to settle he switched the light on again and his fingers found the wristcom. After checking its record of calls he wondered why there didn't seem to be any logged calls from Eleri. He'd been on the ship for days, hadn't he?

He asked his unit to contact hers. No reply. He started to worry. What had happened to her? Then he remembered he could ask the unit to "interrogate" hers. He asked it to confirm whether Eleri had actually *touched* the wristcom within, say, the last Oceanus day or so. If she had, that would reduce the likelihood of any accident having happened up to that particular point. His unit told him she had handled the wristcom approximately 16 hours ago. Okay, that wasn't too bad. He left a message for her. Voicemail only. He didn't want her to see a video or holo of him still lying in the med bay.

****

Approximately two weeks after Mike had recovered his memory Tenak was sitting in his private suite, waiting patiently for the video screen in front of him to activate and show him Professier Muggredge. The link-up was a slow one. He exhaled with some impatience, but just then, the screen lit up and the Professier could be seen at his desk, in his antique looking office, in Janitra.

'Ah, my friend, Mer Admiral,' said Muggredge, 'how are you?'

'The better for seeing you, sir,' replied Tenak. 'Professier, I thought I'd better update you on our situation and was hoping you'd do likewise.' Muggredge nodded affably and Tenak continued, 'First of all, I'm pleased to tell you that Mike Tanniss is much recovered. I know you were concerned about him.'

'Yes, deedly. He helped out vera-much on Fire Island. Do you know why he was yet so badly affected by the grotachalik stings? Gajana Maheshtra could not understand it, and he is a vera-good field medic.'

Yes, I know, and he has our eternal thanks for what he did. The diagnosis is the main reason I'm calling. You see, we were also mystified. The sting toxins should have been neutralised by Gajana's treatment .... but there was something else in Mike's blood. I'm sorry to say he's still got a lot of it.' Tenak paused before continuing, 'It appears the creature infected him with some sort of plasmid storm.'

'Plasmids?' said the Professor. 'Not sure, but yes, I think I do know what plasmids are. We mayst not call them that. But yes, loops of extra-chromosomal DNA that can make a host organism more susceptible to bacteria or viruses. We have very little info' on such. Yet, why a "storm" – and why should that affect Mike? The only infections we've ever had on Oceanus have been from the pathogens the original human settlers did bring in, or yet with things brought in by migrants since-times. And that is, despite our attempts to screen such people.'

'Well, I'm not an expert Professier. I can't add much myself, but I'll download the bio' details from our ship's database, to you. I know that since our teks adapted your comp, it can now take ... most ... of our downloads. Anyway, from what I can gather, Mike was hit by a huge amount of these things; a sort of super-blend of plasmids that worked on his cells over a period of some hours. They were just too small for Gajana to detect with his stuff. I think I'm right in saying they allowed some sort of bacterial infection to get a hold. The point is ... well, I think you see the point Professier?'

'Yes,' said Muggredge, his face falling, 'Only too clearly, by misfortune. What you do say is not good. It means ... I am almost fraid to say, that the super-micro life on this planet has adapted to human tissue – in only 130 years! How is that yet possible?'

'I certainly don't know. Neither do our team. They're continuing with their research, as we speak, but my understanding is that they still think things like this are going to be rare on Oceanus. For a while, anyway. How things go with Mike will be important. I should mention, by way, that I understand there is virtually no likelihood that Mike himself can "pass anything on" to anyone else. The medics had to use nano-size anti-pathogens to search out those things in Mike's bloodstream and try to eliminate them electro-chemically. That's why he's had to stay in the med bay so long. It's been edgy stuff.'

'Poor thingsome,' said Muggredge, with genuine sympathy. 'Yet what is the prognosis?'

'Well, I understand he's doing okay now, but they think he might have some further episodes, maybe some type of attack, in the weeks or months to come. I can't go into a lot more detail Professier, as you can guess. It's confidential – but I know Mike was happy with me telling you as much as I have. I know he's also okay with us releasing the details of the infection process - to you and government scientists, in the best interests of your world. It's something you, and we, all need to keep in mind.'

'Yes, coursry, dear manry. Thank you and please thank Mike. I will look at your team's findings and pass them on to the government's own advisory team ... such as it is.'

'Indeed. There is something else, Professier. Good news this time.'

Muggredge looked up, his eyes brightening as Tenak said, 'Another Home System vessel has entered the Ra system. It's a research vessel this time, called the Antarctica. It entered the outer system a few weeks ago. The good news is that they have much better science equipment than my ship. They may be able to tell us more about the plasmid infection problem but, they're also meant to turn their attention to finding more evidence to prove the instability of Ra.'

'Very good Admiral, but, as I told you, some time since, the best way to convince my people about Ra is for an Oceanus team to find the evidence. That remains true, in my humble-so opinion.'

'Granted, Professier, but your people, *on their own*, might not be able to make a break-through soon enough. I think you might still need some help on that. Afterwards, and assuming we can actually help, then your own team would, of course, take any other steps that are needed. By the way, I have something else I need to tell you. I've been looking for evidence of the missing geology, from up here, in orbit. I hope you approve, but with the greatest respect, I have to tell you I would have done it anyway. If you get me?'

'I am understanding of this. What did you find?'

'Unfortunately, nothing – so far. I launched two automated probes, that's all. They were sent into low orbits over Simurgh and other major islands in the Great Ocean. Regrettably, something went wrong. They didn't provide any data – but I'm not giving up, Professier. I'm sending out some corvettes with artificial intelligences controlling them.'

'Sentient machines?' said Muggredge, his eyes widening with surprise.

'No, not fully sentient. Not like you and me. Even Earth engineers haven't got to that stage of tek yet – though I'm told it's only maybe ten or twenty years away. No, these are just hypercomps that can make autonomous or semi-autonomous decisions about what they think they should do – within certain parameters – of course. It's not really what *you* would call "sentience". But I'm hoping these automated corvettes will do a better job than the probes. If not, we may have to await the arrival of the Antarctica. By the way, Professier, I hope you won't mind me asking you to keep the stuff I told you – about my searches from orbit – *completely* confidential?'

'Deedly, Admiral. You shall yet be glad to know, I do so approve – and I shalt not be telling the government. Just make sure Arbella and her people do not hear about this any other way. Well, was that all, Admiral?'

'Yes, Professier and thank you. Actually, there was one other thing. I wondered if you knew anything about Eleri's whereabouts … and if she's okay? Mike says he's tried to contact her lots of times. He's left messages. No response. We've assumed she's safe because we think we'd have heard by now, if she wasn't. But I am concerned too. She seems such an admirable femna.'

'Yes, thank you, and she is. And – she is fine, Admiral. Mike actually contacted me about a week ago, in fact.'

'Really? He didn't say.'

'He was still in your sick bay at the time. He was lucky to catch me in. He looked a bit befuddly, but tis not surprising. I so set his mind resting. Eleri's family is fine too and she is yet working for me. As for why she hasna-yet contacted him, I carnt really say anything. Some sort of problema. Tis surprising, given how just they melded on Fire Island. Something has changed but tis not my place to comment. I just wish those two would sort something out.'

'Indeed, a mystery. Anyway, I'm glad she's okay.'

'That does remind me, Admiral, I have a favour to ask of you. Will you release Mike from ship's duties again? Just for a few weeks? I would like him to join an expedition I'm mounting – some way in direction of the interior of the continent. Tis just for the collecting of the specimens as we discussed before. He was very helpful on Fire Island. Also, if he's yet in any doubt, you can tell Mike that Eleri is part of the team.' Muggredge coughed somewhat disingenuously and gave a wan smile.

'Of course I'll release him Professier. He's actually getting under my feet. He's been back on duty for nearly a week now but there's not much for him to do here. I'd love to get rid of … I mean … get him to help you. Thank you Professier. Tenak out.'

After the conversation ended and Muggredge's image vanished from the screen, Tenak tapped his wristcom and summoned up a holo of Captain Ebazza. 'Do we have any idea what happened to the orbital probes, yet, Ssanyu?'

'We have not been able to find any intrinsic errors in the deep coding of the probes, Admiral. They should have worked properly but all the images they shot are blank. The engineer investigators have drawn a blank too. I'm sorry to say this

Admiral - and we cannot be sure – but,' and then Ebazza could be seen to flinch, visibly, as she drew breath and continued, 'it's …. starting to look as if someone …. may have interfered with them.'

Tenak's visage clouded over, an unusual sight, and one which fellow crew members rarely saw, nor wanted to see if they had thought about it. He seemed to have to pick his words carefully, then said, almost chewing on them, 'Are you saying – sabotage, Captain? On *this* ship?'

'Well, I am not sure, sir. It's a possibility we can't rule out. Nothing more. I've got to emphasise that. The senior engineers are still looking into it but if it was sabotage, Admiral, it was done with great style and vast knowledge. Whosoever it was certainly knew how to cover their tracks.' Ebazza appeared to catch her breath again and blurted, 'Admiral, I recommend a full lock-down – and the withdrawal of all crew from the planet – for questioning.'

Tenak was silent for a long moment, till Ebazza broke the silence, 'Admiral?'

'No, I don't think so, Ssanyu. At least, not yet. If we lock down now the responsible person – or persons – will dig in deeper than a Prithvian groin worm. No, we'd be best to adopt a "whispering wolf" approach, Ssanyu. Let the quislings think they're safe. See what they do next.'

'Understood, Admiral.'

'And get some of the best tek officers on the job, Ssanyu. I guess we'll see how effective the Second Officer really is.'

'You sound doubtful, Admiral.' There was no surprise in her voice.

'Not necessarily. He didn't serve with me at any time before he joined this ship – which was our last survey trip back home. I don't know the guy, but I understand his credentials as a Security Officer are good – otherwise he wouldn't be on this ship at all.'

'He served as Security Investigator,' said Ebazza, 'when I was First Officer, on the light cruiser Cleopatra. He impressed me then, so I recommended him when he applied. I haven't see him since then, but, I must admit to having some reservations now.'

'He was on the Hood meantime, I think. Anyway, please give him free reign, Ssanyu. Whatever he needs. I want this sorted soon as like. We've enough to contend with here, without quislings of some sort.'

Chapter 22

THE TRIALS OF LEADERSHIP

In one of Antarctica's observation suites Captain Providius stared in disbelief at the huge wall screen in front of her.

'How can that be? What in the galaxies is it?' she asked her companion, a gaunt looking man with a bald head and a goatee beard. Doctrow Argost Utopius Manlington, was barely 1.4 metres tall and even Providius dwarfed him. His hawk like features belied a calm and fun-loving individual beneath them. As a sprightly 109-year-old, he was the oldest research scientist still working on a spaceship, anywhere; unique, even in the 25th Century.

'I wish I knew,' he said, a look of curiosity in his bright eyes, 'but it's a bit like a brown dwarf, sept it can't be as massive as that, or it would induce a noticeable wobble in Ra. More mysterious is that I don't know how it could suddenly turn up here, after people have spent 130 years observing this system from Earth. Something like this should have been seen long times ago, but nothing's ever been tracked approaching this zone, from light years out.'

'Could it be a rogue mega-comet, just becoming incandescent as it approaches Ra?' suggested Providius, looking none too convinced herself.

Manlington stroked his lightly bearded chin with two fingers of his right hand. 'Not really,' he said. 'We would still have detected its presence from light years out. It's probably too big, even for a mega-comet.'

As they watched the screen went into 3D mode and the images appeared to leap off it and hover in the air above their heads. They showed a view of jet-black space splashed with myriad stars, looking like some supernal, omniscient, being had thrown clouds of diamond dust from an impossibly huge, black velvet tumbler. The object that had caught the attention of the Antarctica's scientists was still visible, as a tiny light smudge right at the centre of the deep image. And yet, Providius and her colleague knew it was less than one light month distant, compared to the tens, hundreds, or thousands of light *years* distances of most of the visible stars.

Providius's companion waved a hand at image and alongside the blurry object a view of its rainbow-like spectrum appeared, together with hovering graphs and figures depicting the luminosity and other measurements.

'The science crew aboard The Monsoon analysed the spectrum of the energy burst the thing made – when it first appeared,' said the scientist.

'Yes, they likened it to a gamma ray burst, didn't they?' said Providius.

'And so it was similar, so it was. And now Cap'n, we can see the spectrum which the object was radiating a few weeks ago, as it orbits Ra.' He waved his hand again and the image changed to show hundreds of tiny rainbow strips: the emission spectra of dozens of background stars, shown for comparison.

'You see,' said the scientist, 'the object's own spectrum is extremely faint. It still shows some emission features, but the AI agrees it look suspiciously like the spectrum of Ra itself – or part of it, which makes it seem like – well, some sort of … reflection. A reflection from some sort of solid surface? Maybe. It's also marginally blue shifted because it's still moving slightly toward us, but laterally, as we see it. The hypercomp's calculated it's in an extremely wide orbit around Ra. At its current distance it would probably take about 670 years to complete a full orbit.'

'Thank you, Doctrow,' said Providius, 'I hope I don't shock you now but, from what you say, and by the looks of the animations, it's tempting to think … maybe it's not natural.'

'Really? How could that be, Cap'n?' asked Manlington, a deep furrow creasing his wrinkled brown brow. 'Cos, as far as we know, there's no-one else from the Home System out here. Nothing's been seen from anywhere else in known space. There's no-one out here besides us and The Monsoon.'

'I suppose that's the obvious conclusion,' she said, 'but does that thing seem natural to you, Doctrow? And what about the spectrum?' Her voice had a slightly unsettled edge to it.

'Reflection from ices, maybe? Then again, maybe not, but it's just too early to come to the conclusion you're suggesting, ain't it? Why, the history of astronomy is replete with discoveries of strange objects, things never seen before, which no-one understood - but they always turned out to be natural objects. All of 'em. I advise we take the position that this is also natural – till we have stronger evidence leading us … elsewhere.'

'Granted, my friend. You're probably right,' said Providius. She sounded somewhat relieved, but her face retained its troubled look.

'Look, Cap'n, I won't rule out *anything*,' said Manlington, 'but let's just ask the astrophysics AI. Looking up at the ceiling of the chamber he said, 'Electra? So, what do you think this object is?'

A contralto female voice filled the room, seeming to come from all corners of the chamber, 'It is definitely not a rogue star or a planet, nor is it a standard gamma ray burst object. I also rule out a mega-comet. There is insufficient information to decide, at this time. No reliable conclusions are admissible, Doctrow Manlington.'

'Alrighty, granted,' said Manlington, 'but please give us your best estimate of the object's size and mass.'

'It is estimated to be approximately 4,200 kilometres in diameter, with a margin of error of plus or minus 400 kilometres. The orbit suggests a mass greater than that suggested by extended spectral analysis, but the latter is not trustworthy because of the irregular nature of the spectrum. The Monsoon felt its mass was less than ten to the minus seventh that of the Earth, but my analysis would speculate a mass between ten to the minus five and and ten to the minus three that of Earth's.'

'You see, Cap'n, it's planet sized, yet not really a planet,' said Manlington, 'so roughly speaking, its volume is between that of Mercury and the Earth's Moon, but its mass is clearly indeterminate at the moment. We've got a lot more observation to do before we can narrow it down.'

'Okay,' said Providius. She touched a spot just above her left ear, and said, 'Distance to The Monsoon please – and time to orbital insertion round Oceanus.'

Clearly listening to an electronic voice in her ear, she turned to Manlington after just a second or two and said, 'The nav comp says we're still 4 light minutes from The Monsoon and, given our continuing deceleration, eleven days from insertion around Oceanus. I'll send the Navy what we've got on this object.'

****

Ssanyu Ebazza sat alone at a small table in a cosy little annexe to the main cafeteria in Block four, out on The Monsoon's torus. Sipping a mug of steaming kaffee she stared at the swirling liquid, not taking any notice of the three other crew sitting nearby. She was off duty but still dressed in her uniform. The only concession she had made to being on her own time was to leave the top four buttons of her tunic jacket undone, revealing a magenta tee shirt below.

**

Mike Tanniss was also taking a break and sauntered in, saw Ebazza, smiled politely at her as she looked up, then walked to a bank of drink dispensers, where he pressed a button and waited for the drink. He turned and looked at Ebazza as his glass filled with orange juice. Why was she scowling, he wondered? It's not like her to be morose. Perhaps it's this planet. It seemed to have that effect on outsiders, at first. Perhaps she had something on her mind. Like him. His thoughts turned once again to Eleri, who he couldn't seem to keep off his mind. He was infinitely glad that she was safe but her refusal to return his messages troubled him a lot. That was *not exactly* a first for him, to be ruminating about what a femna might be doing but he was usually better at warding it off. Much better. But then, he thought he and Eleri had found something better than what he, at least, had had before.

He thought about sitting with Ebazza but decided to settle on the table nearest to hers. He was trying to stay positive, despite what was on his mind and he tried smiling at Ebazza again. She ignored him. Ah well, he thought. She can definitely be "like that" sometimes.

'It's a strange place, this planet,' he said, across the gap between them, trying to catch her eye. 'Can be damnatiously dangerous down there. Believe me.'

'Oh, how sad,' she said, her voice thick with ... was that mock concern, sarcasm? Then she finally looked directly at him, but he didn't like what he saw. He actually recoiled from her gaze, his brow furrowing, 'Ssanyu,' he said, his voice tinged with genuine concern, 'what's going on. What's the matter?'

'It's *Captain* Ebazza, to you, young man. You don't have the right to call me by my given name. And please do not look so innocent. You know what the matter is. Just use that brain you've got. I'm told you have one, though I cannot say I have noticed.'

Mike was astonished by her outburst. Several faces around him looked up. 'I don't know what ...' he started to say.

'Here we go,' she said, vehemently, 'the claim of innocence. Okay, since you have not got the wit, let me help you along.'

He could feel his face reddening and he began to feel hot, partly with embarrassment and partly with anger. What in the Universes was wrong with this woman? He stared at Ebazza now, a deadly serious expression on his face.

Ebazza continued, 'For your information *Mister Secretary*, I happen to know you seduced my niece and slept with her – and then you abandoned her. Yes, you heard me. Didn't know she was my niece, did you?'

Mike's face fell and he gave Ebazza a deep scowl. He was going to have to tough this out. He felt acutely aware of the faces nearby, staring. He wanted to snap at them to just go but he wouldn't give Ebazza the satisfaction. He sat back in his chair. 'So that's it. You mean, Abena?'

The Captain nodded, her expression one of satisfaction that she had caught him off-guard yet also slightly surprised that he hadn't claimed ignorance of the femna.

The others in the room then got up and quickly left.

'Actually, I did know,' said Mike, but he was lying. Ebazza started to sneer as Mike continued, 'so, okay, Captain, I understand your concern, being Abena's auntine, I mean aunt, but she's only a year or two younger than me, isn't she?

Twenty-one, I believe? She knew what she was doing. You say I "seduced" her. But how do you know that? Is that what she told you, or did you just dream it up?'

'You are right,' fumed Ebazza, 'she *is* almost as old as you. I am not saying she's not. But I'm responsible for her on this ship. I promised her parents I'd look out for her.'

'So, that's it. The concerned Aunt. Very nice, I guess, but I can assure you I didn't do anything with her that she didn't want me to. I can see why you want to protect her, but she has to be allowed to find her own way in life and yeah, maybe even make some mistakes. She's a member of the crew, Ebazza.' He raised his voice slightly, 'Excuse me, hello there! I said … she's a member of this crew. She might have to get into situations a lot worse than just having some fun with me. And that's all it was – fun.'

Mike had started with the intention of trying to defuse Ebazza's anger but realised this was starting to become something he didn't want. He began to regret it, but it was too late now. Besides, she had started it.

Ebazza looked livid. 'How dare you talk to me like that! You're nothing but trouble, Tanniss. I never wanted you on this ship.' She stood suddenly and seemed to puff herself up larger than life and to Mike, she was, in any case, a formidable presence. He suddenly wondered what she was capable of. But this was getting ridiculous. Ebazza actually then seemed to calm a little but a few moments later she said something which actually shocked him, especially as he wasn't aware that his activities had become so widely known.

'You silly, silly man,' she said. 'It's not just about Abena. And yes, she may be Navy, but emotionally, she is not experienced. You took advantage and *everyone* knows it. The whole crew. And it's more than that. It's about the two other female crew you were bedding at the *same time*. And none of them knew about any of the others. Least of all my Abena.'

'That was last year,' he said, defensive now, 'And it wasn't *two* others. Besides, that's what … I was like then … not now.'

'Pull the other one *Mister* Secretary, it's got bells on it. You should be ashamed.'

Mike stood now as he felt anger rising once more and he grimaced at Ebazza, 'Stop being such a holy mother, *madam preacher*. Who are you to judge? From what I've heard, you've been divorced more times than most men have had hot kaffee. I would also remind you that the Navy doesn't actually discourage liaisons between crewmembers, male-femal, male-male, or any other way. They even think it might encourage solidarity. In fact – I believe that over the years several couples on this crew have actually married. *Despite you.*'

'They were talking about crew forming solid, reliable relationships, you idiot. Not fly in the night sex-charged adventures. And how dare you besmirch my good name, Tanniss. You, of all people. At least I am monogamous. It's what I believe in – and so does Abena. We believe in the old-fashioned idea of The One True God.'

'So,' Mike heard himself say, 'that's the real nublitt of it, is it? Religion. It's all about religion.'

At this point Ebazza started to shout, 'No, you fool. It's about the right way to behave. So many people these days don't seem to know how to behave, especially not you.' She was starting to spit saliva as she raged, 'Well, let me tell you something young man. If you even go near Abena again, or *any* other female on this crew, while I'm around, I'll have you put off on the nearest planetoid. Or I'll put you out of an airlock myself. Is that clear?'

Mike felt he was steaming now. He wasn't taking this from her. His face contorted with rage, but when he spoke, it was quietly and calmly, belying the fury he felt inside, 'Alright. Let me tell you something, Captain Madama. If you spread any more malicious propaganda, about me, around this ship, or if you try to take any official action against me, you'll regret it. I have colleagues and contacts in places you wouldn't imagine possible. I'll have you demoted to lieutenant, or lower, in less time than it would take to whistle "Great Olympus Mons in the Summertime". *Is that clear?*'

Mike was amazed. That seemed to stop Ebazza in her tracks, momentarily, but before she could say anymore, she looked away from him and her eyes widened with surprise. Mike heard a deep but calm voice booming from the doorway of the room, 'As you were, Captain. And you, Secretary Tanniss.'

Arkas Tenak stood in the doorway, his face dark with what looked like feelings of disgust.

'What in the Prithvian slime pits is going on here?' he said, 'that two of my most trusted people should behave like this.'

Ebazza stood to attention but Mike sat back down, or perhaps slumped, would be a better description. He suddenly, inexplicably, felt exhausted inside.

'You,' said Tenak to Mike, with a voice which was very quiet but obviously full of anger, 'Get out. Now. I'll speak to you later.'

Mike stared up at him, considered his limited options and got up to leave. He started to say something but Tenak pre-empted him, 'Enough. I don't want to hear it right now.'

Mike thought better of defying him and left straight away.

Once he'd gone Tenak turned to Ebazza. 'What in galaxy's name was that about?'

'It was about the fact that he …'

'I meant, what was your behaviour about? I don't care what he said. I care about your behaviour – as Captain of this ship. You can't afford to let personal antipathy get in the way of the position you hold.'

'I'm sorry Admiral but I …'

'I was speaking,' he said, almost, but not quite, raising his voice. She went silent and looked down at first, then up at him as he continued, 'I don't ever want to see that sort of display from you again. If I do, I'll bust you down myself.'

She gulped visibly. He waited a few moments for her to compose herself, then spoke more gently, 'Look Ssanyu. I know what he's like but he's right about the crew's shenanigans. I, personally, wouldn't allow it but Fleet Command has the final say. I know you disapprove too, but as the senior officers on this ship, we have to set an example – with the way we lead. The sort of behaviour I've just seen? Well, it doesn't match up.'

'I was off duty, sir,' she said defensively but very quietly. Then she looked him squarely in the eye.

'I don't care,' he said, unyielding sternness returning to his voice. 'As Captain, you're *never* off duty. Thought you knew that. If not, then you'd better get used to it – *or get out of it.* The rest of the crew look to the senior officers to be the examples they should follow. I expect you to be a leader, at all times. On duty, off duty. *Whenever.* Do I make myself abundantly clear?'

She looked down and nodded quickly, 'Please accept my apology for any offence I may have caused you. I will never do it again.'

'It wasn't me you offended, personally, Captain. You know that.'

She looked up and said, 'I understand.'

After a few moments Tenak said, in a more relaxed tone of voice, 'But I accept your apology. And *I know* you'll be faithful to your word.'

****

At the Central University of Janitra, Dracus Muggredge sat at a desk in his wood panelled first floor office, sifting through paper photographs. His computer was switched on and he occasionally tapped at its old-fashioned keyboard, causing pages of data to pop up on his screen. He picked out a set of half a dozen photos before him and held them up to the late afternoon light still flooding through the window near his desk. The pictures were those of a grotachalik; shots taken by a researcher swimming out in the deep ocean somewhere.

Suddenly, there were loud noises from somewhere outside the building. An incoherent babble of many voices. He ignored them and they subsided but returned a few minutes later, louder and more insistent. He rose and moved to the window which overlooked a wide stone courtyard forming a boundary of the University. Beyond a high stone wall was the street which eventually led to the centre of Janitra.

Out on the street he could see a large crowd of people marching back and fore, shouting and waving large placards. Even from his distance he could see what most of those placards said, including things like, "Send navy home", and, "We need the navy NOT! Stop HS interference NOW!"

He tutted to himself and returned to his desk, but the shouts continued to build in volume and harshness. There was a knock on Muggredge's door and upon his invitation to enter, in came Danile Hermington.

'I do guess you've seen the demo' outside, Professier?' he said, sounding edgy. Muggredge nodded, as Danile continued, 'I don't like the look of this. They are starting to look vera-nastie.'

'Nonsensing, Danile. Did you never demonstrate, as a student? I know I didst. On social and political issues and all-sorts. Tis almost obligatory. I do not agree with their sentimenta, on this occasion, but they are entitled to own views.'

'Coursry, but these are not students, Professier. I've been watching them from the ground floor, but yet they seem an aggressive lot. From the town I believe. I am glad our students are not back from their vacation so far.'

'Yes, they would probably join with them,' said Muggredge, with a chuckle.

Hermington smiled thinly and said, 'Alrighting. Sorry to disturb you Professier,' and he left.

After 10 more minutes the shouting seemed to have reached a fever pitch and Muggredge looked sharply up from his desk, his eyes wide with alarm, at the explosive for then he heard the cracking sound of breaking glass – from somewhere downstairs. The shouting from outside was now full of raucous hatred. He got up but his worried expression quickly turned to shock when he looked outside again. Dozens of demonstrators had crossed over the boundary wall and were spilling across the courtyard.

Muggredge watched as a dozen University security guards came running out of the front entrance of the building, directly below his office. His eyes widened even further as he saw the guards remonstrating with the intruders, shouting at them to get back. When they paid no heed, several guards produced stun weapons. Although less powerful than the navy equivalents, these were still reasonably effective weapons, and they brandished them at the crowd. 'No, no! Don't,' said Muggredge, though no-one outside would have heard him.

Most of the crowd now slowed in their movement toward the building but then, they formed a wide arc around the security people, holding out their hands as if trying to calm them – or maybe they were warning them to stand down? Muggredge started to open the window but as he reached for the handle a brick arced upwards toward the glass pane, almost gracefully, seeming to move in slow motion. He spotted it, staggered backwards and ducked as the projectile went through the window, as if it wasn't there. A tsunami of glass splinters washed over him and he heard the brick land and bounce somewhere behind him.

A second later Hermington burst in. 'Professier, you're hurt!' he said, as Muggredge touched his forehead, wiping bright red blood from it.

'Only a scratch Danile. I am okay, but this is yet getting out of hand,' he said, his hands trembling.

Two security men dashed into the room behind Hermington and one of them said, resolutely, 'Listen, Professier and you, young manry, we must be out of here – now!'

Muggredge started to object but Hermington, helping him out of his crouched position, pulled at him and said, 'They are right, Professier. The crowd are trying to get into the building. The security team have pulled back inside. They're such evacuating everyone.'

'Tis for luck there's only one or two admin staff downstairs - and you two up here,' said the guard, as he and his colleague ushered the two academics out of the room. 'The back yards are yet safe,' he said, 'so out you go, through the rear fire escape, please.'

'There are some autocars yet out the back … I hope,' breathed Hermington, as they all rushed out onto the landing and made their way toward a back window at the far end of the long corridor leading from Muggredge's room. As they hurried along they heard terrifyingly loud bangs on the front doors below and the heart stopping sound of splintering, shattering wood.

****

Mike Tanniss paced up and down in his spacious quarters in Block 4, on The Monsoon's torus. He was waiting for his door intercom to buzz, and he was nervous. He knew the buzz was coming but it took a surprisingly long time before it did. Mike thought Tenak must really be giving Ebazza a hard dressing down. Although he had never particularly liked the Captain, and it was obvious she *hated* him, he regretted their altercation. She had started a bitter argument for no real reason, as far as he could see. Surely, Tenak would understand that? Probably not. He was a stickler for proper and appropriate behaviour from all crew but although not crew, as such, ships' Secretaries were included. He would say that Mike should have refused to argue with Ebazza, or withdrawn, or reminded her of their positions, or something. To Mike's mind the fact remained that the Captain had provoked him severely and had impugned his integrity, and in front of other crewmembers.

He decided to sit down. Tenak wasn't going to get there any time soon. And then, there it was: the door intercom. His heart skipped a beat. Well, better to get it over with. Why should he behave like a naughty schoolboy? He had to pull out of that frame. Admitting the Admiral, he immediately saw that Tenak actually looked worried, rather than indignant. Nevertheless, Mike decided to pre-empt things, so he started by saying, 'Okay, Arkas, I know what you're going to say, and I'm sorry. Shouldn't have let it happen. Okay?'

'I'm glad you know what I'm going to say before I say it,' said Tenak but he didn't look amused. 'That's half your problem Mike. You think you're so clever. And yes, I do think you "let it happen" but I'm more concerned about the behaviour that brought that reaction from Ebazza in the first place.'

'She shouldn't talk like that to anyone on this ship,' said Mike quickly, 'least of all in public. I was just minding my own business but then she … Well, you were there.'

'No Mike. I missed the earlier stuff. I walked in when things really started kicking off, but I've looked at the security logs since then. I shouldn't need to tell you this, but the point is …'

'I know. "Unbecoming behaviour", I suppose…'

'No, and don't interrupt me. You're wrong again, Mer Secretary. I was going to say this is a lesson to you, Mike. And that lesson is that you're not as popular amongst the crew as you might think you are.' Tenak paused to let that point sink in and Mike went silent. Then Tenak resumed, 'There's a reason for that and I think you know what it is. I'm aware that Ebazza exceeded the bounds of appropriate behaviour for someone who is, in my absence, the most senior officer aboard this vessel. She knows that, Mike, and she won't forget it. But I want you to take something away from this as well.'

Mike sat down again and sulked as Tenak continued, 'You need to examine your own behaviour, Mike. Not just now but over a long time. Ebazza's not the only one who's complained about your fast and loose sexual exploits, not to mention your arrogant attitude. This is the Navy, Mike, not "civi-state". There are standards to be maintained and by the Maker, I'll see that they are. Now, I know we're friends, and I know you're not officially part of the crew, but I do have authority over you – in matters of general behaviour and discipline. I'm sure you're aware of that. If I get any more serious complaints about you, I won't be able to protect you, nor would I wish to. I'll have to make a written, recorded complaint to the H S Secretariat. Do you understand?'

Mike wanted to say that he wasn't even sure he wanted to remain in the Secretariat. But not now. He knew better than that. He just confirmed that he understood and again said he was sorry. That seemed to placate the man, but Tenak remained where he stood.

'Now to move to other things,' said the Admiral, 'because I've heard from Professier Muggredge and, I decided to come and tell you his news in person. That's when I bumped into your little face-off with Ebazza. Muggredge wants you to join a new science expedition he's mounting – a little way into the interior of the continent, as I understand it.'

Mike said nothing but he felt surprise and yes, flattered.

'Eleri will be on it as well,' said Tenak, 'and I know he told you she's okay. That was a few days ago. I wish you'd said something to me but that's another example of what you're like, I guess.'

Mike looked up and silently mouthed the word, sorry. He had also brightened a little, but he said nothing of his concern over Eleri's apparent refusal to communicate with him personally. Now was not a good time to go into that.

Tenak continued, 'But – I just got another call from Muggredge, on my way here,' he said, his brow creasing. 'He was calling by way of a video link-up from the home of someone called Hermington. It seems there's been some sort of riot at the University. A mob from the town, apparently. The staff had to be evacuated, including the Professier. There was a lot of damage but the mob disappeared before the Janitra Securi-pol got there.'

Mike felt horror at this news and said, 'Are they okay?' and before Tenak could say anything, almost shouted, 'Maker! What about Eleri?'

'No need to get anxious,' said Tenak, 'she's out of town, prepping for the expedition. Muggredge got a minor injury, though. A few of the University's security guards were hurt but nothing too serious. Muggredge doesn't know what sparked all this off but they were demonstrating – *against us*, the navy. What's more worrying is that he says there's been another riot, much worse, in central Janitra. But we've no more about that just yet.' Tenak paused for a moment before continuing, 'Anyway, in the circumstances, Muggredge has announced a change of plan. He originally planned for the science team to meet at the University, but he's now asked that you all meet in "Denebola K". That's a small town about 1100 klicks …'

'I know,' said Mike, '1100 klicks west north-west of Janitra. El told me about it. There's a tiny branch of the University campus there.'

'Yeah, okay. It seems the trouble is confined to Janitra, at least for now.'

'And you want to send me down there again,' said Mike, with mock indignity.

'Eleri will be there, won't she?'

'I hope so.'

'Well, what're you waiting for? Start getting ready. Your landing boat is the "Laurasia", and your pilot is Lew. He leaves for Denebola K, in four and a half hours. And, by the way, I'm authorising the boat to help Muggredge, not to suit your personal convenience. Got it?'

Mike nodded and smiled as he walked to a store cupboard and pulled out a large carry-all bag, already stuffed with clothing. He'd left it like that just in case he was able to get back down to the planet soon. Just as well, he thought. He only had a few things to add.

'It doesn't look like I need four and a half hours,' he said.

'That's when the boat will leave. No sooner, no later. Understand? And Mike. Treat that woman of yours well,' said Tenak, 'or you'll have me to answer to, as well as Muggredge.'

Yeah, but will she treat me well, thought Mike and once again sank into contemplating the mystery of her recent silence.

Interlude

The Fate of Worlds

The Others remain unaware of our true nature, thought Demetia, his meditations flowing through Hermoptica and Percepticon, with whom he had joined.

It may be as you believe, flowed Percepticon, *but reassurance will be gained from the arrival of our vanguard probe at the star's inner zone. The observing station will make planet-fall on the innermost world of Qardestriana, within one fifty thousandth of a cycle. It will observe the Others at close quarters and will communicate with us instantaneously, by way of quantum foam tunnelling. Only by this path may we be apprised of progress.*

Thus, may our autonomous adjuncts be forewarned of the activities of the Others and their true intent understood, thought Hermoptica.

Demetia issued a note of warning, *We may yet be surprised by these quarrelsome anthropoids. The Superadjunct has agreed that they are likely to intervene in the Great Plan. We do not, as yet, fully understand the nature of their aggression, nor the lengths to which they will go, if they decide to interfere. Their nature is alien and hard to fathom.*

That is because they are indeed alien beings and the outcome of different evolutionary pathways. It is incumbent on us to study them and to understand, flowed the thoughts of Percepticon.

Hermoptica glowed with appreciation for Percepticon's wisdom but it also noted thoughts of concern, *We should also be aware that their distant origins are probably little different from our own, though ours stretch back eons further. I estimate their* ancestry is likely to have diverged from the path taken by our own mega-ancestral lineage, within 80 millions of our adjusted cycles, since both they and we evolved on very similar worlds. They still have a long journey ahead of them, I fear.

I adjudge they have greatness within sight but they may yet lose their grip, flowed Percepticon's thoughts, *They may need to leave this world, whose greatness they do not understand, and the system of this, for us, troubled but most wondrous of stars, the Qardestriana Chonis Ektra.*

They wander, are lost and directionless, thought Demetia, the slightest sense of irritation creeping into his thoughts, *as once we did. That we accept, but the Superadjunct has warned that they may need to be rebuked if they partake of interventionist activity. It is right that we should plan for this for we must complete the task our far kin have entrusted to us.*

The thoughts of Percepticon and Hermoptica flowed into Demetia, sharing their concerns. They thought, simultaneously, *We wonder whether the anthropoids could withstand the consequences of the work which we must carry out.*

Chapter 23

APPLIED PRESSURE

The Bhumi Devi Times: Demistre day, 23rd of Quintier month

Special Report on yester-riots:

Janitra is reported yet quiet now-day, after a day which many do say was the shame of decent Devians. It began with demonstrations outside the Central University, a march only, but which quickly moved out-madly. Result t'was several minor injuries, mainly to University security guards. The crowd of demonstrators next rampaged, like a heckle of hungry Agran beasts, all through the main buildings, vacated yet. They are estimated to have caused damage amounting to 200,000 credits. Fortunately, Devian Securi-pol officers arrived before further damage could be done.

However, t'was the centre of Janitra that saw the worst rioting. An anger-crowd of over a thousand people, many-so thought to have been involved in the earlier trouble at the University, stormed through the peaceful streets of our capital, with several shops and businesses yet attacked. The rioters did seek to blame the Home System Navy for recent problems and demanded yet that the authorities throw them off the planet. Such anger seemed directed most-such at the businesses that so do big business with the Navy, including Rolashan's Bank and the Central Hotel.

Worst still, a group of Navy engineers, just arrived to carry out maintenance work on some of the city's geothermal power generators, were chased down the streets and pelted with stones and bottles. Securi-Riot police were able to intervene and take them to safety but sadly, not before one of such engineers received severe head injuries as a result of a thrown brick. Several others reported minor injuries. They were cared for by the Janitran Central Hospital – which, through fortune, the mob declined to attack.

The crowd was yet broken up by the 21st Cohort Ultimate-Securi-pol, and one hundred plus five arrests were made for public disorder offences. It is understood that three rioters were charged with massive-assault and fifty more for unwarranted damage to property. This morn a representative of the Central Janitran Law Enforcement Board said, 'We take these offences such-so serious. Investigations are in hand to determine the ring leaders of the anger-mob. Those who threw the missile, that so injured Navy Engineer Gunderlars, will be prosecuted with the full weight of the law. Behaviour like this is un-Devian and will not be tolerated. Any found guilty of the further serious offences are likely to be sent to the penal colony on Stony Island.

The Blue Planet Chronicle (Editorial)

The city demonstrations that started so peacefully yesternoon could, with just ease, have been a dignified protest of reason, but yet were allowed to degenerate into new-anarchy by what we believe is a minority of misled citizens. There are many rumours circulating, to have us believe the Meta-teleosophists were behind these attacks. We believe that they are only yet just that – rumours. There is not a stripling of evidence that the Meta-teleos, as an organisation, had anything to do with it.

We understand that several politicos from the Oceanus Democratic Congress and even one or two from the Independence Party are suggesting that the Meta-teleos be brought under increased scrutiny and even yet disbanded, or outlawed. We do say, that is outrageous, unfair and undeserved. The Meta-teleos are a legal and popular party and we are sure they will co-operate fully with any police investigation that springs from these trouble-times. It is individuals who should yet answer for these crimes, not organisations, surely, unless there is overwhelming evidence to the contrary.

However, be making no mistake of our purpose. We are of the opinion that the kind of behaviour shown yesternoon, brings no credit to anyone. Whether the crimes were organised or not, we encourage the forces of law and order to exercise full censure and to punish those who are guilty, yet to fullest degree allowed by the law.

****

As he stood before his large ordinary video link screen aboard The Monsoon, Admiral Tenak looked at the image of a po-faced, contrite, Arbella Nefer-Masterton facing him.

'We had no such-way of knowing anything like that would happen and the security forces are doing everything they can to prevent recurrency,' she said, 'and I say, sincere-fully, I hope so much that Navy-man Gunderlars will recover. Please be conveying our very deep regrets to his family.'

'Thank you for your concern, Madama President,' said Tenak. 'and I'm pleased to say that engineer Gunderlars is making … reasonably good progress. Fortunately, his brain damage is very slight, and the senior med team are using super-synthetic tissue to carry out repairs. But it is complex work. The loss of blood, before we we were able to pick him up, has caused other problems. It will be difficult for him for some time but he should be okay. As for his family, I'm afraid it's going to be a long time till we can tell them about this.'

'Yes, of course. I am yet sure,' said Arbella, ashen faced, 'and so I am sorriest that the hospital was not able to find a suitable match – to transfuse blood.' She paused for a moment, then appeared to suck in a deep breath and said, Admiral, I am yet concerned about the orders you have issued withdrawing all Navy and such personnel from the continent. I also understand shore leave has been suspended for your crew-people, wherever they are on Oceanus. Admiral, we have tried to assure you the trouble was confined to Janitra and is now well under control.'

'I'm afraid you are in error, Madam President. It was *the Captain* who made the order, as she is entitled to do in matters like these. And the orders were simply to withdraw all crew members doing work assisting your organisations and companies, in Janitra only. Not elsewhere. But you are correct about cancellation of shore leave from the whole of the planet.'

'I would ask that you please reel-back those orders Admiral. They really be unnecessary. We value the excellent work your scientists and engineers have done and might continue to do still in modernising yet reinforcing our lectrical infrastructures.'

'I'm sorry, Madam President but I am not able to rescind the Captain's orders on this matter. I will speak to her, to relay your wishes, but I can tell you she is extremely displeased by recent developments … as am I.'

'But yet what more can I say? I would …'

'Madam President, I'm sorry to interrupt but I doubt you are able to make the assurances of safety you might suggest. Though, I accept that with time, the situation may change. I can advise you we *are* still active on the planet. Mike Tanniss, together with an engineer and a pilot are on their way down to the surface right now – to a location some distance from Janitra. Their mission is to assist Professier Muggredge with his proposal to collect as many specimens of the biota, gametes and so on, as possible, so they may be preserved against the coming star-storms. And believe me when I say the storms *are* coming, Madam President.'

'I'm pleased to hear you have not ceased all activity on our behalf, though I would prefer the restoration of the other work your engineers were doing. But this will have to do for now, yet I do urge you and your …your staff, to reconsider this matter, Admiral. Well and now I must be saying goodbye, unless you have any other business …'

'Actually, I do, Madam President,' said Tenak, 'as there is one other thing I'd like to raise, if I may?'

Masterton's face dropped a little, as if to say *what's coming next?*

'The Navy would appreciate it if you could extend the permission you gave to us to fly landing boats over the continent, so that we may fly over *any* part of Oceanus.'

It was several seconds before Masterton answered,

'Might I ask – for what purpose?' she said, sounding even more tense.

'One never knows when such permission might become extraordinarily helpful, Madama President. I am attempting to anticipate all reasonable contingencies, as the Navy always tries to do.'

Arbella's frown deepened but Tenak made a show of his impatience as he continued, 'Of course, if you do not wish to assist us in this very small matter ...'

'No, no, I certainly do not so wish to impede you in this, Admiral,' she gulped. 'Normally, I would wish yet to consult with the Inner Policy Committee on such like but, at present-times I am pleased to be able to give you authority, Admiral. I would simply ask that your shuttles should not fly too low, too often, special-so over eco-preservation zones, to avoid distressing the wild biota. Or over heavily so-populated areas – not that there are many.'

'Of course. We'll do our best Madama President, though I should mention something you may not realise. The atmospheric drives of our ships produce less noise – and pollution than the largest of your own passenger turboprops. Just thought it worth mentioning, that's all.'

Arbella Masterton just sat there, glowering.

Chapter 24

RETURNING

It was nightfall when the "Laurasia" touched down 5 kilometres outside Denebola K, a small settlement to the west of a flood plain in the north-western corner of the somewhat limited portion of the continent which was considered to be "populated". The town was so small its centre consisted of a mere three main streets and a tiny residential area, with probably no more than 40 or 50 widely spread buildings.

Tenak had ordered the vessel to be as sensitive as possible to the local inhabitants, so the pilot had given the town a wide berth. Most of the inhabitants probably never noticed anything.

As the pilot, Lew Pingwei, ran through his post-landing checks on the flight deck, Mike Tanniss sat impatiently in his couch, on the left side of the ship's passenger deck, or "lounge", as it was known by the crew. The nickname had stuck because the Navy liked to keep the cabin as spacious as possible. And it was often plush because the Navy frequently used the ships for transport of dignitaries back home. It only changed when military operations were ongoing.

Mike peered out of the large window port, as the thick clouds of dust kicked up by the landing were settling. It must be dry out there, he thought, as he watched the clouds swirl in the gloom, like curtains of fog. But as they cleared, he could see no sign of Eleri, or anyone else, coming to greet them, at least not on his side of the ship.

He glanced across the wide central aisle-way at the man sitting in the seat next to the window, far over on the opposite side of the lounge, one of only two companions on this trip. He saw the short, chunkily built man shift uncomfortably in his seat. This guy had a large, hairy head, and Navy-style beard and moustache combination, and he glanced back at Mike with black, intense, and it had to be said, not particularly friendly, eyes. He seemed totally disinterested in the world outside.

'Can you see anyone on that side, Johann?' Mike called out. Johann Agricola Erbbius, one of the ship's engineers (second class level), had been asked to join the group, on Ebazza's suggestion, to lend technical support, along with Lew Pingwei. Erbbius languidly drew his fingers through his black, glossy hair and lazily glanced out of the window to his right.

'No chance,' said the engineer, with a voice as gruff as road grit.

Mike felt Muggredge's team might resent Erbbius's presence, partly as he was not known to them but mostly as was not particularly gregarious, and often seemed, as now, disinterested in what was going on. However, even Mike had to admit he was good as his job. And he knew that Erbbius's skills might be needed, especially as Muggredge's team had no technical personnel of the same or near equivalent standard. There were better Navy people aborad ship but Johan had been available right now and the Professier had agreed to it. Fortunately, thought Mike, the guy on the flight deck was also coming along. Flight Lieutenant Pingwei had been been Tenak's choice alone and it was a choice Mike was very happy with. The pilot was a good friend.

'Shit, you can't see anything out there,' said Erbbius. 'It's darker than a conduit blankout.'

That's when a rich baritone male voice, with a Chinese inflexion, came over the intercom, 'Mes a' Mers, you may release your safety harnesses. It is now safe to exit the vehicle. I did think of making you "walk the plank", given the problems we've been having with the hatch-avator, but, unfortunately for me, it's been fixed. I will join you as soon as I have completed all post landing cockpit checks. Please make your way to the 'vator.'

He's a wagger-snape, thought Mike, but I'm real glad he's on this trip.

'That's my side,' Mike said to his companion, as he released his waist harness, rose, grabbed his large bag from the storage locker next to him, and strode to the aisle through the wide gaps between the sets of paired seats. On reaching the aft quarter of the vehicle the bulkhead door automatically began to open. As it did so the two men were speedily enveloped by a blast of warm humid air from the Oceanus night, flowing into the landing boat like a tide, bringing with it a rich, sweet, smell which Mike recognised as the scent of Treminius plant blooms. There were wild background sounds as well. Erbbius still looked unimpressed. Seriously?

Both men were decked out in Navy issue, heavy duty, coveralls. Mike hoped the rust- coloured fatigues would blend in with the normal dress of the locals. He was no longer happy to stand out in the crowd.

The door hatch was over 6 metres above ground level so they had to wait a moment while a large metal platform quickly unfurled itself from the deck, which they could then stride onto, while height protection barriers automatically rose up on all sides of it. The whole structure then lowered them smoothly and silently to the ground as it slid down a gantry unfolding itself from below the deck of the passenger cabin. No sooner had they emerged from the ship than Mike and Erbbius were assaulted by the massed chirruping sound of thousands of insectoids, issuing from the bush all around. The dust had largely settled, the sky clear now and studded with thousands of twinkling stars. 'Beautiful, isn't it?' said Mike. His companion grunted.

Two figures unexpectedly stepped from the darkness below and into the pool of bright light from the boat's exit. Mike immediately recognised one of them: Danile Hermington. The other person was a short, plump woman, maybe middle aged, dark haired and round of face.

'Welcome back Mike Tanniss,' said Hermington expansively. 'for I heard you have had a hard-long time of it, friend-mate.'

'Thanks for reminding me,' said Mike, only half seriously.

'Sorry, friendling,' said Hermington, 'please be forgiving my ignorance. I would like to introduce to you Rubia Aalenian Mindara, our senior physicist.' He waved a thin hand toward the woman next to him. She smiled shyly and nodded. Mike thought she had a kind face, a generous face. He liked her immediately. But, right now, she was staring open mouthed at the ship. In fact, she seemed in awe of the size of the shuttle. Even Danile looked surprised but, Mike remembered, it was easy to overlook the fact that the people of this planet had grown up in a very different cultural and technological environment.

Dragging them back to the here and now, Mike said, 'And this is one of our engineers, Johann Erbbius.'

Erbbius just nodded. Mike felt he was almost glowering. Why in the stars did they send *him* on this mission?

'Ah but, yes,' said Danile, 'for you are here to help with tek matters, arint you?'

'Along with our pilot, Lew,' said Mike, 'who'll be joining us soon as he can.'

'We shall yet be walking to our base camp back over there,' said Danile, pointing to somewhere in the thick mass of black forest behind him, 'as tis an old manor house, of very old Earth style. Tis very ornate and very large, Mike, Johann. Should like it. Shall your pilotman be long?'

Mike peered up at the flight deck windows illuminated only by its dim, pale red, operational lights, but from where he stood he couldn't tell if he was in there. Give him a few more minutes, he thought. He asked Hermington to explain the mission in more detail, though he was familiar with the basics, having studied them on the way down.

Hermington said that the next morning they were scheduled to walk to a jetty on the nearby "Dexter" river, to catch a ferry boat that would take them upstream, about 500 kilometres, up to the edge of the "Purple Forest". From there they would all have to hike, with back packs, to the nearest "grow-lodge, or gro-stat," where they would stay another night, before walking on to a second Grow-Lodge. After a week of research in the depths of the forest they would return by the same route.

Mike glanced up at the boat again and touched his wristcom to contact Lew but as he did so the pilot suddenly appeared in the pool of light under the ship. The man had a handsome, lean, athletic look, with amenable, cleanly chiselled East Asian features.

Mike did the introductions and Lew warmly greeted Danile and Mindara with flashing eyes and a friendly smile. Then Lew asked Danile, 'Why take the long way man – by river boat I mean – the landing boat here could take us upriver so much faster?'

Hermington looked surprised, 'I did not yet think that was possible. Arint your ships meant so to keep away from sensitive preservation areas like the Purple Forest?' Lew quickly held one hand up to his right ea, looked away for a moment, seeming to concentrate on something else.

Mike started to explain to Danile that taking the ship wouldn't now be a problem, when Pingwei interjected, saying, 'Ah, no, sorry Mike, I'm afraid I can't take you anywhere. I've just received new orders from the Captain. I have to go straight to the outskirts of Ramnisos. Seems we've still got a number of tek people out there needing transfer *now,* 'fraid. I've got to pick 'em up as well as a few others still on shore leave in different places. Look like the the last ones. Seems like the other LBs are unavailable right now. Captain thinks *Agricola* here should suffice for tek on your mission and … I'm sure she's right.' He shot a half smile at Erbbius, who just grunted acknowledgement. Mike knew the man hated being referred to by his middle name.

'Sorry guys,' continued Lew, 'but I guess you've got some hard walking to do. It'll do you good, boys.' Mike rolled his eyes and said, 'Thanks man,' as Pingwei said his goodbyes and hurried back to the forward end of the craft.

'Okay, we need to move outta here, away from the ship,' growled Erbbius and waved everyone back. When they were around 20 metres distant, they turned and watched as the landing boat rose into the air, slowly and smoothly, more curtains of dust rising around it. Glancing at his Devian companions Mike saw that although Hermington was clearly interested – Mindara was completely entranced.

When the ship reached an altitude of about 150 metres, well clear of any nearby trees, it slowed in its upward motion, started to move forward, then accelerated upwards, at an angle, thrusting up into the night, its sleek delta shape silhouetted black as coal against the dark sky, a small trail of luminescence emanating from its engines. It continued ascending at an increasing speed until the small group on the ground could only see its blinking navigation lights, and, within 20 or 30 seconds, even those lights appeared no brighter than some of the stars above.

Mike and Erbbius turned but saw that Hermington and Mindara still gazing upwards, trying to follow the nav' lights as they slanted off toward the far horizon. But then there followed an unexpected, silent burst of blue and orange phosphorescent light high in the atmosphere – after which the ship vanished altogether.

'Oh, my friendlings,' blurted Mindara, looking frightened, 'what happened just then? Are they alrighty?'

'Don't worry,' he said, 'I know it looked like an explosion, but it wasn't. The boat was just switching to its condensing rocket engines. They'll take it into orbit now.'

Hermington whistled, but quickly turned on his heels and led them away, whilst Mindara faced Mike joyfully and said, 'I hope I can take a ride on one of those things some such day.' Then she gestured for her two guests to follow on.

They walked along an almost invisible path leading into the inky forest. Their guides had no artificial illumination, but Mike guessed they had traversed this route many times. He and Erbbius could only follow the tenebrous shapes of their guides as best they could. Within minutes they emerged from the forest into an open area lit dimly by starlight. In the distance stood a very large house, its windows brightly lit. As they neared it the size of the imposing building became more obvious. Impossibly, it looked as if it might have been lifted from an ancient English country estate, and flown, in one piece, through 123 light years of space, to be set down here. The brilliance from its windows illuminated a broad path to its large portico'd entrance.

****

In the purple-black small hours of the morning Arva Pendocris lay awake in her bed in the Meta-teleo Sanctuary in Ramnisos. Patchalk Remiro lay beside her, twitching and snoring like a rusty wood saw. Wearing a diphonous gown she got up silently and moved to the large picture windows of the room, to part the light curtains. Glancing back at Remiro once, she opened the windows and stepped out onto the narrow, ornate balcony overlooking a small pool, ink black in the darkness, two floors below. A relatively cool breeze was blowing, and she appeared to revel in it as she gazed up at the starlit heavens. Then she glanced back into the room. The snoring had stopped.

'What is yet the matter now, Arva? Are you not well?'

'Go back to sleep Patchalk. I am well.'

Remiro sat up in bed, 'Well, and now I am awake, also. Tell me what is wrong. Please.'

'Alrighting,' she said and with a vehement sounding voice continued, 'but don't forget, you have yet asked for this.'

'What on Devi are you going on for?'

'I told you. Did I not tell you? I told you not to go too far – but you just ignored me.'

Remiro grunted like a Boral creature and lay back on the bed, 'You are now, I am supposing, referring to the riots in Janitra?' He exhaled loudly.

'Coursry,' she spat, 'and now you have brought the Janitran Securi-pol down upon us.'

'Tis a slight exaggeration, Arva,' grumbled her spouse, 'they have yet simply telephoned us to arrange a visit. That is all, Arva.'

'So, tis no problem. They are just wanting to carry out … a full investigation, that is all,' said Pendocris, her voice rising in volume and acid sarcasm, 'and this has stirred up a Metamorph's nest, Patchalk. Be making no mistake. They shall ask lots of awkward questions and they will noselie around. We had better make sure we are ready for them. Why did you not yet listen to me when I asked you to be restrained, Patchalk?'

'Relax such Arva, I beg you,' said Remiro, his tone full of exasperation, 'for tis not the time for all this.'

'So, you think there is nothing to worry about? And so, what if some of the rabble you organised clepp us to the pol? And by the way, just who was it who threw the rock at that navy manry? Who, Patchalk?'

'They are hardly likely to clepp on us, Arva. No-one will give information. There was no intention, on the part of anyone, to injure another. That navy manry was just in the wrong place at the wrong time. Just misfortune, tis all. The manry who did it is yet known to me. He is from Arzona Island in the far north-west. I have sent him back there on a turboprop. He will be there by now – and out of the way. The rest of the mob were organised by him. They do not know anything, believe me Arva. No connections. Now, please go back to sleep.'

'You have really set my mind at rest, Patchalk,' said Pendocris, her voice pregnant with stinging cynicism, 'so, do not you think they can trace someone like that – even to Arzona Island? You're naïve-ness surprises *even me.*'

Turning in the bed, so as to lie facing away from her, Remiro exhaled heavily and said with evident impatience, 'Arva, listen now. He is not known to the police, believe me yet. They do not have any DNA information for him. The brick was one of many thrown. T'will not be found. The manry assures me the security forces have never needed to take samples from him. He is yet a ghost to them, Arva. Ist far away now. You should also know that the navy manry, ... Gunderlars, was it? He has made a well recovery. It said so in the Blue Planet Chronicle.'

'Well, that's alright then. Fine. No need to worry. You are right, Patchalk. I will get back to sleep – but it will be in the bed next door to this chamber. Not in your bed.' She got up, grabbed a negligee and started toward the door at the far end of the room.

He turned toward her and said, 'Arva? You arint listening to me. Please not be doing this. List so please, for even if they do catch up to him, on Arzona Island, or wherever, he is the sort who wouldnar clepp anyway. He would do the jail time for us. He has been paid enough.'

'Paid, Yes, coursry. I am hoping yet that even you would not dare to use bank transfer. Credit notes only?'

Remiro nodded.

'And do you think the credits carnt be traced?' she said as she began to slip out through the door. 'All credit notes are specialry numbered, Patchalk! And all can be linked in time and place. With enough work, they shall trace them.'

'Arva … please do not behave thus,' groaned Remiro, almost to himself and pushed his face into his pillow, as if trying to blank out her bile. The door slammed behind her.

Chapter 25

MISERY

Time dragged along whilst a melancholic Mike Tanniss stood at the edge of a wide, rickety looking, wooden jetty, waiting for the river boat that would take him and Muggredge's team of scientists further inland. At this point the width of the mighty river Dexter stretched out before him, about nine kilometres across. Deeply impressive, he felt, since they were around 400 klicks *inland* from the floodplain and broad delta where it flowed into the eastern ocean. The river rose over four thousand klicks inland but by the time it reached the jetty where he stood the waters flowed relatively sluggishly.

It was an uninspiring grey day. The dull, slack water seemed to match his mood and Mike glumly watched it flow past, pieces of wood and plant debris, including the occasional massive log, floated past.

From his vantage point the far bank appeared only as a hazy grey line on the horizon. On the landward side of the jetty was a small square stone building, standing alone, just like him, and behind that a green-blue bank of bushes and trees rising into a set of low hills. The narrow path they had used to walk from the mansion house wound down, out of those hills, like a thin sandy stream.

As he gazed, transfixed by the slow, steady flow of the river he thought back to the previous evening, when he and Erbbius had met the expedition team in the huge house. Eleri had indeed been there, as promised, but his reunion with her had been mysterious and totally perplexing. Right now she now sat at the opposite edge of the jetty, her back to him. She wore a dark blue coverall similar in style to his own, if you could call it a "style" and her booted feet dangling over the side of the jetty. Mike couldn't stop himself from glancing over at her every few seconds. He was sure he had a forlorn, or, some might say, a 'lovesick' look written all over his face. He had seen this expression an many others. How pathetic, that he should come to this he wondered, and yet it had happened, and the biggest puzzle was why in the galaxies she was ignoring him.

Another woman sat next to Eleri, the 8 remaining members of the team sitting or standing in small knots scattered about the jetty. They spoke mostly in subdued voices, but despite the early hour there were occasional bursts of light-hearted banter and chatter; noises which ricocheted off the face of the sluggish water and the slick grey planking.

Mike stood felt very much on his own. Even Johann, amazingly, seemed to have become engrossed in conversation with two or three other members of the team. Being "alone", like this, was not Mike's style. He was usually in the thick of things, bouncing small talk off colleagues but now his mood was morose, generated by Eleri's rebuffing of all his attempts to try to interact with her the previous evening.

Despite the pain it caused he couldn't help going over the events of the previous night in his mind. Over and over. Hermington and Mindara had introduced him and Erbbius to the team as soon as they'd entered the massive building. The mansion had a number of enormous reception rooms, one of which had been taken over by the team, who used it for the assembly and storage of scientific equipment for use in the field. The place bristled with haversacks, backpacks, packed personal belongings, and the plates and mugs left from several meals at the house. Mike had felt it was a total mess. He'd been surprised at the chaos.

Mindara had briefly shown them the rooms the two "off-worlders" been allocated for the night; large chambers situated off a wide landing reached by the sort of wide staircase that Mike had only ever seen in restored films from the 20th Century.

They had later joined in the hearty meal of local foods which the team had cooked in the cavernous kitchen downstairs, when they got to know some of the team members better. Apart from Eleri, Mindara and Hermington, there was Kenye Neith Sung, an experienced geologist; a large and imposing individual in his 30s, with a wide forehead and a mop of raven hair. Then there was Marcus Taimyr Senestris, the senior geologist previously mentioned by Eleri. Senestris was a tall and thin man, easily the oldest person in the group, and though very amenable, he seemed to wear a perpetual look of uncertainty on his face. There was also Kenning Userkaf Chen, the group's biochemist, a concrete block of a man, probably in his early 20s, who, though of short to moderate height, was very heavily muscled. Mike reckoned he must some sort of body building fanatic. Also on the team was Renton Montastruc Barstow, middle aged, but another fit looking individual who specialised in audio recording and photography. Finally, there was Daniellsa Nitokris Morgath, a tall, lithe and perky OA palaeontologist. Mike had been immediately struck by her attractiveness, something which would have marked her down for "special" treatment at one time but who now held little interest for him, as he dwelt on the mystery of Eleri's current behaviour.

When Mike and Erbbius were being introduced to the team, who had gathered around them in a group, Hermington had waved briefly at Eleri, announcing that, of course, Mike already knew her. Hermington had almost winced, as if in pain, and moved quickly on to the next person. Immediately sensing some sort of problem Mike had tried to behave as diplomatically as possible, knowing many pairs of eyes were on him, so he had acted as though meeting Eleri was no different to greeting an old friend, not one he'd been intimate with. He had extended both his hands toward her, anticipating the double handed shake, traditional on Bhumi-Devi. He had said, as tactfully as possible, 'Yes, Mes Nefer- Ambrell, I'm very glad to make your acquaintance again. I hope you are well.' He had winked at her, slyly, trying to show her that he was just putting on a show of formality for the audience they had. He realised he needn't have bothered. She hadn't extended either of her hands to shake his, but just stared at him, with a look as hard as a flint dagger, giving the briefest of nods, but saying nothing.

Mike's heart seemed to lurch and he felt deflated. It had hurt so much he'd even felt it in the pit of his stomach. The effect of her strange reaction was as new to him as the kind of relationship he'd developed, or thought he'd developed, with her in the first place. And it had left him very nearly gasping for air.

As the group broke up Erbbius had touched him on the shoulder and suggested they join in the meal being laid out on a long table in the "Dining Room". Mike shook him off, saying he wasn't hungry and, instead, had followed Eleri as she left the reception room. He'd soon caught up with her and had said, in a kind of loud whisper, 'I'm sorry, El. I hope I didn't embarrass you just then. I had to say *something*. I tried ...'

She had turned, glared at him and cut him dead, saying, 'Do not bother *"Mer Secretary"*. I am very much aware of what you tried to do. I was not embarrassed – but you were. Now do so leave me alone.' The look she had thrown at him sliced him like a scimitar blade. He realised that whatever the problem was it would have to be left for now. It was probably better not to pursue her against her wishes. He didn't want to make things worse. Still, as she walked away, he had called out, plaintively, 'I don't understand El. What did I do? Please ... tell me. Just ...'

Too late, she had gone.

Mike had sat at the dinner table and, unusually for him, didn't take part in the hubbub of conversation. He noticed that a few of the team seemed to be casting him severe or even hostile glances. The same people had greeted him with unsmiling faces anyway, when first introduced. He'd dismissed it as some sort of paranoia he was experiencing, brought on by Eleri's cold reception.

Nevertheless, he wondered if they actually knew the reason for Eleri's behaviour toward him – because he certainly didn't. He'd been badly injured by the grotachalik, and had been told Eleri had rescued him, though he had no memory of it. Perhaps Oceanus custom demanded that someone with that sort of debt to another was supposed to carry out some sort of ritual act of gratitude. Or perhaps he had done or said something to offend her whilst in the grip of the intoxication induced by the sea creature.

He'd found he couldn't eat much of the meal. His stomach seemed full, but he had watched as Erbbius, who had quietly complained to him that he hated the kind of fish food on offer, chomped his way, with gusto, through three full courses. He and the engineer had been obliged to wash the dishes afterward, as their agreed contribution to the meal.

After a night of poor, fitful sleep, in an iron-like bed, he had been roused by Hermington hammering on his door. At least he felt hungry this morning. Breakfast consisted of local fruits and Janitran baked breads, and he'd wolfed them down. He had packed his bags on the landing, hoping to get a glimpse of Eleri, whs'd been missing from breakfast. Then he'd spotted her downstairs and had rushed to finish packing before racing down, only to find that she had already left for the jetty. A line of team members, all carrying backpacks, had snaked along the wooded path, and he spotted her near the front. He'd considered hurrying ahead to try to catch her up, when a tall, willowy figure drew level with him. It was Hermington.

'I am thinking I know what you intend to do but yet *would not*, were I you,' said the man, 'for have you not got the message, manry?'

'I don't recall asking for advice,' Mike had said, resenting the intrusion, 'and what makes you think you know what I was going to do, anyways?' Hermington's face had become stony and he had started to move faster, moving ahead of Mike, who said, quickly, 'Sorry Danile. Sorry, manry. Please come back. I didn't mean to snap. It's just ... I don't understand what's wrong. If you know anything, Danile, please tell me.'

'Alrighting, Mike. T'was obvious what you were going to do. You have not taken your eyes off her since you got here. I do understand your problem, but don't be asking me what tius about. I do not know. All I yet know is that she is sorely upset about something and it concerns you. That is all I know. Sorry.'

'Listen, Danile, you've known her much longer than me. Can't you ask her what's wrong? She won't let me near. But I have to know. I have to.'

'I'm getting it manry. I really am but I have known her for long times, and I know when not to be skinky with this particular femna.'

'Home System speak, please, my friend?'

'Ah, I mean, I don't want to get into the middle of this, Mike. Leave me out yet, please.' Hermington had cast him a stern look, quickened his pace and loped off ahead. Thanks a lot, mate, thought Mike.

Standing alone on the jetty now, Mike was more perplexed than ever and hurting inside in a way he had not ever really experienced before. He wasn't sure what this trip held in store, but he had to try to find a suitable time and way to talk seriously to

Eleri. He contemplated the team's planned destination: the Purple Forest. This famous area was part of the continent's "Eastern Highlands" and was vast. He'd heard strange things about the place; things about unusual animals and plants, phenomena that were found nowhere else on the continent. There were also disturbing stories about people going missing and never returning from there. On this planet that seemed more than likely he thought.

Despite all that, Mike reckoned the more enclosed environment of the forest might help his agoraphobia, which was starting to surge back while he stood here on the open riverside. It was only his preoccupation with Eleri's behaviour which prevented him feeling physically sick in this exposed place. Taken altogether things seemed so … empty. A kind of nothingness, like the vacuum he felt keenly inside. As he stood his feelings of agoraphobia began to inflame. And he thought he had started to overcome this problem. But no. It was not surprising on this crazy world.

****

The river boat, "Pride of Devi", arrived two long hours after the group had assembled at the jetty, and as it sailed off Mike sat inside the poky passenger cabin, below the open deck, looking through smeared, almost opaque windows. The vessel creaked as if a hundred years old. Perhaps it was, but he was grateful that the journey proper had started and he found solace in the surprising pace at which the boat chuggingly made its way up the river. His understanding was that the vessel's fuel was a mixture of locally produced plant oil, plus power gained from a dozen large and, for this place, surprisingly modern, solar cell arrays, supported on beams above the deck.

There were not many crewmembers but they moved constantly was a constant back and forth, between the deck, reached by a short flight of metal steps, and their workstations, accessed through a hatchway in the passenger cabin, behind Mike. He was alone in the cabin, the rest of the team standing or squatting on the deck above. The openness and sheer scale of the landscape out there was just too much for him to deal with. Through the small dirty windows, he could still glimpse the countryside seemingly flowing by but he felt more insulated from it, making him calmer, but no happier.

He watched the crew carrying out their duties in, what to him, seemed a lacklustre and casual manner, but he reminded himself that this was not a starship, and it certainly wasn't a Home System Navy vessel. Mike felt that most of the crew seemed to bumble around, trying to make it appear they were busy when they really weren't. They could have done something to get the place clean, for one thing. To someone like Mike Tanniss, used to the spick and span conditions of The Monsoon, the place was a disgrace. Where was the captain? He didn't remember seeing one. He begrudgingly allowed himself the thought that Ebazza would have knocked these people's heads together.

As he sat in contemplation, Ra finally burst out from behind the banks of cloud that had hung in the sky like immovable curtains. The boat started to quickly warm. The rainy season was a strange season on this planet, thought Mike. The diurnal temperatures varied so much, compared with the near constant sub-tropical conditions that existed when he and Tenak had first arrived. The heat below deck began to rise and Mike soon started to feel as though he was being cooked. There was little or no ventilation down here and certainly no temp' control. There was also a stench from the plant oil fuel.

Reluctantly he rose, to go on deck, when Mindara stepped through the hatchway. She smiled at him and sat on the dirty seat next to him. She asked him how he was faring and, after he had lied that he was okay, she said, 'I am hoping you willnar mind, Mike, but I carnt help noticing that there's yet a terrible atmosphere t'weenst you and Eleri. Fraid someone told me you and she were supposed to be "paired" – if that is how you say it on your world?'

Mike allowed himself a grim smile. 'Well, I guess I don't mind saying we were "paired", as you put it, or so I thought, but I think something happened down here, when I was up on the ship. She doesn't even want to talk to me now. I don't suppose you know what it's about, do you?'

'No, Mike, I am sorry – and I do not really want to … interfere. But list', if you don't mind some advice, young manry. Most womanry here appreciate complete honesty. Utterly so and from the beginnings. You might try telling her that you are sorry for whatever you did but you just want to put it behind you and move on so. I am sorry, I do not yet know if that does help.' A shy look spread over Mindara's peachy, gentle, features.

Mike liked this femna's freshness, her coyness, but he felt she was off track here. 'I've already tried to apologise, Rubia,' he said, 'for … I don't know …. whatever it was, she just won't hear me out. Won't give me a chance to put things right.'

'I am sorry Mike. I really am, but praps a good time to try again – would be now. She is up on deck, around the stern part. Tis probably better than sitting here, boiling away, like a Denker-spod.'

'A what … oh, it doesn't matter. Suppose you're right,' he said, sighing and walking through the hatch. Mindara followed him and as he set off toward the stern, she looked at him as if to say, *good luck*. He wondered what the Devian vernacular was for that.

Eleri sat back against a railing support and because she had her eyes closed, he hesitated to disturb her. The only other person close by was the burly, positively looming, Kenning Chen, who stared out at the boat's wake. Mike walked over to Eleri and, evidently not asleep, she caught sight of him. She rolled her eyes and said, 'I thought I didst ask you not to talk to me?'

'Sorry, but who said I wanted to talk to you?' Mike retorted, thinking he might try a different tack, but Eleri just said, 'Do not be playing schoolary games, Mike. I am not in the mood.'

'Look, please don't be like this,' he blurted, 'I deserve to be told what it's about, so why don't you just start by telling me. Please.'

'I can tell you where to start, manry. Start by leaving me alone, and still getting on with your own life.'

Mike was about to reply when a deep voice boomed from behind him. It was Kenning Userkaf Chen. The geo-chemist looked menacing, 'I think I heard the femna tell you she did not want to be talking to you.'

'Who asked you?' said Mike.

The next thing he knew was that Chen had grabbed him with his gorilla sized hands, in a motion so fast it was a blur, and projected him roughly to one side. The energy behind the shove was enormous, causing Mike to stagger wildly, so he almost went over the rail of the boat.

'No, do not!' shouted Eleri at Chen, 'There is no need, Kenning. He is not worth it. You are a scientist, Kenning, not a drinks-bar guard.'

'You feg-swill heap-mound,' Mike snarled at Chen, then he glanced at Eleri and said, 'I don't need to be protected by you, either.' He regretted it as soon as he'd said it because Chen's face became contorted with anger and he began to move toward Mike again, but suddenly Hermington was there, in the thick of it, grabbing Mike by the shoulders and saying urgently, 'Hey Mike, be so calm. No need of this. Come to the ship-front with me. I need to talk yet with you.' Turning to Chen he said, 'Tis alright Kenning. I will yet deal with him.'

Mike shrugged off Hermington's hands, but he turned and went with him to the prow of the boat. Hermington turned to him.

'You should not be tangling with Chen,' he said, 'for he would have torn you so apart. He is an expert in many martial arts, and he pulls weights too. About five times a week. For hours.'

Mike felt shaky but tried not to show Hermington. 'I don't care,' he said disingenuously. Inside, he felt deeply hurt and he sighed heavily as he plonked down on the deck, folding his legs. Danile sat next to him.

'What's going on Danile? Is *he* the reason I can't get near her? Something to do with Chen?'

'Oh, I do not think so, Mike. He could not be with Eleri, if that's what you mean.'

'How do you know?'

Mike thought he should have seen it coming when Danile said, 'Because he's homington, like me. I mean … genderie– I think you would say?'

'Not quite, Danile. You mean, gay. So, what's his problem then?'

'Oh, long has he known Eleri. Almost as long as me. Just very protective, that is all. Look, Mike, if you want to know what I think, I say tis yet better to try talking to her when we're off this floating junk yard. Meanwhile, because tis you, I shall do you a favour. Praps I should have done it before. I shall try talking to her, as you did wish, but I can only be asking her to "be putting you out of your misery", I think you'd say?'

'That's fair, Danile. Thank you. I couldn't ask for more.'

Hermington walked off leaving Mike to stare at the river again. The worst thing, he thought, was not anything Chen had done. The worst part of the whole thing was when Eleri had said, "He's not worth it."

Mindara walked past at that moment and glanced furtively at Mike, then away again. She looked very embarrassed.

****

Arkas Tenak watched the full-size, 3D image of Captain Providius that appeared in his office aboard The Monsoon.

So, what do you think it is?' he asked.

'The hypercomp doesn't want to speculate too much but thinks it's a low density super-cometary body,' said Providius, sounding sceptical.

'A what?' said Tenak, 'Ours thinks it's some sort of rogue proto-planet but it accepts that it doesn't have the mass you'd expect, if it were. Shall I tell you what the ship's Secretary thinks?'

'Secretary? Oh, I see. You mean Michaelson Tanniss,' she said and chuckled, 'I've heard things about him. His reputation rather precedes him, I'm afraid. Sorry Arkas, but why are you so concerned with what he thinks?'

'You may laugh Jennifer, but despite everything, I've found him to be an astute thinker in technical matters, and a clever astrophysicist. I know he got his Upper

Research and Mentor Degrees more than three years ago, but he makes it his mission to keep fully updated.'

'Okay, Arkas. If you say he has useful ideas, I'm not going to question that. So, what *does* he think?'

'He reckons it's *artificial*.'

'Really? That's very interesting. Our hypercomps have considered that, but just say there's not enough data. I must admit, the thought's crossed my mind but no-one here seems to agree with me. And they're probably right not to. In all the time humanity's been observing our galaxy and since we've been travelling out to other star systems, we've seen absolutely no evidence for sentience elsewhere. Lots of places with bacterial life or simple life forms, even plants and non-sentient animals, like on Oceanus, but no sentience. No self-aware intelligence. There are some complex animals on Oceanus but nothing you could call sentient – not even in an environment which more earth-like then anything we've ever found.'

'I know,' sighed Tenak, 'But he has a point. We've just started to glimpse what's out here, Jennifer. The conduits can only take us so far. I know our long-range sensors and telescopes haven't seen any signs of socalled "civilisation" elsewhere, so far. Still, Mike is convinced the thing out there in the … boondocks, is a vessel of some sort. And it's worth considering.'

'Well, the AIs haven't ruled it out, Arkas. They just don't think it's probable. I did suggest it to Doctrow Manlington but he … and others … tried to convince me otherwise and have succeeded, I have to say. After all, the clincher could be the sheer size of the object. If it was artificial – a vessel – it's simply massive. Size of a small planet. Like something out of stories of "Wars in the Stars", but even bigger. I suppose it could be an auto- probe, or something, but if it's crewed … well, we better hope they're friendly.'

'It could be dangerous even if it's not crewed. It's a pity the Antarctica can't investigate further – get closer, but it's still nearly 4 light weeks away.' Tenak had a wicked look on his face as he spoke.

Providius chuckled gaily and said, 'Exactly, Admiral. At that distance it would take the Antarctica about *13 years* to reach it by some sort of direct route, if that were even practicable. It would be *35 years* by the most efficient parabolic orbit we could take. But then, The Monsoon is faster, of course …'

'Yeah, so it would just take, what, a mere 20 or so years by the parabolic route?' said Tenak, grinning, 'even ignoring the question of supplies and fuel, and I think the Admiralty might have some awkward questions for us. Sorry, Jennifer. I couldn't resist that. But let's get back to reality. It looks as though we might have to wait a long time to get any decent answers about this mystery.'

'Indeed, but it makes the hair stand up on the back of my neck when I think about it, Arkas. Even if we *could* get there and we found it was artificial, none of us are equipped to carry out any sort of "First Contact" mission, are we? Too risky. If it is artificial, it might just come to us I suppose. But … maybe I shouldn't say that.'

'No, maybe you shouldn't. We can do without *that* sort of complication, Jennifer, no matter how historically important, it would be.'

Chapter 26

THE PURPLE FOREST

The Pride of Devi had dropped off most of its passengers, including Muggredge's team and now, two hours later, the scientists hiked uphill, along a narrow, poorly marked track, winding far into the Devian highlands. They had been cooped up for nearly three days on the river boat and Mike had felt it was like a prison sentence. Sleeping arrangements on board had been very basic, noisy and smelly. There'd been no escape from the vessel, and he had developed a crick in the neck from sleeping on the narrow bed with which he'd been provided, more like a board on tiny legs, with one rough blanket. Not only had there had been no escaping the boat there's been no evading his agonized musings about Eleri's "new" behaviour. He and she had not spoken at all. She hadn't let him.

He had finally begun to realise what he might have put poor Abena through, back on The Monsoon. On the other hand, all the women he had bedded over the years had gotten into an entanglement with him with both eyes wide open. Everyone, or nearly everyone, knew what they were letting themselves in for, and the vast majority had been motivated in the same way as him. That was the day and age they all lived in. But there had been one or two, like Abena, whose natural innocence had made them fall foul of the game, but yet, hurting them had never been Mike's intention. He and Abena had never had the kind of intense relationship he and Eleri had developed but still, he had never realised how innocent Abena was. Who would have, in that era? It was unfortunate that there were unintended casualties and now – that included *him*. It left a bitter taste and he imagined how Captain Ebazza would have whooped for joy, had she known. He became determined to never reveal anything to her, or to anyone who might tell her. Good luck with that, he thought, in a closed community like The Monsoon's.

If it came down to it, he knew he'd have to walk away from this and just accept it. But it had to be worth finding out what happened to change Eleri's mind – though he was beginning to think he knew.

After an hour of feeling uneasy about the environment he was hiking through he began to feel more comfortable, because it had changed quite dramatically. Gone were the wide-open vistas of the lower Dexter valley. The river boat had taken them about 630 kilometres upstream, to the point where the valley was too steep and the water too fast for the boat to go further. It had dropped them off at Fishertons Quay, a wild, wood-built, outpost, a few klicks beyond which were wild river rapids. The hillsides towered up on each side of the valley, wooded with blue-green bushes and tall trees. No bird like creatures could be heard above the sound of the river but they *could* be seen, shooting up, unexpectedly, from the undergrowth and wheeling overhead.

As the group reached the top of the valley, each person kitted out with appropriate outdoor clothing and boots, Senestris, the person Muggredge had placed in charge of the group, called a halt. One or two members of the team were wheezing with the strain of the climb, including Mike, though most of the others were obviously much fitter. Eleri was one of them.

Ra was starting to sink past its zenith and Senestris ordered a rest for 20 minutes before moving on over the ridge, closer to the Purple Forest's edge. Their goal was a "Grow-station", or "Gro-stat": a large tree-like plant that had been carefully grown into a large, complex, living, habitat. The pioneers on Oceanus had learnt, within a couple of generations, to utilise the ability of one species of tree, known as "Ornarend", to be grown to form buildings, sometimes very large. This was done by restricting growth in some areas and encouraging it in others. The technique had been developed over the years until many buildings on the continent; often family homes, had been made this way.

The Gro-stat they were making for was about 38 kilometres into the forest, on a plateau. The station had been designed as a University research station which would blend almost perfectly into its environment, without harm or disturbance to its surroundings. Mike had been told researchers visited it quite frequently, unlike the second one they were to make for, situated another 45 or more kilometres further in. This one hadn't been visited for about two years.

The Purple Forest itself, sometimes called "The Great Purple Forest", extended beyond that second gro-stat, over the lower slopes of a range of tall, jagged mountains, the "great Spiky Mountains". Then it went on for another 1,300 kilometres, across a wide plateau, then a vast, high level lake land, thence to blanket the foothills of a second mountain range, but this time generally lower in height than the first, as the landscape "sank" toward the continental centre. That furthest expanse of the forest, the far mountains and central zone were areas which the humans, who called this world home, had rarely ventured since the earliest astronaut explorers. And most of them had overflown it, occasionally setting down to survey it and carry ot scientific measurements. Mike wondered how much of their data still survived.

Mike was also aware that the second range, the "Snowtooth" mountains, only the very highest peaks of which were regularly snow covered, marked the point beyond which the land was too arid to support forest. The succeeding country was characterised by a broken and desiccated landscape, covered with stunted, thorny bushes, and the infamous, giant, so-called, *"Thorncrush trees"*. Six hundred kilometres of that petered out into a sunken landscape of barren deserts; the so called, "Central Basin". Mike knew that the centre of such a large continent could have been permanently frozen and consequently the climate of Bhumi-Devi vastly different. But several things stopped that happening. The continent had a low latitude in the northern hemisphere of Oceanus and the central zone had a very low altitude, some of the hottest parts of it lying below mean sea level. The continent was also surrounded by water, most of it with warm currents. And the axial tilt of Oceanus was less than that of the Earth's, making seasonal variation less marked. Even so, the central deserts got very cold at night, all year, though boiling hot during the day. There were also widespread frosts there in what passed for "winter" in this land, which was really a partial monsoon season.

Mike wondered at the fact that although the total land mass of Oceanus was much lesss than that of Earth, Bhumi-Devi was larger than any one continent on the home planet. For he remembered that several more ranges of mountains lay beyond the central arid zones and then, as the influence of the oceans returned there were further expanses of dense forest, as strange as the Purple Forest but subtly different, extending for as much as a couple of thousand klicks, before finally reaching the moistly verdant, more open country on the western coast of the continent. And that was just the east to west stretch of Bhumi-Devi. There was a similar series of landscapes stretching the further distance from north to sout. The very thought of all those places and their wide-open nature gave Mike a bad feeling in his gut. Yet, somehow, in some strange way he found it fascinating and exciting, in a way which he thought was rather perverse, for him.

As the group sat near the top of the ridge, people broke out food rations from their backpacks, as well as bottles – organically grown – filled with fresh water. Mike stood in the afternoon sunshine and waited for his breathing to ease and heart rate to settle. Beads of sweat ran freely down his face and bare arms and he was very glad that this time – he'd come prepared. For this time he'd brought a small, personal supply of the ship's special issue undergarments which, with their thousands of nano-size tubules woven into their fibres, helped to control body temperature. They removed heat and moisture, to enable cooling, when hot, or, in cold conditions, to insulate the wearer. He suddenly felt very guilty, reckoning it was a bit like cheating on his O A colleagues, who had nothing like this. He was tempted to think that maybe he shouldn't have brought them, but all these people, except Erbbius, had been born and bred on this world. They were acclimatised. He would take a long time to do that. Most of these people were also fitter – and he knew what he needed to do about that.

He'd also brought protein and energy bars from the ship. But, like most of the others he had bought, whilst on the riverboat, a selection of high nutrition cake or biscuit bars, at high cost, from the vessel's shop. He seemed to be perpetually hungry on that vessel and, wanting to conserve the resources he'd brought along, he'd tried one of the bars, which were called, "Klargi-tomards". They were supposed to be full of nutritious fruits and nuts, grown on Oceanus and it was said they made it unnecessary to eat anything else for hours, after just one bar. He'd tasted one and decided he knew exactly why you didn't want to eat anything else for hours – and it wasn't the nutrition which put him off. Still, he'd persevered and had eventually got used to them. They filled a spot, but now he took on of his own bars from The Monsoon, out of his rucksack.

These were standard navy survival bars, known as, "hyperdensity foodsticks", meaning the ingredients were dense with all the necessary nutrients; a bit like the Klargi-tomards but, not tasting like antique shit. Dense in texture, though dissolving readily into an acceptable consistency once in the mouth, he tucked into the hyper' bar. It had been a while since he'd eaten one and now, he was surprised to find the bar was only just about palatable, but a short while after swallowing it, he started to feel a bit better. Those things worked fast, he thought. Eleri could have had one if she'd allowed him near, not that she seemed to need it.

His strength was returning, very quickly. He wished there was a similar remedy for his emotional problem. Taking a few slugs of water, he spotted Eleri a little lower down the slope. She stood alone, in a clearing, bending over to examine some low plants. Mike quickly made his way down the hill toward her. He could see Kenning Chen some way off to the right, further up the hill. Good, he was out of the way. He had to confront Eleri, possibly for the last time.

She looked up as he neared and gave him a long stare of disapproval. He was trepidatious.

'Is it safe to talk to you this time?' he called out.

'Be taking no notice of Kenning,' she said, with a hint of amusement, 'for he just thinks he needs to look out for me, tis all. He would not have done anything more to you. I would not have let him.'

'That's not what Danile said,' retorted Mike. 'Besides, it's easy for you to say when you weren't the one being thrown around. How would you have stopped him, by the way? I'm just curious.'

'I would have just asked him to stop. He is very … loyal to me, you would say.'

Mike's eyebrows rose with curiosity, but he decided not to pursue this line any further. He didn't want to be considered as being overbearing, so he stood at what he thought was a reasonable distance and said, 'Can we please be honest with each-other?' and he looked her straight in the eye. She nodded, so he continued,

'Why won't you tell me what I'm supposed to have done? This is all a complete mystery to me. One minute we're best of friends. More than that, as you well know. We were intimate, Eleri. As intimate as a man and a woman can be. The next thing I know, you behave as if … well, as if you hate me.'

'Okaidi Mike. You are right. I should have said my mind, and I'm sorry I didnar. I shall do so now – as long as it means you will leave me alone.'

Mike just looked perplexed.

'Tis about what you are *really* like,' she continued. 'My auntine warned me as much.'

That really had Mike puzzled, a feeling betrayed in his face as she continued,

'She said that you were a heartbreaker manry – and she was right.'

'What in Sol's name are you talking about? This doesn't make any sense. I've done nothing to you – or her. Nothing you weren't a willing part of.'

'Do not be playing the innocent, Mike. It doesnar suit you. Let me just say that I was warned off you by others, also. People who actually know you Mike. Know you, apparently, for long times. Some of your own crewmates, in facto.'

Mike's couldn't believe what she was saying. Had Ebazza got to her, somehow?

'While you were in the sick bay, on your ship,' she continued, 'I was yet approached by a two-some of your crewmates, who told me about your adventures "of renown" on The Monsoon. Adventures of a sexual kind.' Mike's puzzlement started to turn to anger. Once again, he had been undermined by those who were jealous of him. People who were prudes. Crewmates! He started to ask Eleri who these snitches were, but she had anticipated this,

'And do not be bothering to ask who they were. First-tides, it doesnar matter. The only thing that matters is whether tis true. But I believe them, because I was approached by yet others, quite separate-like. They it was who told me something so similar. Second-tides, I could not tell you who exactly they were, anywayin.'

Mike felt devastated. It was like the altercation with Ebazza again, but much, much worse – because he genuinely cared what this woman thought of him. As this realisation hit home, he slumped-sat onto a large rock in the clearing. Why were these people; colleagues, no less, ganging up on him like this?

Eleri moved a little closer to him. 'Mayhap I should be telling you a bit of the background,' she said, her voice quieter but edgy with emotion. 'After you were taken up to the ship I was in sheer distress, Mike. I hope you believe that.'

Mike just continued to look at the ground, at nothing in particular. His head was spinning.

'But I was kept busy yet, trying to sort out the storm damage at my parentia's farm,' she continued. 'As it happened, I had some help from some of your engineers. They took me over there on a landing boat and they were of great and best help. They repaired the damage. Got us up and running again.'

Mike looked up at her and he spoke quietly, 'I was told your father was hurt. Is he okay?'

'Yes, he is. Thankly. Yes, we took him to the local hospital. He didnar need to go up to your ship. He is fine now. Anywayin, returning to my story. I travelled back to Janitra, about a week later and went to see my Auntine. After I saw her, I met some of your shipmates in the public concourse. That is when they told me about your "activities" aboard ship – on this journey to our world – and to others, it seems.'

'And just what did they tell you?' Mike felt a rising tide of exasperation but fought to stay calm. It wouldn't help if he lost his cool.

'Well, before I tell you this, I would like to ask you something. Is there any womanry aboard that ship you didnar try to bed?'

'What! Are you serious? That question – it's not fair.'

'Fair? Was your treatment of … Abiena, fair? They told me you slept with 3 other womanry whilst you yet led Abeena to believe you really cared about her.'

'That's a lie,' Mike protested, 'I did … well, I did sleep with one other girl at the time, but I didn't mean to … deceive Abena. She just fell for me too much. She's a crewmember, El. She isn't a child. She knows the score. Besides. What's it got to do with us? That was back then. This is now.'

Eleri's anger seemed to rise at that point. Aping his manner of speaking she said, 'She just fell for me too much. Well, mayhap I fell for you too much, Mike. So, tell now, how many womanry do I have to compete with? By the way, Mer Secretary, they also told me that when you were studying for your higher degrees, on far Earth, you seduc-ed the head of the whole college – who was married – and to one man. Seems it became a scandalry, Mike. She had to resign, did she not? She took the honourable way. But you ... you didst get away with it. They didnar even take your degrees from you. Lucky you, space-boy.'

Mike could actually feel her biting sarcasm, as though it was tearing through his innards.

'Not quite El,' he said, as calmly as possible, though he felt almost like breaking down. He had to stick up for himself though. He continued, 'Some tried to suggest she had a hand in my results, but it wasn't true. In the end they realised they couldn't sanction me. They found she had nothing to do with the results, so they restored them – but I hated what happened to her. And, I could never get a job in scienced, after that.'

'Poor thingso, you. So, you do not deny any of this?' Eleri said and after a pause, pushed even harder. 'Did you love her, Mike? Tell me.'

'No, ... *but she didn't love me.* Listen, I wouldn't deny I've done some lousy things. Things I've regretted. But I never *did anything* that I wasn't invited to. And it doesn't mean that a lot of what you heard isn't just exaggeration. Jealousy. Resentment at my position on the ship. All sorts of things, El.'

'You poor, poor so misunderstood personry. Thing is, Mike, be it yet exaggeration or not, I just do not think I can trust you. Her voice dropped to a barely audible whisper then, as she continued, 'I must keep my sights on this world. Least, as long as I can. I do not know what to think about this Home System of yours.'

'I thought you admired Admiral Tenak?' Mike said, tersely. 'He's from the Home System too. It also looks like you'd rather take the words of my enemies over my own. Is that it?'

'You have not denied any much of what they said, not true?'

'Some of it is, but I keep trying to tell you, I've changed. I feel different about you. I don't know why you're making such a fuss about these … "adventures" as you call them. It happens with people all the time back home.' He winced inwardly. He knew he'd said the wrong thing before that last word left his mouth.

Eleri's face wrinkled in disgust and her voice rose in anger, 'Mayst happen up there,' she said, pointing vigorously to the sky, then down at the ground, 'But not down here – and *not with me!*'

Eleri turned and started to walk away. Mike rose and called after her, 'Eleri, please! I didn't mean it to sound like it did. I just meant things are different over there. But I've changed too. I know it's different down here and I see why.'

She turned back and looked at him, limpid disbelief written all over her face.

'It's true, El,' he pleaded, 'I feel different about you. I knew it right from the start, but it's deepened since we got together properly, you know. On the island. We had a good time, didn't we? Lots of 'em. We "work" well together, don't we? Don't we?'

'Do not dare suggest what I am thinking you are suggesting.'

'You saved my life El. I'll always be grateful to you. But the way I feel hasn't got anything to do with that – because I felt like this before you rescued me.'

In a fit of pique, Eleri said, so sharply it felt to Mike as though he'd been cut in two with a broad sword, 'Praps I should have left you for the 'grotachalik.'

She turned immediately and started walking fast, so that Mike couldn't see the expression on her face. Had he been able to see it, he'd have witnessed a face contorted with the horror of what she herself had just said.

'Yes, you're right,' said Mike. Eleri stopped and turned again to face him.

'What?' she said, a dazed expression on her face. Tears had formed in each eye and they now began to run down her cheeks. She swiped them away with the back of one hand.

'You're right,' he continued, voice hoarse with emotion, 'you should have. You shouldn't have risked your life to save me. I'm not worth it. You said it yourself. I don't deny the truth of it.'

'Oh no. No,' she said, 'you shall not dare to get me feeling sorry for you.'

'I'm not trying to do that. You were right – on the boat. I just want you to know … I also want you to know – I love you.' He thought he'd never say that to anyone. Now, here he was, saying it to someone who was walking away from him. Probably walking out of his life forever. He felt his body starting to tremble, involuntarily. He knew he had to sit on the rock again, before he fell.

'Tis too late for that, Mike,' Eleri was saying, her voiced thick with emotion; probably anger, betrayal, grief, he thought. Just like him.

'Too many doubts, nowtime,' she continued, 'I carnt be distracted again. Not now, not here. But at least I have explained my behaviour. "Put you out of miseries", as you have asked.'

He stared up at her, his pain evident, though there was nothing he felt he could do about it; his feelings ran too deep. She continued, tears continuing to run, 'and you shall just have to get over it. I am sorry but – ask, I will, one last time. Shall you be leaving me alone, now, finally?'

After a silence which seemed to stretch to infinity, he nodded, solemnly. Then his vision started to dissolve in clouds of water, and he had to look away.

****

Ra blazed down with a force which felt like a giant red-hot hand, pressing down onto Erbbius, Mike and the group of Devian scientists, as they hiked through an undulating landscape that might well have been called "mixed savannah", back on old Earth. Finally, the trees started to increase in number as they walked along a narrow, dusty trail that weaved between them. Each expedition member had stripped off their coverall tops but even in their thin undershirts they still sweated under the labour of heavy rucksacks. And they toiled along with the effort of alternately having to climb up, then down the rolling hills which though not particularly high, seemed to stretch on and on.

Since leaving the upper valley of the Dexter they had been exposed to the burning rays of Ra without remit, but now the stands of trees gave some blessed relief. The general trend of the topography began to level out. They had reached the plateau, the vast area covered by the start of the Purple Forest proper. Beyond it could be glimpsed the tops of the highest peaks of the "Great Spiky Mountains", covered with snow, rising out of the far forest fifty or so klicks distant, visible as a kind of white and blue haze.

Mike walked on his own most of the time, as did Erbbius, who was trudging along some way ahead of him. He'd noticed the man seemed increasingly ill at ease. Maybe he was agoraphobic as well. Mike had no idea. Erbbius was a "shut-datapad" to him. He didn't even know if he could trust him. These days it seemed there were quite a few of his crewmates that fitted that appellation. As for his own fear of open places, Mike felt he'd been keeping them under control, but only just. Still, he was relieved that since reaching the plateau he felt a little better. It had to be due to the increasing tree cover. He was thankful. He needed to feel better about something.

Mike's last conversation with Eleri kept bubbling up and pushing most of the rest of the world aside. He'd never felt like this before and he hoped he never would again. He found the words of the conversation kept repeating themselves in his mind, like some holographic movie he'd seen too often. In the depths of his psyche, he knew he'd lost her but some part of him refused to accept this and he still imagined her affection for him might return. *Some chance*, said the more rational part of his mind. When that woman said no, she meant, no. It was better not to think about it, but try as he might to prevent it, it just kept flowing back, like a river in spate.

His thoughts so consumed him he almost failed to notice that they were all now completely submerged in the realm of the Purple Forest. The one thing he had noticed was the change in temperature, moving from fierce heat to cooler, blessed relief, though it remained humid. And this world's sunlight still poured through the occasional gaps in the overhead canopy, blowing intensely bright shafts, burning against the inky forest depths. Minuscule insectoids darted silently hither and thither, quiet in the still air, illuminated like bright, animated motes, as they passed through the occasional brilliant beams of Ra light.

The other thing which struck him was the heady mixture of smells here. Strange, often delightful scents from much of the plant life, sometimes mixed with other, less attractive odours, which reminded him of something like rotting flesh. And, when his eyes adjusted to the lower light levels he was able to see liana like ropes, maybe vines of some sort, dangling from the dense canopy and curling, snake like, between the myriad grey-green tree trunks. But it was the colour of the foliage which made the biggest impact on his senses. It was not so much the "purple" of the name as a mad mixture of green-blue, purple-violet, red-violets and even indigos.

The place was a chaos, a cacophony, of different species of plants. The trees seemed to form almost solid blocks, tightly packed together, but the trees were not all the same size. Most were around fifty or sixty metres tall, though many were as much as a hundred. Those seemed to stretch into the infinite blue above. At forest floor level there was a riot of very small, dark, shrub-like plants everywhere, which surprised Mike since he wondered that the relative darkness would have precluded such efflorescence. But then, also strangely, there seemed a reasonable amount of light available, at *his* level, anyway.

He also could not help but gaze in awe at massive bushes which dotted the whole area, huge things with leaves the size of ground cars, but they grew only where the sunlight pierced the canopy and allowed brilliant beams to reach to ground. Around the bushes and the perimeters of such illuminated areas masses of fungus-like things grew, mushroom shaped structures, rising up to a metre tall.

The team of humans wandered along, and Mike noticed that even his illustrious "native" colleagues seemed in awe of their surroundings. Although impressed himself, Mike felt the whole place was quite eerie, though even he had to admit it was incredibly beautiful.

The group followed a muddy trail of sorts, often forced to walk in single file, because of the dense undergrowth and the huge bush things. The trail was often barely discernible and petered out occasionally, often then becoming clearer after a few dozen metres. Those in the lead, including Chen and Eleri, seemed to be using small, box-like objects to help them navigate. Mike guessed these were old-fashioned compasses; he'd seen them in museums. They also seemed to be using sheets of paper and he guessed, again, that these things were 2D maps. Part of him tutted at the primitive tools but part of him admired them immensely. They could have used Navy tek but they had eschewed Erbbius's offer to use his wristcom and The Monsoon's "nav-direct". Trudging along near the back of the line, Mike hoped their confidence in old-fashioned methods was justified. This was not the place to get lost. Maker only knew how many strange insectoids or weird animals inhabited these woods. In the event of really getting lost, he knew Erbbius would insist on Navy tek, as would he.

On the few occasions he'd been in forests back on Earth he'd always been regaled by birdsong, and, in tropical areas, by monkey screams. The shock was that here there were virtually no animal sounds. Only an occasional grunting or barking sound could be discerned, usually far in the distance, and he knew they had to be made by Borals. As they penetrated deeper in there were occasional loud squawks, very infrequently but, as time went on a slightly disturbing sound, again distant, rather like something very large clearing its throat. It was too raucous to be a boral. An Oceanus version of a monkey, perhaps? He'd never heard of such things.

After 90 or more minutes of walking fairly slowly, for the team's pace had diminished, Mike's question was answered, when an enormous flock of bird like creatures flew, rushing up from a patch of broad leaf bushes ahead, into the torch-like beam of Ra-light breaking through the canopy at that spot. The creatures seemed to rise like a singular being, and as they did so it was their collective vocalisation which made the throat gargling sound, magnified to a might din because they were so close.

'Don't worry! They will not harm you,' came a booming voice from the one of those who had been in the lead. Maybe Chen?

After another hour or two of tramping along, with one 15-minute break, the group emerged, wide eyed, into a more open and flat area, dotted with similar sized pools of water, jewel-like ponds, surrounded by outcrops of greyish white rock and stands of trees even taller than those which filled the dense forest. Ra was sinking fast in an ocean blue sky and the eastern hemisphere was starting to glow with a hazy, light orange, luminance. The group seemed to come to a halt so that the team's geologists could examine some of the rocky outcrops around the pools. They said these were 10-million-year-old limestones that frequently harboured the fossils of gigantic swimming reptiles. While the geologists examined the rock strata, Mike noticed that some of the other scientists seemed to be wandering around with wary expressions, perhaps even anxious ones.

Sung and Hermington warned everyone against spending too long in that place, partly because time was short. They still had 20 kilometres of rough ground to go, and they would be immersed in the utter blackness of night-time in the forest within a few hours. But there was another reason, and for Mike it eventually explained why so many of the group had been casting furtive, nervous glances at the clumps of bushy vegetation.

'All of you, do not be forgetting the metamorphs,' said Sung.

'We have not seen any droppings or yet other evidence of them,' said Marcus Senestris. Eleri spoke up at the front of the group, 'I agree with Doctro Sung,' she said, 'Tis best to be precautionry. Let us move on.'

And so, the group pressed ahead, many still peering into the surrounding undergrowth. Mike had heard of metamorphs but knew very little about them, other than tiny snippets he'd heard from Eleri and Hermington. The ship's data logs had not highlighted them as a particularly dangerous life form here. That had been reserved for several species of sea reptiles, some of which were as large, or perhaps larger than the mightiest of the prehistoric reptiles that inhabited the Mesozoic seas of Earth. But then, he had come to realise that the ShipNet contained remarkably little detail on many aspects of Oceanus and its life forms, as he and Tenak were starting to learn. And there was some truth in the fact that he had not really taken a great deal of notice of the any data on the smaller, furry, creatures of this world, for that's what the metamorphs undoubtedly were. Maybe he should have paid more attention, he thought. He would look it up on his wristcom later, provided the ship was over this hemisphere. He recalled that there were absolutely no communications or signal relay satellites in orbit around Oceanus – and agreed protocols precluded The Monsoon launching any.

They moved on, this time pushing on up a steep, expansive slope, eventually reaching a less steep, lightly wooded area, where a steady droning, and later a rumbling sound, could be heard. There was little or no chatter amongst the group and even if there had been Mike was pretty sure he would not have been a part of it; a very strange situation for him.

The rumbling sounded to Mike like gushing water, a mountain stream perhaps. But the sound swelled to a roar as they mounted a rise in the hill and emerged onto a small plateau. And there, maybe a kilometre ahead of them, lay a veritable wall of rock, probably more than 2000 metres high, from which a narrow waterfall cascaded, crashing down the bluff, feeding a small lake. A mountain torrent ran from there through a steep ravine, down the hill, far to their left, but the cascade evidently fed dozens of smaller streams which spread out and ran furiously down smaller gulleys nearby.

This, Mike realised with pleasure, he knew about. He'd seen a reference, on the ShipNet, to a narrow but immensely tall, waterfall, called "Caradoc Falls", named after a legendary ruler of ancient Wales, back on Earth. There were probably tens of thousands of waterfalls on Oceanus, but given its evident height, he felt it had to be this one; a cascade thought to be the highest found on any known planet. He never thought he'd get to see it for real, but while he was comfortable looking at it from the wooded landscape the team was still passing through, he knew he's find difficulty out on the open territory nearer the cascade.

And surely enough the team wound its way through the trees directly toward the falls, their roar increasing steadily. Mike decided to try to ignore the openness of the vista but was pleasantly surprised to find that the trees continued right up to the lake and along the base of the cliffs. Dense sheets of tiny water droplets, generating white, towering, clouds of water, rising into the sky, cloaked the lower half of the falls as they neared it, giving rise to several wondrous rainbows above them. Mike got the spray even at his distance. It felt wonderfully cooling.

But the noise was almost too much. The crashing cacophony seemed to drown out thought itself, even at a distance of a couple of hundred metres, as the group wandered past, all eyes gazing up, awestruck. The team leaders veered to the right at this point, avoiding the base of the waterfall but instead, trekking on, for several kilometres, along the base of the cliff, the furious sound of the waterfall gradually receding behind them, until the rock wall eventually morphed into a less steep, though still massive, rocky, slope. After a break for food, water and rest, they moved on again, picking up a new, almost non-existent trail, a steep and muddy route, which climbed uphill sharply between groups of stunted, almost dwarf, trees, winding ever higher in a zig-zag pattern. The going was tough, and most of the team were already tired and hot.

Mike gradually became breathless but when asked, refused to acknowledge he was having trouble. He realised, with shame, that he had no right to be this unfit, especially at his age. He noticed Eleri, occasionally, climbing up above, at the front of the group. If she could do this, then so could he. He was beginning to feel real contempt for himself and yet, as he seemed to be observing his own thoughts from a distance, felt his newfound self-dislike to be disturbing. Maybe it was altitude sickness or something. Nah, he thought, they weren't that high. It was just this place. It was starting to get to him. For good or ill, he wasn't sure.

The path upwards became ever steeper until the going became a scramble, hands clawing at rocky outcrops and knees bumping painfully on the same. Mike could feel his leg muscles screaming, but after an extremely long hour they emerged, at last, at the top. They were on a plateau which gave, to those who could apprehend them with alacrity, inspiring views of the whole area from which they had come. The Purple Forest spread out like a carpet before them, the place where they had originally entered lost in the mauve-grey haze of distance. Mike preferred not to look but even he couldn't resist little sneaking, nervous, glances, at the giddy panorama. But the openness made him feel slightly weird. A male voice, Senestris, shouting nearby, shook him out of his reverie, 'Okaid, let us have breath back. Get some refreshments, womanamanry. Little risk of metamorphs up here but be keeping a watch all t'same.'

'We have not got so long, yet,' warned Hermington loudly, then strode toward Mike, as he added, 'Ra sets in about 80 so minutes, team.'

On reaching Mike he sat on the rocky ground beside him and said, 'Are you alrighty Mike? Do you have enough to eat, in your back-packing?'

'Yeah, I'm okay,' said Mike, who sat with his back to nearby edge of the plateau, trying to ignore the view, perhaps an inconceivable thing for most people to want to do. Even so, he felt the skin on his back crawling as he sat there.

'Do not worry, we shall soon be there,' said his companion, as though he knew what was going through Mike's mind. Mike knew he must look rough.

'So, just how far is it now?' Mike asked.

'About 5 klicks, as you would say,' replied the geologist.

'Good. By the way, Danile, why all the fuss about the metamorphs? Aren't they supposed to be quite small critters? I know they have a reputation for fierceness, but …'

'A fierceness that fits them yet well,' said Hermington, with a wry look. 'Praps you do not realise but they are about the size of a felihounds. Sorry, I mean …'

'I know about felihounds. So called, because they're the size of small dog, but have a lot of cat like features.'

'Yes, my friend but the metamorph is no felihound. Both species be quite rare, 'cept praps out here, but though the felihounds just keep away from people and have never been known to attack us, this is not so with metamorphs. The truth is that e'en we do not know much about their behaviour. They are very aggressive when disturbed. They appear as though cute and friendly but if they should come near a person they tend to change into – well – somehows, yet a different animal. Gone yet is the sleek shape, the fur and long whiskers. In about two such seconds. They actually change shape, like magic.'

'What do you mean, change shape?'

'Hard to describe yet, Mike. Coursry, tis not magic. They just do turn, sort of, *inside out*. Change to a thing some do liken to an upright, walking bat. The head will change shape and all you can see is a kind of big mouth. If they get you, they do not let go, so take care. They have been known to kill people by severing important blood vessels. They be the most fiercie creatures you ever knew, but when they calm, they morph back to their previous form. No-one knows their origins, their deep lineage, but tis yet thought they are a newly evolved species which reached their present form over the last two or three million years.'

'Sounds nice,' said Mike, looking sceptical. 'It's all a bit mysterious. Surely, your biologists understand what makes these things tick?'

'So you might think, my friend. Yet, the only ones that have been captured have died very soon afterward and – when they die their insides seem to liquefy, within an hour or e'en less. Such as this makes it difficult to examine properly. They do have such unique biolry to them. There is nothing on your far Earth remotely like them. It has been very difficult to study them but still and such, progress has been made and their internal structure now understood. But not all such details of the process are known, you know biochemic changes, by which they change, nor how they do it so fast.'

'Maybe we should get a specimen up to the ship or something. Except it sounds like it would be a bit difficult, logistically. Well, anyway, you said they shouldn't be disturbed, so, I guess it's best not to disturb them.'

'I know manry, but tis easier said than done. Disturbing them could mean just bumping into one unintended like, on the trail, behind a strapweed or something.'

'Oh, I see.'

'Still, not to worry now,' said Hermington, 'As we said, tis vera-unlikely we shall come across them up here. We are far out of their home-habit, especially in the Upper Purple Forest, which we shall be entering very soon. Alrighting, Mike. I shall see you later.'

As Hermington walked back to the members of the group who seemed to be habitually leading the hike, Mike ruminated on what he'd been told, while he munched on another hyperdensity bar from his pack. This place continued to amaze him. And disturb him. He hoped that none of them bumped into a metamorph in the wild. Ever.

****

An hour and a half after resuming their hike, which finally led across more level ground, the group reached the way station, at last, the famous 'grostat' they'd talked about. The light was almost gone as Ra set behind the plateau in the west, and the dark forest bit deeply into the remains of the deep orange glow of star-down. The group leaders had given out small lanterns which, Mike was told, burned with a type of oil produced by a species of lichen. The lanterns shone with a peculiar silver-yellow colour, but they did the job. The illumination gave the trees and undergrowth an eerie quality. He was reminded of the lights which had illuminated the streets on the outskirts of Janitra. Must use the same principle, he thought. That all seemed a long time ago now.

Lagging behind the rest of the group, near Erbbius and Mindara, Mike climbed a gently sloping sward, emerged from the trees, and a hundred metres beyond him stood a large bunker like structure which resembled a giant, corpulent, tree. It seemed to be growing *sideway*s along the ground - which is precisely what it was doing.

This was one of the famous Ornarend trees. Its branches, like smaller trees in themselves, grew out at crazy angles, and as he neared the main bole light began to shine out of the many port hole shaped windows in the craggy side facing him. Those interior lights resembled that of the "silver" lanterns but must have been much larger and brighter. The group leaders were already there.

Hermington went to greet Mike. He was eager to show him into the "building", through a narrow passage which was completely lined with tiny green and purple plants like mosses. There were irregular rows of thick, coiled, structures lining the "walls" and "ceilings", that looked like roots, for he guessed that's probably what they were, but the "floor" was smooth and reasonably level, marred only by the occasional bump or shallow trough. A labyrinth of tunnels led to a large central chamber, in the middle of which lay a kind of hearth. Two or three team members were already squatting at the hearth, busily setting light to bundles of some kind of kindling, again moss-like. As the flames took hold smoke curled up and out through a central funnel-like chimney above. Danile told Mike that above them stood, what he called, a "hat", of mossy "Tarp plants" covering the funnel outlet, so that rain couldn't get in. The wood inside the chamber was protected from the effects of fire by the linings of moss-like plants.

Mike was utterly speechless. He'd never seen anything like this before. He'd never even seen people setting light to material to make an open fire, let alone doing it inside a tree! He was still warm from the climb, but he knew that this far inland, and at this altitude, it would get cold at night. So, the fire was reassuring.

The Navy Secretary sat down heavily some distance from the fire. His head had started to ache, and he felt slightly dizzy, almost as though he were drunk – but without the euphoria. Hermington evidently noticed something and, that was the first time anyone bothered to tell Mike that, unfortunately, the forest gave off terpenes at night, biochemicals with a slightly narcotic effect, which could prove intoxicating to those not used to them.

'Thanks for warning me *so soon*,' said Mike, with a broad dollop of sarcasm. He had been breathing in the forest's scent for hours. It smelled similar to, what on Earth, could have been a mixture of pine wood and Eucalyptus. Mike knew the latter odour only too well, having been brought up in what was Australia, but that wasn't intoxicating, anyway.

'Sorry, manry,' said Hermington, 'for I'm thinking we just … forgot. Nothing more. Yet the real terpenes are only given off at night, so you shall not have breathed them in all day. And they are not really intoxication then, but tis best not to go out now, unless you wear one of these.' He handed Mike a white mask, a bit like a surgical or dust mask, fairly bulky and with a large metal device inserted into the front, which Mike took to be an "oxygen breather", something like the one he'd used underwater at Fire Island.

'I don't think I'll be going out, thank you,' said Mike, 'cos, yeah, I feel bit weird.' Hermington smiled sympathetically and offered to show Mike to his "occupation chamber"; his bedroom. He said he could offer Mike any of the chambers not already chosen, and there were about 20 of them, all coming off the long main passageway leading from the hearth chamber. As they walked along the "corridor" Mike gestured randomly to an opening on his right, saying, 'Why not here?' In fact, he didn't really care where he stayed.

Hermington nodded and showed him the privacy "door", like a blind, yanked down from the wooden "ceiling" above, and how to fix it to the floor by a short liana like vine. The room had a small side chamber which served as a rough and ready freshment room, complete with an organic digester for waste liquids and solids. The broad leaves of a plant growing out of the walls in the room could be used safely for cleaning the bottom, and yet others could be squeezed to provide a natural hand sanitizer, as well as fluid for washing. Hermington wanted to emphasise that all this had been achieved by means of selective breeding over many years, utilising the natural tendencies of the plant and fungi-like life on this world. But he warned Mike to use bottled water from the store and not to drink the plant fluid. There were plants that stored potable water in the dry interior of the continent, but not here.

Mike asked about any possible "creepy crawlies", that might live in the organic material of the building and Hermington laughed, 'Yes, watch out for them. There are all sorts of insectoids and bi-lobians, of course.' He looked at Mike seriously and the Earthman winced. Then his friend laughed again, 'Just wizzering you, manry. Sorry, you say, joshing? Yes, joshing. Those things are outside, Mike. Not in here. The grostat has been hybridised to keep most of those things out, using mosses and lichens that repel them. We use these stations for lab work, Mike, so they have to be much uncontaminated. In fact, you've got an ultra-dry, micro-length, mossry *bed*, over there, so do not be fraidly to use it. I wish you yet a good night sleep. We shall be up bright and early yet, for breakfast and then a long so hike to the next grostat. We should be able to begin our work proper there.'

A few minutes after Hermington had gone to his own chamber Mike got up from the moss bed where he'd been sitting. It was amazing. The "bed" surface was flat as a pancake and yet, apparently, was formed from millions of tiny moss-like plants, bred for their dryness to the touch. Any moisture was kept well inside the half metre depth of the bed itself. And, Danile had explained, the "bedclothes", if you could call them that, consisted of a flexible thickness of something similar to stromatolite. Stromatolites, on Earth, were colonies of billions of bacteria, usually forming large mats or blocks, in shallow water, completely harmless, as here. But this stuff was markedly different from the things back on Earth. Danile had called them, "stroma-sheets" and they were warm and comfortable.

However, there was nothing in here that could be called a chair. What an oversight, he thought, with a sense of irony. Otherwise, the people who had bred this amazing structure, apparently, several generations ago, seemed to have thought of nearly everything, though the conditions were still relatively primitive compared with what he was used to. He was, though, beginning to acclimatise to this sort of thing, on this crazy planet. But it was okay, he thought. He felt more at ease this evening than he had since the row with Eleri, at the start of the expedition. Yet nothing had really changed. Perhaps the calming was the effect of the terpene fumes, he mused.

As Mike pondered over this he peered out of the strangely incongruent, round, "window" set into the blue-grey wooden wall of his chamber. What material was the window made from, he wondered? It certainly wasn't the transparent duralamium used in The Monsoon. Maybe it was old fashioned glass, still used extensively on Earth. He rose to examine it.

He'd long ago extinguished the lantern, now hanging from a stubby branch projecting from the wall so he was able to easily see the world outside. But there was little light left out there. He was about to sit down again when he noticed movement. Someone or something was still out there. His heart lurched as a shadowy figure suddenly moved into a pool of light coming from the window of a room further along from his own. It was Johannes Erbbius.

Mike watched his colleague with curiosity, as the man stood outside peering at something beyond the gro-stat; something lost in the forest beyond. Then, his colleague just wandered off toward the black mass of the wilds beyond the clearing. What in the galaxy was he doing out there? Then, he realised with horror that the man wasn't wearing a mask. Stupido-flick-wit, he thought. He stood peering out for a while, trying to see where Erbbius had gone and wondered whether he should raise the alarm, or go out and try to catch up with the guy. Give him a mask. But then, if Erbbius wanted to take the risk that was up to him, the hump-jammer. He wasn't responsible for him. On the other hand, maybe Erbbius hadn't been told about the need for a respirator. What then? He was a shipmate, after all, even if Mike found him inscrutable, unfriendly and distinctly odd.

He decided to go after him. Hurrying down the passageway he suddenly realised he had left his own mask behind and had to go back for it. He was on his way toward the Hearth Chamber exit when he almost collided with Hermington and Kenning Chen. Danile was in an extremely light-hearted mood and gently asked what he was doing. After he had told them Danile went back with Mike to the Hearth room, where he grabbed a spare mask and tossed it to the Navy Secretary, shouting, 'Try to make sure he does wear it. He might want to pull it off at firsting.' Danile then joined a small group of his team-mates sitting near the hearth.

Mike was glad Hermington hadn't gone out with him. He didn't think Erbbius would relish the fuss and, for his own part, he was just plain curious about what his shipmate was doing.

He would regret that decision.

When he got outside the cold air quickly hit him, coming as a surprise, though he knew it shouldn't have been. Hurrying to where he had last seen Erbbius he spotted a faint track of flattened Inventrius plant foliage leading away from the gro-stat. He hoped he'd found Erbbius's tracks, but he knew he was hardly some sort of backwoods tracker. Still, he was able to follow it, even in the faint light from the station, into the forest, and after a few minutes realised, with a jolt, that *he,* himself might get lost. Now, who was the hump-jammer? And who knew where Erbbius had gone? Mike wished he'd asked Hermington to go with him after all, but the Devian had seemed more interested in socialising.

The forest felt like a massive, deep, black, glove around him. He *sensed it* more than anything; a sort of prickling of the skin which hinted at childhood terrors, otherwise hidden. He tried to push it out of his mind. He shouted for Erbbius but had to remove his breathing mask for a second, otherwise the man would never hear. The sound of his shout seemed somehow to be completely absorbed into the woods and, he felt, had been useless. He slammed his mask on again quickly.

He noticed, with surprise, that there was a sort of light here, probably from the glimmer of starlight above and the background glow from the gro-stat, but he was no longer able to make out the track, if that's what it had been. He knew the team's base camp would soon disappear from view amongst the trees and he slowed up, as he considered going back for a lantern. Why the feggery hadn't he taken one with him in the first place? What was the matter with him?

But, after a minute or so he noticed there seemed to be more light and then he spotted the source: a strange glow coming through the densely packed trees on one side. Couldn't be another gro-stat out here, could it? It grew in brightness as he walked toward it and soon he found it emanated from somewhere beyond a low rise in the ground, just a few metres away. Threading his way through the tangle of undergrowth between the trees he surmounted the rise and saw that on the other side of it was a glowing trough in the ground, about a metre deep, a trench-like depression, running from his right and to his left, into the distance. And then he saw the source of the glow, for the bottom of the trench was *brightly lit*. Gazing down he could hardly believe what he saw; the trench was alive with a glowing stream, about a metre wide, running all the way along it, winding its way far into the woods.

He felt uneasy about going further but was somehow drawn to the flowing light stream. Stepping closer he saw that the "stream" was made up of hundreds of thousands, or maybe millions, of bi-lobian insectoids, all crawling around and over each-other and all moving along in the same direction, right to left, along the trench. They glowed with an eerily beautiful blue-white phosphorescence and, looking more closely, Mike could see that each constituent creature was about 5 centimetres long, had ten legs – and took absolutely no notice of him at all. If they had started moving toward them, he'd have rushed away from there as fast as he could, but they didn't and, somehow, he still felt strangely drawn to them. They felt somehow benign. Things this beautiful surely couldn't be anything other than benign, could they?

Then, a memory flashed into his mind, about how Eleri had told him stories of this world's equivalent of Earth's glow worms. He recognised this species from a film she had shown him, back on Fire Island. He couldn't quite remember the name of the species, and the only thing he did recall was that they were *not* supposed to be harmful. Thank the Maker. He could observe them safely, for they really were fascinating. In fact, he could hardly take his eyes off them. He could have watched them for hours, but another memory pushed its way into dull focus. Where was Erbbius?

Peering along the length of the glowing stream he noticed a familiar shape, almost a silhouette, bathed in the eerie light of the insectoids. There he was, Johann Erbbius, maybe fifty metres away. Mike risked taking his mask off for a second again and shouted to him but Erbbius also seemed to be gazing at the bi-lobians, and either he didn't hear his colleague, or was ignoring him.

Mike looked longingly at the insectoids once more and had to make a mental effort to tear himself away, slowly making himself move toward his shipmate. As he neared the man, Erbbius also moved off, disappearing over another rise ahead. Mike tried to keep one eye on where he'd last seen him and one eye on the glowing stream. How beautiful the things are, he thought. Where are they going? Why?

Mounting the rise, he saw that Erbbius had halted. He was still gazing at the insectoids, but the stream was veering around the far side of a large flat area; some sort of clearing amongst the trees. As he got closer Mike noticed that at the centre of the flattened area was a set of enormous plant leaves, lying, splayed flat on the ground in a sort of ring. There were six of them; massive, fleshy leaves, lying on the soil, leaf apices pointing outwards. They surrounded a wide, central, brown, moss-like platform, raised a few centimetres off the forest floor. What a peculiar looking plant, he thought. It looked as if some violent storm had hit it squarely in its middle, flattening out all its leaves in a circle. Each bulbous leaf was about two or three metres long and, probably over a metre wide. Strangely, they didn't appear storm damaged at all, but the brown central area did look distinctly singed.

The whole area was illuminated by the glow worms and as he crept closer Mike saw that many similarly splayed-out rings of leaves were dotted around it. He spotted Erbbius again. The man appeared from behind the trunk of a large tree and blithely walked onto the nearest flattened leaf ring. As Mike watched his colleague started to squat at the middle of the plant's central area, the massive leaves arrayed around his silhouette. Erbbius seemed to be staring at the stream of luminous insectoids as they moved along the ground, their stream moving within just a few centimetres of the tip of one of the leaves. Mike thought it curious that none of the tiny creatures crawled onto the leaves themselves.

Despite this the hairs on the back of Mike's neck suddenly stood erect, as a sinister thought entered his head. What if the insectoids attacked people, after all? Perhaps they lured victims onto the circular areas and then attacked them from all around. Mike shouted again at Erbbius, and again, but the man took no notice, so he began jogging toward him, amid a rising sense of apprehension. He didn't want to risk getting too near to the insectoids, but he had to get close enough to raise his colleague's attention.

Reaching a few metres from the man, he pulled away the mask and shouted again – and then it happened. The leaves arrayed around Erbbius came very to shocking and vigorous life. They rose with incredible speed, rising smoothly off the ground, like giant springs, so that they engulfed Erbbius, as he stood in the middle of them. The leaf mantrap made a loud, sickly, sucking sound, as they started to envelope him. Utterly shocked, Mike continued to run forward, thinking he might get to him in time to push him bodily off the leaf base, but he soon realised that Erbbius had been totally engulfed.

In his hurry he failed to see a second set of leaves, smaller and thinner than the first set, which had been lying, unseen, below them, now springing up, threatening to also close over Erbbius. He had reached the plant but noticed the secondary leaves only at the last second and, with a leap of the heart, tried to jump to one side. With horror, he realised that some of them were going to catch *him*. Feeling two of them hit his right leg and right arm, he closed his eyes reflexively as thick glutinous drops of a smelly liquid splashed onto him from the fleshy foliage. They slapped hard against his skin and squeezed in against his limbs, making him howl with pain. He frantically tried to pull them free but could make no headway.

The leaves now formed a tall, blue green, globe. Erbbius had totally disappeared. And now, Mike was partly enclosed as well. His heart was hammering and, adding to his sense of fear and horror, he heard muffled sounds from somewhere deep inside the blue-green globe. They had to be coming from Erbbius – and they were screams. Despite a rising tide of fear Mike knew he couldn't let himself focus on his colleague's cries but needed to put all his effort into trying to lever off the leaves which held him tight.

With a cry of relief, he managed to get his shoulder and his right shoulder out but the leaves kept their sucking like grip on his forearm and right leg. He found it was getting very hard to even think clearly and he had little energy to shout for help. A tide of sheer panic started to rise in him but something at the back of his mind told him that if did give way to panic now, he was lost – and so was Erbbius. It was then that Mike noticed, for the first time, that he'd lost his mask, in the rush to get to Erbbius in time. His head was already starting to swim but he wasn't sure if that might have been to dire situation he was in.

Trying to twist his trapped forearm and leg around he began a kind of "squirming" motion to pull free, but it wasn't long before he ran out of energy again. In one of those curious, detached moments of reflection that are often experienced by people when they are in the gravest of predicaments, Mike was suddenly able to think very clearly and rationally, despite the terpenes. As if he didn't really belong in his mind at all he mused, here we go again. This time, eaten by a fegging plant of all things!'

Chapter 27

TERMS OF ENDORSEMENT

In a large, rambling, 20th century style house on the far outskirts of Janitra, Arva Pendocris led a man from The Monsoon, a senior engineer, called D. Toarcian Mordant, through a maze of shadowed corridors, toward a room the Meta-teleos had assigned for a secret conference. The room was one of many in the house, a secure but largely unused building, half overgrown with strapweed plants.

'Why you people can't have the damnatious lights on, I don't know,' said Mordant, a bulky, middle-aged man, with a flat, square, stone-like face, surmounted by a ginger mop of hair. He carried a similarly bulky bag in his right hand. The darkness of the ramshackle house had already resulted in his bringing the bag into collision with various corners of the narrow corridor, on at least three occasions.

'It happens to be 19.00 hours, Oceanus time, agent "Darkling",' said Pendocris, in perfect Anglo-Span. 'I know the natural light is fading but we try to conserve power here. We do not want to use it unnecessarily – and more important – we try not to draw too much attention to this, our "safe house". The place is usually darkened in the evening. Hardly anyone knows it's in use.'

Her truculent companion gave way to a low throated chuckle; a sound which came across as dry and acidly cynical, and he said, 'So that's why you keep multiple padlocks on all the doors and windows. Yes, I'm sure no-one's attention will be drawn to it. And, since when does a legitimate political party – like yours – need a "safe house"? What in all the galaxies are we coming to? And speaking of safety, please tell me that this place is secure from internal surveillance? Or do I have to go to the trouble of carrying out a full scan, myself?'

'Very little electronic surveillance is currently used on Oceanus, agent Darkling. Generally, there is not the knowledge or will for it. If you knew us at all, you wouldn't need to ask that question. I suppose I understand your concern, of course, and that's exactly why we try not to draw any *unwanted* attention. Besides, my colleague is on duty downstairs, and I, have been over every cubic centimetre of this place, just in case.'

'Of course.' Mordant allowed himself a broad smirk, largely hidden from Pendocris in the darkness. 'Just in case,' he mocked, 'and by the by, I don't care if you call me Darkling or Mordant, or the wicked witch of the west. Just as long as you don't talk to anyone who has dealinbgs with the Navy, about this. But I'm sure you know better than that.'

'And I thought you knew better than to question my loyalty, Mer agent. I have been working long and hard to convince the populari, here, that they cannot trust the Home System.'

'With a little success, I suppose, but you've a long way to go.'

Pendocris frowned, made a snorting noise, but fell silent for a while. Then, she stopped in her tracks, turned to face her colleague and said, almost snarling, 'Since you are so concerned about security, *Mordant,* how do we know we can trust this - Sliverlight?'

'Take it that we can, Arva. I'm not going into details. Believe me, it's better that way. He was sent by Dervello. *You know* how fussy *he* is about who works for him. I don't know the man any better than you. I do know he has a job to do and I'm his official escort, now that crazy Captain Ebazza has finally allowed Navy personnel to come back down to Janitra. She had little choice in the end, because Sliverlight demanded Navy accompaniment. Of course, I volunteered to "assist" him.'

'Very well. I take it he has a function – beyond giving credibility to our cause? That is, after the data sets have been manipulated?'

'How perspicacious of you, Arva. Yes, indeed. In facto, he's been chosen by our "friends" back home, to come here to "assure" you and Remiro that Ultima, and the New Rebels, are firmly on the side of the Meta-teleos.'

'Good, but my husband will not be easily convinced of that. Even I had to work especially hard, just to lay the groundwork for this meeting. But if Patchalk can be convinced - so can the rest of the Movement.' Mordant nodded and the two of them resumed their journey through the deserted corridors. Mordant smiled knowingly to himself, unseen by Pendocris.

'I thought you said even *you* had to work hard to convince him, Arva,' Mordant chuckled. 'You continue to surprise me. By the way, did he have anything to do with those riots a few weeks ago?'

'Well, yes, I suppose. I'm sorry to say I must have been looking the other way. I have warned him about it.'

'How remiss of him, *and you*, Arva. I hope he doesn't go too far and, as you so eloquently put it, "draw unwanted attention to us." If he does, some of my colleagues, aboard ship, may need to do something about him.'

Pendocris faltered in her step as she interjected, 'No. There's no need for that. Please leave it to me. I know how to deal with him. Incidentally, Senior Engineer Mordant, how did you manage to delay Remiro's arrival this eventide? I'll bet it involves your box of tricks, over there.' She pointed at his bag.

'You're right. I used it to synthesise a certain female voice. I rang your husband and pretended to be the Personal Assistant to a "Mes Lockrear, UDec Representative for Janitra North." I said she was thinking of defecting to the Meta-teleos. I asked Remiro to visit my "employer" for a personal meeting, to discuss this, at her home near the city centre. I happen to know from the ship's database, that Mes Lockrear is away on business in Ramnisos, but I'm pleased to say your husband fell for it and decided to give it a higher priority than this meeting.'

'Verily, a neat trick,' said Pendocris. 'He rang me about 30 minutes ago and said he had an urgent meeting but didn't say why. He's coming here straight after.'

'I'm sure he will. How will we know when he arrives? It's important that he gets here but he mustn't see my data manipulations.'

'Don't worry. A trusted colleague of mine, Mer Jeremiah, is on the front desk. He has orders to buzz us as soon as he arrives.'

'Glad to hear it, Mes Pendocris. It's a shame I couldn't have done the data-set work somewhere more convenient but, unfortunately, Sliverlight has the access codes to the Antarctica's computer. And I suppose he needs to be satisfied about the procedure.'

'As do I, Mer Mordant. As do I.'

They had reached the final section of corridor leading to the room where Sliverlight waited. Pendocris knocked the door and and as the two of them entered they saw the Home System Ambassador sitting at a large wooden table which dominated the small, musty, room. Limpid illumination came from a tiny lamp which used an old-fashioned low energy light bulb. There were deep shadows everywhere.

Pendocris introduced Mordant and they sat. The Navy engineer removed a sizeable box of electronics from his bag and then drew some sort of narrow tube from the device.

'Ambassador Sliverlight,' he said, 'may I have the access codes to the Antarctica's mainframe supercomp? I take it you do have them?'

It sounded more like an order than a request.

Sliverlight harrumphed impatiently, reached into the inside pocket of his long coat, producing a small box which he handed to Mordant. The engineer opened the box and removed a tiny cubic shaped chip, no larger than the head of an old-fashioned, small gauge nail.

'The information is on something as ridiculously small as that?' laughed Pendocris. 'It's a wonder you don't lose everything that has any value back in the Home System,' she added. Mordant made a dismissive noise, then dropped the minuscule item into a small device he'd placed on the table, next to the tube. Within seconds a 3D hologram was emitted from the end of the tube. In the gloom the image glowed brightly and generated large, geometric shapes, followed by arrays of figures and colourful graphics that seemed to dance in mid air. The engineer pressed various keys on a mini-pad and the images vanished, to be replaced by another, subtly different pattern of data, this time seeming to fill a shape in the air like a cube.

'These are the data obtained by the Antarctica on their recent pass of Ra, when they entered this star system,' said Mordant, 'so all I do now is to remove the material they accrued prior to arrival. Then I'll upload the substitute, the old stuff, into their AI mainframe memory.'

'Won't they or their AI be able to see that it's the old info - and they'll still have the most recent data set, won't they?' said Sliverlight, his forehead wrinkling. Pendocris nodded.

'Not at all,' said Mordant. 'With this equipment I was able to delete their new material at the same time as I downloaded it to myself. It's disappeared from their databank completely. The best thing is that they won't be able to trace it down here. And this box is AI proof. Latest Ultima tek.' He had a smirk of self-satisfaction on his wide face. Sliverlight looked dubious.

'But they'll just do another scan of Ra and gather the data again, won't they?' said Pendocris, frowning.

'No. I'm afraid not. I just infected their hypercomp with a super-virus I've been developing for some time. They won't know whether they're coming or going, but they'll eventually work it out, and eradicate it. It's not permanent. I wouldn't want to stop them from navigating a return to Earth. It would raise too much suspicion back home and especially in the Navy. But it will slow them down. Should stop them from trying to insert into a closer orbit around Ra – and it'll ruin any attempts to analyse Ra's radiation – for a while. This is where *you* come in, Mer Ambassador.'

Sliverlight shook his head and spoke, with sarcasm evident in his voice, 'The wonders of technology - especially in the *right* hands. Anyway, I suppose I should thank you for making our jobs easier, Mer Mordant. I've seen your own data and I propose that we now make the most of it, together with the data gleaned from the old Home System satellite.'

'Why promulgate that? The satellite belongs to the Home System,' said the engineer.

'Well, the opposition parties will expose it, even if we don't. Besides, it's 20 years out of date,' said the Ambassador.

'Ah, I didn't actually know that,' said the engineer, eyebrows rising.

The other two looked surprised, as if to say, *even we knew that,* and Sliverlight rolled his eyes, 'Don't feel bad,' he said, the words dripping with scarcely hidden sarcasm. 'Perhaps you were busy,' he continued, 'but as I was saying, we must put forward all of this stuff. We, meaning *you*,' he said to Pendocris, 'so you and your husband can appear to be even handed. You've got to appear to be fair to all parties. And don't forget, The Monsoon also has data that can be used. Unless you've done something …' he looked sharply at Mordant, but the engineer shook his head, 'No, I haven't done anything to The Monsoon's databanks. Now that really would be too risky and too obvious. Plus, their stuff is known to be less precise, and open to wider interpretation than the Antarctica's. In this matter anyway, but, never fear, I have instead hampered their attempts to gather geological information from the planet.'

'What geological evidence?' came a deep voice from the far side of the room. Patchalk Remiro stood by the door. Pendocris flushed red, unseen in the gloom.

How long have you been there, husband?' she said.

'Just-so got here. I hope I have not missed much,' he said, with straightforward sincerity. Pendocris breathed a silent sigh of relief and introduced Remiro to the other two men. As he sat at the table Mordant said to him, 'My ship has been looking for evidence of rock strata that could indicate an ancient extinction event. Something that might lend weight to the argument that Ra is unstable.'

'What non-sensery,' said Remiro, 'I have never heard such things.'

Arva Pendocris rolled her eyes. 'Well, I suppose you are not a geologist, Patchalk,' she said.

'Oh, it might indeed lend some strength but, as I said, I've taken care of it,' said Mordant.

'Good manry,' said Remiro and continued, 'and now, should yet anyone tell me what you have been talking about?'

'We have been talking about the weather, husband,' exhaled Pendocris, doing little to hide her exasperation. 'What'ere do you imagine? We've been talking about how we can best put forward our arguments, have we not, Ambassador?'

'Yes, of course,' said Sliverlight, 'for we need to be inclusive in our approach, my friend,' he said to Remiro. 'We've been examining the data sets that are available. You're welcome to look at them yourself, sir. Senior Engineer Mordant and I were just saying that there's little to set anyone else's data in preference to the information the Meta-teleos have gathered. The info The Monsoon brought here is the most "dangerous" thing to your cause. But Mer Mordant feels their data can be argued against, successfully.'

At that, the engineer smiled placidly and nodded.

'Sweet talkie you are,' said Remiro, 'so what ere shall be your own position on this, Mer Ambassador? Arint you a paid employee of the Home System?'

'Put simply, Mer Remiro,' said Sliverlight, 'I feel my position should be seen as one of trying to reach for the truth, whatever that be. Though *we* know what that is, of course. I also bear the news that your Meta-teleo Movement has much more support in the Home System than you might think.'

'Really such?' said Remiro, 'as I have deedly heard that there may be elements in Ultima that appear so to support us, but I was not aware it went any further than that.'

'Of course, it does,' said his wife, 'I thought you didst know it. We discussed it recently, did not? My brother has an important post in The Secretariat to the Navy and has been very helpful. He has sent us news.' Pendocris directed her last comment to Sliverlight and Mordant.

'What you say, my wife, and what your brother says, for that matter, is not of necessity accurate, or up to now-date, is it?' said Remiro. Pendocris glared at him.

'Ah, that's where I come in, dear Mer,' piped Sliverlight. 'I can assure you, from my own association within the renewed organisation, that Ultima is very much of the same mind as the Meta-teleos, barring slight and unimportant variations of emphasis. Their central philosophy is very similar to your own. It is this, that they - and many like minded in the HS government - wish you nothing but success in your drive to take Oceanus in a new direction.'

Pendocris placed a hand, very gently, on Remiro's shoulder and squeezed whilst nodding at Sliverlight's comments. 'I knew it,' she said, her voice bright with enthusiasm and she continued, 'I am so pleased to hear such news Ambassador. Arint you, Patchalk?' She smiled broadly and continued to palpate his shoulder, moving her hand subtly down his arm, caressing him.

'You are so easily pleased, my wife,' he said. 'Still, I suppose we have little choice, at such moment, but yet to go along with this. Tis the only time we have heard this sort of thing from a government official. You are deedly a quisling, arint you, Mer Ambassador? A thornybush in your government's side?'

'Well, I have simply said that ...' Sliverlight blustered.

'I know,' said Remiro, interjecting, 'you are much concerned to show there is support for us back on Earth. I have to say, however, that I, that is, *we* - have many reasons to distrust the Home System. I do not know if you are aware, Mer Ambassador, but tis our deeply held conviction that HS Government want to get us *all* off this planet. That is yet behind the business of this "Ra instability". We and our supporters see that for what it is – a ploy to reverse our independence and remove everyone. This, so they can move in and take this world for its resources. Praps even turn it into a military base - and who knows knows what else? By the time most of the popularia realises what has happened, we shall all have been deported and dispersed throughout that den-zone of iniquity – the Solar System. It makes me sick-so.'

Mordant looked down, with a mock expression of shame on his face but in the darkness Remiro failed to spot the mirth playing on his lips.

'Perhaps, sir,' said Sliverlight. 'as I have no doubt there are elements within the Home System Government that may wish to carry out such plans. That's why I believe in the support we are getting from Ultima, who are vigorously *opposed* to the Allied Government. And I am not alone in this belief. There are increasing numbers, both within and outside the government, who feel it's time for change. Even though I am, as you say, a government employee, I see it as my duty to steer the path of truth through these difficult times and so, I hope you feel you can trust me, dear sir.'

'Sorry, but damnedly, will I do that, sirra,' said Remiro sharply. Then, with an obvious effort, and under the disapproving gaze of Pendocris, he seemed to calm down and said, 'I am yet sorry for that, for … as I said, despite reluctance so to do, we … need the help of someone like you - if you really will intercede on our behalf.'

'I assure you, I shall,' said the Ambassador, 'I attended a reception in your government buildings last night and met some representatives and other dignitaries. It's all informal at the moment, but I've got a formal meeting with Arbella and her Inner Council, tomorrow. The next day I'm supposed to "meet" both of you, formally, and then the leaders of the third party.'

'There's a debate in the Curia in a couplet o' weeks, to decide whether there should be an interstellar conference on the issue of evacuation. Will you be there?' asked Pendocris.

'I shall be there but alas, my lady, I have no locus standi, as an outsider, so will be unable to address the House. My best course is to be persuasive with government officials.'

'See that you are,' said Remiro, sharply, and Pendocris immediately took her hand off his arm. 'I am sorry, Ambassador,' he continued, looking at his wife's face. 'Please be forgiving me. I just grow impatient with this whole issue.'

'Quite,' said Sliverlight, 'but right is on our side. Still, you must realise my powers are limited. I am a stranger on this world, but I will do my utmost to help.'

There was silence for a while, broken only when Remiro suddenly piped up, 'I should say I apologise for my lateness, friendlings. I received a call from someone claiming to be the assistant to the Rep' for Janitra North.' The other three stared at Remiro with mock surprise, as Remiro continued, 'She said Rep Lockrear wanted to defect, to us. Given yet the delicate balance of power that exists at the moment I adjudged it was too good an chance to miss, so I went to see her but – strangely, she wasn't there. Must have been a skankling. Sorry, I should say, prank,' he said, to his Home System colleagues. He continued, sounding very sincere, 'I am yet aggrieved - because I should have known. Didst know something was wrong.'

'How should you have known, husband?' asked Pendocris.

'Because the voice was a fakery-pop. The caller sounded – unreal – somehow. Mayhap was childrine, using some sort of voice muffler device. I do not know.'

'Husband, it sounds much like someone wizzling us around. Pay no heed, yet no real harm was done.'

'True. By the way, Arva, I must say I do not think much of your security arrangements here.'

'Whatso'ere do you mean Patchalk?' There was an edge to Arva's voice.

'Well, I didst arrive, and still was able to walk straight in here. You put old Jeremiah in the front. After I started up the stairway, I saw him coming yet from the washment rooms. Fine security guard, he is.'

'Well now,' said Mordant. 'I'm sorry to hear that my friend but you know, we have a very old saying back home. It goes, "when you gotta go, you just gotta go!'

Everyone except Remiro got the joke.

****

Arkas Tenak, asked his computer desk to patch him through to Professier Dracus Muggredge, who was still at his temporary office outside Janitra. After a few moments the ageing academic appeared on Tenak's desk screen. The Monsoon's technical crew had very recently fitted out Muggredge's office with some more up to date electronic equipment, so he would be able to receive, and send, more complex data than before. They hadn't provided holo capability, Ebazza objecting to this, because of the vandalism which had occurred at the University. After exchanging pleasantries Tenak asked Muggredge whether he'd received a data packet he'd sent the day before.

'Deedly, I looked at it,' said the Professor, 'and thanking you for it. By way, congratulations be yours, Admiral. You have my admiration and gratitude still. You may have succeeded in obtaining video pictures of rock strata of the age we are yet interested in, over on Simurgh. Marvellry!'

'Thank you Professier. I'm glad to say that the corvettes did the job without technical hitches. After quite a few orbits we got the pictures we needed, as well as some thermal data. I noticed you say, "may have succeeded." Some of my people are sure the strata are precisely what we've all been looking for. Aren't you?'

'Sorry Admiral, yet I am not. The thermal data you got from the reflected light is about right, praps, but the colour and location do not seem to fit. Tis a mite too early to be sure. Could you repeat the passes?'

Tenak thought for a second. 'Okay, Professier, I'm not certain of this but maybe your people have a better idea about this than us. Now we know there's something relevant over there it might be more helpful if I get a pilot and scientist to overfly that part of the island. Just to get some close-up vid-science data. I didn't want to try that before because of the restrictions placed on us – and not wanting to draw attention to the location.'

'Yes, good, e'en better,' said Muggredge, 'for that should yet fix the job. I am exceeding glad you would take that risk for us.'

'Glad to oblige. We only recently got consent to fly over the whole of Oceanus, but Arbella is concerned that we don't overdo it.'

'As am I, I must say, Admiral. Still, I think the importance of this outweighs other considerations now, does it not?'

'That's why I suggested it, sir. Now we have this preliminary information we can justify what we do, if necessary.'

'Just one more thing before you leave-yet, Admiral. Have you heard from your colleague, Mike Tanniss? I have not received any single word from the expedition since the day before yestermorn, nor yet have I been able to make out contact with them. Tis so unusual. Everything was okay the last time we spoke. I expect they be busy, but I would like to give them your news, so I shall keep trying.

'As it happens, Professier, I haven't been able to reach Mike either. I've left messages on his wristcom, but he hasn't responded.'

'I doubt there be need to get worried just now, Admiral. The expedition leader, Doctro Senestris, has his head fixedly-firm on his shoulders. He knows what he is doing.'

****

Before ordering a landing boat to overfly Simurgh Tenak commed Ebazza about her investigations into the problems with the original probes, an issue that had vexed them both until recently, leading to worries of sabotage. The Captain told him the ship's Second Officer, Lieutenant Mantford Slevin Cavo Blandin, who was also the Security Chief, had been unable to make serious progress in finding the culprit.

She said that round the clock work, and some lucky chances had enabled the tek teams to make surprisingly fast progress in clearing the previous problems. She thought changes made rendered it less likely that the original perpetrator or perpetrators could carry out any more damage. Any such attempt now would stand out like an exploding fusion reactor. Good results had now been obtained from the corvettes too.

Tenak refused to be complacent about the situation or even overly satisfied with the progress, as he said to Ebazza, 'Whoever's behind this, is obviously some sort of *genius* with hypercomp AIs. Damnable things! These so-called "AIs" are supposed to be tamper-proof.'

'Yes, Admiral. I'm sorry,' said Ebazza's holo-image, with a mournful look. 'It looks as though some new type of subroutine was written into them. Blandin said he has never seen anything like it. I'll get him to update me.'

'Do we have any profiles of crewmembers, who match the capabilities shown by this activity, Ssanyu?'

'Lieutenant Blandin's checked the personnel data sets and says there's no sign of anyone standing out.'

'Alright Captain. It seems we don't know who to trust these days, but I'll tell you this, when I find who's behind this, I'll make sure the Navy makes an example of them. They'll be sorry they ever joined up, and even sorrier they pracked about with me. By the way, it seems we're not the only ones with this problem. Providius contacted me earlier. Seems someone's infected *their* hypercomp with a super-virus. They've lost *all* the data they picked up on the way in.'

Ebazza looked shocked but then a tiny, sly, yet cautious, smile played on her lips. 'At least it makes *us* look a little ... less inefficient,' she said but her face then betrayed immediate regret.

Tenak didn't smile. He just looked sour and strode off.

***

Roughly twelve hours after Tenak's discussion with Muggredge, the landing boat Agamemnon could be sent down to the massive and mysterious island of Simurgh, thousands of klicks from Bhumi Devi, jutting, almost spikily, out of the planet's "Great Southern Ocean".

After the heat of re-entry, the pilot, Lew Pingwei, switched from full autopilot to semi-manual so he could take a greater part in flying the ship down through the upper layers of the atmosphere. Lem Amornius Charnott, a young tek-scientist, new to his job, sat in the co-pilot's seat, evidently lapping up the experience. He hadn't had the chance to do much flying before, the current mission to Oceanus being his first voyage on The Monsoon. The co-pilot's seat had required adjustments to allow Charnot to do this trip, as he was paraplegic, following a severe accident which occurred before joining Naval School as a science cadet.

Pingwei smiled while listening to the whoops of joy coming from his companion as he manipulated the ship's rarely used central control stick protruding from the wide, flat, control interface. He made the shuttle slice down through the layers of the atmosphere and, after breaking through a thin blanket of low cloud, brought them out where they could see the entire south eastern part of Simurgh spreading below them, like a rough hewn, lumpy carpet of brown and grey rock and bluish green vegetation. They were no longer high enough to see the whole of the island, previously obscured by thick, high, cloud.

As they continued to lose height the observable slice of the island gradually shrank until, at only 900 metres altitude, the ship approached Simurgh's eastern coast, travelling at 800 kilometres per hour, and, at that point, still kilometres out to sea. They watched the towering coastal range of mountains draw ever closer, as they approached high buttresses of rock whose pinnacles were lost in an ethereal haze of mist. Charnott couldn't seem to close his mouth as he gazed at them. Lew used the SCAA ramjets to brake the ship a little. In response it dropped a little closer to the wave tops.

'Great view aint it?' said Pingwei. 'We're almost on the coast now. Time to veer North West. Have you got the high-res hypercams running, Lem? We'll be over the target site within about 3 minutes.'

As his crewmate deftly keyed instructions into the computer controlled holocams Pingwei put the power back on, climbed and banked the ship 60° to the left, then, glancing out the windows saw the giant mountains slip underneath, then behind them, disappearing into the haze, aft of the large swept-back port wing. The Agamemnon gained more altitude and after a minute of running parallel to the coast they reached a section where there were soaring high sea cliffs, pounded by crashing, smashing, ocean waves. Then the ship flashed onward over a broad, flat, plateau, until a distant, high massif could be seen.

Pingwei kept an eye on a large screen that continuously advised on the course he should take. He could have used his helmet and its advanced 3D, heads-up display, but after leaving the stratosphere he had elected to do without them and fly "in the old-fashioned way"; much more fun. He and his companion expressed the crazy wish that they could open the windows and let the wind rush in; a refreshing change after many weeks couped up on the mother ship. That, of course, was simply not possible and definitely not a good idea.

Lem announced that the guidance comp had located the target site and Pingwei steered toward it, as they swept over the massif, and on, till they reached a second, gentler slope, above which stood a kilometre-wide shelf of bare rock. The craft banked to starboard again, and the auto-cams started recording data, most of which was fed straight to Lem's own monitors.

'I can see it,' said Lem, with enthusiasm, 'it's a cliff of rock, only about 4 metres high. It winds like a ribbon along the landscape. Looking good to me. I think that's our stuff.' He sounded thrilled.

'Doesn't look like much to me compardre,' said the pilot.

'It looks the right colour, Lew. Spectral characteristics look right. The comp says its reflective index is bang-on and it's in the right place, stratigraphically speaking. Leastways, I think so.'

'You mean you aren't sure? Shame on you,' said Pingwei, smiling at Lem. 'Well, don't ask me. Geology's your thing, ain' t it?'

'Yeah well, I majored in Earth Sciences *and* exo-planetary geology, Lew. Anyway, wherever rock is laid down as sediment, rock is still rock. Stuff, like this, is identifiable, at a distance, by the way it's laid down. The same conditions produce the same kinds of rock. A close-up examination on the ground is what's needed now. Find out what the real age of this stuff is and how it relates to the history of life on this planet.'

'Okay. I believe you, man. Looks like we've got all the recordings we need. Pity we can't just land here and now and check it out ourselves.'

'I know Lew, but this place just doesn't belong to us, does it. So, it's up to the Oceanus people now.'

With that Pingwei nodded and raised the nose of the ship, throttling up the engines. After reaching around 10 kilometres' in altitude he turned the vehicle over to the auto system, to take them into orbit and "home".

On the way up, Lem Charnott reviewed the vid imagery and swung his screen toward his pilot, 'Look at that. See that thin black line?' Look, I'll magnify it on-screen. See now? It's a few metres below the current soil level and runs all the way along the outcropping for a couple of klicks.'

'So, what's it mean?'

'It means we've found what we've been looking for. That line indicates a layer of carbonised material. The comp says it's about 8 or 10 centimetres thick – but it must cover a huge area, underneath the other, more recent, rocks. They've squashed it down in size over a few million years – compressed it. It's a pity we just aren't able to date the stuff, but it looks to me like there was a one hell of a conflagration at some point in the history of this planet, in, I would say, maybe the last 20 or 30 million years. It's down to the politicos to take it further now.'

Chapter 28

OUTSIDERS

In the central chamber of the grostat, deep in the Purple Forest, Hermington and Chen were approached by a puzzled looking Marcus Senestris. Senestris asked them where the "navy manry" had gone. Someone had told him they'd seen Johann Erbbius leave the habitat. That had been a while ago. Hermington told him Mike was going to try to find his colleague. Senestris asked whether Mike or Erbbius had taken lanterns with them. They didn't know about Erbbius but hadn't seen Mike with one.

'You mean you let him go out like that?' said Senestris, irritation in his voice.

'Didnar think about it' said Chen. 'Sorry.'

'Do you not think you should be getting after them? You know about the dangers outside, special so for out-worlders. You are yet responsible …'

Even before Senestris had stopped talking Hermington was already moving and Chen was hot on his tail. They got lanterns out of the storage bins, picked up masks and ran out of the habitat.

'Which way do you think they went?' asked Chen.

'Not knowing,' muttered Hermington. 'Lower your lantern toward the ground. We might pick up some tracks. Soil is slight damp tonight. Might see their boot marks.'

But neither found any tracks. They split up and within minutes Chen started called Hermington over. The big man had already wandered two hundred metres from the station and when Danile caught up he saw Chen, in his own pool of light, standing amongst dense trees near the top of a small rise in the ground. His friend was pointing at a trench-like depression the other side of the rise, where a stream of light seemed to flow along the ground. They were bio-luminescent insectoids.

'What in the six oceans are *they* doing this far north? Do you ...' started Chen. Hermington shushed him.

'Listen. Carnt you hear that?'

'What? Oh, yes. Sounds be someone shouting ... but stopped now. Far distant.'

Both stood listening intently but now there was only silence. They moved on into the forest and after a few seconds they heard it again. The sounds seemed to be coming from several hundred metres further along the ridge, in the same direction as the flow of bi-lobians. Hurrying toward the sound, holding their lanterns high – and taking care not to stare directly at the bi-lobians they tried to locate the noise source. Over the next rise the sounds became clearer.

'Someperson screaming,' said Chen, his face betraying alarm.

'Sounds like Mike,' said Hermington, his voice shrill with alarm, albeit muffled by his mask.

Moving onward then, they saw him. Mike's head could just be seen beyond another rise, and as the men rushed toward him they could see he was standing in a clearing, bathed in a pool of bioluminescence. And he appeared half consumed by a mass of giant leaves.

'Giant spring-trap,' shouted Chen and started sprinting toward Mike, stmbling over the protruding roots of a huge tree and almost falling. Hermington raced up behind him and nearly collided with him.

'Thank the Maker,'shouted Mike, when he spotted them, 'shitting-well get over here now!' As the other two reached him he seemed to calm a little and said, 'Listen to me. Johann is trapped ... he's right in the middle of this thing. You've got to get him out.'

'We've got to get all parts of *you* out first,' said Hermington. 'Don't panic. We'll do it yet. We'll...'

While Hermington was still talking Chen had already gone into action, taking a flying leap at the plant, with both feet, and landing close to Mike, but he simply bounced heavily off the fleshy leaves. Then he started grappling with the leaves with his bare hands, hacking at the seams in the leaf structure enclosing Mike's leg and forearm. He thrust his beefy digits as far as he could, between the leaves, grunting and sweating with the effort.

Hermington looked around for a tool he could use, as Chen sucked in air and heaved with effort. It was just brute force – but it started to pay off. He managed to pull the leaves far enough apart for Mike to yank his right arm out. It came loose with a sucking noise. He shook the limb, which hung limply from his shoulder. 'I can't feel it! It's dead,' he said.

Meanwhile, Hermington had found a long, thick, sharp looking tree branch, big enough to jam between the leaves. He and Chen threw themselves into the fight to lever aside the massive leaves, trying to release Mike's leg. At the same time Mike was relieved to find he had some feeling returning to his arm, and he used his one good hand to hack and pull as well. He was finally able to pull his leg out. It came free, again with an obscene sound. Mike was not surprised to find he had no feeling in his leg but there was no time to worry about that. They had to get Erbbius out.

He began attacking the leaves, shouting Erbbius's name, wildly. Their stick had broken so Danile went to find a larger tree branch whilst Chen resumed his frantic bare-handed hacking at the leaves. Danile came back with a large piece of wood and desperately joined in the fray. All three of them were pulling, smashing and tearing at the leaves, sweating and puffing, purple faced, with the effort. Mike began to feel his energy draining, like water flowing down a plughole, but he felt he had to try to carry on.

A couple of minutes later sheer exhaustion made Danile stop. He tore his mask off as he panted heavily. Mike collapsed with the effort, next to the base of the plant, whilst Chen, grunting with the effort valiantly tried to carry on. Sucking in air, Danile said breathlessly to Mike. 'How long were you stuck before we arrived?'

Mike just stared. What in the planets is he on about, he thought.

'Think Mike! How long?'

'Not sure … seemed like ages. I think … maybe 3 minutes, maybe 4.'

'And we've taken, praps 4, to get you out? Okay, listen. I think this means we are having 5 or 6 minutes more only, before this thing starts in to digest your mate. We have to get the others.'

Chen heard this and abandoned his efforts but without saying anything he started racing back in the direction of the grostat. He also tore off his mask, forgot his lantern and raced back to pick it up.

Danile had sunk to the ground next to Mike and shouted after Chen, 'Do not be looking at the bi-lobians.' But Chen had vanished over the rise.

Danile replaced his mask, picked himself up and renewed his attack on the "seams" in the leaves with his tree branch and Mike, still breathless and feeling distinctly heady with the terpenes in the air, crawled toward the base of the plant and began, uselessly, to yank at the green fleshy material.

'Tis no good,' said Danile, 'for I fear the worst.'

Mike was quickly reaching the point of complete exhaustion – and intoxication.

After what seemed like an aeon, but wasn't, they heard a clamouring noise in the forest and, like the proverbial cavalry to the rescue, a group of people suddenly emerged from the gloom. The whole team were there – wielding crowbars, wooden poles and a miscellany of other tools. They got stuck into the work and soon, the carnivorous plant, as huge and tough as it was, could not resist their combined efforts, for the group hacked and tore down three whole leaves. It left the other leaves to form a sort of half cup on one side. And there, in the middle of the remains of the plant, was Erbbius, covered in white slime, lying in a foetal position. He suddenly twitched, then raised his head and looked up at the gathered group. He had a look of naked terror on his face, appeared soaking wet all over, and smelled of some sort of pungent acidic secretion. As the group went to pull him out his head lolled, and he seemed to lose consciousness.

Within a few minutes most of the group had carried the limp Erbbius back to the grostat whilst Hermington and Chen supported the limping and staggering Mike.

They wiped the slime off him as best they could. Finally, everyone slumped down in the central chamber of the station, emotionally and physically exhausted.

Mindara was the closest thing the team had to a physician, though in truth, she was a "first aider" only. But she set about examining Erbbius as thoroughly as possible, eventually declaring him to be largely unharmed. A chorus of relieved cheers burst from the group. Several team members continued to wipe the secretions off him, with large plant leaves smelling of antiseptic.

Mindara then turned to Mike and said, 'The plant traps large animals for about 10 minutes and during such-time it anaesthetises them, to stop them from damaging the insides of the leaves. Tis only then it starts yet to digest them. The now-rescuing was only just in time. Johann's skin is burned a bit but tis surface damage only. He is mainly exhausted and nervous-shocked. The fumes from the plant's digestion have sent him to sleep but should not such cause long time damage.'

But Mike wasn't really listening. He just watched her lips moving as if in a dream.

Mindara also told the group that Erbbius would likely be asleep for a long time but, he would have to be watched for the rest of the night. So, two of the team volunteered to stay with him all night. He was gently carried him off to his chamber by Chen, Senestris and Hermington.

Mindara approached Mike but he waved her away, looking as though drunk, which, in a way, he was. Trying immensely hard to concentrate he managed to say that he didn't think he'd been harmed. He tried his best to smile, but he said he felt he'd let the "home side" down again. Not taking enough care – again; ignorant of the dangers of this world.

'If and you are sure you are okay, Mike,' said Mindara softly, 'but you have been exposed to the terpinations for a long time, I think. You should be alrighty, if you rest straight away.'

'Yeah, yaeh, man, thanks. You're right. I just … want to get some sleep,' he said, then tried to get up - but nearly fell when he put his weight on the leg which had been trapped.

Hermington reappeared and said, 'Just a second yet, Mike,' and went to the other side of the chamber, bringing back a gnarled, wooden walking stick, said, 'Try this. I think tis a bit short for someone of your height but should yet be for now. I shall look for something better later such. Just get some rest now.'

Mike nodded and then turned to the assembled group. 'I'm really sorry guys. I think I just put everyone in danger again.'

'Non-sensery,' said Kenye Sung.

A lump came to Mike's throat as he said, 'Well, it's nice of you to say that, Kenye, but – I just want to thank you all and – especially you, Danile – and you, Kenning. Without you guys I don't know what ….' Mike left the words dangling as emotion started to overwhelm him. Someone said, 'We had to do something, Mike. Couldn't let the plant get indigestion, could we?' There was muted laughter and even Mike managed to raise a smile, as someone else said, 'That plant had it coming. Trying to eat *two* navy men. That's yet greedy.'

'Okay,' said Senestris, 'that's enough. Let Mike get some rest.'

Mike mouthed a silent thank you to the whole group, again and turned away, limping toward his chamber. For a moment he thought he glimpsed Eleri, standing off toward one side. She had looked distraught. Did she still care? He was sure she wouldn't want him to get eaten by a plant, but did she still really care about him? Nah, just wishful thinking. He put it to the back of his mind. He just wanted to get some sleep before he fell over.

He hadn't got far when he heard a female voice call to him from behind. He recognised it belonged to Daniellsa Nitokris Morgath, the team's senior palaeontologist, who liked to be known as "D.N". She had seemed a quiet and reticent member of the group until recently.

Arriving at the grostat had seemed to galvanise her and she'd been instrumental in getting the station fully habitable for the night. She was very competent in electronics and had taken a lead role in getting the station's large solar panels working, from their previous state of standing open and immobile, on a pole above the grostat. Their electronics had been mostly non functional when the team had arrived. The circuitry materials were so ancient that Erbbius, who had taken a look, had drawn almost a complete blank. Mike guessed that, in any case, the rest of the team seemed keen to show independence from the Home System and might not have appreciated Erbbius interfering.

Mike had also noticed how pretty D.N was, and how easy she was to speak to. Morgath was quite a bit younger than Eleri but, though he liked her, he never considered her to be some sort of rival to the person he'd had the misfortune to fall in love with. However, he had also noticed how, of late, she never seemed to miss any opportunity to get close to him, especially during the latter stages of the long walk into the forest. But was he imagining it? In his current state he thought he probably was. Something had changed in him, quite radically, he mused. What it was, he had no idea.

Daniellsa had caught up with him now, and said, 'Mike, there is yet no reason for you to be sorry for what happened.'

He considered this person walking beside him. She was an impressive height, probably a full 16 centimetres taller even than him. She ran a hand, self-consciously, through her very long dark hair as she approached him.

'Oh, I don't know, Daniellsa,' he said, 'I just seem to have a habit of getting into trouble on this planet. People are getting fed up with it – including me. Know what I'm saying, man?' Mike realised that he still sounded drunk, but it didn't feel as good as that kind of intoxication.

'From what I have yet heard,' she said, 'you were just trying to find your ship-colleagry, Mer Johann. I am believing you also tried to rescue him from the spring-trap. Tis how *you* got trapped, or no? Am I wrong?'

'Well, I dunno, bit … suppose not exactly wrong. But – maybe not completely right. I just don't know what to think any more.'

'Not only heroic but merriam.'

'Sorry, femna?'

'Merriam. That's our word for *modest*, though it probably has a wider meaning. It also means – admirable? Yes, I think that's the right Home System word.'

'Look, I'm not sure …'

'Tis not just I, who say this,' she said, her deep green eyes dragging in his full attention – and holding it, as she continued, 'but the whole of the team thinks so. You are the toasting of the evening, Mike. Praps you could yet come back and have late evening drinks with us? By ways, please do call me – D.N.'

'I'm ... well, I'm sorry, Daniellsa, I mean, D.N. Whatever. Thanks very much, but I'm not feeling too good right now and I'll blank out if I don't get some sleep. Do you mind?'

'No, course not. What must you think of me? I am being selfish. I am wanting your company and you are not well. Please forgive-so. Please do get some rest. Can I be helping any way? Please say.'

'No, thank you, D.N. I'm just happy things worked out tonight in the end. I better get going. I understand we have to move on to the next grostat tomorrow.'

'No, Mike, not so. Marcus has said we will let you and Johann rest till whate'er time you wish. The rest of us will rest later too, morrow-tide, for we are chanckled. We must not expect you and Johann to get going early-time. He also does believe that Mer Johann mayst not be able to move at all on the morrow. We might yet have to stay here. Decision-time then.'

'I guess so,' said Mike, feeling an effort in tearing himself away from that her magnetic smile and he found himself gazing at her generous, moist, lips, and the smooth pink inside of her mouth, behind the gleaming teeth. But he was emotionally drained and physically exhausted. He smiled wanly and started to turn away.

'Okay, Mike,' she said, 'good night-tidings. Please be calling me – should you still need anything.'

'Good night-tidings,' said Mike, smiling and starting back toward his chamber. He failed to notice the furtive figure some way down the tunnel, hugging the shadows created by the natural folds in the organic walls of the corridor.

As he arrived at his chamber, he decided he was too tired to analyse what Daniellsa had meant. He slumped down on his moss bed and looked at his small, wooden bedside table, more of a knee-high block really, with a reasonably flat top;

an object which not only looked as if it that grown right out of the floor, but which really had been.

Lying on top of it was an object that looked strangely out of place here, but which he now sorely wished he'd taken with him when he'd gone to look for Erbbius: the special wristcom that Tenak had given him. The one with defensive capabilities.

****

On board The Monsoon a bright amber light flashed on one of Ebazza's office desks; a piece of furniture made, unusually, of real wood, at great expense. It indicated that someone wanted admittance.

'Come in Lieutenant,' she said, waving one hand in a gesture instantly picked up by the ship's hypercomp terminal, transmitting her voice outside and opening the office's main doors. Lieutenant Blandin, the ship's Second Officer entered, giving the customary salute as he did so. The sallow complexioned, square framed man, who looked older than his actual 34 years, sported a neatly trimmed "combo" of dark brown beard and moustache; a type of facial hair fashion currently in vogue in the Navy, but uncommon on The Monsoon. He regarded Ebazza from small eyes set in a long mournful face. He waited near the door until Ebazza invited him to sit in the chair opposite her hypercomp desk. He removed his peaked cap as he did so, revealing a light brown hatch, as well groomed as his beard.

'Lieutenant,' she said, lightly, 'please tell me we are closer to finding the person, or persons, who are behind the AI hypercomp attacks.'

Blandin took a deep breath and shook his head. 'I regret to say, Ma'am, that no further progress has been made, but I ask that due notice be taken of the fact that the attacks have stopped – altogether. Which is significant, I believe.'

'I have noticed that fact, though I am not as confident, as you seem to be, that they will not resume at some stage – *unless we find the attacker.*' This time she was more emphatic.

'I think you can be assured that they will not,' said Blandin, then added quickly, 'though I suppose we can't guarantee anything in this ....'

'We can dispense with the philosophising for now. But what exactly do you mean by saying, you can *assure* me, Lieutenant?'

Blandin hesitated, looked worried, then said, 'I'm simply saying that the steps ... I have taken have, demonstrably, stopped the perps' in their tracks. I believe they will be fearful that, if they continue, they'll be discovered immediately. Furthermore, the procedures I've put in place will remain – in place – for the rest of the voyage, thereby continuing to deter the perpetrators.'

'I hear what you say Lieutenant, and I've read your full report about what you've done. There's just a couple of things that continue to cause me concern. One, is that you claim you haven't found the culprit, yet you keep saying "perps". You seem convinced there's more than one of them, but you don't say why. Second, you talk about deterrence, but you seem to have forgotten that, in fact, I want the perp, or perps, caught. And jacked out of the damnatious Navy, Lieutenant!'

Ebazza's face had become a mask of displeasure and impatience, and Blandin started to look very uncomfortable.

'I'm sorry Captain. The reason I think there's more than one perp is because of the complexity of what they've done. It suggests more than one *must* have been responsible. And I'm sorry that we've not been able to catch anyone yet, but we are working on it. I'm sure you're aware of how clever they must be. They must also be able to cover their tracks extremely well, but we're still ...'

'Please forgive me Lieutenant, but I think you're talking hogshit. Yeah, you heard me, *Mister*. You keep saying "we're working on it" but listen now. You are supposed to be an expert, cos if you ain't, then what the blood and guts are you doing in that uniform?'

Blandin just stared at her in silence, his face a blank mask, like a slab of stone.

'Okay, I'll lay off for a bit longer,' she continued, after long moments of letting him squirm. 'But tell me, what's got into you Lieutenant? I've known you for a few years, now. On the Cleopatra – remember? Captain Trellis told me she knew you before that. I always thought you gave good service. Maybe not exemplary, but good enough. But I aint pleased mister Second Officer. This is simply not good enough. So, tell me what's wrong? Think of this as a polite enquiry, indicating my willingness to help, if I can.'

Blandin said nothing but continued to look blank. Ebazza, her countenance of irritation growing, continued, 'As you can imagine, the Admiral has put pressure on me about this and I ain't exactly in his good books these days. No harm in you knowing that. I expect the *whole* gracking ship knows. Anyways, if he's putting pressure on me, you can be damnly certain I'm going to put pressure on you, mister. You got that?'

The Lieutenant nodded. Ebazza got up and he followed suit.

'Dismissed. Try again, mister Lieutenant man. Come up with something useful – and soon.'

****

An hour after his encounter with Ebazza, Lieutenant Blandin floated in the microgravity environment of the vast central hub of the ship. As he floated, he used various handholds along the walls, as he moved through a long, twisting corridor and into a small, cell-like, electrical relay inspection chamber. He took care to close and lock the chamber's hatch door after him. Inside the chamber another man floated, waiting; a short, stocky individual with light, sandy hair, who clung to a wall bracket with one beefy hand.

'Are you certain this place is secure, Garmin?' Blandin asked the man.

'Of course, Lieutenant,' Garmin said, 'I wouldn't take any risks.'

'Thank you so much. I'm just a bit jumpy, that's all. I've been char-grilled by Ebazza. Our glorious captain thinks I haven't been doing my job. She's turning up the mixing chamber temperature. That means I'm going to have to turn up the heat as well. So, do you have any new ideas about how we continue to cover our arses? And we need credible ideas, Garmin. You, listening?'

Garmin Calymian Brundleton, Engineer, Second Class, nodded and exhaled noisily through pursed lips. 'She's an interfering asteroid-barge. This is going to be tricky. I suppose we could ask Dravette. Where the feggery is she, by the way?'

'She's busy elsewhere, Garmin. Unavoidable. I was hoping to get more sense out of *you* so don't disappoint me. By the way, Ebazza is entitled to "interfere", and you'd better get used to it. That's what commanding officers do. So, what's your idea and make it good. I don't think we've got as much time as I'd hoped.'

'Straightforward really. You're just going to have to arrest someone.'

'You mean, frame someone? Do you have any likely candidates?'

Brundleton thought for a moment, then said, with a wry smile, 'What about that jackass Petrie? He's been getting on my chewer for a long time. He's a loudmouth and he's lazy. You know what I mean? The sort of tek-assistant who brings this wonderful organisation into disrepute. Can you imagine such a thing?'

'No, not Petrie,' said Blandin, seriously. 'He's much too … unimportant. This is not about private vendettas. Whoever we choose will need to have the necessary tek-skills to be able to pull something like this off. And just so it doesn't look too suspicious, it probably needs to be someone you actually get along with – if there is such a person.'

Brundleton gave Blandin a sour look, then a sly smile spread over his face and he said, 'Well, there is Chepley, otherwise known as, "Chips" Brutelius Havring, I suppose. He's gone no further than mid-level. Like me, I guess, but I'm certain he has my *real* level of hypercomp skills. Maybe not so high as Mordant, but definitely better than *yours*, that's for sure. He probably wouldn't suspect me of dropping him in the shit.'

'Okay, cut the wise-talk, Mer Engineer. We know why you've not gone for promotion, but I wonder why *he* hasn't. Okay, how long will it take to set it up?'

'Hard to say but I'm going to have to carry out some code changes on parts of the system. Plant some evidence on him, or in his quarters, and make sure he can't account for his whereabouts at certain times. Fortunately for us, I happen to know that Chips has a nasty brain-stim habit. Yeah, imagine that. Sneaks off a lot during shifts, just for 10 minutes or so, and he's clever enough to cover it up when he returns – and tries to catch up with his duties. But I've worked out what he's been up to. Been watching him - lots. Even managed to get Shacklebury to pretend some interest in him. Got her to sus' him out for us. Worked great. We can use that info to make sure he can't account for his activities since we began operations in orbit.'

'Excellent. *That* explains why he hasn't reached senior engineer level. Go for it, Garmin but be extra careful. I don't want to see Ebazza's security teams hauling you in – instead of Havring. Cos if they do, I can't help you – and I won't. You know that.'

'Have some faith Lieutenant. Ultima is with us in spirit, always, or so our femna mate would have us believe.'

'Don't talk to me about that. She's weird. But she is loyal, and I expect you to be as well. Just make sure all your skills are with *you*, Mer Engineer. And remember, this idea doesn't have unlimited shelf-life. Sooner or later Ebazza and Tenak are going to realise they've got the wrong man. After that … I'm not sure what'll happen.'

'You'll think of something. Or Mordant will. We'll have to cross that star-bridge when we get to it. The main thing is, that once our other operative has done his work – and our *friend* on the Antarctica as well, this ship will have to go home in shame. And that means more delay to the Allied government's evac' plans.'

Chapter 29

RESOLUTIONS

The Oceanus science team in the Purple Forest were slow to get moving the morning after the giant spring-trap incident. They gave the two "out-worlders" ample time to rest, though in truth, they were all tired and emotionally drained.

The team discussed their findings at length during their communal breakfast around a block-like "table" made of stromatolite. They talked of the fact that the luminescent bi-lobians and the spring-trap plants were common in the hotter, much more humid forests in the southern parts of the continent – but almost unheard of this far north. It was completely unprecedented. Rubia Mindara and Eleri Nefer-Ambrell, the biologists, pointed out that none had been found by the last team to visit the grostat, and that had been only two Oceanus years previously.

Mike hobbled along the hallway toward the central hearth chamber, where he could hear the others assembled, deep in discussion. Emerging into their presence he saw them all look at him with surprised faces.

'Hi everybody. Tis late. What's Erbbius like this morning?' he said almost as though nothing had happened the previous night.

'Mornimbrite Mike. I think he did have a reasonable night,' said Sung, but I think Renton was the last person who didst watch him. I will check, but please, Mike, be partaking of breakinfast.'

Sung and Barstow went off toward Erbbius's chamber. Some minutes later they returned, gently and only lightly supporting Erbbius between them. 'He asked to come to breakinfast, so we brought him,' said Barstow. Erbbius still staggered a little, as if in a dream and his red rimmed eyes had a far-away look about them. Sung said, 'Are you thinking you can be walking with us to the next grostat, Johann? Same goes for you too, Mike, for yet, unfortunately, I have to tell you we have another 30 kilometres to go.'

'Yeah, well, doesn't seem too bad,' said Erbbius, looking embarrassed at having to be supported to sit down properly. He visibly shook the sleep from his head as he began eating the breakfast breads and fruits in front of him. That got everyone's attention.

Thinks he's the tough guy now, does he, thought Mike.

'It's not so simpleful,' said Hermington. 'Most of it is far uphill. Through a muchness of tangl-ed bush country. Further still, into the Purple Forest.'

'Any more of those spring plant thingies?' asked Mike, 'and … please say, no.'

'We hope not,' said Hermington. 'We were yet saying – we have no real idea what caused their sudden appearance here, but it might be something to do with climate change of some sort?' He looked around his colleagues. There were a few nods but lots of shrugged shoulders.

'Maybe it's to do with Ra,' said Mike.

That brought looks of disbelief from the group but Mindara said, 'Mike could be right. So, in truth there has been little change in outpours of "greenhouse" gases from humanry here. And there has been no great volcanic activity for many years. Many millions of years ago, there was yet much more volcanic activity on this planet, but now, almost all the volcanoes are cluster-ed yet in a much more restricted area, in several-many lines almost, right at centre of this continent. Tis because the various crustal plates did move together, over many millions years, to form Bhumi-Devi. Such volcano zones are what normally does produce most greenhouse gasses on Oceanus. But tis estimated there has been little in way of extreme large eruptions in mid-continent, for near on yet 200 years.'

'And,' said Barstow, 'there is no significant change of infra-red radiation, the ordinary solar heating, from Ra, over the period we humanry have been here. And that is despite such changes in the star, as claimed by the Navy, if they be correct.'

Eleri decided to pipe up at this point, 'You say, "if they be correct" Renton. Do you still doubt such findings?'

'Not so necessarily,' said Barstow, frowning defensively.

'Listen now team,' said Sung, 'the point is here, that both Rubia and Renton are right about lack of changes in carbon output and yes, solar radiation, but we all know that the rainy season has been very intense this year. Tis unusually wet, and these plants like humid conditions. Maybe they can respond to temporary changes much faster than we thought.'

'Or praps the measurements we have, of solar radiation and even carbon output, are wrong,' said Mindara, 'after all, that sort of thing is the basis of the Home System message, ist not?'

Mike noticed murmurings of discontent amongst some of the group, particularly from Barstow and Senestris.

'To be fair,' said Mike, 'the particular problems we've seen with Ra don't necessarily imply a general, overall, increase in infra-red radiation. Not *at this stage*. It's more about the flares and how extreme they are and the super-prominences.'

'Anywayins,' said Sung, 'truth is, we do not know why the plants and the bi-lobians are here right now, but they are – and we must be keeping watch for them. The good thing is – they are active only at night, when their symbiants are able to lure in creatures with brains capable of being hypnotised by their oscillations. So, we need to start off to second waystation, if we are to go at all. Personally, I think it makes more com'n sense to modify our goals. Not muchly use in trying to get to the second grostat, to carry out field studies, when we have just now identified a significant change, right here. And it would mean dragging Mike and Johann along, when they are hardly so fit to do the journey. What dost others think?'

There were loud murmurings of general approval. Daniellsa said, 'I think Kenye is right. There is no purpose in struggling on. The next so gro-stat is another 45 lints away. I think we should give our Mike and Johann, still a chance to rest today. We can use the equipment stored here to study the spring-traps and their local-environs. The equipment here mayst not be to the rigor-standards of what is stored in the second grostat but, after all, someone shall have to be coming back here to study the spring-traps, sooner or later. I shall vote – stay here.'

'As a biologist, I would say I do agree with both Kenye and Daniellsa,' said Eleri.

There were no dissenting voices. Mike was relieved.

'Well, I would say we have reached a conclusion,' said Senestris. 'Mike, Johann, I am assumed neither of you would be objecting if we stayed here?'

Mike agreed. Erbbius looked disinterested and Mike rolled his eyes but Senestris announced that the decision was made.

Mike then watched as a transformation overtook the whole Oceanus group. The team seemed suddenly totally galvanised. Laboratory equipment was produced from the grostat's deep storerooms and the team organised themselves into smaller groups who were assigned various, different, tasks, including sampling and analysing parts of what remained of the plant which nearly ate their two colleagues. They sampled and analysed the local soil; photographed and video-filmed the plants and their environment and investigated the smooth defiles the bi-lobians had used in the forest. Mike and Erbbius were told that the insectoids themselves would have gone deep underground during the daylight hours.

Some group members also intended sampling, and analysing, various other plants and trees, and carrying out a full survey, counting and investigating as many of the species that now inhabited the area near the spring-trap field, as possible. That would be a huge undertaking and would likely take days and, for safety, working during daylight only.

For the two off-worlders, it was potentially an easy time, but Mike started to feel like a "spare dick" and became determined to help. He did what he could. Erbbius, however, sat back in the central chamber and slept most of the time. Mike felt he could have done more but believed he was riding on his "injuries" – despite what he'd said at breakfast.

Late in the day Daniellsa Morgath breezed into the grostat and found Mike trying to categorise various still-pictures the team had taken of the spring-traps and the local forest. Mike was impressed to find they were displayed on a screen. The machine used power drawn directly from the large solar panel aerial above the station.

'Thanking you for your help, Mike,' she said, as she joined him at the "table" grown out of the floor of the chamber. She beamed at him – and he felt a familiar sensual "tug" inside him. He glanced around slightly nervously, looking to see if Eleri was near but she wasn't. But so what if she was, he thought.

'It must have been horribilous. Being stuck in that thing,' she said, 'for both of you.'

'Trying to forget about it, really,' said Mike, smiling wryly.

'Oh, deedly, yes, I am sorry. I did not mean to remind you of such an awfrag experience.'

'No. Don't apologise. I've accepted what happened and I'm moving on from it. It didn't have such a bad effect on me as the attack by the … grotachalik, after all. Except, I don't remember much about that. Just bits and pieces. Enough though.'

'Tis a funny thing, memory,' she said, sounding sympathetic. 'My meather was attacked by a metamorph once. Long time ago. I saw it from a distance. I was in teen-years.'

Mike stopped his work and turned to face her, 'That must have been pretty bad. Was she? I mean did she …'

'Survive?' she said. 'Yes, gladling always for that, though I will not ever forget it.' She went quiet for a few moments, then said, 'I am so happy you are getting involved with our work, Mike. Not like your friendling, Mer Erbbius. He seems very unhappy. I suppose tis not surprising so much.'

'Not really,' said Mike, 'he's always like that. I don't think he wants to be here.'

'Oh? Then why is he here?'

'He's a Navy engineer. He has to go where he's told.'

'Ah, coursry. Anywayin, Mike. I am yet glad you seem much happy-so now. Tis important so to me. I am hoping to see you later, very much. Meantimes, I have some more sampling to do.' With that she gave Mike a sweet smile that lingered in his mind as she rose and went outside. Mike ruminated on her words. She was definitely flirting with him. Did she want him to make a pass at her? Surely, he was imagining it - but why so? He knew he'd always been attractive to women. He didn't feel that was false conceit. It was a fact, and it was turning out to be both a blessing and a horrible curse.

He knew he was still feeling down because of Eleri. But perhaps it was time to move on. Eleri was never going to come back to him and he rejected the idea of continuing to chase her. She had made her feelings very clear. In this day and age, it was no longer a viable option to keep chasing a femna after she had done that, if only to avoid the strict no-stalking rules. He understood that these, or their equivalent, were even stricter on Oceanus than on Earth. He also had his pride.

Yet, he still felt the same old way about El. In that moment he suddenly knew, somehow, that he always would miss her. In itself, this was a "first" for Michaelsonn Tanniss. He realised he would have to live with it, the same way he had to live with the knowledge that toxins from the grotachalik would likely return to give him trouble, in unknown ways, at some time in the future. It was all part of a legacy of his experiences on this strange and troubling planet. What else did this world have in store for him, he wondered?

**

After eventidings meal, taken with the group, Mike bade the team good night and hobbled slowly back to his chamber. It was only 20.00 hours, but he was still feeling tired and in low mood. Unnoticed by Mike, Eleri had been watching him and she continued to sit with the others after he left, not really taking part in their discussions. Hermington later moved to sit next to her and, in the subdued lighting of the hearth fire, he whispered into her ear, 'Why do you not yet go after him?'

She pretended to take an interest in something Sung was saying but then whispered back, from the corner of her mouth, 'Because I do not think I should.'

'Who are you kiddering?' he said quietly, and she turned to look at him, wide violet eyes catching the light of the flames licking in the hearth, searching for an answer only she could know.

**

Only a few minutes after Mike had left the group, Daniellsa Morgath got up from beside Sung and quietly wished him a good night.

Meanwhile, Mike sat on his bed and wondered whether he should return the messages Tenak had sent him. Initially, he had felt too upset to bother with them and then a strange plant had tried to eat him. He didn't want to lie to Tenak, but he also didn't want to tell him he'd been in trouble again. This was starting to become very embarrassing. He heard a knock on the thin fold-down wooden partition which separated the chamber from the corridor and called for his visitor to enter.

'What can I do for you, Daniellsa? Sorry, I mean, D.N,' he said, a surprised look on his face, as she quickly pulled up the wooden door flap and walked in.

'Please call me Danry, Mike. Better still than D.N.'

'Yeah, that figures.'

'Sorry. What was that?' she said and laughed lightly.

'Oh, nothing. I'm still trying to get used to the Oceanus dialect, that's all.'

'I might yet say the same about your dialecto,' she said and, without further ado sat on the end of his moss bed. 'Why do we not talk some more, and I will tell you all about our little world?' she continued.

'It so happens … Danry, that I am pretty tired, you know.'

What am I saying, he thought? This was being handed to him on a deck plate. He looked at her and drank in her beauty. But attractive as she was – she was simply not Eleri. He knew he stood no further chance with El, and his mind raced over his whole love life, back home and here, all in a few seconds. The ups and downs. The controversies. The boundless jealousies and rivalries and the constant manoeuvring. Fleeting glimpses of something more, but never allowing himself to get pulled in, or bogged down, in all that. Fun though much of it had been, it was starting to pall on him now.

He was starting to regret much of what had gone before – and maybe now was the time to do something about it. In a flash of insight that shocked even him, he realised there must come a time in everyone's life, when you have to say *enough is enough;* whether that was a question of giving up alcohol or brain-stim, or perhaps some other form of negative or addictive behaviour that earned disapprobation.

'I'm so sorry Danry,' he said, 'but I think you might have the wrong idea about me.'

She looked at him quizzically, as he continued, 'I really like you and all, but I mean it when I say I just want to get some rest. I hope you understand?'

'Oh, that is alrighting,' she said but actually began to move closer to him, edging along the bed, 'I know that you are just yet tired, but I will let you sleep – *afterward*. I do promise.'

This is going to be more difficult than I imagined, he thought, but before he could say any more another figure suddenly appeared in the room, sweeping in under the flap, and she looked very angry. Daniellsa and Mike looked up to see the lithe figure of Eleri Nefer-Ambrell standing there, fixing "D.N" with an intense and hostile glare.

'I think Mike made it clear how he feels Daniellsa. Dost not you think tis time to leave, womanry?'

'Listen, El. I can deal with this,' said Mike but nobody seemed to be listening to him.

'Have you been listening to our private conversationry?' said Daniellsa, an expression of disgust on her face.

'I couldnar help it,' said Eleri, continuing to fix Daniella with a hard stare. 'You didnar put the flap down. I should yet think the rest of the team could hear it. By the way, I said - I think tis best time you leave. How many times do I repeat my message? Mike does nart want you here. Do you Mike?'

Mike wondered what the feggery was going on but he said, 'No. No, I don't. Sorry Daniellsa, Danry ...'

'I do not want to get angry such with you Daniellsa,' said Eleri, her mouth beginning to twist into a snarl.

There was a pregnant pause and then Daniellsa, her face screwing into a furious scowl, jumped off the bed, pushed past Eleri, and out of the door. For a second Eleri and Mike just looked at each-other, wide eyed.

'I am sorry 'bout that, Mike,' Eleri said, 'and yet I should not have pried into your affairs. Tis just that Daniellsa can be very … insisting. I hope I didnar ruin your evening. I shall go now.' She turned but Mike called to her, 'Please don't go, El. Please.'

'You didn't ruin anything,' he said, 'Please come back. Please talk to me.'

Eleri closed the door, carefully tied it down, then sat on Mike's bed, as he said, 'The Maker knows how much I've missed you.' He felt as if he would break down.

She surprised him infinitely, when she blurted, 'Yes, me too. I've been missing you as well. More than you can e're know, manry.' She moved toward his open arms, her lips seeking his. They shared a deep kiss that lingered on and on. Then she pushed him backwards gently, and he pulled her toward him, sighing with huge emotional relief. They needed to talk - but not now. Not at this point.

Their hands roved hungrily over each others' bodies, then began pulling off coveralls, yanking off shoes. Mike felt the wonder of her smooth warm skin and, as she tugged his undergarment off, he slipped between her open legs. He penetrated her and their mouths met again in a deep gratifying kiss. It was just as well that Eleri had closed the door, thought Mike and inwardly laughed with unabashed happiness. Not triumphalism, but pure joy. In that moment all was well now, and forever, it seemed.

**

After Mike and Eleri had satisfied their desires, her head nestled down onto his right shoulder as they lay there.

'Thank you for intervening, El, but I could have handled Daniellsa,' he said, pretending to chide her.

'It didnar sound like it to me, young manry. Are you saying you are sorry I did call in?'

'Of course not! I'm glad you did. She *was* very persistent, wasn't she? I wonder if she's going to be alright.'

'Ah, she yet moved something in you, did she?'

'No, well, yes. Only a little, tiny, tiny bit but …'

'But she is not me, is she?'

'No, she isn't. And never could be.'

'Thanking you for being honest-like. I hope that mode continues in you. And yes, I knowst that you could have resisted her. If t'were not so, I should not be here, with you, now.'

'Talking of honesty, were you really snooping on me, El?'

'Well and so … I was on way to talk to you, anywayins, Mike. I admit I saw Daniellsa yester night and did see she might be after you. Then I saw her come here this night and walk in here and, as I said, I realised she had left the door open. What did you expect me to do? I could hear the two of you yet clearly. I had to know what you would do before I didst intervene. Look, I am deedly sorry Mike - but I had to be sure.'

'Yeah, I know. And are you sure?'

'Maybe,' she said playfully, then tweaked the fine hairs on his chest.

'Ouch! Stop that. El, do you think she's going to be alright?'

Oh yes. Stop your fussery. I've known Daniellsa long times. She will be all-fine, but just watch out for a blade t'ween your ribs from now on.' Eleri chuckled softly. 'Must admit. I have never heard her use that short form of her name. Danry? Strange, I say.'

'I certainly hope you're joking – about the knife blade. Too much has happened to me here to discount *anything*.'

'Hmm. I am not joking now,' she said, and, in one fluid movement, she changed from lying beside Mike, to being on top of him, chuckling as she did so. Her mouth found his again, her urgent moist lips fastening on his. She then turned serious for a moment. 'Mike, I want you to know something. I want you to know how bad I felt when I realised what had happened out there – you know – with the plant.'

'It wasn't your fault,' he said.'

'I know but, well, I sort of yet felt responsible, special-so after what happened on the island. You are still an outsider, down here, and you yet need guidance about this world.'

'Tis okay.'

'By the way, I noticed you yelped on times, in sexual union, earlier. Was it your leg or your arm that hurt yet?'

'Leg,' he said, 'Listen, I'm fine. I can manage.'

'I don't want to hurt ….,' she began.

'Now, who's fussing?' he said, and he gently turned her over onto her back and started gently kissing her breasts and stomach, as she pulled him further onto, then into her. They writhed ecstatically for about for another hour until Mike finally gave in and admitted he didn't think his leg, or his arm, or his stamina, could take any more. She mock chided him again. They finally fell asleep at 02.00 hours.

As Mike dozed off if he thought that all was now right with the world, he was wrong.

Chapter 30

CHANGE OF PLAN

Ssanyu Ebazza commed Arkas Tenak via his wristcom. 'There's something coming out of the planet, on all news casts,' she said, 'and I think you ought to see it.'

'I'm with Lieutenant Jennison at the moment,' said Tenak, speaking to a holo of Ebazza's head and shoulders that had been projected from his wristcom. 'Patch it through to my device. I'll look at it as soon as able.'

He resumed his discussion with his senior scientist. Jennison was saying that the Antarctica had not only lost *all* its recent data, gathered on the way into the Ra system, but further gremlins were now preventing them keeping track of the mysterious object far out beyond the Ra system. The Monsoon had tried to keep track of it instead but their own instrument sensors, inferior to those of those of the Antarctica, were also having problems. The object seemed to have completely disappeared.

'It's strange,' said Jennison. 'After all, it's big enough – and reflecting sufficient light. At least it was a few days ago, so it should still be detectable. It's almost as if it's being obscured by something.'

'Clouds of dust or gas, maybe?' suggested Tenak.

'I think we'd pick up deep-spectral signatures for that, but there's nothing.'

'Can we lend the Antarctica any assistance – with its hypercomp frame, I mean?'

'I anticipated that, Admiral. The Captain ordered Garmin Brundleton over there, on my recommendation but so far, seems he hasn't had much luck. Their data gathering system has well and truly popped.'

'That's odd. But this could have very serious consequences. Will it prevent them from returning to the Solar System or will we have to ship them out of here as well?'

'I don't think so, Admiral. My understanding is that only very specific parts of their hyper frame have been damaged. The navigation and auto-pilot systems, as well as the superconductor, conduit sensing, apparatus, seem okay.'

'Just okay?'

'Well, there's a greater risk of overall failure when parts of the system have been cranked, obviously. But I understand that at least Garmin has been able to continue to isolate the mid frame from the stern frame, so they should be ... okay. They'll have to do lots of tests of course. And we're too far from home to be able to get back-up anytime soon.'

'Hmm. So, we may have to ferry the crew home after all. I hope there's room for them.'

'Your pardon, Admiral?'

'Oh, didn't you know? It's on the Ship-Net now. It seems more and more citizens of Oceanus are applying for permits to migrate back home with us. About 100, so far, and more are being processed. Provided the checks work out, we'll be taking them. And I expect a lot more applications.'

The discussion concluded, Tenak tapped his wristcom and invited his science officer to watch Ebazza's news item with him. It was only available in flat screen mode, as that was the format of the broadcast when picked up from Oceanus. It popped up on Jennison's desk screen. In the transmission a female presenter was speaking, whilst a screen next to her showed a vid-film of a large group of people walking along a street, somewhere in Janitra.

'Such many in the government,' she was saying, into some sort of large thing they took to be a microphone, 'and their opponents appeared surprised today as a massive-such demonstration took place coming yet seemingly out of the blue oceans, all along the streets of the Capital. Some have estimated that up to ten thousand citizenry walked the route, agreed yet beforehand. Most had banners bearing words in *support* of the Home System Navy. After the march, the speakers addressed a multitude, arguing so strongly, for the motion before the Curia Senate at the end of the week. This yet calls for an interstellar conference on the stability of Ra, our sun.'

She continued, 'However, now opponents of the Home System's attempts to carry out evacuation of Oceanus, say they think the government, ailing now in the pole-stakes, had yet encouraged the rally, for politico reasons. A government spokes-womanry has said that proper permissions had been applied for, and permits granted, on grounds of fairness. She said such that if the opponents of the march wanted to demonstrate on another day, full consideration would be given. This, so long as assurances about peacefulness and sure-safety, come forth.'

Tenak and Jennison sat on hearing all of this, wide eyed and speechless. *Support for them?*

****

A polite knock sounded on Mike's door. It was Rubia Mindara. She called, loudly, that it was 10.30, and time for the *two of them* to join the others at mornington-meal. There was to be an important announcement today.

Lordy, there seemed to be no secrets in this place, thought Mike.

The team were assembled, as usual, in the hearth chamber, some still eating breakfast and others huddled around a moss-plant table. Erbbius slouched in a corner, looking disinterested, as usual. Mike and Eleri tentatively entered and made their apologies for being late. Mike felt a tinge of embarrassment as it seemed that all of the team must have known that they had slept together. He knew he didn't need to feel this way but still, somehow, it felt almost mischevious. Oh, to hell with it, he concluded.

The team welcomed them with smiles – except for Daniellsa Morgath. She looked up brefly and appeared disinterested. She yawned widely, quite deliberately. Well, disinterest was to be expected, thought Mike. Erbbius also hardly bothered to looked up at his colleague.

Senestris welcomed them warmly, then announced that they had finally managed to get the radio comms working.

'Pardon me,' said Mike. 'but I didn't know the radio wasn't working.'

'Neither did I, such,' said Eleri. Johann Erbbius suddenly took an interest and chuckled sardonically, adding, 'Neither did I. Now, why am I not surprised?'.

'Fraidling quite a few did not know, Mike,' said Senestris. We didnar want to alarm anyone. I am very sorry for this error. Apologetics in the extreme.'

He actually bowed to all those assembled, apparently wishing to make an ostentatious display of his shame.

'Tis alrighting,' said Eleri. Mike gave her a wry look.

Senestris continued, 'The radio went kruppo about three days ago. Some of us have been trying to fix it but, as nothing untoward happened, til very-recent time, we did not think it was important. We can see that … we were wrong.' He pointed to a large metal box on the nearby stromatolite table. A few of the group had obviously been "working on it". They had smirks of satisfaction on their faces.

'Tis a shame I didn't know,' oferred Mike, 'cos you could have just used my wristcom, or Johann's.' Erbbius cast a sly glance at him.

'Come to think of it, you have a wristcom too, don't you?' Mike added, turning to Eleri.

She looked at him with a slightly embarrassed expression and said, quietly, 'Well, I am yet sorry Mike, but I gave it to Chanda. Twas a thank you gifty, if you like, for all she and Gajana did for both of us. Do you such mind?'

'Oh, I see,' said Mike, 'I guess it's okay. Well, Johann and I certainly have them.'

'Then I am full more, of apologies,' said Senestris, 'for I did not know you had such an device. Can you communicate with the mainland with same?'

Mike was amazed. He thought everyone knew they had them. Some almighty mix-ups going on around here. He nodded to Senestris and, for the benefit of the whole group gave the bare basics of how the wristcom could be used. He did not, of course, mention the "special" qualities of his device and thought it best not to mention that he, himself, had been ignoring messages left by the Admiral,

'Listen, I understand you might want to use these things,' said Mike, 'but I could have asked Johann here, to have a look at your radio. Isn't that right?' He turned to Erbbius.

A sullen look fell on Erbbius's face, and he said, 'Thanks, Mer Secretary, but I don't think I'd necessarily be in the best position to repair something quite as primitive as the stuff *they've* got cos you'd probably need a dealer in antiques.' He nodded toward the group assembled around the radio. Everyone fell silent, frowning and Mike scowled at his colleague.

'There's no need for that tone, Johann. *Their stuff* mightn't be as *primitive* as you think. I've been very impressed by the level of tek innovation here. Well, at … times.'

Sung broke into the conversation, partly to diffuse a rising atmosphere of tension. He laughed and said, 'In facto, this stuff is fairly old, to be sure. We just wanted to bring the basics with us, Mike. Make it easy to carry it, and so on. We would not want to bother you or Mer Johann about here.'

Erbbius chuckled again and said, 'It's just as well I didn't get a serious injury the other night. If the ship's *Secretary* here, and I, didn't have our wristcoms, what would you have done to get me – or anyone, to a proper med centre?'

It was a fair question, thought Mike but he already knew the answer.

Sung looked embarrassed again, but Hermington piped up, 'I must admit, I didnar know about the radio either, but, in fairness, we did not such think anyone would need serious medical attention. Most of us know this area and its dangers, though I accept we did not think of there being giant spring-traps here. We went as such on a calculated risk. We are lucky to have Rubia. She is the nearest you can get to a trained med-doctor. She looked after you well, Mer Erbbius. Did she not – Joahnn?' Danile emphasised his last words and there was no doubt he expected an appropriate response.

Rubbia sat shyly near the back of the group, as usual.

Erbbius seemed to think about it, but then acknowledged, 'Yeah, okay, but you haven't got any advanced med tek here, have you? I see plenty of lab stuff for looking at animal and plant specimens, but no surgical equipment. I gotta put this to you. Could you have got me airlifted out of here?'

There were a few puzzled looks, then Senestris said, 'There is but one way and that is by blimpy airship. I suppose it might have taken a week or so before one could get out here.'

Erbbius looked at Mike and opened his arms out as if to say, *what did I tell you? Primitive, like I said.* There were more frowns amongst the group but also heads bowed with shame.

'It's the pioneer spirit, Johann,' said Mike defensively. 'These people have had to contend with a wild world. It's still not tamed. Means it's full of dangers, all the time. They don't necessarily think the same way we do about "health and safety issues". That's just the way it is.'

Daniellsa Morgath piped up from the back of the main group, 'Who said we want to "tame" this world anyway? We such like it the way it is'

Mike nodded his genuine acknowledgement of her comment, as it was a fair one, but Erbbius retorted, 'I just call it negligent, that's all.'

'Okay, Johann. I think you've made your point,' said Mike.

'Can we move onward?' said Eleri, 'I am assuming you got us out here to tell us more than just the radio is now working?'

'Yes,' said Senestris, 'and we have used it. We have been in touch with Professier Muggredge. He has asked us to finish our work here – right now. He wants us yet to move our operations to the great island of Simurgh.'

Several team members seemed surprised but they also brightened. Senestris then addressed Mike directly, 'Tis fantastico-magic news. Mike, as it so seems your so good Admiral Tenak has found some, at least, of the evidence we were hoping for. He has idntifi'ed a layer of carbonised material in Simurgh. They have no dates for it but his geologist does think it might lie within rock strata of between 4 and 12 millions of years old. Tis somewhere in the east of the island. The Professier wants us to get over there and investigate, soon as can.'

Mike and Eleri smiled broadly. Some positive leads, at last, thought Mike. Erbbius asked how they were expected to get there and Hermington said that the Professier had mentioned there might be help from the Navy. Muggredge had suggested Mike or Erbbius contact their ship to find out. Mike readily agreed to this and started to wander off toward his chamber. In truth, he expected a dressing down from Tenak, and he hadn't packed his sound killing earbuds. He asked Eleri if she minded staying with the others. He was sufficiently embarrassed to want this conversation strictly between him and the Admiral.

He then derided himself for being concerned about a rebuke from the old man. He should be getting used to it, after all. So what if he'd been out of touch? Okay, he really didn't like disappointing Tenak. In any event, the expected "blast" didn't come. Tenak was just concerned about him, or "mindful" of his "tendency to get into sticky situations" as he eloquently put it. Surprisingly, he was not very in fact surprised when Mike mentioned that he'd nearly been consumed by a large plant. Mike said little about his rapprochement with Eleri. That could wait. Tenak wasn't his mother, for Maker's sake.

Rejoining the group he smiled brightly as he announced, a feeling of pride swelling in him, 'Well, I'm glad to say the Admiral has offered us the services of a Navy pilot and the use of the Agammemnon. That's a landing boat. The ship will take us back to Denebola K, first, provided it can land safely out here, to pick us up. We're going to need a relatively flat, tree-free area. I'm told the Professier would like us to refresh our supplies. Maybe pick up new stuff in Denebola, get some rest, and ship out on the Agammemnon first thing tomorrow. How does that grab you guys?'

To Mike's immediate sense of deflation, there was no overwhelming signal of approval from the group. One or two thought it better to wait for an airship! These included Daniellsa, but it was still surprising. Eleri pointed out, forcefully, that it would take many weeks for an airship to pick them up *and* get them out to Simurgh. It was over 10,000 kilometres away. Hermington added his own comment, 'I would estimate the fastest airship available would yet take two weeks to reach the island and there would be nowhere it could land. All our stuff would have to be winched down, and still us too. And we should be at the mercy of that place – even more than here. Tis a lot more dangerous than here, believe me.'

Senestris added, 'There is nothing to say we would even be able to use an airship or be allowed to. I say we use the Navy ship, like the Admiral says. It just makes much comn-sense.'

'Yes, for I have seen these Navy ships and they are marvellry, my friendlings,' said Hermington. Rubia stepped forward and backed up Danile enthusiastically.

Mike decided to push the issue further, saying, 'I should tell you, guys, from the way the Admiral spoke, I would think Professier Muggredge expects us to use the landing boat anyway.'

'Alrighting,' said Senestris, 'I think that does settle it. As Mike said, we will need to re-equip, including getting all-weather tents and camping gear. T'will not be comfortable out Simurgh way.'

'Whoa,' said Mike. 'There's no need for that. Provided there's a flat area where the ship can land safely, we'll be able to use the landing boat as a base. Sleep in it. Eat in it. Everything. Admiral Tenak expects this. By the way, Danile, I think I know what you mean about the dangers. You're talking about the giant birds, aren't you?' Hermington raised his eyebrows in surprise but nodded.

'So, the Admiral has said we'll need the boat for protection,' added Mike, 'but as a further precaution we'll be using an auto-set electrified fence, but don't worry. It won't harm the creatures if they come near. Just deter them. And they're flightless, aren't they? So, they won't be able to get over the fence.'

Erbbius almost exploded with enthusiasm. 'This is more like it. Do it right first time.' This earned him several resentful and surprised looks. Inwardly, Mike groaned.

Senestris quickly stepped into the lull in conversation and suggested Mike accompany him to a nearby forest clearing he'd seen, where he thought the Agamemnon could land. It was about 4 kilometres away, he said, and asked about Mike's injured leg. Mike dismissed the issue. He felt he could get there unaided. And he volunteered to contact Muggredge and Tenak, to finalise arrangements. Erbbius stood up and some people were astonished to see that he seemed completely rejuvenated and ready to go. Mike wasn't really surprised.

Seven hours later the entire group were assembled in a wide clearing, on the brow of a broad hill. It looked like some bald patch in the thick Purple Forest. Senestris had done well to find the area. The tallest vegetation was no more than about two metres high. Though not ideal, Mike knew the ship would be able to cope with this.

Ra was sinking toward the west and bands of brilliant oranges and reds were already splashed right across the sky. I'll miss the starsets here, thought Mike, if I ever get off this pebble alive. So, we have a new problem. Giant flightless birds – up next. He was starting to make a name for himself getting into trouble with the wildlife on this planet. He hoped his run of misfortune would end here and now with the Purple Forest.

He might not be lucky enough to get rescued next time.

Chapter 31

ISLAND OF REVELATIONS

Deep in the Purple Forest the distant first rumblings of the landing boat reached the group, expectantly assembled in the clearing. The sound, welcoming to Mike, emanated from high in the eastern sky. It soon arrived right overhead. The group sat, perspiring in the midday sun, some distance away as the vessel hovered and set itself down squarely in the middle of the flattest, clearest area. The pilot took the landing very slowly indeed. Mike knew the wheels themselves were very tough but the pilot was just taking precautions. The ribbed wheels slowly crushed the upstanding vegetation below them as the ship settled down and Mike half expected to hear some protests about "damage" to the plants, but none came.

In fact, most of the team stared at it with eyes almost on stalks, mostly he felt, with trepidation. Rubia, however, seemed overjoyed. Good for her. She would now get her wish, he thought.

***

The boat had reached most of the way to Simurgh when the pilot, Lew Pingwei, asked Mike to join him on the flight deck. The members of the Oceanus team seemed to be spending the time either wandering around, staring out the large elliptical windows, or else sprawled over the plush seating in the spacious passenger lounge. Mindara, in particular, peered almost ceaselessly out of the windows. The group were actually being spoiled and they loved it. The Agamemnon was the crème de la crème of the four ordinary landing boats carried by the Monsoon.

With a capacity, as an ideal only, of 35 passengers, it usually sported a large conference lounge aft of the main passenger cabin, but for the Oceanus trip this had been replaced with capacity for an extra 30 seats, specifically for the purpose of taking more evacuees. Extra seating could be added to the passenger lounge as well, at a moment's notice, but only to an overall limit dictated by the fuel and weight requirements.

As a concession to the Simurgh expedition there was neither extra seating nor a conference lounge, the latter having been replaced, very quickly, with makeshift living quarters. These included several sets of single and double bed compartments. With modularised interior fittings, conversion processes for the boats were hyper-efficient, so the vessel had been equipped to provide the team with a fully automated galley, all essential facilities, and the capacity for people to live in the ship for extended periods. For Mike and Eleri, the sleeping compartments promised extra privacy; a matter for which Mike now felt indebted to the Admiral.

Aft of the living quarters and galley there was now a capacious storeroom and supply module. On this expedition, the stores held not just food and essential supplies but space for personal baggage and equipment for the expedition, mostly rock drills, geology tools, bags for specimens, camera equipment and a lot more.

On entering the boat Lew had given a short talk to the Oceanus people, advising them of things they needed to know about the boat and Navy requirements. This included information about the aft-most section of the boat, near the root of the high tail fin. There, a large circular shaped module, was fitted, as standard. This was an irremovable, separately pressurised air lock module incorporating an extensible docking tunnel, designed to facilitate escape to any rescue ship which could dock with the device; mainly used for emergencies in orbit. But it could also be used in emergencies during ordinary flight through the atmosphere, to transfer passengers and crew to another vessel, if needed. Lew said it would almost certainly not be needed for their journey, but he felt they needed to be aware of it. Helpfully, he said Mike would instruct them on its use if he, for some reason, became incapacitated! Mike looked askance at this.

Now, as the shuttle progressed toward its goal, Mike was deep in conversation with Hermington and Eleri, when a loud request from Lew came over the cabin speakers, asking Mike to join him. Mike reached the cockpit, punching in the obligatory security codes to gain access, and as he entered, Pingwei signalled for him to sit in the vacant co-pilot seat. Mike deliberately avoided looking at the view out of the forward windshield. Way too much spaciousness out there.

'Thanks, Mike' said Pingwei. 'Wanted to talk to you about this place we're going. Should be there in around thirty mins. You know we surveyed your target zone real recently? Yeah, you did? Well, I reckon that the rock shelf, where the carbonised thingy lies, doesn't look too clever for something as heavy as this baby. It means I'll have to land on a flat hilltop. I saw one about, maybe 10 klicks from the shelf.' He called up a map of the area on his control panel. 'No, make that about 8 klicks. Anyway, is that going to be okay for your group? And by way, how's your leg, man? Heard it got wazzered.'

'Oh, the leg's a lot better, thanks. I managed to get some rest back in Denebola. Rubia gave me some sort of lotion from their stores. Worked wonders. As for the rest of the team, I'm sure they're more than up to the task. Hard as fusion-drive pins, most of 'em. Can't vouch for Agricola, though,' chortled Mike.

'Yeah, why is he here, Mike? There's better engineers on the ship. Erbbius gives me the creeps. Don't know why.'

'I know what you mean. Fact is, most of the senior engineers are occupied elsewhere. I think it was Ebazza's idea anyway.'

'Not sure about that. More like one of the other officers,' said Lew. 'Must have got it past her, somehow. Doesn't matter. Just make sure he stays out of my way, Mike. I won't put up with any shit from *him*.'

'Sure. Strange thing though. Back on the mainland I heard him talking to someone on his wristcom – seemed to be someone senior on the ship, just before we left the mansion at Denebola K. Audio only, and … it was a bit odd. It's funny, but I just heard a snatch of it when I happened to come out of a fresher room opposite. Don't think he expected to see me right then. What's weird is, he sort-of panicked and vanished into his room. Slammed the door.'

'Just a private conversation, maybe?'

'Maybe. The whole thing was just – strange, that's all. Something about the way he was talking. Thought I heard something about," special orders" and … "the master" or something. I don't think it was our quartermaster. I don't know. Must have got it wrong.'

Mike risked a quick glance out of the windshield, during a lull in the conversation. He was surprised to find it didn't make him feel as bad as expected, as he spied a spectacular vista dominated by a rich blue afternoon sky, and kilometres below, a flat plain of billowy white cloud. The only sense of motion came from what seemed like the smooth, slow, movement of the cloud deck below the ship, a movement which belied the true speed of the boat, which, he noticed on the control interface, was about Mach 6.5. Despite his initial satisfaction at being less badly affected than expected, he gradually felt his queesiness at the wide-open spaces ahead starting to get to him, and he had to quickly look away.

'By the way,' he said to Lew, putting his right hand up to shield his eyes from the view ahead, 'It's a shame Lem couldn't be on this mission. I heard he enjoyed the ride last time – and he is a geologist, after all. What happened? I know he wanted to do this trip. So, did the top brass assign him somewhere else or something?'

'Nah. Tomorrow's a big day for Lem.'

'How so?'

'Amazed you didn't know, but I guess you've been out of the ship's loop for a while. He's getting a new spinal nerve inlaid tomorrow. About six new vertebrae as well. Be out of action for at least ten days or so. Has to take it easy for another a few weeks after that.'

'That's great news for him, Lew. Shame he can't be here.'

'Yeah. Hey! I heard about you and the auburn-haired lass out there. Understand you and she, kind of "linked up"? Seems like a real nice person, Mike and I'm not just saying that, man. She seems real genuine, if you know what I mean? Well, course you do.'

'Yeah, Lew, I know. I almost blew it all with her. She's a cert' unique and it's true, she's a very genuine person. None better, I reckon.'

'Way to go, man. You're really serious about her, aren't you?'

'What me? Nah. Can you see that happening?' Mike's tone was mocking.

'yeah, you really *are*, aren't you? Sorry, don't think I'm prying. Just pleased about it, man.'

'It's okay, coming from you. And, like you said, she *is* kind of special. Anyway, better get back there now.'

Mike started to move out of the flight deck and gave Lew a wink, as he left. Lew mumbled, more to himself than Mike, 'Well, just goes to show. The guy had it in him all along.'

As Mike rejoined Eleri and Hermington in the cabin, Sung approached him. Kenye had been appointed, by Muggredge, as the new expedition leader for this trip. Marcus Senestris had stayed behind, apparently because of family reasons but Mike had his doubts. Senestris hadn't exactly led the Purple Forest expedition well. Two new people had joined the team at Denebola K. Apparently, they were "rookers"; beginners, in O A speak.

Sung asked how long it would be before arrival. He could barely believe the answer when told.

'We could have got there even quicker, my friend,' said Mike, 'if Lew had gone for a sub-orbital lob. I reckon he was worried you'd all leave your lunches on the carpet.'

'No, do not like the sounds of that,' said Sung, 'and if he meant we are just not-so used to these sorts of speed, then right he be. Still, this flight is very smooth-flow, shall I say. I can hardly guess we are moving at all.'

'Yeah,' said Mike, 'Lew's got us up at about 14,000 metres, where the air is thin – but stable. And, if you're interested, which you probably aren't, we're hitting Mach 6.5.'

'Scusem me, youngry. I yet know more than you think. Mach 6.5? That would be six and a half times the speed of sound, wouldst not?' said Sung, with mock indignation and added, 'but tis alrighty. I can understand why you would think me not so interested.'

Mike felt genuine shame. He shouldn't make so many assumptions, he thought.

'I'm sorry, my friend, but yes, you're just about right. Anyway, Lew's going to have to land about 8 lints from the target rocks. There's nowhere closer that's safe for the ship. Okay?'

Eleri came forward and tugged Mike around to look at Mindara. 'She's like the cat with the garnwob,' she said.

Mike frowned. A what? He decided not to go there. He could see Mindara was totally absorbed by the experience of flying, standing next to a large observation porthole near the rear of the cabin. She was using some sort of antique camera to image the scenes out the window. He walked over to her.

'You can use my wristcom if you like,' said Mike. 'It would probably take better images than that.'

'Oh, no thank you, Mike,' she replied, a wide smile lighting her face, 'I am happily yet with my video camera. Old fashioned though you might think it. Sorry, Mike.'

Mike smiled broadly, 'No, that's fine Rubia. Please, don't let me disturb you. Best make the most of it, cos we'll be landing soon and I'm afraid you'll need to strap into one of the forward-facing seats.'

'Ah, coursry,' she said, 'tis true I did look at the "Safety Manual for Landing Boat Passengers" on the screen-thing attached to my arm rest. Danile showed me how to use it. The manual was 40 pages long, Mike,' she laughed.

'Well, Johann told you that we take our health and safety issues seriously, I guess, even though we're Navy. And, because we're Navy, everything has to be done "proper like".' Mike stood ramrod straight and stiff and tried to make himself sound like a curmudgeonly senior officer.

'Well so, you are funny-like,' said Mindara, 'but I love this ship, Mike.' A distant look fell over her eyes, as she continued, 'and to think that I am going to visit somewhere as far away as Simurgh. I have never been yet far from home.'

'I'm glad you're enjoying it. So, you haven't travelled much on the mainland?'

'No, Mike.' She looked a little embarrassed at that point, and said, 'I was of twelve years age before I went e'en to Janitra. My parentia were very poor, Mike.'

'Oh, I'm sorry,' began Mike.

'Do not be sorry yet. I am travelling much now, am I not? I have also dreamed of travelling on your mother ship – and it looks as if I will really get the chance – praps soonest. You see, I have been entranc-ed many long years, by stories of old Earth and many times I dreamed of travelling there but … well, I am just a silliest old Oceanus peasant, who got lucky enough to learn some science.'

'Not at all, Rubia. Please don't sell yourself short. It's good to have dreams. Stick to 'em like glue, I say. And I'm sure you will get to go on The Monsoon. Sorry, Rubia, someone over there's calling me.'

Rubia smiled broadly as Mike wandered over to where Renton Barstow was beckoning to him. Chen and Daniellsa were standing with him.

'Mike, you were so saying that we shall have to walk several lints to the rock shelf?' said Barstow, 'but you did know there mayst be giant birds in the area. They are all on Simurgh. What is our protection, Mike? We are not wanting a repeat of anything like the Purple Forest.'

'I know. You're absolutely right,' said Mike, 'and I certainly don't want that, believe me. But I think Lieutenant Pingwei, our pilot, has some ideas about it. And we'll have to keep a watch out for those things. Tell me, are there likely to be … lots of those things?' Mike was starting to feel uneasy about this planet's wildlife again. He wished the subject hadn't been mentioned but he supposed they had to face facts.

Daniellsa moved a little closer to Mike, looked at him through slitted eyes and said, in a quiet, almost sinister voice, 'No, Mike. Do not so worry. Surely, none of us should yet feel fraid? The last survey done, counted no more than 56 breeding pairs but tis also true that they have not been doing so well there. That figure didst show a drop of 40% since the last count.'

'Verily, D.N,' said Chen, very seriously, 'but that survey was done around 25 years ago. No womana- manry has been out there since. We do not really know the situation. We must be on our guard.'

All nodded, then Chen and Barstow wandered off, leaving Mike alone with Daniellsa. Mike felt embarrassed, not knowing what to say.

She moved closer still to him and, though she was smiling, it was, thought Mike, rather grim. Mike remembered what Eleri had said, about knives between ribs. But she had been joking, right?

'Mayst we speak more private-like?' she said, and reluctantly, Mike gestured for them to walk to the quietest spot, near the large observation porthole at the aft end of the cabin, opposite side to Mindara, who still gazed out the window. He caught a glimpse of Eleri, way up front, who'd been watching the two of them, but who then looked away. She was making a pretense of being unconcerned. Seems she really trusted him, he thought, but did she trust Daniellsa?

'Mike,' said Morgath, this time sounding more sincere, 'I wanted yet to talk to you. I near-so did not come on this expedition, because … because of what happened such … back there. You knowst?'

Mike nodded solemnly.

'But I am a palaeontologist and natural historian femna … a scientist, you would say.'

Mike started to say, 'Yes, Daniellsa, I know all about …'

Interrupting him, she said, 'Please just list, Mike. I am interested in this work on Simurgh and tis important to my world. And I deserve to be part of this now team. That is why I came on this trip.'

'Yeah, okay,' said Mike, 'there's no need to explain why you're here, Daniellsa. Professier Muggredge picked you as part of the team. I can't object. Wouldn't. And look, I hope that we can put the past behind us.'

'Yes, deedly,' she said, and then, looking him in the eye very steadily, said with great earnestness, so there could be no doubt in his mind, 'and please now believe me manry, when I say that I do not … want you anymore. I do not know nor ever will know what I was thinking yet, back there, but tis all over now. Facto, I do not know what I did see in you.' She laughed grimly.

Mike actually felt a little hurt by this forthright comment, but he was, in truth, relieved. He knew she was being honest, and this way it all made a lot more sense. And would make life a lot easier.

'Wow,' he said, 'why don't you just speak your mind, Daniellsa?' he said, exhaling slowly.

'Pardon-so?' she said, looking puzzled, then said, 'anywayins, I am sorry, Mike. I do not mean to insult, and I also mean that we can, I am yet sure, be co-operative investigator-pops.'

He thought he knew what she meant, maybe. She walked away solemnly, and he wandered back to Eleri. As Daniella settled in a back-row seat, far behind them, he told Eleri what had transpired, and she laughed out loud. 'Good 'nough,' she said, 'for deedly, she is a member of this team. And shall be useful. Well, she better be.'

****

This time around Lew Pingwei approached the target area from the north. Passing high over the chain of high, rugged, mountains that formed the backbone of Simurgh, Mike guessed he wanted to give his passengers the best possible view. It would have been faster to approach from the east, over the sea, but there was no particular hurry. The team envisaged they'd be on Simurgh for about 5 days, maybe longer. Lew had told Mike that although he thought the Oceanus team seemed a decent bunch, he was also determined they'd stick to accepted procedures. This boat was *his* baby and, given what Mike had told him about the lack of organisation back in the Purple Forest, they needed to know *he* was in charge of Navy facilities.

He asked Mike to sit with him again, as he slowed the ship smoothly, to a "sedate" 600 kilometres per hour, and they lost altitude. Mike took his seat and risked a quick gaze out of the window at the rugged bare tops of Simurgh's so called "Chop Blade Mountains", as they floated serenely past far below the ship. He felt he was able to continue to watch them as they slid aft of the boat, on many of the screens festooning the cockpits's broad control interface.

Lew took the boat lower and much slower, lancing over an impressively deep, dark, ravine between two rocky pinnacles, then onward until they could see a series of green-blue hills far beyond. Mike asked if Eleri could sit in the co-pilot's seat. He would move to the third flight deck seat; the "Observer's" position behind the pilot and co-pilot seats. Lew agreed and, after taking the seat, something she was delighted to do, Eleri pointed out the windshield at a distant hill that appeared much lower than any of the others and sported a wide, almost flat, top. 'Is that our landing site, Mer Lew?' she asked.

Lew congratulated her on her observation skills and taking the ship lower still, arced smoothly downwards, gracefully gliding over the site. When his companions gave him puzzled looks, he explained, 'We have to drop off your supplies at the rock shelf first. I'm going to lower a locker containing enough supplies of water, food, equipment and the rest. Enough to last your team for the likely duration of the mission. I've got the bulk of supplies onboard this ship but the stuff I'm dropping will service you while you're on the shelf. It's so you don't need to come back and fore to the ship all day. It's 8 klicks in the heat, remember?'

'What about the electrical fences?' said Mike, 'I wasn't sure if we had to tote those over to the site.'

'You don't,' said Lew, smiling, 'I'm dropping that stuff off as well. But you guys are going to have to erect it.'

'In that case it's a good thing the fence poles are self-erecting,' said Mike.

'Self-erecting?' asked Eleri, 'Sounds like you,' she said, whispering conspiratorially in Mike's ear.

'Well, not entirely self-erecting,' said Lew, smiling wryly, as though he'd heard Eleri's comment, 'You guys have to set them up straight and vertical first. Then you flick a switch near the foot end of each pole – and it drills itself into the ground. It'll go through most rock. Stuff like granite takes a long time, but that's not the stuff down there.'

Passing slowly over a low ridge Lew used the directional engines to slow the craft to an almost complete halt above the wide rock shelf which formed the target site, bounded on one side by the ocean. On its landward side lay a series of small rock faces that rose to a steeply angled scree slope. On the seaward side the shelf ended in a steep, high cliff, below which lay a narrow beach of large rocks and pebbles. Beyond that the ocean, calm that day, lay like a gently undulating sheet of blue and silver-gold metal, dazzlingly reflecting the Oceanus sun of the morning, in sparkling gold.

The pilot hovered the Agamemnon about 15 metres above the rock shelf and, his hands skimming skilfully over the various large, flat, illuminated panels which covered the control interface. He opened the doors of the ship's capacious cargo bay, situated in the lower half of the fuselage, below the passenger cabins. The cockpit monitors then showed a sizeable container being released from the cargo hold, hanging on four cables, descending slowly to the rock shelf. Lew explained that the "locker" was a simply a large, refrigerated cabinet, sealed, to prevent animals from detecting and getting at the food inside. The team would have to ensure it stayed locked when it was not in use, and at the end of each day.

Once he was satisfied the drop was stable and secure, Lew released the winches and wound up them up, then started back toward the proposed landing site, 8 kilometres away, setting the ship down smoothly on top of the smooth hillock.

The team were able to debark a few minutes later. Most of the Oceanus people were glad to get out but even they seemed to find the heat of the Simurgh day a bit of a shock, after becoming inured to the cool air-conditioned environment on the Agamamnon. As the group spilled onto the dry, sandy ground, someone commented that the mountains further inland were quite different from those found on the continent. Another explained that the island was much younger, the mountains steeper and less forested. Added to that, Simurgh was much further south than Bhumi Devi. And more arid.

Mike wandered around the Agamemnon, trying to avoid gazing too long at the exposed terrain in the direction of the rock shelf. The shuttle itself was sitting, mostly, on level ground, but a hundred meters further inland the ground was covered with a jumble of house size boulders and thickets of trees with huge, sharp, thorns. Mike had forgotten what they were called but he gazed at them because he felt more comfortable looking in that direction. And as for the terrain in the direction of the target site? Well, he was going to have to get used to it. He felt he was a solid member of this team, he wanted them to think well of him and he was determined that Eleri should see this. To cry off now, after all that had happened, was not possible. But his heart still thudded at the prospect.

He brought his attention back to the present and heard members of the team talking animatedly about water supplies, which they thought might be an issue, but Lew advised that the ship's auxiliary power plants could *manufacture* its own water, for about three weeks. But they had plenty in the boat's store anyway. Sung, directing his comments to the team, pointed out that despite the supplies in the locker they would all need to carry some bottled water with them when walking between the ship and the rock shelf. The terrain was extremely rugged and the climate harsh, so they had to stay hydrated.

It was understood that Muggredge wanted this excursion to be a civilian directed effort. Although Sung had been appointed "team leader", Muggredge had gladly conceded that Lew, as pilot, should have as much input as possible. From the Navy perpective, Erbbius, though a second level engineer, was also a Lieutenant in rank, and so, strictly speaking, had the same authority as Lew. But here he was required to defer to Lew, not only because, as pilot, Lew was in charge of the ship, but because, quite simply, he had many more years of experience.

Lew showed the team some holo-maps of their landing site. The images entranced the Oceanus people. The ship's minor AI had a proposed a particular walking route to the rock shelf, which it superimposed on the holo-map. The dangers of the "Macrotargs"; the huge birds of Simurgh, was raised again, this time by Eleri. These flightless avians stood 5 metres tall and sported massive, hook shaped, rock hard beaks. These giants were known to be very aggressive as well as territorial.

For the benefit of the Navy men and anyone else not familiar with the story, Eleri explained the full hsitory of the Macrotargs since human settlement on Oceanus. When the earliest people had arrived the huge birds had lived in all the mountainous areas of the continent, mostly in arid regions. But as time passed they became more adventurous – and troublesome to humans. They kept turning up, with increasing frequency, in the settled areas, where they would harry the livestock being reared, and trampled crops. It was a terrible echo of what had often happened on Earth in the past, with other large animals.

The worrisome thing here was that they had absolutely no fear of humans. All attempts to scare them with noisy horns, and things like powerful cork guns, had failed. No-one wanted to kill them but, after the deaths of several settlers, including a few children, some birds were, unfortunately, euthenazed. The government then chose to take unprecedented action, to protect humans and to conserve the birds themselves. They had them rounded up and transplanted, en-masse, to Simurgh. It had been a truly huge undertaking but one deemed successful at the time.

The island terrain was similar to the areas the birds had originally inhabited and the solution, though not ideal, was considered better than the alternative. That was one reason why Simurgh was, generally, out of bounds to the human population. Its physical isolation did the rest. By law, there was to be no human settlement on the island and only one small airstrip existed, over on the western side, used only by government personnel and scientists. The last visit had been long ago.

Sung then gave a very pointed warning about the birds, though he directed his comments chiefly to the Navy contingent. He said the birds had a tendency to charge, regardless of any perceived danger, and that, despite their size, they were very fast runners. After hearing that Lew decided to break out some weapons. Stun rifles were advised for anyone who wanted one, but they were not compulsory. Everybody took one, except Daniellsa Morgath and Renton Barstow. They refused to partake of anything which might harm the creatures, though it was explained that serious, long term harm was very unlikely. Lew also said he had brought heavy stun grenades, but it was agreed this was to be an absolute last resort, only to be used if the animals somehow got through the fences.

The two new scientists Muggredge had asked to join the team for this trip, had been very quiet on the journey out. Each was a specialist, and each was young and physically fit, having been chosen by the Professier, partly for their fitness and ability to take a full share in carrying out heavy duty work like moving rocks and soil, if needed. The eldest was called Leor Mykarinus Arbinius, about 25 OA years of age. He was a doctorate student of geology. Then there was the 21-year-old, very athletic looking, Janinia Neferkamin Rasmissen, a doctorate student of oceanography. Both had joined the group at Denebola. The new people seemed very enthusiastic, thought Mike, as they thoroughly dived into the job of setting up the perimeter fences around the Agamemnon.

As Lew had promised, it was only necessary to hold each 4-metre pole vertically and, though they were heavy, push them lightly into the sandy soil and press a switch, after which a type of drill-head unit on the base of each screwed the pole deep into the ground. After setting up 40 poles they had to pull a length of flexible wire fencing, rolled up inside each pole, and attach it to rotor pegs inside a cleft in the next pole along. Small motors inside each pole allowed easy reeling out, by hand, of each fence section and similar motors in the pole next along wound it in tightly.

Despite the presence of some automation the whole group sweated profusely throughout the job and, in Ra's heat, most became tired by the time the last piece of fencing was connected. Lew showed them how to pull a length of cabling from the last pole to be set up and connect it to a briefcase size battery generator. Within seconds, the fence was electrified with 200 volts DC; enough to discourage any large bird, even *very* large ones.

'How in the oceans did anyone so come up with this idea?' asked Morgath.

'They used these things a lot in the Rebel Wars, back in the day,' said Lew. 'Don't forget, my friends, every alternate fence pole has a movement detector that can sense anything that moves out to 40 metres. And cameras record it. There's an "R band" feed to a mobile monitor I've put in the cabinet I lowered earlier. The fence also transmits to my ship, of course. That means you and I can monitor anything large which gets near the fence. The sensors point outward, by the way, so if anything has already got into the compound, uninvited, you won't be able to locate it, 'unless it's obvious. We might be out of luck by then anyway, I guess.'

The team sat in the shade cast by the Agamemnon for a while, to rest and drink, but then started moving out as soon as each team member had kitted up with supplies and water bottles. After brief tuition by Lew and Mike, those with stun rifles had shouldered them. Most team members had never touched any sort of armament before that day and Mike wondered how they would fare if they needed to use them.

They set off toward the ridge separating the landing zone from the target site, all of them tired, but in a wondrously light-hearted mood. Mike was startled by this. Some people even started to sing – an ancient rhyme handed down from the earliest Oceanus pioneers:

Come with us, from dark void waves, to lands of silvan glade

O'er misty mountains, thru woods so deep, an' oceans so wild 'neath purple skies

with quintillion stars, void from whence we came, let not resolve fade,

to build for us yet and keep, a new world, which in the firmament lies,

a paradise for all, to show our brethren how we made

And so, it continued for several verses.

Mike thought it a curious little thing, but it had a pleasant, lilting, haunting melody that sank into his consciousness; so much that he found himself, almost without realising, singing along with his companions.

****

Many thousands of kilometres away, in central Janitra, a debate had been raging in the Primary Legislative Assembly for all Oceanus, the so-called Curia Magna, or, in old Earth, western terms, "senate" or "parliament.".

The proposal before the Curia was that an Interstellar Inquiry should be held, to investigate the veracity of the evidence being claimed for the instability of Ra and the consequent danger to the planet. The hope of some was that any Inquiry would find the evidence convincing enough to recommend the wholesale evacuation of Oceanus. Many others hoped for the opposite – and many wanted no Inquiry at all.

The proposal had been drafted by UdeC, the third strongest party on the planet, as agreed by the two main parties, but the Meta-teleos had successfully appended a major condition. This was that if, in fact, there was a vote in favour of the proposal, then the Inquiry should be held in the Ra system; in other words, on Oceanus itself. There was to be a free vote, not subject to any party directive, on both issues.

The "Debating Chamber" was a grand affair, built in the old-fashioned Palladian style, practically copied from an estate in what had once been Great Britain, back on Earth. The Representatives from the dozens of different constituencies across Bhumi Devi, plus those from three, relatively small but inhabited islands, scattered across the six oceans, sat in semi-circular, concentric rows of desks, facing toward a central platform. Arbella Nefer-Masterton sat at the front-most desk, nearest the platform, at one side of the chamber. The place was nearly full and there was a rumbling hubbub of sound from those assembled.

The discussion was debated hotly for hours, with a variety of opinions being voiced. There had been hot headed comments and ones calmly made. There had been tactical and strategic arguments made on both sides of the debate, as well as passionate and emotionally charged speeches. Professier Muggredge and Yardis Sliverlight were observers and not allowed to speak. The Professier hoped his time would come – if, and when, the Inquiry took place.

Three hours was the normal limit for debating proposals of this type but the gravity of this one meant that an application to exceed it was carried, allowing it to continue until six hours had passed. The person charged with recording debates in the Curia, who sat at a wide desk on the front platform, stood, at the six-hour point and hit a small brass gong with a mallet. The debate had to end, and such was the respect accorded to this civil servant, who had no permitted party allegiance, that all those representatives standing in the House, waiting to speak, sat, or if actually speaking, closed their mouths. This way of doing business dated back to the very earliest days of the colony, though the Curia had had fewer legislative powers at that time.

'Thanking you, representatives,' said the Recorder, a short but thickset man in his 60s, 'but yet I think that we must conclude this long-so debate. You have heard submissions from many representatives, including Madama President and leaders still of all the parties. Tis time to put the issues to the vote, unless any 'mongst you be taking argument with such ways this debate has been conducted. If such, speak you now, or be holding your peace.'

He had waited for half of the customary 30 second delay, when a deep voice issued from a desk mic' on the front row. It was Patchalk Remiro.

'Mer Recorder,' said Remiro, 'with respect yet, I have a submission on a point of order, on behalf of the Meta-teleos.'

Arva Pendocris sitting next to him, grimaced.

As was customary the Recorder replied, 'The House does recognise Patchalk Remiro, Representative for Ramnissos West. Please speak, sirra.'

'Thanking you, Mer Recorder,' said Remiro, standing and sneering at some of the representatives he knew had argued in favour of the proposal.

'My point regards now the fact that Rep Deminos, Secretary for the Economy, argued he had carried out research and this tended to support the info-data transmitted by the so-called Argosy probe. This was left, in orbit around Ra, so many years ago, by those who live outside our system. Apart from the fact that this probe stopped working many years ago, I am claiming that its data was never corroborated by any Oceanus instruments. I submit that Rep Deminos should not have referred to any research which he carried out, on his own behalf, or for personal interest. There is no rule, Mer Recorder, against such an member of this House being a professional scientist, so-called, as in the case of Rep Deminos. There is, still, a rule that such an member should refer to the research of others, not his own, which otherwise gives disadvantage to those members without such qualification or resources. That is my point, Mer Recorder.' He took his seat again, looking very pleased with himself. Pendocris looked down at her lap and fussed with a kerchief, as though trying to hide her face.

There were murmurings of approval from some members but hisses and muted invective from others. These subsided as the Recorder stood again.

'Thanking you Rep Remiro. I have located my recorded notes for the matter you raise. I shall yet tell the House what they say and if you continue to object, Rep Remiro, I will ask for such audio recordings be made available to the House immediatingly, so to be broadcast to all members.' He paused as he leafed through a set of shorthand notes, then continued,

'Here is the zone of relevance. Rep Deminos said. I shall read the transcription. It says, "I have myself considered the information relevant to the magnetic cycles in Ra's deep subsurface convection layers. I have researched the conjectures about the core and convective zone, so as to be better able to format the data from the probe, as relevant and cogent, for the time they were made."'

There were murmurings from various directions, but the Recorder continued, 'My interpretation is that Rep Deminos did not put forward his own data, still referred only to the fact that he had undertaken his own research. Mayhap an injudicious juxtaposition of words but, with respect, Rep Remiro, I am believing the point was made fairly.'

Remiro looked around, frowning deeply. Arva Pendocris dug an elbow into his ribs. Remiro stood and bowed to the Recorder, without saying more.

The proposal before the House was then put to the vote by the Recorder. Votes were made by electronic means, registered by the flashing of tiny, bright, orange lights high above the Recorder's desk. But before voting there was a window of ten minutes for members to decide the issues on their own, quietly, and then to cast them on the striking of another bell by the Recorder, after which the opportunity closed.

After the votes had been made the recorder announced the result. There was an awed silence throughout the large hall as he began to speak, his rich baritone voice carrying high and echoing in the sepulchral heights of the chamber.

'Verily, am I able to record' he said, 'that there were 85 votes for the proposal and 78 against. I thereby declare the proposal is passed. On the subsidiary vote of where-yet the Inquiry shall take place, there were 107 votes that the locus be here, in the Ra system and 46 for the locus being in the Home System, with 20 abstains. I shall therefore declare that the Inquiry will be held in the Ra system, the precise place to be decided elsetime.'

There were whoops of joy from many – and groans of disappointment from others, all around the House.

*

On a live-feed vid to The Monsoon, Admiral Tenak, Captain Ebazza and most of the bridge officers had watched the proceedings, played out on a vast 2D screen in the ship's number 14 Common Room. There was palpable relief all around. Shouts of victory rang out from some, gasps of surprise from others.

As crewmembers stood to leave, with, for the most part, broad smiles on their faces, the Admiral gave his Captain a wry look but then spoke out deliberately loud, so all could hear him, saying, 'Don't get too excited. They just voted for an Inquiry. There's a long way to go.'

There were loud murmurs of assent, and Tenak and Ebazza started to leave with the others, when Commander Gallius Statton hurried toward them, speaking in hushed tones, 'Admiral. Captain. I've got some important news. It's urgent. May I speak with you in private? I didn't want to send you a holo and I think it's too early to make a general announcement.' The exprsssion on his gaunt, thin, face betrayed the gravity of his message.

Tenak signalled Statton and Ebazza to move to the back of the room. Some of the other crew hanging about by the screen started to drift toward them but withdrew when they saw the senior officers huddled together. A bridge Officer, Sub-lieutenant Brandon, ushered them out of the room before anyone could eavesdrop.

'We've arrested Havring for interfering with the ship's comp systems,' said Statton, 'and we've put him in the brig for questioning. He denies any wrong-doing but refuses to answer questions.'

Tenak's face clouded over, 'What's the nature of the evidence against him?' he said.

'I don't know all the details yet. Lieutenant Blandin has that. Seems that Chips, sorry, Havring, been acting strangely for weeks. Bogus eye recognition software's been found in his cabin and he can't account for his whereabouts during the times we think the damage was done. There's more, but I'd like to ask that you speak to Blandin about it. I just thought you needed to know immediately.'

'Thank you, Commander,' said Ebazza, a surprised expression on her face. The First Officer withdrew, leaving the Captain and the Admiral in stunned silence.

'I know he's an oddball,' said Ebazza, 'but I wouldn't have thought him capable of this.'

'Don't know huge amounts about him, Ssanyu,' said Tenak, 'but it's time I found out. I'm not convinced he did this on his own. There had to be others. It was a complex operation. We also have to consider whether he's been framed.'

'Agreed, Admiral. I want to talk to him and I'm sure you will, but a full military enquiry needs to be set up as soon as…'

'Not necessarily. Given what's happening on the planet and our overriding mission here, I think we may have to delay that for a little bit. Havring can lie up in the brig for now. Cooling off there may make him re-think his ideas about silence. If he is guilty, he might give us a clue about whoever else is involved.'

'I'm sure you're right, sir, but I'm just concerned to get to the bottom of this yesterday-like.'

'As am I Captain. As am I.'

****

Four days of hard, mainly physical, work on the rock shelf left Mike feeling just a little jaded. At least his phobia had started to abate a little, as the route to and from the site was not as open as he'd thought, the route twisting and turning between steep hillocks and broken masses of rock and rubble. It felt sort of "closed in", *kind of*, though open to the sky and the sun. In any case, he felt or hoped his "condition" was affecting him less often as he became more used to this place, to this world, in fact. At long last, he thought, with relief, though he was still careful not to push things too far too quickly.

All the non-geologists had been lumbered with moving rubble every day, sifting through soil, or just left to carry out "house-keeping" duties. The geologists, Sung,

Morgath, Hermington and Arbinius, were minutely searching for fossils below the carbonised layer, which they would be able to identify as forming a sequence and could then be compared with those found in strata above the carbon rich layer. If there were many species below the layer which were mostly or completely absent *above* it, that would *suggest* that the intervening layer represented a possible extinction event at the time it was laid down. But Mike was dismayed to hear the geologists say that even if there was an indication of an extinction event it might be localised to this area. Of course that made sense. The situation here might not represent the situation over the whole planet at the time of the "event", which it would have to, if the HS theory of Ra's instability was to become more acceptable to the people of Oceanus. This journey, he realised, was only going to be indicative, or suggestive, not the whole answer.

'We do need so to find other places, around Oceanus, which show this carbonised layer too,' said Sung, 'otherwise the Meta's will have field days destroying our credibility.'

'Well, we've only got this place right at the moment,' retorted Mike, 'so we've got to make the best of it for now.'

No-one in the group, apart, possibly, from Morgath, had been unimpressed with the scarce, tiny, snail like fossils discovered at the site over the first two days, finding little of interest in the shale and mudstone strata, but then they began to find a lot of little fossil bones. They thought these belonged to small terrestrial animals, a species not yet unidentified. No sequences as yet, but at least it was a beginning. The thin, dark, carbon rich layer of shales was a different matter. Despite the obvious problems this was something they could all enthuse about having found.

The carbonised layer itself, sitting nearly two metres above the rock shelf, was only about 6 centimetres thick in most places, but was very dense. At this location most of the more recently deposited, overlying, layers had been eroded away, leaving about two to three metres of sandstone to form the top of the step-like cutting above the carbon. The dark material, itself, superficially reminded Mike of coal, but it was highly friable. Clearly, it contained a lot of carbon, as proved by some simple chemical experiments they were able to carry out on-site, and slightly more sophisticated ones on board the Agamemnon later.

Most of the stuff seemed to consist of carbonised plant stems and trunks, which led to the conclusion that there had been very extensive burning of forests here millions of years ago. Mike asked whether they could narrow down the age of the layer, as not even Lew and Charnott had had been able to offer any more than a very wide age bracket for the area.

Even the non geologists understood very clearly that the date of the carbon layer depended on the age of the rocks above and below it. The geologists felt the dating of these layers could eventually be determined by comparison with many others found elsewhere, especially when some of the small fossils in it were identified. Similar rocks and fossils in other locations had reasonably well known ages but Hermington and Sung said they simply could not be certain until finer analyses could be done. It all depended on rates of deposition, in turn depending on the precise environment where they were laid down, and so on and so on… Mike preferred astrophysics. This stuff was palling on him.

And the team certainly couldn't agree amongst themselves. Sung and Morgath said they thought the mudstones dated back about 7 million years, but Danile thought 9 million. So, an accurate age for the carbonised layer could not be made yet either but it seemed to be somewhere between those two estimates – if the geologists were right about the other strata. Precise dating would have to await more chemical analysis and radioisotope dating of the material; something the facilities of the Agamemnon could not provide.

But, thought Mike, if they were right, it was starting to look good for the theory of a massive catastrophe in the "relatively recent" geological past and it fitted with what he knew of the newest astrophysics, which said that stars in their "old age", like Ra, showed a tendency for surface explosions of the type which could cause extinction events on a planet like Oceanus. That meant that when "Ra type" stars, or "Omega Chapman" stars, as they were known in the Home System, reached roughly the same age as the Sun in the Solar System, they developed problems deep in their convective layers and possibly cores, which resulted in the destructive surface explosions.

'The science says, pretty clearly,' he had said to his teammates, 'that after billions of years of stability these types of star kind of, "go wrong" – big time.'

'So, yet,' Morgath had said, 'when, Mikery, are you saying that they do begin to "go wrong"?'

Wincing at her bending of his name, Mike said, 'Well, I haven't carried out any research in this area but I'm aware of the consensus with scientists back home. Basically, it seems to vary from star to star. So, I'm sorry to say it can't be predicted accurately,' said Mike.'But there are clear "markers" seen in the observations – thousands of 'em, which show, pretty clearly, that outbursts – "micro-novae" they call them, start to happen in a series, and the events are, mostly, separated by periods of several million years.'

'They cannot say more accurate-so?' said Danile.

'No, I don't think there's any accurate figure. It varies, but it ain't billions of years.

'And there are a series, you do say, Mike,' said Eleri.

'Yeah. Sorry to say, but it seems there can be anything up to eight of these "episodes", in a row.'

'*Eight!*' Sung, Morgath and others cried.

'Yeah, I know,' said Mike, grimacing, 'and, after all that, seems the stars, sort of, settle down for a few hundred million years, but the physics suggests they start to get nasty again – probably for the rest of their so-called lives.'

'Hmm, sounds like some people I know,' Lew had said.

Now, after a further day at the site Sung and some others were lamenting loudly about not having a mass spectrometer to analyse the chemistry of the rocks, to date them. They were surprised that the landing boat didn't have the necessary equipment. After all, it seemed to have most other things, didn't it? Mike and the Navy crew had no choice but to shatter their illusions. The Monsoon could have done the work but not the landing boats. And, Lew pointed out, forcefully, that this was supposed to be a mission run by the Oceanus people, wasn't it? That was specially to allay the fears of the population that it might be some sort of Navy operation, a Home System "fix". It was enough that the Navy had taken them to the site. Many would find even *that* suspicious.

Lew also reminded the team that The Monsoon would be able to carry out a finely detailed analysis anyway, but only if the specimens were taken up to it. That would, of course, feed into those political sensitivities even more. In the light of this Sung agreed that the work probably needed to be done by other people on the continent, using their own, admittedly less sophisticated, equipment.

When, on the fourth day at the site, the team began to meander back toward the shuttle in groups of ones or twos, Mike took it on himself to remind them of safer practices. Days of working at the site, without anyone ever seeing a Macrotarg, even at a distance, had probably made them all complacent. The agreement, arrived at very early, was that people walked back and forth to the site in groups of at least 3, and one in each group needed to have a stun rifle. The route they had to travel was difficult to check and exposed to Ra light, traversing rough, stony, scrubby country, with just the occasional small copse of larpett trees for shade. The tiring journey also involved several short, but steep climbs, often involving scrambling, followed by equally steep descents, and everyone needed to have their wits about them. It had proved physically draining, especially in 35° heat. To everyone's relief, over the last two days an increasingly strong but cool, soothing wind had begun to blow in off the sea.

The walk "home" in the late afternoon, was still difficult.

When several people started to carry samples of the carbonised deposits back to the shuttle, Erbbius suggested they do themselves a favour and leave the samples on site – in the locked cabinet. Everyone complied with this idea, and Mike was surprised that, for once there'd been a sensible suggestion from his, otherwise, brooding colleague. But Mike couldn't help thinking that Erbbius had been more concerned about his own comfort than the that of the others. He'd long grumbled at the physical effort he'd been expected to contribute.

Although the team were extremely relieved to see no giant birds at any point Lew had fitted a binocular telescope and vid-cam, with 360° vision, high on the boat's vertical fin. He proceeded to monitor the whole area, from his console inside the cockpit, whenever groups were in transit between the site and the ship. Mike was not surprised at the lack of giant birds, given that Simurgh was larger than Greenland, back on Earth. And he had a suspicion that the birds had not done well in recent times. It was a long time since they'd been counted. Even so, he was still relieved. Given his luck on Oceanus, if any turned up around the work site, they'd probably head for him first!

The following day there came a breakthrough – but in a totally unexpected direction. The team made the discovery of their lifetimes; a find which they all thought could be one of the *greatest ever made in the history of astronomical and biological sciences* but not immediately seen as connected with the problem of Ra.

It happened when Mindara was scraping through loose rock chipping and debris, some 400 metres along the "mini- cliff", from the point nearest the route back to the shuttle. She worked at shale like material nearly nearly two metres below the carbon layer. Her eyes widening at what she'd found, she immediately sceamed to the others, who ran over to help her uncover the dusty material obscuring a grime covered fossil bone. Mindara gently brushed the dirt off the object and said that it looked very much like the lower jaw of a reptile – but with a strangely anthropoidal, an ape-like appearance. It was, she said, oddly short and rather gracile; finely shaped, as though highly evolved.

She turned out to be right.

The fossil bone was placed on a soft cloth and gently passed around the team but Mindara was already, very carefully, uncovering more bones with her fine brush. Team members pressed around her and set about clearing away more debris. After two hours of painstaking digging, they were able to extract part of a skull. It looked as big as that of a modern human's. Eleri and the other biologists thought it looked reptilian but totally unlike anything any of them had ever seen, either on Oceanus – or in records from Earth.

But Hermington felt that parts of it reminded him of hominid skulls he'd seen in collections from old Earth; hominids being the ancient predecessors of modern humans. There were gasps and murmerings of agreement.

The whole team congratulated Mindara on her find; something she took with characteristic humility. After that the team's discoveries continued. Very close to the skull their hungry, but careful, hands found small piles of spiky, tubercle like, pieces of fossilised bone, which no-one could see how to match with the first find. They were clearly not part of the skull. Even more astonishing was Hermington's next remark. With nervous hands he measured the skull with dividers and confirmed that it was definitely a little larger than that of a modern human. As it had broken around its longitudinal circumference, from the lower jaw to crown, the team were instantly able to see inside the brain case. Hermington did another quick measurement and announced excitedly that it might just indicate a brain volume comparable, maybe even larger, than in modern humans. A bigger shock followed. Marks on the interior surface of the cranium showed all the signs of a human, or cetacean type of brain having once occupied it.

Unfortunately, the facial bones were in a bad state of preservation but suggested a very pronounced snout, a little like that of some types of short snouted dog. Not so humanoid, then. Sung backed up Eleri, emphasising its resemblance to a reptile. Even so, Eleri, Morgath and Hermington suggested that if it was reptilian then the snout, though protruding, seemed more foreshortened than in any known living reptile, whether on Oceanus, or the Earth. She felt there were some vague similarities to that of Argaran lizards; the type commonly found on the continent. Of even greater significance was that the creature's eye sockets were close to the mid-line; they were forward facing, like that of primates.

The team paused for a moment and gazed at each-other with huge smiles. There were whoops of jubilation. Sung and Hermington danced a little jig of their own. Morgath threw her big floppy hat into the air. Arbinius and Rasmissen stood grinning and laughing wildly. Eleri turned to Mike and grabbed him around his waist, throwing her head back and chortling like a mad thing. Mike winced as she clasped him tightly to her but, as he began to realise, for himself, the significance of all this, he too whooped for joy. Grabbing her hands, he swung the two of them around and around until they almost fell with the giddiness. But then Sung, Hermington and Chen bodily lifted Mindara and triumphantly sat her on their shoulders, whilst she shrieked with the glee and headiness of it all.

'Not a one thing like this has ever been a found on this world,' shouted Hermington.

After a few minutes the excitement began to die down as the whole group got into a huddle and began to animatedly discuss the finds. All, except, that is, Johann

Erbbius. He wandered off to eat some sort of snack and just sat there looking mystified.

****

Garmin Brundleton plonked himself heavily onto a stool on the Antarctica's engineering deck, watching two of the ship's engineers working. One, a male, stood over a wide glass desk with a holographic display hovering over it. He wore a communication ear bud and spoke periodically, almost sub-vocally, to the hyper-comp. To a non-specialist the display before him would have appeared as a flat, smooth, panel showing a mind numbingly complex array of visual displays, patterns shifting and changing almost every second. A second engineer, a woman, stood next to a wall screen display holding a palm sized device at which she spoke, very quietly, every few seconds. The patterns on the two displays, on the desk and the wall, eventually coincided with each-other.

Tabrowska, the male engineer, turned to Brundleton and said, 'It looks like part of the AI is returning to us – finally. I just don't know if the virtual walk you did yesterday, inside the hupercomp brain, made much of a difference. I'm sorry.'

'So am I,' said Brundleton, 'I couldn't see how the Virtual Qubit blocks had changed but it looks like you two have cracked it. My congrat's, gentilhomms. I don't think my presence here was needed after all.' He wore a generous and patient look on his chunky face.

The female operative turned to her colleague. 'We're ready now,' she said, an expression of eagerness on her face.

'Okay, Karlson. Put it through,' said Tabrowska.

He touched his earpiece, peered at the desk display and a loud hum issued from the various screens and control panels. Then, both the desk displays, and the wall screen lit up simultaneously, with a soft golden glow. 'I'm getting the virtual personality coming through,' said Tabrowska, seconds before a vibrant young, male, baritone, voice could be heard throughout the chamber.

'I am sorry, but I think I have been ... away,' the hyper-comp voice said, sounding perplexed, 'I hope that nothing untoward has happened in my absence.'

'No, nothing that need concern you now,' said Karlson. 'We just need you to show us anything in your memory banks which might indicate why your systems went down. We need to know if an operative on this ship did anything to interfere with your functioning.'

'Thank you Doctoro Karlson,' said the comp voice, 'I am retrieving all data packets for the period leading up to the 15 nanoseconds prior to my blackout, when my memory disappeared. The data-plex is still broken but I am attempting to rebuild 200 pico-byte bursts, a billion at a time. Please stand by. Data will stream to your wall display within 4 seconds, 3 seconds, 2 ...'

Brundleton watched, then looked away with a look of dismay unseen by the others, as streams, then seemingly, rivers of numbers and flows of coding ran across the wall opposite him, until a particular array paused and held its place for a few seconds. The comp then stopped the flows and put a brilliant red tag mark on the array. Tabrowska muttered something into his earpiece mic.

*

Ten minutes after the "return to life" of the mainframe and whilst the crew in the "recovery unit" still celebrated, Garmin Brundleton, left behind the congratulatory talk and the pats on the back. He wandered along the largely empty corridors leading from the ship's comp chamber, appearing as though searching for someone.

Then he spotted the young woman standing at the junction of two corridors, about 40 metres from the control centre, apprehension plastering her face. It was Pamela Heracleonn. A technician appeared around the corner further down the corridor. He passed Heracleonn and paid no attention to her, or to Brundleton. He obviously hadn't yet heard they were looking for her.

Brundleton neared Heracleonn and whispered to her, 'The machine flagged up molecules from your skin, on a control surface. Seems it can recognise you from analysis of your protein molecules. You must have had them on your gloves. Hard luck, Pam. They're onto you.'

Heracleon stared wildly at him, 'So what do I do now? Where do I go?'

'Well, I suppose you can't go to The Monsoon,' he said, with an unconcerned voice, 'and you can't stay here. You'd better make yourself scarce, hadn't you? If they catch you, they'll probably take you over to The Monsoon. The Antarctica doesn't have a brig, does it? If you end up on my ship, I can't say I'd be able to stop my friends from … well, let's say, exercising their options, in the interests of "the cause". We have our own operation under way, and we can't have that jeopardised, can we?'

'Thanks very much, *Mister* Engineer,' she hissed at him, 'I don't reckon I've got much info that would make any difference to you, anyway. And the Navy don't use torture, does it? Besides, my mouth can stay shut, any time. Could yours?' She searched his eyes. They were cold and unyielding.

'Well, maybe so,' he said, 'I'm just giving you due warning, that's all. You'd better think of something. And, in case you happened to think of admitting all to Tenak, in hope of protection, I might have to deal with you, here and now.' He reached into his tunic jacket and pulled out the tip of a stun gun butt. It was set on "Extreme". He continued, 'I could say I had to do it. You were trying to escape. I'd rather not, of course. It might put me in the spotlight too much.'

'You're all heart, you feg-pisser,' Heracleon spat.

'Now, what did you expect, Pamela?' he returned. 'You should have done a better job. Cleaned up after you. And, by the way, I can't be seen with you again.'

With that, Brundleton walked briskly away. There were muted voices from further down the corridor. Heracleonn paused for a second, then acted, suddenly and explosively. Racing off along another corridor she heaved open a hatch door leading to a chamber containing a ladder. She climbed up it, as though her pants were on fire, and as she did so she felt the tell-tale signs of gravity leaving her body and the feeling of "weightlessness" taking over. She was proceeding down the emergency access tube of a spoke which led from the ship's rotating torus to the hub cylinder of the ship, where microgravity reigned. As she neared the bottom, she paused near the hatch door, straining to listen for voices the other side.

Chapter 32

BETRAYALS

By the seventh day after Muggredge's team had landed on Simurgh, they had uncovered the flattened remains of a skeleton, to go with the skull parts they'd found – and much more: two other similar skeletons. Each had the remains of arms and legs, attached to a vertebral column, in approximately the same positions as found in humans. The vertebral columns were not exactly as found in humans and – there were traces of a tail of some sort. Eleri, Sung and Morgath claimed that these creatures seemed bipedal, as judged from the layout of the bones. The team's excitement became palpable as they scraped away at the fragmented rock material covering the remains. Unfortunately, one of the skeletons was missing a skull and in the other only the upper and lower jaws were present, together with a few facial bones. More of the tiny pieces of the mysterious tubercles were also found nearby.

The group had tried to determine the height of the creatures, when alive, using the better-preserved skeleton, and estimated it, very roughly, to be around 2.8 metres. When looking at the remains everyone agreed they had the uncanny feeling that they were looking at some kind of humanoid skeleton; almost like looking in a distorted mirror, but it was unmistakeable and disconcerting. The size and shape of the skulls, the slightly odd vertebral column and the strange facial bones marked them as definitely non-human – and there was one other very curious feature. Each skeleton showed unmistakeable remains of a *second* pair of upper body limbs, together with their associated "shoulder" girdle bones.

The biologists said they felt this might have been regular features of this species, rather than any sort of physical mutation limited to these individuals – but there was no way they could be sure. The position of the uppermost arms was approximately equal to the position in humans, but the second, lower pair were situated about one third of the way down the torso and were much smaller than the upper limbs. The bottom third of the lower limbs were damaged in the specimens, so no conclusions there, suffice that they indicated bipedalism, as the team originally thought.

Eleri felt that the bones found next to the backbone, from which the lower arms projected, should be called "support bones", rather than "shoulder girdles". The supporting structure was only complete in two of the skeletons. Sung pointed out that Argaran lizards had three pairs of limbs, as did most reptiles on this planet. But the creatures they'd found here were very different to those and their kin. Despite the strong feeling that these fossils were of creatures who walked upright, Eleri pointed out that this remained to be proved.

And the excitement wasn't restricted to the skeletons. All three bodies had been found lying next to one-other, all lying on their left side, in what almost seemed to be some sort of posed position. And, as if this wasn't sufficient, when the team removed more loose rock they found that the remains were all lying within a rectangular framework of limestone pebbles, all roughly the same size. It looked overwhelmingly like an enclosure, marked out deliberately and not the result of some sort of natural process. The pebbles, apparently ignous rock, had withstood the pressure of the shale and mudstone sediment that had covered the site after the creatures had died.

To cap it all, the end of the day brought what was probably the biggest shock of all; a veritable climax of intellectual joy. They made a discovery they all felt would send shockwaves around the entire planet – and out *as far as the Home System*. Lying between two of the fossil skeletons they uncovered fragments of some objects which, though completely flattened, blackened and fragile with corrosion, suggested such things as the team almost refused to believe were real. It caused most of them to be rebel against returning to the boat for the night. Eventually a group of three pried themselves away to hurry off to the ship, returning, bubbling with excitement, as they carried three medium size arc lamps. In their excitement they didn't even seem to notice the exertion of the journey. Lew had apparently warned against staying out all night, for safety reasons but he could see how animated they were and, after all, they did seem to have made momentous discoveries.

Halfway through the night, blacker than pitch outside the lamplights, they finally relented and returned to the safety of the Agamemnon, leaving the lamps. But none could sleep, the sheer magnitude of their discoveries starting to really sink in, for the strange objects they'd found alongside the skeletons, were not natural objects at all. They were long, thin, metal poles, undoubtedly the product of metallurgists! They might even have been some sort of grave goods or weapons, though none of this could yet be proved.

'They look like things you'd use for digging,' said Eleri as they all sat around the passenger lounge illuminated by wall lights dimmed to a more relaxing half power. Lew sat with them, a look of wonder on his face too.

'No. I think they are yet weapons, probably symbolic such,' said Daniellsa.

'Tis surely too early to tell whether they be tools or weapons, symbolic or otherwise?' said Rubia. 'True, they might be religious or practical. Who can know? Surely yet, the main point is that they are artefacts. Manufacts! Who would have thought? Who would believe it possible? T'will make our names in the world of science on this world, methinks.'

'Praps,' said Eleri, brightly, 'but this find might be the biggest discovery ever made by humanity. So, we must yet be super so careful. I carnt stress that enough. We need to find a way to take this whole thing back to the mainland, soon as possly. Can we do that, Lew?'

'We might have to,' said the pilot. 'If this place is hit by a storm it could wreck the site. But it depends on the practicalities of removing the remains, and the tools you mentioned – and getting them aboard. I reckon it's probably not real practical, at this point, to remove the rectangular frame thing you mentioned. Least, not intact. So, we might have to come back for it.'

'Now you say it, I am reminded I might yet know what the framework is,' said Chen, his face brimming with excitement. They all huddled on seats near to each-other, perched on their edges. The atmosphere in the cabin became hushed. Mike felt it was a magical moment. He and Eleri clung to one another. Mike happened to glance at Erbbius, who sat at the very back of the cabin, and appeared to be taking no interest in the discussion. And yet, Mike felt that this was a visual lie. Somehow, he could tell that his colleague was surrepticiously listening intensely to every word. How odd.

'Tis yet a tomb. A stompry great tombie!' said Sung. 'Oh, sorry for my language.'

'No need to apologise,' said Mindara, her face a picture of joy. She reminded Mike of a small child who'd been given the best toy they had ever known. And why not? She and the rest of the team had earned the right. Mindara was now saying, 'but you are frabbing right Kenning. Oh, now I'm doing it! So sorry. But he is right. Tis surely a tomb, or praps what is left of one? The vertical dimensions of the thing must have yet been squashed right down by the weight of sediment laid upon, long after the beings were buried.'

"*Beings*"? wondered Mike. *Yes. Beings.* She'd said it. Virtually everyone else must have caught Mindara's use of that word and suddenly held onto it for there was another hushed silence, as all contemplated the moment.

Sung injected a note of caution, 'Let us not be skempering too far ahead,' he said, 'since the real meaning of this discovery has such to be laid bare, whence others have the chance to examine it.'

'So,' said Mike, 'I guess that we can't be sure when these beings lived – because you guys say you can't be sure how old the rocks are. That right?' That seemed to have got 'em, thought Mike.

'Hermington rose to the challenge.

'Obvious – so carnt be sure,' said Danile, 'without the right dating equipmento, but a few of us have discussed it …' He paused, looking for support.

'If the other signs – the stratigraphy and the small amount yet of other fossil life we have found,' said Morgath, 'then I wouldst say, could be around seven to ten millions of years – Oceanus years.'

'More work to be done still,' said Danile, 'but yes, I do believe Daniellsa is right. Other fossils in the area, being bones of small mammal type animals and others, do indicate such an date. But there is yet another thing we need to do.'

Most of the team looked to him expectantly. He continued, 'We do need to check, I mean, search, the strata above the carbon layer. Find out if there are other fossils of these beings, or similar such. If there are any, it mayst means that the carbon layer "event" was not so big after all. If they are absent then could mean the carbon event didst wipe them out.'

Arbinius, the young, newest team member, piped up at this point, 'I agree, for the event could be interpreted as being as such, just local to this area. But there is another important point from what you say, Danile. Tis that, even tho' we now know what we are looking for better, there is a cramming great lot of rock to search, just in this area. We could be here many, many weeks.'

'That ain't possible,' injected Lew, standing near the flight deck. 'cos the Agamemnon hasn't got the resources, unless she gets regular supplies from the mother ship. And I, for one, can't afford that time frame, and I don't think even the Admiral would go that far.'

Mike nodded sagely.

'We will yet continue to try to find more of these beings or creatures for as long as we have here,' said Sung.

'And then, we shall have to talk to the Admiral about what should be best from then on,' said Eleri.

The group's discussions continued long into what remained of the night.

Lew had to resort to some pressure, seeming as though he was some sort of parent figure to them all, to get the team members to take some rest. They gradually drifted off, yawning, to their respective bed cubicles in what had once been the Agamemnon's conference room. Mike and Eleri retired to the aftmost section of the chamber and fell into the first double bed compartment which presented itself.

Lying in the double bed with Eleri, Mike could hear other team members standing outside their own booths, still talking about the events of the day and he became acutely aware of the need to keepany "romantic" activity to a minimum, as he still valued his privacy and Eleri's. However, there was little chance of such activity, anyway. They were far too tired but still, Mike found he couldn't sleep. He too was immensely excited, as he knew El was, but, from the sound of her heavy breathing he reckoned she'd gone straight to sleep. In the blackness of the night his mind wandered everywhere, running over and over the day's activities and the momentous discoveries. He pondered the fact that the tools, or weapon things found with the skeletons, meant that the beings had been advanced and were able to shape the world around them, like humans had on Earth. What sort of lives had these beings led? What was this world like in their time? Had their species been extinguished before they had developed advanced tek?

The tomb, if that what it was, also meant that they must have developed a cultural existence. All these things could mean one thing – sentience. In a flash of insight, of a type often encountered in the middle of the darkest hours, he realised how foolish had been his remarks to Tenak the day they arrived on this world. He'd suggested there'd never been anything indicating sentient life on Oceanus. But he hadn't known then. *No-one had. Because of the discoveries today, he and Eleri were now part of this world's history, like the rest of the team and The Monsoon.*

He felt almost shocked to think that this discovery changed everything in current cosmological philosophy. Intelligence and sentience could be proven to have arisen independently, on two separate worlds, over a hundred light years apart. The age-old conundrum had been solved ... provided the Oceanus government didn't mess up this find. That couldn't happen, surely, he thought? It would be criminal.

Also, if sentience existed on two quite separate worlds, then it increased the chances of it existing in many other places too. Although basic forms of life had been found on two other worlds besides Earth, it had been thought that intelligent, sentient life was vanishingly improbable, there being only one exemplar. That is, if you could call humans truly intelligent, thought Mike cynically, and with only partial amusement. The point was, that history had been well and truly made, here, today, in this strange, remote, place.

Mike's mind continued to wander. The "books" would need to be rewritten. No, he corrected himself. Changed, not rewritten. It was a media myth, mere hype, that when any unexpected discovery was made in science, then the "books", whatever that meant, "had to be rewritten". Science actually progressed by way of constantly building on the work of others, adding to the whole sum of knowledge; amending, correcting and refining. Even so, some discoveries were so epochal they were called "quantum leaps" but they were still built on what went before. He felt that the knowledge and ideas flowing from the discoveries made here, this day, must surely fall within that ambit.

Had this newly found species lived on the mainland too? He knew that Simurgh had been a separate land mass for more than 25 million years. So, what had happened to these beings, here on this island? Then, he thought about the carbonised layer and had no doubt he knew the answer. Surely, none of the others had any illusions about that, either? Not now. He lay awake for an unknown time, mulling over events, before exhaustion eventually allowed him to drift off.

He could have no idea at that point where these discoveries would eventually lead him and Eleri.

**

The next day the team consolidated the discovery of the "burial chamber", if that's what is was, taking photographs and vid films, typing - and handwriting - voluminous notes and carrying out a multitude of measurements at the site. More discussions took place in the morning shade of the small cliff. Lew had already contacted Muggredge via the boat's E- band communicators, specially fixed up for the Professier, and the team was able to talk to him about the finds.

Muggredge too, was overwhelmed by the news and gushed with congratulations but he had been very explicit that they should leave the skeletons and artefacts *in situ*. Another, larger expedition, which would include professional conservators, would have to go out to study the site, removing it slowly and carefully. Aside from concern about the preservation of the site he also wanted a wider set of opinions, expressed by people who could see the actual site – as it was now. Lew said he had done some calculations and felt he could try to remove most of the site onto the landing boat, whole, but Muggredge stuck to his decision.

During their breaks the team regularly returned to this subject and it was clear that most people felt the Professier's orders too restrictive. But Muggredge was protecting them. There was a risk of government anger and consequential loss of jobs if they countermanded standard procedure. And so, when they had finished their work the team decided to put all the notes, data logs and camera equipment into a section of the on-site cabinet, before leaving for the boat. That evening many of them returned to the boat with heavy hearts, including Mike and Eleri. The continuation of their work here would likely be down to others.

***

The next day, on board the Agamemnon, virtually all the team decided to take a break for the morning. Lew suggested it first, advising that it would be a good chance to recover from their exertions, rest, and set back to work later in the day, fresh. The ship's supplies would last; no storms were forecast and, after all, the finds weren't going anywhere.

But after an hour or so, Rubia, Daniellsa, Chen and Sung said they wanted to get back to the site to do more sifting of rubble and some preliminary surveying: try to work out the best places to continue digging. They'd only be a few hours, they said, and, in the meantime, the remainder of the group decided they would work on the problem of how best to preserve the site until the next team could get out there. That team might not have a landing boat to hand and the weather could be harsh here. Something had to be done – without disturbing the finds, as per Muggredge's orders.

They felt that the storage bin dropped by Lew might not hold everything. Erbbius surprised everyone by declaring that he was bored with hanging around at the landing site and was happy to accompany the small group back to the rock shelf. Mike noticed, however, that he did not offer to help the others to actually sift rubble. No matter, the team members returning to the site said they didn't mind him tagging along.

And so it was, that five of the group set out for the rock shelf, all toting rucksacks with water and personal provisions. Sung took point with a stun rifle and Lew patiently watched his monitor as they started on their way. Eleri said that it was a wonder he could see anyone walking along the route for any more than a few minutes, because they'd be hidden by the hillocky terrain for long periods. Lew nodded and agreed he couldn't. He was only really able to keep an eye on the situation closest to the landing site. After that, they were effectively on their own. But he could at least keep an eye open for any obvious dangers. Everyone agreed the infamous Macrotargs, whom no-one had seen, no longer seemed to be one of those and dozens of journeys had already been made back and forth without any incident. Lew also said he trusted Sung anyway, as leader of the group, to keep an eye out for everyone's safety, out there. Even so, he said, he'd continue to keep watch.

**

After a hard slog reaching the rock shelf, Sung and the others spent around three hours surveying, until three of them decided the Ra-shine was too unbearably hot that day and they called a halt. Though Erbbius really had taken a small part in the rubble sifting for an hour or so he had eventually drifted away, going off somewhere. Rubia, however, didn't seem to notice the heat and tarried at the far end of the shelf until Daniellsa virtually had to drag her away. Rubia didn't seem to appreciate that. Erbbius reappeared and wandered along with them for a while.

The return journey was largely routine, but Rubia continued to dawdle, examining small outcroppings of rock at different points along the way, pulling a magnifying glass from her large backpack and peering at the lumps of rock she picked up.

At one point the rest of the group sat down on wide, grey, slabs of rock and drank deeply of their water bottles, while Mindara continued her "work".

'Do you mind yet staying with Rubia?' said Sung to Morgath.

'Yet you wouldst think *she* was a geolrist. She be getting onto my nerve-edges,' said Daniellsa, 'but I shall, if you so wish.'

'She is getting on my nerves too,' said Chen.

'No, tis okay,' said Sung, 'tis no great deal. She is just enthusiastico. I shall volunteer to stay with her if you two want to continue. I do believe Mer Erbbius has already walked ahead of us.'

Morgath and Chen agreed and started to walk on while Sung sat near Rubbia, chatting with her while she concentrated on her activities. He saw the others disappear over the next rise and suddenly remembered that he was the only one with a rifle.

'I am sorry Rubbia,' he said, 'but yet I forgot to give the rifle to Chen, for I know Danry will not agree to use it. But we need mayst need the gun too.'

Rubia smiled and said, 'Tis alrightly, Kenye. You know, there really is no need for those gun things, is there? But if you feel happiest, I suggest you get ahead and give them the gun. I will be following on, soonest.'

'You will be safe? You are yet sure?'

'Yes, manry. Definite like. There is no danger out here – and I am, I think, managing the heat yet better than you, am I not? Listen, some of these rocks along the way could be of importance to the team, I think. I shall take some photos and be coming after you all. Do not worry so.' She gave him a sweet, innocent look, then said, 'Little Mindara is yet a big giril now. She has no need of Mer Sung's protection.'

Sung rolled his eyes, nodded and set off, very slowly, after the others. Mindara kept looking at a rock but, out of the corner of her eye, watched him disappear over the hill ahead. Then she turned and speedily moved off back in the direction of the rock shelf site.

Sung caught up to his colleagues after a few minutes and they walked onwards for a kilometre or two but slowed regularly, to look back to see if Mindara was on her way. Sung, worriedly suggested they stop and wait.

'Praps we should go back,' he said.

'She shall not yet appreciate that,' said Morgath, wiping the sweat from her neck and face. 'List, Kenye. She is right. She can yet look after herself. Let her come back in her own time.'

'I am not so sure,' said Chen, 'I am concern-ed she might become lost. This whole area is broken up bad. Though we have worn a pathway of sorts, tis easy to lose yourself. I have nearly done so.'

'Supposing you're right,' said Sung, 'but so is Danry.'

Suddenly Erbbius appeared from up ahead and wandered up to them. His next words made it clear he'd been close enough to hear their discussion. 'Look, it's obvious none of you want to go back for her,' he said, 'so, I'll tell you what. I'll go back. Chivy her up a bit. It's getting toward midday. Even the great Mindara might get over-exposed. And I've now got a good idea of the terrain here. Navy training comes in handy sometimes.'

'There is no need to cause her pressure Mer Engineer,' said Morgath, 'but t'would be good if you just kept an eye open for her. Thank you, Lieutenant.'

'Yeah, that's fine. See you soon,' said Erbbius and waved them to carry on while he turned back along the rough track.

Once out of sight of the others he wasn't able to see Mindara either, as she walked up and down the various hillocks on her way back toward the dig site. But he appeared to pay no attention to the issue anyway, as he hurried over the rough ground, diverging widely away from the route by which they had come, striking diagonally out over the countryside, toward the large hill at the furthest, northernmost limit of the rock shelf itself.

**

Rubia had reached the rock shelf and, hurrying to the site of the main finds, she quickly examined the area where the skeletons were lying, hidden below a securely pegged tarpaulin hung over them. Muggredge had insisted they should not be moved, so she didn't need to get into the storage bins. She carefully picked up some of the creature's tool- weapons, lying next to the skeletons and, placing them in several, large, pieces of clean cloth, she loaded them gently into her rucksack. She glanced around nervously as she did so, then shouldering the rucksack, started to wander back toward the route "home", when she heard the disturbing sound of moving rocks. A miniature avalanche of rocks slithered down the loose scree slope above the rock ledge the team had been working on.

With a look of alarm, she moved away from the small cliff above the shelf, as a small flow of pebbly material skidded down and over its edge, just a few metres away. Frowning deeply, she positioned herself so she could see further up the slope, and saw the figure of a person, a dark silhouette, against the bright sky, far above. A deeply troubled look spread over her face as she squinted against the light and attempted to follow the figure as it walked further up, far above the scree, disappearing over the brow of the hill.

**

Erbbius, hefting his large rucksack on his back, climbed higher, puffing heavily as he ascended the increasingly steep slope. He stopped and removed from his sack a black object the size of a human palm, pressed several buttons on it, which made it bleep twice. He then scooped out quantities of rubble from the loose ground of the slope, just above the scree, and buried the black object inside the hole he'd made. The engineer wandered across the top limit of the wide scree slope, then began to descend, stepping carefully onto the treacherous material itself. As he did so he buried six similar objects, laying them out separately in a kind of zig-zag pattern. After burial each device bleeped loudly in the still, clear air, and he continued to walk and scramble along the ridge, more than 300 metres above the rock shelf – where, below, Mindara was watching.

Having buried the last device, he set off down the slope, sometimes slipping over the loose rocks, sending pebbles and stones downwards in dusty rivulets. He tried to move along the slope laterally to get to the less slippery grassy areas, or what passed for grass on this world, a long way beyond the main scree area, furthest away from the landing boat site.

**

Mindara cautiously made her way up the slope toward the figure, making sure she kept well out of sight amongst the shoulder height "Antiopus" bushes which covered large parts of the lower slope. She moved toward the more stable part of the hillside, toward the far end of the rock cutting, as that's where the mysterious figure seemed to be headed. She watched him bury some sort of device in the ground, high up. She kept climbing, creeping closer, hardly daring to breath and making small, careful movements, staying behind the shelter of plants.

Then – she recognised him. It was Johann Erbbius. She sucked in her breath with surprise. Now no more than 20 metres from him she saw him burying another strange object. He started to move directly toward where she hid. Her eyes widening with alarm, she ducked and kept her eyes on the ground. Erbbius descended, stumblingly, toward the flatter area where she did, and, travelling too fast, he stumbled, almost falling into the bush – and bumped straight into her. Each of them leaped backwards with surprise.

'You! What are you doing out here?' shouted Erbbius, his features contorting with shock and anger, 'I thought you'd got lost back there. But I should have guessed you'd be creeping about over here.'

'I might ask you the same thing, sirra,' she said, spluttering.

'Oh, why don't you people talk plain Anglo-Span? You're not supposed to be here, Mindara. Have you been spying on me?' His manner suddenly became aggressive.

'No,' she said. 'Why? Were *you* doing something you shouldnar?'

'Listen, I haven't got time for this. I've got to get out of this area quick-like. I'll ask you again. Were you spying on me? What did you see? Don't look at me like that. Tell me!'

'There is no need to be aggressive Mer Erbbius. I was just… trying to uncover more of the tomb. That is all. Now, praps you would tell me what you were burying up here, for I did see you, Mer Erbbius.' Mindara pointed up the scree slope and as she did so Erbbius lunged toward her. She saw him just in time and nimbly dodged him, yelped, then turned and raced, sometimes stumbling, out of the bushes and onto the adjacent grassy knoll, where she would be less impeded by the antiopus growth.

'What in oceans is the matter with you, Johann?' she shouted after her, 'so tell me. There is no need of that behaviour. You are yet starting to scarify me. Just stop now, please.'

Erbbius caught up with her and lunged at her again. Again, he missed.

'You weren't meant to see any of this,' he said. 'Why didn't you just stay down on the shelf, or do us all a favour and get lost on the way back?' He paused, then added, 'But, I must say, your decision to tarry back there did me a favour after all. I was wondering when I'd get the opportunity to distribute the sonic charges without the whole team seeing me. Your antics gave me an excuse to come back here. So, if it's just you who's seen me it doesn't really matter much.' A sly and sinister smile played on his lips. Mindara's eyed widened even further, a look of horror on her face.

'What ist sonic charge, Johann? List, I didnar see anything,' she said, flushing red. 'Please believe me. Look, young manry, you can tell me what so troubles you. Why do we not both go back to the ship? We can say nothing happened. I should not be here. You should not be here. Let us just keep this secret together.'

Erbbius suddenly stopped and looked grave. 'It's not as easy as that, Mindara. I have to destroy this site. Got to. That's why I've set the sonic charges. After that *you* won't be able to keep it a secret. That's why I have to do something about you.'

Mindara started backing away, as she said, 'What have you done Johann? What do you mean, "destroy" the site? Why? Be telling me.'

Erbbius stared malevolently at her and started, slowly, to advance again.

'I have to get rid of the evidence you've found – about the creature-beings that lived here. I heard you all talking about it. It's too important. Won't do, Mindara. It's all got to go – and so have you.' He started to move quickly again.

'I am trained in Mykrana-tak, manry,' she said. 'Tis the Bhumi-Devi martial art. I shall warn you.' She put up her hands in a defensive posture.

The engineer laughed, a sneer spreading over his features, 'I don't think so. A podgy little thing like you. When did you last do any training? Well, just in case, I think this ought to do the trick.' He swung the sack off his back and pulled out a thick, heavy wrench longer than his forearm.

'I'm afraid I've got to dispose of you,' he said, 'but, I might even enjoy this. I didn't think I would, but I will.'

Mindara's eyes stood on stalks, as she said, breathing heavily, 'List manry. No need of this, like I said yet. Besides … what would – how would you explain it? I mean, what say you to the others?'

'I never saw you, did I? You don't get it, do you? This whole hillside's going to slide onto your precious rock shelf very soon. I'll put you body down there. It'll be covered by tons of rock and stuff. If they ever bother to get you out, they won't be able to work out how you died, for all the damage done. There might be some chance *on Earth*, maybe, but on this crazy planet, I doubt it. There'll be no evidence. Even the charges are made of a super-gel, so what's left of them, after they blow, will dissolve – and leak away. It's perfect – well nearly. You're the shit in the ointment now.'

He started to advance again, wielding his wrench, like a club.

Moving backwards Rubia suddenly shouted out, shrieking at the top of her voice, calling for help from Sung, Chen, Morgath. The extreme noise made Erbbius flinch and halt momentarily.

When she stopped for breath he chuckled and said, 'They've gone and left you Mindara. They didn't want to come after you, did they? Not surprised. You're on your own. Look, why not let me do it? Get it over with? I'll make it quick and painless. I promise.'

Rubia turned and started to run. Erbbius ran after her but, to his surprise, she was extremely fast – and nimble. She shouted out again, for Sung, Mike, Eleri, anyone.

Still managing to evade his charges at her, she kept talking to him. With tremors in her voice, she shouted, 'Mer Erbbius. I still don't understand why you yet think you have to do this. If you stop this, we can go back and I wil not say anything. I do promise.'

'I've got to do this. Be reasonable. Hell, you people aren't reasonable are you. That's why we have to make sure you don't leave this planet, cos this world will die when the star blows. And it will, you know. We can take advantage of that back home. All the confusion. Recriminations. Mass riots. City States renouncing the Alliance. The embarrassment for the Allied Government. Could even bring 'em down. It's a start you see. Just a start. Come here, now, good girl.' With that he started to advance again, driving her further and further along the grassy knoll, away from the rock shelf and away from the direction of the ship.

Rubia turned and, with a nerve wracked guttural shout, she bent, grabbed a handful of medium size rocks from the ground, then flung them at her attacker. He tried to dodge but Rubia's aim and timing was good. The missiles hit him on his neck and stomach, and he yelped with pain. That made him pause for a moment and she took the opportunity to run again. But where? She could see that the land this side of the shelf was petering out toward the high sea cliff. The dry ground along the edge was pitted and riven with cracks. The scientist soon found herself standing within a metre of the precipice.

She stared out at the ocean with a suddenly faraway look in her eyes as if she could see some inevitable fate, some cruel destiny. A few tears formed and began to run down her cheeks. She wiped them away completely before turning again, to face Erbbius, and saw him walking briskly toward her, blocking the route back to the ship. The wrench was held high. She backed away and seeing a couple of large rocks on the dry soil scooped them up. Erbbius paused.

'There's no point,' he said.

'Oh yes there is,' she said and hurled one at him. He successfully dodged it but in doing so walked straight into the next one. It hit his right leg, just below the knee, making a cracking sound. He yelped again and dropped the wrench. Rubia saw her chance and valiantly ran for the narrow gap between Erbbius and the cliff edge. As she drew level with him Erbbius recovered his composure enough to lunge sideways at her, throwing out his right hand, the ends of his chunky fingers jabbing for her midriff. She saw it and batted his arm out of the way with her own right forearm, but the momentum imparted by striking his hard, sinewy, limb threw her off balance, propelling her toward the cliff edge.

She gasped but her nimbleness saved her again as she began to recover her balance whilst still moving forward. But she'd been forced too close to the edge, her face registering sheer horror, as one of her feet swung over the edge, hanging in mid air. Then a chunk of ground half a metre wide broke under her other foot. The slab went straight down the cliff and took her with it.

She made no sound as she went but Erbbius heard a loud crash when the chunk of rock hit the bottom, over 20 metres below. Erbbius stumbled away from the treacherous edge and didn't even risk looking over it at her broken body. 'Well, that's worked out even better than I thought,' he said to himself, breathing heavily.

The look of satisfaction on his face turned immediately to one of horror as he heard the sonic charges go off above. When he'd set the timers, he had not expected to bump into anyone else from the team. The six charges made only muted thudding noises, the sound he heard being produced by shifting rock, rather than any explosions. The devices transmitted blasts of high intensity infra-sound down through the ground, destabilising the loose rock. Hardly anything could be seen happening above ground when they first blew.

Within a few seconds Erbbius heard a much louder noise, an overwhelming rumble, as the scree slope shook and shivered like an enormous, terrified beast. Looking up with alarm he raced back the way he'd come. Reaching the safety of the far end of the scree slope, nearest the highest part of the cliff, he found some bushes and hid behind them. His face betrayed relief.

If he felt any relief it was short lived.

****

At the landing site, Lew, like some other team members, was lying on a rough cloth laid out on the sandy soil, in the pleasant shade of the Agamemnon. Mike and Eleri sat in the cool afforded by the inside of the ship.

His wristcom bleeped and, with a sigh Lew rose and climbed the steps into the landing boat. Mike, keeping himself shielded from the wide openness of the broad hilltop, looked up.

'Problems?' he asked the pilot.

'Nah. I asked the unit to remind me to take a look at the monitor occasionally,' said Lew, as he stepped up, through the door, onto the raised level of the flight deck.

Someone outside shouted, 'Here they are. They are yet back.'

Lew, Mike and Eleri went to the hatch and saw a group of figures emerging from the rocky, scrubby, land beyond the compound. They were soon unlocking the gate in the protective fence and making for the landing boat.

But there were only three of them.

Eleri dived past Mike and went to greet them.

'Where still is Mindara?' she said.

Sung told her what had happened.

'But you left her out there – on her own?' Eleri sounded angry.

'No,' said Sung, 'Mer Erbbius went back for her.'

'But you're the one with the stun rifle,' said Lew, as he and Mike joined them.

'Mer Erbbius said all was okay. He wouldst look out for her. They shouldnar be far behind.'

'Man, I thought you were the one in charge of this expedition,' said Lew, 'not my … fine colleague Erbbius.'

Sung held his hands up in a resigned gesture and wiped the sweat from his brow. Chen and Morgath reached the boat just behind him and stood in silence.

'Let's hope they're not far behind,' said Mike.

Sung and the others went to the cool water canister Lew had set up in the shade of the ship and slaked their thirst. Then they all waited – in silence. After nearly 30 minutes, Lew went over into the ship and came out with a stun rifle.

'Okay, I'm going to look for them,' he said, 'so, anyone want to come with me? Or I''m happy to go alone.'

Eleri started to say something, when a deep throated rumble hit them all. It came from the direction of the coast. At the same time, they could hear a shrill bleeping noise from inside the landing boat. The noise from the coast rose to a terrifying roar and in the distance a pall of white and grey dust started to rise high into the air. The event could be even be felt through the ground, like a distant quake. It made them all gape with horror.

'That dust must be coming from the rock shelf,' shouted Mike.

'Must be the scree slope,' said Hermington.

Lew had got back on the ship in seconds, racing to the monitors on the flight deck. Sensors continued to trill, but Lew could see only thick dust when he looked at his screens.

Sung and Hermington were starting to make their way toward the gate in the fence but Mike shouted at them, 'Wait up guys. Whoa! We'll go see what happened but listen guys, we need to take provisions and stuff. And stun rifles.'

'And have a plan,' shouted Lew, from the ship's hatchway.

***

North of the rock shelf, Johann Erbbius emerged the bushes, covered by white dust. He still held his hands to his ears, even though the landslide had abated. He shook his head and looked as if he was in pain, screwing up his eyes every few seconds. Dust clouds surrounded him and rose high above, in the warm, still, air. He coughed and spat the dust out of his mouth.

Moaning loudly, he picked up his rucksack and headed for the mass of rubble that had completely buried the team's work site, and almost blocked the route back. He'd nearly reached the debris field when he stopped for a while, waiting for the dust to settle. After a ten minute break, still coughing, he rose and resumed walking in the general direction of the landing boat, the dust pall starting to dissipate finally. He was covered with a fine flour-like powder.

There was a rustling noise off to his right and a couple of seconds later he heard a strange noise, like someone throat gargling, very loudly. He looked around but saw nothing – at first. Then, a movement caught his eye and he turned to see a gigantic bird standing no more than 20 metres away, right behind him.

His jaw dropped open as he gazed up at the creature's head, held a full 2 metres above his own. The bird squawked again and, without any sign of what it was going to do, ran straight at him, its thick powerful legs causing it to bound forward, though, surprisingly, it ran in an agile way. Erbbius seemed transfixed by the creature's head, which was larger than that of a horse; a wrinkled, purple coloured, trigonal block, carried on a thick neck more than a metre long. The creature's blue and brown feathers fluttered in the slipstream it created as it ran, and Erbbius stared, open mouthed at the beak, a thing shaped like a huge, black, shiny, scimitar. It had to be nearly a metre long.

The man finally started to run, his face registering abject terror, but, unexpectedly, the massive creature deviated away from him, turning and heading back the way it had come, racing away over the knoll. Looking over his shoulder Erbbius slowed and breathed a sigh of relief. 'Not so dangerous after all. Must have thought better of it,' he said to himself, breathing heavily.

He turned and hurried onwards – when a shadow loomed over him and made him turn again. Another of the birds was behind him. It was calmly walking, just a just a few metres from him, and as he stared at it the bird's glistening, cold, black, eyes transfixed him with a menacing stare of its own. This one also began to move in on him and as it did so he noticed there were 2 or 3 others running across the grassy slope a few dozen metres away.

Erbbius began to panic at this and, fumbling for his rucksack, dropped it, but then managed to pull out the wrench. He was starting to hyperventilate as he backed away from the bird following him, waving the wrench at it. But it moved nearer, undeterred. He saw the beak making straight for him and he stumbled backwards. Then he took in a deep gulp of air and lunged toward the bird, swinging vigorously at its head with his wrench. The bird merely lifted its head to its full height, out of danger, and looked at Erbbius with something which might have been considered disdain.

It lowered its head again and seemed to be looking for an opening. Its timing and clearly, its eyesight, were superbly acute, and as Erbbius swung again the beak dashed in and pecked at his arm. The man howled with pain – and dropped his weapon, as though he'd been electrified. Blood bubbled from a hole in his right forearm.

Erbbius shrieked in terror and turned to run again but barged straight into another giant bird which had been standing directly behind him while he'd been facing the first bird. His eyes hardly had time to register his dismayed and dread before the animal smashed its beak straight into his face. The first bird also then lunged in and, clamping its beak around Erbbius's neck, lifted his whole body high off the ground.

***

The team hurriedly made their way along their usual route toward the rock shelf while Lew prepared to take off in the ship. The agreed plan, Lew's idea, was that flying very slowly, at about 100 metres altitude, he would criss-cross the entire area of the route to the shelf, to see if Erbbius and Mindara were lost, or in trouble out in the rocky scrubland. The others were to walk directly to the dig site, and Lew would be able to keep track of them from the air. He would contact Mike's on his wristcom if he spotted those missing and direct the team to them. He'd already tried contacting Erbbius's wristcom without success.

The group rushed along the path toward the rock shelf, sweating profusely. Although Mike wondered what had happened to his shipmate his main concern was for Mindara. He liked her a lot. But why had she decided to tarry out here, and why did Erbbius decide to stay with her? He wondered if they had gone all the way back to the rock shelf, but why?

The geologists on the team had said the noise was unmistakeably a landslide. How could that be? But then he remembered the nature of the scree. That slope had always seemed pretty dodgy, he thought. Glancing at Eleri, hurrying along beside him, he saw she was also deep in thought, her face a mask of concern. They could hear the low whistling sound the Agamemnon made, circling above their heads, and he hoped that didn't set off another landslide, but it seemed there was no alternative to their plan.

He was squinting up at the ship flying off northwards, now at its furthest from them, when his wristcom buzzed. He spoke to it, ordering it to relay Lew's transmission on the device's speakers, so everyone could hear. The whole team, breathing heavily, gathered near and heard Lew say, 'Mike, the sensors haven't picked up any sign of Rubia, or Johann. But they have picked up a group of large animals moving north west – away from the coast – away from your position. I'm checking the … and yes, at the largest mag' I can get, they're definitely birds – real big things – keep disappearing from view under trees. But boy, have they got some speed.'

'Lew!' shouted Eleri, 'Please tell how many there are?'

A few seconds later came the reply, 'About … well, looks like 7 or 8 individuals. Why?'

'Sung said, 'They so breed in small colonies of 3 or 4 pairs.'

'That means they were here all the time,' said Hermington, 'somewhere. Tis probably yet a nesting area. But where?'

'Doesn't matter now,' said Lew, 'cos they're on the move. I just hope our teammates avoided them. Listen guys, I'm moving on to the dig site. I'll comm you again.'

Within seconds the shuttle's sleek V shaped body passed almost overhead and off toward the nearest part of the coast.

**

Long before they reached the rock shelf Lew contacted Mike and warned the team to prepare for the worst. He said the entire scree slope had slid down, and now covered the whole area where they had been working. And, much worse – the vidscopes had spotted the infra-red signatures from two, still, bodies. He was getting the ship's hypercomp to magnify and analyse. He warned that it wasn't looking good, and at that point stopped transmitting.

Some minutes later the group arrived at the ruined work site; the mass of rock and stones formed a layer several metres high in the place where they had all worked for many days. Lew commed them again. He confirmed all that they now feared; that their companions were dead. Over the previous few minutes the boat's hypercomp had analysed its images of their bodies, including posture, orientation, and any possible movement. It found everything to be compatible with death. To clinch it the instrument had indicated low temperature in the bodies and rapid, continued cooling. Lew said that, sadly, the images of Erbbius, in particular, showed his body to be, "disintegral", as the comp had put it.

At this point, most of the group drew to a halt. Heads looked down or were thrown up in distress, hands went up in anguish, to cover faces. Mike held his own head in shock. Eleri stopped walking and bent over double, as though with a stomach cramp, muttering, 'Rubia. Little Rubia. What happened to you?' She looked at Mike and asked, 'What the hellsonry could have happened out there, Mike?' He shrugged despondently and went to her. He felt sick to the stomach. She rose to clasp him and they held each-other tightly.

'I don't know what to think, El. But I guess we're going to find out soon enough,' he said, ashen faced, 'but we need to get to them, El. Lew can't land here, so it's up to us now.'

The group began to pick their way ahead over the massive jumble of rocks ahead. Hermington was in the lead but stopped suddenly, shouted and began to walk back to them,

'No, brethry,' he said. 'We must not go this way.'

Lew's voice broke in on Mike's comm unit almost at almost exactly the same time. He said, 'I can see what you're doing, guys. That stuff has to be unstable and the ship's thrusters might even set it off again. Stop immediately. You'll have to double back a bit and walk up the hill on the south west side, then along the top till you get to the knoll at the far end. The one closest to the sea. Erbbius and Rubia are over there. And take care. Have your stun guns ready. We can't be totally sure there aren't birds over there. I'll keep look out up here.' With that the ship rose higher on its vertical thrusters, to put it at an altitude less likely to cause further destabilisation – and allowing Lew to scan a wider area.

Good thinking, mused Mike, sadly. With the ship's instruments he'd be able to keep track of anything in this exposed area and, although they were all feeling shocked to the core it would be necessary to stay on high alert. His thoughts turned to darker matters. What would they find when they reached their teammates? And what would this all mean to Muggredge's plan to prove what had happened on this planet long ago? Even more importantly, what would this mean for the future of this world?

Chapter 33

INQUIRIES

Jennifer Providius paced around the bridge of the Antarctica.

'Why in strepp's name hasn't she been found yet?' she growled.

First Officer Marlon Florian gave her a glance full of dismay. 'We're still trying, Captain,' he said, 'but Heracleonn is clever. She knows her way around very well and she knows we don't have the same personal ID detectors the Navy has.'

'Well, maybe it's time we had them installed, don't you think?' said Providius.

'It's never been thought necessary, Captain. They're expensive and wouldn't go down well with our kind of crew. I'm sorry Captain. I'll make a note to get them installed.'

Providius relaxed then and gave Florian a half smile. 'It's not your fault, Lieutenant. And you're right. Our "kind of crew" would balk at it, even though it's standard issue in the Navy.'

'Maybe so, but *even they* don't use them most of the time,' said Florian, 'except in emergencies.'

'Having said that,' returned Providius, 'I believe our Pamela is probably capable of putting even those kinds of detectors out of action, isn't she?'

'Maybe. She's a very capable tek engineer and she served with the Navy for a few years. Seems she left them cos she got fed up with "routine". She's a high standard physics grad,' too. This posting seemed to suit her well, but her supervisors reported one or two small discipline problems.'

'Yes, I'm aware there were some minor issues, but my recruitment officer seemed quite satisfied with her, when she applied. What could have made her want to frap the comp, though? What's to gain from it?'

'I can't think of a solid gain for her. Maybe it's an idealism thing. Something to do with Ultima, or whatever? We won't know till we catch her – and catch her we will, Captain.'

****

Pamela Heracleonn had hidden in a tiny, claustrophobic storage locker near the central hub of the ship for long enough. She had been in there for nearly two hours, leaving it only once, at great risk, when she returned to her personal locker near the mess. She needed a datacube and its reader, translator, and after retrieving these she returned to the storage unit. She was unwillingly giving the crew time to work out what she might do next. She had to make a move – now.

She opened the locker room door and gingerly floated out, then made a bee line for the deck's outermost corridor, just through the next hatchway. She had floated through when a young scientist almost bumped into her as she emerged into the corridor. He looked startled but Heracleonn reached for a grab rail above the hatch, tightly grasping it with both hands and kicked at the man's midriff with both booted feet. He made a loud coughing sound and sucked in air as he was propelled, in micro-gravity, all the way down the corridor to a bend 5 metres away. He bounced off the wall at that point and out of sight. Heracleonn's own momentum continued unwillingly and she hit the ceiling of the corridor hard, but she'd been prepared for it, her boots in the main colliding with the ceiling. She continued to hang onto the rail and stabilised herself.

'Sorry, Bob. I had no choice,' she offered after victim, then projected herself in the opposite direction along the corridor. She heard groaning and scuffling noises from around the bend, then Bob's shadow running along the wall as he started to return toward her. She continued for 30 metres along then grabbed the handrails near the station she had been making for. It was the first of the ship's two lifeboat stations and, securing herself to wall netting which was designed to hold onto loose objects, she opened a small, illuminated control panel. She plugged a tiny cable into it, reeling it out from a device on her wrist. That device was, in fact, a Navy-issue wristcom, a piece of kit she'd been given prior to this mission, passing as a standard chrono-piece. But the performance of it far outstripped anything used on the Antarctica.

The ship's two lifeboats had already been searched. They thought she would be unable to access them, but she adjusted her wristcom and pressed its outer cover. There was a buzzing sound, the panel sparked, went dark – and her wristcom flashed, sputtering sharp, bright, sparks. Heracleonn pressed her fingers into the panel on the access station and pulled out a set of wires, twisting three of them together. There was another spark, but this time a large hatchway next to the panel slid upwards and she pushed herself through – and into the lifeboat. As she entered, she commanded the small boat to activate, making its internal lights flash on and the control panels burst into life. Reaching back into the corridor, she pressed the panel again and withdrew her arm sharply as the boat's hatch door closed.

In the microgravity environment her action, borne of much needed haste, sent her spinning into the curved lifeboat bulkhead opposite. It caused her to cannonade around the interior until she could clutch at some grab rails. She yowled in pain.

On the Antarctica's bridge, several warning lights flashed. Providius looked up and the hypercomp said, 'Be alerted. Lifeboat Alpha 1, is being launched.'

Both Providius and Florian said, with one voice, 'Heracleonn.' They called up the main outer-hull monitors and the huge screen showed the brilliant blue sphere of Oceanus, set against a blackness thick with stars. A small metal sphere rapidly arced across the field of view. Spinning debris from the structures that had held it in place flew off in all directions as the sphere span away from the ship, heading toward Oceanus.

'Well, that's torn it,' said Florian with disgust.

'I know. We haven't got a dedicated lander to follow her down,' said Providius.

'We could launch the other lifeboat,' said Florian, 'but that would leave us high and dry if we have any sort of emergency.'

'Maybe we should launch anyway. But the recovery of the boats would take a huge amount of work and probably need help from the Navy.'

'And there's something else, Captain. We don't have permission to land. And you know what sticklers the Oceanus authorities are for protocol.'

'You're right. What would I do without you, Lieutenant?'

'We could try asking The Monsoon to intervene. Send a landing boat down there?'

'Maybe. I'd rather not. They've got their own problems. Meanwhile, make sure we track her full trajectory, Lieutenant. We've got to know where she lands. Then, we'll speak to the Oceanus authorities.'

****

At the scene of the landslide on Simurgh various members of the science team stood, shellshocked, in front of the rock jumble, while others sat gloomily on rocks. They had climbed the broad hill, walked along the ridge and reached the knoll nearest the sea, at its north-eastern end, then descended. Despite being forewarned by Lew, nothing could have prepared them for what they had seen then: two wrecked bodies that happened to belong to colleagues they had spent the last few weeks in close contact with. Most of the team had known Mindara for years. Several were good personal friends. She seemed more like a sister to some, even to Mike, who felt he had come to know her well. In the case of Erbbius, hardly anyone could admit to actually liking the man, but none would ever have wanted this to happen to him. And it was his body they reached first.

His torso and legs lay in a ragged heap, but both of his arms and head were completely missing. His torn remains, like much of the immediately surrounding area, was covered with traces of his innards and a large slick of blood was drying fast in the late afternoon heat. Arbbinius, Rasmissen and Barstow seemed unwilling to approach. Chen and Sung lurched behind some rocks and were physically sick.

Mike and Morgath only approached to within a few metres, though Eleri felt able to get a little closer. Mike thought he should look because Erbbius had been his colleague, after all, but he soon realised he couldn't stomach it enough to get closer than a few metres.

It had been obvious of course, from some distance, that Erbbius was totally beyond any help. Eleri was the first to guess that one of the Macrotargs must have killed him. She said that breaking the neck, then tearing off the head was the classic means by which they dispatched their prey.

Then Hermington sucked in his breath and, with a gritty look on his face, moved closer than anyone else, and as he did so he shouted that he'd found a huge claw print less than a metre from the remains. The team started examining the ground all around and suddenly saw dozens of claw prints. As they were clean and undisturbed it became clear that the creatures had attacked *after* the avalanche had occurred, for the prints were clearly impressed in the thick layer of dust from the landslide.

When they had recovered from the shock a little more, Sung and Chen scouted around further away from the body and found a long trail of Macrotarg tracks in the soft soil. They led from the hill down to what little remained of the rock shelf.

The team became edgy again and those with stun rifles pulled them off their shoulders, holding them tightly, nervously glancing all around as they walked toward the cliff edge where they'd been told Rubia could be seen. Mike himself became increasingly alarmed and frequently looked up at the sky, searching for reassuring signs of the landing boat. He could hear it far above, though it might have been above some light cloud that had gathered.

Morgath went straight up to the edge of the cliff, some metres from where Rubia had fallen and shouted back, 'Hoyah, Team! I carnt see her.' But then added, 'Ah yes, I ... Oh no, poor Rubia. No, do not look.'

Unwittingly, the rest of the team, except Mike, sidled up the edge and looked over. Mike felt suddenly overwhelmed by the wide-open nature of the rock shelf above the sea. It was such a bad feeling he decided it was probably exacerbated by emotional distress and it affected him despite the homeopathic remedy poor little Mindara had been giving him: "brackylobe" plant extract.

Despite the long, wide, shadow cast by the cliff itself, they could see Rubia lying on the flat surface of one of the wide slabs of rock all along the foreshore at the bottom of the cliff. The sea lapped, unconcerned, some 30 metres away. Their colleague lay in a pool of congealed blood which appeared, grimly, almost oil slick black, in the lowering light.

Eleri rejoined Mike, bent almost double, a little way from the cliff edge and gathered him to her bosom. She said that poor Rubia looked like a little bundle of rags down there, her rucksack lying closeby. Not only was it obvious she was quite beyond any help, there also seemed no way for them to get down to her. There was a very long silence while group stood around in disbelief. Eleri called everyone to come together.

As they did so there was a sad little debate, filled with anguish, about how Rubia had come to fall. The most likely explanation seemed that she had been attacked by the Macrotargs, like Erbbius, but had fallen, or maybe even jumped off the cliff, perhaps to escape them. That was when Hermington spotted something very alarming. He pointed to a number of cracks and ragged fissures in the hard, dry, ground all along the edge of the cliff. Then Arbbinius pointed to the half moon shaped "bite" out of the edge of the cliff, almost immediately above the site of Rubbia's body. He deduced that it had probably been where she fell and moving closer to the edge, he pointed out something that hardly anyone had noticed when they'd first seen Rubia's body. These were the broken remains of what had evidently been a large chunk of rock and soil lying all around her. Morgath looked around with alarm in her wide eyes and shouted to Arbbinius to move away from the edge. She waved everyone back, well clear of the drop.

So, maybe Rubia had simply gone too close to the edge, surmised Mike, with heavy heart. Yet it was still clear that the giant birds had caused mayhem. Speculation in the group turned back to the question of why Erbbius and Mindara had come out here anyway? It seemed obvious the birds had got in after the fence had been brought down by the avalanche, or was it obvious? The avalanche itself was another mystery. Why had there been no warning of it, nor any problems with landslip in the days before the accident? The questions became overwhelming and frustrating.

Lew comm'd Mike and suggested they all return to the Agamemnon, for the sake of safety. There was nothing more they could do at the accident scene. Lew had already contacted Tenak who had said he would contact Muggredge and the Janitran authorities. Oceanus protocols required this after the suspicious death of any Oceanus citizen. Lew said that Tenak had been deeply saddened by the news but cool headed about what must now be done. He had also ordered that no-one was to touch or interfere with the bodies. The Admiral would get back to Lew with updates within the hour.

Lew also told the group that there was currently no way they could cover the bodies to protect them from the elements. Hermington told him that the elements were the least of their problems. There were a number of species of small animals which came out at night, particularly "ogra rats", and maybe even the macrotargs. Eleri reminded him that the birds were not nocturnal – but the rats certainly were. And there creatures the equivalent of seabirds on Earth, though none were apparent right then.

'I think I know what we can do, guys,' said Lew, 'cos we've got some hypersonic beacons we can use to surround the bodies. They give off ultrasound and infrasound. Gives most animals the grand send-off, or at least Earth type animals it does. They're in the stores at back of the boat. We can get them out here tomorrow, early.'

There were muted grumblings of dissent at the delay, but Lew said, 'Listen up guys. You – and I – we all need some rest and walking about out there in the dark seems kind of risky, with all that loose rock around and all. Makes getting across the route between the sites difficult too. And I don't want to waste ship's energy on unnecessary adventures. Been too many of those already.'

'Praps some of us will …' began Sung, with defiance on his features but Lew cut him short.

'No Kenye, man. Listen guys, I have to tell you something. Admiral Tenak's given me total authority to take over this expedition – completely. Like it, man, or not. I don't care. So everyone, please note the sun is due to set in about an hour. Please start on the way back now. I'm taking the ship back to the hilltop and I want you all to get back there soon as poss'. I'll go slow, and keep the sensors looking for anything big moving around down there. I'm waiting further orders from the Admiral, so stand by.' Mike thought Lew's voice was definitely imbued with a tone which would brook no argument. And Mike didn't blame him one little bit. There'd been too much grief already on these expeditions.

Sung wandered a little way off and sat heavily, holding his head in his hands. Daniellsa and Chen also went very silent. Mike wondered if they were going to throw a "wobbler", or something.

To their credit, he felt, none of the group gave voice to any feelings of anger about the way those three had dealt with the Mindara situation, back before the landslide. He, personally, wasn't at all sure they were blameless, and he guessed most of the others felt the same. They just weren't saying anything. Still, he thought, they'd had no reason to think things would go so wrong, especially when Erbbius had offered to help. But just what had that mascla done, he wondered? Eleri looked at Mike and said, very quietly, that she thought Rubia must have gone all the way back here first and Erbbius must have followed. That was when they had been attacked by the birds. Mike just didn't quite buy all that, for some reason, but he had nothing to go on.

Suddenly, Lew was back on the wristcom. Tenak had been told by the Oceanus officials that they wanted everyone to stick around because the government were going to send a team of pathologists and investigators out. Tenak had agreed the Navy would co-operate with the civilian authorities as far as possible. Mike's heart sank. How long would they have to stay on this godforsaken rock? Then Lew added that the Oceanus officials had agreed to Tenak's offer to use another landing boat; the Laurasia, but they'd said they wouldn't be ready to mount the expedition for a couple of days. The only bright spot for him, Mike felt, was that at least he'd be with Eleri and – after all, the whole team were in the same can.

The team reluctantly left the bodies. It was getting dark as they set off toward the ship's landing site. Mike reminded everyone that they should each have a super-bright light stick in their rucksacks, courtesy of the Navy, and so they broke them out. They were invaluable in helping them to navigate across the riven landscape.

The Agamamnon made for a spectacular sight as they moved out; brightly lit as it sailed back and forth across the dark blue evening sky, but it was pitch black by the time the sad little group emerged onto the hilltop landing site. By that time Lew had just touched down.

They stumbled into their beds, deeply upset and drained. Mike and Eleri lay in each-other's arms, in silence at first. Eleri began to sob so such that Mike couldn't help but give in to it himself, despite his exhaustion. And there seemed they could offer little consolation to each-other about Mindara. She would never get to go on The Monsoon now, thought Mike, tears running freely down his cheeks. Later, as he felt Eleri start to slip off to sleep he wondered how many more things were going to go wrong – badly wrong – on this world, by the time he and Tenak were through with it? He to work very hard to blot out the constant images of Erbbius's body which kept insinuating themselves into his mind but he never really succeeded. It was only his physical and emotional exhaustion which enabled him to get to sleep despite the darkness of his despair.

****

Superintendent Brandron Park-Sekhem Amplin returned the telephone to its receiver, in the small office of the securi-pol station in Alderin, a little town in the far west coastlands of the continent of Bhumi Devi. 'I am just not understanding these personry,' he said, turning to his colleague.

'What was that about anyways?' asked his young male colleague.

'Silly-most womanry I have encountered on the tel-phone,' said Amplin. 'She said she and her partner were out on the moorielands yester-nite. Says they didst see a bright star fall to ground in the east and went out to look for it. Stayed out till darkmost but couldnar find it. Well, I told her t'was probably a meteorite. Get them all the time but no, she insisted, t'was something else. A spaceship, no less. Nearly blasted me ear off me. Says the object they saw got larger and larger as it descended and – get this – she thinks it sprouted a parchute!'

'Did she not say where it went?'

'Nar. Says it disappeared still behind the Lovian Hills. Don't tell me you are taking with seriousness, corporal?'

'Well, tis just mobile patroller Jonas told me half the people in the village saw a bright object in the sky last night, too. Seems they thought there was somethin' very oddso 'bout the way it came down. Not like a meteoritie, Superintendent. They carnt all be wrong 'bout this, can they?'

'Don't know. Praps tis as well I don't live in the village. Anywayin, better get on with the work, eh?'

A few minutes later the sliding door at the front of the office opened and a strange figure stepped in. Superintendent Amplin didn't bother looking up. This town was a very sleepy place. Nothing much ever happened here, and he assumed the visitor was probably someone reporting the loss of some livestock on the moores. Then he heard his corporal say, What in oceans? Super', look. Look!'

Amplin looked up – and saw a young woman standing four metres away. Nothing very strange in that perhaps, but this one was wearing a bulky grey suit which looked totally unlike anything they'd seen before. It was definitely not Oceanus wear and was covered with mud and torn in one or two places. The garment also sported a large breast patch that said, "R V Antarctica". But the biggest clue that she was not from around these parts was the space helmet she held in one hand and the impressive metal suitcase she had in the other. Tubes and cables were draped over her shoulders and around her waist. The woman shook her tousled black hair, gave the two securi-pol men a determined look and said, 'My name is Heracleonn, Pamela Heracleonn, from the Research Vessel Antarctica, arrived here out of the Home System. And I claim asylum on Oceanus.'

****

Jennifer Providius sat back in her chair and sighed. She was speaking to a government official, by way of a standard vid screen. The images she was getting from Oceanus flickered and were shaky.

She sat forward again and, with a determined look on her face, said, evenly,

'Government Secretary Trebert, please tell me there is a way we can come to an arrangement here. One that would suit both the Oceanus Government and ourselves? Pamela Heracleonn is wanted for questioning about very serious offences, including assault on a fellow crewmember, theft and damage of private property. It's vital property in fact, namely, parts of the mainframe hyper-comp aboard this ship.'

'Ah,' said Trebert, 'And I was yet thinking the Antarctica was a HS government vessel. Now you say it belongs as such, to ... what now, a company of some sort?'

'Yes, I'm afraid so, sir. The "Inter-Star Corporation" builds and runs research vessels like ours. The Home System allied government simply hires the vessels, and their crews, to carry out research. And of course there has been interference to them and their aims as well.'

'But still, you run those ships in similar ways to the Navy, will you not admit?'

'Well, only in that we use a command and rank structure that's a bit similar. Just for the safe and disciplined running of things. That's all. We are not Navy, nor are we government servants. But still our employers will be rightly aggrieved by the offences committed by this young crewmember. And so, again, I must gain ask that she be returned to us.'

'And still, you accepted before, Captain Providius, the offences are not proven as of now, and you merely wish to question this, Heracleonn. She says she did not commit the offences so claim-ed, apart from taking the lifeboat, which such she says was the only way she could escape from persecution on your ship.'

Providius's jaw almost dropped. 'Persecution? I have no idea what she's talking about.'

'And madama, tis exactly what she says about such offences on which you charge her. Fraidling, we are unable to comply with your request she be returned to you, as of this time. Mes Heracleonn claims she has many things she would yet like to talk to us about, and we wish to give her every opportunity. Please be clear on this, Mes Captain. The government is not saying they will grant asylum to this femna, as yet.

We wish, as I am sure you shall appreciate, to look into this situation in depth, with a view to finding some such sensible and, let me say ... *justworthy* ...solution. Thanking you for your time Captain. I must be signing off now.' And with that the screen went blank.

'Bullshit, Mer government man,' said Providius, staring at the blank vid screen.

****

Mike Tanniss turned to Eleri, who had just entered the library, at "Main University Building", on the outskirts of Janitra.

'They want what?' he sputtered.

'We have to be so available for the next two weeks yet to be answering questions on what happened at Simurgh,' she said, 'for the Professier just told me. We may still be asked to give evidence to the Prime Investigation Inquiry – and they arint due to sit in this case for some 10 days. I am sorry Mike.'

'Not your fault. What a pain. We've been waiting for 4 weeks already. But ... I suppose it doesn't matter too much. Even if Arkas hadn't granted me extended shore leave he wouldn't have much choice about this anyway. He seems to think I need some recuperation time. There's nothing much the science team can do now, either. It's all a fegging mess. Just shit.'

'Try not to be despondentry, my youngling space boy. We will have to pick up the pieces. That is all.'

'Pick up what pieces, El? We've got nothing to show for all that effort on Simurgh. All that sacrifice, for nothing.'

'Tis precisely for that sacrifice that we need carry on, Mike. Do you not see that?'

'Carry on doing what, El? Where, *precisely,* do we go from here? I know, why don't we just go back to Simurgh and move all that rubble. Then we'll start again. How 'bout that?'

'There is no need of that tone of voice, Michaelsson.'

Using the full form of his given name like that made him realise his whining was starting to antagonise her, so he stopped.

'I'm sorry El,' he sighed, 'I'm just a tadrie down, that's all. I can't get Rubia or Erbbius out of my mind, particularly Rubia. She was so lovely. She didn't deserve that end.'

'No-one does, Mike. E'en I know Johann was the strangest of manry, but what happened to him was horror-full. He didst certainly not deserve *his* end.'

'Yeah, you're right. We lost good people out there. Doesn't alter the fact that we've got nothing to show for their … deaths.'

'I know sweetnie. I feel down as well. My great, wondrous, government made us wait out there – how long? Three days till yet they were ready.'

'Yeah, but they got a surprise when the Laurasia was finally able to pick them up, didn't they? The ship got them over to Simurgh in an hour and a half. They were a bit shell-shocked, I reckon.'

'Yes, love of mine, and there were … how many? Nine, was it not? Let me see. There were yet four securipol officers, three accident investigators and …. Who such else?'

'Two magistrates. Still, they all seemed pretty happy with what we told them.'

'As yet they should be, Mike. For we held nothing back.'

There was silence for a while, then Eleri said, very sombrely, 'I am glad your pilotman, Lew, had those ultra-sound beacons – to guard the bodies – and the ladder, so we could get down to where … Rubia was, so to protect her from more scavengerie. They had already attacked.'

'Yeah, the ogra rats had obviously had a go at poor Erbbius too by the time we got back to him.'

'And … those … shoreline craboids had …'

Eleri started to break down then and Mike went to her, held her, and said soothingly, 'She wouldn't have felt any of it, El. You know that, right?'

She looked at him through tear filled eyes and his own misted over. She said, 'But your Admiral has been so good over all things. He is a diplomat extraordinaire- so.'

'Yeah. He is good. Sticky situation for him, … and us. But, while we're on Oceanus soil, we're subject to its laws, I guess.'

'That-is more like it, space boy,' she said, the tentative beginnings of a smile breaking out on her face, 'And tis good-honour to abide by our rules, I so believe.'

'That's more like it, *ocean girl*. Things have to take their course.'

'Ocean girl?' said Eleri, with wide eyed surprise. They both broke into a light chuckle, albeit subdued. Mike knew they were making an emotional recovery, but he also knew it would be a long time before they got over the episode at Simurgh.

****

Pamela Heracleonn sat on a hard, un-upholstered, straight-back chair made of some sort of metal, in a dark, poky, dirty room, somewhere in Janitra. There were no windows to be seen. She was tied to the chair with old fashioned metal handcuffs that bit into the skin of her wrists. The cuffs may have been old fashioned, compared to Home System methods of restraint, but they were still effective. She wore Oceanus standard prisoner-garb, a beige one-piece coverall, her own flying suit having been confiscated.

A Devian man and woman, wearing civilian clothes, sat opposite her, scrutinising her every reaction from across a wide, grimy table. They had introduced themselves as "Government Investigaria," and tried to reassure her they had her best interests in mind and would detain her no longer than necessary. But they said they expected full and honest answers to all questions.

'I've already told you,' she said, with a tone, borne perhaps not so much of fear, but sheer boredom, 'I had no intention of spying on your people. I have also said that I know the Home System *does* want to spy on you, and has been doing so, using the Antarctica …'

'Yes, yes, we are knowing your say-so on that,' the female investigator said. She was a slim middle-aged woman with a hard-edged face and small, dead looking eyes.

'And still you said you could prove it to us,' the investigator continued, 'using that tiny thing, that "data chip" thing you brought with you. And, what you call a "reader device" – esept such devices do not seem to work, do they?'

'Okay. I know the reader doesn't … seem to be able to talk to your machines. Or maybe it can't translate into your own machine language. I thought it would, that's all. I can't help it if your tek is so far behind ours.' She rolled her eyes after saying that and looked up at the crack-riven ceiling high above. There were groups of little ten-legged things crawling about up there.

The female investigator's cold face took on an even more austere look and her lips curled as though she was eating a raw lemon. Her male colleague took over at this point. A large, spheroidal man with a wide, flat face from which an incongruous beak-like nose projected, smiled at Heracleon. But it came across as an insincere grimace.

'Mes Heracleon,' he said, 'please yet believe us when we say we do not want to keep you here any longer than needed. But believe us still, when we say we shall get deep into all this. We are wanting the truth, simplest put. So, we ask, why did you really abandon your vessel and drop down on us, unbidden? And so, give such surprise? Where is the proof-truth of the things you have told us – about the Home System, and your vessel? List me, Pamelin. We want to help you, mayhap give you asylum but you have to be honest with us.'

'It's Pamela, by the way,' said the Heracleonn, without emotion. 'And I told you. I had to escape when Captain Providius found out I'd stumbled across their spying activities. I'm very proficient with our comp systems and I discovered that the Antarctica has been spying on your planet ever since it entered this system. I wouldn't be surprised if the Navy has been doing the same thing. I've also tried to explain that the Antarctica's been sending automated probes into very low orbit over your world, particularly over Janitra. My ship has detectors of such hypersensitivity as you would *not* believe. They've been using them to listen in to anything of interest, on your radio and telephone traffic, and anything else they can pick up.

She paused, watching their reactions, then continued, 'They also claimed to have lost all the data they gathered about Ra, when they came into this star system. Truth is, the data they picked up was more favourable to those, on your world, who have disagreed with the idea that Ra has become unstable. The crew were astonished to find that the Meta-telesophists were right all along. So, they deliberately deleted all the data. I considered that a heinous and despicable act of info-vandalism. A betrayal of the truth. That's why I "abandoned my vessel". I thought …no, …I *hoped* you people would give me a more positive reception - but you have also now let me down. You should be thanking me, not incarcerating me.'

'Nonsensius, young femna,' said the female interrogator, 'but we have not seen any *proof* of what you say. For all we know, *you* may have been sent down here to spy on us or e'en to commit sabotage – praps acts of terrorism. Or you just may be a deserter.'

'I am not a terroriost and I certainly can't be a deserter. I'm not a member of the military. I'm an employee of a private research company. Science, remember? I'm only guilty of breaching my contract of employment.' Heracleonn threw her head back and exhaled exaggeratedly with impatience.

'You look tired,' said the male interrogator, 'and I am sure you would yet rest, specially after your long journey here. I imagine you are not familiar with trips by propeller air-plane, specialry when they take twenty hours and four stops for refuelling.' A touch of a sly smile broke over his lips, as he continued, 'My collig and I will leave you alone – but only for short whiles. We shall see if we can find someone who might such get your – devices – working. Up to that time, please think hard and long about what really brought you to our planet. If you are thinking we have let you down, praps the answer would be – to hand you back to your Captain. Be knowing, she has definitely asked *for you*.'

A sullen faced Heracleonn nodded with a resigned look and stared at the floor as her interrogators left the room. The only person still in there with her was a tall, brutish looking guard, as broad as he was tall. He stood next to the only door in the room. His arms were folded but in one hand he held a very fat wooden truncheon, one which had sharp metal barbs on it.

Once outside the interrogation room the two investigators spoke in subdued tones as they strolled through a dingy corridor.

'I shall not believe her now, any more than I did when first we interviewed her,' said the woman. 'And I am doubting her *devices* hold anything of value.'

'Tis possible there may still be some truth in what she says about the loss of data on her ship,' said the male investigator, 'as Sargint Darmody told me he heard, from his special contacts, that there was deedly a massive data loss on that ship.'

'I wonder if that info-data came by way of the Metateleos? If she is right about the spying, which I find doubtmost yet, the fact is still, this world has got next-to nothing of any value to spies. Why would the Home System want to spy on us?' said the woman.

'Praps they would be wanting the whole planet,' said her colleague. 'But they know how so many of us feel already, without listening on our conversationry. My understanding is that the government has still to be convinced that Ra will go "nova", or erupt, or whatever. Tis down to the experts to argue out, ist not?'

'True, our job is just to find out why she is really here,' said the woman, 'but I am starting to think she should just be handed back. After all, we are not wanting to aggravate the Home System more than necessary.'

The man sighed heavily and said, 'Do not be forgetting – that is also for others to decide. We might as well keep her here for times being. I can tell she does like it here.' He laughed.

****

'Admiral, my understanding is that Ambassador Sliverlight has been to see the government about Heracleonn, but he didn't get very far,' said Jennifer Providius's vivid, full size hologram standing in front of Arkas Tenak, in his private office suite.

'I know,' said Tenak, 'and it's a shame we can't do any more. Arbella and her Central Policy Committee wouldn't listen to me, or Mike Tanniss, when we first arrived, precisely because we didn't have full diplomatic status. Now we have an Ambassador here, we still don't seem to be getting anywhere. The people down there might be starting to feel differently, though.'

'What do you mean, Arkas?'

'Well, we've had around a hundred and fifty applications from Oceanus citizens, wanting to go to the Solar System. Might not sound a lot, but it's a big step for anyone here to take, believe me.'

'That's encouraging, I guess, but in the meantime, is there anything *you* can do about Heracleonn? At least, you seem to have a bit more diplomatic leverage than me.'

'Nice of you to say so, but I'm not sure you're right. And I'm sorry Jennifer, but there's a whole lot of trouble on my hands right now. Ah, but I'm guessing you didn't know. I … lost a crewman on the planet, a few weeks ago, and I've got another in the brig, under suspicion of doing "a Heracleonn" on us.'

Providius's demeanor changed immediately. 'Oh, Maker, I didn't know, Arkas. I'm so sorry. To lose a crewmwmber? That's terrible.'

'True, but that's an ever present danger in the Navy, Jennifer. Thankfully, it doesn't happen too often. Not these days. We're supposed to be able to take losses like that on the chin, and I've certainly lost more than my fair share of crew in the past. But this one just seems … well, particularly pointless. And these things hurt you. Always. I suppose if they don't then you probably shouldn't be in command.'

'Yes, of course. I know you saw a lot of action in the Rebel War. I apologise for even asking you about Heracleonn, at a time like this. I had no idea what's been happening on your side of the show. Forgive me?'

'No need, Jennifer. No need at all. I'll tell you what I'll do. I'll try speaking to Ambassador Sliverlight. Ask if he can resume negotiations with Arbella, or her Ministers, and I'll mention the matter if I speak to Arbella again directly. That's bound to ruin things for good.' Tenak chuckled mirthlessly, his words heavy with irony. Providius still behaved as though he were serious.

'Nonsense, Arkas. You could probably do a better job than this so-called Ambassador, even if Arbella did give you an initial shove-off. I've heard things about him, Arkas. Not particularly good things. But I'd better shut up about that. It won't help things, and it's probably just rumour. But there is one more thing. It seems a strange co-incidence that both you and I have had similar problems with crewmembers interfering with our hyper-comp systems, don't you think? And both happening in orbit around this planet. They have to be related, don't they?'

'Maybe, but I don't know how to connect them solidly – at least not right now. Hopefully, we will get some intel soon. Just now, we don't have anyone we can link with my arrested crewman. He was a late addition to the crew, but the strange thing is, he came highly recommended. I blame myself for not making it more of my business to look into new crewmembers more thoroughly. Anyway, I'm not convinced this man did it, Jennifer - and if he did, I don't believe he could have done it without help from others on board this ship, or another Navy vessel. Unfortunately, he's not talking, and we don't keelhawl people, or flog 'em anymore, Jennifer.' Tenak allowed a bitter smile to dance on his lips.

'Thank you for sharing your thoughts with me, Admiral. I appreciate your trust hugely. We're still carrying out a full investigation here, too – but we actually *do* think Heracleonn was working on her own. You know, it's a funny thing but, cunning though she is, maybe Heracleonn should have rung alarm bells before.'

'Why do you say that?'

'Well, she was a junior pilot in the Navy, as you know. Brilliant too. Followed in her father's footsteps. He was a big-shot pilot for years. Lieutenant Commander Heracleon, no less. Ring any comm buzzers with you?'

'Not sure Jennifer. Maybe …. Yeah. Some sort of incident, maybe 8 or 9 years ago, wasn't it? I was involved with surveying the Coma cloud cluster at the time. Which cohort was he in?'

'Don't know, Arkas, but I do know he was assigned to duties in the outer Solar System. If you were outside the system most of the time you wouldn't have come across him personally. Point is, he was killed on duty, shortly after Pamela graduated. His corvette crashed on Saturn's moon, Enceladus. Tragically, it also killed a number of civilians on a research outpost. A Navy board found him negligent, but Pamela's family never accepted the verdict. There's not much on whether she actually disputed the finding, but I'll bet hundred to a dollar she did. She left the Navy about a year after. Colleagues on this ship recall her talking about the Navy in disparaging terms, particularly Navy hierarchy. I should have realised, Arkas. She seemed well adjusted to me, at least whilst she served with us.' Providius's face dropped again.

'Don't be so quick to blame yourself. So, maybe she hated the Navy. She left. Sometimes people are a closed book. And nearly *everyone* criticises their employers or their ex-employers, don't they? Doesn't mean they're going to be traitors. For myself, I'm trying to come to terms with the idea there's a quisling in my own crew right now. Alright Jennifer, we'll talk a lot more about this, soon, I hope, but right now I'm afraid I have to go sort some other matters. We'll keep in touch on this.'

'That's for sure.'

Chapter 34

DARK REFLECTIONS

Mike and Eleri strolled along a wide trackway winding through expansive meadow-like countryside, surrounded by low hills covered with blue-green forest. They were nearly 10 kilometres from Chantris, Eleri's hometown, where they had withdrawn, to try to put behind them the nightmare of Simurgh. Seven Oceanus weeks had passed since the tragedy and two weeks since the Inquiry had been held in Janitra.

The four-day hearing had been held under the jurisdiction of the Janitran Inquestor; the Oceanus equivalent of a Coroner. The weeks leading up to the hearing had been a traumatic time for everyone who'd been on the expedition. Mike and Eleri still felt some guilt that they hadn't been more observant, more alert to what had been going on – whatever that was.

Only Sung, as the titular head of the expedition – and Lew, as the shuttle pilot, had been required to give evidence in person; Mike, Eleri and the other surviving team members having made sworn, written statements, accepted by the tribunal in lieu of them being called. But Mike and Eleri had attended the hearing to watch proceedings. There were no surprises, and nothing was revealed which they all didn't already know. Rubia's rucksack was never returned to the team and it was clear that the Oceanus authorities had confiscated it. Erbbius's tools were returned, minus his rucksack. Reference had been made to the full post-mortems, carried out in Janitra, after Erbbius and Mindara had been airlifted to the mainland by the Laurasia. Mike and Eleri had not attended at the reciting of the medical evidence. They'd seen the remains for themselves, and Mike knew he'd never forget it.

A local expert, an "engineer" had given evidence, in which he suggested that the landslide had probably been caused by the general activities of the whole group at the dig site. Fortunately, the Inquestor had ruled it out as speculative. Mike felt that the Oceanus "investigation" had been sketchy, and, frustratingly, they had not allowed the Navy to carry out its own search of the landslide debris.

Forensic evidence had been given, stating that human footprints, matching the boots worn by both deceased, had been found criss-crossing the area to the north of the landslip, together with the claw prints of many Macrotargs. The official conclusion was that the birds had probably surprised the humans and chased them around, before killing Erbbius. Their finding was that Mindara had accidentally fallen off the cliff, the edge of which had given way below her feet, whilst she was trying to avoid the birds. The Inquestor had made a finding that the deaths had been accidental, or "act of Nature". There were wry comments, in the local press, saying the team should not have been allowed to go to Simurgh in the first place; that the expedition was ill founded, and ill advised. But, Mike noted, there was not the tumult of negative publicity which he *had* expected.

Another sad day had been Rubia's funeral, in Demnisos, only a week before, when all the people who'd been on Simurgh had been invited to go to the home of Arelia Blutnose Imromesia, Mindara's sister, with whom she had lived. Only a small number of relatives and friends had turned up. The affair had been surprisingly upbeat, thought Mike; the guests, joining with Arelia, in songs and poetry that gave thanks for Rubia's life.

Erbbius's body had been taken up to The Monsoon and he'd had a traditional naval burial in space. Although Tenak had invited Eleri, she had apologised profusely but said she had not wanted to visit the ship in these circumstances. She promised Mike she would one day let him show her around it. And so, he had flown up on the Agamemnon, with Lew, and returned, sombrely, two days later. He was not used to colleagues dying.

The sun was now low in the sky as the couple neared Eleri's home, a quaint little cottage built of stone and clay, set in rolling meadows dotted with flowering brockeylobe plants and a profusion of low vegetation, known as 'broadies' – so called because of their wide, floppy leaves.

They walked hand in hand, stopping every now and then to sit on some of the small boulders that littered the area, drinking in the scent of the flowering brockylobes. They got to Eleri's home just as Ra was beginning to set and enjoyed a meal of locally produced poultry meat and home grown lapostrap plants. They drank deeply of red wine produced from vineyards to the south east.

Despite the often-distressing times he'd experienced on the planet Mike was genuinely starting to love Oceanus, though he might not yet be willing to admit it to others. But he knew Eleri was aware of it. His agoraphobia still aggravated occasionally and though he had resumed taking the pills Rubia had given him, the truth was, he was beginning to get used to the place. It helped that this particular area did not involve huge, open, vistas but felt a little more enclosed by its surrounding, often high, knolls and deep cut valleys. He felt it was best to keep busy, to take his mind off the wide-open spaces, but truth was, and despite everything, he hadn't been as relaxed as he was now, for years.

The pair sat in easy chairs in Eleri's back garden, watching the sky change from swathes of lush, orangey-pinks and reds, to purples and violets, then indigo. And, as the stars began to shine more clearly and sharply, Eleri stood and walked out onto her broad, flower filled, patio and garden. Mike followed her, taking his glass with him. He felt as if he were in heaven right at that moment. Eleri was smiling broadly. They gazed up at the sky, drinking in the brightening stars.

'It's a shame you haven't got a telescope,' said Mike.

'I'm supposing I did not really look at the sky much before I met you. I do now. All the time,' she said, and drew closer to him.

Chantris was further inland and north of Janitra and, at this time of year the daytime heat readily gave way to cooler evenings and nights than were experienced in places like the Capitol. Mike was grateful for it. He found anywhere near the coast too humid.

'Your star, the Sun, is supposed to be in the northern part of our sky, ist not? Tis up there. That not so?' said Eleri, turning away from the south and pointing to the sky above the house.

'Yeah, but I think it's around the other side of the planet from us at this time of year, at least until much later at night. Anyways, it's not very impressive from out here, El. It wouldn't be any brighter than those stars over there,' said Mike, pointing to a group of faint stars above the north eastern horizon, about half-way up dome of the sky.

'Wizzling! That is faint,' she exclaimed, as Mike suddenly placed a hand on her shoulder and seemed to hang on. He appeared to have a slightly pained expression on his face.

'You be okay?' she said.

'Yeah, just about. Sometimes, when I look too deeply into the sky, I get the feeling it's sucking me in. Like I'm *falling into it*. It only affects me when there's a horizon in view as well. Looking out of the ship's windows doesn't seem to have same effect, least not so much.'

'That is your agoraphobia, I am supposing?'

He nodded and added, 'Yeah, I suppose, but there's more to it than that. It's just … I don't know. It's that when I'm on the ground and I look up, it's like I can see the whole Universe in three dimensions, somehow. Happens a bit on the ship sometimes. Not so often.'

'How canst you say that, Mike? Don't all the portholes remind you of space all the time?'

'My cabin does have a window, yeah. I usually draw a screen across it - and there aren't any windows in the general crew areas. There are huge ones on the observation decks, and the bridge in the torus – and the battle bridge, but I avoid those places. No need for windows much. You can call up vid screens which show the view any time you like. Some still like to look out of windows though.'

'Looking up at all this sky, I just carnt believe you have come to be here, by my side, from such a long-farway place. I carnt foke on such things. Inconceivish.'

'Carnt foke? Oh, I see. Yeah, well, I can't really. No-one can, if they're honest, not even in the Navy.'

'But there must be other worlds out there, just like this one, and like Earth. One farday you can go to see those. I have no relish to travel long times on a starship but if you go, then I will go as well. For, I love you so much, Mike.'

'And I love you too, El. But we probably won't have to travel like that. This world and old Earth are the only ones we can reach. Least, for the foreseeable future. Maybe forever.'

'Real, yet? I am sorry Mike. I did not take astro-science much in college, but I am sure I recall reading that there is another blue world, likely with oceans – praps 150 light years from your Solar System?'

'Um, yeah. You know, you're right. Do you mean Potentia? Yeah, that's it, Potentia Alpha, but I think it's actually, 170, maybe 173 light years from Earth. Beyond the limit of human interstellar travel, I'm afraid.'

'I know there is supposeed to be a limit of some sort, but the conduits stretched for many hundreds of light years, do they not?'

'Well, yeah, but humans can't travel through them further than about 159 light years. Go beyond that and the pain and discomfort become too great – for anyone. Because physiological breakdown starts to happen. Organ failure. Circulation problems. That sort of thing. Some people can just about manage 156 or 157 light years, so I hear, but it's a massive risk. No-one's invented a system to get humans beyond 160. Maybe one day - but there's no point in any case. You see, at 172 light years, organic tissue is destroyed altogether, irretrievably. And around 194 light years, anything we call solid matter, anything that travels through a conduit, starts to dissociate – disintegrates. Sets a pretty strict limit on interstellar travel. Part of the fabric of the Universe. No way past it.'

'That is a soberly thought, but I do suppose someone finds a way to get around this. Maybe a different way of travelling 'tween the stars.'

'Hope so, El. I'll bet there's a lot of people working on it back in the Home System, but it seems pretty far off. Course, the *other* big limit, is that we can't go "laterally", as it were.' Eleri looked a little puzzled, so he explained. 'What I mean is … well, say we wanted to get from this system system to that star over there?' He pointed to a bright star in the northwestern sky. 'Say, that one is about 50 light years from here.

Well, we can't do it if that star system isn't linked directly to the Solar System. That's it. Period. It's to do with the way the dark energy conduits work – which no-one really understands – yet – they only allow travel along *direct* routes, to places like this … and Prithvi and lots of other stars. But you can't go from here, or Prithvi, say, to another star, and another and so on. Damn shame - cos otherwise, you could take relatively "short" hops from one star to another. Then you could exceed the 160 light year limit. Maybe, get to Potentia Alpha and lots more besides.'

'How oddly, ist not? And how do we know about these limits if no-one has been there? Come to thinking it, Mike, how did they work this out in the firsting place?'

'Really want to know? Well, right back when the conduits were first discovered there were loads of experiments, yeah? Starting about 2290, I think. Probes found the throats of the first conduits, opening in the outermost parts of the System. They sent out hundreds of automated probes, and I guess they worked out that the destinations could be achieved by calculation, using a "sum over paths" method, like you get in quantum mechanics. The highest probability measure will take you to where you want to go.'

'You hope! Tis seeming a bit random.'

'No, not really. The highest probability can be trusted but the quantum computers do all that assessment stuff – in seconds, which is a long time for them – but it's vitally important.'

'Are those things the "kewsers", I think they're called? Poor Johann said something about them once.'

'You got it. Mistakes have been made in the past, of course. Nasty ones. Ships ended up in the wrong places – even inside stars. Not nice. But that's real rare nowadays. Practically unheard of. The risk, a slight one, is still there though, and that's why we use *three* kewsers in all interstellar ships, never one or two. That way, if two disagree, the third casts a sort of deciding vote. It really makes the calculation stronger and more precise. Usually, the three of them agree.'

'Thank the oceans for that,' she laughed, her eyes rolling, only partly amused.

Mike chuckled. 'You don't sound too confident in any of this. Listen, El, they've sent literally hundreds of thousands of auto-probes out there and confirmed all this stuff – including exploration of the limits I was talking about. When they send those probes out to the limits and they don't come back or come back damaged – then we know we've reached a limit. But there's been – maybe thousands of crewed flights by now - inside the known limits – without any really serious problems.'

'But it seems yet there are so many places that we humans will never be able to go. Interesting, it is.'

'Yeah. Back home it's usually called, *"The Cage"*. And it's been known of since about, oh, 2312 maybe; a long time before people came to Oceanus. There's talk of using five linked kewers to try to break through …'

'Five?'

'Yeah, five, but it's hypothetical. I can't see it working, myself. Anyway, maybe there's a different way, maybe not using conduits, but we sure can't use faster-than-light travel. The conduits can only take us from one star's sphere of influence to another, by way of dark energy filaments, which … kind of bend space-time when we travel through them. But, in ordinary space-time there's no travelling faster than the speed of light. Outside of the conduits we're still limited by Einstein's Special Theory of Relativity. That's the speed …'

'Ahem, Mike sweedy, I do know about Einstein.'

'Sorry, El. Of course you do. Got carried away,' he said.

'It is alright darlintrie. You know, you should have been a teacher. You would be good at it.'

'I don't think so, *darlintrie*.'

She gave him a playful punch on his arm.

'No need for mockingsham,' she said, laughing.

'I wasn't. Well, not much. I just love the way you talk.'

'I could say the same about you!'

'Anyway. You're wrong about the teaching thing. That's *your* skill, not mine. You taught at the college here, didn't you?'

'Still so, Mike. Tis just that I work for Unkling Muggredge more often now. I still teach at the collegium, but only about 3 days a week in the Fall Time so, I ….'

Just then Mike noticed something peculiar happening in Eleri's garden plot and his jaw dropped with surprise. There were lots of plants with extremely tall stems sporting clusters of large purple flowers, although they looked nearly black in the lowering light. Those blooms had suddenly popped open. Just like that, he thought. As he gazed at them, they seemed to squeeze like miniature bellows, and each blew out a cloud of dust, or something, up into the air; dozens of tiny nebulae, whose movement was caught by the glimmering of soft light from Eleri's house.

Eleri saw his surprise and said, 'Do not be a worrying, Mike. They are my puffrie plants. No harm will come from them.'

'No, it's okay. And what is *that* over them? What's all this about, El?' Mike's face gleamed with wonder.

He watched entranced, as tiny galaxies of tiny lights suddenly materialised out of the darkness and floated down into the little clouds silently rising above the plants.

'Ah, well, those are the so called "dramatae flies". They are yet tiny, like pinhead size. The Puffries open up in the late evenings because that is when the flies are most active and …'

'More bioluminescent things.'

'Insectoids, yes. They are not a worrying you, are they? After your experience in the Purple Forest? For, if so, please come indoors …'

'No, not at all. Those … dramati things are really tiny. They just seem interested in the dust stuff, and they're fading now. They were beautiful.'

'Dust? No, tis a microscopic food, Mike. For that draws the insectoids down to the antheroids in the flowers, and its pollen sticks yet to the flies, who then visit other plants. A bit like your bees on Earth, but just bitso different.'

'Oh, seems very different, and fascinating. I'm sorry it's all over now.'

'Yes, Mike. Tis nearly all over for them and all suchly things. Ist not?'

Mike could see Eleri's glum expression even in the rapidly vanishing dregs of daylight.

He said nothing, not wanting to spoil the magic of the evening, but Eleri continued, 'Mike, please do tell me you understand that yet that none of the creatures of Oceanus meant malice, as such, when they attacked you, or your collig? You know that do you not?'

'Well, I suppose so, El, …'

'All those things, even the macrotargs, were only behaving … well, as they have evolved to. And the landslide obviously disturbed the Macrotarg nest site, and they reacted as expected. Your crewmate and even poor Rubia were in such wrong place, at wrong time. Same with the springtraps and so. All the creatures here are just trying to … get by, to survive, just like we do.'

'Yeah, I know, El,' he said, reaching for her and gently pulling her closer.

'The macro's were put over there, on Simurgh, over 80 years ago and it shows that e'en we can get it wrong. But we try, Mike. We really try.'

'I understand,' he said as he put his arm gently around her waist.

'The founding ancestri who settled this planet had to work hard just to survive,' she said, 'e'en though they used a lot of technology that – well – we have deedly lost, since then. But no-one really cares too much, Mike, because we are learning to get along with the planet. The founders wanted to make a fresh start, but they used a lot of stuff we do not really use now, like genetic manipulation. They had to. They had a wild world such that people were supposed to be able to live in.'

'Yeah, I suppose. I think they had to alter the soil, didn't they? Otherwise, they wouldn't have been able to grow crops. But couldn't they have used the plants already here? For food I mean?'

'No, darlie. Does not work that way. You see, the plants – and the animals have evolved separately here, so t'was not possible, in the early days, to eat anything growing or living here. Humanry digestion and nutrient processes – inside us – would not have worked. Tis why all the foodstuffs had to be imported for long-times, till the founders could be sure that genetically manipulated plants could be grown in these soils without infecting and spoiling the native species.

'Didn't that take a long time, El?'

'No, my mate, for most such work was done on Earth, first. Many records from that time are yet missing. But it makes best sense, yes? I believe they spent years working so upon it.'

'Ah, yeah, I remember now. The "founders" as you call them; the original pioneers, only came out here about 10 or so years after the first exploratory ships landed here, didn't they?'

'Yes, I think you are right. The planning for a full-scale colony must have taken a long time and worked out in much detail. Anywayins, they prepar-ed the soils and planted modified Earth crops but sorely restricted them to small areas – till sure it would all work – without damaging the native environment. But since-times they learned to grow hybrids of native and Earth plants, so more suited to life on this world. Some mistakes there were, but they were contained yet.'

'Didn't they bring out livestock, as well? I suppose they would have to … well, I don't know. How'd they do it?

Mike thought he knew the answer, but he felt that as long as they chatted, Eleri seemed to be avoiding the moments of sorrow concerning the fate of this world which she seemed to lapse into.

'They were brought out in maturation tanks, I am believing,' she said, 'and yet, it took some years before they were able to rear the animals successfully, but even now, the numbers of livestock reared is limited by State Decree. Most populari do not eat such meat anyways. Only such very small numbers of goaties, pigrys and meso-cattle are allowed, but most of the animals reared are free-living poultries anywayin.'

'If we can't eat the animals here, doesn't that mean that the grotachalik thing – and the giant plant couldn't … well, couldn't …?'

Could not have so eaten you? But yes, the grota' could have eaten you, sorry to be saying darlie, and the springtrap could have digested poor Johann. Though they wouldnar get much nutrition – but they did not know that, did they?'

There was silence for a moment, whilst Mike gulped inwardly, astonished again at his close shaves.

Then she said, 'You know, manry, tis strange but it so seems we are adapting to this place, much more than we could have thought.'

'What do you mean?'

'So, there are yet signs, many signs, that populari are gradually able to eat more of the local-grown plant life. That is, local plants not totally hybridised from the past. No-one seems to know why, including me. And I am supposed to be a biolrist. So much for that idea.'

'Don't be hard on yourself, El. You've had a busy work schedule and you can't know the answer to all the riddles. Not even the great Eleri Nefer-Ambrell!'

She laughed then and playfully punched his arm, before continuing, 'But yet, so seriously, another strange thing is what happened to you. Why should you be infected by the grotachalik's injecta, when no-one else has yet been so harmed, not by bacteria nor yet viruses on this world. Special so when life on this planet and on Earth did evolve very separately?'

'I know, El. I guess the guys back on the ship are still working on it.' It was his turn to be morose and Eleri grasped him tightly around his waist.

'They will find out, I am sure,' she said, 'and I am so sorry, Mike. No-one could have foreseen this.'

'Yeah,' he said, 'I know, and now the Antarctica's here, I understand that they're working on it too. I just hope I haven't started a trend.'

She nodded sombrely.

Mike started to feel uncomfortable and, wanting to change the subject, said, 'Anyway, I think your forebears would be proud of what your generation have done here, wouldn't they?

'Praps, but we just follow their first-vision. They wanted a colony that would do things differently from the people of Earth. To their greato-credit, they set forward a process of care of the environment such that later generations developed and built upon it.'

'I'm guessing a key idea was that of restraining population growth, I suppose, and looking after the wildness of this world.'

'Exact so, Mike. Yes. Looking after the world. Care for it. Can you yet imagine? The chance to start new, all over, and to not make the same mistakes. So, part of that is trying to limit city growth and develop cottage industries and still so limiting transport networks. I know your people think we're primitive for using old fashioned aircraft and airships and like, but tis all part of the culture of restraint. Without wanting to completely abandon all advancement. Hard balance. So, yes Mike, tis also why we are seeming paranoid about controlling migration to this world. Many in the Home System have criticised us much for not allowing millions of people to charge out here, on ship after ship, and such, but I hope you now can see why this was not possible?'

'Of course, but I don't think anyone who thinks about it has made that criticism for a long time, El. There's a very solid treaty between the HS and Oceanus. And remember, interstellar travel is limited to the Navy and research ships.'

'Dost your government stop *all* others? I have oft wondered whether there are space-liners, as such, plying the spaces between the stars.'

'Yeah, good point. But, well, there really are "spaceliners" as you call them, back in the solar system, but not many. It still takes many weeks, sometimes months, to get around the solar system. Not much good if you want to just visit another planet for a holiday – and there's not many places people really want to go. Most people just use virtual reality pods. You can travel anywhere with those, in a way – except it's not real. And never will be. I suppose Mars is a popular sightseeing destination – and then there's the general trips around the inner system. That's only really for the super-rich and the ships are just entertainment barges; self contained party palaces. Otherwise, most space flight between planets is deadly boring.'

'So, no party barges out to other stars? I know the treaty says they carnt come here, but what of other star systems?'

'Yeah, your good old treaty. As for other stars? Well, I guess that would be possible, but successive Allied Governments have maintained a legislative ban on interstellar tourism.'

'So why, yet?'

'Guess that one reason is safety. If one of those ships got into trouble – for any reason – there's no easy solution. No easy way to rescue, say, a ship full of, maybe, five hundred or a thousand people? Remember the time it takes to get from one system to another. By the way, there's a similar reason why those ships are not common *within* the Home System. Then there's the question of going through the conduits. Lot of people find it rough going. Some people might be disqualified through health reasons. And, I believe, another reason is – security concerns.'

'Ah, yes, I have yet been reading up on this. The Rebel attack of many years past, was mounted from another star system, was it not?'

'The Rebels built a whole fleet in one of the many uninhabitable, star sytems near the Solar System. Since then, the government's been keeping watch for another trick like that. They're also the guys in charge of issuing the necessary licences, don't forget.'

'Licences for interstellar travel?'

'Not exactly. The licences are issued for – your favourite, and mine – the kewsers, or the linked ones, anyway. They just don't grant them to commercial concerns, or any of the hyper-rich individuals. You know, the rare people who might be able to afford to build an interstellar-capable ship. And we're talking triple kewser systems. No-one is barmy enough to attempt interstellar travel without the triple system. Least, I assume not. It's only the Navy and the Interstellar Research Bureau that have access to the triple kewser system licences.'

'Could companias, or individuals, not be just building their own kewser devices?'

'You *are* curious, aren't you? I suppose the answer is, yes. Without the government's approval, you mean? Yeah, I'm sure it's been attempted. Probably commercial trading blocks, maybe individuals too, I suppose. They have powerful enough quantum computers. The kewsers on board star ships are a bit different though and … I guess it's a complicated story, but as short as I can put it, the ship's kewsers are able to detect and report on the things they're being used for. Add to that the fact that the government has loads of tek reconnaissance methods … Besides, the Navy's own listening networks, and a thing called the multi-band hyper-comp emission detectors, which can keep track of what kinds of vessels might be traversing the conduit zones. I know it's a bit zanerie, but it all goes back to what happened in the Rebel wars. Tenak could tell you more about that. Anyhow, there was a lot of migration out here, to Oceanus, at one time, wasn't there?'

'Deedly. Many thousands each year, for the first, oh, say 50 years. Otherwise, the original colony would not have so survived. They had yet to ensure sufficient numbers of people so to make a genetically viable population. Avoid genetic drift. The population has grown naturally since then, of course and, you mayst know, we *do* allow immigration but …'

'But there's only about 100 to 150 allowed here each year, isn't there? And applicants have to satisfy a pretty rigorous selection procedure to, um, shall we say, convince your people they are committed to the principles of conservation; your world's wildness and …what, your constitution?'

'Again, right my mate. And I thought you but said you did not have the time to study any more than some basic Oceanus historia, when you came out here? Eh, space boy?'

Even in the dark he could see her wide, effervescent smile. It was more to do with feeling than seeing.

'You know, I've had some great teachers while I've been here. Danile Hermington, Professier Muggredge and a funny person called …Elly, no Elri?' teased Mike. She pinched his shoulder. For a while neither spoke. Then, she broke the silence. She sounded suddenly sombre.

'This world means everything to me, Mike. I know there are probably wonders that fill the days of people back in your Solar System, but what we have here is precious and that is why we had to have independence. We had to become self-sufficient and still I know it took a long time, but we did it. We only import some specialised goods from the Home System and we export quality goods – most hand-made. I am thinking there is a lot here, like minerals and raw materials, that HS would like to have and praps their chance has now come.'

'Seriously, El? I thought you didn't go with all that Meta stuff about the Home System wanting to use this planet for themselves?'

Eleri became a little agitated. 'I do not Mike. No. But all of this ... this world I love, and everyone here loves, tis finished. We are going to have to leave. That is why you came here, in first place. True?' Mike looked away from her and nodded, then said, 'You're right, unfortunately. But I guess, on a personal level, I've found a reason to stay. At least, for now.'

'I know, I know,' she said, hugging him again, and after a few minutes said, 'I carnt believe it is all over for Oceanus, darlie, but tis.'

'Forgive me, love, but you seemed to be, maybe a little bit sceptical when I first met you but – not now?'

'Of course not. I was only, how you do you say – sceptical - because I know tis only too easy for alternative interpretations of the evidence to be had, even in science, in complex things. But you saw the stuff on Simurgh. That tomb? I think Rubia was right. T'was a tomb, you know. And that band of black rock? I may not be a geolrist, but I am certain that really it was the sign of a gargrantan conflagration on this planet. Massive calamity - and what happened to those poor creatures, those beings, like the ones we found?'

'Yeah, but Danile told me they probably lived hundreds of thousands of years before the catastrophe, maybe as much as two million ...'

'Dost not matter, does it? They arint here now, are they? No-one has ever seen beings like that here. No-one has ever seen any evidence of self-aware creatures before we came here. They have vanished long-times. I really believe they were wiped out, my love. I am no longer sceptical. And we will also be destroyed if we stay, will we not?'

Mike could see Eleri's mood changing right in front of him, but he could not and would not deny what she was saying. It was no time for false reassurances. She turned her head and the pale, ghostly light from the myriad stars cast a faint blue glimmer on her face – and he saw her tears. He instinctively moved closer and reached for her.

'Everything we worked for is finished, ist not?' she mumbled, and she seemed to pull away from him a little. He hoped he was imagining that.

'El, please. You … and I … We can survive this.'

'And where will the people of my world go, Mike? Do you know?'

'There's plenty of room on Earth and in floating colonies and things. You know the Earth is just like Oceanus. It really is. It's not as bad as you might think. Since the destructions of the late 21st Century, and all that, there's more space. The population is …'

'Still measured in the billions, Mike. *Billions*. And the culture – is totally different. Your world's natural treasures have been pillaged, looted – over centuria. And do you know where will we all go? Praps onto "reservations". Like the places the natives of that America place were sent, five hundreds of years ago?'

'I think you're being too negative, El. It's not like that anymore. There's no reason why the people here couldn't settle down on Earth. I know how you feel but …'

'Do not say that, Mike! I know you mean well and all, but do not say such an thing. Deep shame to you, Michaelsonn. You could not *know*. We will all have to leave our homes and our life-ways, our plans, … and our dreams. We will have to leave our culture and our beautiful world – and we will be spread on the five winds of the space oceans. This planet will be made barren and eventually, no-one will be able to see what we did here; what it meant to us.'

As she spoke Mike felt a pang of guilt and remorse. 'Please El, I didn't mean to upset you. I'm so sorry,' he blurted.

She grasped one of his hands and pressed her lips to it, and he knew she immediately regretted her outburst. But it was completely understandable. Just then warm hands and cool lips sought him. She didn't really blame him. He could only see her outline, but he felt her anguish. The warmth of her tears ran over his own hands, rapidly cooling in the chill night air that suddenly seemed to have gathered around them.

'Tis not your fault. Tis no-one's,' was all she said, and then she withdrew from him, walking silently indoors and out of his presence. He immediately felt an emptiness and thought about following her but felt it best to let her be alone – for now. He stayed on the patio for a long while and stared up at the stars. Tonight, they seemed strangely chill, careless and unpitying. What did human concerns matter to them?

He and everyone else would soon find an answer to that one.

Interlude

EVALUATIONS FROM AFAR

The thought streams of Hermoptica and Percepticon flashed through their respective organic and cybernetic brains; torrents of neural energy surging through their linked flesh. The effect of the organic joining was to generate a thought capacity which was probably equal to that of several dozen human brains; an effect further augmented, when required, by their cybernetic brains, their adjuncts.

The Superadjunct had not advised that there be a further cerebral conjoining of the whole community because the mothership had released her bellyful of robotinoids, and they still required its guidance. There was also the need to pick up vital feedback from that swarm of micro-machines.

The Others remain unaware of our presence, thought Hermoptica and Percepticon. *They are indeed ignorant but are subject to much distress and calamitous decisions, for their actions are uncentred and precipitous. The Superadjunct has learned much about them since we arrived and continues to gather that which enlightens us.*

Then, the nearing presence of Demetia was felt and they warmly allowed his thoughts to impinge, though in a relatively shallow degree, into their deep thought meld. *The outer sensory matrix has warned that the Others are more of a threat than we anticipated,* flowed Demetria. *It has become clear that they use the energy of atomic fusion for transport and may yet use it for aggression, given that they are uninformed anthropoidea; spinners of great dreams, it seems, but also of deceipt. The Superadjunct has predicted that they are not capable of making quantum beam weapons, directed or otherwise, but would instead use archaic devices to produce fusion explosions.

Dangerous of course but the robotinoids will both absorb their radiation and reflect it. And so, we have nothing to fear, flowed Perepticon.

This absorption will be bought at some cost to the robotinoids, and we may readily deal with the anthropoid threat only if correctly anticipated, flowed Demetia's thoughts, *and yet the Others may not be prepared for us, if and when we are obliged to act. They may still be harmed, even by themselves. They seem to be the biggest threat to themselves.*

We must respect their power, of course, flowed Hermoptica / Percepticon, *but the Superadjunct calculates that our swarm of robotinoids shall soon arrive at Qadestriana-Chonis Ekta. We also have interpreted the emissions of the Others, being those emanating from the World of Dreams, which drew us here, and from their strange void-sailing vessels. We are trying to locate the origin point of this species.*

They have not journeyed from a vast distance, I know, mused Demetia, with something approaching contempt, *for their origin has now been located. The Superadjunct, together with the minor adjuncts, have deduced that they have traversed the distance light travels in a mere 77.8 of the cycles our Home Sphere takes to travel around our star-home.*

Percepticon / Hermoptica considered the matter for a lengthy four and a half hundred-thousandths of a second before chiding Demetia, gently. *It is unbecoming to be disdainful, since we know of no others like them in this entire hemisphere of the Great Star Wheel. We know they are not capable of discovering the locus of our origin. Praise we must, our distant ancestors for building our Grand Sphere That Shelters Life, which surrounds and encloses our star, and which cannot be seen by beings like these.*

Demetia flowed a riposte, after a pause of a ten millionth of a second, *They would detect our point of origin were it not hidden by the mighty central dust and gas clouds of the Great Star Wheel, and, it does not emit light that signifies the presence of life, still less sentience. But we need not be concerned thus, for the general Flow has determined that these beings may be utilising the negative energy tendrillons and spiracles that link the stars.*

Lo, the Superadjunct has also now conjoined with us in this matter, flowed Hermoptica / Percepticon, *and has endorsed your conclusion. We may thus pity them, for whilst they may travel between star hyperspheres with some greater speed than even we, they are constrained to travelling to nominal points at equal hyper-complex distances from their home system. We now estimate there may indeed be an aeon of cycles before they could find the means to cross the greater voids, as do we. They may never reach our home star sphere, more than 81,000 light cycles distance from here - and the other side of the Great Star Wheel's central singularity.*

Their limitations have thus been of great cost to them, flowed Demetia, *for they are trapped and might never know of the wonders and greatness beyond their little sphere.*

Chapter 35

FAMILY MATTERS

Arkas Tenak felt his wristcom vibrate against his skin and, from the rhythm he could tell that this was not just an incoming call but a sensitive one and confidential. He quickly checked the device and was surprised to see that it was from Dracus Muggredge.

He tapped his device in a particular pattern, which made it call the Professier back and tell him that there would be a delay before the Admiral could reply. Tenak was in the middle of a Senior Officer's discussion about engineer Havring, the crewmember accused of interfering with the ship's hypercomp.

Tenak sat, with four other officers, around a long, elliptically shaped table, in a sparsely furnished room in one of the command blocks on The Monsoon's rotating torus. Like all of those on the torus, this office enjoyed gravity at nearly the strength experienced on the Earth's surface.

First Officer Statton was saying, in his broad oldworld-French accent, that Havring had been under observation for most of the last ten days. He had received six visits from colleagues and been interrogated five times by ship's officers, including the Captain and the Admiral. Discrete vid surveillance had revealed nothing. He had never given anything away about how, or why, he may have committed the offences, or who else might have been involved. In fact, he had consistently denied doing anything wrong.

And yet, the suspect had been unable to account for his presence, alone, on the mainframe deck at the relevant times. His absences from work were known to be due to his use of a brainstim device, found in his cabin, as well as a variety of chemical drugs also found there. He had finally admitted to various addictions and to dereliction of duty, and he had accepted that his career in the Navy was over. This pleased no-one, and neither would anyone wish to celebrate his downfall, but interference with the mainframe was a different matter entirely. Still he strenuously denied sabotaging the hypercomp, or changing sensor data, or interference with the corvettes sent out to survey Oceanus.

'I can't help but think that he was used as a dupe-man,' said Tenak, 'a bogey-stooge for the real villains. Havring just doesn't seem capable, on his own. He keeps denying that he was ever on the hyper-deck when the sensors say he was, and the sensor data is the only "proof" of that. But we know the sensor arrays have been interfered with, so we're in the proverbial "Klein Bottle"; what they used to call, a "Catch 22" situation.'

'We can't confirm he was in his cabin either, for the same reason,' said Ebazza. 'He certainly wasn't seen in any of the social areas, or mess halls. Not even the exercise decks.'

'Perhaps Havring hasn't told us anything simply because he doesn't have anything to do with the sabotage,' said Statton.

'Maybe,' said Ebazza, sharp-toned, 'but meanwhile, Admiral, all necessary security protocols have been upgraded and strengthened. We are on a level just one micro-grade below battle readiness, sir.'

'Good,' said Tenak, 'and we continue to look for clues, gentilhomms, but I cannot escape the feeling that someone is using Havring. Our job is to find out who. Thank you all for your contributions.' Tenak stood and the assembled officers rose immediately.

'Dismissed,' said Ebazza, and, as the others filed out Tenak remained and paced the far end of the room, speaking to his wristcom. Ebazza closed the door behind her.

As his original communications with Muggredge had involved old world radio waves, Tenak had recently suggested it was time they tried setting up 3D holo capacity for the Professor, which had subsequently been installed into the academic's new office, a few weeks previously. It was the only such system installed on Oceanus, so far, but Muggredge was not keen to reveal its existence to anyone outside his tight circle of trusted colleagues. It probably broke government and university rules, and the professor suggested now was not a good time to aggravate such people.

On Oceanus, Muggredge, having followed the instructions on the manual, specially printed for him by the ship's technician, had signalled to Tenak he was ready. Within seconds of the Admiral instructing his wristcom to access the necessary tek in the University, a holo of him suddenly appeared in Muggredge's office, standing large as life, a couple of metres from the academic's chair.

'Nadder's teeth!' exclaimed Muggredge, almost jumping with surprise, and he tiptoed delicately around Tenak's image, as if wishing to inspect it from many different angles.

'I carnt believe it,' he said, 'for you do look absolute solid and real, though still, I see the odd flickering of light that seems yet to pass through you from your head to your boots. Marvellus. And you are now walking around my office, seeming so to avoid the furniture. But I cannot see your own office.'

'The flickering is just com static, Professier. And yes, I can see most of your office here, on the ship. The pan-holo-emitter net was installed in your office, only. There would be serious breaches of current security protocols if you could see my office, right now. Sorry, Professier.'

'Oh, tis nothing-such, Admiral. I am yet sorry to hear you have security issues so serious.'

'So am I. Anyway, it's good to speak to you again. It's been quite some time. Before we go any further, I just wanted to extend my condolences to you – concerning – the loss of one of your team. I didn't have a chance to tell you, in person, till now.'

Muggredge's eyes were cast down for a few moments, before he said, 'Thankly Admiral, thankly. I have been … devastated. Rubia was quite dear to me. But I should extend the same sentiment to you, regarding your crewmember.'

'Yes, such things ... are difficult. I mean difficult to bear ... but bear them we must, or give up all responsibility.'

'Deedly, Admiral.'

'Now, Professier, I'm sorry to rush you but, unfortunately, I have some pressing duties to perform, so could you ....?'

'Of course, dear-so Admiral. Please forgive me. I have some vera-special news, but this is also a matter of security importance. Ist safe to use this means of communicadio?'

'It's safer than radio but just because I seem to be in the room with you doesn't mean it's as safe as though I was actually there. The only alternative would be for me to come down in an LB. Is that going to be necessary?' Tenak's image gave Muggredge an intensely quizzical look.

'Oh, I am not sure but, as you say, sometimes things carnt be helped. I will amend so my words. Try not to give too much away.'

Tenak's puzzled look deepened into a frown.

'The main thing I proffer is that I have a ... *colleague* in, shall we say – high places. He is more an important ... how you say ... acquaintance, rather than real friendling or colleague. I think you already knew that, yes? This colleague, or praps his personal agent, wants to meet with you, in person. The meeting, face to face, is mainly so to avoid any possible leak of information, Admiral.'

'I suppose that makes sense, but why me?'

'This personry insists so he will not speak to anyone else and if his offer is not taken up, you are losing the information. I am thinking that, of all the Navy personnel on your ship and on the planet, he feels he can be trusting you most-such. I am sorry, Admiral, but I am unable to tell you more, and that is because I just do not know what type of thing this person wants to say. But tis serious stuff. So, I am thinking it would be wise to take up his offer.'

'It seems I am honoured. Alright. Where does he want to meet, and when?'

'The meeting should yet take place on the outskirts of Remnissa. This is a small, out-of-way town, about 2,900 kilometres from Janitra, and t'will be on Farlingsday coming. Tis to be, so I believe, 'tween 23.00 and 23.30. You will be left some kind of sign, as to precisely where to meet. Tis something that you alone will recognise, some cryptical thing, very close to the proposed meeting place. And Admiral, list yet. He insists you *only,* should be there. No other Navy, or people from the Home System. I have been told that if he thinks security has been compromised by this transmission, or in any other way, then such meeting will be off. I am advised that he will be watching … all the time. Admiral, I have been thinking he is well used to this type of subterfugery.'

'Remnissa? Don't think I know much about that place. Must be small, but it's probably on our shipnet. I'll check when I get a chance.'

'Yes, Admiral. Tis small. I know that place is remote. The populari, praps strangemost. I have not been there but have heard much. I understand there is nothing of anything there. But Admiral, my advice is caution. Great caution.'

****

Back in Chantris, Eleri told Mike he'd been invited to an evening meal, at home, with her parents, the next day. This would be the first time for him to meet them. Everyone had been busy with their separate concerns, until then, but Eleri said her folks were desperate to make his acquiantance.

Mike felt slightly awed by the prospect but didn't resist. That wouldn't have been a good idea at all, given Eleri's closeness to her family, and besides, he was curious about them.

The following evening, Mike spruced himself up and wore his white Secretary's uniform, as Eleri had suggested, and they walked the nine or ten kilometres to her parent's house. Mike was getting used to the long walks on this planet.

The white and cream, stone-built, house was a spacious, "old style" farmhouse sitting in beautiful Devian countryside. It seemed to Mike more like an Earth-bound piece of parkland than a farm. El explained that crops were grown on the land to the rear of the building and poultry was raised in large open fields to the sides. They also owned a set of stables nearby, with half a dozen horses, some owned by them, and others by locals.

Eleri's mother, known in OA dialect as a "meether", was, to Mike's surprise, a short, slightly plump, brown haired lady, with a rounder face than Eleri, but with the same intense but kind eyes as her daughter. Her smile was warm and her manner homely, and Mike took an instant liking to her. She was called Elene-Nefer Ambrell, and Eleri's father, or "faether", was known as Marcus of Tharnton. Familial names usually followed those of the female line, the social structure being mainly matriarchal on Oceanus. Marcus was a slim but strong looking, willowy, individual, with a bushy mat of red hair, of similar type to Eleri's. Marcus's thick corded musculature showed the physical nature of much of his daily work. He too, greeted Mike with a huge smile of genuine warmth and he said, in a deep bass voice, that Eleri had told them much about her "favo-manry".

As is usual at times like these, both Mike and El were a little on edge and embarrassed. Mike realised Eleri was keen for her family to impress him and like him and, for his part, he was determined not to let her down. Eleri hugged and kissed her parents and Mike exchanged the Devian style of handshake with Marcus, a double-handed type, and forearm to forearm, but he used the more reserved Home System style handshake with Elene-Nefer. It served to cover the slight embarrassment he felt at meeting another woman almost as good looking as Eleri and related to her.

When they entered the house, Professier Muggredge unexpectedly stepped out from a back room and greeted them. Mike and Eleri were surprised but delighted to see him. Mike was also introduced to Eleri's younger sister, a femna called Meriataten, and her two children, Jod, her son of six and her daughter, Neferikare, aged seven. Interesting names, thought Mike. Jod and Neferikare instantly ran off to play out back.

Meriataten, four years younger than Eleri, looked nothing like her sister, having dark brown hair that cascaded to her waist. She was very thin, almost painfully so, thought Mike, compared with Eleri's smooth and lithe, muscled, build.

'Do not forget childes, twill soon be dinner, so make sure you clean up afore-time,' Meriataten said to the two children as they ran off, 'I am yet sorry,' she said to Mike and Muggredge, 'they are surely tearo-ways, but they are good at heart.'

'Oh, no need to apologise,' said Mike as he and Eleri were invited into the family's large and rustically decorated lounge-room, where they were seated on a spacious and much worn sofa. Muggeredge sat next to them whilst Mer and Mes Ambrell took requests for drinks and hurried into the kitchen.

'Such a great thing to see you again Secretary Tanniss,' said Muggredge, 'I have much to talk to you about, but I think t'will need wait till after we have eaten, yes?'

Mike nodded and Eleri, sitting next to him hugged Mike, then went to join her parents, later returning with tea made from broadie leaves, for her uncle, and water for Mike, as requested.

'Meether doesn't want any help in there,' she told Mike, 'I am thinking I had best yet keep out of the way.' She laughed, the kind of nervous laugh perhaps made by many daughters the first time they introduce their lovers to their families. Mike, for his part, was just as nervous.

'El tells me you write for a living,' said Mike to Meriataten. She nodded rather shyly, explaining that, in the main, she wrote books on history; both textbooks and popular treatments, and mostly for the Oceanus market. But some had been bought by institutions in the Home System. Mike was quite surprised at that. He also remembered not to ask her anything about the father of her children, because he had been primed by Eleri. The man had apparently run off with another woman some years ago. Eleri had said that Meriataten was a home loving femna and now lived with her parents all the time, drawing a small living from selling her books. Her previous manry had owned nothing.

On Oceanus, couples who had sworn to live together, in marriage, were called "combinas". Couples whose combinas failed tended to gather something of a social stigma, for *both* partners, which Mike felt to be rather austere, not to say regressive. An unfortunate throwback to less enlightened times, maybe? But then, was it any worse than the shenanigans that went on throughout most, though certainly not *all,* of the Home System, where so few could keep vows, be they same sex, different sex or transgender couples and groups. He immediately thought of Tenak's unhappiness.

'Meriataten, I can't help but notice that you and your daughter have rather old-world sounding names,' said Mike. 'Are they ancient Sumerian, or something?'

'No, Mike. And yet please call me, Meri. I am glad you have so asked. Our names are taken from ancient Egypt. They are surely very old names, probably not used for thousands of years – but none the worse for that.'

'Absolutely not,' said Mike, nodding vigorously, 'in fact, I think they're really good.'

'Well, thankly, Mike,' said Meri, her face beaming.

'Both I and meether has such a name too,' said Eleri, 'or at least partly. The "Nefer" part. In her case tis linked with her first name, Elene.'

'Of course,' said Mike, cos I was wondering about that.' Sensing some degree of awkwardness at how to follow that up, because he had little knowledge of ancient Egypt, Mike turned to Muggredge and asked him about Admiral Tenak's health, knowing he'd been in touch.

'He is well, I believe,' said the academic, 'though looking something care-worn, praps.' That made Mike feel slightly guilty. He had finally begun to appreciate his special relationship with Tenak. His burgeoning romantic relationship with Eleri had somehow brought to mind all sorts of things like that; things which he had probably buried in his sub-conscious, not wishing to admit to them. Yet his same relationship with her had taken up more and more of his time and of course, had to have total precedence.

A little later everyone was seated around a large, wooden table near a picture window which gave lovely views onto the huge blue-green garden at the back of the house. Mike felt it was idyllic. He guessed he was privileged to be in such company but, most of all, he felt at peace, sitting next to Eleri; a peace that was, in fact, new to him.

Eleri's mother and father shared the job of bringing food out to the family table, serving their guests and replenishing drinks. Mike, being used to food being prepared for him and the rest of the crew, on board The Monsoon, had to be prompted by Eleri into offering his assistance but it was politely declined. The Nefer-Ambrells were perfect hosts, or so Mike felt, and Muggredge, being the most "senior" person present, entertained all, with stories about "the old days" on Oceanus. Only Meriataten seemed to have become withdrawn. Mike wanted to try to bring her into the conversation but Eleri occasionally nudged him to keep silent. That was a bit strange, he thought.

The food, Mike felt, was mostly – okay. It started off with an unusual potato and vegetable soup. Mike was certainly not put off by the sight of blue vegetables, as he was when he first came to Oceanus, but he gulped when a second course of stringy meat and even stringier vegetables was served, covered with a kind of green gravy. The meat was hardly edible, but he dared not offend his hosts, so he tried to eat as much as he could. Eleri saw him fiddling with his dish, like a fussy child. He wondered if she might chide him, but she balanced her right elbow on the table and covered her eyes with one hand, so no-one could see her silent giggling. Mike started to chuckle as well and despite his best attempts to hide it, Elene-Nefer saw him and said, 'Mike, sirra, you really do not need to eat the meat if you do not wish. I am not offended should you not. Please just leave it. The yamkler lizards, out back, will eat it.'

'I'm so sorry. May I ask what it is?' said Mike.

'Yes deedly, Mike. Tis Oceanus hybrid-ogra. Like such a rat thing but hybrised generations ago, with lizard. We farm them, of course, but not for commerce. Tis just for our use – and on small scale.'

Facinating, thought Mike. Pity it tasted like cow shit.

There was a third course, consisting of loaves of genetically manipulated broadie leaves and – just plain, ordinary chicken, with a light gravy. This was followed by a dessert, of strawberries, again familiar, served in a pie, with a cream made from the heat-treated sap of Larp trees. Mike was pleasantly surprised to find he thoroughly enjoyed these particular courses.

Jod and Neferikari sat with them to eat and Mike was impressed by how well they behaved. There was the occasional bout of giggling from them, especially when they saw some of the expressions Mike made, when eating. After the meal the two children started giggling again. 'Do you come from the Homey place?' asked Jod.

'Yes, Jod, I do. And tis called the Home System,' said Mike.

'Tis a long way away?' said Jod.

'A very long way,' said Mike. It took us over six weeks to get here.'

'You are very slow,' said Neferikare. Everyone laughed.

Mike nodded and Jod then piped up again, 'You are deedly slow - and you talk funny.' Neferikare roared with laughter.

'He would probably say *you* talk funny too,' said Eleri.

'Not at all. I suppose I am funny, anywayins,' said Mike.

'Yes, so. You are like a fargie,' said the boy, an impish look on his face.

'And what's a fargie like?' asked Mike, falling into their trap.

'A fargie is funny of course,' said Neferikare.

There was more chuckling around the table, and then Meri told the children to go play outside, but to come in when it got dark as they had some studying to do before bed. The kids raced off, tumbling with each-other in rowdy horse play, giggling all the time.

The adults remained seated and Mike thought this whole occasion so deliciously quaint he decided he rather liked it. Elene-Nefer asked him about Home System technology and said that Eleri had told her about his wristcom. Mike was happy to oblige her curiosity and let her have a close look at the device. As he answered her questions about it, Marcus said, 'What is yet the matter, Elene? Would you want an such like in this house?'

She looked curiously at her husband, 'It might prove useful, at that,' she said, 'and I am curious – tis all.' She looked askance at Marcus, but he persisted, saying, 'Meri tells me that all in the Home System use these devices and similar such, and that they are all addicted to their use.'

Everyone glanced at Meri, who seemed embarrassed at first, but then bristled as Mike said, 'Well, not everyone in the system uses these particular things. They are mostly used by the Navy and …'

'I have studied these things, *Mer Tanniss*,' said Meri, interjecting, 'and have, after all met other folkery from the Home System. I am led to believe that the popularia use all similar devices – and use them to exclusion of their love of nature. Also, such, their environment. They are obsess-ed with them, are they not?'

'I suppose you're right, to some extent,' said Mike, 'but it isn't quite like it used to be in the early days, like the cell-coms, like in the early 21st century. In that case I would certainly agree with you. People had devices they had to hold in their hands. In the first couple of decades after their invention people went really mad for them. That's when I believe many such *"folkery"*, probably got addicted.'

'Praps,' said Meri, 'and by the way, manry, please do not be patronio – sorry, I mean patronising.'

'I think Mike was just teasing you, were you not, Mike?' said Eleri, looking sharply into his eyes. He nodded, obligingly.

Eleri then tried her best to diffuse the tension that seemed to have built up, 'Anywayins, I for one, am curious about the Home System tek. Don't have to get addicted. But now, would anyone like something more to drink or to eat? And praps we should be adjourn-ed to the main resting lounge. Tis more comfortable there.'

Everyone agreed, got up and moved to the next room where they sat on sofas and armchairs arranged in a semi-circle. Mike and Eleri happened to end up sitting on opposite sides of the room, with Elene-Nefer sitting next to Mike. Meri and her father joined them. Muggredge, piped up, 'Ah, now, Mike, why do you not tell us of how you think people have changed their use of, well, "private technology", since such early days?'

'I can if that's what people want to hear, but I am not a historian, like Meri,' said Mike. Meri made a funny noise in the back of her throat and glanced away.

'That is fine Mike. Please go on,' said Elene-Nefer.

'I think a lot changed after the virus pandemics – in 2042, and, as you know, that was followed by the Toba super-volcano explosion.'

'When was that, now?' asked Meri.

'I believe it was 2060.'

'I think you will find t'was 2063, exact-so,' said Meri, earning a warning glare from Eleri.

'I stand corrected,' said Mike. Was this young femna deliberately trying to bait him, he wondered. He continued, 'Anyway, as I' sure you know, the Earth was in a bad way for many decades. A lot of people died, all over the planet, partly from the pandemics but, after that, many more died because of the so-called 'ultra-winter', caused by the super-volcano. Crops were wrecked everywhere. And there were lots of minor wars over resources, all over …'

'I am believing about three billions of people perish-ed,' said Meri, interrupting again.

'Sadly, I think you'll find it was nearer five billion,' said Mike, emphatically, 'over many years and between all the different horrors.' He felt slightly aggrieved that these people didn't seem to know their own ancestors' history, in much detail. He ruminated that civilisation, as known up to that time, had been set back well nearly two hundred years on the home planet, most of the excruciating death toll happening over the first hundred years after the initial disaster, amid famines, tribal conflict, larger wars, and disease. But three billion people *had* survived and amongst them there had been enough enterprise and drive to pull back from the brink.

Even so, it had been a close-run thing and a near miracle that humanity had pulled itself back from total anhiliation, and had recovered its arts, literature, science and technology. Even children of five, back home, knew that it had taken around one hundred and sixty years for humanity to climb out of that deep, sunless pit. For his own part, Mike was proud that so much had been achieved since then, though even he was keenly aware that humanity, as a species, still had a long way to go.

Everyone at the table had gone quiet and introspective. Elene-Nefer broke the spell, as she said, with genuine compassion, 'Mike, sirra, you are right. I am yet sorrymost. We are now unable to comprehend what it must have been like for people living on that poor world during such times.'

Muggredge added, sagely, 'And let us not so forget, that this was all part of *our* historie as well. Tis only our isolation and … our attitude … toward the Home System which now means this historie is not taught as widely in our skoolries as once t'was.'

Nearly everyone agreed with the Professier, though Mike noted that Marcus and Meri seemed reticent.

'Truemost,' said Elene-Nefer, 'but some of our own founders didst set up a monument to the Earth tragedie, here on Oceanus, when they arrived. I am true sorry that, by sad-tiding, I think it became broken down some years back.'

Mike said, 'I hadn't realised that. Back home, there's been a special day of commemorations, held, all across the Earth, every year since then. Every ten years it covers a full two weeks of remembrance events.'

'Deedly, and sad things are remembered therein, though there are also positive things done,' said Muggredge, 'I myself have witnessed such commemoratios.'

Everyone looked surprised.

'I was not knowing you had been to Earth, Unkling,' said Meri.

'Oh, yes,' he said, almost embarrassed by the attention he'd drawn, 'but t'was many, many Oceanus years past. So many, I care not to say, but I shall certainly be remembering that visit forever. But, enough of this. Mike, continue with your story – please,'

'I guess that the story of modern tek comes after the gradual recovery from the so-called "New Dark Ages",' said Mike, 'but, well, as I think you know, most parts of the Earth recovered their science and technology very slowly. At a certain point it took off kind of super quick in many places but not everywhere. But, as advanced as we like to think the tek is now, I reckon that at the present moment, nearly three hundred years later, I'm sure we don't have the advanced tek we would have had if there'd been an unbroken line of development. Do you see what I mean?'

'You mean the tek you have is not good enough for you?' asked Marcus, an expression of cynicism on his ruddy face.

'No, not really, Marcus. I just meant the tek we've got would certainly have been much more advanced than we have now – if there'd been a continuous line of tek development since the mid-23rd century. For example, maybe we would have found a way out of "the cage" by now. Probably long ago. We might have explored half the galaxy by now, or something. Or, maybe we'd be flying ships through space by using … well, thought control, or … .' He stopped, for he was starting to feel a bit uncomfortable from the kind of looks he was getting. Especially from Marcus and Meri, though Elene-Nefer seemed to be enjoying what she was hearing. Eleri and Muggredge looked as though they might have heard it all before, maybe.

But Muggredge nodded sagely and Eleri chimed in, saying, 'And Mike tells me the way interstellar flight is done, though tis a marvellri, is yet restricted. It means that … What did you say, Mike? Humanity is trapped in a bubble?'

'Yeah. It's usually described as a cage, the one I mentioned,' said Mike.

'So, you think we humans, you so say, might have found a way *around or out* of the cage before now – if were not for the New Dark Ages?' said Muggredge.

'If it were not for the break in development. Well, maybe yes, maybe not. I don't know. For all I know, we might have explored the entire galaxy by now. Or something like that.' It had gone quiet again.

'I thinks I am not hearing this proper-so,' said Marcus, with an astonished look on his face. 'You have interstellar flight, *but tis not enough.* You have wizardry communication, *but tis not enough.* Colonisation of all your solar system – the wonderful "Home System" we keep hearing about – yet tis *not enough*?'

'Marcus?' said Elene-Nefer, disapproval etched on her features.

'I never said, tis not enough, sir,' said Mike. 'And in a sense, those things, you know, the interstellar flight, holo-coms and so on, sort of belong to all of us. You, as well. They're a part of all our heritage.'

'Not all of us, Mer Tanniss,' said Meri. 'You people of the Home System think we are backward. Think we have yet dropped behind, when tis *you* who have dropped back – in such terms of culture and understanding of the world and our place within.

And e'en as regards morality, so I understand. Do you not all practice polygamy?' Meri's voice began to rise with indignation.

'Well, yes, but not all of us, Meri,' said Mike. He was just beginning to feel something familiar in the way things were going, here. He thought he'd left the "old style" of Oceanus treatment behind. Maybe not.

'Please do not take that tone with Mike,' said Eleri, unexpectedly and sharply. Eyebrows were raised all around. She glanced at her partner, 'Sorry Mike. I know you can yet fight your own battle-mash but I believe as such, you are too polite to speak as you should.'

'But e'en so,' said Marcus, 'I do yet think Meri has such valid a point and the worst of this is, that *we* are all now expected to leave our homes, and our living-ways. We are to just up and go – to this Home System place.'

Oh no, thought Mike. Now we're getting to the core of the matter. He went silent.

'You – and your people – just want us to leave our homes,' Marcus continued, 'being homes we have such built up for generations. This familia can trace its roots back to the very second group of colonists that came to this world. The *second,* Mikery Tanniss. We have struggled with this place for so long and now we have learned to live in harmony with its nature, at least as far as humanity can do. Now, yet, we have to leave.' Marcus's face went even redder than usual and took on a peculiarly sour complexion. The veins in his neck began to stand out.

'We have no choice faether,' said Eleri, as softly as she could. 'I know you do not wish to hear this, but still we must be leaving – and soon. We should not be waiting too long to book places on HS transport. I am believing there may suddenly be a rush. I am sorry, faether.' Marcus looked angry and his wife looked distraught.

'We will *not* leave this place,' blurted Marcus, 'or, I shall say, leastways, *I will not.*' He looked at his wife of 30 years, mournfully. She reached forward and clasped his hand. 'Do not say these things,' she pleaded.

'I am sorry, Elene,' he said, 'but I cannot leave all this behind.' He swung one large, brawny arm outwards, as though displaying the house and its environs. 'I will so understand if you want to leave.'

'Do not be a fargie, Marcus,' she said, 'you know I would not be a-leaving you. Never.'

On top of the evident sadness of this couple the acidic voice of Meriataten added more misery, as she stared at Mike and said, 'You see. Manry from Earth. This is what it means to us to leave this place. The Home System is mad and so are we – all. Humanity is madness and you say you wish we could break out of our "cage". E'en if we could so do, we should not e'en try.'

'You have said enough, Meri,' said Eleri. Her eyes burning into those of her sister.

'It's okay, El. Let her speak,' said Mike.

Marcus turned back to Mike. 'And where are all our people supposed to go, young manry? Where will they be sent? I have heard many stories about detention centres on the Earth.'

'We will surely be refugees,' said Elene-Nefer, her eyes moist.

'I'm sorry but I don't know very much about this, but I'll tell you what I told Eleri,' said Mike. He felt as if her were skating on ice a millimetre thick. His heart was thumping but he felt he had a duty, to Eleri, if no-one else, to at least try to give these people some reassurance. But could he? Should he even try? He didn't think it would soften the blow. He continued, 'I understand there are about twenty, very spacious, well equipped, reception zones on the Earth. Several on every continent. As well as one on Mars. I think everyone, as they arrive, in groups, is supposed to … to gather in one of the large Earth orbital stations, first. Then they will be ferried down to the Earth. On the station they will, so I believe, find out what everyone wants to do, where they want to go, and what their skills are. Their abilities and so on. I can't be certain, but the idea is to distribute everyone to whatever centres they prefer, on the surface. And eventually, the idea is to get people out to the resettlement areas as soon as possible. The idea is …'

'Lots of ideas, young manry,' said Marcus,' but not much assurances. Nothing so definite …'

'Let the youngst speak!' said Muggredge. Mike sat bolt upright. He had never heard Eleri's uncle speak so sharply before.

'I'm afraid I'm not responsible for what happens, sir,' said Mike, 'I am just the Secretary on The Monsoon. We were just tasked with helping to start getting people off this planet and safely to the Earth. I'm sorry. I'm sure that Admiral Tenak would know more detail. But the evacuation hasn't even begun yet. We didn't think more than a few hundred would be going home, I mean, to the Home System, on this trip. But it's taken this long to … oh, it doesn't matter right now.' Mike was beginning to feel desperate.

Muggredge spoke again, softly, 'Frendling, it dost matter yet. I have still spoken to Admiral Tenak about this, on many occasions, Marcus. There are many areas on the Earth, where the local population is still depleted, following the horrors, as such mentioned. There are large areas available, in several-many city states and surrounding areas. Many such areas within the continents do have a similar climate to this world. One in particular is meant to be our first home, though yet that mayst change. I am told climate is often controlled in some city states, but not in their surrounding zones. Some of us might e'en choose to go to Mars. That planet has a very low gravity yet, but it has been wondrously changed, so its climate is such amenable.

'Anywayins, tis an option. I do not think we will be forced to do what'ere we do not want, Marcus. And as for being refugees, Meri, all I can say is that many social problems were caused in the past because refugees tried to go to already overpopulated countries. Or, other countries refused to take them, gainst good reason. But those poulari wanted to leave their homes, for better lives, or as they were forced out, by bad leaders and bad people. But still, we are different, are we not? We think we do not need to leave. We know better. Seems *we* do not want to leave e'en though we know we must. But we *must*. All of us must leave – or all die. This is not the doing of a tyrant. Nor yet do we need to leave because we are poor. We thought, no, we knew, this world had much, much more to offer us but – no longer. Tis a natural catastrophism that looms. But, on Earth, we are to be offered the chance to go to underpopulated places, where our abilities and talents will be useful. And, so I say, where we will *have to learn to call such places home.*'

Eleri nodded and, with moist eyes looked straight into her father's eyes.

'The thing-such is this, my faether, my meether,' she said, 'we have to adapt. Deedly, t'will not be good for us on the Earth - not at first. With greatest-so respect to him, praps Unkling is being overly-fine about it, because I am not believing we will be able to go where we wish, or do whatever we want. Sorry Unkling. But some of us may, and most of us will, survive. *We* shall adapt. We have to. There is no choice.'

Muggredge stayed silent. Mike knew Eleri was probably right and he reckoned Dracus Muggredge did too.

The conversation seemed exhausted, thought Mike, and so was he. He sat with his head in his hands. Marcus stood quickly and strode outside. They could see him through the window, standing in the garden, with his back to the house, holding onto an iron rail, overlooking the wild blue-green sward beyond.

Eleri started to rise. 'Praps I should go to him,' she said, softly. Elene-Nefer stood, tears running down her face, and held her hand up. 'No, El, I will go to him,' she said and left the house. Meri stood, red faced and angry looking, and, huffing loudly, also left the room.

After 20 minutes Elene-Nefer and Marcus had still not come back in, and Muggredge got up, saying, 'I am thinking tis praps time to go.' Mike and Eleri rose also.

'I cannot leave so without speaking to them,' said Eleri and walked out. A few minutes later she returned, accompanied by her mother and father. Marcus faced Mike and said, 'I am all apologyse. I should not have made harassment of you, Mike.' Making full eye contact with Mike he continued, 'Please be accepting my sincere sorriness. You are not to blame – for any of this. We will still have to decide what we shall do, in full-time. We may not leave still,' he said, glancing at his wife, then back at Mike, 'but I know you are honourable, Mike, and I know you and my daughter will be stronger together than apart.'

It hit Mike then, even more than when he'd had the recent, sad, conversations with Eleri and the power of the insight surprised him. Perhaps for the first time, properly, he could see just how hard it was for these people and how painful it was going to be for them, in the coming months and years. He knew there could be no possible consolation for them.

Eleri went to her father and hugged him tightly, then hugged her mother and uncle. Mike shook Marcus's hand and said, 'There is no need to apologise, sir. I cannot say I *know* what you are going through but I do appreciate how much of a struggle it is for you and everyone on this world.'

'Well said, my boy,' said Muggredge, 'well said. Now, so. Let us thank our hosts for the excellent meal and be leaving them in peace.'

As they went Mike wondered how long Eleri's parents would stay before they decided to give up this place. Would they ever leave? He caught himself even wondering how long Eleri would chance it before she made her escape. He just hoped she would choose to leave in time and that, when she did, it would be with him.

Chapter 36

CLOAK AND DAGGER

After the landing boat Laurasia had burned its way through the friction of re-entry into Oceanus's upper atmosphere, it continued flying, high in the stratosphere, toward the town of Remnissa. Arkas Tenak was scheduled to meet with the mysterious "government agent" in that town. His pilot was a lithe, 35-year-old Brazilian woman, strikingly smart in her light, dusty blue, uniform, the standard for Navy pilots. An experienced flyer, known universally by the moniker, "CH", spoke to Tenak, in the co-pilot's seat,

'Where do you want me to land, sir? The town we want is 760 klicks inland and 2950 north west of the Capital. We're about 50 standard minutes out from the town now.'

'Very good, Lieutenant,' said Tenak, 'I'll need you to slow to around Mach 0.3 when we get to within a hundred klicks of the place, CH. The whole aim is to keep attention away from us, so you'll need to switch to stealth mode. I I guess a lot of people on the eastern seaboard might have got used to seeing landing boats flying around over the last few months – but not up here. I've been told this town is in a sparsely populated part of the mainland. None of us has had any reason to come out here, till now.'

'If that's the case, said CH, grinning at Tenak, 'I guess you don't want to put down in the centre of town?'

Tenak smiled sardonically, 'How did you guess? No, I'm afraid you can't take me closer than about … say, 25 klicks from the outskirts of the town.'

CH's eyes widened. 'That *is* a long way out, sir. Your clandestine meeting is near the centre of that so-called town, isn't it? How will we get there?'

'Good old-fashioned hiking, CH. Fast order. In and out – and I'm afraid there is no "we". I need you to stay with the ship …'

'But Admiral,' said CH, a look of genuine concern spreading across her smooth features. 'This is … Sir, this is against protocols regarding senior officers, isn't it, and …?'

'I know that, CH but my government informant, if that's what he is, will know if I'm not alone. I can't risk losing this information. Whatever it is, it could be vital.'

'I can keep out of sight, sir,' said CH, a look of near pleading, on her face.

'Sorry, CH. I know you mean well, but it has to be done this way. Don't worry.'

'Yes, Admiral,' said CH, and although she smiled, she couldn't quite hide the look of unease that settled on her features.

As they gazed out of the wide wind shield, they saw the sun starting to set in the west, the sky ahead gradually turning from deep azure to a sea of reds and orange, to a dark, metallic blue.

Ten minutes later the shuttle's thrusters slowed the craft very quickly, and its navigation lights winked off. CH took the vessel downwards in a smooth arc, very slowly, finally landing in a safe, flat, open area, on the edge of a forest. CH carried out a landing which was semi-automated, with little need of human visual input. Most shuttle landings were achieved like this anyway, with sparse need for visuals, but in this case, it was especially important as they couldn't risk floodlights for illumination.

As they set down, Admiral Tenak went back ship to get ready. After landing checks were made CH also went back and found Tenak had changed into "civilian" clothing; a one-piece coverall, as worn by most locals, together with a flat cloth cap. He was stuffing a small rucksack with bottles of water and other, minimal provisions. He had even changed his boots from his standard, smart, highly polished Navy issue, for a sloppy, worn looking pair of heavy shoes, similar to those often worn by many inhabitants of Bhumi-devi.

As Tenak readied to leave, CH said, 'Oh, I think you forgot your wristcom, Admiral. It's up there in the luggage locker.'

'Can't take it, CH. It's a give-away.'

'But nobody can see it under your clothing, surely?'

'And what if they body-search me?'

'Now you really are starting to worry me. I thought you were supposed to be meeting one person, clandestinely, not some sort of committee.'

'I don't know what's going to happen, CH. I thought I told you not to worry.'

'Yes, sir, I'm sorry. How long am I to wait here, Admiral?'

'It's 20.00, local time now. If I'm not back by, say 04.30, you're to leave for the ship. And I mean, *leave*. Do you understand?'

'But I can't …. Yes, Admiral.' Her eyes widened further, a look of concern never leaving her face, but she reluctantly nodded in acknowledgement.

'And please don't interact with the locals, CH. Remember, no-one is supposed to know we're out here. It's definitely not an official visit but if someone passes by and sees the ship, … well, there's nothing we can do about that. I think it's a bit unlikely we'll be seen by anyone we need to be worried about, given how remote this place is.'

'Neither the IR instruments nor external cams have detected anyone within two klicks of here. The forest's limiting their effectiveness any further. But I'm pretty sure no-one's out there. Least not right now.'

'Good. From what I hear, I don't think there's what you could call a "thriving" population, in the Remnissa area. Anyway, I'm off now. Keep a look out for anything strange.'

The pilot saluted him as Tenak commanded the cabin's internal lighting to switch off, and for the outer door and auto-stair platform to operate. Then he was gone, away into the muggy evening air. CH closed the door and, leaving the main cabin lights off, climbed back into the cockpit and kept the instrument lights on low vis' red. She was determined to stay awake and alert.

***

After nearly 4 hours of walking, Tenak had reached what appeared to be the outermost buildings of the town of Remnissa. The area seemed deserted. In fact, as he strolled, as nonchalantly as possible, through wide, empty streets, he observed that the whole town seemed unoccupied, though there were lights on in some dwellings. At least that was a welcome sight in a lifeless place of deep grey and black shadows. The clouded sky was now like pitch and there were scant streetlights. The wind blew up the street toward him, a cool zephyr filled with dust.

This far north he became acutely aware that it was much cooler than the climate in Janitra, though it was still not what he considered particularly cold. He was, in any case, very warm from his hike. He saw a mere handful of locals, most of them wandering from house to house. There appeared to be little in the way of entertainment emporia or drinking establishments. Some people stared at him as if they could see straight through his "disguise", but Tenak's tactic was to appear confident, as if he "owned" the place. The locals soon turned their attention elsewhere.

He arrived at a crossroads and hesitated. Reaching into his rucksack he extracted an old- fashioned map, printed on paper. He could hardly see the thing in the tiny glimmer of light from the distant streetlights. He decided to take the road on the right but ten minutes later realised he'd made a mistake and retraced his steps to the crossroads, turning onto the route straight ahead.

As he approached an area which looked like it might be the centre of town, a more built up and brightly lit area than he'd passed through, he noticed that many walls and doors were smeared with graffiti, cryptic markings in reds and greens. He couldn't understand much of it, an unusual form of the Oceanus script, but it looked like it might relate to mining.

He peered at several large buildings which looked empty and as he rounded a corner he saw another, even larger one, up ahead, on the corner of a wide crossroads. No traffic of any sort seemed to traverse any of the roads he had passed along. Suddenly, he heard a strange sound from quite close-by, a kind of cackling, or maniacal laughter. He looked all around but could see no-one. This whole area seemed deserted. The laughter stopped as suddenly as it had started but far away he heard what might have been the sound of Borals – lots of them. That too ceased, only to be replaced with several short-lived screams. It stopped, replaced by utter silence. Tenak wandered around the crossroads area looking out for whatever or wherever the sounds had emanated but they seemed to have come from everywhere and nowhere. And were now gone.

He stopped, peering around with a look of deep unease on his face, when his eye was drawn to a particular piece of graffiti. Its crude white lettering was scrawled over the side of a low wooden fence surrounding the large building, and it said, "Beware HS! Fly faster! Birds of Simurgh spell disaster." The building which the fence enclosed was a two-storey brick place, but it looked very run-down. It had only half a roof and some of the upper storey windows were broken but all the lower floor windows seemed intact. Again, Tenak looked perplexed. The Admiral looked at the strange graffito again, smiled to himself and climbing over the low fence strode stealthily toward the front entrance, a damaged but evidently still usable door. He looked around cautiously, then stood close to the door for some time, listening for any sound that might be issuing from within. Then he opened it slowly. Predictably, it creaked. The sound was sharp in the still air.

Inside, barely anything could be seen in the gloom. He advanced down a long, narrow hallway, stepping lightly. The half rotten wooden floorboards creaked as though they despised his presence and sought to announce his whereabouts to anyone who might be further inside the broken-down building. There seemed to be soot everywhere inside the place.

At the end of the hall he arrived at a stairway leading upwards. There seemed to be some light up there, enough for him to see the stairs themselves and the landing at the top, but nothing else. One bannister was completely missing and parts of it lay all over the hallway floor. Again, Tenak stopped at the bottom of the stairs and listened, then picked up a large piece of broken bannister and held it at shoulder height; a ready-made club.

Creeping then up the stairs, his footfalls were again rang out in the encloaking silence, the stair boards complaining of his presence. Tenak flinched visibly as he climbed. A few of the stairs actually moved sideways as he put his weight on them, so his movements became increasingly tentative.

When he reached the landing at the top the Admiral crouched, instinctively, then crept forward, probably trying to make himself as small a target as possible. His Navy combat training was evidently kicking in fully. He listened and then, there it was! A sound coming from a pitch black space, an open-doored room a few metres down the landing.

'Come in, Admiral,' came a deep bass voice from far inside the room, 'and have no fear. I have been expecting you, suchly.'

Tenak walked slowly through the open doorway, still holding the makeshift cudgel, though he had hidden it behind his back. At the far end of the room the silhouette of a man's head and shoulders could be seen, only visible because of the contrast it made against a feeble beam of light coming through a broken window, from a solitary streetlight somewhere behind the house.

'Hello, Admiral. Fear not. Take a pew-place – on the floor. There is not much of comforty furniture here. I am so sorry.'

Tenak didn't sit but knelt on one knee, keeping his other leg braced and ready to launch himself forward or backward, if necessary. He settled a few metres from the stranger and ensured he stayed out of the distant gleam of the street-light,

'I have to say Mer, I don't think much of your choice of meeting place,' he said, in firm tones.

'And I do not think much of your ability to remain suchly unobtrusive,' said the deep voice, 'as I spotted who you were a lint away. No matter,' he continued, 'for you have got here. I hope you make it back well, else my information will have been given for nothing.'

'What do you mean?'

'Did you not know, sirra? Canst you not see? This town is – how would you say – yes, a ghosting town.'

'Yeah, I'd guessed that.'

'No-one much lives here now, esept nary-do-well folk. This place was a thriving pioneer town one-time. T'was a mining town and did prosper – till the old *colonial* government closed down the mines, because they did want the planet to now concentrate on conservation of resources - totally. But t'was also for pure economic reasons. Mining was yet to be restricted to the most valuable shafts and only bare few, at that. Ways were found to produce what was needed by other methods. This old place was long past its best by such-time. And so, it didst die. No-one stepped in to save it. No-one. Not even my own government. Most folkery moved out. Left it to smugglers and vagabondi.'

'It figures, from what I've seen. Why don't the authorities do something about it? Provide jobs or encourage people to retrain? Set up new businesses?'

'Government does not want to admit this was a failed experiment, sirra. Reluctant-so to come here anywayins. Might have to use force to deal with these people, so t'would be politically ... sensitive. They would sooner put a patch on their collective eye, as t'were. This might be called, a "no-through" area. There is nothing of any use here now. Straight law abiding populari have mostly moved out.'

'That's strange. And a shame. But maybe now you could tell me why I'm here?'

'Coursry. Well, Mer Admiral, I have some good news and some even better news. That is well, no? You might not realise it, but we are not all of the same mind on this world. Some of us have been trying to push the government, and the popularia, toward an acceptance of the ... scientific evidence. First, we did so track down someone who has located for us, or rather, *for you*, more geological evidence which could be showing a global catastrophe in the far past. His name is, or was, Lisdon. I knew our mutual friend, the academic, was searching for him.'

'Ah yes,' said Tenak, 'my ship's secretary and the Professier's niece spent weeks researching this – but they found he'd emigrated to the Home System.'

'He did,' said the agent, 'but he stayed not long over there. Seems he got into some sort of trouble and jarp-winged it out fast as he could. Being a very clever fargie, he managed to come back here under a false identity, despite our so-called space "borders". Some of my staff did pick up yet on this a few months ago, didst investigate him and caught him, and then the Professier spoke to me. Lisdon, though that is not his name now, squeeked to us everything he knew about the research he, and his colligry, did all those years ago. We have given him continued anonymity as a reward, providing that his information bears the truth.'

There was sudden burst of aggressive shouting from somewhere outside and the government agent went silent for long moments. Tenak did likewise but after a few minutes there was no further disturbance. The agent continued, 'As I said, we extracted from Lisdon the name of an island – in the Great Eastern Ocean, a place called *New Cambria*. It has not such been visited since his small team went there, about 20 years past-time. He says they did something called "geophysic" work and found some strangeness in the rocks. You would call them - anomalies. There is also no sign of a …, what did he call it? Ah yes, an unconformry?'

'Do you mean an unconformity? A geological unconformity.'

'Yes. That. Seems yet the full rock record is there. Anywayins, it sounds the same thing your people did find on Simurgh. Lisdon also found some strange items there, but his funding ran out – and his friends did the same when they did not get paid. Seems our Mer Lisdon also had some illegal activities to hide, so he destroyed his records. So now, the Professier could not find anything on paper.'

'How do I, or you, know he's telling the truth?'

'What else have you got to go upon, sirra? Besides yet, if he lies again, he knows we will deport him to be facing charges in *your* system. Believe me, he does not want to go back there. Admiral, I am suggesting you seek permission to take your landing craft to New Cambria, soon as you can. You can say you have detected a clue from the geolry of Simurgh. My friends so, and I, will do our best to ensure that a friend in the ministry of the interior will give permission. We will cover it – for now. I have the co-ordinates of the island with me yet and you will find still more info about the geolry on same sheet. The island is yet very remote Admiral. Tis the other side of the planet but – that should not be an obstacle for such as you. You will surely be reliev-ed to know there are no giant birds there. Just giant, poisonous centipede-worms, but they are easily dealt with. Or so says our informant. Fraid of people, he says they are.'

The enigmatic figure reached forward, and a shaft of dim light reflected off a hand holding a grubby piece of paper. The Admiral took it from him and, squinting, glanced at the numbers on it, then folded it and put it in a pocket.

'I presume,' said Tenak, 'that *we* would be unable to speak to Mer "Lisdon" ourselves. That would show your hand, I guess.'

'You do presume right,' said the stranger, 'for my strategy making would be reveal-ed. I have yet told you as much as can do.'

'Thank you,' said Tenak, 'but is there anything else, before I get back to my ship?'

'Oh yes, Mer Admiral. Something of added interest. Praps you didst realise that the government confiscated the rucksack and belongings of the femna who died on Simurgh, Mindara? Yes, but your populari did not know what was in her rucksack. They were told not to disturb anything, yes? Seems that the bag contained many pieces of spear heads and metal staffs – which *she* must have removed from the dig site. Our laboratri tested them and found they are made of iron, ancient iron, and are approximate so eight or eight and one half million years old. Proof, I should be saying, that there was yet a race of intelligent, praps sentient creatures, living here, all that time past. A quiet revolution in science, you might be saying?'

Tenak whistled through his teeth. 'Yes, yes,' he said, 'that is excellent news, but it doesn't really help our mission, does it? Your government's got the evidence and is *obviously sitting on it*. Of course, there was no data, no proof as to what happened to that species but it's a shame the news is censored.'

'Deedly, but I can help there too. My group is yet prepared to leak this information to certain elements of the press-media over the next few weeks. *Officially,* be understanding, *you do not know* anything about this, and neither does the Professier, so you will not get blamed by the government. Be well understanding of that and so prepared. Do not "blow" this opportun-time. Understand me, sirra?'

Tenak nodded emphatically and sat back, then said, 'And what do you get out of all this? What do you want from me?'

There was silence for a few moments, then the agent said, 'Nothing personally, I am supposing, but I want my all family and friends to live. To survive. To know they have a future-time, mayhap somewhere else in human space, but at least they will survive. And we will be rid of the excessive influence of the Meta-teleos.'

Tenak got up to leave.

'Thank you, Mer agent,' he said. 'I mean that. You and your people are taking a lot of risks to do this – and I appreciate it.'

'Said well, sirra-Admiral,' said the agent, 'but there is still more you should know.'

Tenak stood rooted to the spot as the man continued, 'Remember the femna who escaped from the ship named Antarctica? Yes? So, an agent who interrogated her is one of *my* people. He will recommend that she is of no more use to us. I know the other investigator is of similar opinion anywayin, or can be persuaded, so they will yet both be making such recommendation, that she be handed back. However, I am aware of certain sensitivities in the government, in general, as regards the Antarctica, so the central policy committee will not be wanting to hand her back to *that particular* ship. What happens to her *after* she is handed back, coursry, is up to you.'

'Understood,' said Tenak.

'And, Admiral, mayst I say that while I, nor my group, care not who are commanded to go to New Cambria, there be those in the curia, and yes, some in government, who wouldst desperately not wish to see that any crew from the Antarctica goes there. So, whomever goes, please be ensuring that this news dost not leak out. Understand that, do you?'

'I do. And I guess it means double security on our part Don't worry, if something goes wrong this time – I guess, we'll just have to deal with it ourselves.'

'Deedly. My group will claim no knowledge of the matter. By same token, Admiral, if anything happens in which the Navy is found culpable, *you* and your officers need must take full blame. Now you know why this meeting was yet so ... clandestina.'

'Agreed.'

'So, we do yet understand each-other.'

The agent, suddenly sounding bored by the whole thing said, 'Please run now, good manry. You and all of your people should know what the political game is like.'

'That's certainly the truth.'

'Yes, yes. Thank you for coming, Admiral,' said the agent with a weary, almost disdainful voice.

Tenak rolled his eyes and started back toward the stairs when he heard the agent speak once again, but this time with a genuinely serious tone, 'By the way, Admiral. Be taking care on your ways back from here. There are some very disturb-ed people around these parts. We do not want an *incident.*'

'I might say the same to you. And thank you, again.'

Tenak gave a perfunctory salute and set off down the stairs, treading very quietly.

**

CH pottered anxiously around the spacious passenger lounge of the Laurasia. A com alarm trilled unexpectedly and jolted her out of her reverie. She touched her wristcom and Captain Ebazza flashed out in 3D holo format, in miniature, so that she appeared to be "standing" on the floor beside her, but only about half a metre high.

'Lieutenant,' she said, 'where's the Admiral? I couldn't reach him. Have you completed your mission?'

'He's not back yet, Captain. Been gone more than five hours.'

'You mean you let him go on his own? You know the Protocol for Commanding Officers, Lieutenant.' Ebazza looked furious.

'I'm sorry Ma'am but he insisted. Asked me to stay with the ship,' said CH in a pleading voice.

Ebazza rolled her eyes, 'I guess you're not to blame. That's the Admiral for you. My call is to warn you that we've picked up – or rather – the Antarctica has picked up early warning signs showing part of Ra's atmosphere's going to burst again. Another flare, and it's probably bigger than last one. Time frame is about three days before the full eruption on the star's surface and another 48 hours, Oceanus time, before the proton storm arrives. There's a lot to do before it arrives, and I think the Admiral will want to extract now. So, get out there, Lieutenant and catch up with him. Turn on the Inter-D, secure the ship and find him. *My* orders, this time.' Ebazza's image disappeared and CH started prepping immediately.

In less than 2 minutes she was exiting the craft having switching on the Inter-D; the "Interference Deterrent" – an electrical system that would give a shock to any unauthorised person trying to get into the craft. Mild at first, the shocks would get increasingly severe, until the intruder desisted or suffered injury. CH also changed her clothes, donning a dull, two-piece jumpsuit, to make herself less identifiably Navy. And she took a large stun pistol with her, tucked into the back of her field trousers, beneath her over-jacket. She set off down the road Tenak had taken. It was more of a wide, rough trackway, running through a tall, deep forest. The trackway itself was dotted with clumps of bushes and stumps of trees.

She had been walking, briskly, for nearly a standard hour and as she rounded a wide bend, she saw a familiar figure, jogging toward her. The clouds had cleared, and pearly light flooded down from one of the small, but brilliant, moons of Oceanus; the one called Kruxis. She called out, 'Admiral! It's me. Are you okay?'

'What the heck are you doing here, Lieutenant?' called Tenak as he drew closer, 'I thought I told you to stay with the ship?' He could be heard puffing as he got closer.

'I'm sorry, sir. Captain's orders, I'm afraid. You know what she's like with protocols for high ranks.'

'Very well, Lieutenant. I assume the ship's not far now.'

'Not too bad, sir. About 50 minutes or 60 minutes from here.'

As he drew level with her the Lieutenant told Tenak about the coming solar storm. They continued apace, doing a power walk together, chatting mainly about ship's business. It was as though rank didn't matter. Time seemed to go quickly as they went, but both of them commented on the distinct smell of something burning, wafted on the gentle breeze blowing through the trees lining the trail. CH suggested it might be someone out camping. Tenak said the smell seemed familiar and not like any campfire he'd encountered.

The odour got steadily stronger until it became powerful and acrid. As they reached a wide bend in the trail, which they both recognised as being close to the ship, the cool breeze brought a loud clanging noise to their ears. It came from somewhere beyond the crowded larp trees lining the road.

'That's the ship that's burning,' said Tenak. 'Damnatious. That's why I asked you to stay with it, CH.'

'Sorry sir. The inter-D's armed and I took the precaution of bringing a hyper-stunner.'

'Let's hope you don't have to use it.'

They rounded a final bend in the track and the Laurasia came into view, about 350 metres away. At the same time, they spotted the ivory light from Kruxis glinting off the silvery hull but, alarmingly, spotted a bright orange-yellow glow coming from below the vessel. Someone had built bonfires underneath the main wheels. The flames lit up the area around the Laurasia and they could hear the flames crackling as they licked at the undercarriage.

As they came fully into the open they saw two human figures moving around below the ship, tiny next to the landing boat, silhouetted against the bright glow from the fires. The people were moving agitatedly now, and one was throwing something at the ship's underbelly. The clanging sound echoed off the road and was soaked up by the densely packed trees nearby.

'Why the feggery?' said Tenak.

'I don't think the fires will damage the tyres too much, Admiral,' said CH. 'Those things are composite metal and hyper-synth.'

'I know, but it depends on how long the fires have been going – and their temperature,' said Tenak, 'and it sure looks like they've been burning for a while.' As they drew a little closer Tenak shouted to the figures, 'Hey you there!'

A movement caught his eye and he spoke quickly to his companion, 'Over to the left. Another bogey. Close. Projectile weapon. Watch yourself!'

A third man moved out from under a tree on the other side of them. He was only about 20 metres away and was toting a long-barrelled weapon, like an old-fashioned rifle; the type that used bullets. It glinted sharply in the light of Kruxis.

The man shouted, 'That is yet as far as you get yon strangers! What you doin' round here?' He spoke with a drawl which sounded strange, even for Oceanus. Tenak and CH slowed their walking but did not stop.

'That is our vessel,' shouted Tenak, 'and we need it. Your friends must stop what they're doing.'

'An' you need to shut your saney mouth. If that is your'un "vessel", as you call it, you should know tis on our land. Our land, I says.'

'This land doesn't belong to anyone. We checked,' shouted CH.

'Leave the talking to me, Lieutenant,' breathed Tenak softly, then called out to the armed man, 'We're sorry sirra. We mean not to trespass, if such we did, we did not yet realise. If you just ask your friends to stop, we shall be on our way – and leaving your land.'

'None doin' manry. The boys be having some fun, tis all. Carnt yew see that? Slow down there, stranger-manery. Told yer to stand still, I did say, less you want me to fill your chesties with lead sluggies?'

Tenak and CH stopped immediately and looked around for options. The bonfires around the landing wheels were blazing ever brighter and the two men under the ship were jumping around in a crazy dance, shouting and laughing wildly. The smoke from the fires reached Tenak and CH in pungent gusts. There was no sign that the wheels were about to fail – yet.

'Hey youngers!' shouted the gunman to his friends, 'be bringing yoursems over here. Got us some juicy Meta- whatsits.'

'No, no. We arint Meta-teleos, if that's what you think,' said Tenak, 'We do not want trouble, sirra. Please just let us go upon our way.'

'You sound funny. Not like such Metas - but you look like such Metas. Hates them guys. Like all round here, we hate Metas.'

The men by the ship had stopped dancing and were starting to walk toward them now. CH saw them and breathed, 'Admiral.'

'I know, Lieutenant,' said Tenak.

'What you call him?' said the gunman, 'an what you call her? I know who yous is. Yous is off-worlders arint you?' He huffed loudly and started to walk briskly toward them. 'Don' much like them sort around here either. Think I'll fill yew with …'

At that moment the outer part of one of the ship's large tyres ruptured. The sound rang out like a mortar, bouncing off the surrounding trees. Everyone looked in the direction of the noise but Tenak instantly recovered and barked at CH,

'Break even!' he said, signalling a standard technique practiced in Navy training. Each of them dived, projecting themselves several metres to either side of the rifleman. Tenak had been on CH's right, so he dived to the right as CH flung herself to the left. They rolled as they hit the ground. Still bouncing, with her right hand the Lieutenant pulled her stun gun from behind her, grunting in pain as she did so. The gunman turned, looking bewildered and CH fired immediately, hitting him in the left hip. She cursed herself for being slightly off target. The tightly focused beam of pure sound from the gun had enough energy to knock anyone down at that distance and, on higher settings, would put them out cold for hours. It could even break bones. The highest setting was lethal.

CH had already pre-set the pistol to about 50% power, but the tight sonic punch kicked the gunman sideways. To her amazement he quickly recovered. She fired again, this time holding the pistol with both hands, to compensate for an injured right arm. There was no time to use the auto-target setting but her aim was more accurate this time, the beam hitting the attacker squarely in the stomach. He doubled over, his rifle involuntarily flying from his hands.

Tenak immediately raced up to the man and kicked the rifle out of his reach. The gunman's companions were now running furiously toward them, but one halted suddenly and shouted to the other, 'They got some fancy weapon, Macckie! Leave 'em.' He stood as if rooted to the spot, but his companion kept coming. CH was on it again and levelled her weapon steadily, having more time now. Training the gun's tiny screen sight system on the approaching "Macckie", the weapon sensed the part of the man's body she was aiming for and a red light blinked on at the back of the gun. That indicated the target had been located by the laser red dot. It had chosen the man's lower abdomen. CH evidently approved because she squeezed the trigger and an instant later Macckie went down like a sack of firewood. The remaining would-be aggressor watched with horror, then raced away to the left, soon disappearing into the blackness.

'Well done Lieutenant,' said Tenak and started toward the ship. 'We need to take off soon as…. We'll have to use the ramjet excess vent, on full noble gas flow. It's gone too far for the auto-stinguishers.'

The Lieutenant began to follow Tenak but then stopped next to the prone body of the man who had threatened them with his rifle. She could now see he was a stocky, middle-aged man and that he was gasping for air and retching in his throat. Bending over him she said, 'You should feel better in an hour or so, but if not … well, it's too bad. You shouldn't point guns at people, specially not projectile weapons. Now, I know you can hear me, so listen well, you feg-wit. You were right about us. We *are* "off-worlders" - and believe me when I say we've got more tek like this gun, and more power. More than you can *ever* imagine. And I know what people like you are like. Soon as we've gone, you'll complain to the government that you were attacked, for no reason, by "brutal off-worlders" – or something like that. So, listen up. Don't even think about doin' that. If I get to hear so much as a squeak like that, I'll bring down some of my crewmates – and you'll see how brutal we can be when we're pissed off. Got that, shit head?' There was a moment's silence. 'I said, got it?' she shouted and dug the toe of her right boot into the side of his body. He stared up at her and nodded silently, his face still tightly screwed up with pain.

'Lieutenant! Stop playing with the locals,' shouted Tenak from up ahead. She smiled, unseen, then ran and caught up quickly with him, and seconds later they were both on board the boat, powering up the engines.

'What was all that about Lieutenant?' asked Tenak.

'Just a little insurance, sir,' she said, as they strapped themselves in. 'Some psychology. That's all.'

Tenak said, 'Okay. I can see you're in pain, Lieutenant. You okay to take us up?'

'It's just a muscle strain sir. You don't need to do a thing. Please sit back and enjoy.'

'Nice shooting, by the way,' said Tenak as the craft lifted off on its hyper-jet thrusters and CH operated the ramjet excess bleed nozzles, blasting huge volumes of helium and argon gas onto the tyres, rapidly extinguishing them. Fortunately, only the outermost layer of one tyre had ruptured. There were *another three layers* below that, so a fairly easy repair back on The Monsoon. They were able to withdraw the undercarriage a minute or so after lift-off, then CH opened up the engines, propelling them into the stratosphere and beyond.

'They used some sort of accelerant,' said Tenak, moments after take-off, 'did you smell it?'

'Yes sir,' she replied. 'The bastards.'

PART THREE

THE NATIVE

Chapter 37

DESPERATION

'Thank the galaxies we've been given the licence to send a team to New Cambria, Professier,' said Admiral Tenak, 'and I note the interesting changes you've made to your own part of the team, compared with the Simurgh one, that is. I hope that Doctro Sung is not too disappointed with being replaced? I'm aware what the reports said about his conduct on Simurgh, but I met him briefly on the planet and he seemed to me very efficient and helpful.'

Tenak, with Ebazza, was taking part in a three-way holovid conference between Muggredge's office, The Monsoon and the Antarctica.

'Yes, Doctro Sung is still on my staff but yet I did replace him,' said Muggredge, 'but e'en he didst not think he wanted to take part such, on New Cambria. He still does feel bad about what happened to Rubia, and so do Doctros Morgath and Chen. And they will not be partaking either. And yes, Captain Ebazza, I take agree to your suggestion that I should not tell the participants from my team as to who shall be partaking from yours. They will find out when they so meet on the surface, before flying to New Cambria.'

'I'm glad you realise we only want to keep a lid on it for for security purposes, Professier,' said Ebazza who stood next to Tenak, 'and of course, neither will we advise *our* team of the Oceanus people going.'

At this point Captain Providius, on the Antarctica, spoke up, directing her remarks to Muggredge, 'Professor, I can understand your people might be suspicious, in the circumstances but now that these terms have been discussed, I don't mind admitting that we're certainly going to lend Admiral Tenak and Captain Ebazza all the" tek help" we can muster.' She gave Tenak's holo- image a wicked smile.

'And I'm grateful for it, Captain,' said Tenak, smiling, 'but we'll say no more about this for now.'

'I'm particularly pleased,' said Providius, 'that the government have allowed you to send a boat, Admiral, Captain, given the sensitivities generated by Heracleonn. And, after all, she is responsible for our being … hamstrung on this expedition as well.'

Tenak cleared his throat and said, 'Well, not quite, Captain. I was, let's say, … confident that *we* would be able to send a boat on this occasion too, and, as for Heracleonn, I have some good news for you.' He smiled broadly, as he continued, 'I was told not long ago, by a "government person", that they are releasing Heracleonn to us. They've finally decided to deport her. I also believe, though I can't confirm yet, that the OA authorities were not impressed by anything she told them.'

There was a loud chorus of approval from the other participants, but Tenak signalled, tactfully, that he hadn't finished speaking, and continued, 'However … there are strings attached. As I said, they are releasing her to the Navy, not to yourself, I'm afraid,' he said, directly to Providius, 'and, to honour the agreement I made, I'm going to suggest that she does not return to the Antarctica whilst both ships are in orbit. After we leave here, well, that's entirely different. I hope this will be acceptable, Captain?'

'Yes, of course, Admiral,' said Providius, 'and I know you'll keep her "safe" for us. Besides, you do have the facilities. But I can't see why they're making such a fuss about this. They must know what awaits her in the Home System.'

'Yes, they do,' said Tenak, 'but it's the old game of politics, Captain. It's what they must *be seen* to be doing. Media interest, votes, outward appearances and the rest. Even if most people down there don't know what's actually happening now, they might tomorrow, or the next day – and there's posterity to consider.'

'If there is yet a future for them and us, so to consider it from,' said Muggredge, to everyone's surprise. He continued, gently, 'I am truly pleased that this errant crewmember be returned to you, but now, mayst I yet ask something we have not discussed, about the coming expeditionary?'

'Sorry, Professier,' said Tenak, 'please forgive us. What else do you need? I think we've been able to satisfy the list of equipment you sent us, haven't we?'

'Ah yes, Admiral. Thanking you. But despite our discussion of the other team members, I believe you have not still said who the pilot of the boat will be. Mayst I know?'

'Please forgive us, Professier,' said Tenak, 'especially as that person will be such a focal point for the whole team. Captain Ebazza and I were just discussing this, just before the con.'

'That is so,' said Ebazza, looking at Tenak, almost quizzically, who smiled back at her, as she took over, 'and yes, *I think* we've come to an agreement, finally, that we'll be sending a pilot we all know as, CH. She is a Lieutenant, a great pilot and a fully qualified engineer.'

'Ah. I was rather yet hoping for Mer Pingwei,' said Muggredge. 'for I do know that the Simurgh team members didst get along with him such well and I believe, he rather saved them from more catastrophies out there. But I do not so wish to doubt your judgement. I am sure we will find Mes CH, equally, how you say … amenable.'

Ebazza said, 'Yes, I'm afraid I have some duties for Lieutenant Pingwei which I've assigned to him, here. I only explain because I do not wish to suggest there was anything amiss in his conduct on Simurgh. By the way, following on from our discussions about security, we would also like to send two of our own security guards with you this time.'

'That is yet fine. Most welcome for security,' said Muggredge, 'and mayst I ask when you think the whole team can safest get underway, for I understand there is, awful-like, another solar storm on the way.'

'Yes, Professier,' said Tenak, 'there is, and please, take no chances with this one. It's a grade 10. We have advised the government that people should stay indoors, unless they have to go out for essential reasons. Apart from electrical disturbances, the proton flux might become dangerous to health. Better not to chance it. The severity also means we won't be able to fly anywhere till it's over. This ship and the Antarctica will be fine but ships with less shielding, like the landing boats, will have to stay in our hangars.'

'I think we still have 10.7 hours to go, Admiral,' said Ebazza, 'and so, with your permission, I plan to send CH down to the surface and pick up senior engineer Mordant – and Pamela Heracleonn, before the government has a chance to change its mind about her.' She grinned uneasily as Tenak gave her the go-ahead.

After the holo-con, Tenak and Ebazza, aboard The Monsoon, spoke together conspiratorially. Tenak said, 'We're cutting it a bit fine with this one, Ssanyu.'

'I know,' she said, 'but I want Mordant up here on the double. You're aware, now, that I had misgivings about some aspects of the time logs he filed, regarding his activities on the surface and ...'

'And?'

'And, unfortunately, those misgivings have had some confirmation from the logs put in by some of the other engineers and tekies we've had down there. It might not be anything that can't be resolved but I'd like to hear an explanation from him in person. And I don't want to take the risk of him being on the surface when I put this stuff to him.'

'Are you saying, Ssanyu ... that you don't want him doing another "Heracleonn"?'

'Exactly so, yes, and I know that's unlikely, but we've seen too many weird things happening to take any more chances, haven't we?'

'Of course, and yes, I find it hard to believe. His record has been exemplary. Nevertheless, I agree with your stance. We need him up here, soonest time.'

****

Inside the landing boat, CH glanced at the bright chrono-reading on the cockpit's wide, glass instrument panel and huffed. She asked her wristcom to locate and contact Dempstry Mordant once again. He was now half an hour late for their rendezvous at the town of Emnistra, 130 kilometres west of the Capitol. This time the com was able to make contact and she heard the senior engineer's voice, audio only. 'Yes, I'm sorry, CH. I know I'm late. Couldn't be helped. Been trying to make some last-minute adjustments to the power buffers in the local government building.'

'Then you know how fine we're cutting it. We've got 94 minutes to get up to the ship and I've yet to pick up Heracleonn. How much longer?'

'Don't worry. I should be there in five. Keep a seat warm – in the conference lounge, please. I don't want to sit with Heracleonn. The thought of her makes me sick.'

Mordant arrived at the ship within three minutes and CH took off immediately, making for Darklengton Detention Centre, on the outskirts of the little village of Emnistra, where they'd pick up the quisling, Heracleonn. In the boat Mordant made himself comfortable in the spacious conference lounge aft of the passenger section. The two compartments were only separated by a thin bulkhead and its door. Mordant closed the door and settled onto one of the wide, plush seats studded throughout the lounge. He would be the only passenger here, with Heracleonn under armed guard in the front of the passenger cabin.

He had commed his co-conspirators aboard The Monsoon, using key code cyphers. They agreed that Heracleonn might know who he was and his true function on the mission, and might talk, or otherwise give something away while on the shuttle. She certainly knew Brundleton. She might decide to "blab" when on board The Monsoon anyway, but it would be harder for her there. And he and his colleagues had talked about plans to stop her betraying them.

The boat reached the detention centre in double quick time, settling on a wide concrete apron outside its high walls. They awaited the release of Heracleonn with CH staying in her cockpit, keeping herself busy with maintenance checks. She paced about the spacious flight deck.

'What's the damnatious hold-up?' she muttered to herself with impatience.

Things only got worse, as one of the shuttle's guards commed in from the Detention Centre, to tell her there was some sort of delay in releasing the prisoner. He reported that it was some sort of "bureaucratic thing".

***

Inside Darklengton Detention Centre, Pamela Heracleon stood naked, in front of female warders, as they handed her the clothes she'd worn when she'd first arrived. She asked them for the datacube and translation device she had given the government agents who had questioned her.

'I have been told you are not allowed to have such,' said the shorter of the two warders, a bullish looking woman, with a completely shaved head and wide facial scars.

'But your people can't get them to work,' said Heracleonn.

'I do not know any of this, young woman. Those are my orders. I shall think they will find a use for them things.' The guard chuckled but it was mirthless. 'Though for what, in the seven Oceans yet, I know not.'

Heracleonn spotted her wristcom unit on a shelf nearby; the same shelf her original clothes had lain upon. She asked her guards for it.

The taller of the two guards, a broad-shouldered woman with a thin face and a nose like an ice-pick, grabbed the object and said, 'What is such?'

'It's just a … chrono. You know, a wristwatch. To help you tell the time?' The guard looked closely at the gold coloured device. 'I carnt see any dials or digital number display. Oh, there it is, at the top of the face, still. Smallish numbers. Hardly yet visible. Not much of a time piece.'

'Maybe Shendra and I should keep it,' said short and stocky, glancing at her lanky colleague, who gave a toothy grin and nodded.

'Oh, gentle femnas, please,' said Heracleon. 'My faether gave that to me. He died last year. T'was a special gift – handed down the generations. Surely you could let me have it back? After all, as you said, it's not much of a timepiece. It's just my keepsake. Reminds me of my faether.'

'Yet it could be valuable on Oceanus. You know, a memento,' said short and stocky, 'but I do not know. What are you yet thinking, Shendra?'

'Nar, surely it does not look useful, or valuable, to me Kerala. Let her keep it. Praps she will need it where she is going. Who would want to go to an prison in the Home System?'

Kerala grimaced and reluctantly handed the device to Heracleon. The guards didn't hear the soft sigh of relief breathed by Heracleonn.

At that moment a male guard knocked on the door of the changing room and, when Shendra opened it just a few centimetres, he pushed it further open from the other side and his head snaked around, to peer at the three of them, 'Alrighting. Her paperwork is now ready,' he said, with a gruff tone, 'you can take her out to the lobby, if you have so processed her. There are two HS guards waiting to take over outside.'

Shendra and Kerala grabbed their charge's remaining clothes and made her don them without delay, then bundled her out through a series of double locked metal doors. As they did so, Heracleonn shoved the wristcom into her underpants, just before she was propelled into a reception room where two of The Monsoon's guards stood waiting.

***

Two minutes later Heracleonn was being herded out to the Agamemnon, waiting on the concrete dozens of metres away from the building. It was getting dark and heavy rain was slanting down. Strong winds were whipping up, throwing clouds of spray mixed with dust and particles of woody debris in swirls around the area. It was the start of another seasonal, vicious Oceanus storm, an event which often covered half the continent.

The guards and their charge were soaked by the time she was on board.

'Finally!' said CH over the intercom. 'Do you need to scan her?'

One of the guards, a tall, thick set man, said, 'I doubt it, Lieutenant. The Oceanus guards said they'd cleared her. Do you want me to scan her anyway?'

'There's no time Brady,' said CH, 'so if you think she's okay just get her seated and strapped in. Do the same yourself. It could be a bumpy ride.'

'Rog' that,' said Brady and thrust Heracleonn toward one of a set of three seats, nearest the forward end of the passenger cabin; seats specially installed for this trip, allowing the two guards to be able to sit directly opposite the prisoner, facing her. That way they could keep her under continuous surveillance.

'Hold on!' said Brady's colleague, a small but highly muscled woman. She stopped Heracleonn in her tracks, before she could sit.

'What the fegg is it, Gwan-ji?' said the male guard. 'You heard what CH said.'

'Show me your wrists,' Gwan-ji said to Heracleonn, and when her charge hesitated, she barked her order again. Heracleon reluctantly obliged by pulling up the sleeve of each arm in turn. Nothing to be seen. 'Okay, just sit,' said Gwan-ji and buckled the prisoner roughly into her couch. She and Brady then sat, a mere metre or so away. Brady spoke to an intercom set into the bulkhead separating the passenger cabin from the flight deck, close to their seats, 'Okay. Ready. Please take her up, Lieutenant,' he said.

Within seconds they felt the craft lift from the ground. The rate of ascent was fast, even by Navy standards. In addition to the upward acceleration the passengers could feel the wind buffeting the craft as it climbed. At around three hundred metres the ship stopped its vertical thrust and began to move forward but slanting upward at an increasingly steep angle, until it broke through the lowest cloud deck and emerged into brighter light. But the winds were, if anything, even stronger up there and the vehicle jostled its passengers as it continued its climb toward a higher level of cloud.

Heracleonn gazed at the closed door in the centre of the bulkhead, far down the opposite end of the passenger cabin. A small red light shone above the door, indicating occupancy.

'Who's in the conference lounge, guys?' she said to her guards, grinning. "Some sort of VIP?'

Brady just looked away, a smirk of contempt on his wide face. Gwan-ji said, 'It's nothing that need concern you.'

The vehicle bucked violently. 'Maker!' said Heracleonn, 'these Navy ships aren't as jet stabilised as I thought they were. Haven't moved much with the times, guys, have we?'

'Just shut the fegg up,' said Brady. Heracleonn stared at him sullenly but then leaned forward, a grimace of nausea spreading over her face, as if she was becoming ill. She held her hands to her head, then moved them slowly down to her waist, then her stomach and kept them there, as though in severe discomfort. The guards scrutinised her for a while but as the vehicle continued to shake, they began to stare over her head at the windows behind Heracleonn. The cloud deck looked as though it were see-sawing about but that was, of course, the boat.

The craft suddenly dropped, sinking like a stone, perhaps a thousand metres, or so it felt, sending everyone's stomachs into their chests. The boat stopped its descent but bucked violently and the two guards stared at each-other, anxiously. As security guards, they spent the vast majority of their time aboard star ships. They were probably less used to flying through planetary atmospheres than most people in the Navy.

Heracleonn sat motionlessly, still holding her stomach and when the guards seemed most distracted, she made her move. Suddenly and with shocking speed, she thrust her right hand through the waistband of her trousers and into the tightness of her underwear, where she grasped the wristcom and pulled it into the open, all in one fluid move. Brady saw the gleam of the device's lights and then he too moved like lightning, reaching for his holstered stun pistol. Gwan-ji had also begun to react and simply unbuckled herself, with incredible speed, and started to physically launch herself at Heracleonn.

Before the guards could reach her, Heracleonn quickly turned her face away, as she squeezed her wristcom, twice in succession, and an arc of electric current crackled from it, connecting with both Brady and Gwan-ji, as if drawn to them magnetically. The two guards grunted loudly, Brady crumpling onto the floor. Gwan-ji fell forwards and onto the couch beside Heracleonn, one arm hanging limply over the intervening armrest. Heracleonn unbuckled herself quickly, ripped the stun pistols from each of the guards and raced toward the conference lounge further down the cabin, blowing on a small burn on her left hand.

On the flight deck, CH wrestled with the ship, her hands flying over the surface of the control interface, flitting from one flat geometric section of the control panel to another. She had decided to take over control of the actuators, from the hyper-comp, which normally carried out take-off and the journey into the orbit. There seemed to be a glitch of some sort which had maybe fouled the actuators and prevented them from compensating for the stormy weather. CH merely had to assist the hypercomp to regain stability and within a minute or two the ship was propelling itself up through a high layer of stratus cloud. The Agamemnon shot up and into the thin air of a dark steel blue sky, and out of the severe turbulence. CH had been so busy she hadn't had time to activate the screen that monitored the inside of the passenger cabin.

'I am sorry, Lieutenant,' said a sexually neutral, mechanical sounding voice, speaking into a com bud inserted in her left ear. It was the minor AI, hypercomp, and it continued, 'I believe I may have been adversely affected by a greater than expected ionic electrojet effect, which appeared to have compromised the lateral wing stabilisers. We also experienced wind shear of grade 11, on the Tokogara scale. This is unprecedented.'

'That's okay but ...,' started CH, but the comp interrupted her, saying,

'Red alert! Emergency taking place in aft quarters. Images on monitor, A3.'

**

At the aft end of the passenger cabin Pamela Heracleonn burst through the door into the conference lounge where Mordant had been totally unaware of the drama in the forward compartment. He had been busy gripping his chair arms throughout the noise and disturbance of the turbulence.

'Who the fegfire are ...? Hey, I know you, don't I?' she said as she approached Mordant, who was still firmly buckled in and looking out the window. He turned to her. 'What the shitscrape are you doing back here? Where are the guards?'

'Otherwise detained,' she said and pointed both her stun pistols at him. 'Yeah, I do know you. You're that guy – Mordant. Engineer first class? Supposed to be *one of us*, aren't you?'

'If you say so,' said Mordant, staring at the muzzles of the approaching pistols. 'So, there's no need for those things. It's Pamela Heracleonn, I presume? As you said, one of us. By the way, watch where you're pointing those things.'

'No good talking about "us" anymore,' said Heracleonn, a sour expression on her face, 'Too late for that. I need to escape, and I don't think it's really in your interests for me to do that. Is it, chief Mordant? By the way, the gun in my right hand is on full power, so don't try to be a smart ass. That hand is not my dominant one, so it might just go off without me asking it to.'

Mordant smiled ingratiatingly. 'Come on Pamela. There's no need for this. Besides, where do you think you're going? How can you just – escape? Think about it, Pamela. Just put the guns down and we can talk. We can work something out, I promise you. I can talk to the Captain for …'

'Just shut the feg up! Unbuckle yourself – now! Put your hands in your pockets.' She walked up to him and shoving the pistol in her left hand into her belt, she held the other to Mordant's head. Grasping the thick cloth of his collar she started to pull. 'Up we get, Chief Mordant. We're going to see the pilot.'

As Heracleonn hustled him back toward the door, the cabin intercom activated loudly and CH's voice flooded through the cabin, 'What are you doing, Pamela?'

'You'll find out soon enough,' said Heracleonn, 'but for now, just shut up and listen. I want you out of that cockpit. I'm taking control of this ship and we're all going for a ride and by the way, it's not to The Monsoon.'

'You're way off-kilter Pamela. Where do you think you can go?'

By now Heracleonn had manoeuvred Mordant as far as the couches in the front of the passenger cabin, facing the flight deck bulkhead and its door. She couldn't get access to the cockpit without the code to get in and it was ship's protocol to lock the door on all occasions where security required it, like when carrying prisoners.

'I said, come out of the cockpit, pilot. I don't know who you think you are, but you're going to be responsible for the death of a senior … No, I correct myself, *the* senior engineer of The Monsoon.'

On a large screen in the cockpit CH could see Heracleonn jam the stun gun hard against the side of Mordant's head, and she rolled her eyes.

'You know what'll happen if I shoot him at this range,' said Heracleonn. 'Do you really want his blood and brains all over the place? Listen to me, pilot. Put the ship on full auto and come out of there. I've had complete pilot training – and in the Navy, too, so I know what I'm doing.'

'They all say that,' mumbled CH and sighed, 'but okay, you've got your way, Pamela.' A few seconds later CH opened the cockpit door and emerged very tentatively. The hijacker was standing with her hostage, about 15 metres down the cabin.

'Don't try any nonsense,' said Heracleonn. 'Just get over there and buckle yourself into a seat in the back row, right up near the con lounge. And make that buckle nice and tight.'

Still standing in front of the door to the flight deck CH said, gently and quietly, 'Seriously, Pamela, where are you going to go? There's a grade 10 solar storm about to break over the planet.'

CH then moved down the cabin very slowly while continuing to talk to the hijacker, 'Please, Pamela. Give this up now, while we still have time. That storm is due to hit in about ten minutes. There's just about time to get to the mother ship – but only just.'

'Forget it, pilot. I'm not taking this boat to orbit. I'm heading down, and right round to the other side of this … stupid, crazy world. There's a small island about 12,000 klicks from the continent, right in the middle of nowhere. It's just one of hundreds maybe, thousands of small islands. No-one lives there. No-one has even explored them fully. You see, I read all about them when I was "waiting" in that fegging detention centre. The other prisoners, even the guards, were more than helpful with information about their precious planet, so …'

At that moment Mordant moved unexpectedly, letting out a shocked sound and, turning his head away from Heracleonn, recoiled into her, as if he'd seen some sort of emergency unfold in the direction of his vision. It was a ruse. Heracleonn instinctively looked in the same direction as Mordant, and as she did so he tried to grab her right hand. But he botched it. His sweat soaked fingers failed to get any purchase and Hearcleonn instantly recovered her composure. But CH saw her chance and launched herself toward the two of them, as Heracleonn pulled hard and free of Mordant, making him stumble. She raised her pistol in a blur of movement and brought it down toward Mordant's head. Her aim was nearly out but she succeeded in catching the side of his head, the pistol scraping down his temple. He let out a loud cry and before he could recover, she had brought the pistol up again and, this time, slammed it hard onto the back of his head, where it made a sickening, cracking, noise. CH was nearly on her but Heracleonn had raised the pistol and levelled it straight at her.

Mordant collapsed at Heracleonn's feet, letting out unintelligible noises from the back of his throat. CH winced when she heard him. The quisling looked wildly at CH, who put her hands up in the air, signalling surrender. 'Don't move a centimetre,' said Heracleonn, then sidestepped around the pilot, before lunging at the cockpit doorway, thrusting herself through it, then hitting the panel to close and lock it.

'What're you doing Pamela?' shouted CH into the intercom panel on the passenger cabin side of the door. She knew the hijacker could hear her because the intercom couldn't be switched off. She was also well aware that the ship was turning. It had nearly reached orbit but there was no feeling of so-called "weightlessness".

'Pamela. Listen to me,' said CH, 'Mordant is badly hurt. He's still bleeding and he's unconscious. Making strange noises. We need to get him to medical help – on The Monsoon. The ion storm will hit at any minute, but we might still make it.'

'Forget it, pilot,' came the reply, static interference peppering Heracleonn's voice. 'What's your name, pilot?'

CH looked puzzled but told Heracleonn anyway.

'CH?' said the hijacker, 'I won't bother asking you what it stands for. We pilots have our funny ways, don't we? Listen, I'm sorry about Mordant but I'm still going for the island in Far Ocean. That's what the crazies on this planet like to call it. By the way, in case you're wondering, I'll drop you guys off on the south west side of the continent. The uninhabited part. I'll go on from there, but I'll leave you a wristcom, so you can call for rescue.'

'Nice idea but you're not going to make it. I keep telling you. The storm is about to hit.'

'You're beginning to bore me, CH. We'll be down before then.'

As they spoke the boat reached its apogee, the highest point of its trajectory, and CH found herself starting to float, microgravity beginning to kick in, but to her horror she realised that the ship was heading back down into the atmosphere. After a couple of minutes she could feel her limbs starting to get heavy again. The boat was descending but at an angle too shallow for microgravity to take over. CH saw wisps of super-heated gases beginning to stream outside, past the windows. They were re-entering the denser part of the atmosphere too fast.

The cabin lights suddenly flickered and went out. Then, CH heard loud crackling noises over the intercom, probably violent electrical discharges on the flight deck side of the door. Several actuator sub-assemblies on the main cabin ceiling sparked brightly and sputtered. An acrid smell broke out and the passenger cabin temperature began to increase – much too fast.

'Holy shit,' said CH, 'are you okay Pamela? Even you should realise the storm's just started to hit. Let me in there! Now!'

***

On the bridge of The Monsoon's torus, the First Officer peered over the shoulder of the junior Lieutenant sitting in front of the vehicle tracking station.

'I can't believe it,' Statton said, 'the shuttle's turning through pi by four rad.' He commed Tenak and Ebazza to tell them that the Agamemnon had, mysteriously, turned through an acute angle, away from any intercept course with the mother ship.

Tenak was already on his way to the bridge when the com arrived. 'Hasn't CH commed us?' he asked.

'No and we've stopped getting telemetry from the shuttle,' said Statton, causing Tenak to quicken his pace. He arrived at the bridge a minute later and joined his crew.

'Are we getting anything at all?' he said. Again, the answer was no, and CH wasn't responding to their comms, either. As they watched the flashing white blip, on the screen, that represented the Agamemnon, picked up a red tag as well.

'She's starting to descend,' said Tenak. 'Is she de-orbiting?'

'Yes sir,' said the rating, 'frontal retros are burning to slow it down.'

'Instrument interrogation indicates their comms platforms and telemetry suites are working,' said Statton, 'so it has to be something going on aboard the flight deck.'

'Why do I get the feeling Heracleonn's got something to do with this?' said Tenak.

Ebazza had now arrived and joined Tenak.

'Well, whether she has or not,' said the Captain, 'CH needs to change course - now. Get that ship into orbit,' she breathed, 'cos that ion storm is about to break over them. And there's nothing we can do from here. Maker preserve them.'

****

On board the Agamemnon, following CH's pleas, there were long moments of silence from the flight deck before Heracleonn finally replied, and she now sounded worried. Breathlessly, she said, 'A couple of the panels blew out but … there's something else … much worse. I don't know what … something's wrong. I can't control it. Like … it's got a life of its own. I thought I had this but …'

'Pamela, let me in there now. I might be able to help. I won't try to wreck your plans. But we've gone way past that now. This is survival. You can go to your damn island if you want, but we've got to get this ship down safely and …'

The door to the flight deck suddenly clicked opened and CH dived through, fighting the turbulence now gripping the ship, which forced her to stagger up the two steps into the cockpit. Heracleonn was sitting in the pilot's seat but her mouth was hanging open with shock. CH reached the co-pilot position and said, 'Let me have control, Pamela.'

'You have control,' said Heracleonn, 'but … I don't think it's going to work now …'

CH's hands moved over the banks of hyper-glass interface panels in front of her. Lights flashed and graphics lit up in some of them, but not all, and even the ones that worked weren't showing anything encouraging. Amber and red warning lights flashed everywhere. The minor AI aboard the flight deck spoke out in an unhurried, unconcerned female voice, 'I must tell you the con-panels are mostly non-functional.

There has been unprecedented ionic interference, causing large scale burn-outs, for which the backup units have been unable to compensate.'

They hadn't yet reached the thickest layer of the planet's atmosphere, but the Agamemnon's nose had turned to point downwards at an angle of over 45 °. Then the boat also started to slowly turn around its long axis, rotating prow over stern, so that the ship was then upside down, in relation to the ground below, and pointing backwards. But the rotation continued beyond that so that it began to face forward again.

CH's hands continued to slide over the interface panel, trying to slow the rotation, but the vessel refused to respond and continued revolving, all the time descending fast. The panels showed they were spinning end over end once every nine seconds, but the occupants didn't need to check the instruments to know that. Pamela gripped her stomach with nausea and CH gulped air down in ragged gasps, her eyes screwing up with motion sickness.

'Why can't you stop the spinning?' CH shouted at the control panel. 'Compensate!'

The minor AI said, dispassionately, 'Unable to compensate. Heat from the electrical storm has fused all attitude thruster couplings. They cannot be operated. The ship will continue to spin until …'

'Okay. I get it. Enough,' said CH, her words coming out as stutters, as she gasped with nausea. 'Shut off all power to the interface,' she shouted, 'and give me manual control, assisted by …whatever … actuators still work. Then suspend all your higher functions. Concentrate on all subsystems, particularly life support.'

'Complying,' said the contralto voice and the panel interface immediately in front of CH automatically split into two parts and folded inwards, revealing a new panel which rose from below. A pair of thick control sticks, covered with button actuators, arose in front of CH. They were similar to the ones used on old-fashioned airplanes.

As the control sticks began to appear CH clutched at her stomach and had to screw up her eyes again but when she reopened them she caught movement on the periphery of her vision and noticed the cabin monitor feed, to her left side, was still live. She could still see what was happening back in the cabin. The screen showed a senseless and bleeding Mordant, and the still unconscious security guards, falling from the floor to the ceiling bulkhead, then rolling and all the way down to the conference lounge bulkhead, onto the floor again, and back down to the front in a gruesome type of cycle. As they went, they rolled constantly, into each-other and into the bulkheads, the seating and other objects, tumbling like lifeless rag dolls, though, for all she knew, they might still have been alive.

CH groaned with horror, turned to her right and retched. Managing to control her nausea then, she switched off the screen. There was nothing she could do for them now. A couple of seconds later the manual control sticks became operational and she grasped them, feverishly, manipulating the old-fashioned devices, meant only to be used as a last resort, like right now. She repeatedly pressed the manual thruster rocket actuators - but nothing happened. The controls felt sloppy and lifeless.

Resounding banging noises began to shudder through the ship as it crashed through the mass of the air outside, and a squealing noise began to course through the entire vessel. The stresses on the boat would have caused any airplane or spaceship from the earliest days of rocketry, or aviation, to have broken up a long time ago. But the Agamemnon was still holding together - just.

As the ship continued its rotation CH was forced to tighten her seat webbing as hard as it could go but her head still jerked forward and back again, banging against the headrest. Heracleonn, next to her was like a doll, her upper body flopping forward and back with each rotation. CH tried to tell her to tighten her harness, but she was in a world of her own.

Groaning with the disorientation, CH fixed her gaze on the instrument panels, focussing her concentration on it.

'Come on damn you. Come on,' she gasped.

From the seat next to her Heracleonn groaned, 'I thought I could do it. I thought I could,' and she stared into space in front of her.

CH ignored her and continued to wrestle with the controls for a full two minutes, but then just stopped and let them go. Closing her eyes for long moments, she said, 'Nothing works any more. There isn't time to abandon ship and it wouldn't do us any good, anyway.' Turning to look at Heracleonn, she said, 'Well done Pamela. You've managed to kill us all.'

The two of them watched helplessly as the ship's motion caused the massive, wide blue horizon of the planet to sweep up across the windshield, followed by the pitch black of space, studded with stars, followed again by the planet's reappearance, over and over. But the view was now starting to become obscured by the brilliant red and orange glow of their re-entry into the atmosphere. The glow grew steadily brighter, faster and faster, and was soon accompanied by an intense heat which filled the flight deck. Pamela Heracleonn seemed to be oblivious to everything. She still stared ahead, head lolling, glassy eyed, mouth agape.

CH leaned forward, resting her hands on the useless control panel and, despite the ship's rotation, fought to fold her arms protectively around her head. It was the classic Navy "brace for impact" posture. She closed her eyes.

'Oh daddy,' said Heracleonn suddenly, quietly, eyes glazed over, 'what have I done?'

Seconds later the ship, spinning ever faster, began to lose pieces of its external apparatus. The sensor pylons and aerials and part of the tail fin broke away as the vessel hit the denser, deeper, layers of atmosphere. Then the wings came off. A blue-red glow of super-heated nitrogen and oxygen seemed to completely envelope the vessel and the Agamemnon took on the appearance of a burning meteor. Seconds later it disintegrated completely, flinging outwards thousands of pieces of its fuselage, in flaming shards; multiple meteors, illuminating the skies below.

*

The hemisphere of the planet below the Agamemnon's entry into the atmosphere was beginning to slip into night. Kilometres high, above the northern part of the Purple Forest, hundreds of kilometres from the eastern seaboard the burning wreckage of the landing boat lit the purple evening like a bizarre, gruesome firework display; a brilliant but silent sight. It would have been spectacular for anyone on the ground who happened to be watching, but it continued for no more than a minute, until the flaming streams at last faded and sputtered out in the gathering darkness.

Chapter 38

NEW CAMBRIA

Bhumi Devi Times. Post-Pioneer day, 14th of Erbings month.

Editorial:

Some residentia across the eastern seaboard and northern continent, who didst report seeing an unusual but far-distant meteor shower two nights past did witness the destruction of a Home System Navy Landing Ship. The vessel, a relatively small-so one, by Navy standards, broke up in the high atmosphere of Oceanus, with the loss of all those on board. Unconfirmed reports suggest that as many as twenty Navy personry mayst have died in this tragi-dem.

President Nefer-Masterton has sent her sincere sorrow message to the Navy officers of the mother ship but has asked for a full report be provided, in view that the explosion occurred over the land. She has asked for assurances that no contamination of the land is to result. It has yet been confirmed that no Oceanus citizens were aboard the striken vessel and pieces of wreckage would have fallen in the northern part of the east-central plateau. Tis understood that the sur-Navy have asked permission to send a search party to look for wreckage. Sources say such permission has not been given.

In other dramatical news, an undisclosed source has produced evidence that last month a joint team of scientists from Oceanus, and the HS Navy, made a remarkable discovery on the great Island of Simurgh. If true, such findings may be signalling the most significant finding in all such human history: the discovery of self-conscious beings outside of the human species (barring yet, claims about cetaceans on old Earth).

The small-so team, assembled by Professier Dracus Muggredge, of the University of Janitra, are said to have found carbonised rock layers, and claims show there was yet a massive calamity on this our world, more than eight millions of years past. Tis said to have been due to explosions in the surface of Ra. Sources opposed thereto, claim there is no solid evidence from Simurgh supporting of this idea, and tis convenient that the explorer group claimed the site was destroyed by an avalanche of rocks, leaving no remaining evidence.

Sad yet, our source says also that that two members of such team met their deaths on the island. In view of this shock, there have been calls for the evidence found by an Official Inquestor into said incident, to be made public. The original hearing had been held behind such closed doors.

Our source also says that though the fossil remains on the island were lost, still other things were saved. Now we will announce, we have seen pictures, showing pieces of the primitive weapons yet held by the ancient beings, whose fossils were found. We are told these were made of an alloy of iron, very steel-like, and that were spear heads. If true, and this paper believes it so, it means we humanry were not the first self-aware beings to live on this planet. We shall yet bring more news such when we yet have it.

****

Arkas Tenak pressed Captain Ebazza's private cabin intercom a second time. Ebazza finally noticed Tenak on her screen and let him in. It was downtime for both of them, a fairly unusual occurrence on board The Monsoon, leaving the ship's eminently capable First Officer at the helm.

Tenak walked into the Captain's room, which was in darkness except for one soft, discrete light on the far wall, glowing above a small device that projected a large holo of a scene from the African bush onto the wall. The view changed constantly, as the panorama rotated slowly through 360°.

'Please come in, Admiral. To what do I owe this pleasure?' she said, beginning to rise from the plush upholstery of a chair.

'Please don't get up,' he said, 'I just wanted to see how you were doing.'

'Oh, I am fine, Admiral. Just relaxing – for once. But please join me. I am glad to see you. Can I get you something?'

'Thanks very much but, no. I was at a loose end, I guess. Thinking of CH. Wondering what else we could have done.'

At Ebazza's invitation Tenak sat opposite her, sinking into one of her comfortable armchairs.

'I know you held CH, in high esteem too,' he said. 'You and she were quite close, weren't you? Or, as close as we're allowed to be with our crew.'

'Exactly so, Admiral.' Ebazza offered to switch off the holovid scene but Tenak said he found it soothing.

'She was a fine officer, and Gwan-Ji and Brady were good security guards' said Tenak, 'and, despite our misgivings about Mordant, you have to admit that he was a fine engineer. I just wish I could say there was a good reason for what happened, but it's just, well, it seems … pointless.'

'Yes. I'm afraid this incident tests even my faith, you know. I have always been convinced there is a greater reason for everything, even such terrible things, and I still hope to find meaning in this. Perhaps only the Lord knows. It seems strange to think it happened a whole standard week ago.'

'Yes. It's also shocking to think it's now been five days since the ship's Board of Inquiry. Trouble was, there was virtually no info' to go on. A finding of "Unknown ultimate causation," was the best the board could come up with, but I'm sure, in my own mind, that Heracleonn had something to do with it. I reckon she got loose, somehow. Tried to take over the boat maybe – but we'll probably never know.'

'I am mystified as to why the OA authorities will not let us search for any wreckage,' said the Captain, 'not even to find the *Maser Recording and Location Device*. That would have given us the info we need.'

'It's possible that even the "MARLOD" was destroyed, Ssanyu. Otherwise we would have picked up its signal by now. We could've extracted most of what we need from up here. But those things are supposed to be virtually indestructible, so that's another mystery. My experience tells me that there is no such thing as "indestructible", anyway.'

'But you'd think Arbella's government would have put aside the Injunction the Meta-teleos obtained from the Oceanus Supreme Court. And why do they want to stop us searching anyway? Something about security, was it?'

'I don't think their system can just put aside an injunction, Ssanyu. They can apply, but an assistant of my "contact", the one in the Policy Making Committee, told Muggredge the government would have been embroiled in a problematic court battle. They might have had to disclose documents relating to various permissions already given to us – including the one allowing us to go to New Cambria. The contact advises that with current suspicions running high we'd have to choose between two things: finding the wreckage or going to the New Cambria island. I felt – and you agreed at the time, Ssanyu, it should be the latter. Remember?'

'Yes, of course but it still seems so *petty*. We just want to find out what happened. What's the matter with these people?'

Listen, Ssanyu. When this is all over – which has to mean the people of this world have mostly been shipped to safety, we'll come back to this place – and we *will* find out what happened on that boat. "By hook or by crook", to quote an ancient saying.'

'I hope so, Admiral,' said Ebazza and forced herself to smile. 'Anyways,' she continued, 'in the meantime I have recorded a recommendation that CH, Mordant and the Security detail be awarded posthumous HS Navy Medals of Honour. Do you agree?'

'Absolutely, Ssanyu,' said Tenak and the conversation paused for a while until Tenak said, 'You do realise there'll be a full Board of Inquiry when we get back home?'

'Surely there will. You know, people outside the Navy, or any military force really, think that those in command just take the deaths of personnel in their stride, but it hurts a lot, Arkas. It still hurts. Every time.'

'So it must, Ssanyu. So it must.'

'Sorry, I don't need to tell *you* of all people. You've had mush more experience of this tna me.'

'I suppose. Perhaps too much.'

'It must have been horrendous during the Rebel War. I know you were in the final assault on Mars. Did you ever question what you trying to do, Arkas? Strike that, sir. Sorry, I didn't mean to pry. Or bring back bad memories. Forgive me for asking.'

'Not at all. Sometimes it's helpful to talk. I don't mind. Releases fustiness from the mind. And anyway, I often questioned things, Ssanyu. In this business the most important thing is that you have confidence in your officers – and that those you command have confidence in you. Even if the orders you give don't seem to make much sense, at first. If your crew trust you and respect you, they'll follow you. But of course, you always have to lead by example. Sorry, perhaps I'm lecturing *you,* now. I don't mean to.'

'Not at all, Arkas. I like to listen to you when you talk like this.'

'You flatter me, Ssanyu. But in that particular situation – with the Mars assault, I mean, we were trying to stop the total annihilation of the colony. There were lots of terrible incidents in that push. That's on the record of course but, personally, I lost some close friends. And you don't ever get over that. Not really.'

'There was a classic failure of intel' on that occasion, wasn't there? Weren't you Captain of the battle cruiser, "Cougar?"'

No, I was First Officer. Seems like eons ago now, Ssanyu. And you're right, there was a failure of intel – and sensor tek.'

'Sensor tek? How so? Oh … you mean … there was a failure to detect the Rebels reaching Mars orbit, wasn't there?'

'Exactly. We didn't know the Rebel fleet had inserted around Mars. We were on a trajectory oblique to the ecliptic and still 3 million klicks from the planet. They carried out a burn to elongate their orbits and took us by surprise. Sensors failed to detect their burns, so they managed to let loose a full missile salvo. Full nuclear jobs. At that stage we didn't know that their fleet even had tactical nuclears'. Complete lack of intelligence. Sound familiar to you?'

Tenak's face took on a sour look for a moment, as he paused, then continued long moments later, 'Anyway, they let loose the nuclears' before we could take evasive action. My ship and the "Venture" managed to knock out most of their warheads, using X ray lasers, but the "Viper" and "Vehement," weren't so lucky.' The Admiral's eyes took on a strange look for a second. 'You know, I watched as they just ... sort of flashed out of existence – right there on the screens. Nothing left. All those lives. I knew all the officers and the crew on the Viper and most on the Vehement, as well as a dozen people I'd been through training college with. All gone, in ... what ... a millionth of a second?' Tenak looked at the nearby vid screen for a few seconds before saying, 'There were other incidents, individual ones ... more gruesome than that, but I won't bore you with them.'

'I'm not bored by other people's experiences of command, Arkas. But I think I'm awakening terrible memories in you. I just pray there is no need for such events again.'

Tenak nodded slowly and Ebazza changed the subject, 'By the way, there will be a ship's Service of Appreciation for CH, and the others, in two days. I wondered if you might agree to speak at that, Arkas? I am leading the Service at the ship's Church of the Divine Provider, next week. For those that believe. Not many of those on this ship, I'm afraid.'

Tenak shivered and looked as if were shaking off dust and said, 'Sorry about that Ssanyu. And yes, of course I'll officiate at the Appreciation Service. Listen, Ssanyu, I've got things to attend to right now, but I do need to ask if you've made any progress on reviewing shuttle security arrangements?' Tenak rose to leave.

'Yes Admiral. I am recommending that the remaining two landing boats now carry a back-up pilot on all missions, and a minimum of three security guards on every trip. Enhanced automated monitoring telemetry is to be sent to *this* ship every 30 minutes, without fail, to back up the usual tel' intel.' Tenak nodded his agreement but Ebazza continued, 'And, Admiral, I hope you don't mind, but I do not want any more senior engineers going down to that planet. Mordant was our top engineer, and we've lost Erbbius too. It's getting critical. We can't afford to lose any more specialised people.'

'Quite so. I agree with all your recommendations. Please action them, starting with the mission to New Cambria. I believe the Laurasia will be leaving immediately after the Appreciation Service?'

****

At the same time as Tenak and Ebazza were having their "heart to heart" discussion, three other crewmembers were engaged in a very different type of conversation, elsewhere on the ship. They floated in what they deemed to be their "safe room", deep in the bowels of the micro-gravity dominated hub of The Monsoon.

Mantford Blandin, the ship's Second Officer, anchored by his boots, to a strip of microloop stood next to another of the ship's three remaining top engineers, Garmin Calymmian Brundleton. The other crewmember was newly appointed security guard, Dravette Fulvinia Shacklebury, a short, solid looking woman with a mass of black hair and a quick temper. She simply held onto bulkhead grab rail, as her body floated in the micro-gravity.

'Our little group is getting a "bit thin on the deck-plating" since we lost Mordant,' said Brundleton.

'Is that all you can say about him?' spat Blandin.

'What do you want me to say, Lieutenant?'

'There's no point goin' over all this again,' said Shacklebury, 'Everyone's guessed that bitch, Heracleonn, was responsible for this, but there's nothin' we can do about it now. Just decide what we do next, that's all.'

'Well my friends, we're not likely to inveigle our way onto that New Cambria expedition, that's for sure. Not after Ebazza's new rule,' said the Lieutenant.

'There's no need anyway,' said Brundleton. 'What are they going to find? Another carbonised layer? Big deal. More fossils? Wow! That's not going to change anyone's mind about down there.'

'I wouldn't be too sure 'bout that,' said Shacklebury, her brow furrowing above her intense stare, 'Besides, it's not the discoveries that matter. It's more to do with the interpretations others put on them.'

The two men looked at each-other, puzzled.

Shackelbury rolled her eyes and tried to explain herself, 'I know you guys are non-believers but those of us who adhere to Ultima know that the One True Light would not permit any creature, other than humanity, to be sentient. Those guys down there? They got it all wrong.'

There was silence for a moment, then Brundleton said, with a smirk, 'Sure thing Dravette. Whatever you say.'

'Don't patronise me,' she snapped.

'Okay, that's enough,' barked Blandin. 'We all had our reasons for joining the Rebel Alliance. For some, it's religion. The main thing now, is that we don't do *anything* to draw unwanted attention to us,' he said, staring straight at Shackelbury. 'The top brass, especially the old man, are on the lookout for anything they can use to pin us down. We need to get fresh orders from our taskmasters back home – and we'll do nothing to compromise that, unless the situation gets desperate. Do you both understand?'

The other two nodded sullenly.

****

'Here we go guys,' said pilot Lew Pingwei, 'you should be able to see New Cambria now.' His voice came over the intercom to the group on sitting tightly in the passenger lounge of the landing boat, Laurasia, as it flew, more than 20,000 metres above sea level, toward the island; the latest mission to try to find answers which might convince a recalcitrant government and a stubborn, suspicious population, of the dangers facing them.

Mike's spitits had lifted when he'd learned that Lew was the pilot on this trip. When Tenak asked Mike to join the team for the island, he had been flattered of course, but he'd had a slight case of the jitters, especially given the events on Simurgh. Nevertheless, he had agreed to go, mainly because he felt it extremely likely Eleri would have been asked by Muggredge, and would have accepted, even though she might, he guessed, have similar concerns. But this trip was necessary. And, despite his anxiety he remembered the burgeoning curiosity, the incredible fascination of the discoveries they'd all made on Simurgh which, he felt, had been unleashed in him – before it all got trashed of course .

Mike, obviously unaware of the make-up of the Oceanus part of the team, had been warned by Tenak not to contact Eleri about it. For her part, she had also kept her lips sealed during communications. And, he hadn't even seen her "in the flesh", for a couple of weeks. He'd been engaged on ship's duty all that time.

So, as intended, it was only when The Monsoon members were flown down to the "spaceport" at Janitra, that they met up with their Oceanus counterparts. And there some surprises, for all.

For then, amidst his relief that Eleri was on the mission and his blissful reunion with her, he found out that she had been appointed the leader of the science team of the whole expedition. He was even more surprised to hear, from Eleri herself, that she had had more than a few misgivings about whether to join the team, but decided she'd have to go because she was sure *he* would have been assigned to the mission and would have accepted it. And, like Mike, she was burning with curiosity. Only after accepting had she been told she was to be the scientific "leader", though Tenak, Muggredge and Ebazza had insisted that Lew should be in charge of the all the logistical and tek aspects, and, more importantly, in overall charge of the mission. After the experiences on Simurgh, he had the power to veto anyone else's decisions, though he promised Eleri he would defer to her on the purely scientific matters.

Mike was overjoyed at Eleri's "promotion" and was further pleased to find that Danile Hermington and the Maheshtras were also on the team. Marcus Senestris was also back, perhaps a surprise, given his less than excellent record in the Purple Forest, but Danile later told him he reckoned it was because of the guy's skills as a geologist.

And Mike was made aware of the fact that Sung had been turned away by Muggredge, because of his even poorer Simurgh performance record. Chen and Morgath had also declined positions on the team. Putting personal feelings aside, he genuinely felt the absence of these people was a shame.

But also on the team were Rasmissen and Arbinius, the two young Oceanus geologists. It seemed they had coped well with the events on Simurgh but they were very quiet people. It was hard to get much more than a peep out of them, except when talking about science, when their obvious enthusiasm for the mission couldn't be faked. It was also infectious.

For this trip Mike was classed, temporarily, as a team scientist. He didn't know whether to feel honoured, or disappointed, that the post was considered merely "temporary". He rationalised it by recalling that everything concerning this planet had to be considered "temporary".

But Mike was very happy at the inclusion of another team member. This was none other than hemi-med Padrigg Lomanz. He'd been available for the mission and so, was assigned, mainly on Senior Med Atrowska's suggestion. Tenak and Ebazza had been categorical about the need for a highly qualified medic on this new team, following the events on Simurgh and the Purple Forest.

Mike eagerly introduced Lomanz to Eleri, describing him as the man who had rehabilitated him after the attack of the grotachalik. With typical modesty, though probably accuracately, Lomanz said it had been a team effort.

Also, under Captain Ebazza's new rules, Lew had a co-pilot this time. This was Evressaria Glaphyra Kravikovna, classed as a "upper mid-level" pilot; a mature and lean woman with a round, fresh face that made her seem much younger than her 48 Earth years. Mike knew Everessaria, better known as "Eve", quite well. She had, luckily for him, and given Eleri's presence, not been a "lust partner" of his. She'd had little interest in him that way, but he knew her to be a dedicated pilot who aspired to become one of the Monsoon's best, though she lacked experience. She was a trainee engineer at present and Mike was aware she had volunteered to always stay with the shuttle – if necessary, as per Ebazza's rules.

Also staying aboard, at all times, would be two of the three Navy security guards now supplementing the team, hand-picked by Tenak. This meant that Lew, who had a "lower-mid level" engineering qualification, which, in olden days, would have been called a *first degree*, could provide the benefit of his knowledge and skills, given the absence of a more senior engineer.

And it was concerning the technical aspects of the mission that the final surprise came, for Mike and pretty much everyone else, especially the somewhat mystified Oceanus team. They would be joined by a senior cybernautics engineer, a professor, from the *Antarctica*. He self-consciously introduced himself to Lew and Mike as Alexennder Decius Ventidius Akromo, a tall, thin, slightly grizzled looking man with a glossy brown thatch and a ginger beard. He had intense eyes and the appearance of someone who was perhaps used to having his own way. Neither Mike nor Lew had ever heard of him and after he had spoken very briefly to them he disappeared to the back of the ship and sat down to study a schematics holo' of some kind, produced by his wristcom.

'That looks like an image of some sort of wheeled machine,' Lew said to Mike.

It was later revealed that Tenak felt they might need the technical help Akromo could offer. But, given the stipulations of the OA government it seemed the Admiral was taking a huge risk, causing the need for extra security and the cooperation of everyone to keep quiet about the professor's involvement. It had been Providius's suggestion that Akromo should join the team, agreed by Tenak and Ebazza after much debate, but he came well recommended.

The security meant that Tenak and Providius had ordered no comms with anyone else on the planet during the mission. With Akromo's help, they'd arranged the jamming of all "ship to shore" comms, to prevent anyone deliberately, or accidentally, advising the government, or the Meta-teleos, of Akromo's inclusion. In the end and despite his reservations, Tenak had had enough of pussyfooting around and told Mike of his gut feeling that this mission was too important to jeopardise by *not* including the scientist. If it got out Tenak accepted he'd have to face the consequences.

Now, a few hours after the team had settled down for the flight it was drawing to an end, Lew having again taken the shuttle along what he termed, "the long route", for the comfort of those not used to such journeys, which meant that the journey had taken over three hours. For Mike it might have been a little tedious had Eleri not been with him. Also, there was bubbly chatter around the boat and huge speculation about what might or *might not* be on the island.

**

What actually awaited them on the island was something no-one on Oceanus or in the Home System, could ever have expected.

**

At the outset the team had agreed, for ease of reference, to shorten the name of their island destination to "Newcam". Now they were approaching their target an atmosphere of excited tension became almost palpable. From their altitude and distance they could see the entire island, spread out like a brightly hued, knobbly, carpet, appearing as though it had been fashioned by some powerful demi-god who had simply thrown a gigantic lump of turf and gravel into the sea.

As they drew rapidly closer Lew slowed the Laurasia, reducing altitude to around twelve thousand metres. The ship was in the first stages of preparing to land but now those aboard could better appreciate the target's physical characteristics: a relatively small island, measuring approximately two hundred and seventy kilometres north to south, by one hundred and thirty west to east. It was shaped a little like a tadpole with the "head" part in the north, appearing to their left, a narrow "waist" then another, small enlargement before another, narrower, waist which extended, like a tail curving, to the south west, toward their right hand side. The southernmost tip latter led to a long, trailing archipelago of tiny islands strung far out into the glittering ocean, stretching for more than five hundred klicks. Now, the Laurasia rapidly drew nearer the west coast of "Newcam", and the pilot spoke to everyone over the intercom, banking the ship so they could now see the ragged coastline.

Another Ebazza rule was that no-one, apart from pilots and security guards, was allowed onto the flight deck. It meant, this time, no invites into the cockpit, to get the "best views or "help to look for a suitable landing site". Instead, the views were transmitted, by hologram, directly into the cabin, for all to see. Eleri was able to make suggestions about what she felt were suitable landing sites, with respect to the mission objectives. Lew had the final say.

He now announced, 'The ship's telescopic cameras show the presence of a quantity of that carbonised stuff about 3 klicks from here, way up the west coast but it might not amount to a lot. Eleri, if I can find a safe place to land, do you want me to put us down near that layer?'

Mike showed Eleri a small patch on the upholstery of her couch-chair arm. She just had to touch it and speak. She agreed to Lew's suggestion. Though there was hardly any sound from the engines there was much noise as everyone aboard was talking excitedly. Eleri was still able to speak to Lew without her words being drowned out because of the intelligent mic-receptor, able to attune itself to her voice and *tune out* everyone else's. She was delighted with it.

Within minutes Lew was taking the ship over the part of the coastline with the carbonised layer, landing the shuttle on, what his instruments told him, was a flat but firm stretch of grassland a few hundred metres from the seashore. A plain stretched inland from this point.

Everyone piled out, eager to stretch their legs and breath in the fresh sea air. Even Mike was glad for the change of scene, but he stayed near the shuttle whilst El and the others walked over to a nearby outcropping of low rocks. Eleri had recommended some new tablets for Mike to take, to reduce his agoraphobia but this type of wide-open vista still upset him.

Beyond the silvery-blue grass-like area lay a huge expanse of white beach, stretching far out to pounding surf. In the opposite direction, a distant mountain range beyond the plain; a chain of misty, enigmatic grey-blue peaks, appearing deceptively small at this distance.

The "carbonised layer" itself, formed a wide mass of chaotically scattered chunks strung out everywhere along the shoreface. Eleri joined Hermington as he examined it up close.

'The carbonised deposits,' said Danile, 'look like they have spread out near the top of the strata series.' He had to shout to make himself heard in the strengthening sea wind. Eleri bent closer to him, cupping her right ear.

'These chunks have been dumped here by rivers – outwash sediment,' he continued, 'which means they come from further inland. I so reckons we find a more intact layer on the higher ground, but I would not think they amount to ere' much. I am not sure of the age those mountains, but they do not look so old from here. Mahap less than 8 millions of years? We shall yet see. Also, no shale strata on this beach, like on Simurgh. So, no fossils.'

Professor Akromo could be seen a little way off, picking up small chunks of the dark material and looking confused.

They wandered up to him and Hermington shouted, 'Taking samples, Professier?'

Akromo nodded and said, '*Professor* will do, thank you. And yes, this should be more than enough. I'll feed them to him in the hold. He'll be able to analyse exactly how old they are.' He ambled off toward the ship.

Eleri and Hermington gave each-other puzzled looks. "Him? He?" They returned to the landing boat. The rest of the team followed. Eleri spoke to everyone from the front of the cabin.

'Mer Lisdon did describe the carbon layer here as impressive, but that praps was because he had not been to Simurgh,' she said. 'And Lew tells us the sensors have not detected much in the way of a carbonised layer inland, but he needs to fly further in, to be yet sure. I am more interested in the strange rocks Lisdon said he found further inland, in yonda mountains. He described them as being harder-more than the hardmost of concrete, and a total mysteria. He could not understand their form but yet his funding zoned-out after, so he could not take it further. *We* yet have the luxury of being able to take his work further. So, onward we go. Okay, Lew, thanking you.'

She sat back in her seat and Mike, plonked himself down next to her, looking pleased as punch. He was immensely proud of Eleri, and he found this sentiment in itself to be delightful. It was something he had not felt about anyone since his older brother, Paulanda, had won a poetry medal in his pre-uni school. He knew, instinctively, that his feeling of pride in Eleri would not evaporate into the kind of contempt he had come to feel for his now indolent and feckless sibling.

A few minutes after taking off the ship approached the front range of pinnacles spotted from the shore; the aptly, if colourfully, named, "Dragontooth Mountains". They formed a long, spiky chain, like the backbone of an impossibly large reptile, running up the middle of New Cambria. Lew deployed a special sensor device, which took the form of a large ball. It descended out of a panel underneath the ship, hanging from a stiff tether. It looked like an old-fashioned "glitter ball", of the type once seen in ballrooms of long-ago times. But there was nothing old about *this* device, which Tenak had "borrowed" from the Antarctica. It represented the latest in sensor devices. Only usable at airplane heights, not from orbit, the various telescopic tubes inside the ball were capable of ultra-deep, detailed, very wide- range scans of rock layers, and it could usually "see down" many metres, often a couple of hundred metres.

Lew took the ship over the whole width of the mountain range, flying at 5,500 metres. Some of the central spine of mountains here reached 4,800 metres in height and were topped by large patches of snow. Their elevation was more than sufficient to cause powerful thermals which pushed the ship up, then allowed it to sink again quickly, a little uncomfortably for some of the Oceanus people. Lew and Kravikovna took the Laurasia on a zig zag course up the length of the mountain chain, monitoring the sensor ball feedback, searching for anything unusual. Lisdon had not been very specific about the location, or the extent of anything he'd found.

Half an hour later Lew announced they'd seen a target area, to the enormous relief of some OA people who were feeling a little travel-sick. He banked the craft gently, looking for a suitable landing zone, a task rather more difficult here than at the coast. Everyone peered through the windows, gaping, as he made the ship descend through a saddle between two mountains and, some minutes later, caused it to settle down gently onto a plateau; it   overlooked a wide plain on one side and foothills thickly forested with short, spiky trees on the other. The hills here were small compared with the ones they'd only recently flown over but they could be seen to increase in height into the distance as they marched toward the horizon, like solidified waves.

Lew's holo image suddenly appeared, in miniature, immediately above each of the occupied seats of the craft, using the emitters fitted in each of them. One or two of the OA passengers were taken aback for a second.

'It looks like Danile was right,' Lew's image announced. 'The sensors have picked up precious little in the way of a carbonised layer. There are traces here and there, guys, but the main finding is this …'

The lights in the lounge dimming, so that the images could be seen more clearly. Lew's image was replaced by a new holovid showing the landscape flowing by underneath the shuttle. Superficially it looked like a jigsaw puzzle of multi-coloured pieces. There was absolute silence as Lew's commentary explained that this was the holo trace taken by the sensor ball, from under the belly of the shuttle. The computer had auto-coloured the various layers of rock below, to differentiate them by type.

To the surprise of many, a computer-generated voice then took over from Lew and explained, in rich contralto tones, that they were looking at sedimentary rocks, mainly sandstones and mudstones, which were all more than 8.13 million years old. That was the time when it was posited, more a guess in fact, that a planet-wide environmental calamity was thought to have happened. The Dragontooth mountains, though relatively young, were older than that and near their peaks were traces of a carbonised layer, which the computer pointed out by animated graphics overlying the holo-vid. There was little of the stuff left now and it was clear it had been mostly eroded off the upper layers of the mountain and washed down to the sea.

The even greater surprise – for everyone – was the machine's next announcement. It said that the top of a massive "hemispherical structure" had been found just under the soil, at the foot of the mountain they had just passed over. Most of the structure was underground, but at the level of the soil it appeared to have a convex surface, like the smooth top of a toadstool – except this "toadstool" was a gigantic *thirty kilometres* across.

Excited and loud chatter broke out in the cabin. The auto-voice rose over the hubbub, effectively drowning out the noise. It said the sensor AI had been unable to determine how far down into the rock strata the "artefact" extended, but the "most interesting finding", it said, was that the material of the structure was *not natural*. At this, the cabin chatter rose to a crescendo, punctuated by whistles of disbelief, the auto-voice carried on. It said it could justify its statement because the structure was made, as far as could be analysed, from an unknown type of carbon-boron-nitride material. This could not be a naturally occurring material.

Mike, open mouthed and speechless, recalled that only *humans* had created similar substances – but even then, nothing quite like this. The materials already created in Home System laboratories, were the hardest ever known to humans, many times tougher than diamond. They were also flexible, though resistant to fracturing. But this thing here on Oceanus sounded like it might be superior to all these materials.

According to the computer auto-voice, its sensors had been unable to penetrate more than fifty metres into the dome structure, due to the density of the material but it had determined that below its shell-like outer skin – as much as 40 metres thick – the dome, inside, was mostly empty space. The female voice of the hyper-comp suddenly went silent. Hermington stood and, trying to raise his voice above the hubbub, asked, 'How old would you estimate the dome to be, Mes computer?'

Lew was now standing, in person, at the front of the lounge and he called out, asking people to quieten. Eleri got up and did the same, followed by Mike. As things quietened Lew indicated that Professor Akromo wanted to reply to Danile.

Akromo then stood and said, 'It can't answer your question young man, because it recorded that speech in a hundredth of a second, just before Lew landed, at which time the sensor ball had to be withdrawn. I'm sorry. Any further investigation will have to be done using the "SEV".'

Puzzled looks everywhere.

'SEV? So, what is that, sirra?' asked Gajana Maheshtra gently.

Akromo gave her a broad grin, 'Ah. That's my next trick. It's the "Surface Exploration Vehicle", but it's a lot more promising than it sounds, my friends. Let me explain. The SEV is an automaton we've begun using to explore the surfaces of barren or toxic planets. It's especially useful on my ship because we don't have any vehicles capable of landing people on such worlds. The SEV carries a class 2A, advanced, AI hyper-comp, purely for scientific investigation. When it's required to work alongside humans it responds to voice commands and can engage in analytical conversation. The SEV can also carry more than one *tonne* of human-usable equipment and tools, as well as survival survival and environment suits. We've kitted this one out with a water generating – and recycling unit – and substantial food stocks. Like it? I certainly do.'

Mike was amused. The man sounded like someone selling home help automatons back on Earth. Perhaps he'd done that, once. Some wag at the back, asked, tongue in cheek, whether it had a built-in refresher and made kaffee as well. This produced chuckles though Akromo didn't seem amusemed. He forced himself to smile, but it looked as though he'd tasted sour cream.

'Okay you guys,' said Lew to everyone, 'I need to know what you want to do. Eleri, what do you think when I show you this.' He touched a button on a tiny hand-held device he carried and a different holo appeared in mid-air at the front of the cabin. This time it was a slowly moving, natural though enhanced view of the ground taken from the cameras on the belly of the shuttle. It showed as much of the dome as could be seen from the air. The thing looked like a gargantuan bubble but much of it was covered with dark soil and rocks, as well as stunted trees and undergrowth. It could easily be overlooked from the ground, and even from the air, had it not been for the shuttle's sensor ball. And, thought Mike, this place was obviously somewhere the original human pioneers had never bothered with much, even if they had had this level of tek with them.

Lew superimposed a graphic on top of the natural image, showing the perfectly circular shape of the structure, as perceived by the deep sensors. Radiating out from its perimeter were six straight lines, each arranged at 60° intervals around the perimeter of the dome. A bright red spot was flashing near the south-eastern quadrant of the structure and Lew announced that this spot signalled their current position.

"This is nearest we can get to the biggest area of exposed dome,' he said, 'cos as you can see, most of it is covered with soil, or shitty, sorry ... silty stuff, as well as undergrowth. The rim of the thing is only about fifty klicks away from us now. So, I thought that Eleri, you might want to have a closer look? But listen guys, if it's half as thick as the sensor said, then you won't be able to do much there.'

'What are those lines yet radiating outwards?' asked Hermington. 'They look like the spokes of a wheel.'

'Yes, they are such like the rays of a sun or star,' said Marcus Senestris, 'as a child might draw them. Praps they are symbolic.'

'Could they be entranceways?' asked Mike. Eleri gazed at him and registered a slightly surprised smile.

'Yes,' she said, 'it makes sense, does not? If the structure contains a giant void then praps we can be presuming it to be yet a building?'

'Yes, for you must need have portals, so to gain entry to buildings,' said Senestris.

'We are shooting in the dark here, are we not?' said Danile, 'for we do not know who built this. Or why.'

'Well, humans certainly didn't build it,' said Akromo.

'Not even the earliest pioneers?' said Gajana. 'After all, so much have we lost, of their technology.'

The professor chortled, stifled it and said, 'I am so sorry, young Mes. Even *we* don't have the tek to build this in the Home System.' Everyone looked surprised.

'It's way ahead of us, believe me,' he continued. Mike nodded.

'Yeah, I agree guys,' said Lew, 'the stuff this thing is made of can't have been created by humans. I've never heard or seen anything like it. Materials scientists been trying to create stuff as hard as this for generations. Ships like the Monsoon are made of hyper-duralamium, which is twice as hard as diamond. But even The Monsoon isn't as tough as this thing. And just think of the size and thickness of this baby.' The cabin went silent, for long moments.

'Lord Maker, I am thinking tis the beings we found on Simurgh - again,' said Hermington and at this the hairs on the back of Mike's neck stood proud of his skin. Looking around he could see the realisation of this possibility in everyone, as voiced by Hermington.

'I hate to drag you back but praps we must admit, tis *slightly* more advanced than we saw there, Danile,' said Eleri. 'So, tis vital we find out its age.'

'The SEV might be able drill out a sample and analyse it – to get its age,' said Professor Akromo.

'No! We don't want to damage it,' said Hermington, 'for it might react 'gin us. Praps tis yet booby-trapped. Besides, it does not belong to us.' That brought puzzled looks from Eleri.

'Don't worry young man,' said Akromo, 'the SEV need only take a sample of less than a cubic millimetre, to be able to test it. Though, even that could take some time, given the hardness of it.'

'I think we came here to get answers,' said Eleri firmly, glancing at Hermington. Mike recognised that disapproving look. Danile started to speak but closed his mouth.

'So, I am yet sorry, Dani, but I shall agree to the sample being taken,' she continued. 'We can stop if there are any problems, or any warning signs. I also think Mike might be right when he mentioned the ray lines could be entranceways.'

'The material on those rays might also be thinner. Easier to examine,' said Akromo.

'Okay, I can get us to the nearest "ray", so we can see what's there. Okay?' said Lew and when Eleri nodded, he continued, 'Right, folks. Strap in. It's about forty-five klicks to the nearest, which is the one that points due east but, as I said, most of this thing is covered by muck. I'll fly "low and slow-mo," over it and you can take a good look – and tell me if you think it's worth landing. By the way, if we land, I won't be able to get us very close to it.'

Whilst the others returned to their seats and started buckling in, Lew suggested to Eleri that she move to one of the forwardmost seats, normally used as security seats. After she had done so, Lew tapped the armrest and a very small orange ball on a stalk popped up from the front of it.

This is the holo-emitter for this seat,' Lew said. 'I'm guessing you're familiar with the Navy holo-emitters, but, in any case, you don't need to do anything yourself. The ship's AI will feed the imagery to you.'

'Of course, young manry,' said Eleri, as Mike came to sit next to her.

'Sorry, Mike,' said Lew, 'but I think a geologist should sit next to Eleri for this one, so they can get a good look at the ground and advise if it's possible to get access to the ray, or entranceway, or whatever. Do you mind?' Mike raised his eyebrows, then smiled and nodded, clapping Eleri gently on the shoulder. Then he called over Hermington.

'Okay, let's get going,' said Lew and disappeared onto the flight deck.

****

Navy tek rating Bodram Chaucer Argolid, sat opposite a family of Oceanus citizens in an expansive marquee set up on the outskirts of Janitra.

'Mer Gastornis, please try to understand our position here. Please,' said Argolid, evidently becoming frustrated with the pleas of the local man and his wife. They had irritation, if not anger, written all over their faces and their three small children, standing next to them, wore glum faces with sad, innocent eyes.

When the family said nothing but continued to glare back at him, Argolid said, with hands opened in a plea for understanding, 'I'm sorry, but we just cannot take your flock of new Oceanus goats onto The Monsoon. There just isn't the space.'

Gastornis had applied to evacuate to the Home System, following the latest heavy ion storm. This family was one of several, who, together with a number of individuals, sat or stood in a large group in a screened off section at the far end of the marquee, to ensure privacy for those being interviewed.

The total number of applicants in the tent, including the Gastornis family, was sixty-four, but this number was unusual, the normal daily rate of applications being around fifteen or twenty. Gastornis and his family were the first to be seen this morning. Argolid was one of three junior Navy officers involved in the "processing", none of whom relished the job but who carried out Ebazza's orders to the letter. Two security guards stood at the entrance to the marquee and there were four more on duty outside. The guards were the only ones wearing uniforms; all the other crew wearing civilian garb, ostensibly to put the evacuees at ease.

This was the third week that the Navy had done this work and there had been no trouble, which didn't mean there wouldn't be. A similar team doing the same work in Ramnissos, two weeks earlier, had been abused and pelted with bottles and stones. Unofficially, this had been laid at the door of the Meta-teleosophists and, fortunately, the OA securi-pol had been on hand to prevent things escalating. The Navy were obliged to call on the local police as they were not allowed to carry their own stun weapons. Paradoxically, they were told they could carry *truncheons*. All the Navy security guards were trained in several, quite brutal, martial arts, and Ebazza was unequivocal in giving her permission for them to use whatever means needed, but only if they genuinely felt their lives or those of other evacuees were under immediate threat. Otherwise, a "softly, softly" approach was always to be adopted, or the local securi-pol were to be called.

In general, the business went smoothly at the sessions in Janitra. The migrants were usually genuine and serious minded. They were asked a series of questions designed to weed out the timewasters and charlatans, who were rare. Family circumstances were obtained, including some idea of means. This was part of the Home System's rescue mission, so, naturally, there was to be no charge for evacuation. But financial means could, possibly, be an important factor in determining the futures of evacuees at their eventual destinations; still very mucha sad fact of life back in the Solar System.

At that point, monetary assistance was to be offered to those with the least means, so a test of income and savings was deemed unfortunate, but necessary. Navy personnel had an electronic link to the securi-pol and social security departments on Oceanus, where local civil servants would be the ones to check the data and furnish the details if necessary. A number of necessary health questions had to be asked but great lengths were taken to ensure the evacuees understood this was so that populations back home would not be at risk and so that any needs they had could be catered for, on board ship – and possibly at the destination.

Applicants with a record of serious convictions, particularly those involving murder, violence or sexual assault, were to be held back for further questioning and processing, even though there were assurances that they would certainly not be left behind on the doomed world.

The trouble, for Tenak and the senior officers, was that there were still far too few citizens who considered this world to be really doomed.

As Argolid began to fill in some of the paperwork; old fashioned paper being the necessary concomitant of working on this planet, Gastornis began, loudly, to ask more questions, his voice rising in pitch as he did so.

'I am not seeing why we cannot be taking our miniature goats. What are we to do without them? We have always raised goats. Tis all we know. All I know. This is not good. Not good so much. Firsting, you say we can only take 150 kilomens of luggage and now, no goats! We only want to take our smallest herd after all,' he exclaimed.

'With respect, Mer Gastornis,' said Argolid, 'I advised you that you could not take your animals, right from the beginning, and the government news agencies announced this stipulation on broadcasts made some weeks ago. Only one or two animals are allowed, per family, or per person. This would normally be a pet - but we cannot take herds of domesticated livestock, whether goats, miniature cows or whatever. I'm sorry, but that's just the way it is.'

At this point, Gastornis huffed loudly and slammed a beefy hand onto the table between him and Argolid, sending papers flying. Argolid's eyes widened and a Navy security guard, standing near the tent entrance, began to move toward them. His approach was menacing but Gastornis, now overheated, stood up, apparently ready to deal with him. He couldn't have had any idea of the potential danger he faced. His children, a boy of about seven and two girls, aged ten and eleven, started crying. The man's wife rose, and she barked loudly at her husband, 'Arpe Diatryma Gastornis! Do not do any such foolry. Please, my manry. Please to sit down.'

Argolid himself put up a hand up to warn the Security man not to approach further, and as soon as the guard saw the children he stopped in his tracks, looking around uncertainly.

At that moment, Admiral Arkas Tenak seemed to appear out of nowhere and stepped forward, saying to the Gastornis familty, calmly and firmly, 'What is yet the matter here, sirra? How mayst I help.'

The moment was diffused by Tenak's benign visage, and people calmed. Gastornis turned to Tenak and protested angrily again about his goats. The Admiral beckoned for him to accompany him to a reserved area at the back of the tent, then gently invited the man to sit on a chair which faced his own, with no table between them. Patiently, Tenak asked the man about where he lived, and about his children and wife and the kind of life they led on Oceanus.

Then he asked him to explain his problem in detail and listened seriously. When the man had finished, he said, with genuine compassion, 'I am so sorry Arpe, but my colleague was right. You see, if we were to take your entire herd, we would have to take the next man's herd and the next, and so on, would we not? Do you see my problem? We would have no room for any more people. Imagine if we couldn't take any more children like your own, like Annie, or Kristine, or Andli. All because our cabins and hangars were full of … well, goats – or other livestock.'

He let that sink in before he resumed, 'I have every sympathy with you and I would like to save every animal, every living thing on this world – but, at the moment, we have to give priority to the people. Maybe we can come back for domesticated animals. Please believe me when I tell you that if there was any way to help you take them I would do it. But I can't. Not right now.'

The man bowed his head in misery and nodded, and Tenak gently touched his shoulder gently, then led him back to the main tent. As he returned to his family his wife said to him, 'Arpe, the nice manry here tells me we will probably be able to start goat farming again when we get to Earth, probably in a place called Southern Amerika.' She beamed at him. 'We will a-gather new goats. Our own beloved goats will be roaming free here. They will return to the wild, Arpe – and survive.'

'Till the surface of this world explodes, Anya,' was all he could say as they were led away.

Tenak looked genuinely mournful. 'I expect we'll probably get more of that,' he said to Argolid, who had stood to attention. 'This is an agrarian world, after all,' he continued. Before saying any more, he led the Navy rating to the back of the tent, out of earshot of his colleagues. He said, 'You didn't do anything wrong, rating, but can I suggest that you take a bit more time with them? At the moment we do, at least, have time for individuals. That might change. And listen. You were right in what you said but there's different ways of saying it. Do you understand?' Argolid nodded and Tenak continued, 'Please move the chairs, for the use of applicants, out from the table and around to its side, facing you. It will help if you don't put a barrier up between them and you, Bodie. And it's always best to keep in the forefront of your mind, just what it is they're giving up here. This is a garden world, a kind of paradise for these people, and it's not an easy decision to leave it. Got the idea?'

'Yes sir. Thank you,' said Argolid. The chastened rating walked back to his post.

'Congratulations sir. I got here just in time to see you *in action*' as it were,' said an immaculately uniformed figure, who strode up to Tenak.

'Thank you, Commander Statton, but there's no need for it. It just needs a bit of a humane touch, that's all,' said Tenak. 'Most of these citizens are good people at heart. The ones coming to us here are doing so out of a feeling of necessity, not desire.'

'Yes sir,' said Statton, 'even if the majority of the population are in denial, sir.'

'I know, but they're still to be admired.'

'How so?'

'When you realise what they've achieved here, and in such a relatively short time, and without going to extremes, you can't help admire them. Especially, when you compare it with the Earth. Okay, I know things have changed a lot but for dozens of generations we, effectively, raped the Earth. And we've paid the penalty for it.'

'Yes, sir, but I worry that the people refusing to come to us will pay a penalty too. A pretty extreme one, if they don't change their views soon. There's still too few applications for migration permits, sir.'

'Maybe, but before the last ion storm we were only getting a few applications per week. Now we're getting dozens. That's progress, number one. And the press releases revealing the government's concealment of what went on at Simurgh helped, so I expect a lot more soon.'

'Really sir? You sound like you're expecting the "floodgates to open". I can't really see it happening.'

'Oh, I don't know. I've got a feeling that the team of scientists on their way to New Cambria, right now, are going to produce some good stuff.'

'Like more fossil bones, sir? I know the Simurgh find was startling, from a scientific point of view. The first finding of what might have been sentient beings, outside of the Earth and all that – but, with respect, sir, I can't see it changing the minds of these people. The bones predated the carbon layer by a long way, didn't they? Maybe four or five hundred thousand years, or something? Surely, those creatures could've been killed off by any one of lots of different things in that time gap? Disease, loss of food supply, or some other kind of environmental catastrophe - other than Ra, I mean.'

'Good point, number one. You might be right, but this is an amazing world. I'm confident that this time the team will be able to bring back some solid evidence. Better had. It's our last chance, or theirs, anyway.' Tenak's smile quickly disappeared as a kind of darkness seemed to cloud his features. Statton gave him a puzzled look.

Tenak beckoned to Statton to follow him further into the "reserved" area of the marquee. Checking around them, conspiratorially, he lowered his voice and said, 'There's something you need to know, Gallius. But this is for your ears only – at this point. The Captain and I have just been informed, on the hyper-secure channels, by Captain Providius, that their newest measurements of Ra suggest that its surface is likely to blow around 20 - 25 % earlier than previously thought. They're not sure how much reliance they can place on this finding right now, so they're planning a close fly-past of Ra, to try to confirm the measurement and, hopefully, refine it for us.'

Statton's eyes widened and his mouth turned down with utter dismay.

Chapter 39

STRIDER

The science team on New Cambria trudged along a path forged through an open forest environment, slowly wending their way toward what had appeared, from the shuttle, to be one of the massive dome's "radial line" offshoots. The route wound between scores of massive, gaunt, sandstone outcrops. Giant, free-standing, boulders were scattered throughout the area which meant that the nearest Lew had been able to land was twelve kilometres away. The heat was stifling, and most of the group wore floppy, brimmed UV hats, for protection.

The path they followed had been created by Akromo's SEV, which crawled along ahead of the walkers in the lead. It was a large and curious looking machine, walking on eight, jointed, metal, legs, like a spider, but as the limbs were spread out the length of a long body it more closely resembled a huge, gambolling, scorpion, or a centipede perhaps. Even so, Mike considered it a substantial piece of kit. Everyone, including Lew, had been surprised by its size. Most of the Oceanus people seemed very wary of it.

The main part of its "body" was an elongated boxy shape, about six and a half metres long by two and a half wide, and two metres high, rather like an old-fashioned railway goods car, but the main body articulated in four large segments, shiny and new looking. At its front end were a large number of sensor antennae and four more limbs, or "arms", jointed and sporting an array of pincer-like tools, drill bits and other devices. Its walking legs were all four metres long with each one moving independently. In place of feet, it had thick, padded metal plates, above which sat open slatted wheels, each a metre across. These were currently not in use, the plate feet being more appropriate for this terrain. Akromo said the machine was designed to negotiate almost any type of terrain. That wasn't hard to believe. His pet name for it was, "Strider".

Everyone from the Laurasia, except for two people, were in the group trekking into the New Cambrian foothills, with Kravikovna and one security guard, left to look after the ship. The other two security guards accompanied the team, carrying large stun rifles, ostensibly for protection against the warned of "Kilops worms". Strider, apparently, had no dedicated weapon capabilities, though, mused Mike, his weight and front limbs would make formidable weapons.

Mike, walking next to Eleri, near the back of the group, watched the SEV climb over a massive fallen tree trunk that blocked its path. It was not exactly elegant, but impressive, nonetheless. Akromo had told them that it had been designed mainly for use on rocky, desert like planets, without atmospheres. It wasn't "familiar" with thickly vegetated environments like this, but it would definitely cope, he said. Mike believed the man was possibly over-confident, especially after his experiences on Simurgh. But he knew he had to put those thoughts behind him now.

He remained wary.

*

When he first set eyes on the Strider Hermington had expressed reservations about it, complaining that it would cause too much damage to the environment here, like military tanks of olden days on Earth, or forest strippers. One or two others agreed. Akromo had tried to reassure them that it was programmed, as much as possible, to avoid causing such damage, and that its main procedure was to pick its way over obstacles, not squash them. Mike reckoned that some degree of damage was inevitable, a sentiment echoed by Eleri. She had had to reassure those who grumbled and remind them what was at stake here. Much of the natural landscape here would be destroyed in the coming conflagration anyway. Mike observed all this and, given his experiences on Oceanus so far, wondered how many of the Oceanus scientists, even now, genuinely appreciated this fact.

The Laurasia's hyper-comp had already plotted the main route and fed those instructions to the Strider, as it led them ever deeper into the foothills. The group were eventually climbing a slope which gradually, but inexorably, became steeper. And the going got tougher.

An hour of considerable effort later they finally reached what Lew said was the terminal part of the "ray", as shown on his holo-map. As they mounted a rise they could see part of the artefact some distance ahead, nestled in a mass of blue-green forest. As they neared it the thing looked more and more like a pair of blank stone walls, around four metres high, maybe half a metre thick, with a gap of about three metres between them. On reaching the structure the group got their first close-up look at the curious material from which it was made. There were some gasps of astonishment.

Although the visible parts of the structure had appeared an almost uniform white colour, from a distance, the walls now seemed partially translucent, like frosted glass. Over much of their extent they were covered with a mass of tangled blue undergrowth and a scum of dirt, but there was enough of the walls visible to see that they stretched up the hill ahead of them, climbing at a steady angle of at least 30°. Above a certain point, perhaps three or four hundred metres further up, only partial glimpses of the walls could be seen, poking out of the vegetation and native rock debris.

Gathering around what seemed to be the terminal part of the structure the group noticed that, beneath a veneer of soil and rubble, the ground itself, between the walls, was made of the same odd material. It was quite smooth and looked slippery, but it was ribbed all along it at intervals of three or four centimetres. Was that design meant to allow someone or something to walk along it, in the distant past?

'This material on the walls is yet sediment, wash-ed off the mountain by stream and river,' said Hermington, breaking the astonished silence which had set in. 'From the air all the other rays were completely buried by it, sept this one,' he continued.

Mike was as astonished as anyone else about this structure, which he felt represented a level of development so far above anything anyone had found so far on Simurgh. It could make you giddy he felt. He also began to feel the tickle of nervous excitement inside him and he looked at Eleri in wonderment. She gazed at the structure with a slack jaw.

'Can the Strider clear this stuff off, so we can see more of it?' Lew asked Akromo.

'He might,' said the tek-scientist, 'but we'd best get further up first. Closer to where these walls reach the dome. This part looks a bit like a walkway. I believe it might lead us to where we want to go.'

'That seems a stretch, Professor,' said Lew, 'cos we don't really know what it is, do we?'

'Praps we should examine the stonework of the walls firsting,' said Eleri, 'if deedly, tis stonework at all.'

'We can do better than that,' said Akromo, 'I'll ask Strider to drill out a piece, *if it's possible*, so we can determine its composition – and its age.'

There were sounds of approval from many, but suddenly Hermington raised a voice of dissent, 'I stress much-caution, once again, my friends. We do not know what this thing might do. For it might respond in some way.'

'Carnt see that,' said someone.

'Even if it could have responded once, has yet been here millions of years,' said another.

Eleri piped up, 'I think Danile is right to be cautious. Do not be forgetting, some of us were at Simurgh. We might so have been complacent of the dangers there.'

Mike was a little surprised, given her earlier attitude. Eleri then took Danile's arm and drew him away from the others.

'Look Dani,' she said, quietly, 'I am understanding how you feel but we have to get such job done here. I am sorry, but I will allow Professier Akromo to get his way. But I am glad you did raise the point.' She looked gently but deeply into his eyes and he at last nodded his assent.

'Do not stop warning us, if you must, my manry,' she said to him as they rejoined the group. Mike, who had been looking on with curiosity, clapped Danile on the shoulder, as Eleri nodded to Akromo to let the Strider start work. A surprisingly small but complex looking drill bit suddenly sprouted out of the machine's left, frontal tool arm. It placed the bit, very gently, against the flat inner surface of one of the walls, close to the top. It then stopped and Akromo said,

'Team-mates, I suggest we retire to a safe distance whilst our friend here works. I don't think the wall will "respond", as Mer Herminton suggested but there may be emissions of dust, or debris, which might be harmful if breathed in. Strider has got a vacuum pump sleeve which he is enclosing the drill in, right now. But you never know.'

As the Strider's drill got to work, now invisible inside a sort of black sleeve, the group walked to a copse of large "obeo trees", many metres distant. They sat in the cool shade of the trees and enjoyed snacks and drinks retrieved from a refrigerated bin in one of Strider's rear compartments. Despite the protective sleeve they could still hear a loud whining sound, as the drill worked.

It was about 10 minutes before the Strider had managed to extract a tiny core of material, approximately 1-millimetre-deep, from the face of the wall. Akromo said that the sample had been sucked into the middle chamber segments of his "friend", who would now be analysing it. He suggested, with Eleri's agreement, that they resume the climb up the hill alongside the walls.

The group climbed higher but stopped below the spot where the walls disappeared under mud which had formed a hard crust, mixed with stones, rocks and undergrowth.

'Let's climb over this lot and carry on the other side,' called Akromo. 'The machine only needs to clear the area immediately below the joint between the walls and the dome. But, my friends, be very careful walking on this rubbly material. It might start to shift about underneath us but it should hold.'

With that talk of shifting soil Mike suddenly had a momentary, painful memory of a particular moment on the Simurgh trip.

'This is a bit close for comfort,' he breathed to El' and Danile, as they climbed gingerly up the rubble strewn slope. They nodded sullenly. But Akromo was right, the stuff held well.

Almost an hour later the group, sweaty and tired, had clambered over another two large masses of mud and rock and then, through the trees above, they caught a glimpse of the exposed sections of a curved, smooth, slope, rising above them, made of the ray material. The dome, at last. They clambered toward it and, stopping about fifty metres short of it, resting under the shade of groups of arpet and obeo trees. They broke out snacks again and everyone took in long cool drinks of various flavourful liquids which had been stored in Strider.

Suddenly they saw the gangly machine climbing up to join them, which alarmed some members of the team and then it stopped, the armoured joints of its legs, which Akromo touchingly called its "knees", settling onto its wheel axles. After Akromo had tapped a console on the machine's front end, the group were startled to hear the machine actually talk to them, in a loud, basso-profundo voice.

'My apologies for the delay, me shipmates,' it said, with bonhomie. There were raised eyebrows everywhere and more than a few chuckles.

'But, I am glad to say, mateys, my analysis is now complete,' it continued, very fast, almost as though eager to splash out its news, 'for the sample showed – as expected – a preponderance of long chain, boron carbon nitride molecules – mixed with silicate substrates – forming a super-matrix, into hexagonal carborundum pins have clabrated – creating substance with highest stable density – but hardest and most resilient building material – ever known with ...' The machine had not paused in its spiel, even for a millisecond, but now stopped suddenly. Alexennder Akromo had touched a button on it and now asked it to slow its speech by about 55% and use improved sentence structure. It resumed, obliging him.

'I am so sorry Professor,' it said. 'To continue – and I have carried out radiometric analysis. That is, within the alien material I have found scattered molecular size traces of naturally occurring radioactive "parent" isotopes and their "daughter" products. Therefore, I have been able, using their half-life decay rates, to determine the approximate age of the material. Within a margin of error of, plus or minus 100,000 Oceanus years, I estimate the age to be approximately 8.14 million Oceanus years – equal to 5.9 million Earth years – but remember error bar, please.' After a lilting upwards tone of the last phrase, it finally stopped talking.

Mike felt as stunned as the people around him looked slack jawed. He stared at Eleri and Hermington in disbelief, and it was the latter who spoke first, 'My ancestors' teeth! I am thinking this structure was built at about the same time as the date we have been given for the conflagration on Oceanus. I am yet sure t'was the time when Ra's surface erupted.'

The Strider piped up again, unexpectedly, 'Ahoy there my matey, if you please. I would also advise that my optical and radiometric sensors have examined the surrounding area. I have determined that there are the remnants of a thin layer of the carbonised deposits - on the left flank of the dome structure, above where you now stand. I suspect you have yourselves determined – most of that layer has been eroded by wind and water. Eventually, new deposits of mud will accumulate on top of the dome - swept down from the higher mountain beyond. Thank you, me hearties.'

'Well, that's "dumping it all in the officer's hat",' said Mike, earning him puzzled looks from his Oceanus friends. 'Sorry. Navy figure of speech,' he said. He found himself wondering at the strangeness of it all. He glanced around, with wonderment. To think that some sort of strange civilisation must have existed here so long ago. What would the place have looked like to them? The same as now? He remembered that one of the geologists had said that Newcam would have been joined to a larger island mass and a few degrees nearer the equator, because of crustal plate movements – tectonics. He glanced excitedly out at the distant sea, which lay, grey and vast, between two nearby hills. He had begun to feel comfortable on this wooded hillside, thanks mainly to the tree cover, but catching a glimpse at the sea troubled him and he quickly drew his gaze away. And yet …and yet – it was fascinating. Another sort of "being" might have gazed at the ocean out there – all those years ago. He felt a shiver run up his spine, looked up and suddenly noticed the glowering clouds blowing overhead, swiftly blowing in from the ocean. He also became aware that the temperature had begun to drop as Ra began to be obscured. Weather changes quickly out here, he mused.

Most of the team seemed lost as to what to do next and many looked, expectantly, to Eleri. She shrugged, then simply suggested they continue on up the hill to find the point where the walls joined the dome. That had, after all, been the original objective.

**

Twenty minutes of clambering over further mounds of dirt brought them to the place where the causeway disappeared into a large mass of undergrowth at the base of the dome, some of which could be seen as a larger white mass high above. Fired with curiosity they spent time pulling away clots of the blue-green undergrowth. It looked as though the twin causeway walls simply merged, seamlessly, with the dome. The curve of the dome itself suggested it rose smoothly, covered with the mats of vegetation, at an approximate angle of 60°, but it was difficult to be sure.

Thorny bushes grew in hair-like patches over most of the dome's side, wherever the vegetation could gain a precarious foothold on the thin layers of soil which had adhered to the structure. Even a stunted form of the grass-like broadies, seen on the mainland, grew in isolated places. Akromo, breathless from the climb, joined Mike and the others, declaiming that, 'The vegetation is resilient, but it's probably been helped by some erosion of the structure's material. After all, my friends, even this stuff eventually succumbs to water and air.'

'I should guess so, prof,' said Lew, 'the thing's been here over 8 million years.' He turned to the team members clustered nearby and said, 'Listen up guys, I don't know about you, but I'm fed up calling it stuff, or boron-nitride, or whatever. Let's give it a name of our own, like a new element.' The others looked at him blankly, but Akromo said,

'It's a compound, not an element, but even so, why don't we call it Cambrium? After all, we are on New Cambria. I know it's not official but never mind that.'

Some people smirked, eyes rolled, but no-one objected and so, from that point on it became known, unofficially at least, as "Cambrium".

The Strider was sitting on its "haunches" again, but then, in its deep voice, suggested it should be allowed to start clearing the soil and undergrowth from the junction of the causeway with the dome. That way, they could see whether there was any sort of entranceway into the structure. Hermington looked askance again but Eleri agreed and so, it set to work, while the team sat under the trees for more refreshments.

The sky had now clouded over completely. A grey bleakness settled on the world like a thick pall, but it didn't spoil the group's suddenly buoyant spirits. Akromo said that Strider had ample wet weather gear for all, if needed. A message popped onto Lew's wristcom, from Evressaria, aboard the Laurasia. She said The Monsoon had advised them of a number of deep cyclones moving through this part of the Great Far Ocean. They would be kept updated.

The Strider took no more than 15 minutes to cut and prize away the obscuring undergrowth. It then used spade tools and extensions, in its front arms, to dig out the stony soil. But most of the team had joined in by this time, using tools from the machine's rear storage bins. Standing back, they gazed at the results of the work. Had they found an entranceway at last?

No-one was completely sure, but their efforts had revealed a large, rectangular, vertically flat stone of Cambrium, a metre and three-quarters wide, by three high, set into the dome, precisely where the causeway joined it. Success! The shape was incised into the dome by a few centimetres. Unfortunately, it had no visible means of being opened, if indeed it was even supposed to be opened. After everyone had stared at it for long moments Eleri said, jubilantly, 'I do think that this is it. A door. Must be, surely, such entranceway? Now we just have to get through it.' She sounded very matter of fact, perhaps shockingly so – and confident, thought Mike, even for the ebullient Eleri.

Hermington looked extremely dubious.

There followed a discussion of how they could "open it", or even if they should try. Danile Hermington voiced his unease again. And again, Eleri's opinion was that they should try. Unnoticed, in the background Akromo had been talking to the Strider. Mike realised he was using the personal pronoun again. Suddenly the academic announced the machine might be able to cut through the block with his X-ray and ruby laser drills. This could only happen if preliminary analysis of the block showed it was no thicker than the walls. If it was in fact much thicker then all bets were off. Lew and Eleri chatted briefly and agreed that the Strider could go ahead.

The huge machine took some thirty minutes to carry out preliminary drilling and then the insertion of various mysterious looking sensor instruments, before announcing that the block of Cambrium was around thirty centimetres thick. So, it appeared thinner than the walls of the causeway. Faces brightened. Even more astonishingly, it said it had detected a large void the other side of the block. Even better. Then, it said it would take about three to four hours to cut through to the void. Not so good. At this point Lew approached Eleri and the two were deep in discussion for some minutes before they broke off and addressed the whole group. Lew motioned for Eleri to speak first. Mike was intrigued but he thought he could guess what was up.

'Lieutenant Lew and I have so agreed that we need consult the gento- sorry, true sponsors, I should say, of our mission here, before we try to "open" a gap into yon dome. For this is a big-such step to take. And, if we do so find a chamber in there, we need to know whether our "bosses" will want us to go inside.' She glanced at Hermington, sitting some distance away but who looked on approvingly. Eleri invited Lew to add to this.

Lew stepped up and said, 'Yeah, guys, I know it means waiting around but if we have the go-ahead, the strider machine will take some time to cut through, anyway. And, like Eleri says, we need to know that we've got approval. I doubt if there'd be any problems, but we don't want to release anything, like, maybe, pathogen things, or something that might cause everyone trouble. I guess that's what the Strider is here for, but we want to be as sure as we can be. We'll take it a step at a time. If there's important discoveries in there we want history to judge us … well, favourably, I guess.'

Great evaluation, thought Mike, on both Lew and Eleri's parts. There was a lot of verbalised approval around him, especially from Danile. But it did mean more waiting around. He also mused on the fact that this placed a lot of responsibility on Tenak and Muggredge. Tenak, he knew, was used to it. But Muggredge?

Lew promptly contacted The Monsoon on his wristcom, which Mike knew was linked, for now, to the Laurasia. The new security protocols meant that links to the ship had to be routed through the stronger AI units of the shuttle. Eve then patched them through to the Admiral and to Muggedge simultaneously. Unfortunately, neither were available at that time. Lew said that the Admiral would get back to them within a few minutes; they weren't sure about Muggredge.

Some people wandered around, peering at the local flora. Senestris went to check out the causeway, lower down, examining it closely. Others just sat around and relaxed. Mike chatted with Eleri.

After about 15 minutes Lew, who happened to be standing a few metres away from the main group, got a call on his device. Eleri moved up to join him. After another few minutes they joined the rest and were able to announce that Admiral Tenak had already consulted with Draco Muggredge, after Lew's call. They had given the go-ahead, jointly, for the team to "open up" the dome, with all suitable precautions, and to check in with them once done.

Eleri explained that the main concern was whether, as Lew had mentioned, there could be a pathogen, or gases inside the dome, which could be released into the outside environment. Eleri had suggested that she didn't consider pathogens to be likely, given the extreme age of the structure and the Professier, after careful consideration, had agreed. Lew had said he couldn't, at this point, foresee any other problems that couldn't be dealt with by the Strider, or that it couldn't warn them about. Still, it was agreed that they should all stay well distanced at the moment of "opening".

There were sighs of relief from many, some muted disquiet among others, including, of course, Danile.

Akromo seemed very eager to get on with things and announced that for this thickness of material Strider would use hyper-laser drills, rather than metal bits. And so it began work. As it did so a cloud of white vapour drifted up from the slab, though most of the dust was being sucked up by Strider. Everyone sat or stood some twenty metres away.

Eleri approached Hermington, who sat aside from the others and said, 'What is it Dani? You are still worried-so?'

'Yes, El. I am sorry but I just have a feeling of way zone-out about this. I am worried what we mayst unleash – should we damage this place. Something we know nothing of? And what are you going to do when that thing has cut through the block?'

'I am not sure but, I am supposing, well … we go through it – if we are yet allowed to.' She paused for a moment, then added, 'And if tis safe, and we do so, will *you* also be coming through?'

He hesitated, looking pressured. She continued, 'Please do join us, friending. I need you. We all need you. You have so much to offer. Please tell me you will come in with us.'

'Please do not be thinking I am fraid El. I am just concern-ed that we do the right thing. But … I am supposing I shall go. I am thinking you use these powers of persuasion on Mer Mike all the time, do you not?' he laughed suddenly. She brightened and gave him a playful punch on the shoulder.

The gathering clouds meant it got dark long before Ra-set. The Strider switched on its own floodlights to illuminate the area. The team sat around in the gloom and Lew circulated around the group, advising quietly that they would have to start thinking of finishing for the day and returning to the shuttle. One or two, like Akromo, were disappointed but didn't want to object to Lew's advice. Most seemed relieved, including Mike. He was beginning to feel the cold out here. He, like most of the team, fetched coats out of Strider's very handy rear storage bins. He could be very useful, could Strider. *He*? Now, I'm at it, too, thought Mike.

A little later Lew announced firmly that they should all start hiking back to the shuttle. Akromo announced they could leave the Strider to finish the job overnight. His batteries would easily last long enough, and he wouldn't need bright sunlight to re-charge the next day. Thus satisfied, the team marched off. This way, it would be safer anyway. Mike, tongue firmly in cheek, asked Akromo to ensure he told the Strider not to go through the door till they got back. Akromo looked hurt.

Long after the team had left, the machine switched off its lights and continued to work, deep into the crow dark night, ensuring it cut around the perimeter of the block itself, until there were only three centimetres left to cut through, isolated at the top right corner. All the time that it worked its sensor arrays were analysing any gases that escaped from the interior, through the tiny gap made by its cutting lasers. Then it stopped and, with a gentle sighing of its super-hydraulics, settled down on its eight haunches. The wind started to blow up the slope with increasing vigour, but the Strider paid no heed.

****

'Arkas, friendling, how are you? Thanking you for answering my request to speak,' said Draco Muggredge, standing in front of the holo image of Tenak, which had appeared in his University office.

He continued, 'I just thought I would yet mention something that might interest you – but please keep it guarded, Arkas. Tis for your ears only.'

'Go ahead Draco,' said Tenak, 'this channel is as secure as we can make it. Nothing is totally, 100 % secure, you know. Maybe I should come down, planetside, to meet you?'

'Oh no, Admiral. Not necessary, I do not think. I will trust in your techno' but will be careful. I wanted to tell you that my contact, whose "friendling" – is in such position to know – says that the government is in disarray.'

'What do you mean, Professier?'

'Well, I do not know all such details, but let me say there is a kind of "politico-rebellion" in the Oceanus Independence Party. A lot of people not happy with the way Arbella and the Central Policy Committee have so handled the issue of Ra, and the science concerning such. Specially after the reveals in the media about what was covered up, and deedly, the most recent ion storm. That thing didst cause huge damage, despite the valiant efforts of your teknies.'

'I know but I thought the change of opinion of some in Arbella's party was common knowledge – at least from what we've picked up here.'

'Yes, deedly, but still, what is not so common is the fact that there are attempts, within the "CPC", to overthrow Arbella, and her most-chief ministers.'

'That *is* interesting Draco, and a bit worrying. If there is a transition, I hope it would be peaceful, Draco.'

'Oh, certain-most, certain-most, Arkas. Do not a-worry 'bout that.'

'Good. I would hate to see something nasty happening. Thank you for telling me, Draco, and, as you say, we'll keep it under the fusion shield. We'll wait to see what develops.'

'I shall yet assume that you have not heard more from my nieceling or Mer Lew, on Newcam. I have not. I hope all things go well, there.'

'No, I haven't heard any more but I know Lieutenant Pingwei will contact me straight away with any news on the "grand opening" of the dome. It was late when Lew and Eleri contacted me. I assume they retired for the night.'

'Yes, their discoveries are growing more fascinatio all the time. I just hope they stay safe. Oh, before I have to go, Arkas, I also wondered if you were aware of the demonstrations, in Janitra and Amnissos? The ones *against* the Meta-teleosophists, yestermorn?'

'Yes, Professier, we picked that up from the newscasts, as well. And we were impressed. Perhaps things really are starting to turn our way – and not before time. But I refuse to be complacent about it. Let's keep hoping for the outcome we all need.'

'Yes, Admiral. We are not out of the deeping forest, so far. I am ending transmission now. Mornimbrite to you Admiral.'

'And to you.'

As Muggredge's image began to fade, Tenak turned to leave his office but stopped short when the door intercom buzzed.

'Sorry to disturb you Admiral,' said Commander Statton, over the intercom, 'but I was on my way past anyway, so I thought I'd better alert you, in person ... about Ambassador Sliverlight.'

Tenak groaned. 'What's he done this time?'

'Don't think he's *done* anything, sir. It's what he *wants* to do. He's asking if he can come aboard The Monsoon. Says he's fed up being planetside. He's done as much as he can – or so he says – and wants to return home with us.'

'He's done nothing, Commander, but it's a wonder he doesn't want to claim credit for the demo's yesterday. What did you tell him?'

'That there's no point in coming aboard right now because we won't be ready to leave till we've got a full complement of passengers. That he'd be bored. And, that we're waiting on the results of the Newcam expedition. I think he understood, sir. By the way – he *does* claim credit for the demos. I thought you'd just like to know.' Statton tried to suppress a mischievous grin.

'Very amusing Commander. Thank you. Let's hope we can keep him off the ship for as long as possible.'

Chapter 40

RECOIL

Mike and Eleri, wearing protective suits and integrated headlamps, walked in single file behind Lew Pingwei, in the lead, Marcus Senestris and one of the ship's security guards, a huge man called Morganryn. All the others were strung out behind them as the group progressed very slowly and tentatively through the narrow, strange passageway leading from the Cambrium "doorway"; the block removed by the Strider after they'd all assembled there that morning.

Mike reflected on the fact that when they had reached the machine it had appeared inert, hunkered down outside the stone-like slab. It was recharging its batteries, using ultra-fast solar panels which had sprouted from its dorsal surface, making it look like some gigantic metal flying insect.

Akromo, who seemed to have a strange, almost emotional rapport with the machine, had interrogated it. It reported working on the "door" slab most of the night. This morning, it had taken a mere forty minutes to complete the job, allowing the team to witness the epochal opening of the structure. The machine had reported it had detected nothing radioactive, noxious or anything pathogenic, escaping from the incisions it had made in the skin of the dome. But Lew had advised the group to take cover, away from the slab, as a further precaution. Neither Lew, Mike, Senestris nor Eleri had needed any prompting. They weren't taking any chances. Not after Simurgh.

In the event, the opening went without undue incident, and, as this was, after all, a historic event, Lew had left a wristcom propped on a nearby rock, so that it could record and transmit images to the Laurasia, for onward transmission. He suggested that everyone hide and wait till it was all over, and not to "peek" at the view.

However, some of the Oceanus people ignored the warnings and peered out from behind cover. Eventually, even Lew had discarded his own advice and looked out. They saw Strider press a huge metal claw against the slab, forcing it backwards while the whole group flinched at the loud bang it made as it fell, then a cloud of dust blown outwards, obscuring the automaton.

There were murmurings of alarm from some in the team. But they were reassured as they heard Strider's voice booming from within the dissipating cloud, announcing that it was safe to come forward. So, the group tentatively emerged and saw that a dark tunnel had been revealed behind the fallen slab.

'Staggriten!' said Eleri.

'Amazing!' said Mike.

But nothing further inside could be seen at that point, and Mike began to virtually scream, internally, with excited anticipation. But then he thought, what if it turns out to be a damp squib? The Strider had thought there was a large empty space inside but what if it was wrong? What if the "tunnel" was just a dead end, with no way forward – except to drill through hundreds of metres of Cambrium? No, he didn't think so. He had more confidence in the Strider than that.

*

If he'd been worried about the whole thing being an anti-climax, he was very much mistaken. It would turn out to be something he, nor anyone else, could have bargained for.

*

There had been a long pause as Lew and Eleri again consulted with the Admiral and Muggredge, though it appeared the latter had been absent at the moment of the opening. Tenak had given the team permission to take things further; to go in, if the automaton advised it was safe and if, but only if, Lew and Eleri agreed. He said he would speak to Muggredge as soon as possible - but they could take it that they had authority.

That had been good enough for Mike and as they moved up to the "entranceway", he saw Eleri become hesitant, possibly even anxious, as she peered into the dark reaches of the passageway. He felt it must be the "slight" claustrophobia she had once mentioned to him, when she'd expressed reservations about being on The Monsoon. He had to admit to a general feeling of trepidation about the whole thing right now, but his innate sense of exploration spurred him on.

In profile, the tunnel was like an elongated egg, narrow end touching the ground. It was at least 3 metres tall, though not quite 2 metres wide at ground level, expanded to around two and a half metres a little further up. Then it narrowed again, to around half a metre very close to the top. It looked like it was easy to stand up in it, and just about possible for two people to walk abreast, though uncomfortably. So, no need for any "pothole" style of crawling – at this point.

Mike was pleased about the size of the hole because he knew anything smaller might have caused more problems for Eleri. Or at least, that's what he thought until he spotted that she was becoming visibly more anxious. He had grabbed her hand and squeezed it. She glanced at him and smiled bravely.

The group had ventured in, the two front positions being taken by Jaina, the female guard and Morganryn, both armed with high power sonic rifles. As the team had entered they quickly found that despite their headlamps the further reaches of the tunnel remained inky black. Mike thought it weird but somehow it seemed that the walls were absorbing much of the available light. He realised they would need a lot more illumination if and when they consolidated this investigation. After all, this was not some science fiction scenario, some vid-flick where power and light is magically restored to ancient, dead, ruins at the serendipitous touch of an alien button. In any case, no buttons or control panels were evident anywhere in here.

Mike had wondered how far the tunnel went and how far should they go? As they walked further he'd began to feel some concern at what they might find deep inside. Booby traps for the unwary? Might the roof collapse, or holes open beneath their feet? Arrows, or power weapons, firing unexpectedly from hidden corners? Had he seen too many ancient thriller films?

From snatched conversations with Eleri, and the others, he already knew that nearly everyone was concerned about the same sort of thing. And they were not the concerns of kindergarten children, after all. They were legitimate. No-one had ever encountered anything quite like this on Oceanus, or anywhere else for that matter.

That was why Lew had insisted that everyone must wear thick, heavy, protective, gear. The trousers had stout boots attached to them, featuring special "gripper" soles, and their jackets had sealed zip locks for gloves. They each had a hard hat with in-built headphones and mics, enabling interpersonal comms, if required. And, although the Strider had declared no radioactivity issues, Lew, Mike and the other HS people had primed their wristcoms to be on constant backup alert.

Although providing good all-round protection for the head, the hats were open faced and visor-less, and had only chin straps. They were actually basic grade military helmets, long superseded in the Navy. All of the stuff came out of Strider's storage bins and, evidently, hadn't been updated by Akromo. But full enviro' gear could be very restrictive and there was doubt whether many of the Oceanus team would not have been prepared to use it. They could be sent down to them from The Monsoon, if necessary.

Akromo had contributed to the preliminary health and safety assessment, ratified by Lew. At one point it had been hoped that the Strider machine could have taken the lead – a far safer option, but it was not possible. The machine was simply too large; trying to push into a tunnel with sides of the hardness of Cambrium would have caused it severe damage. Strider was to remain outside the entrance, on guard, shining extra light into the passageway.

Admiral Tenak's authorisation had been based on the assessments by Lew and Eleri, but it wasn't unlimited. It depended on *their* careful and continuous evaluation. Lew, Eleri, Senestris, Mike and Akromo had been prepared to go in but the pilot made it clear that no-one had to do *anything,* if they didn't want to. After some deliberation they all decided to make the attempt. Mike was pleased but he still had reservations of his own. Simurgh kept coming to mind. That place, he realised, would continue to affect him and Eleri and the others who'd been there, for a long time. He just hoped this place wouldn't leave the same legacy.

After a final decision had been made, they had all donned their coveralls and hard hats and had nervously entered the tunnel, their headlights casting brilliant spears of illumination into the blackness, before being swallowed up. They'd reached no more than a few dozen metres inside, when they noticed an even stranger effect than the general absorption of much of the light. The weird wall material also seemed to reflect someof the light, but randomly, causing beams of iridescence to flare from all around them. Akromo, despite the fact he'd been instrumental in encouraging the team to enter, made sure he took the rearmost position. It was, he said, in order to have a clear path of constant communication with Strider, for which he used a special earpiece and mic.

From the rear of the group Akromo now called out that since the Cambrium interfered with light waves as it did, then it would certainly interfere with EM communications too. He added that speech seemed mostly unaffected, so the phenomenon was, he thought, probably restricted to short wavelength EM.

Mike suddenly realised another problem: the Cambrium might have a similar effect on the sonic weapons carried by the guards, if they were used. He was about to speak up when he heard Lew, walking behind Morganryn, mention the same thing to him. Mike knew they didn't need any further warnings *not* to give in to a temptation to use their weapons unnecessarily. These two were experienced people and good at their jobs.

As the group slowly advanced they were unexpectedly helped by the Strider when it performed another trick, using its inbuilt frontal fans to powerfully drive fresh air into the tunnel. The machine had announced that there were no poisonous fumes or gases inside, but the air was stale. It would be wise to force outside air in for as long as necessary.

They hadn't walked in very far before the tunnel began to climb, quickly changing its pitch to that of the causeway outside, forcing the team ascend at a constant angle of around 30°. A nervous hush fell on the group as they ascended, their footfalls being the only sounds they could hear as they trod through a thin layer of gritty dust which covered the floor. Occasionally, when someone spoke, their voice seemed at first to bounce off the walls, yet quickly became absorbed, as though by metres of cotton wool. So, maybe Akromo was wrong, though the distortions weren't excessive, just annoying.

As he glanced around nervously, Mike mused on the fact that he still wore his "special" wistcom. It might come in handy, but then he pulled himself up. Really? After millions of years was it likely that there was anything still alive in here? A creature that might prove to be some sort of danger? And there was no way any of the Kilops worms, or any other island wildlife, could have got inside here. *Unless –* he suddenly realised – there was another way in; one that had opened up elsewhere? Maybe a hole eroded by the forces of nature. Millions of years of storms weathering the dome at a weak spot?

He berated himself for his overactive imagination and mused on the ancient human fear of the dark, hard wired into many of us, perhaps most; once useful to ensure survival, but now usually an impediment. *Usually.* He tried to force himself to think of other things, bu, almost subconsciously, found himself wanting to reach out to Eleri. She was still walking ahead of him but unexpectedly, though gratifyingly, she suddenly turned to look over her shoulder at him. The expression on her face, appearing ghostly white in his headlight, told him she felt very much like him. *Shit scared.* But even so, incredibly curious and excited. They smiled at each other as if to say, *what a pair? Like small children.* He felt very glad to have her company in that strange place at that moment. She slowed up and resumed walking alongside him, slightly awkward for them both though it was.

The group trudged on cautiously, at seemingly glacial rate. It had taken them about forty minutes to advance less than two hundred metres. Thankfully, fresh air could still be felt blowing in from the entrance. And looking back, beyond the people behind, Mike could see a comforting, egg shaped, patch of ordinary daylight.

At the two hundred and ten metre point, the slope came, unexpectedly, to an end, and the tunnel simply levelled out. But going further meant they would lose all sight of the entranceway. The fresh air seemed to diminish as well, and ahead the tunnel appeared to go on forever, straight as a dye, and now level. But up here the passageway was a different shape and size. The end of the ascending stretch had been marked with a kind of raised lip all around the tunnel and the level section they had now reached was almost perfectly circular. Fortunately for Eleri, and any others with claustrophobia, thought Mike, it was also larger by nearly a metre all around.

But then Eleri whispered to Mike that she still felt "bad", especially as the team had lost visual contact with the outside world. Mike tried to reassure her, but if her feelings echoed his own about wide-open spaces, he could certainly appreciate what she might be going through.

Moving onwards the team now noticed the presence of strange, dark stianed, circular markings on each side of the curved roof, each one about eighty centimetres across and covered by a white mesh of some kind. They were spaced out at about one metre intervals all along the tunnel. Akromo suggested they might once have acted as ventilator grills. Then they found, at roughly two metre intervals, straight, rod like, objects, each around 30 or 40 centimetres in length, protruding from the tunnel wall, high up, near its roof. The end of each rod was turned upwards, so they looked like long-handled hooks. Perhaps some sort of long disused lights, wondered Mike?

A loud voice suddenly echoed from behind him, 'I think we should go back and get the light worm,' said Akromo, his voice burbling strangely. Everyone looked back at the Professor with puzzled expressions, until he explained he hadn't thought the tunnel would be so long, so there was now a need for a better and a more permanent form of lighting. The headlamps were flashing around distractingly. The "light worm", he said, was stored in Strider. Where else? It could be reeled into the tunnel and adhered to the walls to provide a continuous, more natural form of illumination. But he needed someone to help him carry the equipment.

Lew volunteered to go with him, so they promptly started back. Without a word, the whole group followed, including Mike and Eleri. Personally, Mike felt he needed some relief from the oppression of the tunnel and he was sure El did too.

Lew said that they needn't all go back but it seemed to be a general feeling in the group. And so it was that the whole team took a refreshment break at the entranceway whilst, guided by Akromo, Lew and the security guards fetched out a large, heavy, spool from a bin in Strider. But the weather had worsened. It felt chilled. Trees swayed alarmingly, buffeted by the wild winds now hitting the island. Lew contacted the boat and Eve reported a warning from The Monsoon that an exceptionally deep cyclone was passing just to the south of Newcam. They would likely be hit but only by the outermost parts of the system. The pilots felt that as the shuttle could anchor itself into the ground, it would be safe whilst for the team, the tunnel would offer good protection.

Or so they hoped.

The "light worm" was, in fact, a flat tape only a few centimetres wide and barely two millimetres thick with one adhesive side. Akromo said it would provide at least 500 lumens of brilliance at every point along its length. One end remained attached to the Strider – which provided the power, and Lew pulled the reel along, carried on a heavy dolly on wheels. Lew soon found he needed the help of Morganryn, to haul it up the tunnel. They were told it had an unfurled length of 3 kilometres but when Akromo tried to stick the light worm to one side of the tunnel, he failed, until Marcus Senestris produced a several rolls of ordinary sticky tape from a capacious pocket. To everyone's astonishment, especially Akromo's, that worked well.

The group followed on Lew's heels, as he and Morganryn pulled the dolly. Senestris and the others proceeded along the ascending part of the tunnel, up into the horizontal one and continued beyond where they had stopped before. They stuck the light worm down with the tape, until they ran out of the stuff. Everyone was astonished at their progess. They had gone three klicks but they hadn't seen anything "new" in the tunnel. There was muted disappointment.

But now, if they were going to continue, they would have to go back to using their headlamps, and so that was how they pressed on, ever deeper, into the massive dome.

*

A large hole suddenly appeared before them. About a kilometre from the end of the light worm it loomed in their vision, rectangular in shape, around three metres long by about two wide. They had evidently reached some sort of crossroads, because another tunnel stretched ahead, across the opposite side of the hole, and there was a tunnel on each of the other two sides. The other tunnels were black maws – and even after shining their lights into them their far reaches eluded the beams.

Even more mysterious was the vertical hole in front of them. Gazing, very gingerly, into the shaft, Lew and Senestris told the hushed group they could not see down to the bottom with their lamps It was another spine-tingling moment for Mike. Now what, he thought? He walking up to the edge and heard Eleri calling to him to take care, but Mike felt comfortable with heights, or so he thought, but then he peered down the shaft. The light from his headlamp was swallowed by its enveloping darkness and he drew back.

'What do you think's down there?' he asked Lew.

'A refresher? A sanitation pit?' said Lew, grinning. 'How should I know?'

Subdued, but distinctly nervous laughter at that.

'Did not the ancient civilisations on old Earth, build tombies at the foot of such shafts?' called out Chanda Maheshtra.

'You mean tombs?' asked Lew, 'so, do you really think this dome is one massive tomb? Or maybe lots of them?'

'No, not of necessity,' said Chanda, 'but yet I speculate.'

'Seems too big for that,' said Mike and anticipating possible objections, said, 'so, I know the Egyptian pyramids were massive, and the tomb of the first Chinese Emperor and so on. But this place way exceeds those.'

'What this whole structure says, I reckon,' added Lew, 'is that these beings were technically super-advanced. Wouldn't they have developed beyond such things as grand tombs? Places to bury "important" people, and their goods?'

'Not of necessity, and could be yet,' said Danile, 'for we know nothing of their culture. Nothing. They may have deed thought such things important. What do *you* think, Eleri?'

'I know not,' she said quietly, almost whispering, 'for tis much too soon to say. Might be nothing down there. Nothing of import.'

'Still praps there could be *things* down there,' said Gajana, her eyes widening, 'but how should we go down, if we so decide? I am not sure it is pratic-most.' Mike wasn't sure if she was afraid of the possibility or was offering to go down.

Another debate ensued. Lomanz thought it not worth the risk of going down, at that stage, but Akromo wanted the team to descend. There were, he reminded them, winches and "auto A" frames, plus pulleys, all in Strider but, of course, they would have to carry the components up the tunnel. Some pieces were heavy. Eleri said she would welcome another break at the entrance, where they could discuss their options, but Akromo seemed to be desperate for an instant decision.

'Hold on, prof' man, said Lew. 'For maximum safety, we should fly an airo drone-bot down it.'

'We didn't bring any from The Monsoon,' said Mike.

'Professor?' said Lew.

Akromo looked embarrassed. 'We didn't bring any either,' he said. 'Okay, so I thought we were going to be looking at rock strata. Probably thin rock strata, judging by Simurgh. Not, going through … manufactured tunnels.'

'Okay,' returned Lew, 'but we can order some down from the ship. It'll take time. A few hours maybe, given the need to equip a bot first. Maybe more. And don't forget the storm will disrupt things. And I guess we can't be sure how well we could control a drone-bot in here. What do you guys want to do? Eleri, what do *you* think?'

'I say … yes, we go down now,' said Senestris, before Eleri could reply. 'So long as the Professier thinks the A frames are safe? Is time not of the essential?' he continued.

Lew frowned and said, 'I asked Eleri.'

She looked uncertain.

'We have got to go back to the entrance hole and bring that stuff up anyways,' she said.

'That shouldn't take long,' said Lew. 'You know, the other thing we could do is to bridge the shaft and carry on along the tunnels. Might be best to split up in that case. Smaller teams to take each tunnel at the same time.'

There was a loud murmur of disapproval.

'Okay. So, we go down the shaft?' Lew said, looking slightly frustrated at the group, 'as long as you approve, Eleri.'

She continued to hesitate, but Mike knew she was just being adversely affected by the restricted space of the place, so he turned directly to her and said, softly, 'It's okay if you don't agree, El. Just say.'

'No, my love,' she said, with sudden resolve, 'for I am thinking we should be getting further on with this. Going down yon shaft.' Mike felt she was trying to be the confident leader everyone expected her to be. But he guessed none of them, or not many, had her claustrophobia.

'Thank you,' said Lew softly. 'Good decision. Okay. Let's go back for the stuff.'

They all set off and when they arrived at the entrance, found the weather getting much worse. But they bent to the task of bringing out the winches and other equipment. Lew advised Eve of their intentions. They all munched eagerly on snacks as they returned up the passageway, Lew having reminded them they should keep up their energy levels.

An hour later the team were staring once more into the shaft. Led by Lew and Akromo, the team assembled the winch and A frame, assisted by the frame's automated hydraulics. Things were going well, thought Mike, but he felt a certain nervousness clutching at his stomach.

Akromo had said that the hard part was over now and going down the shaft relatively easy. But Mike predicted Akromo wouldn't volunteer to be the first down it. And he was right.

***

At the same time as the team carried their equipment up the tunnel, Eve, the shuttle co-pilot, was playing electro-chess with Jarimy, the remaining security guard, sitting in the comfortable surroundings of the Laurasia's cabin. Relaxing neo-temporal jazz, the latest music craze in most places, played in the background. A bleeping sound from the flight deck signalled an incoming message from The Monsoon. The minor AI patched it through to Eve. The transmission, on audio only, was from The Monsoon's hyper-comp, warning that the nucleus of the massive storm, approaching from the east, was now predicted to turn north-west over the next half hour. It would reach their precise location within forty minutes. It was potentially damaging. But both The Monsoon's and Laurasia's comps agreed that it posed very little threat to the boat itself, as long as standard precautions were taken.

Eve went to the flight deck and operated the boat's "anchors". Large tubes were deployed from the oleo legs of each of the ship's three wheels, from which large, heavy duty harpoon-like drills were fired into the ground, burrowing in deeply. A fourth harpoon was fired from the underside of the ship's tail, behind the trailing edge of the V wing, and buried itself in the ground astern the ship. The craft was firmly tied down. It was fortunate, however, that the ground was soft enough for the harpoon drills to penetrate deeply, but firm enough to hold the ship tight, or so it was hoped. Hard igneous rock might have been a different story. Eve would have had to lift off and hunt around for a better spot.

Several times, she tried to contact the exploratory team, but even the shuttle's powerful transmitter couldn't penetrate the dome. But the Strider picked up the com stream and replied that it would extend its radio boom into the tunnel entrance. It said it was "confident" it would be able to bounce a signal through the tunnel, so it could reach its "ship-mateys".

'Ship-mateys?' Eve said to Jarimy, a bemused look on her face.

***

Back in the tunnel the exploratory team was trying to set up the winch and pulley system for descent into the shaft, the "auto A" frame having bridged the hole. The large device was unable to drill itself into the Cambrium, so Lew reprogrammed it to instead brace itself rigidly against the shaft edges. To ensure full rigidity Lew unfolded additional frame members from the device and extended them so they auto-braced against the remaining two edges of the shaft aperture. The whole structure finished up looking like a large metal tepee.

While Lew used a control panel to interrogate the device on its stability and safety margins, the others watched in fascination. Akromo sidled off to pace up and down the nearest part of the tunnel, distancing himself from the others. He put a hand to his right ear, which had its com-piece link inserted, and, looking around furtively he quietly said something into it. He returned to the group.

Eleri was turning a bit greenish and swung to face Mike. 'So sorry Mike, but do you yet mind if I go back to the start of the bottom tunnel? I am feeling slight queasy in here, but I am alrighto. I just want to be able to see the natural light, back there.

Get some air? And yes, I did take my own tabs, like the ones I did give to you. But they do not seem to be working so well,' she said morosely.

'Of course, I don't mind you going,' he said. 'I'll come with you if you'd like?'

'No, there is no need of. I know you want to see what is happening here. I will not be long.'

Mike fretted as she went off. He, of all the people in here, might have the best idea of what she was going through. She was being extremely brave even *coming* in the place. Hermington surprised him by announcing that he also felt a little claustrophobic, so he would keep Eleri company. Mike nodded and re-joined the main group.

Lew was saying they'd be ready in another few minutes. Once they were sure the auto-frame, winch and pulleys, were fully secured, they could think about descending. He wanted them to decide who was going down first. He wasn't going to decide for them.

The group had started discussing this when there was a very loud "twanging" sound. It was like some sort of gigantic elastic band being released but it turned into a piercing, scraping sound, coming from behind them. Everyone turned around and saw the light worm reel and dolly whipping up in the air and shooting away down the tunnel at high speed. Mouths dropped open and everyone stood motionless. Mike's brain took a couple of seconds to turn the situation over, and with utter horror he realised what was happening – and, more importantly, what was going to happen next. He found himself racing back to where the circular tunnel joined the egg shaped one – the place where his lover had gone. He screamed Eleri's name at the top of his voice, his brain warning him it was probably too late.

Eleri had been chatting to Danile, standing right at the lip of the circular tunnel, staring down at the egg-shaped glimmer of light below, when she saw the light worm seemingly come to life, whipping around like a luminous, demented, snake. It cracked like a bull whip as it was yanked toward the tunnel entranceway. Then she heard a booming sound from behind her and, turning reflexively, saw the reel and dolly smashing against the tunnel walls, barrelling toward her and Danile. She glanced at Hermington, who was still staring at the whipping light worm – and standing squarely in the middle of the tunnel. Eleri leaped at him and, despite his superior weight, slammed into him, pushing him to the other side of the tunnel, and over into the raised curve of the lip the other side of the circular tunnel.

The best they could do was to close their eyes and hope. Over a second or two the booming noise got deafeningly loud as the dolly hit the bottom lip of the tunnel, rebounding onto the curve of the ceiling, before being pulled into the lower passageway. The device then separated from the reel, which skittered down toward the entrance. The remains of the dolly itself splintered, with an ear-piercing crack, flinging pieces of itself around Eleri and Danile.

Mike, racing along the tunnel, still shouting Eleri's name, skidded and fell on his backside, sliding to a stop near the lip of the tunnel. He tried to scramble up and looked at his girlfriend breathlessly. She and Danile stood slack jawed, but they were clearly in one piece. Both they and Mike were starting to tremble with shock as the rest of the group breathlessly caught up with them.

Mike said he was okay as Eleri threw her arms around him. She hugged him so tightly he couldn't breathe. Danile leaned against the tunnel wall and said, with husky voice, 'El, you saved me! Oh, my Maker. That was close too much. Thank you El, thank you verily.'

Mike's heart was thumping but he calmed down as soon as he saw that El and Danile were okay. He couldn't help thinking, *it's Simurgh all over again,* and he continued trembling. He could feel Eleri shaking too.

'What the feggery just happened?' said Morganryn, in a booming voice.

Lew said, with ashen face, 'Shit man. I think something happened to the machine out there. You know, Strider thing.'

Most members of the team gathered around Mike, Eleri and Danile, touching them gently, on their shoulders and arms, as people who care are wont to do, just to prove to themselves that all was okay. Mike noticed that Eleri seemed to be in pain. She said she thought she might have hurt her back when she tackled Danile. He needlessly apologised. Lew gathered everyone together and gently ushered them down the tunnel toward the entrance. As they began walking Eleri noticed Mike limping. He had, he said, bruised his "pally-ass".

On reaching the tunnel entrance they surveyed a scene of devastation. Several small trees had come down nearby, one partially covering the walls of the causeway. There were bits and pieces of wood scattered everywhere, but more shockingly, Strider had disappeared completely. The causeway itself had turned into a water channel down which a river now ran. Water was pouring off the slope above them, like a newly created waterfall, and more water ran off the surrounding land, sloughing off mounds of mud and vegetation that had piled up around the causeway walls. The whole area down-slope was awash with rivulets of mud and floating debris.

'Oh Maker,' said Mike, 'now this really *is* like Simurgh. How can it happen twice? What's this planet got against us?'

Everyone stared at the devastation; ashen faces looking numbed. Mike immediately thought about the Laurasia. He prayed no-one had been hurt over there but Lew was already using his wristcom to contact the ship. The anxiety on his face soon turned to relief and he told everyone that the boat was okay. Eve, he said, had tried to warn them about the storm. They hadn't got the message.

Lew turned to Akromo, a deeply troubled look on his face.

'Professor,' he said, 'Eve just said that your machine was going to warn us.'

Akromo, started to look very uncomfortable.

'Guess it didn't,' Lew continued darkly, 'so any idea why?'

Akromo looked flustered and said, 'I'm concerned about what happened to him. He must have been washed away. Good job he's got flotation bags. We'll have to find him.'

'Damn and shit your machine, Professor,' said Lew, loudly, 'two of our group nearly got killed in there. Did you know anything about the storm?'

'Well, I'm not sure,' said Akromo, looking flustered. He was a bad liar, thought Mike.

'I shall think we deserve to know the truth, Professier,' said Eleri, her face reddening with frustration.

Morganryn moved closer to Akromo, and he took on an intimidating stance, while there were loud stirrings among the whole team. Marcus Senestris stepped forward and, pointing at Akromo said, 'I didst see him put his hand to his ear – the one with the earpiece thingry.'

'Well, maybe … Well, yes,' said Akromo, finally. 'He, Strider, that is … did contact me to say the storm …might come this way.'

'And you – you chose not to tell anyone?' said Lew.

'Well, I didn't think it was necessary at the time. But, well, I see now, I was wrong.'

There were shouts of anger amongst the group and Lew stared malevolently at Akromo. 'I lost good people on Simurgh and I nearly lost two more just now, and you say you "didn't think it was necessary"?'

'Guess he's just an idiot,' shouted an irate Padrig Lomanz, the quietest member of the team till now.

'Well, I didn't know there would be a flood. Well, did I?' said Akromo loudly, his eyes registering fear at the storm of anger coming at him. 'I didn't think Strider would be washed away. It must have been a … a really massive storm to do that.'

It still is, thought Mike, looking out at the devastation and feeling the cold of the whirling wind whipping around the group.

Sneering at Akromo, Lew turned to the rest of the group, 'We won't be able to get back to the Laurasia yet, but I think we should try to go as soon as it's relatively safe. We need to re-equip if we're going back in the tunnel.'

'When we return, I suggest we all bring back a rucksack with provisions,' Lew continued, 'food and water and whatever. We don't know how deep the shaft is, or what it leads to. I want to fix holo-vid cams to everyone's helmets, as well. We can set up a relay transceiver at the entrance here, now that the Strider's gone. That way we can transmit our activities to the boat; they'll transmit them to The Monsoon. *But we don't come back until the weather improves.* I take it you agree, Eleri?'

'Yes, courserie,' she said. 'At least your way someone will see what happens – if something goes wrong.'

'I want to make as sure as I can that *nothing* goes wrong again,' said Lew, glaring at the Professor, 'but I guess you can't guarantee anything. I was thinking more along the lines that we'll have two-way comms with The Monsoon. We can get advice from them – if needed. You happy with that?'

Eleri nodded her approval. 'I think still today's events yet prove we could do with some help and advice.' There were mutterings of approval from the others as the group sat down near the entrance and waited for conditions to improve.

Two hours later the group was finally able to set off, having been advised by Eve that the worst of the storm was over. The landscape seemed to settle remarkably fast; the flood water and debris dying down quickly. Fortunately for them, the route to the boat, directly to the east, seemed the least affected by the storm. But they still had to pick their way very slowly and gingerly, down the debris strewn hill, and were forced to wade across several streams, knee deep in water, in places where there had been none before. They got soaked but they had a good leader in Lew, who somehow, unerringly, always managed to pick out the safest routes.

There was no sign of the Strider anywhere, but a large mud slide led off from the base of the walls, where he'd been, and out to the south, then down through some forest.

Akromo moaned of his concern for the machine and speculated that maybe it had gone down in the mudslide. That brought calls for him to just shut up. On the way back Mike couldn't get images from Simurgh out of his mind. Lomanz had treated their physical symptoms with "flash-spray" he'd carried with him, to stop the pain and inflammation, but said he needed to examine them fully back at the boat. They were able to walk normally but he advised Mike and Eleri to support each-other, to prevent further injury. No-one spoke to Akromo on the way back.

The team finally reached safety and were eventually able to rest in relief in the welcome shelter of the Laurasia. Though splattered with mud and some woody debris it looked quite unaffected by the storm. Most of the team rested for a while, then heeding Lew's suggestion, started packing rucksacks full of provisions. While this was happening, the pilot approached Akromo, at the back of the ship.

'*Professor* Akromo,' said Lew, his voice dripping with sarcasm, 'you're banned from going back with us. I can't take the risk of having you along. You're a liability.'

A few of the others gathered around and there were mutterings of approval.

'You cannot do that,' said Akromo.

'You think?' said Lew. 'I'm sorry man, but I can, and I say you stay here. You shouldn't have been on this expedition anyway. Not suitable.'

'I was invited by your commanding officer – and mine,' blustered Akromo, 'and I'm glad you mentioned that, because if you ban me, I'll make sure the prime council of the OA government knows your ship brought me here – which I suspect was pretty much against their wishes. And that would throw a few kinks in your path, wouldn't it?'

Lew's eyes narrowed with anger. He grabbed Akromo by the shirt lapels and the man shrank from him. Mike grew alarmed. Though Lew was not a particularly large man he knew what he was capable of. This was not good for Akromo, or for Lew.

'Lew, take it easy,' Mike said, 'it's not worth the hassle, man.'

Eleri intervened too, 'There is no need of this. Please, Lew, I am alrighting. I could have been hurt but yet was not. Same for Danile. No real harm done. Can we reach some sort of compromise, please?'

Lew backed off a little and stood with his arms folded, as Mike piped up, 'El's right. Listen, man, I agree this guy's a liability, but we don't want the consequences of banning him, do we? Let him come along if he wants, but we'll all keep an eye on him. Or at least, maybe rating Morganryn can. You'll do that, won't you, Morgy?' he said, glancing at the security guard, who immediately moved closer, menacingly, toward Akromo.

'Oh yes, sir. That'll be my pleasure,' said Morganryn, and began stroking the barrel of his stun rifle in a very peculiar and alarming way. Akromo's eyes widened yet further.

'Okay,' said Lew, finally, 'I don't like it, but … I guess he can come.'

The cybernetics man straightened himself and flattened out his lapels, 'If I had been a Navy man I could have … well, reported you, for assaulting someone in the ranks,' he said to the pilot.

'Yeah, but you're not Navy and not "in the ranks",' said Lew, 'and if you were, I'd have put you on a charge and had you drummed out in disgrace. So be grateful you aren't one of *us*.'

Akromo looked away, as Lew turned and marched off. Mike approached Akromo and said, quietly, 'Take a tip from me. If I were you – I'd shut the feg up and leave it at that.' He glared at the cybernetics man, then got busy picking equipment out of the Laurasia's storage lockers.

Interlude

PREPARATIONS

The alien ship continued to coast along its wide orbit of the star, known to humans, as Ra. It was two light months distant from it so any EM signals would take that long to reach the innermost part of the star system. The ship's occupants now took measures to reduce that delay, so they might communicate more quickly with the multitudes of semi-robotic vehicles they had set loose into the system.

The massive ship, the size of a small planet, had been rotating lazily as it accelerated along its orbital path, but then the lazy turn stopped as the hemisphere facing the orange-yellow beacon of Ra began to open. Like the petals of a flower of truly gargantuan proportions peeled outward, like six enormous segments of an orange. The sections moved languidly and as they opened outwards revealed, deeper inside the vessel, a morass of spiky pinnacles, complex projections and spires. Thousands of directional thrusters kept the orientation of the whole sphere steady while these projections, each hundreds of kilometres long, began to extend themselves from within the headily cavernous interior. They thus unfurled to nearly four times their original length, all of them pointed, unswervingly, directly at Ra.

And then tips of the projections began to glow, a faint pink at first, then a bright cherry red, continuing on through the visible spectrum until they reached a blazing white.

Chapter 41

DESCENT

Back on New Cambria the joint Oceanus – Home System team peered, in palpable silence, down the enigmatic shaft they'd found deep inside the enigmatic dome. Marcus Senestris broke the silenceand voiced what everyone else was probably thinking,

'Does look so … bottomless. Absoluto bottomless.'

'Looks so - inviting, do you not think?' added Hermington, a sharp edge to his voice.

'Nah, I'm sure it ain't bottomless,' said the ever-pragmatic Lew. 'But we have to hope it's not deeper than the winch line will go – and in case anyone's wondering – that's three hundred and fifty metres.'

'That winch ropey thingry seems awefull thin,' said Gajana Maheshtra. 'Are you sure it will hold the weight of – well, one of us?'

'Yeah,' said Lew calmly. 'Don't worry. These "ropey things" are the Navy's finest "neoline". Only one millimetres thick, but fifty times stronger than tensile steel. I know it's "thin" but if it weren't, we would have needed a pulley reel so big we wouldn't have got it in here.' He smiled reassuringly at the throng of anxious looking individuals from Oceanus and got mostly blank stares in return.

'Been tested thousands of times by the manufacturers, but Navy Special Forces have used it lots of times – in action,' said Mike. The Oceanus contingent still didn't look convinced. To be fair, thought Mike, they'd had their faith tested by what had happened earlier, especially the disappearance of the Strider.

'I am beginning to wish I had followed Akromo,' said Gajana, tongue firmly in cheek.

'Yeah, he's missing all this … the lucky fegger,' said Mike.

'Tis a pity for him, that he yet decided to opt out,' said Eleri, 'as I am thinking we might be about to discover amazing things – well, maybe.' Mike thought she didn't really appear to have convinced herself.

'That was his choice,' said Lew. 'So, he changed his mind. I didn't make him. He's the one who decided to try and find his damn machine. Seems more concerned about that thing than is healthy, I reckon. We're probably better off without him.'

'Praps. I carnt believe that he change-ed his mind, after all that he did say,' said Eleri, 'Still, I do not think he did neglect to tell us about the storm through a malice. He just did not think right,' she continued. Mike nodded his agreement. She's compassionate indeed, he thought and smiled at her.

'Everyone makes mistakes. Sometimes big ones,' said Mike, 'but it doesn't mean they shouldn't get a second chance.'

'Okay guys,' said Lew, 'and while I think it's all very nice to be forgiving of that mascla, I just wonder if there's some delaying stuff going on here? So, who's first down?'

There were shrugs all round, as each person looked about them, expecting someone else to say something.

'I'll make it easy,' said Lew. 'I'll go *last*. I'd love to go down first, and I think you all know that. But I'm the only engineer here, now. Someone's got to make sure there's absolutely no problems with the machinery. I'm not expecting any, but I'm just trying to cover all bases. That's all guys. And someone has to operate the winch. Someone who knows how it works. Okay?'

No-one challenged him as they all knew, Mike thought with confidence, that Lew wasn't bluffing when he said he'd be first down there if he wasn't needed at the top. There was still silence, so Lew continued, 'While you're thinking about it, I'll set up the cascade hyper-amp, and transceiver, right here. That way, we can see what the "volunteer" can see, via the headcam – and so can The Monsoon.' They had all agreed to use Home System advanced headcams fixed to the "volunteer's helmet.

Lew started to attach a light weight-looking sphere of shiny metal, about the size of a baseball, onto the A frame, near the winch. When they had earlier returned to the tunnel Lew had brought the device to be used in place of the missing Strider machine. Mike had seen this amplifier before and hoped it would be good for the job, but there had been some doubts. The team were finding lots of difficulties with signal transmission down there. It had to be due to the Cambrium, particularly its thickness. Since they weren't sure how deep the shaft was it was vital that all could see that the person descending was safe, and to be able to advise that person. Lew's device would pick up the AV cascading signal from the headcam, amplify it, and transmit it to the team and to a transceiver at the entranceway –thence to the shuttle and finally to the ships in orbit. Whoever went down first would find themselves at the centre of a lot of attention. They'd better be good, he thought and realised he didn't really know what that meant.

After he had fixed up the amplifier Lew again asked who was going down first. And again, no-one spoke.

'Okay, don't get me wrong here, but I'm guessing most of you are a bit, well, maybe claustrophobic?' he said, gently and quietly, 'and some more than others. That's why I think it should be … you Mike. Then Eleri.'

Mike's heart jumped and he felt as if he'd been poked with a long, sharp, pin. 'Me? Why me?'

'Because you're not claustrophobic, man. Or maybe because you deserve to see whatever's down there. Hey, it's probably the toilet-fresher the ancient aliens used,' he said, to a muted chorus of edgy laughs, 'so you'll love it.' he winked at Mike. For his part Mike didn't want to discuss his own particular brand of phobia and hoped Lew would stop talking about these things in case he inadvertently raised it. He quickly realised he should have known better, and most of them present knew anyway.

Morganryn, at the back of the group, said, 'Good choice, sir. Go on Mer secretary! You can do it, sir.'

Lew nodded and continued, 'And I think you, Eleri, also deserve to be one of the first to see – what's down there – and, if Mike's already down, I reckon you might draw some support from that. Up to you, though. You can go *first* if you want.'

El shook her head, the light from her lamp swinging about. 'Out there in the open lands, in the wild woods, maybe,' she said with burning honesty, 'in the places I oft go? Very likely, I would. But here?' She turned and clapped Mike on the shoulder, drawing chuckles from the group, as she said, 'Off you be going, my love. Enjoy it so.'

Mike tried to look brave because he knew he was saddled with this whether he really wanted it or not. No way out. Besides, Lew was making sense. Smiling wryly, but with the hair on his neck standing up like pins, he nodded and said, shakily, 'Okay. Okay, man. Let's do it. Now, before I change my mind.' There was instant applause. Mike could see Eleri was forcing a confident look onto her face. She could be the next down after all. He again wondered at her courage for just being down here in the first place.

Lew held onto Mike as they stood at the edge of the shaft. He advised him to take off his rucksack and strap it onto his chest, just in case he needed to get something out of it – a tricky manoeuvre if it remained on his back while in his harness. They also decided to stick with the convenient use of the headcam, rather than using Mike's wristcom. Lew wanted Mike to concentrate on the task in hand, not to be fiddling with, or issuing instructions to the com unit.

Lew fitted the tight harness for him and as he did this he drew closer to Mike and said, very earnestly, 'I need you to stay alert and remember, if you get into trouble, or anything goes wrong, just sing out. In particular, watch out for water down there, or any other liquid. You'll go down real slow but even so, if you miss seeing any bodies of liquid you could be up to your neck before you can tell us. We might not get such a good view, so don't rely on us up here to keep an eye on everything. If there's any problem like that or anything else, we'll bring you back up fast. Max rate is about 3 metres per second.' Mike nodded, trying not to look nervous. His mouth had gone as dry as a bone.

Then the pilot finished strapping the harness around Mike's waist and under his arms, pulling a wide piece under his buttocks and clipping it onto the harness by way of an uncomfortably large strip which went between his legs. Gajana was right, Mike decided; the winch line, which split into three pieces which attached to points around his harness, was extremely thin, but he tried to keep its proven strength at the forefront of his mind. He knew the vidcam on his hard hat was already transmitting images to The Monsoon, via the Laurasia. He felt he couldn't afford to look afraid at this point, but his stomach churned like a spinning water wheel. He glanced nervously at Eleri. She smiled at him, but he knew she had serious misgivings. And was that the hint of a tear or two he saw in her eyes? Probably not. She was keeping her emotions pretty much in check, he thought.

Before he even realised it, Lew had touched a control pad on one of the winch braces, and Mike was descending. He tried to think of something important to say but all he could come out with was, 'Well, toilet refresher or not, I'm going down.'

There was muted laughter and a chorus of well wishes and, within a few seconds, he was below the level of the floor, descending into blackness – only partially relieved by the light from his headlamp. That Cambrium stuff again! He had snatched a good look at Eleri as he'd gone down and hoped it wouldn't be his last. She had smiled back, though it seemed a little forced.

As he descended now, he felt his heart thumping as though he'd just run a two-minute mile. He was sweating and starting to breathe rapidly. Get a grip, he kept telling himself. He realised it was lucky that his audience of shipmates – and he had no idea how many were watching – could not, at that point, see his face; the advantage of a headcam over a wristcom

There seemed no end to the shaft but then he realised he'd only been going down for about twenty seconds, descending very slowly, at about 50 centimetres per second. He heard Lew's voice in the headphones of his hard hat.

'You okay, Mike?' asked the pilot; his voice a reassuring sound.

He answered yes, breathlessly. Strangely, it seemed hard to talk. A minute went by and Lew asked if he could see anything below. No, nothing yet. Just more blackness. What were they expecting, he wondered? What was he expecting. His logical brain said it would just be more and more shaft.

A few minutes later he began to relax into the journey. He must be getting calmer, he realised, because he was even starting to get bored. Looking down into the void, his lamp showed no change at all. His heart rate slowed, and he felt tempted to start daydreaming, but resisted. He was still too much on edge for that. Once the neo-line ran out they'd have to just bring him back up. End of story. Except he knew this planet, this amazing world, better than that. Didn't he?

Nasty little thoughts started intruding. What if he did hit water, or oil, or acid or something? What if the winch couldn't reverse and he got stuck down here? He started to feel very relieved that Eleri wasn't coming down here yet. Even so, at that point he missed her sorely. And yet, he didn't want to talk to her personally. Not just yet. He didn't know if the prying ears of the ships' crew might detect the lack of true courage in his voice. He'd betray himself. He didn't mind what the Oceanus people thought, but the Navy mob was a different matter.

More than eleven minutes passed, which seemed more like eleven hours, and Mike, though looking down still, realised he had indeed started to daydream. With a jolt, he noticed, though he didn't know how, that he must have emerged from the shaft. But, into what? He shouted into his mic, 'Lew! Stop. I've come out – somewhere.'

**

At the top of the shaft the rest of the team had gathered around Lew, watching a screen he had taken out of his pocket and unfolded to a full metre squared. Everyone had followed Mike's descent, glued to the view on his head cam but it hadn't been very exciting. Mostly, it had shown a wide patch of illuminated, featureless, shaft wall, moving vertically upwards. Disappointingly, and slightly alarmingly, after about five minutes the picture on the screen had become disrupted by static noise in the AV signal, which began to deteriorate more and more. Lew said it must be effects of the Cambrium. No-one welcomed it but the audio signal from Mike came through clearly, at that point.

**

A few seconds after Mike's call to Lew the winch was brought to a stop, jarringly. Mike didn't have any idea where he was, but he looked around, as he hung in mid-air, swaying slightly. The random movement made his headlight swing back and fore, but nothing was revealed by its beam. There was just an empty abyss. Not good, he thought. A sense of disorientation set in; the feeling of hanging in a massive black void making his nerves jangle.

He knew the nerves would probably be heard in his voice, but that was just too bad. He wondered how much the vidcam was picking up. 'I can't see anything yet, guys,' he said, 'but, I don't know, I just get the feeling I'm in a huge … maybe a cavern or something.'

A voice – Lew's, he thought, told him to look downward and try to focus the light beam. The man's voice was starting to get broken up by static. He did as suggested and by reaching up to use the light's limited degree of focussing capability, he slowly began to resolve something out of the darkness below. Was that a floor? Yes, a dusty grey floor. He shouted out but realised the vidcam had probably already picked up the visual clues.

'How high above it do you think you are, Mike?' asked Lew.

'Hard to tell, Lew. A good few metres, I think. Well, no. Maybe three metres? How much line left?'

'None,' came the abrupt response. 'If you released your harness, could you jump down, *safely*?'

Mike looked down and swung his lamp about, 'I think so,' he said, 'do you want me to try it?'

There was worsening static interference as Mike awaited instructions. He couldn't hear Lew's answer, so asked for a repeat.

'Only if you're pretty sure it's safe, Mike,' came the crackling reply, 'because if you're injured it might be difficult to get you back up quickly. And try to check if the floor's solid. Hey, why don't you drop something from your rucksack, first? See what happens. Don't take any chances. I mean it, Mike. By the way, we're not getting good visuals up here and ...'

Mike almost laughed and thought, why in the galaxies does he think I'm going to take chances? Down here? And *now* he decides to tell me it could be difficult to get me out.

Mike was suddenly very aware of the butterflies in his tummy. They began to gnaw at him, but, he realised with astonishment, he was as much excited as he was fearful. Possibly more. He tried to relax and reached into the rucksack in front of him. Searching for something suitable he pulled out a standard, Navy issue, miniature multi-tool. It was not large but certainly heavy enough for this test, so, holding his breath, he dropped it and a split second later it clattered loudly onto the floor. The effect was almost startling in that utterly silent place. He saw the object bounce once, raising a little cloud of dust, then clatter to the floor again, lying there, gleaming, in his lamplight. Yeah, the floor was solid, and it was about two, maybe two and a half, metres below.

He made his decision, then took a few minutes to compose himself. He triple checked, then quadruple-checked his estimate of the distance of the drop – and thought again aboutthe wisdom of *releasing his harness at all*. Then, sucking in a deep breath and holding it, he flexed his knees and assumed a crouching form, then started to release his harness. It was fiddly and seemed to take ages to release the buckles – but it was meant to be like that, to prevent accidental release. The he was free and barely a second later he was almost surprised to land squarely onto the floor – of ordinary Cambrium. The impact splashed pain through his feet and legs and made a resounding noise in that dark place, kicking up dust in a small cloud around his boots. But he immediately overbalanced and stumbled forward, somehow managing to recover. That was nearly embarrassing, he thought, remembering the vidcam on his helmet. He took a second or two to recover, checking that no damage had been done. No, he was okay, he thought, with huge gratitude.

The headlight seemed to illuminate very little, except a massive expanse of floor. Mike felt as though the enveloping darkness just swallowed the light wholesale, seemingly insulted by some sort of challenge to its integrity. His thoughts were jolted by the sound of Lew's voice, suddenly loud, and very crackly, in his helmet, 'Mike, … Mike, are you okay? What's happening? You are okay, aren't you?'

'Visuals still affected?' he asked.

'Ah, so you *are* okay! That's right, Mike. We can't see anything at all.' Despite the static there was evident relief – and frustration in his voice. Then Lew said, 'We got a bunch of people going purple up here.'

Mike smiled. He was instantly reminded of the significance of the phraseology, from his history classes: the first moon landing by humans. Not as significant as that event had been he thought, humbly, and *he* wasn't exactly of the calibre of the Apollo astronauts. Lew continued, 'Eleri's jumping around up here. Mike, the image went down just when you jumped. I think the jolt of your landing might have fegged it up, once and for all.'

'Sorry lew. Sorry El,' said Mike. 'Well, I'm down,' he said, 'and, as if you hadn't guessed, I'm okay.' Before he could say any more, he heard cheers in his earphones.

'Well done Mike, my man,' Lew crackled.

'Thanks,' said Mike. 'Glad to hear El's happy now. It seems strange to be without the harness. But at least now I can walk around. But where to, I don't know. This place feels kind of … huge, and the light's being swallowed up a lot, but still good at short range. There's an ordinary Cambrium floor down here, so no surprises in that. There's a lot of dust on the floor. Okay, I'm starting to walk round now. Kind of cold in here. Colder than where you are. Glad I've got this thick suit on. I'll tell you when I can see anything significant.'

'Mike,' said Lew, his voice crackling worse than ever, 'it's time to switch to your wristcom, please. It might not work any better than the headcam but it's worth trying.'

The wristcom, *of course* Mike thought. In all the excitement he'd forgotten about it. It was deeply buried in a sealed pocket of his coveralls. He fetched it out but as he did so, thoughts returned to him about some of the nasty surprises that Oceanus wildlife can throw at you. What about those large lizards? Or the kilops worms? He caught himself. Wild animals? Really? Not down here, surely? And then there were the small, dangerous things, like metamorphs, but they were more than 16 thousand klicks away. Well, as far as anyone knew. No strange creatures were likely down here – unless there was another way in. Though he'd not noticed at first, he became aware that his breathing had quickened, and his heart rate had again risen rapidly.

He held the wristcom in one hand and told it to begin transmitting to the corridors above, and to record everything, for posterity. His headlight fell very faintly on something many metres distant. A wall? Yes, but at its foot there was something else. A large block of some kind. Maybe more than one. He walked toward it and soon confirmed there were a number of large objects. They seemed totally inanimate. The nearest block looked like a large cabinet, with its top half, at about shoulder height, angled away from him at an angle of maybe 135° to his line of sight. The surface on the angled part was covered with coruscations and stick-like projections. Some of the protrusions were in the form of strange spiral structures but others were topped by large, bulbous heads, like enormous pommels. How odd, he mused. Decorations? Or controls of some kind?

'Are you getting all this?' he said, imagining the others, far above, watching the scene with bated breath.

'No, Mike,' came Lew's voice over the wristcom, again crackling. Mike hadn't bothered asking the unit to either transmit a holo-view. The earlier experiments, up above, had shown that full 3D holo imagery was not possible in this place. Now, even 2D imagery seemed out.

'Nothing at all?' he said.

'We got some vid when you first switched on, but it's gone now. No, wait, it's back again. You can't do anything about it now, Mike, so just keep filming and we can hope that …' Lew's voice vanished in the static.

Mike described the scene in front of him, as best he could, hoping that at least some of the audio would get through. Then he just resigned himself to the thought that he was very much on his own down here. He thought of Eleri and wished she was with him. Soon, perhaps.

He continued to survey the scene and as he looked around saw that not only was there more than one "control stick cabinet" but dozens of them, all in a long line, stretching into the murky darkness, to his left side and his right. They seemed to be lined up against the wall he'd first spotted, itself disappearing into the gloomy distance. So, the wall evidently marked a boundary in this place, and it hadn't been far from the shaft. Looking up he saw the wall vanish vertically into the void above.

He wondered whether he should touch the nearest cabinet. What if it was booby trapped? But after all this time? Nervously, he edged closer, and peered at its surface, ready to pull back if something moved, or jumped out of it. He decided he'd been watching too many science fiction holo-movies, particularly that one with the face-clutching thing in the egg. Fantasy, surely? But then again this was Oceanus. Home of the weird. Very much the unearthly.

He hesitated again, then decided to touch the angled surface gently, and very lightly. Instead of something jumping at him, the surface just felt – ordinary. Hard and very cold. It was not made of Cambrium but was more like some sort of metal. He pulled his fingers back sharply and examined them in his head light. Just some dust on his skin. Was it dust or some sort of chemical? No, it was more dust and he found he could blow it easily off. *Skin?* With a jolt he realised he had forgotten to put his gloves on before touching this thing! Such was the power of excitement and an unfamiliar environment – and stupidity, he thought.

He wondered why, if this place was eight million years old, there wasn't even more more dust than there was; more decay. But then, presumably, there hadn't been anything living down here for that length of time. He decided to move on. Excitement tugged at him but also a strange tingling of foreboding. No, worse than that. A slight sense of … doom?

∎∎∎

At the top of the shaft Eleri, Lew and the others could only listen and wait. There wasn't much coming over the audio channel.

Senestris piped up, 'He does keep forgetting to talk to us. Praps we should winch up the harness yet and be sending down another of us?'

'No,' said Eleri, firmly. 'That would cut off Mike's only route of escape. We carnt know what is down there still. Praps we should tell him to come back up. Now.'

'I know you're worried, El,' said Lew, placing a reassuring hand on her shoulder, 'and I am too. But I'm sure he's okay. Anyway, this place looks like it's been kind of inert, for a real long time. He'll tell us, somehow, if he wants to come back up, and the harness isn't too high for him to reach it, if he needs to. He'd have to jump a bit, I reckon, but if I think he's a lot fitter than he admits. We need to be ready. Let's give him a chance.'

**

In the mysterious chamber hundreds of metres below Mike continued to walk, uneasily, along the line of cabinets, going steadily further from the shaft by which he'd entered. At one point he suddenly realised what he was doing and fretted he might get lost. He paused, tried to get his bearings, yet he was drawn to move on. After a few minutes he ran out of control cabinets. In their place was a line of other cabinets of a different type, wider than the previous ones and with flat not angled tops. And, to his amazement, each had a convex, transparent covering, like a bubble of glass. He didn't know why he found that so strange. It was just – unexpected. Then he realised he had neglected to give any commentary to the crew up top. He apologised and updated them.

It was all so alien and yet, somehow, strangely familiar. He waited for a reply from above, but nothing came – just static. Then, the wristcom unit itself, spoke, in the suave contralto voice he'd long ago asked it to use, 'The stream signal from the tunnel above cannot be received at the moment. I am attempting to amplify by drawing power from the holo-micro-tube emitter. Please stand by.'

Mike waited for a few seconds, but nothing happened. He still felt uneasy and soon found his eyes drawn magnetically back to the scene around him. He peered at the nearest glass topped cabinet. He knew he shouldn't do it, but he just couldn't resist the urge to touch it this one too and, well, the top certainly *felt* like glass. Inside the cabinet, about half a metre below the covering sat a range of objects sitting on a shelf-like surface. They all had strange and weird shapes. Looking beyond this cabinet he saw there were dozens more stretching into the blackness beyond, the glass tops glinting in the light from his lamp. There could be hundreds of these units.

He wondered what the others were thinking, right now, and was concerned Eleri might be worried about him.

The hairs on his neck hadn't stopped standing straight up since he got down there, but the feeling was exacerbated now because he suddenly felt as though there was a presence close-by; someone watching him. His heart started to pound yet again as he glanced over his left then right shoulders. He turned fully and with relief he saw there was no-one there but as he moved his light fell dimly onto the surface of another, distant, cabinet.

This one was much larger than the others and isolated, far out from the wall. There was something odd about it. Like a large box the thing was again rectangular in cross section but he estimated this one stood more than four metres tall and, maybe, three metres on a side. And it was mounted on a raised rectangular platform, like a plinth, which had small flights of low steps cut into it, one flight on each side. Mike somehow found himself drawn to the cabinet. He began to walk toward it.

His wristcom suddenly burst into life. His heart leapt straight up into his mouth.

'Okay Mike, your unit's telling me that you should be able to hear me now? Mike? Mike, are you okay?' It was Lew's voice again.

'Man, I'm really glad to hear your voice. But you gave me a shock right then,' said Mike. He told Lew about his discoveries up to that point.

'Be very careful about approaching that … cabinet thing you've described,' said Lew, 'but I reckon you're doing the right thing investigating it. Just keep your wits about you.'

As if he wasn't going to be cautious! Mike thought.

'And don't forget to keep talking to us.'

He neared the corner of the cabinet nearest to him and noticed that the two sides forming the corner were very dark in colour. They seemed somehow different in texture from the wall cabinets he'd seen. Thicker stuff, maybe? Then he made an astute guess. They're probably made of Cambrium this time, not metal., he thought. Slowly, he began to walk around to the other sides of the cabinet but then something in the way his headlight glinted off the far corner struck him as strangely different.

Coming round fully he had a surprise: the whole of the previously hidden side of the cabinet was faced with a transparent glass-like sheet. But what was that inside the cabinet?

As he gazed at the contents of the cabinet his jaw went slack, his eyes widened, and he felt himself suck in air reflexively as his pounding heart jumped again.

With a dry throat and in tones evidently filled with awe, he announced to all those assembled somewhere above, 'I think you need come down here. In person. See this for yourselves. Right now.'

*****

In her private office aboard The Monsoon, Captain Ebazza glanced at her guests, Admiral Tenak and Doc Jennison. They had been watching an enormous fold out screen and although the AV signal flow from the expedition on Newcam, had long since stopped, they continued to look at the now blank screen, listening to audio only. But above the annoying static they could hear mere snippets of the conversations down on the island.

They had witnessed the view from Mike's headcam as he had descended into the chamber inside the alien dome. The picture had been poor from the start, partially due to the movement of Mike's light as he swung his head this way and that but the interference had increased as he'd descended further, until the video stopped altogether. Transmission had only resumed when Lew had asked Mike to switch to his wristcom, and then, after mere seconds it dropped to audio only, badly broken up at that.

'That Cambrium material is … well, it's amazing,' said Jennison during one of the many gaps in the transmission, 'so I think it's vital we get it fully analysed up here. It could revolutionise materials science in the Home System.'

'I believe the Strider machine already analysed it, Lieutenant,' said Tenak, 'and the results were transmitted to the Antarctica. I'm sure Captain Providius will send us the data-cache as soon as she's had a chance to look at it properly.'

Jennison nodded glumly, then left in order to pay a visit to the fresher unit.

'I'm more concerned about Mike's safety right now,' said Tenak to Ebazza. 'That young man is at the heart of … I guess, astounding things going on down there. But he's also very vulnerable, on his own, down that shaft.

'Yes, he is, so why in the galaxy did it have to be Michaelsson Tanniss who was first down?' said Ebazza, wrinkling her brow.

Tenak looked askance at her and shot back, 'Really? Why not, Ssanyu? From what I recall, he didn't exactly volunteer for it. Lew *chose* him and I, for one, trust Lew's judgement. I also applaud Mike's courage.'

Ebazza looked slightly embarrassed and said quickly, 'Of course, Admiral. I did not mean to cast any doubt on Lew's judgement. It's just … well, Mike Tanniss? Really?'

'Don't let your personal views cloud your judgement, Ssanyu. He's made big strides since he's come to this world, especially since meeting that young femna. And you'll surely agree he's in a tricky situation down there? We have absolutely no idea what it's really like in that place.'

'Okay, yes, Admiral, granted,' said Ebazza and gave a genuine smile of apology. 'In fact,' she continued, 'he's doing well in the circumstances. Better than I expected.' After a long pause, and just as Jennison returned, she said, with genuine frustration, 'And this wonderful material you're so desperate to get your hands on, Lieutenant Jennison, is a nightmare for comms. The preliminary data we got from Lew was that it could even stops hard gamma rays. It's got to be something weird if it can do that. It takes doped-duralamium and the the full power of our EM super coils to do that for our hulls.'

'Exactly,' said Jennison, 'and anyway, I hate the idea of audio transmission only. I want to see what's going on down there.'

'Well, aside from my concern for the personnel involved,' said Tenak, 'I actually think there's a sort of charming retro' quality to all this. Almost romantic, I guess.'

In response to the blank looks he got from his colleagues Tenak said, defensively, 'You know, back in the Home System most people are too used to living their whole lives through the medium of electro-gadgets, holos and the like. There's a school of thought which says that too much of that diminishes the value of personal, individual experience. Maybe they have a point.'

■■■

Jennison gave a slight nod of concession, but Ebazza looked unconvinced.

'With respect, this is not a "private" event, Admiral,' she said. 'If I interpreted what you said before, correctly, this is epoch-making, isn't it? So, isn't there a sort of duty to all humankind?'

'Sure,' replied Tenak, 'and I believe it's all being recorded by Mike, on his wristcom. Don't you think that with audio only … well, it increases the mystery, the remoteness of it all, the alien nature of all this. And we'll all get a chance to be a part of it soon enough.'

'If he gets through all this safely, Admiral. If,' said Jennison but that earned him scowls from Tenak and Ebazza.

'He will,' said Tenak.

'May the Lord allow it,' said Ebazza, almost to herself, still staring uselessly at the blank screen. Tenak allowed himself a sly smile which he hid from her.

Just then, the audio channel burst back into life and the three of them jumped in their seats. They heard Lew's voice blurt, '*Okay Mike, your unit's telling me that you should be able to hear me now? Mike? Mike, are you okay?*'

The three officers listened intensely as, over the next few minutes they heard continuing brief exchanges between Mike and Lew – then silence for a couple of minutes. Tenak stared anxiously at his wristcom chrono' and both Ebazza and Jennison seemed to screw up their faces as if willing the ship's Secretary to continue his commentary about the large cabinet he'd seen. Then, they actually heard Mike's gasp of astonishment and stared at each-other with bewildered looks, which deepened when they heard Mike's next words.

■■■

He had known it could happen. Anxiety, fright. That place was so dark, weird, and *gigantic*. It was starting to get to him. If he could have seen the full extent of the chamber, he knew he would have been badly affected by it. The fact that he couldn't lessened the effect somewhat; just enough so that, together with Eleri's pills and his intense curiosity, he was just about managing to keep control. For some while he'd had something else to occupy his mind, his senses. He now realised he felt lost in that cavernous place and suddenly felt he had try to relocate the shaft by which he'd entered.

'Lew, I can't find the shaft. I just can't find it,' he said to his wristcom, 'I should have left some sort of marker system. Basic error. Sorry guys,' He was desperately trying not to sound panicked.

'Don't worry,' said Lew, his voice still being broken up, but not so badly now. He continued, 'I reckon it's safe enough to put someone else down there. So, we've brought up the harness and we're sending Eleri down right now. She was willing to do it but I know she's got problems. So, I've asked her to concentrate real hard on looking down, not at the shaft walls. You should start to see her light in a few minutes. Just keep looking up for it and you should get a fix on the shaft.'

Great idea thought Mike. Lew had probably anticipated what would happen. He hoped Eleri would heed Lew's advice and try to ignore the nearness of the shaft walls moving past her face, only a metre or so away. He was eager for her to arrive, knowing he'd probably feel a lot better when she got there, but there was no sign of her light. He wandered along, unsure as to which direction to go and then, some way off, directly to his right, he saw the first glimmerings of a light beam flickering, almost mystically, shining out from a point in the blackness above.

In a fit of joy, he hurried toward it, not paying attention to what his own headlight was reveaing, and walked straight into a very hard object; some sort of sculpted rock crystal, rising over a metre from the ground. He yelped with pain. Fortunately, his heavy suit had given adequate protection, mostly. But it still hurt. Rubbing a spot on his right, just below the crotch he continued, hobbling with lameness, until he was directly below the shaft, now suddenly illuminated like a searchlight, by Eleri's helmet.

Seconds later his own light picked out her figure as she emerged high above.

'Mike. Mike!' she shouted, 'where are you? Oh, sorry, you're down there. I can see your light now. Thank the Maker. Get me off this thing. Get me off!'

'Eleri. Thank the galaxies,' he shouted, as he watched her descend further, until she came to an abrupt halt above him. He told her she would have to release the harness and jump down. He was pleading with her to be careful, but he then saw she had already released herself, and was dropping gracefully. Like a gymnast she landed neatly and safely, a couple of metres from him. Well, I guess that's how it's done, he thought.

He heard her exhale heavily with relief, then she rushed toward him and, somewhat ironically, fell over her own feet as she did so. He stopped her fall, grabbing her as she stumbled forward, and they laughed with abandon as they hugged each-other.

He could feel her sweat soaked face as they kissed. She said, 'Manry, am I yet glad to be down. That shaft! Did hate-so it.' He could feel that she was trembling very slightly.

'That was super-brave of you, El. You're fantastic. And you're okay. You're down now,' he said.

After a few moments trying to steady herself, she looked around.

'This place … is … amazrie. Staggrinten. Spookie-so though. And Mike, what didst you see, my manry? Sounded awe somuch. Please, take me to see it too.'

'Yeah, okay,' he said, 'but don't you think we should wait for the others? Then we can all go. Besides, well …I'm not entirely sure how to find it again.' He felt embarrassed again.

'Oh Mike,' she said, chuckling. 'Alrighting, I am guessing we really should wait for the others. Our combined lights should help. We must get some decent lighting down here, some stage soon.'

'Yeah, but just think. Our light, yours and mine, is the first this place has seen in millions of years, so I reckon.'

'I know. I know,' she said, lowering her voice as if she were speaking too loudly in a place of worship. She continued, unnecessarily whispering, 'Mike, we might yet be the first self-aware beings to be entering here at all, in all that time. Since whoever built this place. And do you realise what that makes us?'

'Idiots?' said Mike.

She grinned, then, a look of joy on her face, 'No, Mike. It makes us pioneers. Especially you. You, Mike. *You were the first.*'

'And you,' he said, 'you've always been a sort of pioneer. She shook her head, her eyes signalling genuine modesty, embarrassment, He continued, 'I've only gone where The Monsoon has taken me. You've always forged your own way.'

'Nonsense so, Mike. You do not realise what you have done here and the other places we have been. Well, never do-mind at the moment. Main thing is that we are together now. And we are the only ones all the ways down here.' She drew out those last few words for emphasis.

'Not exactly, El. We're not really the *only* ones down here.'

And with that Mike glanced off into the darkness surrounding them.

****

Alexennder Akromo walked gingerly across a sea of mud, struggling toward the bank of a swirling river. He had seen a few bits of Strider, mainly parts of it's antennae, strewn across the mud flats. He had been clambering about, scrambling in the dirt for about two hours, wending his way through the New Cambrian forest, searching for signs of the machine's location. Following a trail of woody debris that wound down the foothills below the dome structure he had begun to pick up small pieces of the machine. The weather had calmed, and the roaring wind had dropped to a whimper. The sun came out and the mud trails started to dry quickly.

When he reached a large flat area of mud and debris he stopped and looked around, the only sound being the churning and rushing of the water some metres away and a strange sort of chirruping of – something – in the branches of the nearby trees. Then, a movement caught his eye and he turned to his right – as the bizarre sight of a long metal pole slowly emerged from the thick mud, about 10 metres away.

'Strider!' he said, 'I knew you were down here somewhere. I knew it.'

He gazed as a set of solar panels, shaped like an umbrella, unfurled from the pole, now standing three metres clear of the mud and a kind of deep throbbing, humming noise could be heard.

'Come on, me beauty,' he said to himself. 'Get yourself re-charged. You'll need to pull yourself out of there. I'm afraid I can't help you.'

And sure enough, within a few minutes a huge area of soil seemed to heave and bulge upwards in front of him, suddenly ballooning upwards and outwards. He immediately stepped back out of harm's way, as the machine wrenched and pulled itself from its muddy prison. Several of Strider's legs appeared first and hauled the main part of its body out of the silt, like some sort of catastrophically large, alien, spider arising from its underground lair. It appeared to be a titanic struggle and took a good fifteen minutes, but the Strider didn't stop until it had hauled itself completely free. Then it crawled away onto more solid, leaf covered, ground some metres from Akromo.

The scientist could see the remains of its yellow flotation balloons, still stuck to its mid-body, and he noticed areas of damage, mainly to the legs. Some antennae were missing, as expected. It seemed to look around for several seconds and, appearing to suddenly spot him waiting, said, 'Welcome Professor, welcome. You came to find me. I am glad to see you, me- hearty, but please do not approach me. The mud is still dangerously deep near my location. Please be a land lubber and proceed directly up the hill behind you, keeping to the tree cover. I will join you there when I have recharged fully. I seem to have sustained some damage.'

The scientist nodded and did as advised. 'I am also very glad to see you,' he said, 'and I think we can repair you quite easily. I knew you'd be okay. I think your services may still be needed up at the dome.'

'Thank you, professor, my friend and ship-mate. I will be very glad to help in any way I can,' it said in a steady voice.

Chapter 42

FAME

Deep inside the enigmatic dome the entire group had now, finally, descended through the shaft, one or two needing a small amount of assistance to dismount from the winch line. All were now assembled in the cavernous chamber, except for the guard, Morganryn, ordered by Lew to operate the winch and keep the area secure. He was tasked with ensuring that nothing walked, scuttled, crawled or otherwise intruded into the tunnels from outside.

The combined headlights of the group made the job of finding their way to Mike's mysterious "cabinet" much easier. At first, he nearly led them the wrong way until he remembered the general direction and eventually got them to a point where their light beams could pick it out. They all finally assembled before the strange, monolithic thing, which, Mike saw, clearly generated the same sense of wonder and raw excitement as it had in him.

The tension was palpable as they had approached the cabinet and then they were able to gaze up at the apparition held inside it, when Mike said, with understandable and entirely appropriate melodrama, 'Behold, I give you the lord of the dome!'

If there was a name for a collection of dropped jaws, such a word was needed now, as Mike's team-mates stared at the alien *being* which appeared to be standing erect behind the glass in the cabinet. For it appeared to be nothing less than a large bipedal, slightly grotesque, creature standing within. The creature was humanoid in appearance, though it was clearly *not* human, and yet its pose couldn't be interpreted as anything other than a proud one, if not a commanding one. Blue skinned and large, the group's estimate being around 3 metres, it stood as if frozen in a moment, almost as if in the act of walking, or rather, striding forward, one of its "feet" placed a short distance in front of the other. In fact, it looked as though about to burst out of its the cabinet though it was definitely frozen in motion in a moment of time. Mike, for one, was grateful for that. And that was because the creature this statue, and they all agreed that was what they thought it was, depicted a being that might have been very intimidating indeed in real life.

The core of its lithe-looking frame was a highly muscled torso, from which *two* pairs of upper limbs sprouted; the uppermost being in the position they would normally occupy in a human. The upper "arms" were evidently massively muscled and toned they sprang from thick shoulders, which looked similar to those of a human, but were, somehow, subtly different. The lower pair of arms was much smaller, though more, in fact, similar in size to those of human arms. But they appeared weaker looking than the upper arms and lacked shoulders. They just emerged from about mid-way down the creature's torso, from a swelling in the torso at those points.

The being's neck, from which the upper shoulders sloped steeply, was extraordinary. It looked about three times longer than a human neck and so, deceptively, appeared relatively thin. But, on closer examination they could see that once again, it was thicker than that of a human being's and evidently powerful, as evidenced by its corded sinews.

Various members of the team made strange noises of curiosity and loud exhalations of surprise and no-one spoke as they continued to peer at the statue. The proportions of the creature's body were around the same as those of a human, though the legs seemed slightly longer in proportion. They were stout, thick and corded with muscle again. They appeared to bear "knee" joints, exactly where they would be expected, but about two thirds of the way down the "calves", another joint appeared in each leg, oppositely articulated, like a horse's hock, with the lowermost portion of the legs tapering down in an almost bird-like way. These lower limbs ended in large, leathery looking feet that resembled a human's only vaguely, but which also had a claw-like appearance. On the back of the "hock" was a kind of dew claw, projecting out backwards. That looked, to Mike, as if it must have been positively deadly in a "live" being of this kind.

Everyone continued to stare, mostly open mouthed, for what seemed like hours, though it was not. Looking around him Mike saw the awe change gradually to expressions of delight, on some but something approaching horror on others. Eleri was wide eyed and had an open-mouthed grin. The whole group then began to crowd in together as close as they could, pressing up to the glass so as to get a better look at the statue, their headlamps illuminating the humanoid in a brilliant pool of light. Mike noticed that some of the light was reflected and some refracted by the cabinet material, which cast strangely moving patterns in the darkness around about the team. Mike's earlier assessment, that it was not "glass" was, he felt, vindicated.

Eleri seemed unable to stop gasping, though she managed to utter, with almost child-like excitement, 'Look so, look at its hands.' Everyone looked as one.

Each of the being's uppermost arms ended in narrow, long hands, each with *six* very long fingers. Intriguingly, each hand sported what appeared to be *two* opposable thumbs, one above the fingers and the other below them. Despite the obvious differences with humans the hands seemed the features most similar feature to those of a modern human. And the hands were not empty. In the left was a sort of rod or stick, perhaps a metre in length, with a bulbous orb of sparkling pink crystal at its end, almost like a ceremonial mace. And, in the right the being held a roll of shining metal, a little shorter than the rod, with slightly fluted ends, which made it appear like a parchment scroll, from Earth's ancient times. The lower pair of arms ended in hands which were more like claws and which, although they held nothing, still appeared capable of articulation.

The group continued to gape the being, making strange cooing sounds. That, in itself, was unusual, thought Mike. He wanted to say so much but didn't want to disturb their awed concentration.

Hermington pointed to the garments the being wore, for it was not naked, though, in truth, the clothing was scant. It appeared to have burnished leather-like plates covering both the upper limb shoulders and its upper arms The plates looked like they extended down the creature's back, but the back panel and sides of the cabinet being non opaque, it was difficult to tell. The being also wore a wide belt around its midriff, sporting pocket-like structures and pouches.

But more than all this, there was something drew the attention of the whole team like a magnet, and that was the being's head and face, up atop that long neck. It was much larger than a human's head and more ovoid, the widest part being at the peaked top of its cranium, where it ended in a sort of wedge shape. Six spines extended several centimetres from the back of the wedge, giving an overall impression of a kind of backwards facing bony frill. Some in the group speculated it might have been important in courtship displays. Another piece of apparel, which looked like a length of diaphanous cloth, hung from the wedge and spines, at the back of the skull and the bottom of it could be seen hanging behind and below the being's upper legs, hanging well above the floor. It reminded some people of a type of cape.

But it was the creature's face, by far, which everyone in the group seemed to find the most striking – and for good reason. Several people expressed the view that it was quite intimidating. For the face before them was bulbous and pointed forward much more than that of modern humans. Despite that and the fact that the face angled backward toward the upper cranium, it was flattened sufficiently so that its two, widely set, narrow, eyes were forward facing. Everyone agreed its eyes would have given good stereoscopic vision. The eyes themselves were wholly jet black and flashed eerily as the team's headlights caught in them.

The reason for the impression of "pointedness" of the face was that, below those beady eyes the face protruded to a snout like nose; a long nasal protuberance narrowing to a set of *four* flattened nostrils, set above a prominent area of maxillo-facial cheek and jaw bones. A small mound could be spotted on the top of the snout. Below the nostrils the jaws protruded, significantly more than in humans, and the mouth was wide, with thin lips slightly parted, revealing a tiny glimpse of serrated, ivory like, teeth. Mike could barely keep his eyes off the face.

As the group members gradually overcame their initial sense of awe, they began to discuss the statue, animatedly. Some team members bent over, stood on tip toe, or contorted themselves to be able to peer through the "glass", at various features. As they did so it became apparent that "it", was actually a "he". In a spot close where the genitalia would be found in human males, a broad penis-like structure could be observed. It was spade shaped, protruding downwards from the join with the torso, then tapering into a triangle with a sharp looking tip. The first surprise was that the structure was several centimetres to the right of the body's mid-line and was actually in the being's right groin. It was around 4 centimetres long, so, the second surprise was how comparatively small it was, purely in relation to the size of the rest of the body. No structures like testicles could be seen.

'Their testicles might have resided wholly within the body cavity,' offered Lomanz, and he continued, 'And that suggests a very different body temperature to that of humans. Or maybe a different temperature control system.'

'Indeedo,' said Eleri, 'and that structure most definite seems to be a penis, or penile mechanism. And be not forgetting that this may be a representation of a detumescent penis. Many male animals have apparently tiny such peniles but yet they become hose like when … arous-ed.' She flushed as one or two subdued chuckles were heard. Aren't we humans strange when it comes to such things, thought Mike.

'Eleri's right,' said Lew, and moving the subject quickly on from erectile penises, added, 'but what strikes me, guys, is that if this thing is a male there's no attempt to cover that organ or, for that matter, to *protect* it.'

'Different social or cultural mores, obviously,' suggested Mike. Maybe they were less bashful than us.'

'Less repressed, are more like the words you need, Mike,' said Lomanz, with a grin.

'And why is the penile so far away from the mid-line,' said Rasmissen, from the back of the group.

'Yes, didst wonder. That is a surprising variation in bilateral symmetry on this world,' offered Eleri.

More animated discussions blossomed. Little debates broke out over various features of the statue. Mike saw how deeply engrossed Eleri was in it all, and after a few minutes she turned to him and beamed such a smile of satisfaction that he thought he'd never forget it.

Then she said, to the group as a whole, that she felt the overall appearance of the being was undeniably reptilian but there was also a vaguely simian element to the cranium, despite the protruding face and lack of prominent external ears. There were things which appeared to be ear canals but there were two on *each* side of the swept back skull. And could that slight prominence above the four nostrils, possibly be a *horn*? Someone offered that some lizards have horns, but no simian ever did.

Some people felt that if the being was fully reptilian, it would not have had a chin, not even the small one it did apparently possess, which was smaller than that in a human. How would that affect it's powers of speech, assuming, as they thought they must, that this species simply must have had speech. And yet, the overall shape of the face was still very reminiscent of a reptile. Another surprise was a cluster of what seemed to be feathers appearing to have grown from that knob-like "chin" below the mouth. On closer inspection, the team could see that the sides of the head, the neck and the area around the stomach, *if it was the stomach*, all had a fine, downy covering.

Eleri suddenly gasped and said, 'Overall, do you not realise what this being is yet like?'

'Yeah. I can guess what you mean. It has to be,' said Mike, as if he'd read her mind, his eyes lighting up again.

'Tis like the creatures we saw *on Simurgh!*' burst Gajana Maheshtra, before he could speak.

'Yes, the skeletos on the rock shelf,' said Danile, 'but this one is yet somehow different. Bigger, for certain.'

'Presumably, it's a later version. Sorry, I mean, a more evolved species,' said Mike.

'Well, at least this sculpture shows a complete creature …whatever it is,' said Lew, 'cos the skeletons were kind of mashed up. And now we can see it fully, this mascla looks formidable to me.'

'Deedly,' said Hermington, 'and just be looking at the way tis depicted. Tis full bipedal-like in humans, not so much like a therapod dinosaur, such as on old

Earth. You know – they were the fierce ones that did run round on two long legs and yet ate other dinosaurs. T'were such things such as carnotosaurus and terrosaurs. Sorry, I should say, tyrannosaurs.'

'I thought there were fossils of things like that on Oceanus, too?' said Mike.

'Deedly,' said Eleri, 'but what you might call "dinosaurs", such like the therapods or other, are different on Oceanus, though do look similar.'

'But this thing is *very different* from that type of creature, guys,' said Lew.

'Should we yet refer to him as a "thing", must we?' said Eleri and there were murmurs of approval in the group. 'Look,' she continued, 'we see that skull is so big but tis in proportion to the rest of the body. It probably held a brain as big as ours, praps even bigger.'

'Yes,' said Gajana Maheshtra, 'I agree but would say tis the brain case which is large, not the whole skull. Tis not yet like the skull of a gorilla, from old Earth's wildlife parks. They be huge, yet the brain case is small. This being is much refined, like a gracile version of a dinosaur.'

Several team members chorused approval of his comment.

'Precise-right,' said Senestris. 'Tis what you would expect, if the dinosaur, or archosaur line, had not died out on Earth and had evolved onward, for further millions of years – instead of being replaced by mammals.'

'You mean, it's what might have happened if the dinosaurs hadn't been wiped out by a meteorite, or climate change, or whatever?' said Mike.

'Lomanz voiced a note of caution, 'Hey guys, aren't we moving ahead a bit fast here? If this is a statue you might have a hard time proving any of this, but there could be other things, maybe even other statues of this being, or maybe other species, somewhere else in here. After all, we can't be certain that the creature this statue represents was typical of the beings which inhabited this world.' Sounds of approval at that.

'Sure,' said Lew, 'and by the way, are we sure it's a male? I mean, I know it's got male genitals – but what are those?' He pointed to two rows of what looked like tiny teats, which ran up the belly of the being, from the level of the belt, until disappearing under a wide chest strap which tied the two shoulder coverings together. Everyone looked amazed. How did they miss that? Eleri pressed herself up against the glass.

'Looks so very like teats,' she said, 'but I do not understand.'

'Praps tis hermaphrodite,' said Hermington.

'Praps,' said Eleri, 'but not of necessity. There are examples of males of some species suckling the young, in our world. And one or two on Earth. Like seahorse and pipe fish and here, on Oceanus, the land darbodem. And at least four sea reptile species. Praps these beings evolved from those?'

'Or more likely, a common ancestor,' said Chanda, 'but we have never found any fossils of such like.'

'So, I guess it's what confirms that dinosaurs, or rather, your version of dinosaurs, lived on Oceanus for longer than on Earth?' said Mike.

'How long are we talking about?' asked Lomanz.

'Oh, praps about three to three and one half, *hundred million* of years,' said Danile.

'So, if that's how long your age of reptile age lasted,' said Lomanz, whistling loudly, 'there was probably ample time for a more gracile and intelligent form to evolve. And there were no catastrophic asteroid strikes or super volcano explosions, like on Earth. At least not since that time.'

Another astute observation, thought Mike. There seemed no limit to that man's intellect. He added a question,

'So, are you saying that there were dinosaurs, or dinosaurians – on this planet till the … what did the Professier call it …?'

'The unconformity,' said Danile, 'but – on the land – the biggest-most of the dinosaurians had been dying out for some many million years. Were nearly gone some two or three million of years *before* the unconformity. We yet think that climate change was the cause, or reduction of suitable food-prey.'

'And I think tis right to say that there were still dinosaur types on Oceanus,' said Eleri, glancing at Danile, for confirmation, 'after the big-most ones were gone? Yes, and they were just much smaller. And there were many species.' Hermington nodded his agreement.

Danile continued, 'And that is where the unconformity dost come in. For several million of years we know little about, from the rocks on the land, what happened in the times leading up to the eruption of Ra's surface event.'

'And it looks like that's where our friend here, comes in,' said Lew.

'And still, as no fossils like our friend have been found,' said Danile, 'these beings must have evolved, if so they did, during the time represented by the unconformity, ... the so-called, "missing time".'

'Agreed,' said Eleri, 'and going back to his form, his bearing-so, and ... well, this place, praps we can all agree, surely such, that this being was not only intelligent? He, if t'were a he, was *self-aware*. If his appearance is not enough to convince you, look most of all to the things he dost carry. They must be symbols, physical symbols. All point to him saying praps, "Observe! This is yet who I am. Be afraid-so.' Eleri spoke in a falsely deep voice and, meolodramatically, struck a pose like the being in the cabinet. The group around her burst into laughter. It lightened the mood somewhat.

'I'm certain you've hit the spot, Eleri,' said Lew, still chuckling, 'but, right now, maybe we should move on and have a look at whatever else is down here. Mike said something about "control cabinets". I'm going to take a look. Who's coming with me?'

'Most of the team nodded, amidst murmurings of soon returning to the "statue cabinet", and so they followed Lew, leaving Mike, Eleri and Danile still standing by the cabinet.

'Who do you think this being was?' asked Mike. 'Maybe you're right El, was he one of the builders of this place, maybe? Or a leader of some kind. The "king" of the dome?'

'We cannot know,' said Danile, pressing his face to the case again. Mike did the same, then, with embarrassment, he remembered his wristcom. He turned and shouted back to Lew's group before they had gone too far, 'Hey guys, I just realised. We'd better start acting like professionals here. I'm going to use my wristcom to record all of this. Lew, I suggest you do the same, man. Cos we can't transmit out. I've checked my device works and I did a bit of recording earlier on but sort of forgot to do anymore in all the excitement. I reckon the rest of you could use your headcams, if you want. Lew can show you how.'

'Excellentia,' said Eleri.' She called to the others, 'Mike is yet right. And Lew, is it possible to take physical measurements?'

Lew turned back toward her and said, 'Mike and I will be able to take enough images with our wristcoms for them to produce a 3D model. I guess measurements could be calculated by the computers. But there is a molecular scale measuring device in the Laurasia. We need to go back there soon, anyway. It will be nearly dark outside. Danile tells me the Kilops worms come out at night. I know we can stun 'em, but he tells me we could cause them a lot of damage if we did that. We should try to conserve things, if possible, after all. Shouldn't we?'

Eleri looked pleasantly surprised, agreed with him and said they should come back the next day. But they might have to leave the entranceway open, as they would have difficulty closing the stone block.

As Lew's group moved off Mike started recording again. Eleri called to him and Danile.

'Look, over there, below the hock of the being's left leg. Does look to me like plaster dust or powder.'

They pressed their noses against the glass. Eleri was pointing to a pile of white material on the floor of the cabinet.

'Yeah, you're right,' said Mike, 'it looks very granular.'

'Seems to point to it being a statue after all,' said Mike, looking disappointed. 'I was kind of hoping it was maybe some sort of preserved body. It's so *real*.'

The three continued to film the figure in the cabinet whilst Lew's group ranged widely, examining the banks of other cabinets. After about twenty minutes all, except Lew, returned to the statue cabinet, pulled there almost magnetically. Lomanz suggested they find a proper name for the animal inside, albeit a nickname, rather than keep calling it, "the being". Eleri nominated Mike's suggestion, "the Lord of the Dome or maybe the Lord of the Mountain," but most people didn't seem to like that. Other names were suggested but rejected. Finally, Eleri said,

'Surely now, this being is a native of this world. He and his kind were here long before us. He is yet an example of, I am supposing, a true native.'

'That's it,' said Mike, 'we should call him, "the Native".' There was general approval, though Lomanz muttered, 'Still think the mountain king's best'.

And it was Lomanz who, using his own wristcom to record, then magnify, sections of the Native's skin, manipulating the images and extrapolating, announced to his colleagues that not only was there a sort of feathery down on parts of the body but most of the Native's skin seemed to be covered with something very tiny feathers. But he reported getting some sort of interference, like static, on his device, when trying to get a better resolution in his images. Lew and Mike said they'd had similar problems. Another issue with the Cambrium, perhaps?

At that point Lew said, 'Listen up guys. While you were busy, I stood under the shaft and managed to get a better cascade signal from Morganrynn, but just for a few seconds. He's been contacted by Eve. Says Akrommo is back at the Laurasia.' There were sighs of relief from virtually the whole group, which surprised Mike, given how angry everyone had been about his earlier behaviour.

Lew continued, 'I think there was also something about the Strider being found intact. There was a chorus of approval at that. The machine seemed to have made some friends, thought Mike.

Danile had wandered further afield and called out that he had found more of the glass top cabinets. Most of them contained interesting but truly bizarre artefacts, like metal spheres balanced on sharp spikes, and trigonal shapes, tetragonal ones and more complex shapes. What he found astonishing was that all the metal was shiny, looking as though made yesterday – not eight million years ago.

'Yeah,' said Lew, 'fascinating stuff I agree, but I think we should be getting along now, folks, if it's okay with you. My wristcom says nightfall is about one hour away and we've got to get back up the shaft first.'

Some began to shuffle slowly off, with Lew at the front, but Mike saw Eleri lingering near the Native's case. She seemed almost transfixed by the being, impatient to know more about him, such as who he was supposed to be and why he was down here. What became of him and his kind.

'I'll bet I know what you're thinking, El. But could be some time before we get any answers, and some we might never know.'

She said, 'Yes, I do know that, Mike.' They suddenly noticed Danile had joined them.

'His eyes are so – intense,' he said.

'Yeah,' said Mike, 'like the ones you get in ancient picture portraits.'

Eleri looked spooked. 'I have never so heard that,' she said, 'but tis certainly true of this being. I wonder what his eyes are made of. Rock gems? They are created so well.'

Further discussion was cut short when they heard shouts of alarm coming from a distance. For some reason most of the team had wandered over toward the wall of the cabinets. They were peering upwards, headlights trained on one particular section of the uppermost part of the wall. Mike thought he noticed movement there. Was someone or something up there, watching them?

Mike's heart started to pound again, as he, Danile and Eleri joined the others. Yes, there was movement. Even more bizarrely, it seemed the movement was *inside* the walls. Strange silhouettes and shapes, possibly weird animals, some large, some small, some fleetingly luminescent, seemed to pass along silently, inside the wall, from right to left and vice-versa, many crossing past each-other. The mutterings of alarm continued. Lew had drawn his stun gun.

The whole group went tensely silent until it became apparent that whatever the shapes were, they were not a threat. Nor could they have been real creatures.

Danile said, 'They must yet be images. They are not real beings but those things must be nearly the same size as our friend, the Native – but tis hard to make out whether they are reptiloids. Tell me I am right yet. They are not really here, are they? I mean …'

'No,' said Lew, holstering his weapon. 'Looks to me like some sort of automated imagery. There might be a device in the wall or something. I can't make out what they're doing but they don't seem dangerous. They're a bit like our holo images but – well, different. More primitive tek, I'd guess.'

'I can't believe we never saw them till now,' said Mike.

'They weren't there before,' said Padrigg Lomanz, 'I was watched my light shining on the top of the walls as I came out of the shaft.'

'Maybe they're only activated,' said Mike, 'if light hits them from down here, on the floor. Maybe at a specific angle. Anyway, they don't seem to be a problem. Got me going for a moment.'

'I think that speaks for all of us,' said Lew, 'and it kind of shows how much we humans are "pre-programmed" to react in certain ways. Pity, they're not real. Would have been interesting if they'd been real aliens – natives – whatever – up there – alive.'

That drew gasps of surprise from many in the group.

Danile said, 'No, I am yet glad they are not live creatures like our friend over there. He is a just a tensh bit scary-like.'

'More hard wiring,' said Lomanz, 'because we might be hard wired to react that way to large reptiles. Personally, I didn't think the shapes were that much like our friend in the box.'

The group finally seemed to acknowledge Lew's renewed, gentle, herding of them toward the shaft, all agreeing that there was enough work to do down there to keep many research teams, from Earth *and* Oceanus, busy for decades. That feeling seemed tempered by the sure knowledge that life on this planet didn't really have many more decades to go. After that a sullen silence settled on the group, at least for a while.

The guard at the top of the shaft was brimming with questions as each rose out of abyss and Lew promised him that he and everyone else on the expedition would get a chance to see the hall.

Walking back down the egg-shaped tunnel, Mike found he had to support Eleri, as she seemed forced to recover from another bout of claustrophobia on coming through the shaft. He joshed with her and teased her, talking her round, and she began to recover. She said she thought her own pills were perhaps finally starting to help. Too little, too late, thought Mike.

As the group emerged into the outside world Eleri stood still and breathed in and out deeply for a couple of minutes, then said to Mike, 'I am yet so glad to get out in't freshly air.'

Mike breathed a sigh of relief too and they set off for the landing boat. As they walked, she said, loudly enough for all to hear, 'Yet I was thinking, my lovely friendlings. Do you not realise that this day … this very day – we have become *famous*?'

There were muted chuckles and chatter amongst the group. Someone up front said, sarcastically, 'If you like that sort of thing.'

Danile piped up, 'Do not have much choice, unless the government does hush this up.'

'Oh no,' said Lew, something like venom in his voice, 'No way they're doing that.'

Then Lomanz said, 'Guess you're right, Eleri. And you Lew. It's amazing to think we are the first *humans* to ever set foot in that place. The first to see those artefacts. And, I guess, the first to see the Native. It's a privilege for sure.'

'It's like the first explorers into King Tut's tomb, in ancient Egypt, or Xian's tomb in China,' said Lew, 'except it isn't a tomb, is it?'

'I am not thinking so,' said Eleri.

Mike waxed philosophically, 'No, guys. This is way bigger, I reckon. Don't forget, King Tut and the other guy were humans. The Native, down there, definitely is not.'

Eleri grasped his arm as they walked in the cool evening air and said, 'I am also glad that the Professier Akrommo, and the Strider machine are safe, for, in reality, if t'weren't for them, we would not have been able to see those things.'

No-one contradicted her.

As the group wended their way back toward the shuttle Mike silently reflected on the day's events and wondered if things would ever be the same again. For anyone.

*

In truth, none of them had any idea how different things would be.

****

'In short, Draco,' said Tenak, 'she and her Inner Policy Committee are now prepared to allow a full team of scientists *from the Antarctica* to fly down to New Cambria. They can take as much equipment as they need, so the dome and its contents can be investigated properly. And she's happy with a large contingent to go from this ship. It's a huge concession, Professier, and a great chance for science. And, in reality, progress on the main thrust of our own mission.'

The Admiral's holo image "stood" in the middle of Professier Muggredge's University office again. The academic was beaming at Tenak's image, 'Yes and tis mostly due to your persistence that we have such progress. I am glad so much that Madama President is now beginning to see it our way. However, she did surely attach conditions, didst not?'

'Yes Draco, of course. She wants at least three of her own government's "official" scientists there – at all times. I'm sorry to say she insisted on people who aren't associated with your University.'

'So suspicious, she is,' sighed Muggredge.

'Yeah, I suppose, but that's not all. She's put a ban on any findings being released for general transmission or publication. At least, not till her own people have analysed the possible impact.'

Muggredge's face reddened a little and he blew heavily through his nostrils, like an angry bull.

'I am not believing this, Arkas,' he said, 'yet she is prandling, surely? This is nothing but a muzzle order'.

'I know Draco. I'm sorry, but it's the best we could get. I felt it was more important to have people from the Antarctica down there than to insist on publication freedom. She was very insistent. Maker knows why.'

'Lots yet, of internal politics going on, Arkas. Power struggles inside the government, as I did say to you, e'en though she has survived politically, so far.'

'Have you had any further details from your "sources"?'

'Not so much, Arkas but – yes, there has yet been lots of pracking going on behind the scenery.'

'As I thought. Anyway, I've informed Captain Providius, and her staff are putting together a team now. I'm withdrawing some of our own team and sending down two other scientists, including our chief scientist, Doctrow Jennison. I'm happy for Mike Tanniss to stay down there with your team, and I'm sure your niece will want to stay.'

'Good. Yes, those two are virtually inseparable, friendling.'

'Guess so, Draco. I also hope those two stay out of trouble down there.

Chapter 43

REVELATIONS

When the door to his private office buzzed, Arkas Tenak didn't ask his comp to issue an invitation or invite the caller inside. Instead, he walked to the door with brisk enthusiasm.

'Mike, it's good to see you in person. Come inside. It's been a long time,' he said as he greeted his friend with a traditional, but now extra warm, Home System handshake.

Mike had worn his best blue uniform jacket and black trousers with blue side stripe. He'd been looking forward to this meeting but not for the same reasons as Tenak might have. He knew the Admiral wouldn't like what he had to say.

'It's good to see you, Arkas,' Mike said, warmly. 'How long has it been?'

'Too long my friend. Too long. It's been hard enough getting hold of you by holo or synth screen, let alone in person. You've been real busy down there. Is everything okay?'

Mike walked to a pair of Tenak's comfy armchairs as the effusive Admiral invited him to sit. Mike declined the offer of a non-alcoholic drink and he knew Tenak did not imbibe. He began to feel increasingly on edge.

'Yes, everything's … fine Arkas. As you said, just been busy. Or at least Eleri has.' Mike tried to relax into the plush seat. He had to admit to himself, it felt good to be back aboard the ship.

'Is everything okay between you two?' asked the Admiral, his brows knitting.

'Yeah, of course. More than okay. That's partly why I've come to see you. It's just that, with her anthropology training, El is getting a bit more, well, a lot more than me, I guess, out of the research down there. Oh, I can help with the physics to do with artefacts, and you know, we've made some progress but it's slow right now. No, it's the palaeontologists and anthropologists who are having the fun. Still, it's all fascinating stuff.' Mike paused for a moment, then added. 'To be honest Arkas, I miss the ship a bit. But only a bit, you understand. Well, a really *small* bit.' He smiled as Tenak rolled his eyes. He knew the Admiral enjoyed the teasing.

Tenak sipped his hot kaffee and said, 'Okay Mike. I get the picture. In fact, I have some news for you as well, and it's connected with what you're talking about – but please, give me yours first.'

Mike considered the Admiral, the man he felt he owed so much to, and wondered, with rising trepidation, how he would react to the next thing he was going to say.

'Well, there's no easy way to put this, Arkas,'

Tenak looked concerned for a second, as Mike hesitated, then he said, 'Just spit it out, Mike.'

'Eleri and I are … going to get married. And I mean married, not merri-bonded, like back home. I hope we'll have your blessing.'

'Wow! That is something great. Congratulations young mascla – but, in truth, it's not really unexpected. Not after the way things have been going between you two. Still, it's wonderful news. Maker, how you have changed.'

Mike frowned then smiled, 'I'm not sure how to take that, Arkas – but I suppose you mean well. The bad news is that, well, we're not marrying on the ship. Eleri wants to get married on Oceanus itself. That's why it's what she thinks of as marriage, and me, and not … well, you know. But it wouldn't be until next year – Oceanus time.'

'That's fine, Mike. Don't worry. Listen, I'm not upset I won't be able to perform the ceremony. But, galaxy's edge, why wait a year? Won't that interfere …? Ah, I think I see where this is headed.' Tenak's eyes narrowed as he leaned forward.

Here we go, thought Mike and gulped, 'Well, it's just that marriage rules are complicated on Oceanus. We have no choice but to wait a year from betrothal, apparently. But what it means is …. well, what I'm saying is that I want to hand in my resignation. I'm sorry Arkas. Really sorry.'

Tenak sat back in his chair rather more heavily than Mike expected.

'Yeah,' said the Admiral, 'well, I thought it might mean something like this. I guess it's understandable, Mike. I know you want to be sure El's family are going to make the transition to the Home System in good shape. Not being in the Secretariat would enable you to do that. It's a good idea.' Tenak forced a smile.

That went better than he'd anticipated, thought Mike, but it didn't stop him feeling bad. He withdrew a small alumina-plast box from his dress jacket and handed it to Tenak.

'The microblock inside this contains my formal letter. I wanted to hand it to you personally, not send the text by cascade. Look, I'm sorry about all this, Arkas.'

'You keep saying that Mike. No need. I told you, I do understand. We'll miss you of course. Good Secretaries are hard to come by these days. But I can tell you now. There's something else happening, so I'm going to give this block right back to you. You see, I can't accept it. Not yet.'

Mike looked him, puzzled. 'Why not? I thought …'

'I had some news too, remember? Just hear me out. Jennifer Providius is taking the Antarctica in a spiral orbit around Ra. To get really close in. She wants to repeat the run she did before. Take close up observations of the star. Replace the data they lost before Heracleonn did her thing. Seems they've also found some weird gravity wave signals emanating from a source way out beyond this system. We think it may be the object we saw when we got here. Mike, she has asked specifically for *you,* to go along with her and her team.'

Mike's heart leaped. A chance to go on a mission with the Antarctica. But there were complications. He had to think of someone else's wishes now, as well.

'She asked for me?' he spluttered. 'Amazing. I suppose I'm tempted Arkas, Really. But why ask for me?'

'Why do you think? I guess she likes your astrophysics credentials. Listen, I know this comes at an awkward time and you don't have to decide right this minute, but you should know she wants to leave pretty soon. If you're too busy on New Cambria then just tell her, no. But I thought it'd be a change for you. Plays to your strengths. Gravity waves – and all that. Course, you'll … have to leave EI, for a while.'

'Yeah, too right. She won't like that. How long, would you say, roughly?'

'Suppose it depends partly on what you find, but around 18 to 20 standard weeks.'

'Won't you need to set course for the Home System before then?'

'Not really, Mike. You've been out of the loop for a while, haven't you? There's been a drop in the number of migrants for the Home System, since the flurry that followed the last proton storm.'

Mike looked puzzled for a moment but then he remembered how fickle the people of Oceanus could be.

'Also, I'm guessing,' said Tenak, 'that you were at least aware that news about Newcam was leaked to the Oceanus Press. Not by us, I might add.'

Mike nodded, and the Admiral continued, 'What you might not know is that someone in the government leaked it to the mass media here. Seems that someone's back on the continent is on the receiving end of data about Newcam. Who knows? Anyway, the result is that the Meta-teleos have become resurgent and re-strengthened. Yeah, I know. They're accusing the government of conspiring with *us* and with the Home System. They're also aggrieved that the government didn't invite any of their *natural philosophers* to join the teams on New Cambria. I've had to send one of our few remaining data-probes back home, to advise the allied government of developments.'

'So, we're back to square one.' Mike felt deflated and angry.

'Not quite. There are still more applications to leave than there were *before* the last storm. They're just not increasing so fast, right now. We're still trying and, on that score, by the way, Professor Muggredge is a participant in a live televised debate, down on Oceanus, next week. Seems he's up against some sort of media raconteur called, Madam Galleane.

'That should be interesting.'

'Yeah. So – what do you say to Jennifer's invitation?'

Mike sat in silence for long moments. Tenak was right, he thought. This would be a chance to use his skills and knowledge in a way the work on Newcam didn't. But it would mean being away from El, for some time. He had hardly left her side for months.

Tenak leaned forward and spoke very earnestly, 'Listen Mike. I don't want to influence you one way or the other. It's entirely up to you. But the offer is a good one – whether you decide to get a job, kind of temporary, on Oceanus, or come back early to the Solar System, maybe with El and her family. Whatever. You're going to need to work – if you're giving up this job. I said I won't accept your resignation yet. That's because I think the trip on the Antarctica could give you the time to consider what you want to do in the future. You can still work as a ship's Secretary - even if you're "married" - and you could also look out for El's family too. I suppose I'm just asking you to think about it for a while – whether you go on this trip or not. Just don't say I tried to push you, Mike. But, sometimes, it takes others to point out the options you might not have thought of.'

Mike whistled long and low. 'I'd like to discuss it with Eleri before I say anything.'

'Of course. I would say you'll *have to* discuss it with her.'

****

Mike floated in one of the Antarctica's well-appointed observation lounges, a bubble shaped bulge on the surface of the craft's tubular hub; a zone where microgravity ruled. A large observation window gave a view back along the outside of the hub, toward the wide skirt of the fusion engine shield. Just like The Monsoon, this ship had an aneutronic fusion power plant, meaning it didn't produce large amounts of potentially damaging neutron radiation. Unlikely as it was, some stray neutron flux couldn't be ruled out entirely, and the skirt was a precaution, to deflect or absorb it.

In addition to the fusion shield the lounge, like every other crewed part of the ship, was inside the bubble of protection afforded by the ship's powerful electromagnetic and atomic nucleon wave shields. Fitted on all starships, these fields were generated by large coils and mast antennae, sited in clusters at the back end of the engine module, around the shield, and at the extreme prow.

The generators enveloped the vehicle with a flux field designed to keep out cosmic and solar radiation and had the effect of deflecting the millions of small particles of dust and rock which would otherwise hit the ship as it flew at exceptional speed through space. At such speeds even a soot sized particle of dust could hit a starship with the force of a miniature explosion. Decompression, even if it could be localised, would be the result.

Because of the presence of the engine shield, Mike couldn't see much of the glow from the giant engine bell, which he knew would be pouring out a seething inferno of ions hotter than the surface of Ra, busily pushing the Antarctica into a wide parabolic path, away from Oceanus. He chuckled inwardly when he thought of the way that the folklore of space had, for dozens of decades, depicted spaceflight. Almost invariably the impression given to the public was given that when you wanted to get to a specific destination in space you just had to keep firing the engine, with the ship pointing toward your objective. Off you would go, usually with someone manually piloting the craft, *directly* to the destination.

The reality was that all the guidance was done by computers, fed by masses of sensor data. These days humans simply gave approval for guidance operations, if required, and monitored progress. If necessary, they could order adjustments and refinements – but still under computer guidance. Gone were the days when humans played any real part in the actual flying of large ships and, even in the early days, guidance and many other tasks were computerised. The first ships to land on the Earth's Moon were manually piloted down in the final stages and that was because of the limitations of computers of the time. Ships like the modern landing boats could still be manually flown, in planetary atmospheres, of course, albeit with computer augmentation. And the vessels which landed on planets without atmospheres could also be piloted manually over some stages, including landing. Mike thought that this could only be a good thing. It was nice to know that humans weren't a completely redundant part of the process.

But in space proper, you got where you wanted to go by firing your engine so as to insert you into an *orbit;* the most efficient orbit, which would bring you to your goal. In a star system, constantly firing an engine opposite to your intended line of travel, or perhaps more accurately, your *arc* of travel, did not propel you in completely the opposite direction. It simply pushed you into a wider or "higher" orbit in the gravity well of the star or planet that was the destination. You would stay in that orbit until another engine burn was carried out. If that was in the same direction as before that would push you into an even wider orbit, or possibly out of the star system altogether. But if the burn was made in the direction of your travel, it would slow you down, so narrowing, or "lowering", your orbit, bringing you closer to your destination. More burns would get you to that goal, until insertion into orbit.

In the case of the Antarctica, now, the ship needed to accelerate to escape the gravity well of Oceanus, to push it further away from Ra. It would later turn around and fire the engine in the opposite direction, to slow down, and allow Ra to drag the ship deeper into its own gravity hole. Later, the plan was to use a gravity assist sling shot, around Ra, together with an engine burn, to accelerate the ship back toward Oceanus, which would have moved further along in its own orbit around Ra.

Right now, Mike gazed at the pearlescent blue and white orb of Oceanus, as the ship sped away from it. Fortunately, he didn't usually get agoraphobic at such times, perhaps because of the blackness of space, admittedly star spangled. He more used to this anyway.

In fact, Mike never got tired of such sights and was always, perhaps unaccountably, amazed by the speed at which planets shrank when ships accelerated away from them. Inevitably his thoughts turned to Eleri. What might she be doing now? But "now" was different for her than it was for him, of course. He imagined she might like this view but then again, maybe not. She had never been off-world. He was still not sure he she would take to spaceflight.

As he gazed still at the receding orb, the Great Middle Ocean of Oceanus faced toward him. Somewhere "down there" was New Cambria, an inconceivably tiny, essentially invisible speck, at this distance. The terminator stretched around the planetary globe, so half of the Middle ocean was hidden by darkness. He thought the terminator had covered Newcam, so it was likely Eleri was asleep. He wished he was with her, next to her. Sleeping on his own seemed an almost distant memory, though it really wasn't that long ago. He would have to get used to it for at least the next two or three standard months.

As there was no-one else in the observation lounge Mike had a chance to just float there, tethered loosely to a handhold, and reflect on how he came to be here. He had expected Eleri to be very unhappy about Tenak's suggestion that Mike go on this mission, but, in the event, she hadn't been too upset. He had teased her that she must have lined up someone to spend *friending- time* with, once he'd gone. He was, of course, confident that Eleri would remain solidly loyal, but it had come as a surprise to be told that she also trusted him – implicitly. His surprise was not because he intended being untrustworthy, but because it marked such a difference from the way his life had once been – not so long ago.

Once El became aware that he was actually excited by the mission, she had encouraged him to go. 'They shall yet benefit from your skills and knowledge, Mike,' she had said in her Oceanus brogue. 'After all,' she'd added, 'there must be such good reason for you to be on that ship, otherwise Mes Captain would not have asked for you – specialry.'

She had also felt the relationship between the two of them might even be strengthened. How so, he had asked?

'On Oceanus,' she'd said, 'there is a saying that "the ocean winds blow a stronger love from thee to me and back, e'en though we be at separate ends of the world". Besidings, what is yet a few weeks apart, when we have the whole of our lives to be together?'

He had agreed, there and then, that he would go ahead. It would be good to get off- world again. And, as she said, they were talking about nineteen weeks, or so, Earth time. After all, she had suggested, if their love couldn't survive that long maybe there was no hope for them. She'd also reminded him that they would be able to communicate, using 'the 3D –wizzery thing,' as she'd put it. He'd reminded her that holo-vids weren't the same as being in someone's presence and, worse, as the ship's distance increased, conversation would become impossible, due to the time lag. She'd said they would manage.

Still, he knew it would be hard when the time came to say goodbye. Both he and El, had fought back the tears in their eyes as they kissed, a last bittersweet moment. Then, they had left the scientists' accommodation, set up near the dome, prefabricated though it was, and he had boarded the Laurasia.

Watching her from the shuttle as she tried to stifle a few tears, and with a welling-up in his own eyes and a lump in his throat, he watched El walk back to a safe distance and gaze up, waving, as the boat had lifted off. He had tried to keep her in sight as long as possible, as she and everyone on the ground, shrank rapidly until only the blue-green sward of strapweed meadows and the New Cambrian forests could be seen. The speedily shrinking globe of Oceanus he now gazed at, reminded him too much of that moment, and he decided to leave the observation lounge.

****

'I am resenting the implication-such that I my academic credentials be too influenced by the Home System Navy,' said Professor Muggredge. He sat in a large armchair, on a stage, in a type of theatre which was partly a TV studio. A live audience of around a thousand people sat on basic, uncomfortable chairs, staring at him. Opposite his was another chair, occupied by the colourfully named Madama Galleanne, a media personality, a rare thing on Oceanus. She was also a current affairs critic, was considered a formidable intellect – and known to have leanings toward the Meta-teleos. Galleanne sat imperiously, an ingenuous smile plastered all over her flat, round face.

The Professor was taking part in the much-vaunted live televised debate in the Bhumi-devi TV Company studios, in central Janitra. It was a few days after Mike had left on his expedition and Muggredge had returned, courtesy of the Navy, from a trip to New Cambria, to see 'The Hall of the Native' for himself. He had been overwhelmed by the place.

The debate was meant to be an informal discussion. The fact that it was a television debate perplexed people from Earth, where that type of thing was long extinct. Today's debate was part of a series this TV channel ran, to discuss topical issues, and had been organised after the news about New Cambria had been leaked to the press. Muggredge had told Tenak of his fury that the government had not published the news themselves, leading inevitably to the suggestion they were, yet again, trying to cover up things. Tenak had opined that there were other forces at work here.

The television series was popular, and the program was being hosted by a woman called Tremanion, a TV host and raconteur, a popular figure, at least to the extent that Bhumi-Devi society took any notice of such people; perhaps quite a lot in Janitra but less elsewhere, though apparently increasing. Tremanion, a thin woman with a shaggy mien of hair, sat behind a wide desk between the two debaters. She spoke now, in velvety smooth tones which usually belied the ferocity she often showed to guests she didn't like,

'I will say I am believing Madama Galleanne did not so suggest you were so influenced, Professier.'

'No,' said Galleanne, 'I simply did say you may be too close to the Navy to be completely objective yet. After all, will you be denying you have had many meetings with the Admiral of the ship in orbit, and that your niece, who all know you hold dear, is engag-ed to be married to someone from that ship?'

Muggredge could be seen to be stifling a sense of outrage but managed to say, as evenly as he could, 'I am not believing such things as that, should form any part of any discussion of this sort. Tis private. All I do try to establish is that the existence of the Native and the massive building where he is housed, shows that a species of powerful and sentient beings once lived on this world. And, tis quite clear so, that those beings are no longer in evidence. Something must have destroyed them and - when this is combined with what we know to be true of the variancy of our star, and such carbonised deposits on the dome covering the Hall of the Native ....'

'Yes, we know what you are trying to say,' said Galeanne, 'and I have some sympatico but, with respect, Professier, we have no real idea why these beings disappeared. It could have been anything. Special-so considering how long ago this happened. How many times have *we*, as a species, still come near to destroying ourselves?' Galeanne turned to look at the audience and murmurs of approval could be heard.

She continued, 'I believe you said, Professier, that a time gap of several *hundreds of thousands* of years separates the beings found on Simurgh – from the being on New Cambria. And, by the way, should anyone think I am overly influenced by the Meta-teleos, I will say here and now, that I *do* believe that early examples of these creatures were actually found on Simurgh. Anywayin, the point is that *we* went from the Stone Age to the Nuclear Age in a matter of – what – 6,000 Earth years? If these beings didst have three or four hundred thousand years to evolve a technology, what might they have been capable of? Seems very likely, to me, that they extinguished themselves by their own foolery, as we nearly have. Or, praps it was disease or environmental change. Look at what we did to the Earth.'

Someone shouted from the audience, 'What the Earth people did, not we!'

'Excusing us. I will have order here,' said Tremanion in surly tones, staring out of intense black eyes, at the audience, and added, 'The debate is between our distinguish-ed guests.'

Muggredge said, 'Thanking you. You are right, Madama, but still, we do not see evidence of ancient war. Nuclear war would have left traces of radiative isotopes in the rocks. I accept that disease is possible, and we would not need see any physical evidence of that nowtime. However, we would surely have found, by now, more evidence of the buildings, or roads praps, or yet something else they would have left. The dome on New Cambria seems to have been purpose-built to withstand some sort of environmental disaster. There is also the carbonised layer which covers parts of the dome and was found on Simurgh. Sad to say, the geolry history of our planet means that most of the rocks of that age are probably underneath the seas.'

'I agree with you that to some degrees, Professier,' said Galleanne, 'but I am not as confident as you about the variances of Ra. I do not think the small amount of carbonised deposits are very convincing. They could, again, be accounted for by something the Native's popularia did.'

Muggredge smiled and said, 'But perhaps you forget that the carbonised layer has now been confirmed to contain significant quantities of Beryllium 10 radioisotopes. Tis exactly what would be expected if Ra's surface were to erupt and throw down massive amounts of radiation upon us.'

'Praps, Professier, praps,' said Galleanne, 'but I am believing much more work needs to be done before we can be certain, Professier,' she said, her downturned mouth betraying her inability to answer the point fully.

'That seems to have clinched it,' said Lieutenant Commander Statton, who was sitting in the studio audience, alongside Admiral Tenak. Muggredge had obtained two seats for them. They had come from a distant drop-off point and had been careful to wear local civilian clothes, to blend in.

'I hope so,' said Tenak, 'because I sense a kind of mood swing in the people's attitude. I hope our people on The Monsoon are watching.'

'Oh yeah,' said Statton, 'I'm sure they are, and I believe the Antarctica were tuning in too. And *they* should be well on their way toward Ra, by now. I envy them, sir. They're doing the really exciting stuff, diving into the great unknown.'

'So are we, Lietenant,' said Tenak.

****

The Antarctica's one canteen wasn't as good as any on The Monsoon, Mike decided. Apart from the glass he had in his hand he felt the drinks tasted like fusion engine coolant, not that he had actually tasted any of that! He sat on a high stool in the Antarctica's one and only refectory, sited on its rotating torus, which allowed occupants to eat and drink in the comfort of about three fourths Earth gravity.

Around 10 of the ship's current complement of 25 people, also populated the small canteen; mainly research scientists and a few tekies from the crew, a group who numbered, Mike was surprised to hear, numbered only about 10. All the scientists aboard, a group of multi-disciplinary people at the top of their game, had been hand-picked to go to Oceanus.

Mike had got to know a few of the regular scientists and tekies since the ship broke out of orbit three days earlier. They seemed a friendly bunch and he noticed that all the researchers took their work extremely seriously. When visiting the canteen, they didn't even bother to remove their "zarmas" – headband-like devices used instead of wristcoms. The zarmas received full cascade level comms and projected everything, when required, in holo-format, to a focus to a suitable distance in front of their eyes. A type of visor could also be worn in order to visualize the full cascade.

The zarmas were an improvement on wristcoms, so Mike had been told, supposedly being particularly sensitive to incoming wide-band EM and comms, via a massive range of frequencies. They were even vaunted as having the ability to interpret quantum field fluctuations to a degree that, apparently, put most AIs in the shade. Of less immediate practical use was their supposed ability to pick up, not just alpha waves but a wide variety of other brainwaves from their users without the use of fine skull-penetrating wires. These, it was theorized, could eventually make them suitable for direct communication with Kewsers. Mike knew, however, that this aspect of their use was still in the very earliest stages of development and the concept was not without its critics.

Mike foresaw a number of issues concerning perception and, maybe, brain function, which could cause problems for users, if this function was developed more fully. But he reecognised he was not a neuroscientist, so he wasn't sure. He noticed that the ship's officers didn't use them, just relying on wristcom devices. Many of the scientists on board said the zarmas helped with more efficient collaborative work. Mike had tried a zarma and, though he felt they were quite effective he doubted the accuracy of many of the claims made for them. In addition, they just looked plain silly. He hadn't really investigated any further, nor did he intend to. Using them worried him for reasons he couldn't quite fathom and surprised him because it was not like him to eschew new tek.

Right now, Mike sat on his own in the refectory. He missed Eleri badly and was not in the mood to try to humour some of the rather intense scientists aboard, though the tekies were okay. And despite making some interesting acquaintances, Mike still felt he was not yet an accepted part of the ship's working group. He knew he'd be able to turn things around and would get used to this place soon. Or had being with Eleri – and even the people of Oceanus, for a long time, brought about more far-reaching changes in him?

He was draining the last drops of his slynberry juice when he spotted the approach of a large, stocky man. He knew the mascla though they were not particularly well acquainted. He appeared to be in his late thirties but had a very fresh-faced look that belied his real age. He didn't seem much older than Mike himself but he knew he was. Mike smiled and nodded when the man asked if he could sit with him. Mike wondered what was going on. After all, this guy had not seemed particularly concerned with conversing with him on the way over to the Antarctica, even though it had been just a very short hop from The Monsoon. For the man who now sat next to him was the pilot who had transported him over to the research ship, on a Navy corvette named *Bosporus*.

Mike knew he had transferred to The Monsoon fairly recently and he seemed to have kept to himself for the most part, but Mike was happy to try to use this opportunity to get to know him better. His name was Sanders Utopius Dagghampton II, a junior engineer with, it appeared, excellent piloting qualifications, but lacking some experience. Mike almost felt sorry for him. Dagghampton's current assignment was non-descript, consisting solely of carrying Mike over to the Antarctica, then staying aboard for the whole mission and ferrying The Monsoon's Secretary back afterwards. Mike wasn't surprised the guy had not bothered to chat much on the way over. This must all have been very boring for him.

Ebazza had not been easily persuaded to release another pilot for a long period like this but eventually agreed, in the spirit of mutual co-operation with Jennifer Providius. This was doubly important now because their scientists formed the backbone of the current research work on New Cambria. In any case, Tenak had suggested that the assignment would do the pilot good, to spend some time on a civilian ship. And he said he could even be of use because, since the Heracleonn incident the Antartica now had only one lifeboat remaining. Mike had had a sneaking suspicion that Tenak was providing some "insurance" for the research ship, because maybe he thought there could be some sort of incident on this very research mission. If that's what he thought Mike just hoped he was wrong.

Mike watched the pilot sit next to him, wearing a big smile.

'Good to see you, Mike,' said Sanders, 'so how's it going?'

'Fine, Sanders, fine. First time I've seen you in here. Seem to keep to yourself quite a bit, don't you?'

The man's brow wrinkled at that and – something else maybe, Mike thought. Indignation, perhaps? But the pilot just said, 'Oh, it's not that. I just like to read and use the ship's gym a lot, you know. But I did notice that *you* tend to come in here a lot, usually around the same time, and I wanted to ask you something.'

Mike had a nagging feeling that Sanders might have been watching his movements. 'Do you always watch what I'm doing?' he said, and Mike's wish not to sound overtly hostile or to begin an altercation, made him say it lightly and easily. Nevertheless, he wanted to know the answer.

'Oh … no, sorry Mike. Not at all. There's just not that much to do around here, except maybe work out in the gym hall. It's just down the corridor from here – in case you didn't notice. It's just that I keep seeing you walking past – down this way, that's all. Please forgive my curiosity.'

'That's okay. After all, it must be pretty boring for you to have to bring me over here and hang around for the whole mission.'

'No, not really, Mike. I see every "mission" I'm assigned as a particular challenge. This is just another one, I guess.'

Mike hadn't expected that but at least it sounded very positive. Mike had already observed the large size of his companion when he first saw him on The Monsoon and no-one could fail to notice the lean rippling muscle under the casual sport garments. He was not surprised that the guy worked out in the gym a lot.

'Just wanted to ask you something,' said his companion. 'You knew Johann Erbbius, didn't you? Quite well, I'd imagine. I'm sorry about what happened to him down on Simurgh. I met the guy a few times and I must admit to being a bit concerned about his … motives, I suppose. There's lots of unanswered questions about his part in the Simurgh "affair", if I can put it like that. I wondered what you thought.'

'You've only been with the ship since we started off for Oceanus, haven't you?' said Mike, trying again not to sound too hostile, but it was becoming difficult. 'Still pretty new to The Monsoon, I guess?' he continued.

'Well, that's true, Mike, but does it really matter?'

'It just seems odd to be talking about Johann like that, when you couldn't have known him much. I knew him for a couple of years.' Mike didn't bother to reveal that he didn't actually like the man and had never really got to know him.

'Yes, I see your point,' said Dagghampton, 'and yeah, I admit I didn't know him too well. It's just that I'm – quite observant Mike. And I noticed he seemed to zone in with a group that were often – well, not to put too fine a point on it – unhappy with things.'

'Unhappy with things?'

'Yeah. Sorry Mike, I'm not being very clear, am I? I mean, there's a group on the ship - our ship - who seem maybe a little bit … over-critical … of the officers. Maybe a bit … I don't know, subversive? Just makes me jumpy that's all. Muttering stuff about the Admiralty, the Home System Government. That kind of stuff. And I'm talking serious stuff, Mike, not just the usual gripes, you know, like everyone has. Seems maybe they're not as committed as the rest of us. Know what I mean?'

'Not sure I do, Sanders. Sorry, man. Look, I can't say I got on with Johann very well. As far as I know he just zoned about with the other engineers. And I never heard any of them being "overly critical" of the officers, or the Admiralty. In fact, they seemed to get on very well with Lieutenant Blandin, the Second Officer. Besides, it's not a crime to criticise the HS government – is it?'

'No, it isn't Not at all, Mike. Sorry. I didn't mean to imply that. As for Lieutenant Blandin. Did you know he got a roasting from Ebazza, a little while back?' Mike shook his head.

'Yeah,' Sanders continued, 'word on the fusion pipeline is that she threatened to relieve him if he didn't shake up his act. Shortly after that he and his men arrested that guy, Havring.'

'No, I didn't know that, Sanders. I've been busy elsewhere and it's not really my business is it?'

'Well, I guess security on the ship could be said to be everyone's business, couldn't it? And you are the ship's Secretary.' Sanders smiled thinly. Mike felt he was being tested in some way. By this mascla? Surely not?

'I suppose, yeah, of course,' said Mike, 'but I don't keep a close watch on these things, unless there's a good reason. That's why we've got a Security Officer. And a Captain.'

'Oh, okay. It's just that – Havring? Seriously? Come on Mike. You don't really see him as the saboteur type, do you?'

'Suppose not.' Mike was starting to feel uncomfortable, but he didn't know why.

'That's why Admiral Tenak's looking into that matter as a priority,' added Mike, 'and I hope you're not going to say you think Tenak is somehow …'

'No, no, of course not, Mike. I have nothing but the greatest respect for the Admiral – and Captain Ebazza, too. The First Officer strikes me as one neat-type guy, as well. Thoroughly respectable. No, I wouldn't dare. Difficult for the top uniforms though, what with trying to convince the whole population of Oceanus of the need to move to another world. Takes up a lot of time, doesn't it? Still, at least the hypercomp problems seem to have stopped. That's the main thing, I suppose.'

'Good to know you trust the Admiral, Sanders. Guess you just don't like some of the engineers, though. Well, we've lost two of the best, so you don't have to worry about them anymore.' Mike couldn't help his tone of sarcasm.

Sanders looked slightly offended and his voice rose only slightly but noticeably, as he said, 'I didn't say I was worried about the engineers, Mike. I just have my doubts about one or two crewmembers, and one of them was Johann Erbbius. And I'm sorry he's dead. I really am, but after all, what was he doing out at your dig site that morning? The morning he and that poor femna, the local one, died? That's never been explained. Do you have any ideas Mike?'

'No, I'm afraid I don't, but it's not really my job to find out.'

'No, but you have your doubts, don't you?'

Mike didn't say anything. Sanders gave him a wry smile, suddenly stood and made for the door. He said, 'Anyhow, thanks for the chat. Got to go now. Hope to see you around.' He walked briskly to the door.

Not if I see you first, thought Mike. And he decided he would vary the times when he visited the canteen from now onwards. What a strange character. Well, he'd done his own research as well. Tenak had told him Sanders had come highly recommended, by the Captain of the Argonaut, the light cruiser he'd served on previously. He'd been in the service for only two years but had excelled at his duties and was regarded as an Alpha-class pilot, albeit lacking operational experience. But he felt there was something strange about Sanders that he couldn't quite put his finger on. Something distinctly odd.

Sanders had been right about one thing, though; Johann Erbbius's antics. Mike had never liked Johann and the man's behaviour had been disgraceful, particularly on the journey through the Purple Forest. He'd never even thanked anyone for rescuing him from the man-eating plant.

***

In the evening of the day he'd been approached by Dagghampton, Mike was contacted by Eleri. It was her second call, made by holo-vid, using the wristcom she'd been given. Mike always took her calls in his private cabin, a small but well-appointed room in the ship's rotating torus. In the holo-transmission Eleri appeared horrified at the cramped quarters, though, as yet, holo-comms still gave a relatively poor idea of the real reception location. Eleri would have been even more horrified, had she been there in reality, thought Mike.

Her first communication, on the ship's first day out, had enabled them to converse almost normally, with only a two second delay between one's person speaking and the other's reply. Today, the time lag was fourteen seconds; the ship now shooting away from Oceanus at around 28,000 kilometres per hour. That delay was growing irksome but Mike had warned her about this. From now on, and despite a steep drop in the ship's acceleration, the time delay would make two-way conversation impossible to manage. He suggested they resort to just sending each-other holo-vid messages, sometimes called "H-lets", emotionally straining though they both knew that would be.

Right now, Eleri appeared to stand a mere metre or so from his small bedside chair. So close and yet, so very far, he thought. Her lovely face, though slightly hazy, due to the increasing distance, was beaming with excitement as she told him of some amazing news from New Cambria. She was evidently brimming to tell him it had been found that the figure of the Native was *not a statue,* after all. They had discovered that it was an embalmed body. Mike gaped with surprise. It had also been confirmed to be a male after all. Eleri explained that the scientists had been unable to get deep body scans at first, the crystalline Cambrium of his case preventing it, interfering with the frequencies of most of the EM and sonic waves. The Antarctica's group had then, at great cost and effort, brought in positron and muon analysers, plus the heavy shielding required by that – and had finally obtained good quality images of the whole body. They showed that all the being's internal organs were intact, as well as the skeleton and musculature. There was no hint as to how he had died and it was not yet known how he had been so perfectly preserved, but Eleri said the detail in the images was astounding, going right down to the cellular level.

They also confirmed the Native was, as they'd guessed, much more like a reptile than a mammal, though his species was a very advanced, or, more correctly, a more highly evolved form of reptile, the like of which was completely unknown on Earth or Oceanus. That said, it turned out that he also had some mammalian characteristics, such as the extensive nipples. It seemed likely that while the females gave birth to live young, not eggs, the males may have played a part in suckling the young.

Perhaps more importantly, the being's brain was intact and as suspected, was very large and remarkably similar to that of a human brain. But its cortex appeared to have even more gyri and sulculi than in a human; these being the deep folds and fissures which hugely increased the cortical area. There were also several structures in its brain which completely defied identification at present.

Eleri said the teams were due to carry out more detailed scans of the brain. The one thing they didn't want to do was to try to get inside the crystal casing and disturb the body. That wouldn't be legalised for a long time, if ever; something the OA government scientists had emphasised, though there had been no real opposition from HS scientists.

Given that bthe Native was a body Mike found himself wondering whether Chanda had been right, in a way, when she'd said that a tomb might be at the bottom of the shaft. But it was clearly much more than just that.

The news about New Cambria poured out of Eleri in a constant stream, and Mike felt himself almost overwhelmed. He wanted to ask her to slow down but trying to interrupt, given the time lag, was pointless. He was, he had to admit to himself, a little envious of her but mostly he just missed being with her.

The next thing Eleri told him was that some of the tek people from The Monsoon and Antarctica had managed to open some of the strange cabinets in the hall of the Native. They'd done so without damage to the crystalline casings because they had found, only after many attempts to beam various EM frequencies at the objects, that simply running a suitably protected hand around some of the edges and corners caused a mechanical latch to release. It had been as simple as that. Sadly, this method had not worked on all the cabinets.

She said that the larger, angled cabinets, contained masses of what looked like circuitry – but composed of a crystalline substance which seemed like the transparent Cambrium. They appeared to be some sort of optical electrical system – but quite unlike the optical circuitry that was standard on all Navy ships.

Mike anticipated what she next said, when she advised, in her inimitable dialect, that the teks felt, 'The best so-guess is that the cabineties are computers, Mike darlie. But yet the mystery should now be as to why, if that they be, they should be so large, specialry as the natives do seem to have been so advanced.' Mike himself had guessed their true purpose and believed that the crystal circuitry itself pointed to the highly evolved nature of the "Native culture", since no-one had any idea how to make such materials. He also felt that the size of the computers must relate to some quality or properties, of which humans have absolutely no idea at present.

'I'll bet they'll be fighting like mad to reverse engineer those materials,' said Mike, when Eleri paused for breath. She had started to speak again but when it was obvious the signal from Mike had finally reached her she stopped, with a look of surprise – born of unfamiliarity with these comms.

Another, even longer time lag and then she said, 'Do you mean such they will be wanting to build something similar, darlie?' Mike just nodded.

Time lag again, then, 'Yes,' she continued, 'but I am yet thinking the main aim at the moment, is so to find out more about the Native's culture.'

He started to say, 'You, me and the rest of the team want to understand it but I'm sure there'll be many who want to use …. Never mind. Please carry on El. I can tell you haven't reached the end of your story.'

Long time lag, then, 'Pardonry? Yes, I thank you, darlie. The point is – they got into the cabinets which do hold the strange metal objects, too. You know, the ones you called "display cabinets", Mike? After taking caresome for the objects, and making 3D recordings of them, in place, they have actually been able to remove some.'

Time delay. 'Remove them?' said Mike, 'so what are they doing with them?'

Again, the frustrating delay, then, 'I am not sure my love. I think they are probing them yet with some light waves or something. I am not entirely still sure of how these things are done, Mike. I am sorry. They have not removed the objects from the Hall. The government scientists will not allow this.'

After a while Mike replied, but had almost forgotten what she last said, 'They're useful for something then. The government people, I mean.' He waited for her reply. Though he didn't want to see her transmission end, he was getting very worn down by the time lag and he was sure she was, too.

'Tis very excitingly Mike,' she said presently. 'but still, I wish you were here, or I was there, with you.' Eleri's eyes seemed to fill up, though it was slightly difficult to tell. The resolution was often fuzzy when there was rapid relative motion between sources. Mike didn't need to see detail too well, anyway. He could tell most things from his fiancée's body language. His own probably said, *why did I agree to this trip?*

They ended the frustrating conversation with a promise, from her, to keep him updated, and from him to say he had yet to feel he was really needed on this journey. She berated him when she thought he was suggesting Tenak was at fault, for trying to persuade him to go.

'Please do not be saying that about Unkling Arkas,' she said.

He said, '*Unkling Arkas*? Are you serious?'

Eventually she was heard to say, 'Oh, but yes, Mike. I think of him like that now. I have felt he is suchly good friend, to you as well as me, for long times now. He has been to Newcam a twice in the last few days. Wants to keep an eye on things on this island, he said. He has become a great friend Mike – but only that, Mike. Nothing more, so do not be getting any strangey-type ideas. Just an genuine unkling.'

Mike grinned. Good old Tenak. He's just keeping an eye out for her, he thought. All for the good. They wound up their conversation, holding back the emotion as best they could, till they could converse properly. That probably would not be for quite some time. Meanwhile, they would each have to be satisfied with just watching H-lets from each-other.

Chapter 44

ENIGMA

The research ship had turned so that it could fire its engines into its direction of travel, to decelerate. It was a long burn which caused the vessel to slow down enough so that Ra was able to pull it in close into it. En-route, the vessel came within a mere 5 million kilometres of Seth, the innermost of the three rocky planets in Ra's retinue. Beyond that, at a much greater distance, was Oceanus itself and then the last rocky world, the planet called Kumudu. Beyond that lay three gas giants forming the outermost part of the Ra system.

Named after the Ancient Egyptian god of chaos, Seth was a mere 41 million kilometres from its primary. Although appreciably larger than the mercury in the Solar System, Seth was just as hot and desolate, it's scarred and ragged surface sporting a gigantic furrow all around the northern hemisphere of the planet. It looked as though, many eons ago, a cosmic chisel of unimaginable proportions had scraped through its top layers.

The Antarctica's engine firing had been four and a half weeks ago, and as the ship sped along in its new orbit, one that would take it around the hemisphere of Ra not currently visible from Oceanus, a cluster of tiny objects were let loose from it, as though flung in a fit of anger. The objects glinted in the brilliant light from Ra, tiny sparks against the utterly black silence and loneliness of the interplanetary void. The tiny objects left the ship along wide, curving, trajectories; orbits which would take eventually them to their goal, Seth.

The result of the encounter was to prove an enduring mystery.

**

Mike was more than pleased to feel he was finally playing a part in this mission. The core science group on the Antarctica had, at long last, invited him to participate in their deliberations. And now he was sitting in at a meeting of the group, at a large oval table in the ship's main conference room. He was even wearing a dratted zarma.

And he was anxious. Not because of the zarma. He just hadn't done this for a long time. Not as a scientist. Would he be able to contribute in a valid and useful way? Maybe, maybe not, but it was better than being left out altogether. He'd been invited for a reason, after all. He still had the feeling he was just being impossibly impatient.

They group were looking at holos of a zone of space a long way out from the section of the ship's projected orbit, further along its wide arc; a zone which it would not reach for some two weeks. The holos were enhanced by AI, so they graphically showed the many kinds of radiation which had been detected; different frequencies all collected in layers, illustrated, in colour, like a cake with marbled layers.

One of the ship's scientists spoke. 'Well, this is your chance Mike. I'm sorry you haven't had a lot of time to study these but neither have we,' said Fardham Cicero Trammel, one of the ship's leading physicists, a man who wore a permanently ironic smile on his round, puffy, face. There were sage nods from most of those assembled. Trammel continued, 'So, to what do *you* attribute that type of gravity wave?'

Some sort of test, or just genuine curiosity, wondered Mike? Okay, he could deal with that. He took the time to look long and hard at the data before saying, 'Hard to be sure. I've never seen that sort of thing before.' He expected some gruff comments, possibly lampooning him for a lamentable lack of knowledge but, to his surprised relief there was a muted chorus of agreement. He was suddenly glad he hadn't jumped in with some half-baked theory, instead of admitting he just didn't know.

Captain Providius herself sat at the head of the table. She turned to him, and with a genuine smile said, 'That's what we all said before you arrived.'

She continued, 'The AI thinks we might be looking at a massive cloud of gas of some sort or, more likely, dust soot particles. Nothing like that seen before, in this system. And it is truly enormous. But the AI won't speculate about exactly what it is or why it's there. Does anyone here have any ideas about what it might be? Don't be afraid to speculate, Mike. At this point, I'd just like ideas.'

'That's the trouble with AI's,' said Mike, 'they're good at analysing but not so good at guessing, especially if there's a few, biggish gaps in the data. As for these waves, I'd say the AI may be right. Probably soot, but the spectral data sets make it look like the stuff – well, it looks like it's *incoming*, doesn't it?'

'Yes, yes, well, I think we already said that, did we not?' said Margus Vipsanius Marvelli, a thin, gaunt faced astrochemist, sitting opposite Mike. A few people shook their heads. 'No, we didn't?' he said. 'Oh alright. Sorry Michaelsonn. But, in that case, the real question is – where is it coming from?'

'There's nothing out there except … maybe …,' started Demestina Citheris Arkooda, a gaunt looking female planetary geologist. She stopped mid-sentence.

'Except … maybe … that vessel we saw some time ago out in the boondocks,' said Mike gently, smiling at Arkooda, 'you know, the one that produced the huge splash of gamma rays?'

She nodded, accompanied by a good- natured smile.

Marvelli piped up, 'I thought we all agreed that that was a natural event? What's this about a "vessel", suddenly?'

Providius spoke, preventing Mike from giving an immediate answerand gesturing toward him, 'This young man speculated, right at the start of the gamma ray event, that it was some sort of vessel. An alien vessel. I don't think it's as far-fetched as it might seem, but, naturally, I'd like to have more evidence. Lots more, I'm afraid. But we shouldn't rule it out.'

Mike nodded. She was a perspicacious woman, he thought.

'I'm far from convinced of the need for such an extravagant theory at this stage,' said Trammel, somewhat grumpily, 'but I accept that, unfortunately, we can't rule it out.' He paused for effect, then said, 'Though we probably will soon be able to.'

'I think that sounds pretty much like an unwarranted assumption, sir,' said Mike, drawing a surprised look from Trammel, who seemed, begrudgingly perhaps, to acquiesce.

'I'm assuming that the AI has done a quantum cascade spectral analysis of the incoming cloud?' Mike added. These guys are pussycats, he thought, compared to Navy staff, let alone Navy officers.

We're a bit too far from it, as yet, for that sort of sophisticated test,' said Providius, 'but the bad news, Mike, is that the cloud is on an intercept course with our own orbit, about two weeks from now. It's so big it covers a significant proportion of our orbit so we can't avoid it. But we'll certainly get a better idea what it is then. If it's soot, we needn't worry. If it's radiation of a type previously unknown…? Well, let's hope the ship's EM shields can deal with it.'

Mike suddenly felt very uneasy.

****

On a remote island back on Oceanus, Danile Hermington, standing in the now celebrated "Hall of the Native", was observing experiments being carried out on one of the solid geometrical objects taken from a so-called cabinet. This was a flawless tetrahedron; a three-sided pyramid, with equilateral edges, obviously constructed of some sort of metal alloy, composition unknown, and still shiny – after 8 million years! The object was one of scores found in dozens of cabinets. Most were in the form of the well known "platonic solids"; regular, geometric, 3D shapes, first described, in detail, by the ancient Greeks on Earth. All the cabinets and objects in the Hall had been found to be non-radioactive; essentially, inert.

The researchers had found that some of the other artefacts found had edges of unequal length and of these the longest edges were invariably no more than 40.7 centimetres long. The significance of that precise length was another mystery, albeit a small one. But then, all the artefacts were mysterious things. They were considered objects of some wonderment, simply because it seemed the beauty and the perfection of their proportions might be unrivalled. Not true, of course, but it was how it *felt*. There was a great eagerness to probe them, to discover their chemical compositions and investigate their crystalline structures.

However, there were to be, by dint of the Oceanus government, no attempts to drill into, or otherwise physically sample any of the objects. As it happened, most of the Janitra University and Home System scientists and engineers were similarly minded. No-one wanted to damage the things. And all experiments were to be done inside the Hall itself. None could be taken out of the environment in which they'd been found. Not yet.

The mysterious objects could be investigated only by probing them with various frequencies of light, mainly ultra short-wave X rays, and analysing the diffraction patterns produced in sensor equipment. Amazingly, these experiments had been able to penetrate only a few million layers of atoms deep into the few objects so far tested; merely "scratching their surfaces", in effect, but this had revealed the presence of giant, highly complex, molecules, arranged in a crystalline form similar to the mineral perovskite, back on Earth; a magnesium silicate which formed most of the planet's mantle.

To probe more deeply it was decided to move one of the objects onto a test bed and to use heavier equipment. Once the Oceanus government people had finally given permission they chose the tetrahedral object, absorbing Danile's attention, which had been transferred gently onto a large experimental bench, sited some distance from its cabinet. A small, tracked, robot had moved it and at the same time weighed it, very accurately. Strangely, the result didn't tally with the estimate derived from earlier measurements using X rays. It was much heavier. The conclusion was that it did not have a consistent crystalline structure throughout its interior.

Protective shielding in the form of screens made of a duralamium derivative, similar to the material making up starship hulls, had already been installed by scientists from The Monsoon and Antarctica. Much effort had been expended to get the screens down into the Hall and to set them up, but they were eventually placed around 3 metres from the test bench, completely surrounding it. Hermington had initially expressed worries about much of the testing but Eleri had done a good job of persuading him to go along with it. The government scientists had, in any event, not objected, so they were good to go.

Now, for some strange reason, Hermington seemed to have become more eager to participate than any time before. So he, Eleri, the other Oceanus scientists and a number of HS scientists, now assembled under the guidance of Professor Akromo and his senior from the Antarctica, Professor Thadian. Thadian, a large, square shaped man in his fifties, looked like an archetypal mad professor, sporting prematurely white hair and beard.

It had been Thadian's idea for all the participants in the experiments to wear zarmas.

Akromo expressed reservations about that, suggesting they were too sensitive and could cause problems for the wearers. He was overruled.

*

Senestris, Eleri and even Danile, had wanted to show their willingness to participate, so agreed to be trained in the use of the zarmas, despite their initial "Oceanus scepticism." Using them they could observe experiments in close-up, even from outside the screens, along with the others. They might also be able to contribute to the work being done on this object, after all.

And so it was that they all watched through the large protective windows of the screens, data also being fed to their zarmas, as the tetrahedron lay on the bench on one of its faces, with one vertex sticking up in the air. It was bombarded with X rays from a small machine no more than a metre away from it. Anyone hoping for immediate results was disappointed. The tests went on for several hours and Hermington admitted to Eleri that he'd given up on the thin streams of minimal data being sent to him, through the holo-vid feeds of his zarma. He said they seemed to dance perpetually in front of his eyes, but he stuck it out, as did Eleri.

The tetrahedron didn't seem to want to give up its secrets easily, so, again with permission, the Antarctica people decided to probe it more deeply the following day, by using an electron probe. The larger than life, and very persuasive, Professor Thadian, got the Navy scientists to bring down their compact "Distance High-depth

Scanning Electron Microscope". Known simply as a "DEM". The machine had to be brought into the Hall in pieces and assembled inside.

'It certainly isn't as accurate as ours,' Thadian had said, imperiously, 'but it's lighter and more compact and I believe it might have a wider frequency range.'

In Mike's absence, Lew had been tasked by Tenak with keeping a wary eye on the use of Navy equipment. The pilot observed the proceedings, zarma free, from some distance and he now whistled at Thadian's evident arrogance.

The probe, a device which fired a stream of electrons, was set up, like the X ray machine, one side of the bench, about a metre from the tetrahedron, with the probe's sensors on the other side. The machine then fired a powerful, tightly focussed, beam of electrons at the object, starting at the thinnest section, the tip of the object's upwardly projecting apex. The electrons in the beam, were, of course, invisible, as were those which left it but the streams leaving the object had been diffracted and the patterns they made were picked up by the sensors. The zarmas picked up the stream as well and generated data for their users, in the form of complex and garishly coloured images, overlain with graphics. Hermington's jaw dropped at the apparent beauty of it. But he and Eleri agreed they understood little of it.

The beam was to be slowly tracked down through the progressively thicker part of the object – but the process took a long time, even with the zarmas analysing the results as the process continued. Eleri, Danile and the many of the other participants started to take breaks.

Work had just resumed after a break when the whole apparatus shut down unexpectedly. It was said to be a problem with the electron gun. As a team of engineers went to work on it Eleri turned to Hermington and said,

'I am yet so thirsty, Dani. I need some slynth-juice.' She started off for "the refuge", a temporary structure put up some distance away. It was a reasonably spacious structure and contained some soft furnishings and refreshments. It had been built for the teams of scientists, engineers and other workers who now were full time investigators of the Hall, having well insulated walls. It provided welcome relief from the hubbub going on outside it.

'Want yet to join me?' she said to Hermington, who shook his head, smiling, as he sat on a small bench near the screens.

'Sorry, but I think they shall be continuing, soonest,' he said, 'and this is so fascinatio. Do you not think so?'

'Well now, yes and no. But I am yet pleased to hear you say such. I am not so into geolry, or physica, as are you. Yet look, I shall keep my zarma thing on, in case you want to bring me back quick.'

'I will,' he said, 'but you know the zarma will not be able to feed the full images to you. You will be behind two sets of protection – the screens here, and the walls of the refuge.'

'I know, but I am happy to be away from that object thing for a while.'

'You can tone down the imagery too, if you so want.'

Eleri smiled an acknowledgement as she wandered off.

The beam was restored, and Hermington and the others watched anew but as the beam tracked lower and lower down the object, Akromo could be heard, blurting into everyone's headset, that there was a clear change in the crystal structure. It was showing smaller and smaller crystals, indicating a different group of elements, seemingly embedded inside the larger structure.

'These atoms' he said, 'must be packed together more tightly than in the crystals at the apex,' he said, 'but they're too tightly packed, surely? What about the nuclear repulsive force?'

'But that explains the higher density that we calculated, first off,' said Thadian.

'Looks so that the images are deteriorating,' said Hermington, his zarma picking up his voice for the others, 'for the view seems ...dimmer ...'

'The beam can't probe so deeply into these layers,' said Akromo, 'so we might as well stop and ...'

'No, wait,' said another scientist, 'Look at that! What the hell is happening, now?'

'The thing's giving off ... particles,' said Thadian, with a voice full of shock.

'It's taking a while to analyse but …my zarma's suggesting they're … protinium particles!' came Akromo's voice.

Someone else said, 'Yeah, that's it. Anti-protonic hydrogen. Amazing.'

'So, what now is that?' said Hermington.

'Thadian answered, excitement mounting in his voice, 'It's … an exotic particle, where a proton and an anti-proton orbit each-other. A bound system.'

'Yes, yes, t'was known that these things can sometimes be produced by low energy collisions. Not so?' said Marcus Senestris, who now was also one of the Oceanus investigators.

'Yes,' said Thadian, 'and I can see they're producing decay particles around the equipment.'

'Just as well *some of us* insisted on these screens,' said Akromo, biting sarcasm in his voice.

'Alright, point taken,' said Thadian, 'but, don't you see what's happening here? This can't be right.'

Akromo gasped audibly, and said, 'Yes, my zarma's showing it now. The protinium particles … are … They're being projected a couple of metres before decaying. They're supposed to annihilate each-other in billionths of a second! What sort of tek? What can do this?'

'Whatever it is, the effect's dying down,' said Thadian.

Then, more surprises. The object on the bench gave off a bright amber glow in ordinary light, and, within the glow itself, an image bigger than the test bench itself, flashed into the air and hovered a short distance above it.

'What now? It looks like a …kind of … a sort of holo-vid scene,' said Akromo, his jaw, like that of most of the other participants, dropping loose.

'Yes, my zarma's magnifying it,' said Thadian, 'but it … looks like buildings of some sort. Yes, I can definitely see buildings in there. And something else.'

'It is, it is,' shouted Akromo, in a voice fairly trembling with excitement. He continued, 'but … it's a whole landscape … a whole landscape in miniature. Must cover ... well, looks like a wide area – on that scale. The zarma's suggesting about 20 klicks being represented over about 5 metres, here in the hall.'

'It's yet an urban landscape. Is that smoke? Can you see columns of smoke ... coming out of that ... from different places in it,' said Senestris, his voice brimming with excitement.

'Yes,' said Hermington, as excited now as the others, 'columns yet of smoke. I can see tiny fires burning ... different places. But the buildings. They look so weird. Wait, I can see ...'

*

He didn't finish his sentence because that's when everything went crazy.

*

From Danile's point of view, one second he was standing before the thick glass-like screen, gazing at the image of the miniature urban landscape being projected in front of his eyes by his zarma. The next, everything changed – spectacularly.

++++

[In the personal diary recording which Danile Senusret Hermington later completed, he described his experiences in full. He said that his view of the Hall of the Native seemed to disappear, and he gasped as he found himself standing on parched, compacted soil. The Cambrium floor of the Hall had vanished, as had the Hall itself, in a mere fraction of a second. He had no idea where he was, or how he got there. He remembered uttering an unintelligible cry of disorientation and bewilderment as he tried to take in the scene around him. Then cast his eyes down, trying to blot it out. But he couldn't.

He felt a deep, almost nauseating disorientation and instinctively pulled the zarma off his head. Removing it made no difference. He still stood on the burning hot sod and then was aware of a roaring cacophony raging all around him. Clouds of dust ravaged his skin and stung his eyes. The burning sun smote him, and a wild wind lashed him. He swayed. He certainly wasn't on New Cambria anymore. Couldn't be. His racing heart felt like it might burst from his chest at any moment, as he raised his head and saw a host of large, bipedal creatures swirl around him. They were strangely human-like, yet definitely not human, and they rushed around him, careening in every direction. Panicking? Yes, panicking.

These things were much bigger than a human and seemed to run with an unlikely gait. He said he eventually realised, in his febrile state, that they were nothing less than *living* examples of the preserved Native they'd found. But that being was long dead. These were very much alive. But Lord above, how could that be? How in all the Oceans could that possibly be? He clapped his hands on the sides of his head. Tried to shut it all out but still he couldn't.

The noise increased and Danile stood rooted to the spot, starting now to tremble with fear, as these beings, who he himself had named, "Reptiloids", gambolled about him. He described relief as he saw that they didn't seem to notice his presence. He could hear the fall of their claws on the ground, kicking up dust, as they ran around him, but yet the beings sounded remarkably light footed for creatures of their size. It would have been an entrancing spectacle were he not in the middle of it. But the whole thing was too much to take in. The heat, the dust, the sounds and sights. *The differentness.* He wanted to blot it all out and scream but inordinate curiosity forced him to keep watching.

He was grateful that the reptiloids had not noticed him. They were a frightening size, and their large mouths sported some fearsome teeth. But even so, ... what he took to be expressions of anger were not that at all. They were grimaces of sheer terror.

An incredibly loud noise hit him then, like that of a giant bullwhip cracking nearby, and it tore his attention away from the reptiloids, forcing him to gaze out, to the horizon beyond, straight ahead. Several hundred metres in the distance he could see a huge vehicle – possibly a spaceship? Yes, it was a spaceship – starting to lift off, amidst a dark brown pall of sand and dust. It was nothing like a Home System Navy ship. At that distance the thing was certainly large; perhaps eight, or maybe ten times the size of a Navy landing boat. The noise from its screaming engines seemed to pierce Danile's chest and a deep, disturbing, vibration rattled through the ground and filled his feet and legs.

Then, an horrific event. A huge, deep, shadow flashed over him and he looked up instinctively, spotting another vessel of the same sort, flying maybe only fifty or sixty metres above him. It looked even stranger from this angle, a thing full of facets and metallic excrescences. He watched it glide overhead and his eyes suddenly became unaccountably wet with emotion, even before the craft abruptly sprouted from one side a massive cloud of black, sooty, smoke. Seconds later there was an ear-splitting boom, and the sky went totally black. The ship had been hit by something. Bright orange flame billowed from it, the vessel exploding before his very eyes. He shut the sight out, but he could still somehow *feel* it happening, seemingly only metres above. He was overwhelmed with emotion and he knew he'd go mad if he couldn't find a way to block it all out.

An instant later he was aware of hands touching him – human hands. They were holding his arms, dabbing his forehead with a moist cloth. Dimly, slowly, he began to emerge from the place where he'd been and then he heard a familiar voice.

'Danile, Danile. Are you alrighting?'

It was Marcus Senestris. Hermington slowly opened his eyes and realised he was slumped on his knees on the cold floor under the bright lights which recently had been installed in the Hall. Around him stood colleagues from the combined science teams. Pandemonium seemed to have broken out. Everyone's face was etched with concern. Between them he spotted, further away, several other individuals, looking ashen and as confused as he was. They stood unsteadily, or, like him, remained slumped on the hard Cambrium floor.]

+++++

'How didst I get back here?' breathed Hermington, wide eyed, and continued, 'Did you fetch me? How did you find me?'

A few metres away Professor Akromo was being helped into a sitting position by two of his colleagues from the Antarctica, attending him fussily. Remarkably, he seemed able to collect his senses very rapidly and his face suddenly became animated with excitement.

'Those, those holo-vids must be some sort of transportation device,' he said, panting as though he'd been sprinting, 'but it was … instantaneous. God-all, that was so strange. Real disturbing.'

'But Professor,' said a young woman helping him, 'you didn't *go* anywhere. You've been here all the time. All of you, the ones ... affected, have been here all the time.'

Akromo started to argue but Lew Pingwei had reached them from where he'd been observing everything from a distance.

'She's right, Professor,' he said, 'I was some way from you, but I saw the whole thing ... from the point when you said you saw a holo-view. All you guys participating in this ... experiment thing ... well, you all just went sort of frozen and silent. Then you all just ... keeled over. Didn't know what to think. I got someone to pull the power on the whole rig. I reckon that's when you guys started to recover.'

Hermington said loudly, 'But manry, I be telling you, I was somewhere else. I was.'

Heads around him shook and Lew said, 'I'm sorry, Danile, but no, you didn't, man. None of you *went anywhere.*'

Lew then turned as someone emerged from the refuge some metres distant; someone looking dazzled. Everyone turned to see Eleri walk toward the group, holding her zarma in one hand. She seemed dazed. Lew rushed over to her.

'Okay,' she said to him, 'yet I am ... fine, I so think. What didst happen?'

Akromo was on his feet now. 'Did you ...? Were you taken somewhere else? Did you see ... things?'

'No, no Professier,' she said, with a confused expression, 'I was not ... taken anywhere. What e'er do you mean?'

Danile had struggled to his feet as well and, though he staggered a little, as if intoxicated, he went over to Eleri.

'El, what Professier .... means is that we ... well so, we thought we were somewhere else – for a while-time. I don't understand it but ...' he said, stumbling a little over his words.

Her brows knitted with concern. She went to him and hugged him.

'No Dani, I am fine,' she said, 'but now, what did happen to you? You look fargied. Come over to the refuge and sit down.'

But Lew approached the pair, saying he was keen that everyone connected with the "event", should go straight to the med bay – another small, prefabricated, building which had been set up close to the entrance shaft. He wanted everyone to get checked out and, by the looks of things, he wasn't taking no for an answer.

The team from The Monsoon, both those who had been "affected", and their anxious colleagues, who had not, began to wander over to the med bay. Lew had no authority over the people from the Antarctica but Thadian asked everyone to comply. The Oceanus people seemed to comply without question.

Everyone closely involved with the experiment soon gathered in the med centre, but Lew and Thadian contacted all the other scientists and tekies, from wherever they had been in the Hall, and asked them to join them. So it was that a crowd of about 30 gathered inside the prefab, filling it to capacity. The few med personnel there, mainly from The Monsoon, wound their way around all who had been affected and swept diagnostic e- instruments over their heads and bodies. The checks proved negative for everything except for anxiety and a few injuries caused by people collapsing where they had stood. The medics said they were lucky that none of those were serious. Some observers said that the afflicted appeared to have gradually "folded" onto the floor, rather than collapsing.

Lew announced that he was not going to describe the experiences of those affected as being "hallucinations", or anything similar, but instead he suggested they talk about "mental imagery". He asked all those concerned if they would be happy to describe their experiences. A few seemed reluctant but most were ready to speak and they told their tales, albeit self-consciously. They outlined their experiences as best they could, and it became clear that everyone's "vision" seemed to have had similar intense emotional content. This included Danile, one of those worst affected and nearly the last to speak. After giving his account he said to Eleri, nearby, 'I know that you didst have some experience too, El. Will you tell us about it too?'

'Yes, yes, I saw ... something,' she said, 'but t'was yet familiar to me, not strange-like. Not like yours. T'was a scene from my childhood. Like ... a flash of reminiscence. Only what you get when you hear or smell something that reminds you of a time ... a place in your past – but was more ... more real than that. Like reliving it completely, in the now-time.'

'A memory?' said Akromo, 'but can you tell us what memory? Will you share that?'

'Well, yes, okay so. I think t'was … I was running. Sort of skipping along. Like I did always when I was a tinie youngry. I was on my parentia's farm – as it used to be. That was good, felt good, but there was … something else. Something not so good … something in our barn, but …I do not remember more.'

'You didnar see the alien things? I mean, the things like the Native … the Reptiloid, here, … in this place?' asked a wild eyed Senestris. She shook her head, confusion still evident on her face.

'I experienced a sort of memory too, like Eleri,' said another scientist, a Home System tekie, who, like her, had decided to take a break. He'd been in the entranceway to the refuge at the time of the incident. 'It was nothing more than a sort of "flashback",' he said, 'but nothing much. A sort of … memory from one of my journeys through a conduit. Lasted a few seconds. Nothing more.'

'Were you wearing a zarma?' said Lew. The man nodded. 'Was everyone in here, *except me,* wearing a zarma?' he persisted. Everyone who had been affected in some way, confirmed they had.

'Of course!' exclaimed Akromo suddenly, causing one or two individuals nearby to twitch nervously.

'Nothing "transported" us away from here,' he said, 'nothing like some sort of … transporter beam thing. Something from yester-year science fiction. It was to do with the zarmas.'

'Yeah. I agree with that,' said Lew emphatically, 'and I'd say that the holos of the alien scene, or Native scene – whatever you want to call it – the one being projected by the tetrahedron, was the same scene as you all describe in your experiences. Okay, so maybe you all "saw" it from different perspectives. Danile, you saw a ship exploding. Marcus, you saw some sort of tower collapsing very close to you. You all saw different scenes, but they could all have been different parts of the alien holo vid which appeared. That holo popped up just before your …experiences.'

Hermington seemed to be staring into space but suddenly said, very loudly, 'Yes, deedly! Lew is yet right. I think I do know where we, sort of … went, in our minds.'

Akromo blurted out his agreement and Eleri chipped in, her own face a mask of shock, as she pointed to the experimental set-up, 'And I think I know too, Dani. I am thinking that you – no, your mind – your consciousness – was in there – *inside* the holo-vid, itself.'

******

Jennifer Providius spoke softly to the Antarctica's AI, as she stood on the ship's research deck,

'So, we've haven't re-acquired any data cascades, or any sort of signal, from two of the probes, after they disappeared behind Seth. They're effectively lost. Where are the other two?'

In a smooth, baritone, voice, seemingly emanating from all around the deck, the ship's AI said, 'We still have contact with them. As they were launched slightly later, they were 400,000 klicks behind the first two. Due to the apparent loss of the first probes those following have decided to vary their orbital paths toward Seth. They have also moved into higher orbits, so they will be twenty-five thousand kilometres above the surface, before we lose signals from them, as they pass behind the planet.'

'To what, do you – and they – attribute the loss of the first two probes?' asked Providius, her brow furrowed.

'The loss may have been caused by the planet's magnetic field, though my scans, and all previous ones, indicate that the field is very weak compared to that of the Earth, and Oceanus. But there may be some magnetic anomaly not previously detected, possibly exacerbated by the anomalous behaviour of Ra. Alternatively, there may be volcanism on the far side of Seth, which we cannot see as yet.'

Several members of the science team, including Mike, standing nearby, wore sceptical looks.

'Volcanism seems equally unlikely,' said Mike, 'cos there's been no detection of any activity in the mantle of this world since humans came to this system.'

'Yes, but Mike, no studies have been done in many, many years,' said Marvelli, 'and we, and The Monsoon, have been concentrating our efforts of Ra. Previous studies suggest that volcanism on Seth was very powerful in the deep past. If it has restarted, it could have disrupted the low fly-bys of the probes, especially in the absence of an appreciable atmosphere.'

'Well, maybe,' said Providius, 'but when Seth *was* studied its molten core was found to be tiny. It must have cooled enormously since its formation. Hence, the weak magnetic field.'

'It looks like we might have some answers soon,' said Arkooda, as they all watched a huge holographic globe of Seth appear, courtesy of the AI, which made it hover in mid-air, a couple of metres above the deck. Surrounding the group were wrap-around, hyper-definition screens, which enhanced the views of the planet, in close-up, churning out streams of graphic data. But the holo-globe was a historical view the planet which gave it the appearance of a bright amber and ochre coloured world, pock marked with impact craters of myriad different sizes. Wisps of haze clung to the planet's limb: the visible outer edge of the world. Contrasting with the pitch black of space beyond it the limb view betrayed a thin haze, a tenuous atmosphere, once much thicker but driven off by the heat from Ra, long ago.

The present, *real time* view of Seth appeared on one of the screens which ran from the floor to the ceiling of the deck, and this showed Seth as a huge, blisteringly bright crescent, the current view from the ship. That crescent showed the wispy atmosphere as a thin but roiling layer, illuminated by Ra from behind Seth. It made the crescent even brighter and left the bulk of the hemisphere facing the Antarctica, the largest part of the planetary disc, a dark, mysterious, inky mauve.

The ship's team had originally been looking for signs of damage on Seth's surface; anything which might have been caused by eruptions of Ra' upper layers in the distant past. The surface had likely not changed in five to ten million years, because of the cool core and solidified mantle. But, from more than five million klicks out, the science team had been, days earlier, surprised by flashes of light picked up from a single point on Seth's northern hemisphere.

The AI announced, 'As you will notice, the planet turns on a slightly inclined axis, once every 49.7 Earth-equivalent hours,' which was not something they needed to be told, but continued, 'and the bright flashes have been located as emanating from close to the planet's eastern limb, on the first and only sighting, and so, the locus will have quickly moved onto the side hidden from the probe's scanners as they travelled toward it. The eleven minutes of views they transmitted have not resulted in a resolution of the source of the light, nor in any solid data.'

This surprised everyone. Mike could also see that the scant sensor data had been badly distorted by some sort of interference, like static noise. Again, a surprise, given current technology. Mike pondered how it could be that the leading two probes had swung behind the planet and yet no signal had been received from either after the period of approximately twenty minutes it should have taken for them to re-emerge from behind Seth. Although the holo-view showed all parts of the planet's globe, based on data already known, the representation couldn't show the positions or progress of the probes, then a matter of probabilistic prediction, until they reappeared. They never had.

Now, over the globe holograph, and on the flat screens, the positions of the two remaining probes were highlighted with large, bright blue markers, or "tags", the spacecraft themselves being invisibly small in comparison with the planet.

'I could, I suppose, order them to deviate,' said Providius suddenly, 'then make them do a burn to put them into a wide parabola around Ra, but it seems very unlikely we'll lose these two as well.' There were nods of approval.

I wonder, thought Mike.

Their orbits had already taken the probes over the eastern limb of the planet and they were five minutes away from disappearing over that horizon. The blue tags suddenly winked out. There was a soft chime and combined graphics and data streams flashed up in the air above the HD screen views, but they were distorted and broken up, like tossed confetti.

'What just happened?' said Providius, looking shocked again. 'What was it this time?'

'Unknown,' said the AI, 'as all cascade data, and contact, has been lost with the probes.'

'We can see that,' said Providius, with some impatience, 'so speculate!'

'The signals were distorted 4.304 seconds before all contact was lost. The most likely explanation is electrical failure of the on-board comm buses. Cause of failure, unknown.'

'The same failure on both vehicles at the same time? Are you being serious?' said an irritated Providius.

'You asked me to speculate,' said the computer, in an almost, but not quite, indignant tone.

Mike had never seen the captain looking so agitated. She was normally a model of almost practiced serenity. There had been many strange anomalies on this mission and, despite his painful separation from Eleri, he was, at this moment, immensely excited, almost as much as he'd been in the Hall of the Native. And he was very glad that he was here, now, on this vessel, playing a part in this.

He'd have time to regret that soon enough.

*

Everyone on the bridge of the Antarctica stood in stunned silence, eventually broken by Marvelli.

'I'm supposing,' he said, looking relatively composed, 'that we're going too fast in our own orbit to brake – to swing by Seth. High by-pass, maybe? Stay out of trouble?'

Mike felt a pang of alarm. Looking askance at the scientist he said, 'Really? Do you want us to "disappear" as well?'

'Thank you, Mike,' said Providius, 'exactly right and, in any case, we're going too fast to divert at this stage without using up an unacceptable proportion of our fuel. I'm afraid the mysteries of Seth will have to wait for another pass, some other time. Besides, there's something even more mysterious dead ahead. Something that a diversion won't change.'

'Precisely,' added Fardham Cicero Trammel, 'Didn't you know, Professor? Mike? The inbound cloud of soot particles has broadened out. It's about two hundred million klicks across now and nearly five hundred million long. Which means that the ship's orbit will intercept it much earlier than anticipated.'

Mike had that horrible feeling of doom again, as he'd done when he first found out about this strange cloud. He'd been concentrating so much on the encounter with Seth over the last few hours, he'd almost forgotten about it. He saw the responses of the others around him and his own enthusiasm for this mission began to slip, as he thought more deeply about what might happen during the intercept.

'But any damage, well, that would depend on the density of the cloud, right?' he said, feeling slightly shaky, 'and the fields from our superconducting coils should shield us pretty well, shouldn't they?'

People began silently filing out of the science station, including Providius, who smiled wryly at Mike and as she passed him, said, 'I'd agree with you, if we juat knew what those particles were.'

Mike had guessed this trip was going to be eventful, but he'd never guessed just how much.

Chapter 45

FINAL CONFIRMATION

It was during Eleri's fifth transmission to Mike when she related the shocking news about the "incident" involving the holo-vids, in the Hall of the Native. Her message was a "H-let", as Mike and most people labelled them; they represented a super-advanced HD, fully 3-dimensional format, using cascade tek. But the name harked back, partly, to the days of paper letters of old; the old "notelets".

Eleri's athletic figure appeared to stand squarely in front of him, in his cabin, but her eyes were focused on the holo-camera before her, for she could not see Mike, or his surroundings. That would have to wait for his reply.

So, Mike had been unable to do anything other than listen, albeit raptly, to her astounding story. She related how an experiment had caused a holo to mentally envelope members of the investigating team and how the holos had revealed disturbing scenes from what was thought to be the history of the Natives; scenes which evidently happened in the very distant past but may have been the "most recent" history of the beings who had inhabited Oceanus. But first, she related, in a rush of words, which seemed to leave her almost breathless, the disturbing nature of the "mental imagery", suffered by Danile, Senestris, Akromo and the others. She described how it was first thought that their minds, or consciousness perceptions, had somehow been *pulled into* the holos, themselves. They had experienced the scenes as if they had actually been there when they were filmed, physically seeing it and hearing it all happen around them. But more than that, it was as though they could feel the whole thing, through their senses, their skin, their bones and muscle. Most of those affected had even been able to *smell* their surroundings.

Perhaps most distressing, was the experience most of them had, of feeling the emotions which could be said to be appropriate to what they witnessed, as though they had been placed inside the minds, or perceptions – of the Native beings. Eleri said that Hermington and most of the others would probably have been emotionally affected anyway, to some degree, by the disturbing scenes, if they had been there at the time, but everyone had found the imagery difficult to understand and confusing. And yet, they still reported feeling emotions far beyond what could be expected. It was, they'd said, almost as if they *knew* the Native beings who were a part of those events all that time ago; surely an impossibility? But seemingly not.

After the "incident" the decision had been made to abandon the use of the zarmas, as they seemed to have mediated the "real life" holo transmissions from the alien artefact, in ways not yet understood. Akromo and Thadian were working on the assumption that the astoundingly long lived protinium streams had been the wave carrier, which had been picked up by the zarmas, then perhaps converted, electromagnetically, into something like brain-stim. It was theorized that an as yet unknown form of subliminal, psycho-active effect had been produced by quantum tunnelling within the brain. It was being theorized that the brains of the Natives must have had certain similarities with those of humans. But shielding and distance from the experiment, definitely had had an ameliorating effect.

Mike was completely entranced and momentarily forgot about the forthcoming threat to his own existence, as he listened to Eleri's story. She said progress had been made when the team had set up auto-cyber holo-cams, which could operate within the shields, and were always now kept in place. The robotics transmitted the alien "scenes" to ordinary holo projectors, which, after extensive testing, were found to be safe for viewing by humans.

As Eleri's story continued Mike became alarmed as to how badly *she* might have been affected by the Native's holos. Eleri had gone on to say how Akromo had blamed himself for not spotting the potential dangers earlier, yet it was Thadian who had insisted on the use of the zarmas, against Akromo's advice.

Finally, Mike almost breathless with a mixture of curiosity and anxious concern for her, Eleri admitted, reluctantly, that she had also been affected but, thankfully, only marginally. She had been wearing a zarma but had been sheltering some distance away in the team's refuge. That had "saved her," she said. Mike wondered about that. But, she said, people without zarmas, and even more distant, had been completely unaffected. An AI unit from the Antarctica had calculated that the disturbing effects produced by the alien holos probably varied with the inverse of the cube of a person's distance from the hologram. So, a person twice as far away as the nearest was affected eight times less than them. At least, that was the guess, because no machine could be precise about how much any one person had been affected. It was all based on interrogation and psychometric assessment of those concerned.

Eleri said that the long-term psychological effects on the human mind had become a matter of great concern and tests were currently being carried out by Home System Psychromotherapists. Eleri said that Danile, with whom she had had most contact, seemed fine. Although he had experienced some nightmares since the event, he had not dwelt on them. He'd said they hadn't involved the Reptiloid beings.

When Eleri's detailed missive had finished, she said her heartfelt farewell, asking for his early reply. Mike sat quietly thoughtful for a long time. He felt stunned. This whole mission, the reluctance of the Oceanus people to accept the truth about their star; the discoveries on Newcam; the weird happenings *out here;* all seemed too strange and disturbing to begin to comprehend. His mind began to spin with it all. And on top of that, he missed Eleri like he was missing an arm. He shook himself out of his reverie and set about recording a reply to her. But he worried how much he should say about *his own* situation. Should he warn her about the potentially impending disaster faced by the ship?

His message began, naturally enough, with his regret at not being with her, a sentiment given added poignancy by the current predicament of the ship, and his concern over her experiences. But he wanted to know more about what she had seen, in the flashback she'd described. He wanted reassurance but was also hungry for more information. As for his own situation he hinted only that those on board were a little concerned about a vast cloud of particles in the ship's path, which it must cross. He said little more, though, in reality, he'd wanted to warn her to expect the worst. But there was nothing she could do anyway. There was no point in worrying her.

At the end of the missive he pondered aloud on the question of whether the momentous discoveries on Newcam, and those being on board the Antarctica, were, in some strange way, linked. Then, moments after concluding his transmission, he dismissed such thoughts. A long time after the holocam switched off, he felt the physical gulf between him, and his lover, as if it were a huge hole in his own heart – and it hurt like hell.

He didn't yet realise it, but it would only get to hurt more in the coming weeks.

**

Three weeks after Eleri's first piece of incredible news, Mike picked up a new H-let from her. This time, El's image appeared to be sitting on a low stool, in her own office. She was somewhere on Newcam, but she didn't say where. She was more upbeat about herself than before and there was some very good news. Home System medics had carried out exhaustive tests on her and all the others affected by the alien holo-vids.

Those worst affected, including Danile, were announced as having no detectable physical brain trauma and no apparent psychological damage. It was thought there would probably be no lasting, deep seated, psycho- disturbance. Eleri had complained a little about the intrusive nature of some of her psycho-evaluations but had accepted it as necessary. They had compared tests done a few hours after the incident with others done a couple of days before her H-let. They felt there were no lasting effects and no damage. Despite their prognoses, they warned that very long-term effects still couldn't be ruled out completely – for any of them – particularly those who'd seen themselves "inside" the holovid field. In her case, they had asked her report anymore "flashbacks", or anything she thought strange, immediately.

Full of admiration for her upbeat report Mike then saw Eleri's face turn bleak as she gazed down, then she stared up at the holo-camera, His heart jumped. More bad news, he thought. What now?

She then related a story so bizarre that the thoughts it engendered remained with him for a long time. The science teams, she said, had been examining the Native holos for weeks, by way of the "filtering" process of the cyber-cams. It had taken a long time before they'd replicated the *precise* conditions which had led to the first Native holo "eruption" and they had taken things slowly. Finally, they had done it and had controlled the experiment enough to be able to produce coherent holos, which were then robotically filmed and reproduced in "flat" form.

By the time of her transmission they had examined about 30% of the geometrical artefacts in the Hall and most had "contained" as many as twenty holo-vid sequences. Some were approximately two hours long; others only two minutes. Many had been watched and catalogued but many were still to be studied. All had to be interpreted but all seemed to tell a long and detailed visual story of what had happened to the Native's own civilisation, long ago. It was starting to get easier to follow the story, as a chronological sequence. Each artefact produced one kind of sequence, but the events in the different artefacts were being linked to each-other, by the AIs, to produce a coherent and consistent "history".

The Native people's narrative was thought to cover a time period of many decades and included hundreds of different scenes. The Reptiloids were seen in many different situations, ranging from working in some sort of control room setting to more "civic" types of scene. There was no sound but there were straplines containing hundreds of different, very complex, data and what were evidently language symbols. Though not yet interpreted, said Eleri, there was confidence the AIs would solve it soon.

The vids included views of a star which had been positively identified as Ra, Ra, often appearing through instruments of some sort. It appeared to swell very slowly in the sky and it was assumed the observations had taken place over a lengthy period of time. But the images could not be more indicative of Ra's instability.

There were also extensive scenes of a visually disturbing nature, similar to those "experienced" by Hermington and others but now no longer having the deleterious effects, of course. There were scenes of social disruption, including conflict, possibly wars, between different groups of Reptiloids and there were often scenes of Natives who appeared to be firing large-scale energy weapons at each each-other.

Although first seen as internecine struggles it had become apparent that this was looking more like the results of planet-wide panic and ensuing anarchy. Many scenes featured deserted settlements; towns and cities of the ancient Reptiloids. And many holos showed the beings trying to shield themselves from the fierceness of the sun; others showed distressing scenes of crowds suffering from radiation burns. The story in these scenes was at once horrifying but fascinating; the detail of the Native civilisation thus revealed, both breathtaking and heart-rending.

Although intrigued, Eleri was sad because of the suffering the Natives had endured. As she spoke of this her image started to break up because of the ever-increasing distance from Oceanus and because of the ship's closeness to Ra. She said it was obvious to all that the Natives had been unprepared for the damage let loose by the star, and she shuddered at the scenes of destruction on the planet's surface. Most of the scientists and analysts felt, however, that the Natives were aware of the dangers much earlier than humans in the present era but may still have been caught out by the fierceness and speed of the changes.

After a particularly irritating couple of minutes of severe interference, Eleri's image, much deteriorated, came back on-line. She was saying, '…. telling you, my love, that despite the excitement, I am growing weary of seeing so much utter destruction as so depicted in the Reptiloid films. In 'tween the vid activations we can go down and do our work in the Hall itself, but I yet hate going down in that one - personry elevator they have installed in the shaft. They did not wish to disturb such dome structure by trying to dig a larger shaft. Said it would take too long to cut into the cambrium, anywayin. But I have still to hold my breath so hard and think of other things every time I go down. Think of nicely things – like you and me, together, as we were. And will be again, darlie.

'Tis now time for me to say good-morrowbright, Mike, love. I must yet say, first, I think every person with common-right sense, knows that this planet is doomed. Tis certain that the last time Ra erupted its surface, it fair did wipe out much of the land life and some in the seas. Most recent of Native holos do make it clear that they did leave this star system, but these holos are still being worked upon. Your people were right all along. True that I, myself, have not doubted it since first I met you, tis terror-some to see the evidence "in the real". Wherever you are in space, I wish you safety in what you are doing, my great-love. You know how much I miss you. I would still gladly give away all this excitement and all this knowledge to see you and hold you to me again.'

Eleri's image faded then, her whole body seeming to evaporate in front of him. Anyone using holo-vid communication was used to this and before he'd found Eleri, it had never seemed disturbing to Mike. But that wasn't true any longer. He found he was cursing himself for deciding to go on this mission and sat for a long time in moody contemplation. But he knew he was stuck with it. He worried he'd go insane – if there was time to do that, given what was coming.

******

A week after Eleri's extraordinary message, the Antarctica passed behind Ra, as seen from Oceanus, and that made any EM transmission, to or from the planet, impossible, for some hours. Mike began to feel cut off from what he had come to think of as "home", in a sense he hadn't experienced before. It would be over soon, of course, but not before the ship had encountered the massive cloud of "soot". Except that it no-one really believed it was soot.

As the ship neared the "zone of encounter" the Antarctica's AI confirmed that the particles were not, in fact, soot. What a surprise, thought Mike, grimmacing inwardly. The machine suggested, though it gave a warning that this was speculation, that the particles might be made of a transuranic element, one of those very heavy but normally very short-lived elements beyond mass number 92 in the Periodic Table. The alternative possibility was an alloy of exotic elements from the inner transition metals. The particles appeared to vary in size from a nanometre, up to a millimetre across and seemed to be covered with molecular carbon deposits – which is why they'd originally been classified as "soot". It was agreed by those on-board the ship that the cloud's extremely high speed, of nearly twenty thousand *kilometres per second,* and the organic carbon, had hidden the true nature of the particles very effectively. The ship's AI was clearly still unclear about it and that spooked everyone.

Mike continued to suggest that the particles might have an artificial origin and he accrued more followers in this, but no-one could even begin to come up with a credible idea as to why a massive cloud of artificially produced particles would be out here. And why should they behave like a soot cloud of the sort given off by the atmospheres of very ancient stars. But such a cloud, if driven off the atmosphere of a star, would have become a rarefied, expanding shell of dust. It would have been dissipated to the point of almost being unnoticeable by the time it reached the Ra system – certainly not the dense mass this one was – and not travelling at such a phenomenal velocity. This cloud thing was travelling so fast Mike was sure its component particles would have become slightly enlarged in size and mass by early relativistic effects.

A bigger surprise shook the crew when the Antarctica's powerful EM shields were switched on. These were normally engaged when the ship travelled at high velocity, on the way out to transit zones. They prevented potentially disastrous collisions with small particles, such as micro-meteoroids and yes, soot, and they deflected dangerous radiation. They'd been used recently, around Oceanus, to protect the ship from the storms from Ra. Now, it was hoped they would deflect the soot particles but, given the unknowns, no-one could be sure.

This was still, potentially, a life-or-death situation, thought Mike, who, though not considering himself a religious person, found himself wondering whether he should pray to his "Maker" in the days leading up to the encounter with the cloud. He berated himself for that – and for using that term, "Maker" in the first place. It was a throwback to what was considered by many, more superstitious times, yet again like many, he used it mostly without thinking. All the same, times like these made him wonder.

As the time of encounter neared a kind of hush descended on the entire ship's complement, most people appearing to keep to themselves. Everyone spoke in muted tones and many spent a lot of time in their own cabins. This was not the first time Mike had been in a sticky situation in the Ra system, but he hadn't felt quite so helpless as he did now. The ship had to pass through the cloud, whether those on board wanted it or not, since its orbit would intersect at some point or another, regardless of whether they widened or narrowed the vessel's orbit.

As the time of "intersection" drew closer and, despite the sense of doom, most of the scientists seemed determined to bury themselves in the scientific aspects of the event. It was unprecedented, after all. As the event drew near two of the ship's complement; a male scientist and a female tekie, had nervous breakdowns and had to be confined to the sick bay, heavily sedated. Although it hardly helped general morale, no-one despised them for their "psycho-crashes". Only the desire and hope to return to the arms of Eleri kept Mike sane, he felt, and forced him to retain a small degree of optimism.

For the actual encounter Mike had elected to sit with the main group of scientists, who gathered in the primary conference room once more, ready to watch the situation unfold on the Antarctica's external vidcams. He felt his nerves building as the cloud approached but, like most of the others, he tried to focus on the science. Inside him he was screaming, though he didn't want to show it to these people. They all seemed much braver than him.

Captain Providius and most of the senior officers had decided to stay together on the bridge hoping against hope that if something went wrong, they and the AI might be able to "pull a rabbit out of a hat".

Mike found himself pondering that descending the shaft in the dome on New Cambria, had been a cinch compared to this. Yet, as there, he found himself becoming more and more excited by the discoveries that might fall out of this incident, if the ship survived.

With seconds to go, he began to reflect on all the mistakes he'd made in his life but – again berated himself. There was no point in going through this sort of mental exercise, but, somehow, he just couldn't help it. By the glazed looks in the eyes of most of the others present he guessed they were probably having similar thoughts. No-one spoke – at all. That didn't help in any way, but what was there to say?

He watched the screens as the ship's AI counted down to collision with the leading edge of the dust cloud. The tension in the room and aboard the whole ship couldn't have been split with a hatchet. Mike felt his stomach knotting and twisting like a demonic boa constrictor. But he tried to ignore it. He suddenly wished he'd been able to say goodbye, properly, to Eleri, but these kinds of thoughts were no help now.

**

Although there is no sensation of motion aboard a spacecraft travelling along an unvarying trajectory, Mike could almost feel, almost visualise, in his mind's eye, the ship speeding, rushing, toward this massive, palpably dense, cloud of particles.

Then something extraordinary happened. The encounter was still nearly eight seconds away when the AI announced that the cloud had changed its shape. It had broken apart, effectively splitting into two parts, such that a plane of clear space had opened up! Not daring to breath, everyone looked at each-other, puzzled and astounded expressions all around.

As the time of encounter came – and went, the AI announced that the ship had, in effect, passed between the two parts, which had formed "sheets" on either side of the Antarctica. And neither of the sheets had hit the ship's outermost EM shield. The expected bow shock had simply not happened. As if that weren't enough, the hyper-comp then reported that the cloud sheets had simply joined back together, forty thousand klicks "behind" the Antarctica, as the vessel continued on with its journey, unhindered. A few seconds later the AI said it had lost the signal from the cloud in the radiation glare from the star.

The relaxation of tension in the room was as physically tangible as the twanging release of an arrow from a bow. A palpably solid feeling of collective relief emanated from everyone.

'What in the fegging galaxy d'you make of that?' said Marvelli, ashen faced.

Expletives abounded then. One or two people looked like they were going to be physically sick.

'Shit me,' said Mike. He hoped he hadn't, though.

The Captain's voice came over the intercom, 'Alright everyone, that was rather close. But I think we just got lucky. I know I'm just amazed to be still - here, and I'm sure you are too. But it would have been nice to have got some real data – if only for the trouble we've all gone through. Unfortunately, it looks like the hyper-comp wasn't able to get any good close-up data on the cloud. Either it was travelling too fast or … well, I don't know. The signs are that, somehow, it radiated some sort of signal ahead of itself, to confuse the hell out of our instruments. I'd say I imagined that, but the AI seems to think so too.'

'Maybe it produced some sort of quantum super-foam,' said Mike, almost bubbling with released tension. 'You know, a kind of macro-projection of the quantum foam that fills the Universe at the Plank scale' he continued, 'but it's just a wild guess, I suppose.' He knew he was reaching in the dark but, to his surprise, his suggestions weren't dismissed out of hand.

'Thank you, Mike. I'm willing to take anything right now,' said Providius. 'and just so you know, the AI says you may have a point. What it can't say is where in the shit-verse the cloud's gone now. Back into the quantum foam? It hasn't had time to reach the star's outermost atmosphere, so it can't have been swallowed by Ra. We'll have to keep the whole of the star, and the zone all around it, under constant obs'. One thing seems clear. That "cloud" was just really – obliging – like it wanted to avoid hitting us. I just hope we can get to learn more about it. Meanwhile, please relax gentilhomms. I applaud your courage and fortitude throughout this matter. We will start an engine burn in thirty-four minutes – and … counting. With the gravity assist from Ra, that should kick us back toward rendezvous with Oceanus.'

****

A few days after the encounter with the cloud Mike received another transmission from Eleri. In the meantime, he'd sent her one, telling her all, or *almost all*, about the particle cloud. At this distance, being the furthest the ship had gone from Oceanus, the holo-vid signal had become too weak and dispersed to be received in 3D format. It was a blow to Mike to be able to see her in 2D only, on a flat screen, but that situation would probably persist for only a few weeks.

In her transmission Eleri expressed horror at the situation Mile had found himself in. She would not have approved his journey, she said, had she known about beforehand. It was easy to say that with hindsight, he thought. Unfortunately, the cloud had just turned up out of nowhere, like most nasty surprises.

For her part, Eleri surprised Mike again, by saying that she was speaking from the estreme eastern side of somewhere called "Jungle Island", not from New Cambria.

He'd suspected a change of location because of the unfamiliar background he'd spotted outside her window, as seen on the screen.

Then she revealed where she was. She had been ferried to Janitra first, by Lew Pingwei, and had then flown herself to the island, over 900 klicks south east of the mainland. She was delivering laboratory supplies there. Jungle Island, she said, was a large, heavily forested island, as its name suggested, and populated only by a few natural historians and scientists. As she had hinted previously, she'd had enough of the Dome and Newcam, but she was keeping in regular contact with the discoveries there.

One strange bit of news was that a couple of scientists from The Monsoon had "volunteered" to be directly exposed to the alien holos, so they could learn even more about the Reptiloids and their world. They thought it would be a worthwhile experiment, but Tenak had not approved it. Some of the Antarctica's scientists left on Newcam, had wanted to do it too and had, at first, protested that they were not bound by Tenak's authority, but the Admiral had threatened to withdraw the co-operation of the Navy and use of their equipment. That had ended the matter – for now. More generally, there was a consensus that a better understanding of the way the holos had been produced was first needed. That was likely to take some time.

The science teams were, she said, still having problems accessing the data stored in the metal spheres, so she had decided she needed to get away for a while. It was not just because of her anxiety at using the shaft elevator. She also found the Hall gloomy and now, rather sad. It was the last remnants of a once proud and hugely advanced civilisation.

Mike felt she was selling herself short when she added that she felt she couldn't contribute any more to the question of the Reptiloid's biology, though she might be right when she opined that the artefacts and the astronomy were beyond her ken. However, he reckoned she was simply fed up at Newcam and wanted a change.

So, at long last, she had decided to return to studying the biology of Oceanus, as it is in the "here and now-so", as she put it. There was much work to be done, and it seemed more important than ever.

Perhaps now the authorities would finally endorse evacuation as well, she said.

But, knowing these people, thought Mike, who could tell?

Eleri's last bit of news concerned the mystery of how the large machinery and cabinets of the Natives had been put into the Hall in the first place, when the only access seemed to be that narrow shaft. Obviously, there was another entrance. But where?

Now, using powerful tools, she said the science teams had found another void beyond the Cambrium wall at the far end of the Hall, and an even bigger void directly underneath it. All the walls of the Hall were forty metres high and most of the far wall was many metres thick, but in one small location sensors indicated it was only about half a metre thick, with a void was the other side.

The HS teams had wanted to drill a small hole in the wall to test the atmosphere the other side, then send a probe through, but the OA government scientists had been obstructive again. But she said, sounding more upbeat than for a while, they'd all sort it out between them. Mike thought that maybe the change of location might be doing her some good, after all.

She was enjoying her flying and although "Unkling Arkas" had offered her the use of the landing boat to get between Jungle Island and the mainland, she had insisted on doing her own flying. It was typical, thought Mike, that she wanted to do things her own way. Whilst he admired her he wondered if she might be better off, in the long run, taking up "Unkling Arkas's" offer.

It appeared she was flying a much larger aircraft than the one she'd taken to Fire Island; this one being a twin-engine ship, called "Arcingbird", after the large, graceful, swooping birds that populated the coastal cliffs off Bhumi-Devi. The Arcingbird was especially useful for carrying large crates full of specimens, plus lab' supplies, and containers of tissue and gametes, frozen in liquid gases.

Mike was amazed by the way she didn't seem to mind the confines of an aircraft's cockpit on long flights. The one to Fire Island had been a relatively short hop and the cockpit quite large. She had once explained that she was okay with long duration flights, because she was concentrating on the flying. And, in any case, she could see the whole wide world just outside the windshield.

Mike felt pleased that she was now doing something she felt was a significant contribution to the future of the flora and fauna of Oceanus. The thing that had to be done now was taking care of the safety of the human population. As he left his seat to walk to the refreshment locker he hoped there would be no more holding back on that, but then he suddenly felt queasy. Pain, which quickly became severe, began to course through his chest, like liquid fire, and there was a sudden, horrible, dizziness in his head. What the feggery was going on? He sat down again with a thump. He hadn't drunk any alcohol for weeks, so it wasn't that. The crew of this ship frowned upon intoxication as much as the officers on The Monsoon.

Perhaps it was something he'd eaten? He tried to stand up again and the pain in his chest got worse. A heart attack? Surely not, he thought, but, with a rising sense of panic he felt the pain worsen dramatically until he found it difficult to breath properly. Then the pain began to course into his stomach. Doubling up, he slumped to the floor. Despite the rising sense of panic, the pain and discomfort, he had the presence of mind to tap his wristcom four times, in quick succession; a code to make it transmit an emergency call to Captain Providius. Then he folded up on the floor and passed out.

Chapter 46

ARCINGBIRD

Eleri Ambrell's image appeared on Arkas Tenak's 2D screen, as he stood in his private quarters aboard The Monsoon. The restriction on holo imagery from the planet was still in place and, in any case, Eleri's current base on the eastern tip of Jungle Island was not equipped to carry holo-tek.

'Tis so good to see you, Unkling,' said the young woman, smiling widely, with a genuine warmth.

'My goodness,' said Tenak, 'did you say, Unkling? I don't think …I didn't… Uncle?' He actually blushed.

'Oh, I am sorry yet,' said Eleri, 'I am thinking I have embarrassed you. I thought Mike had probably told you … but yet … no. Please to forgive me.' She looked down momentarily.

'Nonsense, Eleri. No need to apologise. I feel very honoured you should think of me as an uncle. Oh, and that puts me in some very distinguished company, I believe. Not sure I deserve that.'

'In certaince you do. And I do think of you as an "uncle". Twas not mere jest.'

'Well Eleri, I don't actually have a niece but if I could choose one, I can't think of anyone I would rather have.'

'I do thank you, Admiral. Anyways, so now, may I ask why you have honoured me with a call to my wristcom? So sorry, I should be saying, *your* wristcom.'

'No, the wristcom is yours to keep, Eleri. As for the call, well, I'm sorry but I have to be the bearer of some bad news.'

Her face fell immediately.

'Tis not Mike, is it? What'ere's happened, unkling?'

'Don't panic. I'm sorry, I didn't mean to scare you. But it is about Mike. He's okay – well – going to be okay. It looks like he got ill again. Probably the after-effects of the grotachalik attack. Remember – our med bay warned that he might suffer recurrences?'

'Oh, my Maker. Are you yet sure he is okay? Is he …in another hypso-sleep? I mean, coma?'

'He is … unconscious – most of the time but he's comfortable. There were a few nasty moments but he's making a slow and steady recovery, so please try not to worry. I don't have a lot of info myself, right now, but I'll describe it the way it was put to me. The med-surgeon said, "he is stable and certainly out of danger". They wouldn't say that if it weren't true, Eleri. And El, we have a lot to be grateful for. He's in good hands. Padrigg Lomanz says the Antarctica's chief med-surgeon is as good as they get. And that's real praise, coming from him. Mike is just about in the best place he could be right now.'

'I had no idea anything was wrong. Could not know. I recently did send him a message I have received, myself, from Newcam.'

'Yes, I'm sorry, but I only just heard from the Antarctica. They said he fell ill about two days ago. They've been a bit busy with – various troubles of their own. As I said, El, please try not to worry too much. I'll keep you informed as best as I possibly can. Now, please tell me your own news. I've been out of touch as well, you know.'

Taking a few moments to compose herself again, Eleri began her story about the latest developments on New Cambria but Tenak could see she was struggling to concentrate.

'The news is,' she said, 'that there have been more amazery developments – but tis a bit groop. Sorry, tis our word for … I think you say, grisly? Anyways, seems the government finally gave permission for the teams to drill through to the void behind wall "Gamma", as they do call the backmost wall of the Hall. The Antarctica scientists drilled a small hole the day before yestermorn. Deedly, they found a vacuum in the void t'other side and, in thanks, no poison gases were found. They cut a larger hole yestermorn, so they could walk through, and they did find a very large tunnel. Seems it does lead all the way to the other side of the dome, nearly thirty lints.

'That's extraordinary. So, was that the main way into the Hall?'

'Yes, unkling. We did wonder about the other "ray" anyways, the one diametrically opposite the one we entered is much larger by far. They sent a robot down the tunnel and it did find the entranceway at other end, but tis now blocked by millions of tons of rubble and sediment. But listen to this, unkling. They also yet found a set of stairs in the tunnel just opened, a few hundred of metres in. These stairs, being some huge stairs, descend many metres down to another void. This one goes right under the dome – almost as far as its other side.'

'That's fantastic. So, what's down there. El? Another hall of Natives?' asked Tenak, his voice crackling with excitement.

Eleri frowned. 'Well, yes, tis a hall, unkling. Massive yet. *Five times bigger* than the one we entered – but tis filled with … dead bodies.'

Tenak stared at her, his brows wrinkling in horror.

She continued, 'They are the desiccated bodies of Natives. They look some like the one in the crystal case – but not embalmed, like him. Rather now, they are skeletonised or, I am told, naturally mummified. Shrivell-ed. It does seem there was no oxygen down there to cause decay, so there was degree of preservation. They are, it so seems, like dried husks.'

'That's unfortunate but it's also very interesting,' said Tenak, 'and the discoveries just seem to keep rolling in. Do they know why those beings died? Was it the lack of oxygen, itself, or … some sort of … genocide? I suppose it's too early to tell.'

'Many questions there are, yes. There are thousands of bodies, unkling. Thousands, where before we had but one. Imagine that. Sept these are poor-so specimens, compared to the one we found. They are all sizes. There are male and female, and yet little ones. The team are doing much research on them. Could be many months before they finish but yes, they think they suffocated. Probably not some sort of mass murder. There is yet nothing which be suggesting such an thing. Some are saying mayhap they were hiding from Ra's temper and something went wrong. Tis terrible and sad, uncle.'

'Yes, Eleri. Tis that, but it all happened a long time ago. I wonder if they were left behind when Ra's surface erupted. Or maybe they chose to stay. Seems to me that *we* must not repeat that mistake.'

Eleri nodded solemnly. After a few moments she said, 'Talking yet about those poor creatures ... does not make me happier – about Mike. He will be alright, will he not?'

'Yes, of course he will. I can make sure you can stay in touch with his situation, El. If you ask your wristcom it will record the code I'm about to send to it.' Tenak fiddled with his own wristcom, as he continued, 'It's Captain Providius's private comm code, so you can talk to her directly. Otherwise, you won't get through to her and you could be tied up for ages. She has given full permission for you to use it, so please do, El.'

'That is yet good. Thank you uncle. I will yet make sure I stay in touch but will not pester her such, when not necessary. I am going to fly to Janitra morrowmorn. I will contact her when I get there.'

'That's a long journey, isn't it? Why didn't you tell me before, El? I could have got Lew and Kravikovna to take you there, if I had known. If you leave it a few days I could free up the boat then. I'll get Lew to pick you up.'

'No thank you, uncle. No need. Yet you have been too kind already. Tis better for me to keep busy, in such now-times as these, and I have some important samples to get to the University. I am yet already behind schedule. Besides, did not Mike tell you I have been flying for nearly ten years? I am so very used to such. Flown all sorts. Even flew right across the continent once, using extra, under-the-wing, tanking.'

'Okay, El, if you say so. Take care. I hope I'll hear from you again soon. Love you.'

'I love you too, uncle. Bye for now.' Her image vanished.

****

Ra blazed from an azure sky and the birdlings chittered all around as Eleri carried her personal bag out to the apron on which her aircraft stood – the so called "Arcingbird". It was not really her aircraft. It belonged to the University, but she was allowed almost exclusive use of it on several occasions throughout the year, so she could carry out various aspects of her research work.

She walked back to the hangar, where an assistant, a tall, middle aged, muscular man, was busy gathering crates and dumping them onto long metal trolleys.

'Tis such an wonderful mornimbrite, Cal,' she said. 'Tis yet hard to believe the sun can be so ... destructive to all life on this planet. And that we shall all have to leave soon.'

'I know, Mes,' said her assistant, his brow furrowing, 'still not now, eh? Let us enjoy the place while we can.'

'Deedly,' she said. 'Did you see Frank at all? Or is it his away-time?'

'Day off, Mes. Tis just me and thee to load up. If you do not mind me to say, I wonder if you should have loaded up last night.'

'I am sorry Cal. Just didn't have time. I'm late again this morning. I've been trying to find out more about Mike. I know they have been out all night, but the crates should be alrighting, should they not be? The vital ones are self- refrigerated.'

'Yes. Supposing so. But I was just worried about Metamorphs. I know Frank was too.'

'But come now Calanish, they have-nar been seen around this part of the island for years. The presence of people up here seems to have made them stay in the southern areas.'

'I be not so sure, Mes. With respect, you haven't been to these parts for a long time. There were many sightings of them down at the Mabri Gorge last year. Looks like you didnar know. Frank hi'self saw one, in his hyper-noclars, about 200 hundred metres away, last week. Down by the river bridge, it was.'

'No, I didn't know, Cal. Still, they are not likely to sniff around the air-drome, are they? I would not have yet thought they would try to eat into any of the crates, either. Best check though, after what you say.'

'I have checked, Mes,' smiled Cal, 'but the ones out on the apron need checking as well.'

'Listen, Cal, please, I need you to get the liquid nitro' cannisters out of the stores above the office, so I will check the crates outside. But first, I have to check the latest weather forecast on the rad-tuner.'

Twenty minutes later Cal joined Eleri, as she stood near her aircraft, checking it for any visual problems. They looked around at the vibrant blue greens of the lush, tropical vegetation beyond the apron. 'I am glad I decided to take a break, out here,' she said.

'Did you yet check the crates?' asked Cal.

'Some, yes, but I did not have much time. There was much interference on the airo-radio. Took forever to get the forecast. Doesn't seem too good out there. Big cyclonic system off the eastern part of the continent. I haven't got time to fless round here anymore. Tis a long way from this side of the island to Janitra but if I yet leave now, I should get there before the weather system. Well, thanking you for all help, Cal. I will see you in a few days.'

Cal nodded and smiled broadly as Eleri climbed up through the large door behind the cockpit and settled into her seat. She grinned at him as he withdrew beyond the wings and watched her start up the twin propeller engines. The blades span and she throttled up to test them. Then she powered down for taxiing to the end of the runway. Five minutes later she was gone, the plane sweeping gracefully into the air at the far end of the compacted dirt runway. Cal raised one hand to shade his eyes so he could watch the aircraft rise into the distance. But as he walked back to the hangar he saw a small metallic object lying on the tarmac where the crates had been. It glinted in the sunshine. It was some sort of chronometer. Something that used to be called a "watch"?

****

FINAL REPORT OF DEPARTMENTAL SCIENCE GROUP ALPHA 2 (Ex 3)

TO SECRETARY TO THE MINISTER OF THE INTERIOR,

MER TANEMBAUM

12/8/02 (anno. Ind). 2492 CE

Transmitted by Electro-transfer. EL 1.

Ref: ARMO 2 (New Cambria)

We do refer to our first-yet and interim reports (Ex 1 & 2). As reported previously, we are pleased to verifie that all precautions have been taken to assure safety of participantes in the further exploration of the tunnels and deep-so chamber of the alien dome. The research work on the mummified alien bodies continues yet and will likely so consume many months of effort.

Our now-report seeks to summarise (see appendicie below) the key features of the discoveries made to date and the timescaling involved.

We have seen many scenes yet from the Native artefacts, as summarised in earli-so reports. These do show many disturbed yet images. But many more have been produced and, though still confusing to some degree, they do appear to show images shot through the windows of spaceship. Many do seem to be from vessels ascending into orbit and still in orbit as well. The teams we work with have so-identified the planet thus shewn, to be Oceanus itself.

We are slight divided about this interpretation, since the scenes do show the surface of the planet as slightly different from what we do know today. However, most of us are so inclin-ed to agree with the Home System Team that this is because crustal plates have moved since those long-past times.

There also seems yet little doubt that the Native civilization here did suffer complete disrupting of their times, by way of increasingly violent particle storms and radiation which we feel didst cause planet surface wildfires and destruction massive-so.

Further even, we have now witnessed video scenes which seem to show the Natives leaving this world, in many large space vessels. HS sources are quoted as saying that many such ships are estimated to be more than ten times as large as "The Monsoon", in orbit above us now. Most of us do believe yet that as many as millions of the Natives may have left this world, to avoid the worst of the catastrophe from Ra.

Some of us have witness-ed videos which, as far as we can say, the departure of dozens of giant ships, firing huge engines and disappearing far to the limits of this sytem. Long range views in said holos do suggest, and the Muggredge team, and HS team, do say they believe these craft didst leave the Ra system totally. Most of us are of the opinion that this is a correct interpretation. The HS team do also believe that the Native ships used a different means of interstellar travel than do they (and as didst our ancestors), but we speculate no more on this aspect as it is irrelevant to the purpose of this report.

As to that, we must now give the conclusions of the majority of this group, being 4 out of 6 of us. Be noting that the dissenters do not feel so strongly that they yet wish to produce their own, separate report. We are thus confident of our recommendions, set out below:

We wish to state <u>we have no hesitation in endorsing the findings of the Off-World science teams in this matter, in the question of the fate of the beings who lived on this world far long before human arrival.</u>

The sentient reptiliano animals, being in- fact, the original natives of this planet, were subjected to the destruction of their environment by upwellings and violent eruptions of the surface of Ra, approximately 8.14 millions of years ago. We are convinced that the violent instability of Ra, induced by the irregular "tying" of the so-called Karabrandon Waves (see Appendic 4) did result in such overwhelming of the surface of Oceanus, with ionic and proton plasma, as well as excessive ultra-violet radiation. All teams and we, set out the suggested results detail as in Tabel 10, Appendicie 6.

We are, too, convinced, that most of the sentient Native inhabitants were able to escape before the vast majority of the destruction happened and evacuated this entire stellar system. As the Native holograms do not continue beyond the confines of the Ra system we currently have no idea where these beings went, or what became of them. We are told by our HS colleagry that no convinving-yet signs of any such intelligent life has ever been discovered within the boundaries observed by their best astronomic instruments, over the last 420 years. But, again, this is yet beyond the scope of this report and so we have no comments of any significance to add.

What we can and do comment, is, <u>we have no doubt that Ra is exhibiting the same patterns of behaviour now </u>(and, we accept, has yet been doing so many years) which are, in our consideration, likely lead to greater instability and so, to widescale destruction again of the surface environment of beloved Oceanus Alpha. We are not in doubt this will lead to the same consequences as did happen 8.14 million years ago. In short, we endorse the advice and information given by the Home System scientists in the dataprobe NRX 010, received 1.8 OA years ago. We also yet endorse the findings of The Monsoon specialists in this matter, since their arrival 14 months ago. We are aware yet that other naturalist-scientists – and others – may continue to dispute these findings of ours, and we humbly accept yet that we are but four in number, discounting the scientists of the HS and Research ships. Yet we also humbly exhort you to accept our conclusionry.

<u>FINAL NOTE:</u>

It is not our place to form policy and so we can recommend only that the Native / Alien holograms should not be shown (if this e'en proves possible tek-ways) to the people of Oceanus, by way of television or otherwise. We believe it would cause wide-scale panic and disturbance. It is, of course, in ultimato, down to the President and her government, how to explain the content and import of the holo-vids to the people and to prepare them for leaving this world of ours but we humbly believe the people must so be told.

****

After flying for over three hours Eleri picked up a signal from "Sea-squaw", a part time Air Traffic Control Point, set up on a small island, some 150 kilometres off the east coast of Bhumi-Devi. She had timed her departure to coincide with the operating regime of the Control Point, so she could get up-dated weather reports. It had been one of the reasons she'd been in such a hurry to get off Jungle Island that morning.

She was flying at around 3000 metres altitude, above a brilliantly white layer of fluffy cotton-wool-like clouds. A thinner layer of cloud floated far above her, looking like white lace. There were no strong winds to note, so it was an easy flight and she was enjoying herself, humming to herself some of her favourite Oceanus folk tunes. The beacon from Sea-squaw broke her reverie, badly broken by static noise.

'Omega, Victor 9, Sea-squaw, ... have now your transpo-marker. We have your heading and speed. Please ... confirm your intended landing-point?'

'Sea-squaw, Omega Victor 9,' said Eleri, speaking into the mic' of her headset, 'I do intend landing at Janitra, Glennistry One. Please yet advise on most recent met-notifications.'

'Omega Victor, Sea ...,' said the controller, calmly but firmly, as the staic started to subside, 'but we do not agree your course, Janitra One. Incoming storm currently north by north east, current vector is 190 to 210 degrees, heading west south-west at 250 lints from your position. Storm worsening over last three hours. Estimated arrival, at continental coast – three hours. Tis a force 8 storm with a cold front on leading edge, forming heavy cumulo-nimbus, up to 10,000 metres. Estimated to cause class 9, electric storms. Advise you return to point of departure, or, only if absolute necessari, change your heading to 240 degrees, and proceed as far as Arrowman Islands. Then change to heading 232 degrees to land at South Tanglemoss.'

Eleri replied, equally calmly, 'Sea Squaw, Omega Victor. Negative to course change. That will take me too far out of my way. I will be unable to refuel at South Tanglemoss.'

'Omega Victor, Sea Squaw, we are having problems receiving you. …. as advised, best alternative is to yet turn back to point of departure. We repeat, we do not advise you continue on your present heading.'

'Sea Squaw, Omega Victor, thanking you for advice. Will comply with advised new heading but will review as necessary.'

Sea-squaw signed off and Eleri studied her fuel gauges once more. The fuel tanks might, possibly, get her all the way back but it was a risk. Even if she returned to Jungle Island it would delay her mission by several days, given the need to refuel and allow the storms to move inland, out of the way. Continuing on her present heading was clearly not a good idea but South Tanglemoss, in the "Southern Swamplands", had only a small, rudimentary, air strip, used in emergencies only, mainly for inbound flights from the Southern Ocean.

South Tanglemoss was a tiny hamlet, with poor transport links to the outside world. The reference to "Southern" meant simply that it was located in the southernmost sector of the settled eastern seaboard area of Bhumi-Devi. The southernmost section of the continent itself was many thousands of kilometres further away. Even so, the southern swamplands zone was a sparsely populated place, dotted with occasional "back-woods" towns. The area was infested with insectoids and arachnolids, the latter being mildly poisonous, worm-like, creatures. These things were very small but had ten clawed legs at the front and the rear and hurt a lot if they bit. But it wasn't really such creatures which bothered Eleri, but rather the poor transport infrastructure in that part of the continent. Her radio was not functioning well because of interference from the storms, so she'd need to wait until landing and try to charter a plane or an airship to fetch her. Otherwise, she would have a grinding journey of around 250 kilometres, mostly by pony and trap, out of the swamplands. Then there'd be another 300 klicks, over the Pentorian Plateau, which lay between the swamps and the nearest large town, a place called Teramium. That impoverished settlement had only a slow autocar link, of around 200 klicks, to the larger towns of the south-eastern lowlands, where she could pick up a maglev train to Janitra.

She could use her wristcom to charter a flight out of Tanglemoss, of course, but this option would still be extremely expensive and the earliest she could expect to be picked up – by a cumbersome air taxi, or a blimp, was probably about 7 days. It was quicker to use the wristcom to contact Uncle Tenak, but she didn't want to admit she'd been wrong. Besides, she would still have to wait for at least 3 days to be picked up because she'd left it too late. After mulling over the options, she decided to turn left, as advised, and take the suggested heading. She would wait to see what the conditions were like nearer the Arrowman Islands – about 100 lints to the south-west. Eleri stopped singing to herself.

The meteorological conditions deteriorated as she flew onward. She spotted distant storm clouds, far out to her right, and the aircraft began to be jostled by more turbulence than was usual on this run, even given that this was the wettest, stormiest part of the year. The turbulence produced occasional but wide swings in pitch and roll. Most people, unused to flying in relatively small aircraft, would have been horrified, made queasy, by such conditions. Eleri considered the turbulence easily manageable and was satisfied it did not threaten the integrity of the aircraft.

She saw the Arrowman Islands, up ahead, difficult to spot through the haze below. The cloud cover at low level was thickening. As she neared the Arrowmans, Eleri decided not to follow the suggested flight plan. On Oceanus, such directions as she'd been given were advisory only, not mandatory. She was closing on the coast very rapidly, so she banked right and changed to a heading of 210 degrees, a direction that would take her toward Teminisirios, well north of South Tanglemoss, further up the coast of the continent. She had the necessary fuel and she knew it had a small but serviceable airport. And the capital city was easily reached from there.

She decided to keep a careful eye on the weather conditions and if necessary, change heading for South Tanglemoss later. The only so called "flamefly in the soupo", was a chain of 2000-metre-high mountains, rising up from the coast, between her current position and Teminisirios, but she knew she could fly well above them. The Arcingbird had two sixteen-cylinder engines, each with 12,000 horse-power rating, and so, for a mid-size propeller plane, it had a whopping ceiling of 9,000 metres. But she would need to keep a wary eye on her fuel levels if she had to go very high.

An hour after turning onto her new heading she ran into heavy cloud at her altitude and had to climb to 4000 metres. The rain rattled against her canopy as she flew through the dense cloud, but she noted that her fuel gauges showed her engines had more than eight hours of flying in them. Off to her right she could see more storm clouds building but she'd expected that. What she *hadn't* expected was that she would encounter them this early. Sea-squaw's forecasts were generally accurate, but even they had underestimated the speed of this cyclonic system. Perhaps she should have taken that into account.

Of more concern was the height to which the clouds had built. She gazed to her right and had to crane her neck upwards in order to see the wispy tops of the hammerhead, way above her. They must have been at least 12,000 metres high – more than 10,000 metres above their black-as-soot bases. The masses of water started to blot out the light from Ra in a staccato-like way, her cockpit going dark, like pitch, then brilliantly bright, then dark again, in rapid succession. Soon, the gloomy towers seemed to encircle her plane completely, plunging her into continuous darkness, and a huge drop in temperature, so she was obliged to switch on her illuminated instrument panel and turn up the cockpit heating.

She now knew she couldn't rise above the hammerheads and needed to consider turning toward South Tanglemoss after all. She cussed at herself for going against her accumulated, not to say hard-won, flying experience. She pulled a map from below her instrument panel. Keeping the steering yoke steady, she pored over it, periodically checking her instruments. She had to work out how far she had already come along her present heading. With a layer of cloud below her she had to use her instruments and some quick mathematics to work out her current position. And she knew she should have heeded Sea Squaw's advice, but, for Maker's sake, she had been in difficult situations many times before! She was still confident and kept her cool. Panicking in this situation could be disastrous and she was determined she would not do *that*.

Okay, she now had the heading she needed. Leaving the map on the empty co-pilot's seat to her right, she banked left and headed, reluctantly, toward the swamplands area. There were, she knew, two possible problems. One was her diminishing fuel but she knew she could reach New Tenby, near the coast, which also had a tiny air strip, but it was even more difficult to get from there to Janitra, than from South Tanglemoss. And she didn't want to change course again. The other problem was that there were yet more coastal mountains, the "Pentorian Chain", between her and New Tenby, smaller ones these, none of them more than 1,000 metres high, and easily surmounted.

The storm cloud giants were at her back now and a wide belt of azure sky opened up, lime a belt along the horizon. Her mood lightened again, and she wondered and worried about how Mike was doing. She realised she could have asked Tenak to persuade Captain Providius to let her go along with Mike, but, apart from the nasty thought of being cooped up on a ship for several months, she'd felt she had important work to do planet-side. But she missed Mike as though some part of her own body was missing, as though amputated and, despite everything, she now remonstrated with herself for not asking to go along on the Antartica.

But there had also a part of her that had wanted to "test" their relationship, to some extent, to see how well they managed with separation, albeit a fairly short one. She now felt that was probably silly. Outside of her own family, she had never felt so close to anyone and, before Mike, had certainly never had such a deep emotional relationship with any man. Though she knew she'd see him in a month or two, right now she wanted to be with him very badly. She allowed herself some self-pity, for a short while, before she steeled herself and determined she would get to New Tenby safely. The eventual reunion with Mike was going to be all the better for their separation. It would be special; very special indeed.

She was starting to tire, and so opened the instrument panel vents to allow fresh air to flow into the cabin and she lowered the heating. As Eleri held the plane straight and steady she suddenly thought about an incident from her childhood. In her mind's eye she was running barefoot through the soft broadies, back on her parent's farm. The memory was very vivid. It was almost as if she were actually there, all those years ago.

Within seconds the aircraft's cockpit seemed almost to disappear, and she felt the joy and freedom of running through the meadows of the farm, the wind whistling in her long, fair hair. She was squealing with delight in the brilliant sunshine, for she was very young. She saw the big barn where she knew her father was working and decided she would run to him, but almost slipped on a muddy patch of the track which ran between the meadow and the shed.

Eleri involuntarily bit her lip as she suddenly remembered where she was. The cockpit appeared again, and she tasted blood, as she stared out of the canopy. Where had she been? A flashback? She'd been warned about those. How long had she "been away"? Luckily, the plane was still in straight and level flight, but the skies ahead were once again growing dark with cumulus clouds. Trying to ignore the incredibly lucid feel of the memory of that day, on her parent's farm, so long ago, she checked the instruments and reassured herself she was still on course for New Tenby.

She was back on the farm again and she forgot all about her adult life and where she was. She trotted into her father's barn, tripping through its large doors. But as she slowed to a walk, she found her eyes wouldn't allow her to see much of the interior. They hadn't yet become dark adapted but, at seven years old she didn't realise that. Just then she heard her father's deep bass voice. It was coming from far inside the barn, a large and mostly empty building, apart from some farm equipment.

But no, there was something else there. She thought she caught a glimpse of her father but there was another thing in there, with him, or *near* him. Something growling. With horror she realised it was a metamorph – crouching in a corner. Her father saw her approaching and shouted to her to keep away, but she was fascinated by the creature, and just stood and stared at it. The thing was quite small, about the size of a young dog but extremely hairy; shaggy, in fact. Most of the time these were slow moving, harmless, creatures, disinclined to be aggressive, but when they felt threatened, or cornered, they turned virtually inside out, revealing a massive, "secondary mouth", with disproportionately large, black teeth. They could attack with a ferocity unequalled anywhere in known space.

Eleri's father must have bumped into this one accidentally. They usually kept well away from humans but when their plant and small mammal food sources were not abundant, they were known to stray into human settlements. One OA Administration had been about to pass legislation allowing them to be hunted and culled but this had caused a political storm. Many were quick to remind everyone of the ethos of the colony's founders: to protect and preserve the planet's indigenous wildlife – even the parts considered to be dangerous. Although very young, little Eleri had understood the need for conservation. She had relished studying all the wildlife and the plants, on her parent's farm and all around it.

But now, never having seen a metamorph this close, she stood wide eyed and rather scared, especially as she saw that the creature appeared about to charge her father. Marcus had no weapons to hand, and he cast his gaze wildly around. Seeing a chance for him and his daughter to survive he grasped a large sheet of scrap metal which lay nearby, propped up against the wheel of an electro-tractor.

He shouted at Eleri to drop to the floor and, clutching the sheet, dived toward her, then threw the makeshift shield over the two of them, the sharp edges cutting into his hands and splashing little drops of blood on her dress. But it worked. The metamorph shot toward them, bounced heavily on the metal sheet and then, growling and screaming, it scampered out of the barn at high speed. Her little heart was thumping so much she thought it would burst – and she suddenly came to – looking wildly out of the canopy of an aircraft.

Her heart was still hammering, and when she remembered where she was, she saw, with alarm, that the Arcingbird had lost height. They were no longer in straight and level flight but about 1,000 metres below optimum elevation. She must have pushed the plane into a shallow dive. She started to correct it, gently pulling the yoke toward her and pushing the two throttles forward, increasing power to the twin engines. Making her heart jump, she was startled to hear two loud bangs from somewhere near the back of the aircraft.

She threw open the door that divided the cockpit from the cargo bay behind and looked through into the darkness. On this aircraft the interior of the hold had no windows. The light switch wasn't on her panel but was in the rear cabin. She couldn't reach it without leaving her controls. Convinced that the sound had come from somewhere in the hold, she nevertheless ran a full check on her instruments and a visual check through the large canopy windows, just in case. There was nothing untoward on the outside the plane, at least as far as she could tell. Perhaps it was the cargo shifting behind her?

She turned her attention back to flying, becoming concerned about the building cloud. She felt a little disorientated as to her heading and, when she caught an all too brief glimpse of the ground below, she frowned. Meadowland? There should be low foothills. Where was the meadowland? Rather than check her map again she suddenly had the idea of using her wristcom to contact The Monsoon. Of course, why hadn't she done that before? She was so used to the "old ways" of doing things. She laughed at herself and pulled up her left sleeve but – no wristcom! After a moment of sheer bewilderment, she remembered a crate banging into her wrist, when she and Cal had been moving the cargo onto the plane. She had felt something move on her wrist but had been in a hurry to get things sorted and had failed to check it. How stupid was that?

But then again perhaps the device was in the store-box, the compartment used for personal items, directly under the panel, to the left. She opened it and glancing down, fumbled for the wristcom. She felt her fingers touch a large cold object, but it wasn't the wristcom. It was a stun pistol. Mike had given it to her, to be used simply for personal protection. It was probably, she guessed, against navy rules and maybe she should have refused it. She looked and fumbled again. No wristcom? Never mind. She would have to manage without it.

Another loud bang came from the back cabin. What in the Oceans was going on back there? Unfortunately, this model of aircraft had no autopilot, so she couldn't leave the yoke to go back and check. This was another disadvantage of flying solo. Holding the yoke with her left hand she half stood and stretched across to her right, to get a better look through the door, into the back. She still couldn't reach the light switch and made a mental note to ask about getting a switch installed on the damned instrument panel.

As she peered into the darkness of the hold, she was jolted again by another disturbance, more like a thumping, scampering sound this time, followed by a peculiar scraping. Something about the sounds made her think they were being made by an animal, or maybe a person, back there. Something alive. Surely not? Her heart rate, already high, climbed further and she called out, 'Who ist back there? Come out such, where I can see you.' There was no reply. What was the matter with her? Whatever made those sounds wasn't a human. It sounded more like some sort of creature – but what was it? How did it get in?

With a realisation that made her heart leap wholesale into her mouth she remembered something Cal had said. And in the next second she actually saw it.

Barely illuminated by light from the cockpit a dark shape crawled out of the shadows a couple of metres inside the hold, right in the middle aisle-way. A metamorph? No, surely not? This was just insane. Things like this didn't happen, did they? Cal's words rang out in her mind. "… I was just worried about metamorphs. I know Frank was too …" Cal been concerned about crates being left out overnight. But they'd checked them. Well, Cal had checked some of them. She was supposed to have checked the others but had been – in a hurry. Damnatious.

At least the metamorph was staying put. She could see one claw; a forelimb, she thought. The rest was still in shadow. It was essential she didn't panic. Very carefully, she reached into the space beyond the door, to try to pull it shut. She concentrated on making as little noise as possible because it was essential the creature had to be shut into the hold. She thought about trying to open the store-box again so she could get the stun gun but closing the hold door was probably the better option. These critters could move like lightning.

Hold on. What if this was some sort of flashback? Except, no, it wasn't. She'd never seen a metamorph on an aircraft and hadn't seen *any* close-up, since the barn incident, when she was seven. Even if it were some sort of distorted flashback, or illusion, she couldn't take the chance it was not real. She had to act – and fast. If it turned out to be an illusion, no harm done. Eleri continued to reach for the door latch.

She found herself uttering a strange, involuntary, squawk, when her hand, slick with perspiration, slipped off the door latch and the door banged against the side panel of the hold. The metamorph had heard it and came fully into view. It was still in its normal rodent-like form, its shiny, black, and perversely cute looking snout snuffling as it moved forward toward the cockpit. Good. It hadn't morphed into the aggressive form – yet. Eleri moved bodily toward the door latch again but the animal looked up, its small black, shiny eyes fixed straight on her. And then its eyes started to bulge, as if extending out of its head. They changed colour to a dull red.

Eleri gave up all pretence of subterfuge and just grabbed at the door, pulling it toward her as fast as she could – but the creature had already turned dark shades of mottled pinks and reds. It seemed to unfold itself before her eyes as it pulled its own skin from its rear end, right over its head, like som some sort of bizarre hood. Large brown and black fangs, stained with something white and pink, appeared, jutting out from under the "hood" – and then, in silence, it launched itself straight at her. The creature was already through the entrance into the cockpit before she could grab the latch, forcing Eleri to abandon the door. She threw herself at the instrument panel and fumbled for the storage box.

As she did so the metamorph bounded forward again, jumped at her and bounced off the cockpit canopy, making a wet slapping sound, then it landed on its back on the co-pilot seat next to her. With valiant calmness of purpose, she somehow got the storage box open and grabbed inside for the stun gun, but the metamorph launched itself at her again. She saw it coming out of the corner of her eye and, instinctively, threw her head back, out of its way. Fortunately, the creature sailed past her face but by mere centimetres, hitting the canopy window to her left.

Again, instinctively, she threw herself out of the way, toward the co-pilot seat, while the metamorph glared at her with eyes that had now risen right, on red stalks, right out of its "hood". Strangely, it seemed to hesitate, and she dived for the store-box again. Concentrating on not fumbling. She tried to concentrate on not fumbling, though she still did but then she found the stun gun. With relief that was immeasurable, she turned and launched herself backwards into the hold. Getting back there seemed to be hard to do, almost as though she was trying to run uphill. She had no time to dwell on this because the enraged metamorph now shot sideways, bouncing off the right hand canopy and, with a chilling scream, it rammed itself into a bulkhead and bounced back toward the hold.

The stun gun Mike had given her was preprogramed to remain on mild stun only. He had given her basic training in its use and now, Eleri tried to hold it steady and aim, but the creature came at her too fast, but whistled past, disappearing into the darkness of the hold. It had completely missed her. She couldn't believe it. With a wildly pumping heart she jumped forwards into the cockpit and, now deftly grasping at the door handle slammed it shut behind her. She heard a loud thumping noise as the creature barged against the other side of the door but, throwing the latch, she collapsed into the pilot's seat. Blessed relief. She was through the danger, safely. And she had come through it without so much as a scratch from that creature. How amazing was that?

Another realisation hit her. Oh, Maker, the plane! What was happening?

Staring out of the cockpit windows she saw that the aircraft was enveloped in thick cloud. Even before she had a chance to check the altimeter, she sensed the craft was descending through a low cloud layer. She grabbed the yoke and, with trembling hands, started to pull it back, and, at the same time, pull the throttle out. As she did so she managed to check the altitude and the attitude indicators. The Arcingbird was banking at about 15° from horizontal and had descended, quite steeply, by around 500 metres. Not too bad after all, she thought, but she had no idea how far she'd come since last checking her position and had no idea of her whereabouts.

As she increased engine power and began to climb the cloud and mist cleared and right then saw something all pilots dread seeing, for the best of all possible reasons. In a second her heart rate leapt, sweat seemed break out from every pore but yet her blood seemed to freeze in her veins. to With bulging eyes, she saw, straight ahead, and completely filling her view, the deep green-blue sward of a vegetation covered mountain side. Something instinctive, deep within her troubled mind, told her what, with all her heart, she didn't want to believe: the game was up. She only had time to draw a short, sharp, breath as the plane closed with the hillside at over 250 kilometres per hour. The last thing she ever saw was a brilliant flash - but she didn't feel the impact at all.

THE STORY OF 'CRADLE OF DESTRUCTION'

CONTINUES IN BOOK TWO:

'ANGER OF THE GODS'

Printed in Great Britain
by Amazon